When
you're

Summer Seductions

Find all your holiday romance in this irresistible
volume – passionate love affairs guaranteed!

The Contaxis Baby
plus BONUS story *The Greek Tycoon's Baby*
by Lynne Graham

The Unlikely Mistress
plus EXCLUSIVE story *In Bed with the Boss*
by Sharon Kendrick

His Pretend Wife
plus EXCLUSIVE story *Wedding in Venice*
by Lucy Gordon

MILLS & BOON
100 YEARS
of pure reading pleasure

100 Reasons to Celebrate

We invite you to join us in celebrating
Mills & Boon's centenary. Gerald Mills and
Charles Boon founded Mills & Boon Limited
in 1908 and opened offices in London's Covent
Garden. Since then, Mills & Boon has become
a hallmark for romantic fiction, recognised
around the world.

We're proud of our 100 years of publishing
excellence, which wouldn't have been achieved
without the loyalty and enthusiasm of our
authors and readers.

Thank you!

Each month throughout the year there will
be something new and exciting to mark the
centenary, so watch for your favourite authors,
captivating new stories, special limited
edition collections…and more!

The Contaxis Baby

Lynne Graham

Summer Seductions

Lynne Graham
Sharon Kendrick
Lucy Gordon

M&B™ and M&B™ with the Rose Device
are trademarks of the publisher.
Harlequin Mills & Boon Limited, Eton House,
18-24 Paradise Road, Richmond, Surrey TW9 1SR

SUMMER SEDUCTIONS © by Harlequin Books S.A. 2008

The Contaxis Baby © Lynne Graham 2002
The Unlikely Mistress © Sharon Kendrick 2001
His Pretend Wife © Lucy Gordon 2002

The Greek Tycoon's Baby © Harlequin Books S.A 2000
In Bed with the Boss © Harlequin Books S.A 2001
Wedding in Venice © Harlequin Books S.A 2003

ISBN: 978 0 263 86665 0

24-0608

Printed and bound in Spain
by Litografia Rosés S.A., Barcelona

Lynne Graham was born in Northern Ireland and has been a keen Mills & Boon reader since her teens. She is very happily married with an understanding husband, who has learned to cook since she started to write! Her five children keep her on her toes. She has a very large dog, which knocks everything over, a very small terrier which barks a lot, and two cats.

Sharon Kendrick started story-telling at the age of eleven and has never really stopped. She likes to write fast-paced, feel-good romances with heroes who are so sexy they'll make your toes curl! Born in west London, she now lives in the beautiful city of Winchester – where she can see the cathedral from her window (but only if she stands on tip-toe).

Don't miss Sharon's brand-new Mills & Boon®
Modern™ romance, *The Greek Tycoon's Convenient Wife,* available in July 2008!

Lucy Gordon cut her writing teeth on magazine journalism, interviewing many of the world's most interesting men, including Warren Beatty, Richard Chamberlain, Sir Roger Moore, Sir Alec Guinness, and Sir John Gielgud. She is married to a Venetian, whom she met while on holiday in Venice. They got engaged within two days.

Don't miss Lucy's brand-new Mills & Boon®
Romance, *The Italian's Cinderella Bride,*
available in June 2008!

CHAPTER ONE

WHEN Sebasten Contaxis strode to Ingrid Morgan's side to offer his condolences on the death of her only son, she fell on his chest and just sobbed as though her heart had broken right through.

A ripple of curiosity ran through the remaining guests in the drawing room of the Brighton town house. The tall, powerfully built male, every angle of his bronzed features stamped with strength and authority, looked remarkably like…but surely not? After all, what could be the connection? Why would the Greek electronics tycoon come to pay his respects *after* Connor's funeral? But keen eyes picked out the long, opulent limousine double-parked across the street and then judged the two large men waiting on the pavement as the bodyguards that they were. Heads turned, moved closer together and the whispers started.

Stunning dark eyes veiled, Sebasten waited until Ingrid had got a grip on that first outburst of grief before murmuring, 'Is there anywhere that we can talk?'

'Still looking after my good name?' Ingrid lifted her blonde head and he tensed at the sight of the raw suffering etched in her once beautiful features. Then he knew that even her love for his late father had in the end been surpassed by her devotion to her son. 'It doesn't really matter now, does it? Connor's gone where he can never be embarrassed by my past…'

She took him into an elegant little study and poured drinks for them both. Always slim, right now she looked emaciated and every day of her fifty-odd years. She had been his father's mistress for a long time and some of the few happy childhood memories Sebasten had related to her and Connor, who had been five years his junior. For all too short a spell, Connor had been the kid brother he had never had, tagging after Sebasten on the beach, a little blond boy, cheerfully and totally fearless. As an adult, he had become a brilliant polo player, adored by women, in fact very popular with both sexes. Not the brightest spark on the block but a very likeable guy. Yet it had been well over a year since Sebasten had last seen the younger man.

'It was murder, you know…' Ingrid condemned half under her breath.

Sebasten's winged dark brows drew together but he remained silent, for he had heard the rumour that Connor's car crash had been no accident, indeed, a deliberate act of self-destruction, and he knew that there was no more painful way to lose a loved one. She needed to talk and he knew that listening was the kindest thing he could do for her.

'I liked Lisa Denton…when I met that evil little shrew, I actually *liked* her!' Ingrid proclaimed with bone-deep bitterness.

The silence lay before Ingrid continued in a tremulous tone. 'I knew Connor was in love when he stopped confiding in me. That hurt but he was twenty-four…that's why I didn't pry.'

'Lisa Denton?' Sebasten was keen to deflect her from that unfortunate angle.

Her stricken blue eyes hardened. 'A spoilt little rich brat. Gets her kicks out of encouraging men to make an ass of themselves over her! It's only three months since Connor met her but I could tell he'd fallen like a ton of bricks.' The older woman swallowed with visible difficulty. 'Then without any warning, *she* got bored. She cut him dead at a party two weeks ago…made an exhibition of herself with another man, laughed in his face…his friends told me *everything*!'

Sebasten waited while Ingrid gathered her shredded composure back together again.

'He begged but she wouldn't even take a phone call from him. He'd done nothing. He couldn't handle it,' Ingrid sobbed brokenly. 'He wasn't sleeping, so he went for a drive in his car in the middle of the night and drove it into a wall!'

Sebasten curved an arm round her in a consoling embrace and seethed with angry distaste at the ugly picture she had drawn up. Connor would have been soft as butter in the hands of a manipulative little bitch like that.

'You're going to hate me for what I t-tell you now…' Ingrid whispered shakily.

'Nonsense,' Sebasten soothed.

'Connor was your half-brother…'

Sebasten released his breath in a sudden startled hiss and collided with Ingrid's both defiant and guilty gaze.

'No…that's not possible,' he breathed in total shock, not wanting it to be true when it was too late for him to do anything about it.

Ingrid sank down in a distraught heap and sobbed out a storm of self-justification while Sebasten stared at her as though he had never seen her before. She had never told his father, Andros, because she had known how ruthless Andros would be at protecting the good name of the Contaxis family from scandal.

'If Andros had known, he would've bullied me into having a termination. So I left him, came back eighteen months later, confessed to a rebound relationship, *grovelled*…eventually he took me back!' For a frozen instant in time, Ingrid's face shone with the remembered triumph of having fooled her powerful lover and then her eyes, fell, the flash of energy draining away again.

'How could you not tell me before this?' Sebasten bit out in an electrifying undertone, lean, strong face rigid with the force of his appalled incredulity. In the space of seconds, Connor's death had gone from a matter of sincere and sad regret to a tragedy which gutted Sebasten. But he knew why, knew all too well why she had kept quiet. Fear of the consequences would have kept her quiet throughout all the years she had loved his father without adequate return.

'I'm only telling you now because I want you to make Lisa Denton sorry she was ever born...' Ingrid confided with harsh clarity as his brilliant gaze locked to her set features and the hatred she could not hide. 'You're one of the richest men on this planet and I don't care how you do it. There have got to be strings you could pull, pressure you could put on somewhere with someone to *punish* her for what she did to Connor...'

'No,' Sebasten murmured without inflection, a big, dark, powerful Greek male, over six feet four in height and with shimmering dark golden eyes as steady as rock. 'I am a Contaxis and I have honour.'

Minutes later, Sebasten swept out of Ingrid's home, impervious to the lingering mourners keen to get a second look at him. In the privacy of his limo, he sank a double whiskey. His lean, dark, handsome face was hard and taut and ashen pale. He had no doubt that Ingrid had told him the truth. Connor...the little brother he had only run into twice at polo matches in recent years. He might have protected him from his own weakness but he hadn't been given the chance. Certainly, he could have taught him how to handle *that* kind of woman. Had Lisa Denton found out that, in spite of his

popularity and his wealthy friends, Connor was essentially
penniless but for his winnings on the polo field? Or had
Connor's puppy-dog adoration simply turned her off big
time? His wide, sensual mouth curled. Was she a drop-dead
babe who treated men like trophies?

He pitied Ingrid for the bitterness that consumed her. Yet
even after all those years in Greece, she *still* hadn't learned
that one essential truth: a man never discussed family honour with a woman or involved her in certain personal matters…

Maurice Denton stared out of his library window and then
turned round to face his daughter, his thin, handsome face set
with rigid disapproval.

'I can't excuse *anything* you've done,' he asserted.

Lizzie was so white that her reddish-blonde hair seemed
to burn like a brand above her forehead. 'I didn't ask you to,'
she murmured unevenly. 'I just said…we all make mistakes…and dating Connor was mine.'

'There are standards of decent behaviour and you've broken them,' the older man delivered as harshly as if she hadn't
spoken. 'I'm ashamed of you.'

'I'm sorry.' Her voice wobbled in spite of all her efforts
to control it but that last assurance had burned deep. 'I'm
really…*sorry*.'

'It's too late, isn't it? What I can't forgive is the public embarrassment and distress that you've caused your stepmother.
Last night, Felicity and I should have been dining with the
Jurgens but it was cancelled with a flimsy excuse. As word
gets around that your cruelty literally *drove* the Morgan boy
to his death, we're becoming as socially unacceptable as you
have made yourself—'

'Dad—'

'Hannah Jurgen was very fond of Connor. A lot of people

were. Felicity was extremely upset by that cancellation. Indeed, from the minute the details of this hideous business began leaking into the tabloids Felicity has scarcely slept a night through!' Maurice condemned fiercely.

Pale as milk, Lizzie turned her head away, her throat tight and aching. She might have told him that his young and beautiful wife, the woman who was the very centre of his universe, couldn't sleep for fear of exposure. But what right did she have to play God with his marriage? She asked herself painfully. What right did she have to speak and destroy that marriage when the future security of her own little unborn brother or sister was also involved in the equation?

'Do you think it's healthy for a pregnant woman to live in this atmosphere and tolerate being cold-shouldered by those she counted as friends just because you've made yourself a pariah?' her father demanded in driven continuance.

'I broke off my relationship with Connor. I didn't do anything else.' Even as Lizzie struggled to maintain her brittle composure she was trembling, for she was not accustomed to hearing that cold, accusing tone from her father, and in her hurt and bewilderment she could not find the right words to try and defend her own actions. 'I'm not to blame for his death,' she swore in a feverish protest. 'He had problems that had nothing to do with me!'

'This morning, Felicity went down to the cottage to rest,' the older man revealed with speaking condemnation. 'I want my wife home by my side where she ought to be. Right now, she needs looking after and my first loyalty lies with her and our unborn child. For that reason, I've reached a decision, one I probably should have made a long time ago. I'm cutting off your allowance and I want you to move out.'

Shock shrilled through Lizzie, rocking what remained of her once protected world on its axis: she was to be thrown to the wolves for her stepmother's benefit. She stared in sick disbelief at the father whom she had adored from childhood, the father whom she had fought to protect from pain and humiliation even while her own life disintegrated around her.

Maurice had always been a loving parent. But then the death of Lizzie's mother when she was five and the fifteen years that had passed before the older man remarried had ensured that father and daughter had a specially close bond. But from the day he had met Felicity, brick by brick that loving closeness had been disassembled. Felicity had ensured that she received top billing in every corner of her husband's life and his home.

'Believe me, I don't mean this as a punishment. I hope I'm not that foolish,' the older man framed heavily. 'But it's obvious that I've indulged and spoilt you to a degree where you care nothing for the feelings of other people—'

'That's not true…' Lizzie was devastated by that tough assessment.

'I'm afraid it is. Making you go out into the world and stand on your own feet may well be the kindest thing I can do for you. There'll be no more swanning about at charity functions in the latest fashions, kidding yourself on that that's real work—'

'But I—'

'—and after the manner of Connor's death, who is likely to invite you to talk about generosity towards those less fortunate?' Maurice enquired with withering bite. 'Your very presence at a charity event would make most right-thinking people feel nauseous!'

As the phone on the desk rang, Lizzie flinched. Her father reached for it and gave her a brusque nod of finality, spelling out the message that their meeting was at an end. The distaste he could barely hide from her, the angry shame in his gaze cut her to the bone. She stumbled out into the hall and made her way back to the sanctuary of her apartment, which lay behind the main house in what had once been the stable block.

For a while, Lizzie was just numb with shock. Over the past ten days, shock had piled on shock until it almost sent her screaming mad. Yet only a fortnight ago, she had been about to break the news of the fabulous surprise holiday in Bali she had booked for Connor's birthday. She had not even managed to cancel that booking, she acknowledged dimly, must have lost every penny of its considerable cost. But then when had she ever had to worry about money? Or running up bills on her credit card because she had overrun her monthly allowance? Now, all those bills would have to be paid...

But what did that matter when she had lost the man she had loved to her own stepmother? Sweet, gushy little Felicity, who was so wet she made a pond look dry. Yet Felicity, it seemed, had also been the love of Connor's life and, finally rejected by her, he had gone off the rails.

'I didn't mean it to happen...I couldn't help myself!' Connor had proclaimed, seemingly impervious to the consequences of the appalling betrayal he had inflicted on Lizzie. The guy she had believed was her best friend ever, maybe even her future husband, and all the time he'd just been using her as a convenient cover for his rampant affair with her stepmother—the whiny, weepy Felicity! A great, gulping sob racked Lizzie's tall, slender frame and she clamped a hand to her wobbling mouth. She caught an unwelcome glimpse of herself in the mirror and her bright green eyes widened as she scanned her own physical flaws. Too tall, too thin with not a shadow of Felicity's feminine, sexy curves. No wonder Connor had not once been tempted all those weeks...

And Connor? Her tummy twisted in sick response. What a ghastly price he had paid for his affair with a married woman! Connor…dead? How could she truly hate him when he was gone? And how could she still be so petty that she was feeling grateful that she had never got as far as offering her skinny body to Connor in some ludicrous romantic setting in Bali? He would have run a mile!

Mrs Baines, the housekeeper, appeared in the doorway looking the very picture of discomfiture. 'I'm afraid that your father has asked me to pack for you.'

'Oh…' In the unkind mirror, Lizzie watched all her freckles stand out in stark contrast to her pallor before striving to pin an unconcerned expression to her face to lessen the older woman's unease. 'Don't worry about it. I'm all grown now and I'll survive.'

'But putting you out of your home is *wrong*,' Mrs Baines stated with a sharp conviction that startled Lizzie, for, although the housekeeper had worked for the Dentons for years, she rarely engaged in conversation that did not relate to her work and had certainly never before criticised her employer.

'This is just a family squabble.' Lizzie gave an awkward shrug, touched to be in receipt of such unexpected support but embarrassed by it as well. 'I…I'm going for a shower.'

Closeted in the bathroom, she frowned momentarily at the thought of that surprising exchange with Mrs Baines before she stabbed buttons on her mobile and called Jen, her closest remaining female friend. 'Jen?' she asked with forced brightness when the vivacious blonde answered. 'Could you stand a lodger for a couple of days? Dad's throwing me out!'

'Are you jossing me?'

'No, talking straight. Right at this very moment, our housekeeper is packing for me—'

'With your wardrobe…I mean, you *are* the original shop-till-you-drop girl; she'll still be packing at dawn!' Jen giggled. 'Come on over. We can go out and drown your sorrows together tonight.'

At that suggestion, Lizzie grimaced. 'I'm not in a party mood—'

'Take it from me, you *need* to party. Stick your nose in the air and face down the cameras and the pious types. There, but for the grace of God, go I!' Jen exclaimed with warming heat only to spoil it by continuing with graphic tactlessness, 'You ditched the guy…you were only with him a few months, like how does that make *you* responsible for him getting drunk and smashing himself up in his car?'

Lizzie flinched and reflected that Jen's easy hospitality would come with a price tag attached. But then, where else could she go in the short term? People had stopped calling her once the supposed truth of Connor's 'accident' had been leaked by his friends. She just needed a little space to sort out her life and, with the current state of her finances, checking into a hotel would not be a good idea. Maybe Jen, whose shallowness was legendary, would cheer her up. Maybe a night out on the town would lift her out of her growing sense of shellshocked despair.

'Work?' Jen said it as if it was a dirty word and surveyed Lizzie with rounded eyes of disbelief as she led the way into a bedroom mercifully large enough to hold seven suitcases and still leave space to walk around the bed. '*You…work?* What at? Stay with me until your father calms down. Just like me, you were raised to be useless and decorative and eventually become a wife, so let's face it, it's hardly your fault.'

'I'm going to stand on my own feet…just as Dad said,' Lizzie pronounced with a stubborn lift of her chin. 'I want to prove that I'm not spoilt and indulged—'

'But you *are*. You've never done a proper day's work in your life!' A small, voluptuous blonde, Jen was never seen with less than four layers of mascara enhancing her sherry-brown eyes. 'If you take a job, when would you find the time to have your hair and nails done? Or meet up with your friends for three-hour lunches or even take off at a moment's notice for a week on a tropical beach? I mean, it would be *gruesome* for you.'

Faced with those realities, it truly did sound a gruesome prospect to Lizzie too, although she was somewhat resentful of her companion's assertion that she had *never* worked. She had done a lot of unpaid PR work for charities and had proved brilliant at parting the seriously wealthy from their bundles of cash with stories of suffering that touched the hardest hearts. She had sat on several committees to organise events and, well, *sat* there, the ultimate authority on how to make a campaign look cool for the benefit of those to whom such matters loomed large. But nine-to-five work hours, following orders given by other people for some pocket-change wage, no, she hadn't ever done that. However, that didn't mean that she *couldn't*…

Four hours later, Lizzie was no longer feeling quite so feisty. Whisked off to the latest 'in' club, Lizzie found herself seated only two tables from a large party of former friends set on shooting her filthy looks. She was wearing an outfit that had been an impulse buy and a mistake and, in addition, Jen had been quite short with her when she had had only two alcoholic drinks before trying to order her usual orange juice. Reluctant to offend the blonde, who felt just then like her only friend in the world, Lizzie was now drinking more vodka.

'When my girlfriends won't drink with me, I feel like they're acting superior,' Jen confessed with a forgiving grin and then threw back a Tequila Sunrise much faster than it could have been poured.

When Jen went off to speak to someone, Lizzie went to the cloakroom. Standing at the mirrors, she regretted having allowed Jen to persuade her to wear the white halter top and

short skirt. She felt too exposed yet she often bought daring
outfits even though she never actually wore them. While she
was wondering why that was so, she overheard the chatter
of familiar female voices.

'I just can't *believe* Lizzie had the nerve to show herself
here tonight!'

'But it does prove what a heartless, self-centred little—'

'Tom's warning Jen that if she stays friendly with
Lizzie, she's likely to find herself out on her own with *only*
Lizzie!'

'How could she have treated Connor that way? He was so
much fun, so kind…'

Lizzie fled with hot, prickling tears standing out in her
shaken eyes. Returning to her table, she drained her glass
without even tasting the contents. Those female voices had
belonged to her friends. One of them had even gone to school
with her. *Ex-friends.* All of a sudden everybody hated her, yet
only weeks ago she had had so many invitations out she
would have needed a clone of herself to attend every event.
Now she wanted to bolt for the exit and go home. But she
wasn't welcome at home any more and Jen would be furious
if she tried to end the evening early.

Yes, Connor had seemed kind. At least, she had thought
so too until she went down to the Denton country cottage and
found Connor in bed with Felicity. Her skin turned cold and
clammy at that tormenting memory.

She had been thinking about inviting a bunch of friends
to the cottage for the weekend. Believing that the property
had been little used in recent times, she had decided to check
out that there would be sufficient bedding. Connor must have
come down from London in her stepmother's car and it had
been parked out of sight behind the garage, so Lizzie had had
no warning that the cottage was occupied. She had been in
a lovely, bubbly mood, picturing how amazed Connor would

be when she told him that he would be spending his twenty-fifth birthday in Bali.

Lizzie had been on the stairs when she heard the funny noises: a sort of rustling and moaning that had sent a momentary chill down her spine. But even at that stage she had not, in her ignorance, suspected that what she was hearing was a man and a woman making love. Blithely assuming that it was only the wind getting in through a window that had been left open, she had gone right on up. From the landing, she had got a full Technicolor view of her boyfriend and her stepmother rolling about the pine four-poster bed in the main bedroom.

Felicity had been in the throes of what had looked more like agony than ecstasy. Connor had been gasping for breath in between telling Felicity how much he loved her and how he couldn't bear to think that it would be another week before he could see her again. Throughout that exchange, Lizzie had been frozen to the spot like a paralysed peeping Tom. When Felicity had seen her, her aghast baby-blue eyes had flooded with tears, making her look more than ever like a victim in the guise of a fairytale princess.

But then crying was an art form and a way of life for her stepmother, Lizzie reflected, striving valiantly to suppress the wounding images she had allowed to surge up from her subconscious. Felicity wept if dinner was less than perfect… 'It's my fault…it's my fault,' she would fuss until Maurice Denton was on his knees and promising her a week in Paris to recover from the trauma of it. In much the same way and with just as much sincere feeling she had wept when Lizzie found her in bed with Connor Morgan. Tears had dripped from her like rain but her nose hadn't turned red and her eyes hadn't swelled up pink.

When Lizzie cried, it was noisy and messy and her skin turned blotchy. That afternoon, Connor and Felicity had enjoyed a full performance to that effect, before Lizzie's pride came to the rescue and she told them to get out of the cottage. After they had departed, she had made a bonfire of their bedding in the back garden. Recalling that rather pointless exercise, she forced herself upright with an equally forced smile when Jen urged her up to dance.

Up on the overhanging wrought-iron gallery above, Sebasten was scanning the crowds below while the club manager gushed by his side, 'I recognised the Denton girl when she arrived. She looks a right little goer…'

Derisive distaste lit Sebasten's brooding gaze. The very fact that Lisa Denton was out clubbing only forty-eight hours after the funeral told him *all* he needed to know about the woman who had trashed Connor's life.

'Although *little* wouldn't be the operative word,' the older man chuckled. 'She's a big girl…not even that pretty; wouldn't be my style anyway.'

His companion's inappropriate tone of prurience gritted Sebasten's even white teeth. Beyond the fact that he had a very definite need to put a face to the name, he had no other immediate motive for seeking out Lisa Denton. She would pay for what she had done to Connor but Sebasten never acted in reckless haste and invariably employed the most subtle means of retribution against those who injured him.

At that point, his attention was ensnared by the slender woman spinning below the lights on the dance floor below, long hair the colour of marmalade splaying in a sea of amber luxuriance around her bare shoulders. She flung her head back with the kind of suggestive abandonment that fired a leap of pure adrenalin in Sebasten. Every muscle in his big, powerful length snapped taut when he saw her face: the exotic slant of her cheekbones below big, faraway eyes and a lush, full-lipped pink mouth. Her beauty was distinctive, unusual. Her white halter-neck top glittered above a sleek, smooth midriff and she sported a skirt the tantalising width of a belt above lithe, shapely legs that were at least three feet long. Bloody gorgeous, Sebasten decided, sticking out an expectant hand for the drink he had ordered and receiving it while contemplating that face and those legs and every visible inch that lay between with unashamed lust and wholly dishonourable intentions. Tonight, he would *not* be sleeping alone…

'That's *her*…the blonde…'

Recalled to the thorny question of Lisa Denton by his companion's pointing hand, Sebasten looked to one side of *his* racy lady with the marmalade hair and, seeing a small blonde with the apparent cleavage of the Grand Canyon, understood why the manager had referred to his quarry as a big girl. So *that* was the nasty little piece of work whom Connor had lost his head over. Sebasten was not impressed but then he hadn't wanted or expected to be.

On the dance floor below, Jen touched Lizzie's shoulder to attract her attention. Only then did Sebasten appreciate that the two women knew each other and he frowned, for such a close connection could prove to be a complication. It was predictable that within the space of ten seconds Sebasten had worked out how that acquaintance might even benefit his purpose.

Jen reached the table she had been seated at with Lizzie first and then turned with compressed lips. 'I've been thinking that…well, perhaps it's not such a good idea for you to stay with me…'

Remembering the dialogue that she had overheard in the cloakroom, Lizzie felt her heart sink. 'Has someone been getting at you?'

'Let's be cool about this,' Jen urged with a brittle smile. 'I have every sympathy for the situation you're in right now but I have to think of myself too and I don't want to—'

'Get the same treatment?' Lizzie slotted in.

Jen nodded, grateful that Lizzie had grasped the point so fast. 'You should just go to a hotel and keep your head down for a while. You can pick up your things tomorrow. By this time next week, everybody will have found something other than Connor to get wound up about.'

And with that unlikely forecast, Jen walked without hesitation into the enemy camp two tables away and sat down with the crowd, who had been ignoring Lizzie all evening. For an awful instant, Lizzie was terrified that she was going to break down and sob like a little baby in front of them all. Whirling round, she pushed her way back onto the crowded dance floor, where at least she was out of view.

It was an effort to think straight and then she stopped trying, just sank into the music and gave herself up to the pounding beat. Her troubled, tearful gaze strayed to the male poised on the wrought-iron stairs that led down from the upper gallery and for no reason that she could fathom she fell still again. He was tall, black-haired and possessed of so striking a degree of sleek, dark good looks that the unattached women near by were focusing their every provocative move on him and even the attached ones were stealing cunning glances past their partners and weighing their chances.

He looked like a child in a toy shop: spoilt for choice while he accepted all those admiring female stares as his due. He was also the kind of guy who never looked twice at Lizzie except to lech over her legs and then wince at her flat chest and her freckles when he finally dragged his Neanderthal, over-sexed gaze up that high. Story of my life, Lizzie conceded. An over-emotional sob tugged at her throat as self-pity demolished a momentarily entrancing fantasy of said guy making a beeline for her and thoroughly sickening Jen and her cohort of non-wellwishers.

Ashamed of her own emotional weakness, Lizzie headed for the bar, for want of anything better to do.

A hand suddenly closed over hers, startling her. 'Let me…' a dark, deep, sinfully rich drawl murmured in her ear.

Let him…*what*? Flipping round, Lizzie had the rare experience of having to tilt her head back to look up at a man. She encountered stunning dark golden eyes and stopped breathing, frozen in her tracks by shock. It was the guy from the stairs and close to he was even more spectacular than he had looked at a distance, not to mention being very much taller than she had imagined. Male too, very, *very* male, was the only other description she could come up with as she simply stared up at him.

Beneath her astonished scrutiny, he snapped long brown fingers, tilted his arrogant dark head back to address someone out of view and then began to walk her away from the crush at the bar again.

'I've got freckles…' Lizzie mumbled in case he hadn't noticed.

'I shall look forward to counting them.' He flashed her the kind of smile that carried a thousand megawatts of sheer masculine charisma and her heart, her *dead* and battered heart, leapt in her chest as though she had been kicked by an electrical charge.

'You *like* freckles?'

'Ask me tomorrow,' Sebasten purred with husky amusement.

CHAPTER TWO

AS SEBASTEN approached the table where Lizzie had been seated, his bodyguards, who Lizzie assumed were bouncers, shifted the people about to take it over with scant ceremony. Two waiters then appeared at speed to clear the empty glasses.

Watching that ruthless little display of power being played out before her, Lizzie blinked in surprise. Was he the manager or the owner of the club? Who else could he be? The bar was heaving with a crush of bodies but the bouncer types only had to signal to receive a tray of drinks while others less influential fumed.

Looking across the table as her companion folded down with athletic grace into a seat, Lizzie still found herself staring: he was just *so* breathtaking. His lean, bronzed features were framed with high cheekbones, a narrow-bridged classic nose and a stubborn jawline. He had the kind of striking bone structure that would impress even when he was old. Luxuriant black hair curled back from his forehead above strong, well-marked brows, his brilliant, deep-set dark eyes framed by thick black lashes. Her heart hammered when he smiled at her again but she could not shake the lowering sensation that his choice of her with her less obvious attractions was a startling and inexplicable event.

'I'm Sebasten,' Sebasten drawled, cool as glass. 'Sebasten Contaxis.'

His name meant nothing to Lizzie but, as what she had already seen suggested that she *ought* to recognise the name, she nodded as if she had already recognised him and, having finally picked up on the sexy, rasping timbre of his accent, said, 'I'm Lizzie…you're not from London—er—originally, are you?'

Taking that as a case of stating the obvious with irony, Sebasten laughed. 'Hardly, but I'm very fond of this city, Lizzie? Short for? The obvious?'

'Yes, after my mother…it's what my family and closest friends call me.' As Lizzie met the concentrated effect of those spectacular dark golden eyes, a *frisson* of feverish tension not unlaced with alarm seized her: he was not the sort of straightforward, safe male she was usually drawn to. There was danger in the aura of arrogant expectation he emanated, in the tough strength of purpose etched in that lean, dark, handsome face. But perhaps the greatest threat of all lay in the undeniable sizzle of the sexual signals in that smouldering gaze of his.

'I take it that you saw at one glance that we were likely to be close,' he said in a teasing undertone that sent a potent little shiver down her taut spine.

Her breath snarled up in her throat. Caution urged her to slap him down but she didn't want him to walk away, could not, at that instant, think of clever enough words with which to gracefully spell out the reality that she was not into casual intimacy on short acquaintance. But for the first time in her life, Lizzie realised that she was seriously *tempted* and that shook her.

In surprise, Sebasten watched the hot colour climb in her cheeks so that the freckles all merged, the sudden downward dip of her eyes as she tilted her head to one side in an eva-

sive move that was more awkward than elegant. For a moment, in spite of her sophisticated, provocative appearance,
she looked young, *very* young and vulnerable.

'Smile…' he commanded, suddenly wondering what age
she was.

And her generous mouth curved up as if she couldn't help
herself in an entirely natural but rather embarrassed grin that
had so much genuine appeal that Sebasten was entrapped by
the surprise of it. 'I'm not the best company tonight,' she told
him in a tone of earnest apology.

Sebasten rose in one fluid movement to his full height and
extended a hand. 'Let's dance…'

As Lizzie got up she caught a glimpse of the staring faces
at that table of ex-friends that she had been avoiding all evening and she threw her head back, squaring her taut bare
shoulders. It felt good to be seen with a presentable male,
rather than being alone and an object of scornful pity.

Just as it had once felt good to be with Connor? Lizzie
snatched in a sharp gasp of air, painfully aware that Connor
had smashed her confidence to pieces. She had thought that
he was as straight and honest as she was herself. When he
had made no attempt to go beyond the occasional kiss, she
had believed his plea that he *respected* her and wanted to get
to know her better. In retrospect that made her feel such an
utter and naïve fool, for his restraint had encouraged her to
make all sorts of foolish assumptions, not least the belief that
he was really serious about her. When she was forced to face
the awful truth that Connor had instead been sleeping with
her much more beautiful stepmother, she had been devastated
by her own trusting stupidity.

A strong arm curved round Lizzie and tugged her close in
a smooth move that brought her into glancing collision with
Sebasten's lean, muscular length. A shockwave of heated response slivered through her quivering body.

'What age are you?' Sebasten demanded, an aggressive edge to his deep, dark drawl, for he had seen the distant look in her eyes and he was unaccustomed to a woman focusing on anything other than him.

Putting that tone down to the challenge of competing against the backdrop of the pounding music, Lizzie told him, 'Twenty-two…'

'Taken?' Sebasten prompted, a primal possessiveness scything up through him at the sudden thought that she might well be involved with some other man and that that was the most likely explanation for her total lack of flirtatiousness.

He was holding her close on a floor packed with people all dancing apart but as Lizzie looked up into his burnished lion-gold eyes she was only aware of the mad racing of her own heartbeat and the quite unfamiliar curl of heat surging up inside her.

'Taken?' she queried, forced to curve her hands round his wide shoulders to rise on tiptoe so that he could hear her above the music.

Indifferent to the watchers around them, Sebasten linked his other arm round her slender, trembling length as well, fierce satisfaction firming his expressive mouth as he felt the tiny little responsive quivers of her body against his. 'It doesn't matter. You're going to be mine…'

And with that far-reaching assurance, retaining an arm at the base of her spine, Sebasten turned her round and headed her up the wrought-iron staircase.

You're going to be mine. Men didn't as a rule address such comments to Lizzie and normally such an arrogant assumption would simply have made her giggle. She got on well with men but few seemed to see her as a likely object of desire and her male friends often treated her like a big sister. Perhaps it was because she towered over most of them, was usually more blunt than subtle and never coy and was invariably the first to offer a shoulder to cry on. Until Connor, her relationships had been low-key, more friendly than anything else, drifting to a halt without any great grief on either side. Until Connor, she had not known what it was to feel ripped apart with inadequacy, pain and humiliation. Sebasten—and she had already forgotten his surname—was just what her squashed ego needed most, Lizzie told herself fiercely.

He took her up to the VIP room, the privilege of only a chosen few, and her conviction that he owned the club increased as she spread a bemused glance over the opulence of the luxurious leather sofas, the soft, expensive carpet and the private bar in the corner.

'We can hear ourselves think up here,' Sebasten pointed out with perfect truth.

Lizzie stared at him, for the first time appreciating that his more formal mode of dress had picked him out as much as his looks and height. His superb grey suit had the subtle sheen of silk and the tailored perfection of designer-cut elegance.

'Do you own this place?' she asked.

'No.' Sebasten glanced at her in surprise.

'Then who are you that you get so much attention here?' Lizzie enquired helplessly.

'You don't know?' Amusement slashed Sebasten's lean, bronzed features, for not being recognised and known for who and what he was a novel experience for him. 'I'm a businessman.'

'I don't read the business sections of the newspapers,' Lizzie confided with palpable discomfiture.

'Why should you?'

Lizzie coloured. 'I don't want you thinking I'm an airhead.'

A tough, self-made man, her father had refused to let her

take any interest in the family construction firm. As a teenager she had told him that she wanted to study for a business degree so that she could come and work for him and Maurice Denton had hurt her by laughing out loud at the idea. But then, that he had done well enough in the world to maintain his daughter as a lady of leisure had *once* been a source of considerable pride to him.

'I think you're beautiful…especially when you blush and all your freckles merge,' Sebasten mocked.

'Stop it…' Lizzie groaned, covering her hot face with spread hands in reproach.

He lifted a glass from the bar counter and she lowered one hand to grasp it, green eyes wide with fascination on his lean, strong face. Did he *really* think she was beautiful? She so much wanted to believe he was sincere, for she was more used to being told she was great fun and a good sport. Her fingers tightened round the tumbler and she drank even though her head was already swimming.

'Very beautiful and *very* quiet,' Sebasten pronounced.

'Guys like talking about themselves…I'm a good listener,' Lizzie quipped. 'So what was the most exciting event of your week?'

Sleek black lashes lowered to partially screen his shimmering dark eyes. 'Something someone said to me after a funeral.'

Lizzie's soft lips parted in surprise and then sealed again.

'Connor Morgan's funeral…' Sebasten let the announcement hang there and watched her tense and lose her warm colour with quiet approval. He was no fan of cold-hearted women and her obvious sensitivity pleased him. 'Did you know him?'

Lizzie's tummy muscles were tight as a drum but she kept her head high and muttered unevenly. 'I'm afraid that I never got to know him very well…'

It *was* true: she had barely scratched the surface of Connor's true nature, had been content to accept the surface show of the younger man's extrovert personality, had never once dreamt that he might lie to her and cheat on her without an ounce of remorse.

'Neither did I...' Sebasten's dark, deep drawl sent an odd chill down her spine.

'Let's not talk about it...' Taut with guilty anxiety over the near-lie she had told, Lizzie wondered if he was aware of the rumours and if he would have approached her had he known of her previous connection with Connor.

Aware he ought to be probing for some first-hand information on the voluptuous little blonde who had ditched his half-brother, Sebasten studied Lizzie's taut profile. However, his attention roamed of its own seeming volition down over her long, elegant neck to the tiny pulse beating out her tension beneath her collarbone and from there to the delicate curve of her breasts. By that point, his concentration had been engulfed by more libidinous promptings. Below the fine fabric, her nipples were taut and prominent as ripe berries and the dull, heavy ache at Sebasten's groin intensified with sudden savage force. Without hesitation, he swept the glass from her grasp and reached for her.

As she was sprung with a vengeance from her introspection, Lizzie's bemused gaze clashed with his and the scorching heat of his appraisal. She trembled, her body racing without warning to a breathless high of tension. Excitement, naked excitement flared through her, filling her with surprise and confusion. Dry-mouthed, pulses jumping, knees shaking, she felt his hand slide from her spine to the fuller curve of her behind and splay there to pull her close. She shivered in contact with the lean, tight hardness of his muscular thighs, every inch of her own flesh suddenly so sensitive she was bewildered, embarrassed, *shocked*.

'This feels good...' Sebasten husked, revelling in the way she couldn't hide her response to him. He could feel every little quiver assailing her, recognise the hoarseness of the breath she snatched in, read the bright luminosity of her dilated pupils and the full enticement of her parted lips.

'I hardly know you.' Lizzie was talking to herself more than she was talking to him. But that attempt to reinstate her usual caution didn't work. Being that close to him felt like perching at the very top of a rollercoaster a nanosecond before the breathtaking thrill of sudden descent and she was incapable of denying herself the seductive promise of that experience.

'I'll teach you to know me...' Sebasten framed with thickened emphasis, the smouldering glitter of his pagan golden eyes fixed to her with laser force. 'I'll teach you everything you need to know.'

'I like to go slow...'

'I like to go fast,' Sebasten imparted without hesitation, letting a lean brown hand rise to stroke through a long silken strand of her amber-coloured hair before moving to trace the tremulous line of her mouth with a confident fingertip. 'So fast I'll leave you breathless and hungry for more.'

Mesmerised, her very lips tingling from his light touch, Lizzie couldn't think straight. He might have been talking a foreign language, for right at that instant her leaping hormones were doing all of her thinking for her. She just wanted him to kiss her. In fact, she was so desperate to have that wide, sensual mouth on hers that she had to clench her hands to prevent herself from reaching for him first and, since she had never felt anything quite like that shameless craving before, it felt as unreal as a dream.

But when his mouth found hers, teased at her tender lips with a series of sensual little nips and tantalising expertise, no dream had ever lit such a powder-keg of response in

Lizzie. Suddenly she was pushing forward into the hard, muscular contours of his powerful frame, hands flying up to link round his neck to steady her wobbling knees and from deep in her own throat a tiny moaning, pleading sound emerged as frustration at his teasing built to an unbearable degree.

He reacted then with a hungry, satisfying urgency that pierced her quivering length with the efficacy of a burning arrow thudding into a willing target. Suddenly he gave her exactly what she had wanted without even knowing it. As he drove her lips apart in a devastating assault of erotic intensity, her very skin-cell seemed to spontaneously combust in the whoosh of passion that shockwaved through her. Her own excitement was as intoxicating as a drug and all the more dangerous because raw excitement in a man's arms was new to her.

'Theos mou,' Sebasten groaned as he lifted his arrogant dark head. 'You're blowing me away…'

Bereft of his mouth on hers, Lizzie blinked in confusion. Only then conscious of the urgent tightness of her nipples and the pulsing ache between her thighs, she was surprised by the painful effect of both sensations. Her body didn't feel like her own any more. Her body was sending out frantic signals that the only place it was happy was up against *him*.

Sebasten flipped her round, curved her back to him again and let his hands glance over the pointed invitation of her sweet breasts, feeling her jerk and shiver and gasp as though she was in the eye of a storm. He eyed the nearest sofa. He didn't want to wait. He wanted her here, now, fast and hard to ease the nagging throb of his aroused sex. Sleazy, his mind told him while his defiant and fertile imagination threw up various explicit scenarios that threatened that conviction. No, he preferred to take her home to his own bed, where he could take his time, and he already knew once wouldn't be enough.

On fire from sensation, Lizzie broke free of him and dragged in a great gulp of oxygen. It was an effort to walk in a straight line to the table where he had set her drink. Lifting it with a shaking hand, she tipped it to her swollen lips, needing to occupy herself while she came to terms with the amazing feelings gripping her. She wanted to know everything about him from the minute he was born. She wanted to know him as nobody else had ever known him and a crazy singing happiness filled her when she looked back at him over the rim of her glass.

'I've never felt like this before,' she whispered with an edgy laugh that screened her discomfiture.

'I don't want to hear about how it felt with anyone else.' Burning golden eyes slammed into hers and he extended a commanding hand. 'Let's go…'

Lizzie moved and let him engulf her fingers in his. 'Are you always this bossy?'

'Where did you get that idea?' Sebasten purred like a very large and amused jungle cat because she had just leapt to do as he asked without even thinking about it. But then women always did. In his entire adult life, Sebasten had never met a woman who was *not* eager to please him.

He swept her back down the stairs, past a welter of curious eyes and on towards the exit. Her nerves were jumping like electrified beans. She relived the bold caress of his sure hands over her breasts and her cheeks flooded with hot self-conscious colour. Not the sort of familiarity she normally allowed. What was she doing with him? Where on earth was he taking her? *He* thought she was beautiful. *He* wanted to be with her, she reminded herself with feverish determination. Nobody else did, not her father, who had cut her out of his life, not a single one of her friends.

On the wet pavement outside, a uniformed chauffeur extended an umbrella for their protection and hurried to open the door of a long, opulent silver limousine. Lizzie was impressed and she got in, refused to think about what she was doing and turned to look at Sebasten again. The dizzy sense of rightness that had engulfed her only minutes earlier returned. 'Where were you born?' she heard herself ask.

In the act of tugging her close, Sebasten grinned at what struck him as an essentially feminine and pointless question. 'On an island the size of a postage stamp in the Aegean Sea…and you?'

'In Devon,' she confided, heart skipping a beat over that incredible smile of his. 'My parents moved to London when I was a baby.'

'How fascinating,' Sebasten teased, lacing his fingers into her hair and kissing her. She drowned in the scent and the taste of him, head falling back on her shoulders as his tongue darted in an erotic sweep between her lips and made her gasp with helpless pleasure.

At some point, they left the limo, climbed steps, traversed a low-lit echoing hall, but true awareness only returned to Lizzie when she swayed giddily on the sweeping staircase she found herself on. His hands shot out to steady her. 'Are you OK?'

'These stupid shoes…' Lizzie condemned in mortification and she kicked off her spike-heeled sandals where she stood as though her unsteady gait had been caused by them.

'How much have you had to drink?' Sebasten enquired with lethal timing, a dark frown-line forming between his ebony brows.

'Hardly anything,' Lizzie told him breathlessly while making a conscious effort not to slur her words. She was taut as a bowstring, suddenly terrified of receiving yet another rejection to add to the many she had already withstood.

As he received that assurance Sebasten's tension evaporated and he swept her on into a massive, opulent room rejoicing in a very large and imposing bed. She was jolted by the sight of the bed and a rather belated stab of dismay made her question her own behaviour. She barely knew Sebasten and she was still a virgin. But then she had never been tempted until she met Connor and she had expected *him* to become her first lover. As the degrading memory of finding her boyfriend and her stepmother in bed together engulfed Lizzie afresh, she rebelled against her own moral conditioning. After all, hadn't her old-fashioned principles let her down badly when it came to men? A more experienced woman would have been suspicious of Connor's lack of lusty intent.

Eyes flaring like emerald-green stars on that bitter acknowledgement, Lizzie spun round and feasted her attention on Sebasten. He was gorgeous and tonight he was hers, *all* hers, absolutely nobody else's. She had never met anyone like him before. He was so focused, so sure of himself that he drew her like a magnet and the heat of his appreciative appraisal warmed her like the sun after weeks of endless rain.

Lizzie tilted her head back, glossy marmalade hair tumbling back from her slanted cheekbones. 'You can kiss me again,' she informed him.

With an appreciative laugh, Sebasten claimed her parted lips in a long, drugging kiss that rocked her on her feet. Lifting her up into his arms with easy strength, he brought her down onto his bed. What was it about her that made her seem so different to other women? One minute she was quiet and mysterious, the next tossing an open challenge, glorious green eyes telegraphing pure invitation.

Lizzie surfaced from the mindless spell of her own response and stared up at him. 'Are you as good at everything else as you are at kissing?'

Sebasten tossed his jacket on a chair, enjoying the wide,

wondering look in her face as she watched him. 'What do you think?'

That she could barely breathe when those shimmering dark golden eyes rested on her and her mouth ran dry as a bone when he unbuttoned his shirt. From his broad shoulders to his powerful, hair-roughened pectorals and flat, taut abdomen, he was all sleek, bronzed skin and rippling muscles.

'That you're very sexy,' Lizzie confided helplessly.

'We match…' Sebasten strolled lithe as a hunting animal and barefoot towards the bed.

'Do we?' Her heart hammered behind her ribs. She felt like an infatuated teenager confronted without warning by her idol: butterflies in her tummy, brain empty, teeth almost chattering with nerves. Every lingering strand of caution was urging her to acknowledge her mistake and take flight but those prudent promptings fell into abeyance at the same instant as Sebasten rested shimmering dark golden eyes of appreciation on her.

'*Ne*…'

'No?' Lizzie was confused.

'*Ne*…is Greek for yes.' Sebasten came down on the side of the bed with a smile that lit up his lean, strong face and melted her.

'You're Greek?'

'Ten out of ten,' Sebasten gathered her close and threaded lazy hands through her tumbling mane. '*I love* the colour of your hair…but I still don't know your surname.'

In the expectant silence, Lizzie tensed. Fearful of his reaction were he to recognise the name of Denton, she heard herself quote her late mother's maiden name. 'Bewford.'

'Now I can't lose you again,' Sebasten asserted.

'Would it matter if you did?' Heart racing so fast now that she could barely speak and keep her voice level, Lizzie curved an uncertain hand round his arm.

'Absolutely, *pethi mou*.' Sebasten reflected that he might even make it to the three-month mark with her, a milestone he had yet to share with any woman. Unsettled by that uninvited and odd thought, he kissed her again.

He made love to her mouth with devastating virtuosity, plundering the tender interior she opened to him. Lizzie pressed forward, unsteady hands linking round his neck, fingers uncoiling to rise and sink into the depths of his luxuriant black hair. It was sweeter and wilder and more intense than anything she had ever known. He bent her back over his arm so that her bright hair trailed across the pillows and let his lips seek out the tiny pulse going crazy beneath her collarbone.

Lizzie quivered in surprise and what little grip she had left on reality vanished. When he then located the tender pulse spot below her ear, her body thrummed into a burst of life so that not one part of her was capable of staying still. She was not even conscious of the deft unsnapping of the clasps on her halter top, only of the air grazing her distended nipples and cooling the swollen sensitivity of her flesh. He eased off her stretchy skirt to leave her clad in only a pair of white lace panties.

'You're perfect,' Sebasten groaned, cupping the ivory-pale rose-tipped mounds he had unveiled with possessive hands, easing her back against the pillows to direct his attention to the tender tips straining for his attention.

Capturing a throbbing peak between his lips, he flicked it with his tongue and she moaned out loud at the surge of tormenting sensation that made her tense and tremble and jerk beneath his ministrations. Nothing before had ever felt so good that it almost hurt and she was lost in the shocking intensity of her own response. She was breathing in fast little pants, aware of her body as she had never been before, feeling the charged readiness of wild anticipation, the crazed race of her own pounding heartbeat, the damp heat pulsing between her thighs.

'Talk to me…' Sebasten urged.

'I…can't find…my voice,' Lizzie tried to say after a bemused hesitation in which she had to struggle just to force her brain to think again. Even to her own ears, the words emerged sounding indistinguishable and slurred.

Sebasten stilled and, scanning her dismayed face, he removed his hands from her. 'You're drunk…'

As that harsh judgement came out of nowhere at her, Lizzie flinched. Bracing herself on one awkward hand, she sat up. His lean, powerful face was taut, stunning golden eyes betraying angry distaste.

'I'm—'

'Out of your skull on booze…*not* my style!' Sebasten incised, springing upright to his full intimidating height.

Dragged with little warning from the breathtaking hold of unbelievable passion, Lizzie found herself in need of a ready tongue. But there was nothing ready about her tongue when her brain was in a haze of confusion. 'Not your style?' she echoed.

It was a terrible strain for her to try to enunciate each word with clarity. She reeled off the bed in an abrupt movement, suddenly feeling horribly naked and under attack.

As he watched her stagger as she attempted to stay vertical Sebasten's wide, sensual mouth clenched even harder, his whole body in the fierce grip of painful frustration while he questioned how he could possibly have failed to register the state she was in. 'The consent issue,' he breathed with icy restraint. 'No way would I even consider bedding a woman too inebriated to know what she is doing!'

Her toes catching in her discarded skirt where it lay, Lizzie tipped forward and only just managed to throw out her hands to break her own fall. As she went down with a crash, punctuated by a startled expletive from Sebasten, she just slumped on the soft, deep carpet.

With a mighty effort of will, Lizzie lifted her swimming head again and focused on Sebasten's bare brown feet. Even his toes were beautiful, she thought dimly as she tried to come up with something to say in a situation that had already gone far beyond embarrassment. 'Do you think…do you think you could sober me up before we continue?' she muttered hopefully.

CHAPTER THREE

SEBASTEN surveyed Lizzie with thunderous incredulity and then he wondered what he *was* going to do with her.

After all, he was responsible for her, wasn't he? He had pressed more alcohol on her when she must already have had enough and he had brought her into his home. In the condition she was in, he could hardly stuff her into a taxi or ask his chauffeur to cope with her and, since he too had had several drinks, he could not drive her anywhere.

In the tense silence which would have agonised Lizzie had she been sober, she surveyed his carpet fibres and then looked up. Sebasten was down on one knee, contemplating her with an expression of fierce frustration.

'I could just sleep here on the floor,' Lizzie proffered, striving to be helpful.

Sebasten collided with huge green eyes.

The beginnings of an irreverent grin pulled at her full, reddened mouth because she was suffering from a dreadful urge to succumb to uncontrollable giggles. 'You see…I don't think I can get up…can't feel my legs.'

Sebasten experienced a sudden near-overwhelming desire to shake her until he could force some sense back into her head. Had she no idea how much at risk she could be in a stranger's house? Or of how dangerous it was for a woman to drink so much that she could neither exercise caution nor defend herself? The very idea of her behaving in such a way with another man filled him with dark, deep anger.

'Do you make a habit of this kind of behaviour?' he demanded rawly.

As she was assailed by that gritty tone, all desire to giggle was squashed at the source. 'No…you're the first…sorry,' Lizzie slurred, sinking back to the carpet again.

Vaulting to his feet, Sebasten strode over to the phone by the bed and lifted it to order a large pot of black coffee and sandwiches to be brought upstairs. Then he contemplated his victim with brooding intensity and his long, powerful legs carried him over to the windows. Depressing the locks, he thrust the French windows back to let in the cold night air.

As that chilly breeze touched her slender bare back, Lizzie gave a convulsive shiver. Sebasten surveyed her without remorse. He would sober her up and *then* have her conveyed home. Wrenching the top sheet from the bed, he flung it over her prone body and gathered her up with determination to carry her into the adjoining bathroom.

'Sleepy…' Lizzie mumbled.

'You need to wake up,' Sebasten informed her, settling her with some difficulty onto the seat in the spacious shower cubicle and hitting the buttons to switch on the water. Only as the water cascaded down did he appreciate that he hadn't removed the sheet. Then he no longer felt quite so comfortable with her semi-clad state.

As the water hit her, Lizzie opened bewildered and shaken eyes. 'No…don't want to be wet,' she framed weakly.

'Tough,' Sebasten told her, barring the exit in case she made a sudden leap for freedom.

Far from making a dive for it, in slow motion and wearing an only vaguely surprised expression, Lizzie slithered off the seat like a boneless doll into a heap on the floor of the cubicle.

'Up!' Sebasten urged in exasperation.

Lizzie curled up and closed her eyes, soothed now by the warm flooding flow of water. 'Sleepy,' she mumbled again. 'Night…night.'

Teeth gritted, Sebasten stepped into the shower to hit the controls and turn the water cold. She uttered a satisfying yelp of surprise as the water went from warm and soothing to icy and tingling. However, Sebasten got so wet in his efforts to haul Lizzie's uncooperative body back up onto the seat, he ended up squatting down to hold her up and suffering beneath the same cold gush.

'C-cold!' Lizzie stammered.

'I'm freezing too!' Sebasten launched, shirt and trousers plastered to his big, powerful body as the same chill invaded him. He withstood the onslaught with masochistic acceptance. Served him bloody well right, he thought grimly. She was way too young and immature for him. What had got into him? Bringing her home had been a mistake and he had never sunk low enough to take advantage of a stupid woman.

'Very…cold,' Lizzie moaned.

'And you said you weren't an airhead,' Sebasten recalled out loud with a deep sense of injustice, watching her wet hair trail in the water, looking down at her miserable face which was now—aside of the odd streak of mascara—innocent of all cosmetic enhancement. She still had perfect skin and amazing eyes, he noted. But he could not credit that he was trapped in his own shower with a drunk woman. He didn't get into awkward situations like that.

'Not,' Lizzie pronounced with unexpected aggression, her chin tilting up.

A loud knock sounded on the door in the bedroom beyond. With a groan, Sebasten put her down but she slumped without his support. A vision of having to explain a drowned woman in his shower overtaking him, he switched off the water.

'Don't move…' he instructed Lizzie as he strode back to the bedroom, dripping every step of the way.

A faint flush over his hard cheekbones as the member of staff presenting the laden tray of coffee and sandwiches stared in open stupefaction at his drenched appearance, Sebasten kicked the door shut again and set down the tray beside the bed.

When he returned to the bathroom, Lizzie was striving to crawl out of the shower on her hands and knees and being severely hampered by the trailing sopping sheet.

'Feeling a little livelier?' Sebasten quipped with dark satire.

'Feel…*a-awful*!' Lizzie stuttered through teeth chattering like castanets and she laid her head down and just sobbed in weakened rage. 'Hate you!'

She looked pathetic. Sebasten snatched up a big bath towel, crouched down to disentangle her from the sheet and wrapped her with care into the towel. Hauled up into a standing position, she fell against him like a skater on ice for the first time and he lifted her up and carried her through to the bedroom to settle her back on the bed. Keeping a cautious eye on her in case she fell off the bed too, he backed away to strip off his own wet clothing and pitch the sodden garments onto the bathroom floor.

It was like babysitting, he decided, his even white teeth gritting. Not that he had ever *done* any babysitting, for Sebasten was not in the habit of putting himself out for other people. But the comparison between his own erotic expectations earlier in the evening and reality was galling to a male who was accustomed to a life than ran with the smooth, controlled efficiency of an oiled machine.

'Close the windows…' Lizzie begged, deciding there and then as cold dragged her mind from its former fog that she had fallen live into the hands of a complete sadist.

'Yes, you're definitely waking up now.' Sheathed only in a pair of black designer jeans, Sebasten crossed the room to pull the French windows shut.

Lizzie blinked and then contrived to stare. The jeans fitted him as well as his own bronzed skin, accentuating his flat, muscular stomach, his narrow hips and long, hard thighs. Colouring, she looked away, sobered up enough already by the shock of that cold shower to cringe with mortification. Sebasten tugged her forward, tossed pillows behind her to prop her up and proceeded to pour the coffee.

'Don't feel like coffee—'

'You're drinking it,' Sebasten told her and he laid the tray of sandwiches down beside her. *'Eat.'*

'I'm not hungry,' she dared in an undertone.

'You need food to soak up the booze in your system,' Sebasten delivered with cutting emphasis.

Squirming with shame and embarrassment, Lizzie reached for a sandwich. 'I don't get drunk…I'm not like that…I just had a hideous day—'

'So you decided to give me a hideous evening,' Sebasten slotted in with ungenerous bite. 'Count your blessings—'

'What blessings?' Lizzie was fighting hard to hold back the surge of weak tears that that crack had spawned.

'You're safe and you're still all in one piece. If you'd picked the wrong guy to spring this stunt on, you might not have been,' Sebasten pointed out.

Chilled by what she recgonised as a fair assessment, Lizzie swallowed shakily and made herself bite into the sandwich. It was delicious. Indeed, she had not realised just how hungry she was until that moment. In silence, she sipped at the black coffee, wincing with every mouthful, for she liked milk in her coffee, and worked her way through the sandwiches.

Sebasten watched the sandwiches melt away and noted

that for all her slenderness she had a very healthy appetite. 'When did you last eat?' he finally asked drily.

'Breakfast,' Lizzie worked out with a slight frown and that had just been a slice of toast. Lunch she hadn't touched because just beforehand her father had phoned to say that he was coming home specially to talk to her and her appetite had vanished. As for supper, well, Jen hadn't offered her anything but her first alcoholic drink of the evening.

'No wonder you ended up flat on your face on my carpet,' Sebasten delivered as he topped up the cup she had emptied.

Lizzie paled. 'Not the world's most forgiving person, are you?'

'No.' Sebasten made no bones about the fact. 'What did your "hideous" day encompass?'

Lizzie looped unsteady fingers through her fast-drying hair to push it back from her brow and muttered tightly. 'My father told me to move out and get a job. I was *very* upset—'

'At twenty-two years of age, you were still living at home and dependent on your family?' Sebasten demanded in surprise. 'Are you a student?'

Lizzie reddened. 'No. I left school at eighteen. My father didn't *want* me to work. He said he wanted me to have a good time!'

Sebasten scanned the delicate diamond pendant and bracelet she wore, conceding that they might well be real rather than the imitations he had assumed. Yet she didn't speak with those strangulated vowel sounds that he associated with the true English upper classes, which meant that she was most probably from a family with money but no social pedigree. He was wryly amused that Ingrid, who was obsessed by a need to pigeon-hole people by their birth and their bank balance, had taught him to distinguish the old moneyed élite from the *nouveau riche* in London society.

'And, *no*…having a good time did not cover my behaviour tonight!' Lizzie advanced in defensive completion. 'That was a one-off!'

'So you were *very* upset at the prospect of having to keep yourself,' Sebasten recapped with soft derision and innate suspicion that her apparent ignorance of who he was had been an act calculated to bring his guard down. 'Is that why you came home with me?'

Startled by that offensive question, Lizzie sucked in a sudden sharp breath. As the fog of alcohol released her brain, she had already absorbed enough of her surroundings to recognise that she was in the home of a male who inhabited a very much wealthier and more rarefied world than her own. She lifted her chin. 'No, to tell you the truth, now that I'm recovering my wits, I haven't the foggiest idea *why* I came home with you because I don't like you one little bit.'

A disconcerting smile flashed across Sebasten's dark, brooding features. Angry green eyes the colour of precious emeralds were hurling defiance at him and her spine was as rigid as that of a queen in a medieval portrait. Unfortunately for her, though, her tangled hair and the bath towel supplied a ridiculous frame for that attempt to put him in his place.

The instant that incredible smile lit up his lean, strong features, Lizzie's heartbeat went haywire and her mouth ran dry and she knew exactly why she had come home with him. If he kept his smart mouth closed, he was just about irresistible.

'You're angry that you made a fool of yourself,' Sebasten retaliated without hesitation. 'But I may have done you a big favour—'

Hot colour burned in Lizzie's cheeks. 'You call throwing the windows wide and torturing me in a cold shower doing me a *favour*?'

'Yes…if the memory of that treatment stops you drinking that much again in the wrong company.'

Unused to a woman fighting with him, Sebasten savoured the sheer frustrated rage in her expressive face and his body hardened again in sudden urgent response. He wanted to flatten her back onto his bed and remind her of how irrelevant liking or anything else was when he touched her. His own reawakened desire startled him. Then her tangled torrent of hair was drying to gleam with rich gold and copper lights and that exotic and passionate face of hers still kept drawing him back. The intimate recollection of her lush little breasts and that lithe, slender body of hers shaking with hunger beneath his own was all the additional stimuli required to increase Sebasten's level of arousal to one of supreme discomfort.

In the midst of swallowing the sting of that further comment destined to humble her, Lizzie felt the burn of Sebasten's stunning dark golden eyes on her and what she had been about to say in an effort to save face died on her tongue. Stiffening, she shifted forward onto the edge of the bed. Suddenly aware of the high-voltage tension that had entered the atmosphere, she felt too jittery to handle her discomfiture and she settled her feet down onto the carpet.

'It's time I went home,' she announced but she hesitated, afraid that the awful dizziness might return the instant she tried to stand up.

'Where is home?'

'No place right now,' Lizzie admitted after a dismayed pause to appreciate the threatening reality. 'I still have to find somewhere to live. Right now my luggage is parked at a friend's place but I can't stay there.'

Sebasten watched her stand up like a newborn baby animal afraid to test her long slim legs and then breathe in slow and deep. She plotted a passage to the bathroom and vanished from view. Closing the door, she caught her own reflection in a mirror and groaned out loud, lifting a trembling hand to her messy hair. Any pretence towards presentability was long gone, she reflected painfully. It was little wonder Sebasten had been sprawled in an armchair at a distance, talking down to her as if he were a very superior being.

And she guessed he *was*, she conceded, snatching up a comb from the counter of a built-in unit to begin disentangling her hair. He could have thrown her back out on the street. He could have taken advantage of her…well, not really, she decided, reckoning that Sebasten would prefer a live, moving woman to one showing all the animation of a corpse. And he *had* prevented her from making a very big mistake! Why didn't she just admit that to herself? Her life was in a terrible mess and she shouldn't even have been looking at Sebasten, never mind behaving like a tramp and coming home with him. She ought to be really grateful that nothing much had happened between them…

Only she *wasn't*. Tears stung the back of Lizzie's eyes and she blinked them back with stubborn determination. The ghastly truth was that she still found Sebasten incredibly attractive and she had blown it. Really blown her chances with him. There was nothing fanciable or appealing about a woman who had to be dumped in a shower to be brought out of a drunken collapse, naturally he was disgusted with her. But she was much angrier with herself than he could possibly have been. She had never been so attracted to any guy and she was convinced that alcohol had had very little to do with her extraordinary reaction to him. Why had she had to meet the most gorgeous guy of her life on the one night that she made a total, inexcusable ass of herself?

Wishing that she had thought to reclaim her clothing before she entered the bathroom and embarrassed to death as stray memories of her wanton behaviour broke free of her subconscious to torment her, Lizzie crept back into the bedroom.

Dawn was beginning to finger light through the heavy curtains. She had hoped that Sebasten would have fallen asleep or taken himself tactfully off somewhere else to allow her a fast and silent exit but no such luck was hers.

Sebasten was watching the television business news but the instant the door opened he vaulted upright and studied her. Still wrapped in the towel, hair brushed back from her scrubbed-clean face, she looked even more beautiful to Sebasten than she had looked earlier. Even pale, she had a fresh, natural appeal that pulled him against his own volition.

'You might as well sleep in one of my guest rooms for what's left of the night,' Sebasten surprised himself by suggesting.

'Thanks…but I'd better be going.' Strained eyes centred on him in a look so brief he would have missed it had he not been watching her like a hawk. 'I've taken up enough of your time.'

His mouth quirked. She sounded like a little girl who had attended a very bad party but was determined to leave saying all that was polite. He watched her stoop in harried movements to snatch up her clothes and shoes, mortification merging her freckles with a hot pink overlay of colour. Her inability to conceal her embarrassment was oddly touching.

'How sober are you?' Sebasten prompted lazily, eyes flaring to smouldering gold as her lush mouth opened and the tip of her tongue snaked out in a nervous flicker to moisten her full lower lip. Hunger, fierce and primitive as a knife at his groin, burned through him.

'Totally wised up…' Lizzie tried hard to smile, acknowledging her own foolishness.

'Then *stay* with me…' Sebasten murmured thickly.

Thrown by that renewed invitation, Lizzie gazed across the room, green eyes full of surprise and confusion. 'But—'

'Of course there *are* conditions,' Sebasten warned, smooth as silk. 'With your eyes closed, you have to be able to touch the tip of your nose with one finger and you only get one chance.'

An involuntary laugh escaped Lizzie as she looked back at him. Still clad only in the jeans, he was drop-dead gorgeous: all sleek, bronzed, hair-roughened skin, lean muscle and masculinity. Even the five o'clock shadow now roughening his strong jawline only added to his sheer impact. Feeling just then that it would be more sensible to close her eyes and deny herself the pleasure of staring at him as though he had just dropped down from heaven for a visit, Lizzie strove to play the game and performed the exercise even though at that point she had every intention of leaving.

'Then you have to open your eyes again and walk in a straight line to the door,' Sebasten instructed.

Growing amusement gripping her, Lizzie set out for the door.

'Full marks,' Sebasten quipped.

Lizzie spun round. 'You've got to do it *too*.'

Disconcerted, Sebasten raised a brow in scornful dismissal of that challenge.

'You take yourself very seriously.' Lizzie watched him with keen intensity because it was one of the most important things she had learnt about him. 'You don't even like me to suggest that you might be anything less than totally in control.'

'I'm a man. That's normal,' Sebasten drawled.

Not to Lizzie, it wasn't. She was used to younger men who were more relaxed about their image and the differences between the sexes but she could see that Sebasten inhabited another category altogether. The strong, brooding, macho type unlikely to spill his guts no matter how tough the going got. Not her type at all, she told herself in urgent consolation.

Sebasten strode in a direct line to the door but only because where she was was where he wanted to be at that instant. 'Satisfied?'

'Yes…we are two sober people…and I need to go and get dressed.' Breathless at finding herself that close to him again, Lizzie coloured, heartbeat thumping at what felt like the base of her throat.

'I'll only take it all off again,' Sebasten threatened in a dark, deep undertone of warning that sent a tingle of delicious threat down her taut spine.

'Walking in a straight line to the door when you asked was just my effort to lighten the atmosphere,' Lizzie shared awkwardly.

'While every lingering look you give me tells me how much you still want me,' Sebasten delivered without an instant of hesitation.

'You've got some ego!' Lizzie condemned in disconcertion.

'*Earned*…like my reputation,' Sebasten slotted in, closing his lean, sure hands to her slender waist to tilt her forward. 'We'll conduct an experiment—'

'No…*no* experiments,' Lizzie cut in on a higher pitch of nervous stress. 'I don't *do* stuff like this, Sebasten. I don't have one-night stands. I don't sleep with guys I've only just met…in fact, I haven't got much experience at all and you'd probably find the business news more riveting—'

Sebasten recognised one of the qualities that had drawn him to her but which he had failed to identify: a certain degree of innocence. Fired by the rare event of being challenged to persuade a woman into his bed, he focused his legendary negotiating skills on Lizzie. 'I'm riveted by *you*,' Sebasten incised with decisive conviction. 'Right from the first moment I saw you at the club.'

'Stop kidding me…' Skin warming, Lizzie connected with his stunning golden eyes and trembled, wanting to believe, her battered self-esteem hungry for that reassurance. That close to him, it was difficult to breathe and the warm, clean male scent of his skin flared her nostrils with a familiarity that tugged at her every sense. She wanted to lean into him, crush the tender tips of her swollen breasts into the hard wall of his chest, feel that wide, sexy mouth ravish her own again.

'I'm not kidding. One look and I was hooked.' Sebasten gazed down at her from below the dense fringe of his black lashes and just smiled and that was the moment she was lost, that was the moment when any pretence of self-control ran aground on the sheer strength of her response to him. Her pulses racing, Lizzie felt the megawatt burn of that smile blaze through her and she angled into him in a helpless movement. When his mouth came down on hers again, the heat of that sensual assault was pure, addictive temptation.

In the midst of that kiss, Sebasten carried her back to the bed and peeled away the towel. He cupped her breasts, bent his arrogant dark head over the pale pink distended peaks and used his knowing mouth and his even more knowing hands to give her pleasure.

'Are you protected?' he asked.

'Yes…' She had started taking contraceptive pills a month after she had begun dating Connor but she crushed that unwelcome association back out of her mind again, the bitterness that had haunted her in recent weeks set behind her. A fresh start, a new and more productive life, Sebasten. She was more than ready for those challenges when Sebasten was giving her the impression that *he* felt much the same way that *she* did.

As he slid off the bed in one fluid movement to dispense with his jeans, her cheeks reddened and she turned her head away while wicked but self-conscious anticipation licked along her every nerve-ending.

He came down beside her again and she let her hands rise

up over his powerful torso. She had never really wanted to explore a man before but she could not resist her need to touch him. Her fingers roved from the satin-smooth hardness of his shoulders to graze through the short black whorls of hair hazing his pectorals to the warm tautness of his stomach, feeling his muscles flex in response.

'Don't stop there, *pethi mou*,' Sebasten husked.

Lizzie got more daring, let her fingers follow the intriguing furrow of silky black hair over his stomach and discovered the male power of him with a jolt of mingled dismay and curiosity. He was smooth and hard but there was definitely too much of him.

'*This way*,' Sebasten murmured with concealed amusement, initially startled by her clumsiness and then adapting to teach her what he liked. It was a lesson he had never had cause to give before but it sent his desire for her surging even higher.

That intimate exploration made Lizzie feel all hot and quivery and she pressed her thighs together on the disturbing ache stirring at the very heart of her. When he teased at her swollen lower lip before letting his tongue delve into the tender interior of her mouth in a darting foray that imitated a far more elemental possession she trembled against his lean, strong body, feverish hot craving gripping her.

His breathing fractured, Sebasten dragged his mouth from hers to gaze down at her with fiery golden eyes. 'I don't think I've ever been so hot for a woman as I am for you.'

He pulled her to him and his expert hands traced the beaded sensitivity of her breasts. She couldn't stay still any more. Tiny little tremors were racking her. Her breath was rasping into her dry throat, pulses thrumming, heart pounding. At the apex of her legs he traced the moist, needy secret of her femininity and she moaned out loud, couldn't help herself. The pleasure was dark and deep and terrifyingly intense. He controlled her and she didn't care; she just didn't want him to stop. The bitter-sweet torment of sensation sizzled through every fibre of her writhing body with increasing intensity until she was on the edge of a desperation as new to her as intimacy.

'I need you...*now*,' Sebasten growled.

Rising over her, he tipped her up with strong hands and came down over her. She barely had time to learn the feeling of his urgent demand for entrance before he plunged his throbbing shaft into her slick heat and groaned with an earthy pleasure at the tightness of his welcome.

The momentary stab of unexpected pain made Lizzie jerk and cry out but the passionate urgency controlling her allowed no competition. Too much in the grip of the feverish need he had induced, she gave him a blank look when he stilled in questioning acknowledgement of that cry. Her whole body craved him with a force of hungry excitement that nothing could have haltered and she arched up to him in frantic encouragement until he succumbed to that invitation and ground his body into hers again, sheathing himself fully and sending another shockwave of incredible desire through her. His pagan rhythm drove her to the edge of ecstasy and then flung her over the wild, breathtaking peak before the glorious, peaceful aftermath of fulfilment claimed her. As he reached his own shuddering release, she wrapped her arms round him tight.

'Sublime,' Sebasten muttered hoarsely in Greek and then he rolled back and hauled her over him to study her flushed and shaken face, the unguarded softness and warmth in her green eyes as she looked back at him. He pushed his fingers into her tumbling hair and tugged her back down to him so that he could kiss her again. 'I think we're going to do this again and again...and again.'

'Hmm...' Lizzie was more mesmerised by him than ever

now. She scanned his lean, strong face and let her fingertips roam from his shoulder to curl into his tousled black hair instead. His features were *so* masculine: all taut angles from the clean slant of his high cheekbones to the proud jut of his nose and the blue-shadowed roughness of his hard jawline. His stunning gaze gleamed lazy gold beneath the semi-screening sweep of his spiky lashes. She just wanted to smile and smile and smile like an idiot.

She had been a virgin, he was *sure* of it, Sebasten thought, but he wasn't quite sure enough to broach the issue. He recalled her clueless approach to making love to him and amusement filled him. A split-second later the renewed ache of desire prompted him to kiss her again and it was the last even semi-serious thought he had for some hours.

Lizzie wakened with a start, feeling horribly queasy.

Sebasten was asleep. Sliding as quietly as she could from the bed, she fled to the bathroom, where nature took its course with punishing efficiency. Humbly grateful that Sebasten had not witnessed the final reward for her own foolishness, Lizzie got into the shower and used his shampoo to wash her hair. Even the already familiar smell of his shampoo turned her inside-out with intense longing. She felt weak, frighteningly vulnerable and yet crazily happy too. Yet hadn't she honestly believed that she was in love with Connor? What did that say about her? Connor had never lowered her to the level of sniffing shampoo bottles. Connor had never turned her brain to mush with one smile, never made her feel *scared*…

Yes, she *was* scared, Lizzie acknowledged as she made use of the hair-dryer and surveyed her own hot, guilty face in the mirror. She was in wholly uncharted territory and she was scared that Sebasten would just think of her as a one-night stand and would not want to see her again. Wouldn't that be just what she deserved? After all, how much respect could he have for a woman who just fell into his arms the very first night she met him? A woman, moreover, whom he had had to sober up first from the most disgusting state of inebriation. Shame and confusion enveloped Lizzie as she recalled how she had behaved *and* how he had reacted: angry and sardonic but essentially decent in that he had looked after her.

In the bedroom next door, Sebasten asked himself if he ought to be sympathetic towards her being ill and decided that support or sympathy might only encourage her to repeat the offence in the future. No, he definitely didn't want to risk that. He might be almost convinced that she was not an habitual drunk but it was his nature to be cautious with women. So they had a future? He could not remember ever thinking that with a woman before and it really spooked him.

Springing out of bed, Sebasten lifted the phone and ordered breakfast and might well have made it into the bathroom to join her in the shower had he not stood on her tiny handbag where it had been abandoned on the floor the night before.

With a muttered curse as he wondered whether he had broken anything inside it, he swept it up and the contents fell out because the zipper hadn't been closed. Reaching for the items, he thrust them back into the bag and in that rather impatient handling her driver's licence slipped out of her purse. He studied her photograph with a smile and was in the act of putting it back when he saw the name.

Liza Denton.

What the hell was Lizzie doing with another woman's driving licence in her possession? Sebasten stilled with a dark frown until he looked back at the photograph and the truth exploded on him with all the efficacy of an earthquake beneath his feet. Lizzie was usually short for Elizabeth but mightn't it also be a diminutive for Liza? In thunderous disbelief, he recalled the club manager pointing out the small blonde on the dance floor the night before. It dawned on him then that the man might well have been pointing at Lizzie instead, for the two women had been standing together.

In a rare state of shock, Sebasten stared back down at the photo. Lizzie was Liza Denton, the vindictive, man-hungry tramp who had driven his own kid brother to self-destruction. Sebasten shuddered. Not only had Lizzie pretended to have only the most tenuous acquaintance with Connor, but she had also outright *lied* by giving him a false surname! Her awareness of the notoriety of her own name and her deliberate concealment of her true identity was, in his opinion, absolute proof of her guilt.

Lizzie Denton was a class act too, Sebasten acknowledged as he threw on clothes at speed, ferocious rage rising in direct proportion to the raw distaste now slicing through him. That he should have *slept* with the woman whom poor Connor had loved to distraction! That he himself should then have been taken in to the extent of believing her to be a virgin! Sebasten snatched in a harsh breath.

On top of that first shattering discovery the conviction that the judgement and intelligence that he prided himself on should have fallen victim to a clever act was even more galling. Of course, it had been an act calculated to impress! So calculating a woman would be well aware that, for a male as cynical and bone-deep Greek as he was, a pretence of sexual innocence had immense pulling power. For he *had* liked that idea, hadn't he? The idea that he was the *first* to make her feel like that? The first to stamp that look of shellshocked admiration on her lovely face?

And why had she done it? Well, hadn't she told him that herself? And very prettily too with tears glistening in her big green eyes. Her adoring daddy had pulled the plug on her credit line and she had to be desperate to find a rich and generous boyfriend to keep her in the style to which she was accustomed, sooner than accept the hard grind of the daily employment that others less fortunate took for granted as their lot in life. Then Lizzie Denton had not bargained on dealing with Connor's big brother, had she?

In the fiery space of a moment, Sebasten knew exactly what he was about to do and little of his usual caution was in evidence. He would play her silly games until she was wholly in his power and then when she least expected it he would dump her as publicly as she had dumped Connor. He would repay lies with lies, hurt with hurt and pain with pain. It might not be the towering revenge he had quite envisaged but then why should her entire family suffer for her sins when it was evident that her father had already repudiated his daughter in disgust? It would be a much more *personal* act of vengeance…

With a chilling smile hardening his handsome mouth, Sebasten knocked on the bathroom door, cast it open only a few inches, for he did not yet trust himself to look her in the eye without betraying the sheer rage still powering him. 'I'll see you for breakfast downstairs…'

CHAPTER FOUR

HAVING stolen one of Sebasten's shirts from a unit in the dressing room to cover her halter top, Lizzie descended the stairs in hopeful search of a dining room. She was a bag of nerves, her heart banging against her ribs.

Sebasten had not even waited for her to emerge from the bathroom and he had sounded so cold and distant when he had said that he would see her downstairs. After the night they had shared, it was not the way she had naïvely expected him to greet her and now she was wondering in stricken embarrassment if he was eager just to get her out of his house. Perhaps only some refined form of good breeding had urged him to offer breakfast at noon.

One look and I was hooked...wasn't that what Sebasten had told her the night before? For an instant, she hugged that recollection to her and straightened her taut shoulders. But then maybe that had only been the sort of thing the average male said when things got as far as the bedroom. When she had no other man to compare him with, how would she know? Furthermore, he *wasn't* the average male, was he? Lizzie stole an uneasy glance at the oil paintings and the magnificent antique collector's cabinet in the huge hall. Everywhere she looked, she was seeing further signs of the kind of stratospheric wealth that could be rather intimidating.

A manservant appeared from the rear of the hall and opened a door into a formal dining-room, where Sebasten was seated at the end of a long polished dining-table. Colliding unwarily with veiled dark golden eyes as he rose upright with the kind of exquisite manners that she was unused to meeting with, she felt a tide of colour warm her pale complexion, and broke straight into nervous speech. 'I pinched one of your shirts. I hope you don't mind.'

'I should have sent out for some clothes for you,' Sebasten countered, throwing her into a bewildered loop with that assurance and then the unsettling suspicion that he brought a different woman home at least three times a week. 'My apologies.'

As the unfamiliar intimate ache at the heart of her tense body reminded her of just how passionate and demanding a lover Sebasten was, Lizzie dragged her tense gaze from his in awful embarrassment and sank down fast into a seat.

Sebasten was very tempted to give her a round of applause for her performance. The blushing show of discomfiture was presumably aimed at convincing him that she had never before spent a night with a man and faced him the next morning.

'I have an apartment you can use,' he murmured evenly.

Startled by that sudden offer of accommodation, Lizzie glanced up. 'Oh…I wouldn't dream of it.'

'I can't bear to think of you being homeless,' Sebasten quipped.

'Well, I won't be after I've found somewhere of my own, which I intend to do today,' Lizzie hastened to add, grateful for the distraction of the food being presented to her by the manservant.

'It's not that easy to find decent accommodation in London,' Sebasten countered.

'I'll manage. Thousands do and so will I. In fact, I'm

looking forward to proving to my father that I can look after myself,' Lizzie admitted. 'I did offer to leave home after Dad remarried but he wouldn't hear of it. He had a self-contained flat built in the stable block at the back of the house for me.'

Settling back in his antique rosewood carver chair, Sebasten cradled his black coffee in one lean brown hand and surveyed her with a frown-line dividing his level ebony brows. 'I can't understand why the indulgent father you describe should suddenly go to the other extreme and practically *throw* you out of your home.'

Visibly, Lizzie lost colour and after some hesitation said, 'Dad thinks he's spoilt me rotten—'

'Did he?'

'Yes,' Lizzie confided ruefully. 'And I have to be honest and admit that I *loved* being spoilt.'

'Any man would feel privileged to offer you the same treatment,' Sebasten drawled, smooth as glass.

Lizzie laughed out loud. 'Stop sending me up!' she urged.

Grudging appreciation flared in Sebasten's veiled gaze. She was clever, he conceded. She had not snatched at the apartment he had mentioned and was determined to demonstrate an appealing acceptance of her reduced circumstances. 'So what *are* your plans?'

Lizzie thought of the number of bills she had to settle and almost flinched. Before leaving home she had trotted up the sum total of her liabilities, and she was well aware that without her father's generous allowance only the sale of her jewellery and her car would enable her to keep her head above water on a much smaller budget. However, she had no intention of startling him with those uncomfortable realities.

'Somewhere to live is my first priority and then a job.'

It was evident that he had made use of another bathroom while she hogged his own. His black hair was still damp, his strong jawline clean shaven and she couldn't stop staring at him. Inherent strength and command were etched in his devastatingly attractive features and, regardless of the little sleep he had enjoyed, no shadows marked the clarity of his dark golden eyes. Even in his mood of cool reserve that increased her own apprehension as to how he now saw her, she was fascinated by him.

'On the career front, try the Select Recruitment agency.' Sebasten not only had a controlling interest in the business but also used it to recruit all his own personal staff. 'I've heard that they're good.'

'They would need to be,' Lizzie remarked with a wry twist of her lush mouth. 'I have no references, only basic qualifications and very little work experience to offer.'

'I'm sure you'll manage to package your classy appearance and lively personality as the ultimate in saleable commodities. It all comes down to presentation. Concentrate on what you can do and *not* what you can't,' Sebasten advised.

Grateful for his advice and the indirect compliment, Lizzie nibbled at a delicious calorie-laden croissant spread with honey and sipped at her tea. Did he want to see her again? She thought *not*. As her hand trembled, the cup she held shook and she set it back on the saucer in haste. Don't be such a baby, she urged herself furiously, willing back the stinging moisture at the backs of her eyes. Indeed she might console herself with the reflection that what had been so special for her had probably been *equally* special for him in that she could not credit that he made a regular habit of sharing cold showers with a drunk.

As the grandfather clock in the corner struck the hour, Sebasten rose to his feet again with a sigh. 'I'm afraid I have a lunch engagement I can't break at my club but my chauffeur will drive you back to wherever you're staying. Please don't feel that you have to hurry your meal.'

'It's OK…I've finished anyway.' With a fixed and valiant

smile, Lizzie extracted herself from behind the table with un-cool speed and walked back out to the hall ahead of him, her hand so tight on her bag that her knuckles showed white. No, she wasn't very good at this morning-after-the-night-before lark and possibly it was a lesson she had needed. Never, ever again would she drink like that, never, ever again would she let a squashed ego persuade her to jump into bed with a guy she had just met.

Possibly being awkward and gauche came naturally to her, Sebasten reflected in surprise, raising a brow at her headlong surge from his dining room. She was behaving like one of his dogs did when he uttered a verbal rebuke: as though he had taken a stick to her. He was pretty certain that Connor had not exercised similar power over her and grim amuse-ment lit his keen gaze.

'I might as well give you a lift,' he proffered equably, de-termined to drag out her discomfiture for as long as he could. 'What's the address?'

Ensconced in the opulent limousine while Sebasten made a phone call and talked in Greek, Lizzie was just counting the minutes until she could escape his company. She watched him spread the long, shapely fingers of one lean, bronzed hand to stress some point that he was making and her tummy flipped at the helpless recollection of how he had made her feel in his bed: driven, possessed, wild, ecstatic. All unfamil-iar emotions on her terms and mortifying and painful to ac-knowledge in the aftermath of an intimacy that was not to be repeated.

Having made arrangements to have her followed every place she went, Sebasten flipped open a business magazine out of sheer badness until the limo drew up outside the smart block of flats where she was staying. Only as she leapt onto the pavement like a chicken fleeing the fox did he lean for-ward and say, 'I'll call you…'

Lizzie blinked and her long, naturally dark lashes swept up on her surprised eyes as she nodded, staring back at him while his chaffeur hovered. 'You don't have my number,' she suddenly pointed out and before he could be put to the trouble of asking for it, she gave him the number of her mobile phone.

When Lizzie finally sped from view, slim shoulders now thrown back, marmalade hair blowing back like a banner in the breeze and long, perfect legs flashing beneath her short skirt, Sebasten was recovering from the new experience of being told that *nobody* had a photographic memory for numbers and then directed to punch hers straight into his phone so that he didn't forget it because she wouldn't be at her current address much longer.

Without a doubt, he was now recognising what might have drawn Connor in so deep, Connor, who had had strong protective instincts for the vulnerable: that jolly-schoolgirlish bluntness she practised, that complete seeming lack of a cool front, that seductive, what-you-see-is-what-you-get attitude she specialised in. And it was novel, different, but it *was* indisputably a pose designed to charm and mislead, Sebasten decided in contemptuous and angry dismissal.

Did I really make him put my number straight into his phone? Lizzie asked herself in shock as she stepped into the lift. Oh, well, he already knew how keen she was and at least that way she deprived herself of the time-wasting comfort of wondering if he had just forgotten her number when he didn't call. And he wouldn't call, she was convinced he wouldn't call, because he had been polite but essentially aloof.

At no stage had he made the smallest move to touch her in any way and yet he was a very hot-blooded guy, the sort of male who expressed intimacy with contact. Indeed, looking back to the instant of their first meeting the night before, she was challenged to recall a moment when he had not automatically maintained some kind of actual physical contact with her. Yet in spite of that, when she joined him for breakfast he had been as remote as the Andes around her. Then why had he offered her the use of an apartment? Maybe such a proposition was no big deal to a male who might well deal in property, maybe it had even been his way of saying thanks for a sexually uninhibited night with a total tart. After all, weren't all single men supposed to secretly crave a tart in the bedroom?

As Jen answered the doorbell, Lizzie was pale as death from the effects of that last humiliating thought.

'You have a visitor,' Jen informed her in a disgruntled tone, her pretty face stiff with annoyance. 'Your stepmother has been plonked in my sitting room since twelve, waiting for you to put in an appearance.'

At that announcement and the tone of it, Lizzie stiffened in dismay. What on earth was Felicity playing at? All that needed to be said had been said and it was still a punishment for her to even look at her stepmother. And did Jen, who had invited her to stay in the first place, really have to be so sour?

'Look, I'll get changed and get rid of her and then I'll be out of here just as fast as I can get my cases back into my car,' Lizzie promised, hurrying down to the bedroom, refusing to subject herself to the further embarrassment of greeting Felicity in an outfit that spelt out the demeaning truth that she had not slept anywhere near her own wardrobe the night before.

Clad in tailored cream cotton chinos and a pink cashmere cardigan, Lizzie walked into Jen's sitting room ten minutes later. Felicity spun round from the window, a tiny brunette, barely five feet one inch tall with a gorgeous figure and a tiny waist that Lizzie noted in surprise was still not showing the slightest hint that she had to be almost four months pregnant. Her classic, beautiful face was dominated by enormous violet-blue eyes. Predictably, those eyes were already welling with tears and Lizzie's teeth gritted.

'When your father told me what he had done, I was devastated for you!' Felicity gushed with a shake in her breathless little-girl voice. 'I felt *so* guilty that I had to come straight over here and—'

'Check out that I would continue to keep quiet about you and my former boyfriend?' Lizzie slotted in with distaste, for the brunette's shallow insincerity grated on her. 'I gave you my word that I wouldn't talk but it's not something I want to keep on discussing with you.'

'But how on earth will you cope without your allowance?' Felicity demanded. 'I've been thinking…*I* could help you out. Maurice is very generous and I'm sure he wouldn't notice.'

Hush money, Lizzie found herself thinking in total revulsion. 'I'll manage.'

Felicity gave her a veiled assessing look that was a poor match for her tremulous mouth and glistening eyes. 'You've never been out there on your own and you don't know how hard it can be. If only I didn't have our baby's future to think of, I *swear* I would have told your father the truth.'

The truth? And which version would that be? Lizzie thought back to the conflicting stories that Felicity and Connor had both hurled at her in the aftermath of her inopportune visit to the cottage which had become their secret love-nest. Her stepmother's priorities had been brutally obvious. Felicity had had no intention of surrendering her comfortable lifestyle and adoring older husband to set up home with an impecunious lover. As he had listened to the brunette lie in her teeth about their affair and accuse him of trying to wreck her *happy* marriage, Connor's jaw had dropped, his disbelief palpable. When her stepmother had followed up that with the announcement that she was pregnant, Lizzie's shock had been equal to Connor's devastated response.

Dredging herself back from her disturbing recollections of that day, Lizzie was so uncomfortable that she could no longer stand to look at the other woman. 'Dad will come round in his own good time. And with Connor gone, you have nothing to worry about.'

'That's a wicked thing to say…' Felicity condemned tearfully.

But deserved, Lizzie reflected. It would be a very long time before she forgot the flash of relief that she had seen in the brunette's face when she had first learnt that Connor had died in a car crash. But then what was the point of striving to awaken a conscience that Felicity did not have? The brunette had few deep emotions that did not relate to herself.

As soon as Felicity had gone, Lizzie got stuck into repacking her luggage. Jen appeared in the bedroom doorway and remarked. 'If it's any consolation, we were all eaten alive with raging envy when you landed Sebasten Contaxis last night…'

Encountering the sizzling curiosity in the pert blonde's gaze, Lizzie coloured and concentrated on gathering up the cosmetics she had left out on the dressing-table.

'Mind you,' Jen continued, 'I hear he's a real bastard with women…lifts them, *lays* them, then forgets about them. But then who could blame him? He's a young, drop-dead gorgeous billionaire. Women are just arm candy to a guy like that and of course he's happy to overdose on the treats.'

Even as a chill of dismay ran over Lizzie that Sebasten's reputation should be that bad with her sex, she angled up her chin. 'So?'

'When you get dumped, everyone will crow because you weren't entitled to get him in the first place. He dates supermodels…and let's face it, you're hardly in that category. It's my bet that, once he gets wind of all the nasty rumours there have been about you and Connor, you'll never hear from him again!'

'Thank you for the warning.' In one move, Lizzie carted two cases out to the hall in her eagerness to vacate the blonde's apartment. 'But I wasn't actually planning on *dating* Sebasten. I was just using him for a one-night stand.'

Twenty minutes later, Lizzie climbed into her Mercedes four-wheel-drive and the startled look on Jen's spiteful face travelled with her. It had been a cheap, tasteless response but it had made Lizzie feel just a little better. So where did she go now that she was truly homeless and friendless? Well, she had better try to sell her little horde of jewellery first to get some cash so that she could pay upfront for accommodation.

One week later, Lizzie dealt her new home a somewhat shaken appraisal. Six nights in an overpriced bed and breakfast joint and then *this*…

Her bedsit was a dump and, as far as she could see, a dump with no secret pretensions to be transformed into a miraculous palace. But then neither her car nor her jewellery had sold for anything like the amount that she had naïvely hoped, and until she had actually trudged round the rental agencies and checked the newspapers she had had no idea just how much it actually cost to rent an apartment. Any solo apartment, even the *tiniest* was way beyond her budget and, since she had been reluctant to share with total strangers, a bedsit had been her only immediate option.

But on the bright side, she had an interview the next day. When she got a job she would make new friends and then possibly find somewhere more inspiring to live, and in the meantime life was what you made of it, Lizzie told herself sternly. She would buy herself a bucket of cheap paint and obliterate the dingy drabness of the walls rather than sit around drowning in self-pity!

Sebasten had *not* called. Well, had she really expected him to? An aching wave of regret flooded Lizzie. It was so hard for her to forget the sense of connection that she had felt with him, that crazy feeling that something magical was in the air. Indeed she had slept with her mobile phone right beside her every night. However, the something magical had only been her own stupid fantasy, she conceded, angry that she still hadn't managed to get him out of her mind. After all, if what Jen had said about Sebasten's reputation was true, she had had a narrow escape from getting her heart broken and stomped on. In any case, how could she possibly have explained why she had lied and given him a false surname?

Reading his security chief's efficient daily bulletins on Lizzie's fast-disintegrating life of ease and affluence had supplied the major part of Sebasten's entertainment throughout the past week.

Lizzie had been conned into flogging her six-month-old-low mileage Mercedes for half of its worth and then ripped off in much the same way when it came to parting with her diamonds. Having run a credit check on her, Sebasten had appreciated the necessity for such immediate financial retrenchments and could only admire her cunning refusal to snatch at his offer of an apartment. Evidently, Lizzie was set on impressing on him the belief that she was not a gold-digger or a free-loader. Now in possession of both her Merc and her jewellery and having paid very much more for both than she had received for either, Sebasten was ready to make his next move.

When her mobile phone sang out its musical call, Lizzie was standing on top of three suitcases, striving to get the paint roller to do what it was supposed to do as easily as it did in the diagram on the back of the pack. It had been so long since her phone rang that it took her a second or two to recognise the sound for what it was. With a strangled yelp, she made a sudden leap off the precarious mound of cases, the roller spattering daffodil-yellow paint in all directions as she snatched up her phone with all the desperation of a drowning woman.

'Sebasten…' Sebasten murmured.

Lizzie pulled a face, suddenly wishing she knew at least three Sebastens and could ask which he was. At the same time, she rolled her eyes heavenward, closed them and uttered a silent heartfelt prayer of thanks. He had called…he had called…he had *called*!

'Hi…' she answered, low-key, watching paint drip down from the ceiling, knowing that she had overloaded the roller and now wrecked her only set of sheets into the bargain and not caring, truly not caring. Her brain was in a blissful fog. She couldn't think straight.

'You'd better start by giving me your address,' Sebasten told her before he could forget that he wasn't supposed to know it already.

Lizzie rattled it off at speed.

'Dinner tonight?' Sebasten enquired.

Her brain peeped out from behind the romantic fog and winced at that last-minute invitation. Breathing in deep and slow, she dragged her pride out of the hiding place where it was eager to stay. 'Sorry I can't make it tonight.'

'*Try…*' Sebasten suggested, a wave of instant irritation gripping him. 'I'll be abroad next week.'

Lizzie paled at that additional information and then surveyed the devastation of the room which she had only begun to paint. 'I really *can't*. I'm in the middle of trying to decorate my bedsit—'

'I've had some novel excuses in my time but—'

'If I leave it now, I'll never finish it…are you any good at decorating?' Lizzie asked off the top of her head, so keen was she to break into that far from reassuring response of his.

'Never wielded a paintbrush in my life and no ambition to either,' Sebasten drawled in a derisive tone of incredulity, thinking that she was taking the I'm-so-poor façade way too far for good taste. Decorating? *Him?* She just had to be joking!

Wishing she had kept her mouth shut, Lizzie felt her cheeks burning. Of course, a male of his meteoric wealth wasn't about to rush over and help out. But it was hardly her fault that she wasn't available at such very short notice, and for all she knew he had only called because some other woman was otherwise engaged. 'Oh, well, looks like I'm on my own. To be frank, it's not a lot of fun. I'd better go…I've got paint dripping everywhere but where it should be. Maybe see you around…thanks for calling. Bye!'

Before she could weaken and betray her anguished regret, she finished the call. Maybe see you around? Lizzie flinched. Some chance! Her fashionable nights out on the town in the top clubs and restaurants were at an end.

In outraged disbelief, Sebasten registered that she had cut him off. Who the bloody hell did Lizzie Denton think she was? When the shock of that unfamiliar treatment had receded, a hard smile began to curve his wide, sensual mouth. She was trying to play hard to get to wind him up and increase his interest. He phoned his secretary and told her to find him a decorator willing to work that night.

By six that evening, Lizzie was whacked and on the brink of tears of frustration. Practically everything she possessed including herself was covered with paint and the first layer on the ceiling and two of the walls had dried all streaky and horrible. When a knock sounded on the door, she thrust paint-spattered fingers through her tumbled hair and tugged open the door.

Sebasten stood there like a glorious vision lifted straight from some glossy society-magazine page. His casual dark blue designer suit screamed class and expense and accentuated his height and well-built, muscular frame. A flock of butterflies broke loose in her tummy and her heartbeat hit the Richter scale while she hovered, staring at him in surprise.

'What are you wearing?' Sebasten enquired, brilliant golden eyes raking over what looked very like a leotard but his true concentration absorbed by the lithe perfection of the female body delineated by the thin, tight fabric. Instantaneous lust ripped through him and smouldering fury at his lack of control over his own libido followed in its wake.

'Exercise gear…I didn't have anything else suitable.' She was unsurprised that he was staring: she knew she had to look a total fright with no make-up on. 'I'd have been better doing it naked!' she quipped tautly, her mind a total blank while she tried to work out what he was doing on her doorstep.

Naked; now there was an idea… Sebasten stopped that forbidden thought dead in its tracks but lust had a more tenacious hold still on his taut length.

'I've brought a decorating crew…and we're going out to dinner,' he informed her, scanning the chaos of the room and the horrendous state of the walls with elevated brows of wonderment, certain that should he have taken the notion he could have done a far more efficient job. 'Grab some clothes. We'll stop off at my place and you can get changed there, leaving the crew to get stuck in.'

'You've brought…*decorators*?' Lizzie was still staring at him with very wide green eyes, striving to absorb his announcement that he had drummed up decorators to finish her room for her. She was stunned but even more stunned by the manner in which he just *dropped* that astonishing announcement on her. As if it was the most natural thing in the world that he should hire decorators so that she could be free to join him for dinner. This, she registered, was a male who never took no for an answer, who put his own wishes first, who was willing to move proverbial mountains if it got him what he wanted.

'Why not?' Sebasten turned his devastating smile on her and, in spite of her discomfiture at what he had done and what it revealed about his character, her heart sat up and begged and sang at that smile. 'You did say painting wasn't a lot of fun.'

'And I'm not exactly brilliant at it,' Lizzie muttered, head in a whirl while she reminded herself that it was also a compliment that he should go to such extravagant lengths just to spend time with her. He might not be willing to wield a paint-brush for her benefit but he was certainly no sleeper in the practicality stakes.

'So?'

Aware of his impatience and even while telling herself that she ought not to let herself react to that or be influenced by his macho methods into giving instant agreement, Lizzie found herself digging into the wardrobe and drawing out a raincoat to pull on over her leotard. 'I'm a complete mess,' she pointed out anxiously, grabbing up a bag and banging back into the wardrobe and several drawers to remove garments.

'You'll clean up to perfection,' Sebasten asserted, plant-ing a lean hand to her spine to hustle her out of the room.

'Are you always this ruthless about getting your own way?' Lizzie asked breathlessly after she had passed her keys over to the businesslike-looking decorators waiting by their van on the street below and had warned them that she had bought rubbish paint.

'Always,' Sebasten confirmed without hesitation, lean, powerful face serious. 'I work hard. I play hard. And I didn't want to wait another week before I saw you again, *pethi mou*.'

Clutching her raincoat round her, Lizzie tried to keep her feet mentally on the ground but her imagination was already soaring to dizzy heights. Presumably he had been really, really busy all week but couldn't he at least have called to chat even if he hadn't had the time to see her sooner? Squashing that unwelcome reflection, she discovered that she couldn't wait to tell him about the highlight of her week.

'I've got an interview for a job tomorrow afternoon,' she told him with considerable pride.

'Where?'

'CI...it's a big City Company,' Lizzie advanced with a grin.

Sebasten veiled his amused gaze with dense black lashes. Select Recruitment had come up trumps on his request and even faster than they had promised, for the agency had not yet come back to him to confirm that she had paid them a visit. CI was *his* company and the fact that she hadn't even registered yet that CI stood for Contaxis International did not say a lot about the amount of homework she had done in advance of the interview. Or was she just pretending and did she know darned well that it was his company?

'Of course, it's only a temporary position where I fill in for other people on holiday and stuff but I gather that if I do OK it *could* become permanent,' Lizzie continued.

'You sound as if you're just gasping to work,' Sebasten mocked, knowing that there was no possibility on earth that the position would become permanent as it had been dreamt up at his bidding and styled to deliver the maximum pain for the minimum gain. He couldn't wait to see her application form and discover how many lies she had put in print.

'Of course I am...I'm skint!' Lizzie exclaimed before she could think better of it.

As she encountered Sebasten's enquiring frown, a wave of colour ran up from her throat to mantle her cheekbones. 'Well, don't tell me you're surprised,' she said ruefully. 'I'm not living in a lousy bedsit so far out of the city centre so I'll need to rise at dawn to get into work just for the good of my health!'

'I can't understand why you didn't accept the apartment I mentioned…but then the offer remains open,' Sebasten delivered.

'Thanks…but I've got to learn to look after myself. I was so annoyed when I screwed up the painting project,' Lizzie confided truthfully. 'I didn't appreciate that it wasn't as easy as it looked and I *hate* giving up on anything! I should have stayed and watched those guys work and learned how to do it for myself.'

'Let's not go overboard.' Sebasten reckoned that the number of fresh challenges awaiting her at CI would prove quite sufficient to occupy her in the coming weeks.

An hour and a half later, Lizzie scanned her appearance in the mirror in the opulent guest room she had been shown into in Sebasten's beautiful town house. She had enjoyed freshening up in a power shower, for it was slowly sinking in on her that a thousand things that she had once taken for granted were luxuries she might never get to experience again. Her dress was leaf-green with a cut-away back and a favourite, but in the rush to leave her bedsit she had forgotten all her cosmetics.

As she descended the stairs she thought about how much she had appreciated not being shown into *his* bedroom as if how the evening might end was already accepted fact. It wasn't. She had her interview tomorrow and she wanted to be wide awake for it and, furthermore, she suspected that it might be unwise to fall into Sebasten's arms too soon, at least not before she had got to know him better.

When Sebasten watched her descend his magnificent staircase, he stilled.

Feeling self-conscious, Lizzie pulled a comic face. 'Want to change your mind about being seen out with me? I forgot my make-up.'

'You have fabulous skin and I like the natural look.'

'All men say that because they think anything artificial is somehow a deception being practised on them but very few of them are actually *wowed* by the natural look if they get it!' Lizzie laughed.

Their arrival at the latest fashionable eaterie caused a perceptible stir of turning heads and inquisitive eyes. Afraid of seeing any familiar faces and meeting with an antagonistic look which would take all the gloss off her evening, Lizzie looked neither to her right nor her left and stared into stricken space on the couple of occasions that Sebasten broke his stride to acknowledge someone, for she was terrified that he might try to introduce her using the false name she had given him. Mercifully he did not but she saw that there was no escaping the unpleasant fact that she would *have* to admit to lying and give him an acceptable explanation for her behaviour.

As soon as the first course was ordered, Lizzie breathed in deep and dived straight in before she could lose her nerve. 'I have a confession to make,' she asserted, biting at her lower lip, green eyes discomfited. 'And I don't think you're going to like me very much after I've told you. My surname isn't Bewford, it's—'

'Denton,' Sebasten filled in, congratulating her mentally on her timing, for few men would contemplate causing a scene or staging a confrontation in a restaurant where, whether she had noticed it or not, they were the cynosure of all eyes. Yes, he had definitely found a foe worthy of his mettle.

Taken aback, Lizzie stared at him. 'You already *know* who I really am?'

Never one to tell an untruth without good reason, Sebasten explained that he had seen her driving licence that morning a week ago.

Lizzie paled. 'Oh, my goodness, what must you have

thought of me?' she gasped in shamed embarrassment, recalling his failure to await her emergence from his bathroom and his subsequent coolness on parting from her and now seeing both events in a much more presentable light. 'I'm really sorry…and I'm just *amazed* that you wanted to see me again after I'd told a stupid lie like that!'

'As to what I thought…I assumed you would explain when the time was right and that you must have a very good reason for giving me a false name. As to not seeing you again…' Brilliant dark golden eyes rested with keen appreciation on her lovely, flushed face, absorbing the anxiety stamped into every line of it with satisfaction. 'I'm not sure that was ever an option. We shared an incredible night of passion and I want to be with you.'

Relief and shy pleasure mingled in Lizzie's strained appraisal and she decided that she owed him the fullest possible explanation in return for his forebearance. 'I was—er—sort of *involved*,' she stressed with reluctance, 'with Connor Morgan up until a few days before he died. I don't know whether you're aware of the rumours—'

Sort of involved? Sebasten wanted to laugh out loud in derision at that grotesque understatement. The troubled plea for understanding in her beautiful eyes was an even more effective ploy. Lounging back in his seat as the head waiter appeared to refresh their wine glasses, Sebasten endeavoured to ape the role of a sympathetic audience. 'I had heard the suicide story but I also understand that he never made any such threat and that he left no note either.'

Relieved to hear him acknowledge those facts, Lizzie clutched her wine glass like a life belt and then put it down again, her hands too restless to stay still. 'If I tell you the whole truth, will you promise me that you won't repeat it to anybody?'

His contempt climbing at that evident request not to carry

the lies she was about to tell to any other source, who might fast disprove her story, Sebasten nodded in confirmation but then murmured. 'Connor called you Liz, not Lizzie…didn't he?'

'That was typical Connor,' Lizzie sighed. 'He had an ex called Lizzie and he always insisted on calling me Liza.'

'So tell me about him…' Sebasten encouraged.

'I first met Connor just over three months ago. I liked him; well, we all did. He was the life and soul of every event.' Lizzie frowned as she strove to pick her words, for inexperienced she might be, but she knew that discussing her previous relationship with the new man in her life might not be the wisest idea. 'I suppose I developed quite a crush on him but I never expected anything to come of it. When he grabbed me one night at a party and kissed me and then asked me out, I was surprised because I didn't think I was his type…and as it turned out, I *wasn't*.'

'Meaning?'

'That four days before he died, I discovered that Connor had been using me as cover for his steamy affair with a married woman.' Lizzie winced as Sebasten's intent appraisal narrowed in disbelief. 'I know it doesn't sound very credible because Connor always seemed to be such an upfront guy but it's the truth. I found them together and nobody could have been more shocked than I was.'

'Who was she?' Sebasten enquired, impressed by her creativeness in a tight spot, for her tale was a positive masterpiece of ingenuity. In one fell swoop, she sought to turn herself from a heartless little shrew into a cruelly deceived victim and Connor into a cheat and a liar. His anger on his late half-brother's behalf smouldered beneath the deceptive calm of his appraisal.

'I can't tell you that. It wouldn't be fair because I gave my word to the woman involved that I wouldn't. She was very distressed and she regretted the whole thing and she broke off with him. All I can tell you is that he believed he was crazy about her but I think that for *her* it was just a little fling because she was bored with her marriage.'

'I'm curious. Tell me her name,' Sebasten prompted afresh, ready to put her through hoops for daring to tell him such nonsensical lies.

Her persistence made her squirm with obvious discomfiture. 'I'm sorry, I can't. Anyway, now it's all over and behind me, I can see that Connor really just treated me like a casual girlfriend he saw a couple of times a week…we didn't sleep together or anything like that,' she muttered, her voice dwindling in volume, but she had wanted to let him know that last fact. 'But it was still a very hurtful experience for me and I didn't like him very much for making such an ass of me.'

'How could you?' Sebasten encouraged, smoother than silk.

'It wasn't until I drove down to Brighton to try and pay my respects to his mother that I realised that *I* was getting the blame for his death. People just assumed that he'd got drunk and crashed his car because I had ditched him,' Lizzie shared heavily.

Ingrid had not admitted that Lizzie had made a personal visit to her home, Sebasten recalled, hating the way women always told you what they wanted you to hear rather than simply dispensing all the facts. 'What happened?'

'Mrs Morgan said some awful things to me…I can forgive that,' Lizzie stated but she still paled at the recollection of Ingrid Morgan's vicious verbal attack on her. 'I mean, she was just beside herself with grief and naturally Connor hadn't admitted to his own mother that he was carrying on with someone else's wife. She said that if I tried to go to the funeral she'd have me thrown out of the church!'

'So you've been getting the blame for events that had nothing to do with you. That's *appalling*,' Sebasten commented with harsh emphasis.

'It's also why all my friends have dropped me and my father showed me the front door,' Lizzie confided, grateful for the anger she recognised in both the taut set of his hard bone-structure and the rough edge to his dark, deep drawl, for she believed it was on her behalf.

'Surely you could have confided in your own father?'

Lizzie tensed, averted her gaze and thought fast. 'No—er—he knows the woman concerned and I don't think I could rely on him to keep it quiet.'

'I'm astonished *and* impressed by your generosity towards a woman who doesn't deserve your protection at the cost of your own good name,' Sebasten drawled softly.

'Wrecking her marriage wouldn't bring Connor back and I'm sure she's learned her lesson.' Lizzie studied her main course without appetite, certain that she had just put paid to any sparkle in the evening with her long-winded and awkward explanation.

Sebasten reached across the table and covered her clenched fingers where they rested with his own. 'Relax…I understand why you lied to me. You were seriously *scared* that after one extraordinary night with you I might make a real nuisance of myself.'

After a bemused pause at that teasing and laughable assertion, Lizzie glanced up, amusement having driven the apprehension from her green eyes, and she grinned in helpless appreciation, for with one mocking comment he had dissolved her tension and concluded the subject. He was clever, subtle, always focused. Meeting his dark golden gorgeous eyes, she felt dizzy even though she was sitting down.

They had a slight dispute outside the restaurant when Sebasten assumed she was coming home with him.

'Where else are you going to go?' he demanded with stark impatience. 'The decorators aren't finished yet!'

'How do you know that? By mental telepathy?'

'I only needed to take one look at the havoc you wreaked with a paintbrush. They'll be lucky to finish by dawn!' Sebasten forecast.

'Call them and check.' Lizzie smothered a large yawn with a hurried hand, for she was becoming very sleepy.

'I can't…don't know how to reach them. Even if they had finished you couldn't sleep in a room full of paint fumes,' Sebasten spelt out, getting angrier by the second because the very last thing he had expected from her was an exaggerated pretence of *not* wanting to share his bed again, most particularly when *he* was determined not to repeat that intimacy. 'The bed I'm offering you for the night doesn't include me!'

'Oh…' Lizzie computed that surprising turn of events and gave him full marks for not acting on the supposition that her body was now his for the asking. 'That's fine, then. Thank you…thank you very much.'

Never had Sebasten snubbed a woman with so little satisfying effect. With an apologetic smile, Lizzie climbed into his limo, made not the smallest feline attempt to dissuade him from the rigours of a celibate night and then compounded her sins by falling asleep on him. He shook her awake outside his town house.

'Gosh, have I been asleep? How very boring for you,' she mumbled, stumbling out of the car and up the steps, heading for the stairs with blind determination but pausing to remove her shoes, which were pinching her toes. 'I'm almost asleep standing up. I shouldn't even have had *one* glass of wine over dinner.'

But for all her apparent sleepiness, Lizzie was thinking hard. She might have been pleased that he had no expectations of her, but when it dawned on her that she was heading for his guest room and that he had still not even attempted to kiss her she was no longer quite so content. Telling him about Connor, it seemed, had been a horrible mistake. It had turned him right off her.

On the landing her stockinged feet went skidding out from under her on the polished floor and she fell with a wallop and hit her knee a painful bash. 'What is it about your wretched house?' she demanded, the pain hitting her at a vulnerable moment and bringing a flood of tears to her eyes. 'It's like… booby-trapped for my benefit!'

In instinctive concern, Sebasten crouched down beside her. Tears were running down her face in rivulets and he assumed she had really hurt herself. 'I'd better get an ambulance—'

'Don't be stupid…I only bumped it…I'm just being a baby!' Lizzie wailed in mortification. 'I'm tired and it's been a tough week, that's all.'

And when she cried, she really cried, Sebasten noted. There were no delicate, ladylike sniffs, no limpid, brimming looks calculated to induce male guilt. She just put her head down and sobbed like a child. She was miserable. He *should* be happy about that. Lean, powerful face taut, he snatched her up off the floor and into his arms. Reasoning that sticking her in a guest room alone with her distress would not only seem odd but also suspicious behaviour for a male supposed to be interested in her, he carried her into his room, where he deposited her on the bed and backed off.

With a tremendous effort of will, Lizzie gulped into silence and squeezed open her swollen eyes. It was true that she was very tired but it was her over-taxed emotions which had brought on the crying jag. In the frame she was in, she didn't think that she was capable of having a relationship with anybody. She missed her home, she missed her father.

'I'm sorry you met me last week,' Lizzie confided

abruptly. 'You're never going to believe that I'm not normally like this.'

From the shadows outside the pool of light shed by the bedside lamps, Sebasten strolled forward. 'Have a bath. Get some sleep. You're exhausted.'

'Not very sexy… Exhaustion, I mean,' she muttered, plucking at the sheet with a nervous hand, peering out from under her extravagant torrent of hair, which shone with copper and gold lights.

'I'll be up later…I've got a couple of calls to make.'

'Kiss me goodnight,' Lizzie whispered on a breathless impulse before he reached the door.

Sebasten stopped dead and swung round, emanating tension. 'Surely, feeling so tired, you're not up for anything tonight?'

'So if there's no—er sex, you don't kiss either,' Lizzie gathered and nodded, although she was cut to the bone at his rejection.

'Don't be ridiculous!'

'You don't fancy me any more?' Lizzie was determined to get an answer.

Sebasten strode across the room, closed firm hands over her arms and hauled her up onto her knees on the mattress. She could have drowned in the pagan glitter of his splintering golden eyes. He brought his mouth plunging down on hers and it was like being pitched into a stormy sea without warning. Excitement shivered and pulsed through her in answer, heat and craving uniting at the thrumming heart of her body until she went limp in his hold, all woman, all invitation.

'I hope that answers that question,' Sebasten breathed thickly, dark colour accentuating his fabulous cheekbones as he let her sink back from him in sensual disarray.

Lizzie had a soak in his sunken bath, let the water go cold

while she waited for him to join her. Then, ashamed of her own wanton longing, she took advantage of another one of his couple of hundred shirts and climbed into bed. That fiery, demanding kiss had soothed her though and she drifted off to sleep with a dreamy smile on her face…

CHAPTER FIVE

LIZZIE opened her eyes just when morning light was spilling through the bedroom and found Sebasten wide awake and staring down at her.

She didn't feel shy or awkward; she just felt happy that he was there. Indeed, so right and natural did it feel that she might have been waking up beside him for absolute years. But then had she been, she might have been just a little more cool at the effect of that all lean, bronzed, hair-roughened masculinity of his poised within inches of her. With a languorous stretch, she gazed up into the dark golden eyes subjecting her to an intense scrutiny and her heart fluttered like a frantic trapped bird inside her.

'Good morning,' she whispered with her irrepressible smile. 'You shouldn't stare. It wakes people up.'

Three brandies and a cold shower had failed to cool Sebasten's ravenous arousal and he had never been into celibacy. It was just sex, he reasoned, thought and integrity had nothing to do with it and denying himself was a pointless sacrifice when he had already enjoyed her.

He threaded caressing fingers through a shining strand of her amber hair and then knotted it round his fist to hold her fast, his stunning eyes semi-screened by his lush black lashes to feverish gold. 'Lust is keeping *me* awake, *pethi mou*.'

'Oh…' Breathing had already become a challenge for Lizzie.

'*And* you've been nicking my shirts again…there's a price to pay.' Long brown fingers flicked loose the topmost button and she quivered, melting like honey on a hot plate and mesmerised by his dark male beauty.

'Will I want to pay it?'

'I *know* you will,' Sebasten husked, releasing another button with tantalising slowness, watching her spine arch and push her pert little breasts up tight against the silk, delineating the straining pink buds already eager for his attention.

'How do you know?' Lizzie prompted unevenly, mortified by his absolute certainty of his welcome.

'Your exquisite body is screaming the message at me…' Sebasten parted the edges of the shirt with the care of a connoisseur and bent his arrogant dark head to graze his teeth over a pale pink swollen nipple.

Her entire body jackknifed up towards his, a low, moaning cry breaking from her lips.

With a groan, Sebasten lifted his head again. 'Different rules this time. You lie still…if you move or cry out, I stop.'

'S-sorry?' she stammered.

'You get too excited too fast.'

'That's wrong?' Lizzie had turned scarlet.

A shimmering smile flashed across Sebasten's lean, bronzed features. 'I want an excuse to torture you with sensual pleasure…*give* me it.'

A quiver of wild, wanton anticipation sizzled through Lizzie. 'I'll just lie back and—er—think of painting then—'

'It's going to be a lot more exciting than watching paint dry,' Sebasten promised with a husky laugh of amusement, scanning her expressive face.

And she found out that it *was* within minutes. The tension of struggling to stay still and silent no matter what he did electrified her with heat and desperate craving. He shaped her tender breasts, toyed with the throbbing peaks until every muscle in her shivering length was whip-taut and then switched his attentions to other places that she had never dreamt had even the tiniest erotic capability. But she soon found out otherwise. Sebasten ran his mouth down her spine and she was reduced to a jelly. He sucked her fingers and she was ready to flare up in flames, wild, helpless, terrified he might stop as he had threatened, turn off that wholly seductive, enslaving flow of endless exciting pleasure.

'You're doing really good,' Sebasten groaned and it was an effort to find the words in English as a telling shudder racked his big, powerful frame. The challenge he had set her from the pinnacle of his own bedroom supremacy was gnawing with increasing savagery and ego-zapping speed at his own self-control.

Lizzie gave him a smile old as Eve, leant up and ran the tip of her tongue in provocation and encouragement along his sensual lower lip and he growled and pushed her back against the pillows and drove his mouth down on hers with raw, hungry demand. Literal fireworks went off inside her. She was with him every step of the way, ecstatic at the change of pace that matched her own fevered longing and impatience.

'I want you...*now*!' Sebasten ground out hoarsely, hauling her under him with an incredible lack of cool when she had not the smallest intention of arguing.

And then he was there where she had *so* needed him to be, coursing into her and burying himself deep. Her climax was instant, shattering. Shorn of all control, she was thrown to a fierce peak and then she splintered into a million shell-shocked pieces in an experience so intense she was left in a daze.

'You're a lost cause,' Sebasten bit out with a sudden laugh

and then he kissed her, slow and tender, and her heart gave a wild spin as though it were a globe on a hanger.

'Sorry,' she muttered but that was the exact moment that she realised that she was in love, head over heels, fathoms-deep in love as she had never been before.

'Don't be…you're incredible in bed,' Sebasten assured her, reminding himself that tomorrow was another day to re-instate restraint before he took her to heaven and back again.

Exactly a fortnight later, Lizzie experienced her first day at work.

Her concentration was not all that might have been: Sebasten was due back that afternoon from his *second* trip abroad since she had met him. In the intervening weeks, he had only managed to see her twice, once meeting her for dinner when he was actually *en route* to the airport, and on the second occasion taking her to the races to help him entertain a group of foreign businessmen in his private box. As neither event had entailed anything in the way of privacy, Lizzie was counting the hours until she could see him again and could indeed think of nothing else *but* Sebasten.

True love, she recognised ruefully, had taken a long time to hit her. What she had felt for Connor had just been a practice run for the main event. Connor had damaged her pride, her self-confidence and her blind faith in others more than her heart. With Sebasten, she had discovered an entire new layer of more tender feelings. She worried about the incredible hours he seemed to work. She cherished every tiny thing she found out about him but Sebasten could be stingier than Scrooge when it came to talking about himself. His different moods fascinated her, for the cool front he wore concealed a volatile temperament controlled by rigid self-discipline. He was full of contradictions and complexities and every minute she spent with him, even on the phone, plunged her deeper into her obsession with him.

Even so, the poor start she contrived to make at CI on her first day annoyed and frustrated her.

'A couple of little points,' Milly Sharpe, the office manager on the sixth floor, a whip-thin redhead in a navy business suit, advanced with compressed lips. 'Getting off at the wrong tube station is not an acceptable excuse for being late. Please ensure that you arrive at the correct time tomorrow. Did you receive a copy of the CI dress code?'

Lizzie almost winced. 'Yes.'

'The code favours the darker colours, suits—longer skirts or trousers—and sensible shoes. The key word is *formal*, not casual.'

There was a pause while a speaking appraisal was angled over Lizzie's fashionable green skirt worn with a matching fitted top that sported *faux* fur at cuff and neckline and the very high sandals on her slender feet. Lizzie reddened and wondered if the woman honestly believed that she had the wherewithal to rush out and buy a complete new wardrobe. She had never bought dark colours, had never owned sensible shoes that were not of the walking-boot variety and her trouser collection consisted of jeans, chinos and pure silk beach wear.

'I would suggest that you also do something with your hair. It's a little too long to be left *safely* loose when you're working with office equipment.'

It was worse than being back at school, Lizzie thought in horror, waiting to be told to take off her earrings and removed her nail polish as well.

By the time Lizzie was shown to the switchboard and taken through a bewildering number of operations while various messages flashed up lightning-fast on the screen in front of her, sheer nervous tension had killed her ability to concentrate on the directions she was being given or remember them.

The hours that followed were a nightmare for her. She learnt that if she pressed the wrong button, she created havoc. She put calls through to lines that were engaged, cut people off in the middle of conversations, connected calls to the wrong extensions, lost others in an endless loop which saw them routed round the building and back to her again. The amount of abuse she got was a colossal shock to her system. Furious callers raged down the line at her and several staff appeared in person to remonstrate with her.

'A switchboard operator must remain calm,' Milly Sharpe reproved when Lizzie was as wrung out as a rag, jumping and flinching at the mere sight of an incoming call and ducking behind the screen if anybody walked past in case they were about to direct a volley of complaints at her.

She was weak with relief when she was switched to photocopying duties after lunch. Although the machine's sensors gave her a real fright by buzzing into sudden life the instant she approached, she felt better able to cope. In addition, something more than mere nerves was afflicting her: the longer she stood, the more light-headed she felt and her queasy tummy had put her off eating any lunch. She prayed that she was not developing summer flu.

Having access to a computer that was linked to the colour photocopier, while she waited for the copier to finish printing she succumbed to the temptation of doing an online search for information on Sebasten. But the very site she found brought up a to-die-for portrait photo of Sebasten and she never got any further. Her heartrate quickening at first glimpse of that lean, strong face, she drank in his image with intense appreciation. The stress of her difficult day seemed to evaporate as she hit the print button to get a copy of that photo to take home.

When *more* than one photo began to pile up in the copier, she did not initially panic. In fact she just thought she would have a photo for every handbag, would indeed not need to go an hour without a frequent fix of studying Sebasten. However, as the pile began to mount beyond the number of bags that even *she* possessed she tried to cancel the print run. But nothing she did would persuade the wretched machine to cease the operation. As luck would have it, Milly Sharpe arrived at that point.

Scooping up the first picture of Sebasten, she held it up like an exhibit at a murder trial, icy condemnation in her challenging gaze. 'Where did you get this from?'

'I only meant to print one—'

'You mean…there's *more* than one?' the redhead demanded and swooped on the fat pile in disbelief, checking the print run with brows that vanished below her fringe. 'You have printed four *hundred* copies of this photo?'

Lizzie reddened to her hairline, feeling like a kid caught languishing over a secret pin-up. 'I'm really very sorry—'

'Have you any idea how much this special photographic paper costs per *single* sheet?'

Lizzie was shattered to be informed that she had wasted a couple of hundred pounds of very expensive stationery.

'*And* on company time!' The other woman's voice shook with outrage. 'I would also add that I consider it the height of impertinence to print photos of Mr Contaxis. I think it would be best if you spent the rest of the afternoon tidying up the stationery store room across the corridor.'

Just when Lizzie was wondering why it should be 'impertinent' to print images of Sebasten, a wave of such overpowering nausea assailed her that she was forced to bolt for the cloakroom. After a nasty bout of sickness she felt so dizzy that she had to hang on to the vanity counter before she felt steady enough on her feet to freshen up. While she was doing that, a slight, youthful blonde came in.

'I'm Rosemary. I'm to check up on you and show you to

the sick room,' she explained with a friendlier smile than Lizzie had so far received from any of the female staff.

'I'm fine now,' Lizzie asserted in haste, thinking that if she ended up in the sick room on top of such a disastrous work performance, her first day would definitely be her *last* day of employment in the building.

'You're still very pale. Don't let Milly Sharpe get to you,' the chatty blonde advised. 'If you ask me, she's just got a chip on her shoulder about how you got your job.'

Lizzie frowned. '*How*…I got my job?'

Rosemary shrugged a carefully noncommittal shoulder. 'There's this mad rumour flying round that you didn't come in by the usual selection process but got strings pulled for you by someone influential on the executive floor—'

Lizzie coloured in dismay. 'That's not true—'

'The average temp doesn't wear delectable designer suits either and we're all killing ourselves over what you did with the photocopier,' Rosemary confided with an appreciative giggle as they left the cloakroom. 'Four hundred copies of our hunky pin-up boss, Sebasten. I bet Milly takes them home and papers her bedroom walls with them! Glad you're feeling better.'

'*Boss?*' Lizzie queried that astonishing label several seconds too late, for the blonde had already disappeared into one of the offices and Lizzie was left alone, fizzing with alarm and confusion.

She hastened into the stationery store room and yanked her mobile phone from her bag to punch out Sebasten's personal number. When he answered, she broke straight into harried speech. '*Am* I working for you?'

'Yes…did you finally get to read a letterhead?' Sebasten murmured with silken mockery. 'CI stands for Contaxis International.'

'Did you *fix* this job for me?' Lizzie demanded with a sinking heart, devastated by that first confirmation.

'You wouldn't have got it on your own merits,' Sebasten traded, crushing her with that candid assessment. 'Personnel don't take risks when they hire junior employees even on a temporary basis.'

'Thanks…' Lizzie framed shakily and then with angry stress continued. '*Thanks* for treating me like an idiot and not telling me that this was your company! *Thanks* for embarrassing me to death by doing it in such a way that the staff here know that I got preferential treatment!'

'Anything else you want to thank me for?' Sebasten enquired in an encouraging tone that was not calculated to soothe.

'I needed a job but you should have told me what you were doing!' Lizzie condemned furiously. 'I don't need your pity—'

'Trust me,' Sebasten drawled, velvety soft and smooth. 'The one emotion I do not experience in your radius is…pity. I'll pick you up at eight for the dinner party…OK?'

Lizzie thrust trembling fingers through the hair flopping over her damp brow. 'Has one thing I've said got through to you?'

'I'm not into phone aggro,' Sebasten murmured drily.

'I don't want to see you tonight—'

'I didn't hear that—'

'I…don't…want…to…see…you…tonight,' Lizzie repeated between clenched teeth, rage and pain gripping her in a vice that refused to yield. 'If you don't care about my feelings, I shouldn't *be* with you!'

'Your choice,' Sebasten breathed and cut the call.

After work, Lizzie returned to her bedsit in a daze. She stared at her fresh, daffodil-yellow walls, completed to perfection by the decorators he had hired. It was over, finished…just like that? Without ever seeing him again? Had she been unfair? Even downright rude and ungrateful? How long would it have taken her to find a job *without* his preferential treatment? She had no references, no office skills, no qualification beyond good A-level exam results gained when she was eighteen. In the following four years she had achieved nothing likely to impress a potential employer, although she had gone to great creative endeavours to try and conceal that fact on her application form.

When her father phoned her on her mobile phone out of the blue at seven that evening and asked her if she would like to meet him for dinner she was really pleased, for they had not spoken since she had left home. Over that meal, she made a real effort to seem cheerful. Felicity, Maurice Denton then confided wearily, had demanded that he dismiss their housekeeper, Mrs Baines, and he didn't want to do it. The older woman had worked for the Dentons for over ten years and was very efficient, if somewhat dour in nature.

'I thought possibly you could have a quiet word with Felicity on the subject,' her parent completed hopefully.

'No, thanks. It's none of my business.' But, even so, Lizzie was curious as to what the housekeeper could have done to annoy Felicity and she asked.

'Nothing that I can see…' Maurice muttered with barely concealed irritation. 'To tell you the truth, sometimes I feel like I don't know my own wife any more!'

Sebasten went to the dinner party alone, smouldered in a corner for an hour with a group of men, listening to sexist jokes that set his teeth on edge, snubbed every woman who dared to so much as smile at him and left early. On the drive home, he decided he wanted to confront Lizzie.

When he pulled up in the street he was just in time to see Lizzie, sheathed in a little violet-blue dress that would have wowed a dead man, in the act of clambering out of a Porsche. Smiling as if she had won the lottery, she sped up onto the pavement to embrace the tall, well-built driver.

Maurice Denton returned his daughter's hug and sighed. 'Let's not leave it so long the next time. I'm really proud that you're managing on your own. I can't have got it as wrong as I thought with you.'

Lizzie was so busy keeping up her happy smile as her father drove off again that her jaw ached from the effort. In truth it had been an evening that provoked conflicting reactions inside her. Her father had let her see that his marriage was under strain. Once she would have been selfishly overjoyed by the news, but now she was worried, wondering if she had been a mean, judgemental little cat when it came to her stepmother. Felicity was pregnant and stressed out and surely *had* to be labouring under a burden of guilt and unhappiness?

'Busy night?' a familiar accented drawl murmured, breaking into Lizzie's uneasy thoughts with sizzling effect.

In bemusement, Lizzie spun round and just feet away saw Sebasten lounging back against the polished bonnet of a fire-engine-red Lamborghini Diablo. Instantly, she went into melt-down with relief: *he* had come to see *her*. Shimmering dark golden eyes lanced into hers.

'Sebasten…?' Lizzie tensed at the taut angularity of his hard features.

Like a jungle cat uncoiling prior to springing, Sebasten straightened in one fluid movement and strode forward. '*Theos mou*…you staged a deliberate fight with me today, didn't you?'

Her brow furrowed in confusion. 'Sorry?'

'You had *other* plans for tonight,' Sebasten grated, ready to ignite into blistering rage and only holding on to his temper while his intellect continued to remind him that he was in the street with a car-load of his own bodyguards sitting parked only yards away.

'I really don't know what you're talking about.' And Lizzie didn't, for she had already forgotten her father's brief pres-

ence while her brain strove to comprehend what Sebasten
was so very angry about.

'You slut!' Sebasten bit out, lean hands coiled into powerful fists. 'I should've been waiting for this!'

Acknowledging that the volatile side of Sebasten that she
had once considered so very appealing was in the ascendant,
Lizzie sucked in a sustaining breath and murmured with determined calm. 'Could you lower your voice and say whatever it is you just said in—er—English?'

When Sebasten appreciated that he had spoken in Greek,
incandescent rage lit up in his simmering gaze. He gave her
the translation at sizzling speed.

So taken aback was Lizzie by that offensive charge that
she just stared at him for a count of ten incredulous seconds.

'And you're coming home with me so that we can have
this out in *private*!' Sebasten launched at her between even
white gritted teeth.

A shaken little laugh with a shrill edge fell from Lizzie's
parted lips. Even as pain that he should attack her out of the
blue with such an unreasonable accusation assailed her, she
could not credit that he should imagine that she would now
go *any* place with him.

Without warning, Sebasten closed a purposeful hand to her
elbow.

Temper finally igniting, for caveman tactics had never
had even the smallest appeal to her, Lizzie slapped his hand
away and backed off a pointed step. 'Are you crazy? What's
got into you? I have a stupid argument with you and you
come out of nowhere at me and call me a name like that?'

'I saw you smarming over the jerk in the Porsche! How
long has *he* been around?' Sebasten raked at her, all awareness of surroundings now obliterated by a fury stronger than
any he had ever experienced.

At that point, clarification was shed on the inexplicable for

Lizzie: he was talking about her father. Green eyes sparkling, she tilted her chin. 'Since before I was born. My father looks well for his age, doesn't he? But then he keeps himself very fit.'

'Since before you were *born*...your father?' Sebasten slung before the proverbial penny dropped, as it were, from a very great height on him.

'Goodnight, Sebasten,' Lizzie completed and she swanned into the terraced building behind him with all the panache and dignity of a queen.

Out on the pavement, Sebasten turned the air blue with bad language and then powered off in immediate pursuit.

When a knock that made the wood panels shake sounded on the door of her bedsit, Lizzie opened it on the security chain and peered out. 'Go away,' she said fiercely. 'How dare you insult me like that? And how dare you call my father a jerk?'

Before Sebasten had the opportunity to answer either furious demand, the door closed again in his face. Her father. What he had witnessed was the innocent family affection of a father and daughter. The mists of rage were dimming only to be replaced by a seething awareness that he had got it wrong. And she had *laughed*. Lean, whipcord muscles snapping to rigidity as he recalled that shrill little laugh, Sebasten went home and collected a speeding ticket on the way.

In the bath that Lizzie took to wind down, she ended up humming happily to herself. True, she had been furious with Sebasten, but Sebasten had been beside himself with rage only because he was *jealous*. No man had ever thrown a jealous scene over Lizzie before and she could not help but be impressed by the amount of emotion Sebasten had put into that challenge. For the first time in her life, she felt like an irresistible and dangerous woman. Just imagine Sebasten getting that worked up over the belief that she was two-timing him! Lizzie smiled and smiled. But he just had to learn what was acceptable and what wasn't. He wasn't very trusting either, was he? However, he did seem pretty keen. He would phone her, wouldn't he? Should she just have let him come in?

The following morning, Lizzie wakened feeling out of sorts again and groaned with all the exasperation of someone rarely ill. Perhaps she had picked up some bug that her system couldn't shake off. About that point, she registered that, although she had finished taking her contraceptive pills for that month, her period had still not arrived and she tensed. No, she couldn't possibly be pregnant! Why was she even thinking such a crazy thing? All the same, accidents did happen, she reasoned anxiously and she decided to buy a testing kit at lunchtime just to *prove* to herself that she had nothing to worry about.

When she arrived at Contaxis International, she was taken down to the basement file-storage rooms with an entire trolley-load of documents to be filed away. As Milly Sharpe smiled after showing her the procedure with her own personal hands, Lizzie had the sneaking suspicion that the subterranean eerie depths of the building were where she was destined to stay for the remainder of her three-month contract.

Footsteps made a creepy hollow sound in the long, quiet corridors and Lizzie had a rich imagination. She peered out of the room she was in: there was a security guard patrolling. As she worked, she heard occasional distant noises and indistinct echoes. With the exception of the older man parked at a desk with a newspaper at the far end of the floor, there seemed to be nobody on permanent duty in the basement. It was boring and lonely and she hated it but she knew she had to stick it out. Not having made a good start the day before, she reckoned she was still lucky to be employed.

When she heard brisk footsteps ringing down the corridor just before lunchtime, she assumed it was the security guard again until she heard her own name called loud and clear and setting up a train of echoes. 'Lizzie!'

It was Sebasten's voice and he was in no need of a public-address system, for, having done an initially discreet but fruitless search of half a dozen rooms for her, he was out of patience. He had ensured that a magnificent bouquet of flowers had been delivered to her early that morning and he had expected her to phone him.

Lizzie ducked her head round the door. 'What are you *doing* down here?'

'This is my building—'

'Show-off,' she muttered, colour rising into her cheeks as she allowed herself to succumb to the temptation of looking at him.

'Isn't this a great place for a rendezvous?' Sebasten leant back against the door to shut it, sealing them into privacy.

'I don't think you should come looking for me when I'm at work,' Lizzie said with something less than conviction, for in truth she was pleased that he had made the effort.

From the crown of his proud dark head to the soles of his no doubt handmade shoes, he looked utterly fantastic, Lizzie acknowledged, the flare of her own senses in response to his vibrant, bronzed virility leaving her weak. His charcoal-grey business suit exuded designer style and tailoring. His shadow-striped grey and white shirt would have an exclusive monogram on the pocket: she ought to know, after all; she had two of them in her possession and had no intention of returning them.

As Sebasten began at her slender feet and worked his bold visual path up over her glorious legs to the purple silk skirt and aqua tie top she wore, sexy, smouldering intent emanated from every lithe, muscular inch of his big, powerful body.

'Miss me…?' he enquired lazily.

'After the way you behaved last night? You've got to be joking!' Lizzie dared.

'How was I to know the guy with the Porsche was your father?' Sebasten demanded, annoyed that she was digging up a matter that he believed should be closed and forgotten.

'You could have given me the benefit of the doubt and just come over and spoken to us.' With unusual tact, Lizzie swallowed the 'like anybody normal would have done' phrase she had almost fired in addition.

Sebasten dealt her a level look golden eyes now dark, hard and unapologetic. 'I don't give women the benefit of the doubt.'

Lizzie stiffened. 'Then you must've known some very unreliable women but that's still not an excuse for throwing a word like "slut" at me!'

'What I saw looked *bad*,' Sebasten growled, evading the issue.

'Did you have a really nasty experience with someone?' Lizzie was dismayed by his stubborn refusal to apologise but far more disturbed by that initial statement of distrust in her sex.

'Oh, just a mother and three stepmothers,' Sebasten imparted with acid derision, dark eyes burning back to gold in warning.

'Three?' Her lush mouth rounded into a soundless circle and slowly closed again, for she was so disconcerted she could think of nothing to say.

'One gold-digger, two sluts and one pill-popper,' Sebasten specified with raw scorn, for he loathed any reference to his family background. 'I suppose you now think you understand me.'

No, what she understood was how deep ran his distrust and his cynicism and she was shaken by what he had kept hidden behind the sophisticated façade. Well, you admired the complexity and now you've got it in spades, a dry little voice said inside her head. This is the guy you love: running in the opposite direction is not a realistic option. What was in her own heart and the reality that she already ached at the thought of the damage done to him would pull her back.

'No, I think you'll do just about anything, even spill the beans about the family from hell…*anything* rather than apologise,' Lizzie quipped, making her tense mouth curve into a rueful grin.

Thrown by that unexpected sally, Sebasten stared down into her dancing green eyes, the worst of his aggressive tension evaporating. 'The flowers were the apology—'

'What flowers?'

'You should've got them this morning—'

'I leave for work at the crack of dawn.' Lizzie tossed her head back. 'Was there a card with a written apology included?'

'Just a signature,' Sebasten admitted, sudden raw amusement sending a slashing smile across his lean dark face. 'You're very persistent, aren't you?'

The megawatt charm of that smile made Lizzie's knees wobble. Her body was held fast by a delicious tension that made her skin prickle, her breasts swell and her nipples tighten with sudden urgent and embarrassing sensitivity. 'Don't try to change the subject,' she warned him shakily.

'Or persuade you into silence?' Sebasten questioned, closing his hands to her narrow waist and lifting her up to bring her down on the table at which she had been sitting sorting documents just minutes earlier.

'Sebasten…' she gasped, disconcerted by that sudden shift into lover mode but secretly thrilled by it too. 'Suppose someone comes in?'

'The door's locked—'

'That was sneaky—'

'Sensible…' Sebasten contradicted, bracing long fingers either side of her and leaning forward to claim a teasing kiss. But the instant his mouth touched the lush softness of hers, he remembered how he had felt the night before when he had seen her in another man's arms and a sudden primitive need that was overwhelming swept him in stormy reaction. Instead of teasing, he forced her willing lips apart with the hungry driving pressure of his own.

Her heart banging in both surprise and excitement at his passion, Lizzie only worked up the will-power to tear free when her lungs were near to bursting. 'We have serious stuff to talk about—'

'This is *very* serious, *pethi mou*,' Sebasten broke in with fierce intensity, brilliant eyes locked to her as he let his lean hands travel with possessive appreciation up over her slender thighs. 'It was two weeks since we'd made love…two weeks of indescribable frustration…I think that must be why I lost my head last night.'

With a mighty effort of will Lizzie planted her hands in a staying motion over his, even though every weak, sinful skincell she possessed was thrumming like a car engine being revved. 'We haven't even discussed you fixing up this job for me—'

'But I'm so bloody grateful I did…it keeps you within reach,' Sebasten groaned, escaping her attempt at restraint with single-minded purpose and sinking his hands beneath her hips instead to tug her to the edge of the table and lock her into contact with him.

Brought into tantalising connection with the virile thrust of his potent masculine arousal, Lizzie uttered a sudden moan and plunged both hands into his luxuriant black hair and kissed him with all the wild hunger she had suppressed during his absence unleashed. Sebasten sounded a raw, appreciative groan low in his throat. Throwing back his broad shoulders to remove his jacket, he jerked loose his silk tie with a distinct air of purpose and cast both away.

Her mouth ran dry even as shock gripped her that he intended to take their lovemaking further.

'I'm so hot for you, I *ache*,' Sebasten spelt out hoarsely, golden eyes smouldering over her with burning intent, any hope of restraint wrested from him by the sheer charge of shaken anticipation he could see in her feverishly flushed face.

'Yes…me too,' Lizzie muttered, instinctively ashamed of the intensity of her own hunger for him but unable to deny it.

With deft fingers Sebasten undid the tie on her aqua top, spread it wide and then tipped her back over one strong arm to claim a plundering kiss of raw, sensual urgency while he unclipped the front fastening on her white bra. 'I'm not used to frustration…I've never felt this *desperate*,' he grated truthfully.

That same seething desperation had Lizzie in an iron hold. She was trembling, already breathing in short, shallow little spurts. The bra cups fell from her tender breasts and a lean brown hand captured an erect pink nipple to toy with first one throbbing peak and then the other. The pleasure was hot, heady and so immediate that all the breath was forced from her in a long, driven gasp. The maddening twist of craving low in her belly was a growing torment.

Sebasten sat her up, sank impatient hands beneath her and peeled off her panties. She was helpless in the grip of her own abandonment. An earthy sound of approbation was wrenched from him when he discovered the slick satin heat already awaiting him, and from that point control no longer existed for him either.

'Please…' Lizzie heard herself plead in helpless thrall to the pleasure and to him.

Sebasten straightened, hauled her back to him at the point where she had all the resistance of a rag doll and sank into her silken sheath in one forceful thrust. She clung to him on a wave of such powerful excitement, she thought she might pass out with the sheer overload of sensation. It was wild, wilder than she had ever dreamt it could be even with him. When she finally convulsed in almost agonised ecstasy, he silenced her cry of release with the hot demand of his mouth, stilled the writhing of her hips and ground deep into her one last time.

In the wake of the most explosive climax of his life, Sebasten was stunned. He took in his surroundings, his attention lodging in disbelief on the bland office walls, and he was even more stunned. Feeling as though he had just come out of a blackout, he raised Lizzie, smoothed her silky, tumbled hair back from her brow with a hand he couldn't keep steady and began to restore her clothing to order at speed.

The loud staccato burst of knocking on the door froze him into stillness.

Dragged from the dazed aftermath of their intimacy, Lizzie opened shattered eyes wide on the aghast awareness of how impossible it would be to hide a male of six feet four inches in a room full of wall-to-wall filing cabinets. 'Oh, no…there's someone wanting t-to get in here—'

'Ignore it.'

'We can't!' she whispered frantically.

'We *can*—'

'I'm calling Security if this door is not unlocked immediately!' a furious female voice threatened from the corridor.

CHAPTER SIX

SEBASTEN swore under his breath, swept up his jacket and dug his arms into it while Lizzie leapt off the table, smoothed down her mussed skirt and retrieved the one item of her clothing which Sebasten had removed with a face that burned hotter than any fire.

'This is Sebasten Contaxis…the lock's jammed and I'm stuck in here! Call Maintenance!" Sebasten called back, all ice-cool authority.

Five seconds later, high-heeled shoes were to be heard scurrying down the corridor. As soon as the racket of the woman's retreat receded, Sebasten stepped back and aimed a powerful kick at the lock. The door sprang open all on its own but the lock now looked damaged enough to support his story. Lizzie was still paralysed to the spot, transfixed by his speed and inventiveness in reacting to what had threatened to be the most humiliating encounter of her entire life.

'After you…' Sebasten invited with the shimmering golden eyes of a male who enjoyed a healthy challenge and enjoyed even more turning in a gold-medal performance for the benefit of an impressed-to-death woman. 'Grab a few files and lose yourself at the other end of the floor. I'll pick you up at half-six. We're entertaining tonight at Pomeroy Place, my country house, so pack a bag.'

'Sounds great,' she mumbled, revelling in the coupley to-getherness of that 'we' he had employed.

'I forgot about the blasted party,' Sebasten admitted with a frown over that same slip of the tongue as he swung away.

'Sebasten…?' In a sudden surge of emotion that Lizzie could no more have restrained than she could have held back floodwater, she flung herself at him as he turned back with an enquiring ebony brow raised. Green eyes shining, she linked her arms round his neck and gave him a hug. 'That's for just b-being you,' she told him, her voice faltering as he tensed in surprise.

'Thanks.' Sebasten set her back from him, his keen dark gaze veiling as he read the soft, vulnerable look in her expectant face. 'I should get going,' he pointed out.

Lizzie gathered up some loose papers and found another room in which to work. From there she could hear the rise and fall of speculative voices as maintenance staff attended to the damage door further down the corridor but she was incapable of listening. She pressed clammy hands to her pale, stricken face, unable to combat the deep inner chill spreading through her. Even after the incredible passion they had shared, even while her wretched body still ached from the penetration of his, her affectionate hug and declaration had been received like a step too far. He might have attempted to conceal that reality but his lack of any true response had spoken for him.

But why? For a split-second, Sebasten had looked down into her eyes and what had he seen there? *Love?* She felt humiliated, foolish and scared all at once. Whatever he had seen, he had not wanted to see. It was as though she had crossed some invisible boundary line and, instead of moving to meet her, he had turned his back. But then what had she been thinking of when she threw herself at him like that? The wildness of their lovemaking had shattered her and perhaps she had wanted reassurance…emotional reassurance.

At that awful moment of truth, Lizzie regretted her first night in Sebasten's bed with an angry self-loathing of her own weakness that nothing could have quenched. She had been reckless and now she was paying the price for not resisting temptation until she knew him better. Even more did she suffer at the recollection of her own wanton response to him only thirty minutes earlier. What Sebasten wanted it seemed Sebasten got. He touched her and she demonstrated all the self-will of a clockwork toy. For the first time, she understood with painful clarity just how cruelly deceptive sexual intimacy could be. Was she at heart the slut he had called her? She winced, her throat aching, because she was just so much in love with him. But did Sebasten see her as anything more than a casual sexual affair?

In the mood Lizzie was in, the prospect of devoting her lunch hour to buying a pregnancy test had scant appeal. Where had the insane fear that she might have conceived come from in the first place? It wasn't as though she had felt sick or even dizzy since she had come into work. She was just being silly, working herself up into a panic because she was involved in her very first intimate relationship. All the same, oughtn't she to check just to be on the safe side?

She bought the test kit, buried it in her bag, tried to forget it was there and discovered she could not. Then that afternoon, when she sprang up in a sudden movement after leafing through a bottom file drawer, her head swam and she swayed. As soon as she got home she knew she would use the test because a creeping sense of apprehension was growing at a steady rate at the back of her mind.

On the top floor of the CI building, Sebasten stared out at the city skyline with a brooding distance etched in his grim gaze. He was in a state of angry conflict that was foreign to him. *What was he playing at with Lizzie Denton?* When had his own motivations become as indistinct to him as a fog?

Since the morning he learned her true identity, he had not once stopped to think through what he was doing in getting involved with her. That reality shook him at an instant when he was still striving without success to come up with an adequate explanation for what he had already labelled the 'basement episode'. He felt out of control and he didn't like it.

How could he keep on somehow neglecting to recall how cruelly Lizzie had treated his half-brother, Connor? Or the number of sweet studied lies that had tripped off her ready tongue on that same subject? What was he suffering from? Selective-memory syndrome? Did that glorious body of hers mean more to him than his own honour? Or even basic decency? From start to finish, his intimacy with her had defied every tenet he lived by.

He could no more easily explain why he had bought her diamonds and her car back for her. Did Lizzie deserve a reward for demonstrating that buckets of winsome pseudo-innocent charm could conceal a shallow nature? After all, most women made a special effort to impress and hide their worst side around a male of his wealth. Furthermore, he was very fond of Ingrid Morgan but he was bitterly aware that on the day of Connor's funeral he had made the rare mistake of letting emotions cloud his judgement. It was past time he ended what should *never* have begun…

While Sebasten was coming to terms with what he saw as an inevitable event, Lizzie was seated on her bed in shock, just staring at the little wand that had turned a certain colour ten minutes earlier. She picked up the test kit instructions and read the section on false results for the third time. Maybe the kit had been old stock. She checked the sell-by date on the packaging but there was no comfort to be found there.

Although it seemed incredible to her, she *was* going to have a baby…Sebasten's baby. If he reacted to a hug as if it were a marriage proposal, how would he react to a baby? She paled and shivered and wrapped her arms round herself. That first night she had told him that she was protected, had fully, confidently believed that she was, but hadn't she also known that no form of contraception yet existed that was a hundred per-cent effective?

The concept of having a child in her life transfixed Lizzie. As yet none of her former friends had children and discussing babies had always been considered deeply uncool. Lizzie had always kept quiet about the fact that she adored babies, had had to restrain herself from commenting in public about how seriously attractive some of them were and how insidious was the appeal of the shops that sold tiny garments. She stood up and studied her stomach in the mirror, sucked what little of it there was in…was there just the very faintest hint of it not going in quite as far as it once had? Registering what she was doing, she frowned in dismay at her inability to think sensible thoughts.

She wasn't married, she wasn't solvent, she didn't even have a proper job, and on being told the father of her baby would most probably demonstrate *why* he had such a bad reputation. He might try to deny that he was the father or he might assume that she would agree to a termination that would free him from the responsibility for her child. In fact, it would be extremely naïve of her to expect anything but a shocked and angry reaction from Sebasten. This was a guy who had told her that he *never* gave women the benefit of the doubt. In her situation that was not good news.

Here she was, living in a crummy bedsit, having come down in the world the exact same day she met a very rich man, and lo and behold…a few weeks later she would be telling him that she had fallen pregnant by him. Even to her that scenario did not look good. The least suspicious of men might have doubts about conception having been accidental in such circumstances, so the odds were that Sebasten would immediately think that he had been deliberately entrapped. An anguished groan escaped Lizzie.

She might really love Sebasten but she was getting acquainted with his flaws and her pride baulked at the prospect of putting herself in such a demeaning position. There was no good reason why she should make an *immediate* announcement though, was there? Wouldn't it make more sense to wait until she had at least seen a doctor? Furthermore, that would give her more time to work out how best to broach the subject with Sebasten...

As Sebasten drove over to collect Lizzie, he cursed the necessity of their having to spend the night under the same roof at Pomeroy.

He was about to break off their relationship, so where had his wits been when he had made an inconvenient arrangement like that? But then he had since worked out exactly where his wits had been over the past three weeks: *Lost in lust*. Indeed, recalling his own extraordinary behaviour that same morning, his strong jawline took on an aggressive cast. Unbelievably, he had staged a clandestine sexual encounter at Contaxis International in the middle of his working day. All decent restraint had vanished the same instant he laid eyes on Lizzie's lithe, leggy perfection: he had had that door shut and locked within seconds.

So, in common with most single males with a healthy sex drive, Sebasten reasoned, he had proved to be a pushover when it came to the lure of a forbidden thrill. But that angle was cold consolation to a Greek who prided himself on the strength of his own self-discipline. Yet in that file room he had behaved like a sex-starved teenager who took advantage of every opportunity, no matter how inappropriate it might be. That demeaning image rankled even more.

It just went to show that a guy should never, *ever* relax his guard round a woman, Sebasten conceded in grim conclu-sion. Lizzie was an absolute powder-keg of sexual dynamite. Why else could he not keep his hands off her? Why else had he dragged her home with him only hours after meeting her?

After all, he had never been into casual encounters. Had anyone ever told him that he would some day sink to the level of sobering up a drunk woman and then falling victim to her supposed charms afresh, he would have laughed out loud in derision. Only now he wasn't laughing. After all, he had only got through the previous couple of weeks of self-denial by virtually staying out of the country and seeing her only in public places, he acknowledged with seething self-contempt.

When he picked up Lizzie he would be really cool with her and she would register that the end was nigh for herself. Exactly *why*, he asked himself then, was he agonising about something that had cost him only the most fleeting pang with other women?

Relationships broke up every day. She had ditched Connor without an ounce of concern, he reminded himself. But then how did he judge her for that when he had done pretty much the same thing himself? The rejected lover was hurt and what could anybody do about that? He recalled Lizzie's shining, trusting green eyes clinging to him and something in his gut twisted. He didn't want to hurt her.

Lizzie was still getting ready when Sebasten arrived.

'Are you always this punctual?' she groaned, hot, self-con-scious colour burning her cheekbones as she evaded his gaze, for all she could think about at that instant was the pregnancy test that had come up positive.

'Always,' Sebasten confirmed, shrugging back a cuff to check his Rolex for good measure, determined to be difficult.

He looked grim, Lizzie registered, her heart skipping a beat as she noted the tautness of his fabulous bone-structure.

'I'll wait in the car,' Sebasten said drily, striving not to notice the way her yellow silk wrap defined her slender, shapely figure. For a dangerous split-second he thought of her as a gaily-wrapped present he couldn't wait to unwrap and the damage was done: his body reminded him with ferocious and infuriating immediacy that their stolen encounter earlier had only blunted the edge of his frustration.

'Don't be daft…I'll only be a minute.' Lizzie watched the faintest hint of dark colour score his chiselled cheekbones and wondered in dismay what on earth was the matter with him.

Desperate for any form of distraction that might lessen his awareness of the ache in his groin, Sebasten studied the open suitcase festooned with an enormous heap of garments as yet unpacked. He frowned. She was very disorganised and he was quite the opposite, so why was there something vaguely endearing about the harried, covert way she was now trying to squash everything into the case without regard for any form of folding whatsoever? He hated untidiness, he hated unpunctuality. Tell her it's over *now*, his intelligence urged him just as Lizzie looked up at him.

'You've had a lousy day, haven't you?' she guessed in a warm and sympathetic tone that snaked out and wrapped round Sebasten like a silken man-trap. 'Why don't you just sit down and chill out and I'll make you a cup of coffee?'

Disconcerted, Sebasten parted his lips. 'I—'

'I bet the traffic was appalling too.' Lizzie treated him to the kind of appreciative appraisal that implied he had crossed at least an ocean and a swamp just to reach her door and disappeared behind the battered wooden screen that semi-concealed the tiny kitchen area in one corner.

'Lizzie…' Sebasten felt like the biggest bastard in creation but what hit him with even more striking effect was the sudden acknowledgment that he did not *want* to dump Lizzie. Shattered by that belated moment of truth with himself, he snatched in a deep, shuddering breath.

'Yes?' She reappeared, her wide, friendly smile flashing out at him as she handed him a cup of coffee. 'What's your favourite colour?'

'Turquoise,' Sebasten muttered, struggling to come to terms with what he had refused to admit to himself all afternoon. It was as if she had put a spell on him the first night: he and his hormones had been haywire ever since. Yet there was no way on earth that he could add to Ingrid's grief by keeping the woman she blamed for Connor's death in his own life. And did he not owe more respect to his late brother's memory? Lizzie's only hold on him was sex, he reminded himself angrily. She was also an appalling liar and he ought to tell her that before they parted company.

Lizzie rustled through the wardrobe, grateful for the opportunity to occupy her trembling hands. She just had a bad feeling about the mood Sebasten was in. She could only equate his presence with having a big black thundercloud hanging overhead. Clutching a turquoise dress, she went behind the screen to change.

Never had the audible rustle and silky slither of feminine garments had such a provocative effect on Sebasten's libido. Out of all patience with himself, infuriated by the threatening volcano of opposing thoughts, urges and emotions seething inside him, he paced the restricted confines of the room until she was ready and said little after they had driven off in the Lamborghini.

'Do you like—children?' Lizzie shot at him then right out of the blue.

Already on red alert, Sebasten's defensive antenna lit up like the Greek sky at dawn. The most curious dark satisfaction assailed him as his very worst expectations were fulfilled. After just weeks, it seemed, she was dreaming of wedding bells. But that satisfaction was short-lived as it occurred to him that, possibly, he had given her grounds to believe she had him hooked like a fish on a line.

Hadn't he made a huge prat of himself when he saw her hugging her father? And what about all those phone calls he had made to her when he was abroad? Why had he felt a need to phone her every damn day he was away from her? And sometimes *more* than once. Not to mention activities that were the total opposite of cool and sophistication in the CI basement. She might well believe that he was infatuated with her.

'Children are all right…at a distance,' Sebasten pronounced, cool as ice.

Lizzie lost every scrap of her natural colour and caution might have warned her to keep quiet but she was quite incapable of listening to such promptings. 'What sort of answer is that?'

'They *can* look quite charming in paintings,' Sebasten conceded, studying the traffic lights with brooding concentration. 'But they're noisy, demanding and an enormous responsibility. I'm much too selfish to want that kind of hassle in my life.'

'I hope your future wife feels the same way,' was all that Lizzie in her shattered state could think to mutter to cover herself in the hideous silence that stretched.

'I'm not planning to acquire one of those either,' Sebasten confessed in an aggressive tone. 'If even my father couldn't strike gold *once* in four marriages, what hope have I?'

'None whatsoever, I should think, with your outlook,' Lizzie answered in a tight, driven reply. 'Of course, some women would marry you simply because you're loaded—'

'Surprise…surprise,' Sebasten slotted in with satiric bite.

'But personally speaking…' Lizzie's low-pitched response quivered with the force of her disturbed emotions and she was determined to have her own say on the subject…'not all the money in the world would compensate me for being deprived of children. I also think there's something very suspect about a man who dislikes children—'

'*Suspect?* In what way?' Sebasten demanded with wrathful incredulity, exploded from his already unsettled state of mind with a vengeance.

'But then, as you said, you're very selfish, but to my way of thinking…a *truly* masculine man would have a more mature outlook and he would appreciate that a life partner and the children they would share would be as rewarding as they were restricting.'

Sebasten was so incensed, he almost launched a volley of enraged Greek at her. Who was she calling immature? And when had he said that he *disliked* children? A truly masculine man? His lean brown hands flexed and tightened round the steering wheel as he sought to contain his ire at her daring to question what every Greek male considered the literal essence of being.

'Your mind is narrow indeed,' he gritted, shooting the Lamborghini down the motorway at above the speed limit.

'You're entitled to your opinion.' Lizzie was wondering in a daze of shock how she could have been so offensive but not really caring, for what he had told her had appalled her. Dreams she had not even known she cherished had been hauled out into the unkind light of day and crucified. 'But please watch your speed.'

Deprived of even that minor outlet for his rage, Sebasten slowed down, lean, bronzed features set like stone. 'The minute my father, Andros, suffered a setback in business and her jetset lifestyle looked to be under threat, my mother demanded a divorce. She traded custody of me for a bigger settlement,' he bit out rawly. 'Although she had access rights, she never utilised them. I was only six years old.'

In an altogether new kind of shock, Lizzie focused her entire attention on his taut, hard profile. 'You never saw her again?'

'No, and she died a few years later. A *truly* feminine, maternal woman,' Sebasten framed with vicious intent. 'My first stepmother slept with the teenager who cleaned our swimming pool. She liked very young men.'

'Oh…dear,' Lizzie mumbled, bereft of a ready word of comfort to offer.

'Andros divorced her. His next wife spent most of their marriage in a series of drug rehabilitation clinics but still contrived to die of an overdose. The fourth wife was much younger and livelier and she was addicted to sex but *not* with an ageing husband,' Sebasten delivered with sizzling contempt. 'The night that my father suffered the humiliation of overhearing her strenuous efforts to persuade *me* into bed, he had his first heart attack.'

After that daunting recitation of matrimonial disaster, Lizzie shook her head in sincere dismay. 'Your poor father. Obviously he didn't have any judgement at all when it came to women.'

Not having been faced with that less than tactful response before, Sebasten gritted his even white teeth harder until it crossed his mind that there was a most annoying amount of truth in that comment. Throughout those same years, Ingrid, who would have made an excellent wife, had hovered in the background, at first hopeful, then slowly losing heart when she was never once even considered as a suitable bridal candidate by the man who had been her lover on and off for years. Why not? She had been born poor, had had to work for a living and had made the very great strategic error of sharing his father's bed between wives.

But how the hell had he got on to such a very personal subject with Lizzie? What was it about her? When had he ever before dumped the embarrassing gritty details of his background on a woman? He was furious with himself.

Given plenty of food for thought, Lizzie blinked back tears at the mere idea of what Sebasten must have suffered after his greedy mother's rejection was followed by the ordeal of three horribly inadequate stepmothers. Was it any wonder that he should be so anti-marriage and children? Her heart just went out to him and she was ashamed of her own face-saving condemnation of his views earlier. After all, what did she know about what *his* life must have been like? Only now, having been given the bare bones, she was just dying to flesh them out.

However, Sebasten's monosyllabic responses soon squashed that aspiration flat and silence fell until the Lamborghini accelerated up a long, winding drive beneath a leafy tunnel of huge weeping lime trees. Pomeroy Place was a Georgian jewel of architectural elegance, set off to perfection by a beautiful setting.

Before the housekeeper could take Lizzie upstairs, Lizzie glanced back across the large, elegant hall and focused with anxious eyes on Sebasten's grim profile before following the older woman up the superb marble staircase. Shown into a gorgeous guest room, she freshened up, a frown indenting her brow. In the mood Sebasten was in, he felt like an intimidating stranger. But then, it was evident that she had roused bad memories, but did he have to shut her out to such an extent? Could he not appreciate that she had feelings too?

Downstairs, receiving the first of his guests, Sebasten was discovering that a bad day could only get much worse when the vivacious gossip columnist Patsy Hewitt arrived on the arm of one of his recently divorced friends. Aware that Lizzie had been attacked by one of the tabloid newspapers for not attending Connor's funeral, the very last person he wanted seated at his dining-table was a journalist with a legendary talent for venom against her own sex. He did not want his relationship with Lizzie exposed in print just when he was about to end it. In fact, he was determined to protect Lizzie from that final embarrassment.

Quite how he could hope to achieve that end he had no clear idea, and then even the option seemed to vanish when Lizzie walked into the drawing room. He watched Patsy look at Lizzie and then turn back to the other couple she had been chatting to and he realised with relief that the journalist had no idea who Lizzie was.

'And this is Lizzie,' he murmured with a skimming glance in her general direction, drawing her to the attention of his other guests in a very impersonal manner.

'Do you work for Sebasten?' a woman in her thirties asked Lizzie some minutes later, evidently having no suspicion that Lizzie might be present in any other capacity.

'Yes.' The way Sebasten was behaving, Lizzie was happy to make that confirmation but an angry, discomfited spark flared in her clear green eyes.

Another four people arrived and soon afterwards they crossed the hall to the dining room. Pride helped Lizzie to keep up her end of the general conversation but she did not look at Sebasten unless she was forced to do so. What she ate or even whether she *did* eat during that meal she was never later to recall. She started out angry but sank deeper into shock as the evening progressed. Had she really expected to act as his hostess? Certainly, she had not expected to be treated like someone merely invited to keep the numbers at the table even.

'So…which luscious lady are you romancing right now?' the older brunette, who had entertained them all with her sharp sense of humour, asked Sebasten in a coy tone over the coffee-cups.

Lizzie froze and watched Sebasten screen his dark eyes with his spiky black lashes before he murmured lazily. 'I'm still looking.'

With a trembling hand, Lizzie reached for her glass of water. Feeling sick, betrayed and outraged, she backed out of her chair without any perceptible awareness of what she was about to do, walked down the length of the table and slung the contents of her glass in Sebasten's face. 'When I find a real man, I'll let you know!' she spelt out.

Sebasten vaulted upright and thrust driven fingers through his dripping hair.

The silence that had fallen had a depth that was claustrophobic.

And then, as Lizzie went into retreat at the shimmering incredulity in Sebasten's stunned golden eyes, one of the guests laughed out loud and she spun to see who it was that could find humour in such a scene.

'Bravo, Lizzie!' Patsy Hewitt told her with an amused appreciation that bewildered Lizzie. 'I don't think I've *ever* enjoyed a more entertaining evening.'

'I'm glad someone had a good time,' Lizzie quipped before she walked out of the room and sped upstairs with tears of furious, shaken reaction blinding her.

Had that guy talking been the guy she thought she loved? The male whose baby she carried? Denying her very existence? He was *ashamed* of her. What else was she to believe but that he was ashamed to own up to being involved with Connor Morgan's ex-girlfriend? He needn't think she had not eventually read the significance of his having neglected to speak her surname even once or his determination not to distinguish her with one atom of personal attention. So why the heck had he invited her? And how did she ditch him when she was expecting his baby?

But such concerns for a future that seemed distant were beyond Lizzie at a moment when all that was on her mind was leaving Sebasten's house just as fast as she could manage it. So it was unfortunate that while she had been downstairs dining her case had been unpacked.

She was in shock after the evening she had endured and

the shattering discovery that Sebasten could turn into a male she really didn't want to know. Why? *Why* had he suddenly changed towards her?

In a flash, she recalled his cool parting from her that morning at Contaxis International and stilled, comprehension finding a path through her bewilderment. Nothing had been right since then. He had been in a distant mood when he came to pick her up and then in the car she had asked that stupid question about whether or not he liked children and the atmosphere had gone from strained to freezing point. He wanted *out*. Why had she not seen that sooner?

With nerveless hands, she dragged out her case and plonked it down on the bed. She remembered the way he had made love to her earlier in the day and she shivered, almost torn in two by the agony that threatened to take hold of her.

When Sebasten strode in, she was gathering up the items she had left out on the dressing-table earlier and in the act of slinging them willy-nilly into her case.

'What do you want?' Lizzie asked, refusing to look higher than his snazzy dark blue silk tie.

'Perhaps I don't like having water thrown in my face in front of an audience,' Sebasten heard himself bite out, although that had not been the tack he had planned to take. 'And the audience didn't much enjoy the fall-out either…it's barely midnight and they've all gone home.'

'If I had had anything bigger and heavier within reach, the damage would have been a lot worse!' Lizzie's soft mouth was sealed so tight it showed white round the edges.

'Do you even realise who the woman who last spoke to you *was*?'

'I don't know and I don't care. There is just no excuse for the way you treated me tonight!' Lizzie was fighting to retain a grip on her disturbed emotions and walk out on him with dignity. Deep down inside she knew that if she allowed herself to think about what she was doing or what was happening between then she might come apart at the seams in front of him.

'Patsy Hewitt is the *Sunday Globe*'s gossip columnist. No prizes for guessing which couple will star in her next lead story!'

The journalist's name had a vague familiarity for Lizzie but so intense was her emotional conflict that she could not grasp why he should waste his breath on something that struck her as an irrelevant detail.

'I didn't flaunt our relationship tonight because I wanted to protect you from that kind of unpleasant media exposure,' Sebasten completed angrily.

That *he* should dare to be angry with *her* after the way he had behaved added salt to the wounds he had already inflicted. In the back of her mind, she discovered, had lurked a very different expectation: that he might grovel for embarrassing her in such a way, for denying her like a Judas before witnesses. And nothing short of grovelling apologies would have eased the colossal pain of angry, bewildered loss growing inside her.

'Why the heck should a guy with *your* reputation care about media exposure?' Lizzie demanded and looked at him for the first time since he had entered the room.

And it hurt, it hurt so much to study those lean, devastatingly attractive features, note the fierce tension etched in his fabulous bone-structure and recognise the hard condemnation in his scorching golden eyes.

'And why the heck would I care anyway?' she added in sudden haste, determined to get in first with what she knew was coming her way. 'We're finished and I want to go home. You can call a taxi for me!'

'You can stay the night here. It would be crazy for you to leave this late at night.' Instead of being relieved that the deed he had been in no hurry to do had been done for him, a jagged shot of instant igniting fury leapt through Sebasten.

'The very idea of staying under the same roof as you is offensive to me. You're an absolute toad and I hope Patsy whatever-her-name-is shows you up in print for what you are!' Lizzie slung back not quite levelly, for a tiny secret part of her, a part that she despised, had hoped that he might argue with her announcement, might even this late in the day magically contrive to excuse his own behaviour and redress the damage he had done.

'Perhaps had you considered telling me the truth about Connor *this* might not be happening,' Sebasten heard himself declare, his jawline clenching hard. 'Instead you lied your head off to me!'

'I beg your pardon…?' Settling perplexed green eyes on him, Lizzie stared back at him, her heart beginning to beat so fast at that startling reference to Connor that it felt as if it was thumping inside her very throat. Why was he dragging Connor in?

'Connor's mother, Ingrid, is a close family friend.'

Her gaze widened in astonishment at that unexpected revelation, pallor driving away the feverish flush in her cheeks, an eerie chill tingling down her spine. 'You didn't tell me that before…you *said* you hardly knew him—'

'I knew Connor better as a child than as an adult.' On surer ground now, Sebasten let true anger rise and never had he needed anger more than when he saw the shattered look of incomprehension stamped to Lizzie's oval face. She was so pale that all seven freckles on her nose stood out in sharp relief. 'You also said you didn't know him well and then told repeated lies about your relationship with him.'

'I *didn't* lie,' Lizzie countered in angry bewilderment, her tall, slender body rigid as she attempted to challenge the accusation that she was a liar while at the same time come to terms with the shocking reality that Sebasten had close ties that he cherished with the Morgan family but that he had not been prepared to reveal that fact to her. 'I actually told you a truth that nobody other than myself, Connor and the woman involved knew!'

'*Theos mou*…the *truth*?' Sebasten slammed back with raw derision, infuriated that he had noticed her freckles in the middle of such a confrontation and outraged by the unfamiliar stress of having to fight to maintain his concentration. 'Your most ingenious story of Connor's secret affair with a married woman that would be impossible to disprove when you declined to name the lady involved. That nonsense was a base and inexcusable betrayal of Connor's memory!'

'You *didn't* believe me,' Lizzie registered in a belated surge of realisation and she shook her bright head in a numbed movement. 'And yet you never said so, never even mentioned that Ingrid Morgan was a friend of yours. Why did you conceal those facts? If you believed I was lying, why didn't you just confront me?'

'Maybe I thought it was time that someone taught you a lesson.' No sooner had Sebasten made that admission than he regretted it. 'That was *before* I understood that what I was doing to you was as reprehensible as what you did to Connor.'

Lizzie only heard that first statement and her blood ran cold in her veins. *Maybe I thought it was time that someone taught you a lesson.* That confession rocked her already shaken world and threatened to blow it away altogether. He had gone after her, singled her out, and it had *all* been part of some desire to punish her for what she had supposedly done to Connor? She was shattered by that final revelation.

'What sort of a man are you?' Lizzie demanded in palpable disbelief.

Anger nowhere within reach, Sebasten lost colour beneath his bronzed skin and fought an insane urge to pull her into his arms and hold her tight. 'The night I met you, the first night, I didn't *know* who you were. I didn't find out until the following morning when I saw your driving licence.'

Lizzie dismissed that plea without hesitation. 'I don't believe in coincidences like that…you went on the hunt for me.'

'Had I known who you were I would never have gone to bed with you,' Sebasten swore half under his breath.

A wave of dizziness assailed Lizzie. She could not bear to think of what he had just said. Blocking him from her mind and her view, she sank down on the foot of the bed and reached for her mobile phone. Desperate to leave his house, she punched out the number of a national cab firm to request a taxi.

'Hell…*I'll* take you back to London!' Sebasten broke in.

Having made the call, Lizzie ignored him and breathed in slow and deep to ward off the swimming sensation in her head. The guy she had fallen in love with had embarked on their relationship with the sole and deliberate intent of hurting and humiliating her. She could not believe that he could have been so cruel, and why? Over the head of Connor, who had already cost her so much!

Sick to the heart, she stood up like an automaton and headed for the dressing room, where she assumed her clothes had been stowed away. She dragged garments from hangers and drawers, dimly amazed at the amount of stuff she had contrived to pack for a single night. But then she had been in love, hadn't she been? Unable to make up her mind what she might need, what would look best, what *he* might admire most on her. A laugh that was no laugh at all bubbled and died again inside her. Her throat was raw and aching but, in the midst of what she believed to be the worst torture she would ever have to get through, her eyes were dry.

Sebasten hovered, lean, powerful hands clenching and unclenching. 'I should never have slept with you,' he admitted with suppressed savagery. 'If I could go back and change that I *would*—'

'Try staying out of basements too.' Her tone one of ringing disgust, Lizzie quivered with a combustible mix of self-loathing and shame that he could have been so ruthless and wicked as to take advantage of her weakness. 'There could never have been an excuse for what you've done. That you should have set out to cause me harm is unforgivable.'

'Yes,' Sebasten conceded in Greek, snatching in a deep-driven breath and switching back to English to state. 'I *do* accept that two wrongs do not make a right, but in the heat of the moment when I was confronted with the depth of Ingrid's despair my mind was not so clear. I was appalled that first morning when I discovered your true identity and what took place today was indefensible. But from the outset I was very much attracted to you.'

Heaping clothes into the case, Lizzie made herself look at him, hatred in her heart, hatred built on a hurt that went so deep it felt like a physical pain. 'Is that supposed to make me feel better? I met you when my whole life had crashed around me. I was very unhappy and you must have seen that…yet you waded in and made it worse,' she condemned. 'How could you be such a bastard?'

'I lost the plot…isn't that obvious?' Sebasten threw back at her with a savage edge to his accented drawl as he swept up the couple of garments she had dropped on her passage from the dressing room but held on to them because he did not want to hasten her departure. 'I got in deeper than I ever dreamt and I'm paying a price for that now too.'

Lizzie thought in a daze of the child she carried and a spasm of bitter regret tightened her facial muscles. She was no longer listening to him. 'Connor cheated on me and he didn't spare my feelings a single thought. I lost my friends and my father's respect. I paid way over the odds for being the fall guy in that affair. But this is something else again…I *loved* you…' Her voice faltered to a halt and she blinked, shocked that she had admitted that and then, beyond caring, she snapped her case closed with trembling hands and swung it down off the bed.

'I don't want you to leave in this frame of mind…' Sebasten declared as much to her as to himself.

'I hate you. I will never forgive you…so stop saying really *stupid* things!' Lizzie slung at him with a wildness that mushroomed up from within her without any warning and made her feel almost violent. 'What did you expect from me? That I was going to shake hands and thank you for wrecking my life again!'

Sebasten had no answer, but then he had never thought that far ahead and just then cool, rational thought evaded him. 'If you want to go back to London tonight, let me drive you,' he urged, taking refuge in male practicality.

'You're wired to the moon,' Lizzie accused shakily, hauling her case past him.

His hand came down over hers and forced her fingers into retreat from the handle. She just let him have the case. She walked to the door, threw it wide and started down the stairs while she willed the taxi to come faster than the speed of light.

Sebasten reached the hall only seconds in her wake. As a manservant hurried from the rear of the hall to relieve him of the case, only to be sent into retreat by the ferocious look of warning he received from his employer, Lizzie wrenched open the front door on her own.'

'Give me my case!' she demanded, fired up like an Amazon warrior.

With pronounced reluctance, Sebasten set the case down. 'Lizzie…Connor was my half-brother…'

Lizzie spun back to him in astonishment and an image of

Connor surged up in her mind's eye: the very dark brown eyes that had been so unexpected with her ex-boyfriend's blond hair, the classic bone-structure, his height and build. She did not question Sebasten's ultimate revelation. Indeed, for her it was as though the whole appalling picture was finally complete.

'*Two* of you…' she muttered sickly as she turned away again to focus with relief on the car headlights approaching the front of the house. 'And *both* of you arrogant, selfish, lying rats who use and abuse women! Now, why doesn't that surprise me?'

Sebasten froze at that response. The cab driver got out to take her case. Within the space of a minute, Lizzie was gone. Sebasten looked down at the flimsy white bra and red silk shirt he was still grasping in one hand and he knew that he was about to get so drunk that he didn't know what day it was.

CHAPTER SEVEN

LIZZIE didn't cry that night: she was reeling with so much shock and reaction she was exhausted and she lay down on her bed still clothed and fell asleep.

After only a few hours, she wakened to a bleak sense of emptiness and terrible pain. She had fallen in love with a sadist. Sebasten had got under her skin when she was weak and vulnerable and hurt her beyond relief. Yet he was also the father of her baby. Her mind shied away from that daunting fact and her thoughts refused to stay in one place.

If Sebasten was Connor's half-brother that meant that the still attractive Ingrid must have had an affair with Sebasten's father. A very secret affair it must have been, for Connor himself when she asked had told Lizzie a different story about the circumstances of his birth.

'Ingrid met up with an old flame and the relationship had fizzled out again before she even knew I was on the way,' he had confided casually. 'He was an army officer. She did plan to tell him when he came back from his posting abroad but he was killed in a military helicopter crash shortly before I was born.'

Had that tale been a lie? Her brow indented as she dragged herself out of bed to look into her empty fridge. What was the point of thinking about Connor and the blood tie that

Sebasten had claimed? She needed to keep busy, she told herself dully. She also had to eat to stay healthy, which meant that she had to shop even when the very thought of food made her feel queasy. In addition, she reminded herself, she had to make an appointment with the doctor.

Without ever acknowledging that she was still so deep in shock from the events of the previous twenty-four hours that she could barely function, Lizzie drove herself through that day. She got a cancellation appointment at the doctor's surgery. She learned that she was indeed pregnant and when she asked how that might have happened when she had been taking contraceptive pills was asked if she missed taking any or had been sick. Instantly she recalled that first night with Sebasten when she had been ill, stilling a shiver at the wounding memories threatening her self-discipline, she fell silent. Concentration was impossible. Behind every thought lurked the spectre of her own grief.

From the medical centre she trekked to the supermarket, where she wandered in an aimless fashion, selecting odd items that had more appeal than others, but she returned to her bedsit and discovered that she had chosen nothing that would make a proper meal. She grilled some toast, forced herself to nibble two corners of it before having to flee for the bathroom and be ill.

Sebasten rose on Sunday with a hangover unlike any he had ever suffered. He had virtually no memory of Saturday. Any thought of Lizzie was the equivalent of receiving a punch to the solar plexus but he couldn't get her haunting image out of his mind. Was it guilt? What else could it be? When had any Contaxis ever sunk low enough to contemplate taking revenge on a woman? What the hell had got into him that he had even considered such a course of action? And now, when he was genuinely worried about Lizzie's state of mind, how could he check up on her?

Over breakfast, he flipped open the gossip page of the *Sunday Globe* and any desire to eat receded as he read the startling headline: 'CONTAXIS 0, DENTON 10.'

For all of his adult life, Sebasten had been adored and fêted and flattered by the gossip-column fraternity but Patsy Hewitt's gleeful account of events at his dinner party was very much of the poison-pen variety and directed at *him*. She made him sound like a total arrogant bastard and recommended that Lizzie keep looking until she found a man worthy of her, a piece of advice which sent Sebasten straight into an irrational rage.

Of course Lizzie wasn't about to race off on the hunt for another man! She was in love with him, wasn't she? But since their affair was over, ought he not to be keen for her to find a replacement for him? Just thinking about Lizzie in another man's bed drove Sebasten, who ate a healthy breakfast every morning without fail, from the breakfast table before he had had anything more than a single cup of black coffee.

He went out for a ride, returned filthy and soaked after a sudden downpour and got into the shower. After that, he tried to work but he could not concentrate. Why shouldn't he be concerned about Lizzie? He asked himself defensively then. Wasn't he human? And why shouldn't he give her the Mercedes and the diamonds back? After all, what was he to do with them? She was having a hard time and possibly getting back the possessions which she had been forced to sell would cheer her up a little.

As for her father, Maurice Denton, *well*, Sebasten was starting to cherish a very low opinion of a man he had never met. Family were supposed to stick together through thick and thin and forgive mistakes. Instead the wretched man had deprived his daughter of all means of support when it was entirely *his* fault that she was quite unequal to the task of supporting herself in the style to which her shortsighted parent had encouraged her to become accustomed.

Inflamed on Lizzie's behalf by that reflection, Sebasten snatched up his car keys and arranged for the Mercedes to be driven back to London to be delivered. He could not wait long enough for his own car to be driven round to the front of the house and he startled his staff by striding through the rear entrance to the garages and extracting his Lamborghini for himself.

After attending church, guiltily aware that it was her first visit since she had left home, Lizzie wondered why her father and Felicity were absent from their usual pew and realised that they must be spending the weekend at the cottage. Buying a newspaper before she went back to the bedsit, Lizzie read what Patsy Hewitt had written about that evening at Pomeroy Place and assumed that the journalist had decided to take a feminist stance for a change. She frowned when she perused the final cliff-hanging comment that advised readers to watch that space for a bigger story soon to break and then assumed that it could be nothing to do with either her or Sebasten.

Studying Sebasten's lean, dark, devastating face in the photo beside the article, her eyes stung like mad. Angry with herself, she crushed the newspaper up in a convulsive gesture and rammed it in the bin. Then she opened the post that she had ignored the day before and paled at the sight of a payment request from an exclusive boutique where she had a monthly account. She had barely had enough cash left in her bank account to cover travel expenses and eat until the end of the month, when she would receive her first pay cheque. She would have to ask for a little more time to clear the bill. Furthermore, she would have to exert bone and sinew to try and find part-time evening or weekend employment so that she could keep up her financial commitments.

The first Lizzie knew of the mysterious reappearance of the Mercedes she had sold was the arrival of a chauffeur at her door. 'Miss Denton…your car keys,' he said, handing them to her.

'Sorry?' Lizzie stared at him in bewilderment. 'I don't own a car.'

'Compliments of Mr Contaxis. The Merc is parked outside.'

Before Lizzie even got her breath back, the man had clattered back down the stairs again.

Compliments of Mr Contaxis? What on earth was going on? In a daze, Lizzie left her room and went outside. There sat the same black glossy Mercedes four-wheel-drive which her father had bought her for her twenty-second birthday. She couldn't credit the evidence of her own eyes and she walked round it in slow motion, her mind in a feverish whirl of incomprehension.

Where had Sebasten got her car from and why would he give it back to her? Why would a guy who had dumped her only thirty-six hours earlier suddenly present her with a car worth thousands of pounds? Oh, yes, she knew that—technically speaking—she had dumped him first but in her heart she accepted that she had only got the courage to do that because she had known that he intended to do it to her if she did not.

Having reclaimed the diamonds from the safe in his town house, Sebasten arrived on Lizzie's doorstep, feeling much better than he had felt earlier in the day, indeed, feeling very much that he was doing the right thing.

Lizzie opened the door. The sheer vibrant, gorgeous appeal of Sebasten in sleek designer garments that exuded class and expense exploded on her with predictable effect. Just seeing him hurt. Seeing him dare to *almost* smile was also the cruel equivalent of a knife plunging beneath her tender skin. Even an almost smile was an insult, a symptom of his ruthless, cruel, nasty character and his essential detachment from the rest of humanity.

Lizzie dealt him a seething glance. 'You get that car taken away right now!' she told him. 'I don't know what you think you're playing at but I don't want it.'

Engaged in looking Lizzie over in a head-to-toe careful appraisal that left not an inch of her tall, shapely figure unchecked and thinking that he might like the way turquoise set off her beautiful hair but that she did something remarkable for the colour red as well, Sebasten froze like a fox cornered in a chicken coop and attempted to regroup.

'I don't want your car either…it's no use to me,' he pointed out in fast recovery, closing the door and, without even thinking about what he was doing, leaning his big, powerful length back against that door so that she couldn't open it again.

'Exactly what are you doing with a car that I sold?' Lizzie demanded shakily, temper flashing through her in direct proportion to her disturbed emotions.

'I bought it back for you weeks ago…as well as these.' Sebasten set down the little pile of jewellery boxes on the table. 'I had you watched the first week by one of my bodyguards and I knew everything that you did.'

'You had me watched?' Lizzie echoed in even deeper shock and recoil as she flipped open a couple of lids to confirm the contents and the sparkle of diamonds greeted her. 'You bought my jewellery as well? *Why?*'

Sebasten had been hoping to evade that question. 'At the time I planned to win your trust and impress you with my generosity.'

'You utter bastard,' Lizzie framed with an agony of reproach in her clear green gaze. 'So that's why you offered me the use of an apartment! You thought you could tempt me with your rotten money. Well, you were way off beam then and you're even more out of line *now*—'

'I just want you to take back what's yours,' Sebasten slotted in with fierce determination.

'Why? So that you can feel better? So that you can *buy* your way out of having a conscience about what you did to me?' Lizzie condemned in a shaking undertone. 'Don't you even have the sensitivity to see that you're insulting me?'

'How…am I insulting you?' Sebasten queried between gritted teeth, for he was in no way receiving the response he had expected and he wondered why women always had to make simple matters complicated. He was trying to make her life easier. What was wrong with that?

'By making the assumption that I'm the kind of woman who would accept expensive gifts from a guy like you! How dare you do that? Do you think I was your mistress or something that you have to pay me off?' Lizzie was so worked up with hurt and anger that her voice rose to a shrill crescendo.

'No, but I never bought you a single thing during the whole time we were together,' Sebasten pointed out, one half of his brain urging him to take her in his arms and soothe her, the other half fully engaged in stamping out that dangerous temptation to touch her again.

'I suppose that's how you get so many women…you pay them with gifts for putting up with you!' Lizzie slung fiercely, fighting back the tears prickling at the backs of her eyes.

Determined not to react to that base accusation, Sebasten was staring down at the bill from the boutique that lay on the table and then studying the little column of figures added up on the sheet of paper beside it. Was she *that* broke?

'I could give you a loan. You would repay it when you could,' he heard himself say.

Lizzie wrenched open the door and said unsteadily. 'Go away…'

'It doesn't have to be like this.' Sebasten hovered, full of angry conflict and growing frustration. 'I came here with good motivations and no intention of upsetting you.'

Lizzie scooped up the jewel boxes and planted them in his

hands along with the car keys. 'And don't you dare leave that car outside. I can't feed a parking meter for it on my income.'

'Lizzie—?'

'You *stay* away from me!'

'All I wanted to know was that you were OK!' Sebasten growled.

'Of course I'm OK. A visit from you is as good as a cure!' Lizzie hurled, her quivering voice breaking on that last assurance.

Sebasten departed. He should have thought about her not being able to afford to run a car, he reflected, choosing to focus on that rather than anything else she had said. However, the disturbing image of her distraught face and the shadows that lay like bruises beneath her eyes travelled with him. She didn't look well. Was he responsible for that? For the first time since childhood Sebasten felt helpless, and it was terrifying. He could not believe how stubborn and proud she was. He saw Lizzie in terms of warmth and sunlight, softness and affection, and then he tried to equate that belated acknowledgement with the character that Ingrid had endowed her with.

Lizzie threw herself face down on the bed and sobbed into the pillow until she was empty of tears. What must her distress be doing to her baby? Guilt cut deep into her. She rested a hand against her tummy and offered the tiny being inside her a silent apology for her lack of control and told herself that she would do better in the future.

As for Sebasten, did she seem so pitiful that he even had to take her pride away from her by offering her a loan as well as the car and the diamonds? Why had she ever told him that she loved him? And why was he acting the way he was when all that she had ever known about him suggested that a declaration of love ought to drive him fast in the opposite direction? How dared he come and see her and make her feel all over again what she had lost when he wasn't worth having in the first place?

When was she planning to tell him about the baby? She drifted off to weary sleep on the admission that she was not yet strong enough to face another confrontational scene.

CHAPTER EIGHT

ON MONDAY morning, Sebasten thought his personal staff were all very quiet in his radius and he assumed that the *Sunday Globe* gossip column had done the rounds of the office.

He swore that he would not think about Lizzie. At eleven he found himself accessing her personnel file. When he discovered that she had been reprimanded for the printing of four hundred copies of a photo of himself, all hope of concentration was vanquished. He was annoyed that he liked the idea of those photos.

Sebasten did not believe in love. He was crazy about Lizzie's body…and her smile…and her hair. He had enjoyed the way she chattered too. She talked a lot, which in the past was a trait which had irritated him in other women, but Lizzie's chatter was unusually interesting. He had also liked the easy way she would reach out and touch him; nothing wrong with that either, was there? It didn't mean he was infatuated or anything of that nature, merely that he could still appreciate her good points.

On the other side of the equation, she was a rampant liar and she *must* have slept with his half-brother and he could not work out how he had managed to block that awareness out for so long. At the same time, he could no longer credit the dramatic contention that Lizzie had driven Connor to his death. Ingrid had needed someone to blame. But Connor had got behind the wheel of his car, drunk. That car crash had been the tragic result of his half-brother's recklessness and love of high speed.

At that point, without any prior thought on the subject that he was aware of, Sebasten decided to settle that outstanding bill he had seen in Lizzie's bedsit. She couldn't prevent him from doing that, could she?

That same day, Lizzie went into work and found herself the target of covert stares and embarrassing whispers. Only then did she recall the article that had been in the newspaper the previous day. In a saccharine-sweet enquiry, Milly Sharpe asked her where she would like to work and Lizzie reddened to her hairline.

'Any place,' Lizzie answered tautly and ended up at a desk in a corner where she was given nothing like enough to keep her occupied.

She saw then that continuing employment in Sebasten's company could well be less than comfortable for her. During her lunch break, she called into the employment agency across the road from the CI building and enjoyed a far more productive chat with one of the recruitment consultants there than she had received at the establishment which Sebasten had recommended a month earlier.

'You have a great deal of insider knowledge and experience in the PR field,' the consultant commented. 'I'm sure we can place you in a PR firm. It would be a junior position to begin with, and of course you're entitled to basic maternity leave, but if you prove yourself you could gain quite rapid advancement.'

On Tuesday, Sebasten took sudden note of how very long it had been since he had staged a meeting with the accounts team on the sixth floor and he instructed his secretary to make good that oversight. That Lizzie worked on that floor was not a fact he allowed to enter his mind once. On Wednesday, he was infuriated by the announcement that the accounts meeting could not be staged until Friday, as key personnel were away on a training course.

On Thursday, Ingrid phoned Sebasten and demanded to know if it was true that he had been seeing Liza Denton. Sebasten said it was but that it was a private matter not open to discussion, and if Ingrid's shock at that snub was perceptible Sebasten was equally disconcerted by the very real anger that leapt through him when the older woman then made an adverse comment about Lizzie. On Friday, Sebasten arrived at the office even earlier than was his norm, cleared his desk by nine, strode about the top floor unsettling his entire staff and checked his watch on average of once every ten minutes.

On the sixth floor, Lizzie's week had felt endless to her. She was craving Sebasten as though he were a life-saving drug and hating herself for being so weak. She knew she had to tell him that she was pregnant, but while she still felt so vulnerable she was reluctant to deal with that issue. Midweek, during the extended lunch break she hastily arranged, she had an interview for a position with a PR firm but had no idea whether or not she was in with a chance. On Friday morning, Milly Sharpe greeted her arrival at work with a strange little smile and put her on the reception desk.

When Sebasten strode out of the lift, the first person he saw was Lizzie. Lizzie, clad in a yellow dress as bright as sunshine. He collided with her startled green eyes and walked right past the senior accounts executive waiting to greet him without even noticing the man.

'Lizzie…' Sebasten said.

Taken aback by his sudden appearance, Lizzie nodded in slow motion as though to confirm her identity while her gaze welded to him with electrified intensity. His sheer physical impact on her drove out all else. She drank him in, heart racing at the sudden buzz in the atmosphere and there was not a thought in her head that was worthy of an angry, bitter woman. His luxuriant black hair gleamed below the lights and her fingers tingled with longing. His brilliant golden eyes, semi-screened by his spiky lashes, set up a chain reaction deep down inside her, awakening the wicked hunger that melted her in secret places and made her tremble.

'So…' His mind a wasteland, his hormones reacting with a dangerous enthusiasm that made lingering an impossibility, Sebasten snatched in a deep, sharp breath. 'How are you?'

'OK…' Lizzie managed to frame after considerable effort to come up with that single word.

'I have a meeting…' Sebasten swung away, her image refreshed to vibrance in his memory.

As he strode down the corridor, Lizzie blinked and emerged from the spell he had cast. A slow, deep, painful tide of colour washed over her fair complexion. A burst of stifled giggles sounded from the direction of Milly Sharpe's office, which overlooked Reception, and her heart sank. Had she somehow shown herself up? Well, what else could she have done when she had just sat staring at Sebasten like a love-sick schoolgirl? Squirming in an agony of self-loathing and shame, Lizzie decided she would not be around when Sebasten emerged from his meeting again.

That afternoon the recruitment agency called and informed her that Robbins, the PR firm, were keen for her to start work with them the following week. Deep relief filled Lizzie to overflowing and she accepted the offer. Away from Contaxis International, she would be better able to put her life together again and possibly it would be easier to face telling Sebasten what he would eventually *have* to be told.

On Friday evening, for the sixth night in a row, Sebasten

stayed home and brooded. He didn't want to go out and he didn't want company.

Lizzie called her father for a chat. He seemed very preoccupied and apologised several times for losing the thread of the conversation. She asked what he had decided to do about Mrs Baines, the housekeeper, whom Felicity had wanted dismissed.

Maurice Denton released a heavy sigh. 'I offered Mrs Baines a generous settlement in recognition of the number of years she'd worked for us. She accepted it but she was very bitter and walked out the same day. Felicity was delighted but I must confess that the whole business left a nasty taste in my mouth.'

'How is Felicity?'

'Very edgy…' the older man admitted with palpable concern. 'She bursts into tears if I even *mention* the baby and when I suggested that *I* ought to have a word with the gynaecologist she's been attending, she became hysterical!'

Lizzie raised her brows and winced in dismay. Was her stepmother heading for a nervous breakdown? All over again, she felt the guilty burden of the secret knowledge she was withholding from her father. Then she wondered how Maurice Denton, never the most liberal of men and very set in his traditional values, would react to a daughter giving birth to an illegitimate child and paled. Such an event might well sever her relationship with her father forever…

On Sunday morning, Sebasten again lifted the *Sunday Globe*, which he had always regarded as a rubbish newspaper aimed at intellectually-challenged readers. However, he only wanted to check out that Patsy Hewitt had not picked up any other information relating either to himself or Lizzie. The front page was adorned with the usual lurid headline offering the unsavoury details of some sleazy affair, he noted, and only at that point did he recognise that the article was adorned with a photo of Connor.

And Sebasten was gripped to that double-page spread inside the paper with a spellbound intensity that would have delighted Patsy Hewitt, who had found ample opportunity to employ her trademark venom after doing her homework on Lizzie's stepmother, Felicity Denton. Mrs Baines, the Denton housekeeper, had sold her insider story of Felicity's affair for a handsome price and Connor, even departed, still had sufficient news value to make the front page with his once tangled lovelife.

Lizzie was still in bed asleep when her mobile phone began ringing. Getting out of bed to answer it, she was bemused to realise that it was a former friend calling to express profuse apologies for misjudging her over Connor.

'What are you talking about?' she mumbled.

'Haven't you seen this morning's *Sunday Globe* yet?'

Learning that Mrs Baines had sold her story of Felicity's affair with Connor shook Lizzie rigid. No longer did she need to wonder why her stepmother had been so eager to get rid of the family housekeeper: Felicity had been justifiably afraid that Mrs Baines knew too much. Had Connor visited the Denton home as well? Lizzie wrinkled her nose with distaste. The housekeeper had probably known about that affair long before she herself did.

Over an hour later, Lizzie arrived at her family home to find it besieged by the Press. A half-dozen cameras flashed in her direction and she had to fight her way past to get indoors. Her father was sitting behind closed curtains in a state of severe shock.

CHAPTER NINE

'FELICITY walked out late last night. A friend in the media phoned to warn her about the story appearing in the *Sunday Globe*,' Maurice Denton shared in a shattered tone as Lizzie paced the room, too restive to stay still. 'Felicity isn't coming back. She made it clear that she wants a divorce.'

'But…but what about the baby?' Lizzie pressed, disconcerted by the speed and dexterity of her stepmother's departure from the marital home.

The older man regarded her with hollow eyes. In the space of days, he seemed to have aged. 'There *is* no baby…'

Lizzie's mouth fell wide. 'You mean, Felicity's lost it…oh, *no*!'

'There never *was* a baby. She wasn't pregnant. It was a crazy lie aimed at persuading you not to tell me about her affair with Connor.' Her parent shook his greying head with a dulled wonderment that he could not conceal. 'Felicity thought that if she *tried*, she could get pregnant easily and then pretend she'd mixed up her dates. But it didn't happen: she didn't conceive. As time went on and she was forced to pretend to go to pre-natal appointments she decided that she would have to fake a miscarriage…thank heaven, I was spared that melodrama!'

'Do you think…er…Felicity's having a breakdown?'

Lizzie suggested worriedly. 'I mean, maybe it was one of those false pregnancies that come from *genuine* longing for a baby—'

'No.' Maurice Denton's rebuttal was flat, bitter. 'Last night, she informed me that she didn't even like children and that she was fed up not only with the whole insane pretence that she had foisted on us all but also sick and tired of living with a man old enough to be her father! She wasn't even sorry for the damage she did to you, never mind me!'

Lizzie flinched. 'I'm so sorry…'

'Perhaps when a man of fifty-five marries a woman more than thirty years younger he deserves what he gets. Why didn't you come to me about her and the Morgan boy?'

'I…I told myself I couldn't tell you for the baby's sake…but possibly, I just couldn't *face* the responsibility.' Listening to the mayhem of raised voices outside the front door, Lizzie said gently, 'Look, maybe the reporters will go away if I make a statement to them…what do you think?'

'Do as you think best,' Maurice Denton advised heavily. 'Felicity is gone and it can only be Felicity or you that those vultures are interested in. I've never had much of a public profile.'

Lizzie went outside to address the assembled journalist and parry some horrendous questions of the lowest possible taste. 'Was Morgan sleeping with both you and your stepmother?'

'Connor and I were only ever friends,' Lizzie declared with complete calm.

'What about you and Sebasten Contaxis?' she was asked.

'Oh, I'm *not* friends with him!' Lizzie asserted without hesitation and there was a burst of appreciative laughter at that response.

It was only later while she was making a snack for her father that she truly appreciated that her own name had been cleared. Would Sebasten find out? Sooner or later, he would discover that he had targeted the wrong woman. How would he react? But why should she care? What he had confessed to doing was beyond all forgiveness. She looked into the fridge, where a jar of sun-dried tomatoes sat, and her taste-buds watered. Sun-dried tomatoes followed by ice-cream. She shut the fridge again in haste, unnerved by recent food cravings that struck her as bizarre.

An hour later, Sebasten sprang out of his Lamborghini outside the Morgan household in the leafy suburbs. A lingering solitary cameraman took a picture of him. Waving back the bodyguards ready to leap into action and prevent that photo being taken, Sebasten smiled. Sebasten had been smiling ever since he read Patsy Hewitt's hatchet job on Lizzie's stepmother. The wicked stepmother, a typecast figure and a perfect match to Sebasten's own prejudices. He could not imagine how he had contrived not to register that Lizzie's father had a very much younger wife who bore more than a passing resemblance to the evil queen in *Snow White*. He could not imagine how it had not once crossed his mind that Lizzie might be engaged in protecting a member of her own family.

'Lizzie's not friends with you, mate,' the cameraman warned Sebasten.

'Watch this space,' Sebasten advised with all the sizzling, lethal confidence that lay at the heart of his forceful character. He just felt happy, crazy happy, and all he could think about was reclaiming Lizzie.

'She's a gutsy girl...I wouldn't count my chickens.'

Sebasten just laughed and leant on the doorbell and rattled the door knocker for good measure.

CHAPTER TEN

IT WAS very unfortunate for Sebasten that Lizzie had watched his arrival from the safe, shadowy depths of the dining room.

Even at a distance, the slashing brilliance of his smile rocked Lizzie where she stood. He was so gorgeous but that he should *dare* to smile, sure of his welcome, it seemed, before he even saw her, lacerated her pride, fired her resentment and drove home the suspicion that he lacked any sense of remorse. He was tough, ruthless and hard and no relationship with Sebasten would ever go any place where she wanted it to go, she acknowledged with agonised regret. He had already spelt that out in terms no sane woman could ignore.

Hadn't she already got through the first week of being without him? She would get over him eventually, wouldn't she? It dawned on her that on some strange inner level she had not the slightest doubt that Sebasten was about to suggest a reconciliation and that shook her. But once she announced that she had already conceived his child and in addition had every intention of raising that child, Sebasten would surrender any such notion fast. So really, what was she worrying about?

Sebasten had killed his smile by the time Lizzie opened the door. 'Come in…'

'I suggest we go out, so that we can talk,' Sebasten murmured levelly. 'I imagine your family aren't in the mood for visitors today.'

'Only my father is here and he's having a nap in the library.' A quiver assailing her at his proximity, Lizzie pushed wide the door into the drawing room.

'Where's the…' Sebasten bit back the blunt five-letter word brimming on his lips in the very nick of time and substituted, 'your stepmother?'

'Already gone,' Lizzie admitted, tight-mouthed with tension. 'They'll be getting a divorce.'

'Your father's got his head screwed on,' Sebasten asserted with an outstanding absence of sensitivity. 'Booting her straight out the door was the right thing to do.'

'Actually Felicity left under her own steam,' Lizzie declared, making the humiliating connection that she had once been booted out of Sebasten's life with the same efficiency that he was so keen to commend.

'Even better…she won't collect half so much in the divorce settlement,' Sebasten imparted with authority.

'Right at this moment, my father has more to think about than his bank balance!' Lizzie hissed in outrage. 'He's devastated.'

'I was thinking of you, *not* your father. Not very pleasant for you, having to put up with a woman like that in the family,' Sebasten contended, allowing himself to study her taut, pale face, the strain in her unhappy eyes, and then removing his attention again before he was tempted into making the cardinal error of a premature assumption that forgiveness was on the table and dragging her into his arms. 'Why the blazes didn't you spill the beans on your stepmother weeks ago?'

'I believed she was pregnant with my little brother or sister…only it turns out now that she was lying about that to protect herself and keep me quiet.' A tight little laugh fell from Lizzie's lips as she thought of the baby that she carried.

It seemed so ironic that the conception which Felicity must initially have been desperate to achieve should have come Lizzie's way instead.

'It sounds like she was off the wall. If it's any consolation, Ingrid Morgan is shattered too and feeling very guilty about the way she treated you,' Sebasten revealed. 'She called me this morning.'

'I don't hold any spite against Connor's mother.' Taut as a bowstring, Lizzie hovered by the window.

'I don't understand why you couldn't tell me the *whole* truth. If you had named your father's wife, I would never have disbelieved your explanation and I could have been trusted with that information.'

Lizzie noted without great surprise that Sebasten was playing hardball and landing her with a share of the blame for *his* refusal to have the smallest faith in her. 'I'm not so sure of that. You and your old friend Ingrid wanted your pound of flesh, regardless of who got hurt in the process!'

Sebasten did not like the morbid tone of that response at all. 'I misjudged you and I'll make it up to you.'

'Was that an apology?'

'*Theo mou*…give me time to get there on my own!' Sebasten urged in a sudden volatile surge that disconcerted her and let her appreciate that he was not quite as cool, calm and collected as he appeared. 'I am sorry, truly, deeply sorry.'

'I can't be,' Lizzie confided shakily.

'I'm not asking *you* to be sorry,' Sebasten pointed out in some bewilderment, wondering whether the shine of tears in her eyes was a promising sign that the very first humble apology he had made to a woman in his entire life had had the right effect.

'You see, I *can't* be sorry that you misjudged me because if I hadn't found that out, I would never have discovered what a ruthless, conscience-free louse you are,' Lizzie completed in a wobbly but driven voice.

Sebasten spread lean brown hands in a natural expression of appeal. 'But I'll never be like that with you again,' he protested. 'I want you back in my life.'

'Oh, I'm sure you'll find another dumb woman to take my place,' Lizzie snapped out brittly and turned her back on him altogether while she fought to rein back the tears threatening her.

'Yes, I could if I wanted to but there's one small problem…I only want *you*.'

In his bed, that was all, Lizzie reflected painfully, her throat thick with tears. She forced herself back round to face him again and tilted her chin. 'I think you'll give up on that ambition when I tell you what I have to tell you.'

'Nothing could make me give up on you,' Sebasten swore, moving forward and reaching for her without warning to tug her forward into his arms.

Lizzie only meant to stay there a second but Sebasten had come to the conclusion that action was likely to be much more effective than words that appeared to be getting him precisely nowhere. He framed her flushed face with two lean hands and gazed down into her distraught green eyes. 'Why are you looking at me like that?' he was moved to demand in reproach. 'I will never hurt you again.'

Trembling all over, Lizzie parted dry lips and muttered, 'I'm pregnant…'

Pregnant? That announcement fell on a male quite unprepared for that kind of news. Sebasten tensed, not even sure he had heard her say what she had just said. 'Pregnant?' he echoed, his hands dropping from her.

'Yes,' Lizzie confirmed chokily.

'Pregnant…' Sebasten said again as though it was a word that had never come his way before and innate caution was already telling him to shut up and not say another single sentence. But he was so shattered by the concept of Lizzie being pregnant that not all the caution in the world could keep him quiet. 'Is it Connor's?' he shot at her rawly, savage jealousy gripping him in an instant vice.

Watching the flare of volatile gold in his stunning eyes, the fierce cast of his superb bone-structure, Lizzie was backing away from him and she only stilled when her shoulders met the china cabinet behind her. 'No, it is not your half-brother's child. Even Connor was not low enough to try to get me into bed while he was making mad, passionate love to my stepmother behind my back. I never slept with Connor,' Lizzie spelt out shakily.

Sebasten recalled his own belief in her inexperience the first night he had shared with her but Sebasten was always stubborn and not quite ready in the state of numb shock he was in to move straight in and embrace the possibility of a child he had never expected to have. 'How do I know that for sure?'

Temper leapt with startling abruptness from the sheer height of Lizzie's tension. 'You're the only lover I've ever had…is it *my* fault you were too busy taking advantage of me to even notice that I was a virgin?'

'I didn't take advantage of you and if you're telling me the truth you're the only virgin I've ever slept with,' Sebasten launched back, playing for time while he mulled over what she had said but all his anger ebbing at miraculous speed. Even so, that did not prevent him from finding another issue. 'You said you were protected.'

'I was sick the next morning…it might have been that or it might just be that I fall into the tiny failure-rate percentage…but the point *is*,' Lizzie framed afresh, 'I am pregnant and it's yours.'

'Mine…' Sebasten was now unusually pale at the very thought of what he saw as the enormous responsibility of a baby. All he had to do was think about his own nightmare childhood, the misery inflicted on him by self-preoccupied adults who left him to the care of unsupervised staff when it suited them and isolated him in boarding schools, where he had also been forgotten with ease. Nobody knew better than he that even great wealth was no protection when it came to a child's needs.

'I appreciate that this is a shock for you,' Lizzie conceded when she could hear that ghastly silence no longer. 'But I should also add that I'm going to *have* this baby—'

Emerging from his unpleasant recollections. Sebasten frowned at her in complete innocence of her meaning. 'What else would you do?'

Silenced by that demand, Lizzie blinked.

'I suppose we'll have to make the best of it,' Sebasten breathed, squaring his broad shoulders in the face of his inner conviction that life as he knew it had just been slaughtered. But much of his gloom lifted on the sudden realisation that, of course, Lizzie would come in tow with the baby. With Lizzie back in his life and him ensuring in a discreet way that the baby was never, ever neglected for even a moment, he could surely rise to the challenge?

'And what would making the best of it…entail?' Lizzie prompted thinly.

'Sebasten expelled his pent-up breath in an impatient hiss. 'Obviously, I'll have to marry you. It's my own fault. I should've taken precautions too that night but we're stuck with the consequences and I'm a Contaxis…not the sort of bastard who tries to shirk his responsibilities!'

During that telling speech, Lizzie almost burst into a rage as big as a bonfire. She went lurching from total shock at the speed with which he mentioned marriage when she had never dreamt he might even whisper that fatal word. Then she truly listened and what she heard inflamed her beyond belief.

'I don't want to marry you—'

'You've got no choice—'

'Watch my lips—I do not *want* to marry you!'

Sebasten dealt her a grim appraisal in which his powerful personality loomed large. 'Of course you do. Right now, we've got a bigger problem than me being a ruthless, conscience-free louse!' he countered with sardonic bite. 'Can we please focus on the baby issue?'

'You don't want to marry me…you don't want the baby either!' Lizzie flung at him in condemnation, feeling as though her heart was breaking inside her and hating him for not being able to feel what she felt.

'I want you and I'll get used to the idea of the baby,' Sebasten declared.

Intending to show him out the front door, Lizzie yanked the drawing-room door wide and then froze. Her father was standing in the hall, his face a stiff mask of disbelief. It was obvious that he had heard enough to appreciate that she was carrying Sebasten's child. He looked at her with all his disappointment written in his eyes and it was too much to her after the day she had already endured. With a stifled sob, Lizzie fled for the sanctuary of her old apartment in the stable block.

Sebasten could see 'potential ally' writ large in his future father-in-law's horror at the revelation that his unmarried daughter was expecting a baby. 'I'm sorry you had to hear the news like that. Naturally, Lizzie's upset by the circumstances but I'm just keen to get the wedding organised.'

Maurice Denton was relieved by that forthright declaration. Unfreezing, almost grateful for a distraction from his own personal crisis, he offered Sebasten a drink. Sebasten accepted the offer.

He had never been more on edge: he felt as if Lizzie was playing games with him and that was not what he expected from her. It took time to concede that he might have been a little too frank about his reactions and that perhaps lying in his teeth would have gone down better. After a third drink to Sebasten's one, Maurice informed Sebasten that should he himself live until he was ninety-nine he had no hope of ever hearing a marriage proposal couched in less attractive terms. He then asked his son-in-law-to-be if he was shy about being romantic.

Sebasten tried not to cringe at the question but he was honest in his response: he had never made a romantic gesture in his entire life.

'I think you'd better get on that learning curve fast,' Lizzie's father advised before going on to entertain Sebasten with stories of how devoted a mother Lizzie had been to her dolls and how much she had always adored fussing round babies.

While the older man began to find some solace not only in those happier memories of the past but also in the prospect of a grandchild after the humiliation of his own disappointed hopes of another child, Sebasten began to imagine the baby as a miniature version of Lizzie tending to her dolls and relax and even warm to the prospect.

A copy of Lizzie's birth certificate having been supplied helpfully by her parent, Sebasten drove off to apply for a special licence that would enable him to marry Lizzie within the week. Mindful of that galling advice about romance, he went on to pay a visit to a world-famous jewellery store. He chose the most beautiful rare diamond on offer and a matching wedding ring.

Late that evening, Sebasten returned to the Denton household as confident as he had been of his reception earlier in the day, only on this second occasion convinced he was infinitely better prepared to deliver exactly what was expected of him. Lizzie could hardly doubt the strength of his commitment to marrying her when he had already made *all* the arrangements for the wedding on his own.

That afternoon, Lizzie had had a good cry about Sebasten's crass and wounding insensitivity. She had tried hard to respect his honesty but in point of fact it had hurt too much for her to do that. She might love him but there were times when furious frustration and pain totally swallowed up that love. With the best will in the world, how could she marry a guy who didn't want a wife and could only stick children at a distance or inanimate on a painted canvas? No crystal ball was required to foresee the disaster that would result from Sebasten making himself do what he had always sworn he would not do.

Sebasten took the steps up to Lizzie's apartment three at a time. The door wasn't shut and he frowned. It was dangerous to be so careless of personal safety in a big city. She really *did* need him around. He let himself in. Lizzie was curled up on a big, squashy sofa, fast asleep. She was wearing a pale pink silk wrap, another colour to add to the already wide spectrum of shades which Sebasten considered framed Lizzie to perfection. He crouched down by her side.

Lifting up her limp hand, he threaded the engagement ring onto her finger. Now she was labelled *his* for every other man to see. As that awareness dawned on him, Sebasten finally saw the point of engagements. She got the little ring, he got to post the much more important hands-off-she's-mine giant ring of steel. He liked that. This romantic stuff? Easy as falling off a log, Sebasten decided.

With a sleepy sigh, Lizzie opened her eyes and focused on Sebasten and thought she was back in bed with him again, which she very often *was* in her most secret dreams. Enchanted by the pagan gold glitter of his intense gaze, she let appreciative fingers drift up to trace a high, angular cheekbone. He caught her hand in his and captured her lips in a sensual, searching exploration that was an erotic wake-up call to every sense she possessed. She leant up the better to taste him, breathe in the achingly familiar scent that was uniquely his, close her arms round his neck so that she could sink greedy fingers into the depths of his luxuriant black hair.

Sebasten made a low, sexy sound of encouragement deep in his throat. Scooping her up, he sank back with her cradled in his arms and let his tongue dip in a provocative slide between her lips. Lizzie jerked and strained up to him, wanting, needing, possessed by helpless excitement and hunger for more.

'You still want me, *pethi mou*,' Sebasten husked, pausing to trail his mouth in a tantalising caress down the line of her long, elegant neck. 'But I can't stay long. Your father has been very understanding and tolerant but I won't risk causing offence.'

Emerging for the first time since she had wakened to proper awareness, Lizzie snatched in a quivering gasp of shame and embarrassment: she had fallen like an overripe plum into Sebasten's ready hands. 'This shouldn't be happening,' she bit out shakily and flew upright to smooth down her wrap.

Only then did she register the weight of the ring now adorning her hand. In disbelief, she raised her fingers to stare at the fabulous solitaire diamond sparkling in the lamplight.

'Like it?' Sebasten lounged back on the sofa with the indolent, expectant air of a male bracing himself to withstand fawning feminine approbation.

'What is it?'

'You really need to be told?'

Lizzie jerked her chin in an affirmative nod, for she could not credit that the male she had flatly refused to marry could have bought her an engagement ring and what was more put in on her finger without her knowledge or agreement.

'It matches the wedding ring. I got it too.' Well-aware of her shaken silence and proud of that seeming achievement,

Sebasten rose to his full height so that she could fling herself at him and hug him.

'You...*did*!' Lizzie parroted, a swelling forming in her tight chest that she did not immediately recognise as rage.

'In fact, I've been extremely busy,' Sebasten extended in his rich dark drawl. 'I've got a special licence. I've got the church booked and a top-flight wedding-planners outfit burning the midnight oil on the finer details even as we speak. You have nothing to do but show up looking gorgeous on Saturday—'

'You mean...I get to pick my own dress?'

'I contacted an Italian designer...they're flying over a team on Wednesday with a selection for you.'

'Oh...*this* Saturday?' Momentarily Lizzie's rage took a back seat to shock at the sheer level of organisation that had taken place behind her back and the news that her own wedding was to be staged in just six days' time.

'Your father agreed that we shouldn't hang around.'

'Did he really?' Lizzie queried in a rather high-pitched tone. 'Sebasten...cast your mind back to my answer to your declaration that we should marry.'

'You said no but I knew you didn't mean it,' Sebasten informed her.

'D-did you?' Lizzie's response shook with the force of her feelings but she looked again at the ring on her engagement finger. Her eyes stung and she spun away, remembering the guy who had hired decorators to leave her free to dine with him. He did what *he* thought best and if that meant refusing to credit her refusal, using her own father as back-up and going ahead and arranging a wedding all on his own, he was more than equal to the challenge.

And more than anything else in the world she would have loved to have faith in that blazing confidence he wore like an aura and rise to that same challenge. But he didn't love her, was only offering to marry her because she was pregnant and he had *never* wanted a child. Where would they be in a few months' time when she was more in love and more dependent on him than she was even now and he discovered that good intentions were not enough? He wouldn't find her so attractive once her slender figure vanished. He might even be downright repulsed by her fecund shape. He might get bored, he might even stray and she would be destroyed…absolutely, utterly destroyed by such a rejection.

'I can't do it,' Lizzie whispered.

Sebasten linked strong arms round her and slowly turned her round. 'Bridal nerves,' he told her with a determined smile.

'I can't do it,' Lizzie whispered again, white as milk. 'I *can't* marry you.'

Sebasten freed her and took a step back. He was making a real effort to control the stark anger threatening his control but he could not understand what was the matter with her. He had done every single thing he could think of to please her and she had not voiced one word of appreciation. She had not even appeared to register his enthusiasm for something he had never, ever thought he would do.

'The baby *must* have the Contaxis name and my protection,' he spelt out. Eyes dark as the night sky pinned to her taut, trouble face. 'That's not negotiable.'

'Commands don't cut it with me,' Lizzie snapped, feeling the full onslaught of his powerful personality focused on her and rebelling.

'Then tell me what *does* because I sure as hell have no idea!' Sebasten raked back at her in sudden dark fury.

Trembling, Lizzie whirled away again. Although she loved him, she had a deep instinctive need to keep herself safe from further hurt and disillusionment. He had too much power over her, and how could she trust him when only his sense of responsibility had persuaded him to offer marriage? She saw the sense in his insistence that they marry to give their baby his name, for the law as it stood did not recognise less formal relationships. Yet to marry him and live with him as a wife felt like a giant step too far for her at that moment.

If *only* there was something in between, a halfway house that could answer her needs and the baby's without trapping Sebasten into immediate domesticity and commitment before he could judge whether or not he could meet those demands in the long term. A halfway house, she thought in desperation, and then the solution came to her in a positive brainstorm.

'I want an answer,' Sebasten told her fiercely.

A flush on her cheeks, excitement in her eyes, for Lizzie was eager to come up with a blueprint that would allow her to marry him. 'I have it. We don't live together…you buy me a house of my own!'

'Say that again…no, *don't*.' Sebasten warned, studying her with laser-like intensity, shimmering golden eyes locked to her in disbelief.

'But don't you see it? It would be perfect!' Lizzie told him with an enthusiasm that could only inflame. 'You could visit whenever you liked.'

'Really?' Sebasten's bitten-out response was not quite level while he wondered if she was feeling all right, but he was reluctant to risk asking that question in case she took it as an insult.

'We would each hold on to more of our own separate lives than married couples usually do. You'd have your business and I'd have my new PR job—'

'What new PR job?' Sebasten interrupted faster than the speed of light.

'I'm starting tomorrow—'

'But you're pregnant—'

'Pregnant women work in PR too—'

'You were working for *me*, Sebasten remind her, taking a new tack as his raging frustration rose to almost ungovernable heights. He didn't want her working any place and certainly not in some freewheeling PR firm where she would be engaged in constant interaction with other men and a frantic social life.

'Not any more and it wasn't a good idea, was it? Other people don't feel comfortable working around a woman who may be involved with the boss. So, as I was saying…if we lived in separate houses we wouldn't crowd each other.'

Dark colour now scored Sebasten's rigid cheekbones. 'Maybe I fancied being crowded.'

Lizzie breathed in deep. 'And I think,…the first couple of months anyway…you shouldn't stay overnight.'

'I can tell you right now upfront that I won't buy a separate house and either you take me overnight or you take me not at all!' Sebasten launched at her with savage incredulity.

Lizzie swallowed the thickness of tears clogging her throat. 'You can't blame me for trying to protect myself. I don't want to be hurt again and it's going to take time for me to be able to trust you.'

Sebasten spread rigid hands and clenched them into tight, angry fists in silence. So it was payback time. Oh, yes, he understood that. She wanted to put him through hell to punish him and it would be a cold day in hell before he accepted humiliation from any woman!

'You're taking this the wrong way,' Lizzie said anxiously.

'I don't like being taken for a ride—'

'I just want us both to have the space and the freedom to see whether or not we want to live together—'

'I know that now…what is the matter with *you*?' Sebasten demanded rawly.

'I won't agree to any other arrangement before Saturday,'

Lizzie countered shakily, crossing two sets of fingers super-stitiously behind her back and offering up a silent prayer.

A sexless, endless probation period during which she made him jump through hoops like a wild animal being trained? Sebasten could barely repress a shudder.

'Forget it…' he advised between clenched teeth, outraged, stormy dark eyes unyielding.

The silence lay thick and heavy and full of rampant under-tones of aggression.

'Is it…well, is it the lack of sex that makes this idea of mine so unacceptable?' Lizzie finally prompted awkwardly.

'Where would you get a weird idea like that?'

'OK…sex is included,' Lizzie conceded, reddening to her hairline at her own dreadful weakness in failing to stand firm.

So he would buy her a house which she would never, never live in, Sebasten reflected, sudden amusement racing through him at the speed with which she had removed the ban on intimacy.

'I suppose it might be rather like keeping a mistress,' Sebasten mused, watching her squirm at that lowering con-cept with immense satisfaction. 'OK…it's a deal. I'll go for it.'

But when Sebasten climbed into his car minutes later, neither satisfaction nor amusement coloured his brooding thoughts. She didn't love him. If she had ever loved him, he had killed that love. She would accept the security of mar-riage but she was set on having a separate life. Yet he had al-ways been separated from other people, initially by wealth and being an only child, later by personal choice, when keep-ing his relationships at an undemanding superficial level had become a habit.

Yet somewhere deep down inside him Sebasten registered that he had had a dream of living a very different life with

Lizzie, Lizzie *and* the baby. A life where everything was shared. He did not know when that had started or even how it had developed and that such a dream even existed shook and embarrassed him. Especially after his bride-to-be had spelt out *her* dream of two separate households, talked about space and freedom and only included her body as a last-resort sop to his apparent weak masculine inability to get by without sex.

Intellect told him that he would be insane to accept such terms.

Only a guy who was plain stupid would accept such terms. Or a guy who was…desperate?

At supersonic speed, Sebasten reminded himself that their main objective was taking care of their future child's needs and that it was better not to dwell on inconsequentials.

CHAPTER ELEVEN

LIZZIE discovered the hard way that embarking on her first career job the same week she planned to get married was a very great challenge.

On the balance side, she thrived in a more informal working environment where a designer-clad appearance was a decided advantage and she was earning almost twice the salary she had earned at CI. She got on great with her new colleagues, was immediately given sole responsibility for organising a celebrity party for the opening of a new nightclub and spent the entire week wishing there were more hours in the day.

Having to slot in choosing her entire bridal trousseau in the space of one extended lunch hour, however, annoyed her. Spending two evenings drumming up interest in the new club by frantic socialising with acquaintances now all too keen to be seen in the company of the future wife of Sebasten Contaxis was even worse. Being pregnant also seemed to mean that she tired much more easily and she just paled when she thought of how difficult it would be to fit ante-natal appointments into such action-packed extended work hours.

She thought about Sebasten with a constant nagging anxiety that kept her awake at night when she most needed to sleep. He spent the first half of the week away on a business trip, and although he called her he seemed rather distant. She asked herself what more she had expected from him. What had seemed in the heat of the moment to be the perfect solution to her concerns about marrying him now seemed more and more like a mistake.

What real chance was she giving their marriage or Sebasten by insisting on separate accommodation? What true closeness could they hope to achieve if they lived apart? It was also much more likely that, shorn of any perceptible change in his life, Sebasten would continue to think of himself as single. That was hardly a conviction she wanted to encourage. And, in telling him upfront that she didn't trust him and yammering about space and freedom, wasn't she giving him the impression that he would be wasting his time even *trying* to adapt to the concept of a normal marriage?

In the light of those unsettling second thoughts on the issue, Lizzie's heart just sank when Sebasten phoned her forty-eight hours before their wedding to announce that he had found the perfect house for her requirements.

'Gosh, that was quick!' was all she could think to say in an effort to conceal her dismay at the news.

Lizzie had not seen Sebasten since the night they agreed to marry. Yet when he picked her up that evening to take her to view the house, he proved resistant to her every subtle indication that she was just dying to be grabbed and held and kissed senseless. After a week in which she had missed him every hour of every day, one glimpse of his lean, devastatingly handsome features and lithe, powerful frame and she was reduced to a positive pushover of melting appreciation.

'I really love my ring,' she told him encouragingly. 'And the wedding planners you hired are just fantastic.'

'I didn't want you overdoing things when you were pregnant. How's the PR world shaping up?'

'It's demanding but a lot of fun,' she said with rather

forced cheer, not adding that after only four days she had reached the conclusion that it was the perfect career for a single woman without either a husband or children.

'You'll be able to rest round the clock on our honeymoon,' Sebasten informed her drily.

'*What* honeymoon?' Lizzie gasped. 'A week into the job, I can't ask for time off!'

'Then it's just as well I asked for you. Your boss was very accommodating—'

'He was…?'

'Naturally. You're an enormous asset to the firm. As my wife, you will have unparalleled access to the cream of society and the kind of contacts most PR companies can only dream about. You could dictate your own working hours, even go part-time.' Sebasten dropped that bait in the water and waited in hope of hearing it hooked.

'Quite a turnaround from my working conditions at Contaxis International,' Lizzie could not resist remarking while cringing with shame at the reality that she had almost leapt on that reference to part-time work. Wouldn't he be impressed if she took that easy way out at such speed?

His strong profile tensed. 'Blame me for that. I wanted the spoilt little rich girl to learn what it was like to have to work for a living. Yet I would never have been attracted to you had you been what I believed you were.'

The Georgian town house he took her to see was only round the corner from his own London home and Lizzie did not comment on that reality when he did not, but her heart swelled with hope at the proximity he seemed keen to embrace. It was a lovely house, modernised with style and in wonderful decorative order. His lawyers, he explained, had negotiated a compensation agreement with the current tenants, who were prepared to vacate the house immediately. In a similar way, the owner had made a very substantial profit from agreeing to sell quickly.

'You always get what you want, don't you?' Lizzie muttered helplessly, struggling to admire the elegant, spacious rooms but increasingly chilled at the prospect of living there alone. She must have been crazy to demand such an eccentric lifestyle, she decided, close to panic. Feeling horribly guilty and confused by her own contrariness, she talked with gushing enthusiasm about how much she was looking forward to moving in.

Sebasten had been on keen watch for withdrawal pangs from the separate-house commitment. After all, the house would be a bit large perhaps but perfect in every other way for his future father-in-law, who had already mentioned a desire to sell the home he had shared with his estranged wife. As Lizzie complimented all that she saw, his hopes that she might never move into the house suffered a severe setback.

On her wedding day, Lizzie donned a gown fit for a fairy tale. The exquisite beaded, embroidered bodice bared her smooth shoulders and the flowing full skirt made the utmost of her tall, slender figure.

Surprise after wonderful surprise filled her day. A gorgeous sapphire and diamond necklace and earrings arrived from Sebasten as well as a blue velvet garter for good luck. Although she had never indicated any preference for certain flowers, her bouquet was a classic arrangement of her favourites. The equivalent of Cinderella's coach drawn by white horses came to ferry her the short distance to the church. Seeing everywhere the evidence of Sebasten's desire to make their wedding match her every possible fantasy, she was a radiant bride.

Her heart swelled when she walked down the aisle and Sebasten turned to watch her with a breathtaking smile on his lean dark features. Surely no guy marrying against his own will could manage a smile that brilliant? Hugging that belief to herself, she cherished every moment of the ceremony and sparkled with quicksilver energy in the photos taken afterwards.

'You look stunning,' Sebasten groaned in the limo that whisked them away from the church and, tugging her close, he ravished her soft raspberry-tinted mouth under his, awakening such a blaze of instant hunger in Lizzie that she clung to him.

'I'm wrecking your lipstick…your hair,' Sebasten sighed, setting her back from him with hands that he couldn't keep quite steady.

Loving his passion, Lizzie awarded him a provocative look of appreciation. 'It was worth it.'

There was an enormous number of guests at the reception. Introductions and polite conversations continually divided her and Sebasten and it was a relief for Lizzie to glide round the dance floor in the circle of his arms, safe from such interruptions.

'I feel awful…I just can't feel the same about friends who dropped me after Connor's death because of those stupid rumours,' Lizzie confided ruefully.

Sebasten stiffened, realising he disliked even the sound of his half-brother's name on her lips and discomfited by the discovery. 'Are there guests here who did that to you?'

'Loads of them. A good half of them I've known since I was a kid, and Dad's acquainted with their families too, so I didn't feel I had the option of leaving them off the guest list.'

'I wouldn't have given *one* of them an invite!' Shimmering dark golden eyes pinned to her in clear reproof. 'You're too soft. If someone crosses me once, they don't get a second chance.'

Lizzie tensed. 'Didn't I cross you too?'

Sebasten wrapped her even closer to his big, powerful frame, infuriated by the knowledge that she had been snubbed and ignored by people she had considered to be her friends and then been so forgiving. 'Continually...but then you inhabit a very special category, *pethi mou*.'

Lizzie looked up at him with her irreverent grin. 'Remind yourself of that the next time I cross you...you know,' she added impulsively, 'if I look very hard I can see that you *do* bear a slight resemblance to Connor.'

Taken aback by that sudden assurance, Sebasten's superb bone-structure tensed. 'Why are you even looking for a resemblance?'

At the coolness of that demand, Lizzie coloured in surprise. 'Only because you told me that you were half-brothers...and there is only a vague similarity. In your height and build, around the eyes, that's all.'

Without the smallest warning, Sebasten found himself wondering whether she had been drawn to him in the first instance because he reminded her of his younger brother. Until that same moment, he had not actually thought through what he had finally learned about his half-brother's relationship with Lizzie. Connor had cheated on her with another woman, Connor had essentially done the rejecting and wasn't it possible that Lizzie had been left carrying a torch?

'What's wrong?' Lizzie asked because Sebasten had fallen still in the middle of the dance.

'I should've warned you that Connor's true parentage is a secret. Ingrid had her own good reasons for successfully fooling my father into believing that Connor was another man's child. Connor himself never knew the truth.' His lean dark features were taut. 'Nor does his mother want it known even now.'

'I haven't mentioned it to anyone,' Lizzie swore, assuming that fear of her having already been indiscreet had roused his concern on Ingrid Morgan's behalf. 'To be frank, after what I had to put up with on his and Felicity's behalf, he wouldn't be my favourite conversational topic.'

Although Connor was most definitely not Sebasten's favourite topic either, Sebasten discovered that his thoughts continued to circle back in that direction. He sacked his memory in an effort to recall every word that Lizzie had said the night he took her out to dinner and she told him her side of the story on Connor. But he hadn't been listening, not the way he *should* have been listening, for at that point he had believed that her every word was a lie.

'So you can finally tell me where we're going for our honeymoon?' Lizzie carolled with rather contrived sparkle when they boarded his private jet some hours later.

'Greece.' Sebasten reflected that there had to be some evil fate at work, for he was taking her to the one place in the world that held once fond memories of Ingrid and Connor.

Still striving gamely not to react to his brooding aura, Lizzie smiled so wide her jaw ached. 'You're taking me to your home there?'

'A private island.' Not the brightest spark of inspiration he had had this century, Sebasten decided with grim irony.

'Whose island?'

'Mine.'

'You own your own island?'

'Doesn't every Greek tycoon?' Sebasten shrugged.

'So I'm being dead vulgar and I'm impressed!' Lizzie quipped, a glint of annoyance flaring in her green eyes.

They had enjoyed the most fabulous wedding. Sebasten had seemed to be in the best of humour and nothing had gone wrong that she knew of. So what was the matter with him? Was it only now sinking in on him that he was a married man? Was being married to her *that* depressing? Tears prickled at the backs of her eyes but her expressive mouth tightened and she lifted a magazine, enjoyed the superb meal she was served and said not another word.

Late evening, they arrived on the island of Isvos. The helicopter set them down within yards of a long, low, rambling house built of natural stone. Sebasten carried her over the threshold. 'Bet you're glad there isn't a flight of steps!' Lizzie giggled.

His brilliant gaze centred on her lovely laughing face and suddenly he smiled.

The interior enchanted Lizzie: polished terracotta floors, stone walls and rough-hewn support pillars of wood contrasted with glorious sheer draperies and pale contemporary furniture. In every main room, doors opened direct on to the beach and the whispering, soothing sound of the surf seemed to flow through the whole house.

'I love it,' Lizzie murmured with an appreciative smile. 'It's so peaceful.'

'Ingrid Morgan helped to design it.'

Lizzie glanced at him in surprise. 'I thought she used to be a very superior PA.'

'She was but she was also my father's mistress.'

Lizzie blinked and then her lush mouth rounded into a soft silent 'oh' of belated comprehension.

'She ended it before Connor got old enough to suspect the truth and moved back to England.'

'Has she ever come back here?' Lizzie asked.

'No. Ingrid's not into reliving the past.' His jacket cast on the chest at the foot of the handsome beech bed, Sebasten lounged back against the pale wood door frame, six feet four inches of glorious leashed male power and virility. 'Neither am I as a rule. But, as I'm sure you'll recognise, Connor is a subject we've never really discussed in any depth.'

'Connor…?' Lizzie repeated after a startled pause. 'You want me to talk about Connor…*in depth*?'

Lean, powerful face taut with determination, Sebasten

shifted a broad shoulder in a fluid movement. 'We should get it out of the way.'

'Well, excuse me…' Green eyes wide with annoyance and discomfiture, Lizzie tilted her chin. 'I wasn't aware there *was* anything to get out of the way!'

'I know next to nothing about your relationship with him,' Sebasten countered with immovable cool.

'This is our wedding night and you want me to rehash unpleasant memories of another man…is that right?' Lizzie demanded, snatching in a sustaining breath in an effort to control the incredulous resentment splintering through her but failing. 'Go take a hike, Sebasten!'

Sebasten straightened, beautiful dark eyes flaring stormy gold. 'I might just do that.'

At that threat, fear touched Lizzie deep and that very fear that he might walk out only increased her fury. 'Wasn't it bad enough that you spent most of the trip here hardly speaking to me? I put up with that but I can't stand moody people. You never know where you are with them—'

'I am not moody,' Sebasten grated in an electrifying undertone. 'But when you admitted that you saw a likeness between me and Connor, yes, it did give me pause for thought. It made me wonder just what you *first* saw in me…'

Understanding came to Lizzie and she studied him with angry, hurt condemnation, for she could not change the reality that she had met his brother first. 'You have to be the most possessive guy I've ever met—'

Sebasten shot her a fulminating look. 'I'm not and I have never been possessive—'

'Volatile…possessive…jealous. Pick any one of them and they every one fit! If I'd just popped out of a little locked box somewhere the first night we met, you'd have loved it! How *could* you ask about Connor tonight of all nights? Do you honestly think I want to talk about how I found him and my stepmother in bed together?' Lizzie slung at him in furious reproach. 'You haven't got a romantic, sensitive bone in your body!'

The bathroom door slammed and locked on Lizzie's impassioned exit. Sebasten strode out onto the beach, angry with her, angry with himself, angrier still with Connor, now that he finally knew how brutal an awakening she had had to that affair. But he was not volatile. Nobody had ever accused him of that before. He was a very self-controlled guy. As for being possessive, what was wrong with that? *Theo mou*…she was his *wife*! A certain amount of possessiveness was a natural male instinct. As for that other tag, he wouldn't even dignify that suggestion with consideration.

Lizzie's frustration was overborne by tears of sheer tiredness. Where did Sebasten get the energy to be so volatile? At least though she now understood what had been riding him since the reception. She should never have mentioned that bit about there being a resemblance between him and his half-brother. She sank down on top of the comfortable bed, thinking that in just a moment she would go and track Sebasten down and smooth things over. After all, it was kind of sweet: Connor couldn't have held a candle to Sebasten in looks, personality or desirability.

When Sebasten strolled back in off the beach half an hour later, Lizzie was sound asleep. Clad in something filmy the colour of rich honey, she was curled up on top of the shot-silk spread. When he saw the faint track of a tear stain on her cheek, he suppressed a groan and raked long brown fingers through his tousled black hair. Why did he go off the rails with Lizzie? Connor had caused her a lot of grief. On the same score, his own conscience was hardly whiter than white *and* she was carrying his baby…

Lizzie wakened with a start and sat up. The doors on to the beach were still wide but now framed a spectacular crimson and gold sunrise over the bay. The indented pillow beside hers indicated that at some stage of the night Sebasten had joined her and she groaned out loud: she must have slept like a log. Sliding out of bed, she went into the *en suite* bathroom to freshen up and wondered where the heck Sebasten was.

When she returned to the bedroom, she stilled in relief. Sebasten was sprawled on the floor cushion by the doors watching the sun rise and her mouth ran dry. His strong brown back was bare and his well-worn jeans outlined every line of his narrow hips and long, powerful thighs. When he turned his arrogant dark head to look at her, deceptively sleepy golden eyes accentuated by the darkness of his lashes, he just took her breath away.

'Hi…' he said softly, extending a lean hand to her in welcome.

'You should've woken me up last night—'

Sebasten tugged her down beside him and pulled her back against him. 'Be honest…you were exhausted. A siren wouldn't have wakened you—'

'But *you* could have,' Lizzie whispered, curving back into the sun-warmed heat of him and tightening his arms round her for herself.

'Call it the first selfless act of a lifetime *pethi mou*,' Sebasten teased huskily, brushing her tumbled hair from one slim shoulder and pressing his expert mouth to her exposed skin in a caress that sent a helpless shiver of response coursing through her.

She twisted round in a sudden movement that took him by surprise and locked her lush lips to his with a hunger she couldn't hide.

'And this is the *second* unselfish act…' Sebasten shared with a ragged edge to his dark, deep drawl as he lifted her and set her back from him. 'Breakfast awaits you…'

'B-breakfast?' Lizzie stammered in total disconcertion.

'You can have me for dessert if you want,' Sebasten promised with husky amusement, vaulting upright with easy grace and pulling her with him to walk her out onto the terrace, where fresh rolls, cereal and fruit were already laid on the table.

'Are the staff invisible?' Lizzie asked as he tugged out a seat and tucked her into it.

'I made it. The staff will be very discreet and only show up when necessary—'

'And where do they hang out the rest of the time?'

'In the main house across that hill.' Sebasten nodded in the direction of the thick pine grove that ran on steep sloping ground right down to the edge of the sea.

'There's *another* house?'

'This place wasn't impressive enough to satisfy my father's wives. I use the main house when I'm entertaining. When I'm on my own, I come here.'

That he had brought her with him made her smile. When she had finished her tea, he peeled a peach for her, fed her with it segment by segment. She collided dizzily with smouldering golden eyes and licked his fingers clean of the peach juice. He closed his hands over hers and tugged her upright.

'Ready and willing,' Sebasten husked.

The well-worn denim of his jeans made that so obvious that her cheeks burned with colour but her awareness of his rampant arousal only heightened her own. Driven by the taut sensitivity of her breasts and the ache stirring at the very heart of her, she pushed into connection with every hard, muscular angle of his lean, powerful frame. He knotted his fingers into the tumbling torrent of her hair and claimed her ready mouth with explicit passion.

'I make a really *mean* breakfast,' he teased as he swept her quivering body up into his arms and carried her back to bed.

'But can you do it…every morning?' Lizzie mumbled, trying to hold her own in the breathless dialogue while struggling with his zip.

'Try me…' Sebasten took care of that problem for her by ripping off his jeans with single-minded purpose and dexterity. 'You wouldn't believe how sexy it feels to know that your woman carries your baby inside her.'

'Honestly?' Lizzie opened wide, uncertain eyes, met the fiery confirmation in his intent gaze, and relief and appreciation filled her.

'Honestly,' Sebasten confirmed with the slashing charismatic smile that always made her heart lurch inside her and he deprived her of her nightdress with smooth expertise.

Empowered by that declaration, Lizzie began, 'About last night, what you said about Con—'

'Shut up,' Sebasten warned without the smallest dip in that blazing smile. 'I was way out of line—'

'But—'

'Close your eyes and pretend we have only just arrived,' he urged, finding the tender peak of her breast with caressing fingers and depriving her of both breath and concentration.

He took her into a sensual world where all that mattered was the next sweet, drugging high of sensation. He let the heat of his mouth trail over her tender, pouting flesh and a long sigh was driven from her lungs. He lingered over the distended little buds until her sigh had become a moan she wasn't even aware of making and she was shifting her hips in a restive movement, unable to stay still.

'Sebasten…' she gasped as he worked his erotic passage down over the quivering muscles of her tummy. 'I want you…'

'Not yet,' he asserted, parting her slender thighs with ease and embarking on an intimacy that was new to her.

Shaken as she was, her eyes flew wide. 'No…'

But he transformed her negative into a helpless positive within seconds and drove her crazy with a pleasure that came close to torment. She was out of control, abandoned to the urgent need he had driven to an ever greater height. At the instant that her heart was a hammering thunder-beat in her ears and her whole quivering body was sensitised to an almost unbearable degree, he came over her and entered her in a single smooth-driving thrust. Excitement flung her so high, she couldn't catch her breath. She lifted herself up to him, moved against him in a helpless frenzy of need and then cried out as the shock waves of climax took her to an ecstatic peak and then released her again.

She felt soft with love, weak with fulfilment. Revelling in the peaceful aftermath of passion, she rubbed her cheek against a satin-smooth muscular brown shoulder. Happiness cocooned her as he hugged her close. He might not love her but he was very affectionate, she acknowledged, suppressing the inner sense of loss that that first acknowledgement threatened.

'Just to think, *pethi mou*,' Sebasten murmured with raw satisfaction as he gazed down into her warm green eyes, 'nobody but me is ever going to know how fantastic you really are.'

'Trust you to find a new slant on marriage,' Lizzie whispered with amusement.

Dark golden eyes welded to her, he brushed a kiss across her lush reddened mouth and breathed rather like a guy steeling himself to make a major statement. 'What we have is special…*really* special.'

'Is it?' she muttered, wanting more, striving to silence that need inside her and be happy with what they had.

'Yes.' Sebasten was just a little annoyed that she seemed so indifferent to his attempt to impress on her how much he valued her. 'We're so close, I can *feel* it.'

'Oh…' Lizzie snuggled into him.

'I've never been that great at getting close to women,' Sebasten confided, soothed by the fact that she was now wrapped round him like a vine. 'But you're different. You're very open.'

'Have you ever been in love?' she muttered in as casual a tone as she could muster.

Sebasten tensed. 'No…'

And with that Lizzie had to be content.

Two weeks later, Lizzie shimmied into a dress the shade of copper and noted how well it became the very slight tan she had acquired in the heat of the Greek sun.

Emerald drop earrings dangled from her ears and an emerald and diamond necklace encircled her throat. Sebasten had given her the earrings at the end of the first week and the necklace just the night before. Lizzie smiled. She had never been so happy. Even the reality that her beautiful dress was just a tinge too neat in fit over breasts that had made an inconvenient gain in size as her body changed with early pregnancy couldn't cloud her good mood.

They had had lazy golden days on the beach, eating when they felt like it, swimming when they felt like it, staying in bed when they felt like it and talking long into the night over the exquisite dinners the staff served on the terrace in the evening. On a couple of occasions they had walked down to the sleepy little village at the harbour and dined in each of the two taverns, where they had been treated like guests of honour. Other days they had flown over to the bigger, busier islands like Corfu to shop or dine or dance.

She had learnt a lot about the male she married. She had also been both disconcerted and touched when he had said he would be cutting back on his trips abroad so that he would be able to spend more time with her and the baby.

'It'll be difficult for you,' she had remarked.

'It's my choice, just as it was my father's choice to be a stranger to me throughout my childhood. He was never there,' Sebasten had admitted, his strong jawline squaring as he voiced a truth that his sense of family loyalty had always forced him to repress. 'He expected his wives to do his job for him but they didn't. It was much easier to leave me in the care of the staff or pack me off to boarding school.'

For the first time, Lizzie had recognised the strength of his sense of responsibility towards their unborn baby and her heart had gone out to him as she understood that his own experiences had made him all the more determined to ensure that his own child would receive very different treatment. But for the early loss of her mother, her own childhood had been secure and loving and she began to grasp the source of Sebasten's innate complexity. He had been forced to depend on his own inner resources at too early an age.

Yet throughout those two glorious weeks they shared, Sebasten continually surprised and delighted her with the unexpected. The night that he found her eating sun-dried tomatoes with a fork direct from the jar she had brought out to Greece with her, he had laughed at her embarrassment over her secret craving and carried both jar and her back to bed. But within twenty-four hours a ready supply of Greek sun-dried tomatoes had been flown in.

'It's a Greek baby,' he had pointed out cheerfully.

She would never have dreamt of telling Sebasten but she truly believed he was a perfect husband. He was romantic, although without ever seeming to realise that he was being romantic. He was also incredibly passionate and tender as well as being the most entertaining male she had ever been with. In short, he was just wonderful. She could not credit that she had been so worried that he might not be ready for the commitment of marriage. She was convinced that at any moment he would open the subject of their living in separate houses when they returned to London and talk her out of what she had already decided had been a very stupid idea.

It was the last night of their honeymoon. Sebasten had selected it as the night they would cast off their newly married seclusion and host a party at the big white villa over the hill. He wanted to entertain all the Greek friends and business acquaintances who had not been able to make it to a wedding staged at such short notice.

'You look fantastic in that dress,' Sebasten informed her as he entered the bedroom.

Lizzie encountered the appreciative gleam in his gaze and just grinned. 'You picked it. The emeralds look spectacular with it too. Thank you.'

'Gratitude not required. Those emeralds accentuate your eyes and I had to have them, *pethi mou.*'

She looked so happy, Sebasten thought with a powerful sense of achievement and satisfaction. He could not believe that she would insist on living apart from him when they got back home again. If she had begun to care for him even a little again, she would surely change her mind.

'How did you get so friendly with Ingrid Morgan?' Lizzie asked as she kicked off her shoes to walk barefoot across the sand. The path that led up through the pine wood to the main house was on the other side of the beach. 'You never did explain that.'

'Between the ages of eight and eleven, I spent every vacation here with Ingrid and Connor. My father would just fly in for a few days here and there,' Sebasten explained wryly.

'*Every* vacation?' Lizzie queried in surprise.

'It suited Andros. He was between wives. Ingrid treated me the same way she treated Connor and I began to think of them as my family.' Sebasten grimaced as if to invite her scorn of such a weakness on his part. 'It ended the day I asked my father when he and Ingrid were getting married.'

'Was marriage so out of the question?'

'By that stage they had already had a stormy on-and-off relationship that spanned quite a few years. He never thought of her as anything other than a mistress and he'd convinced himself that I was too young to ask awkward questions. But he took me back to our home in Athens that same evening and I was an adult before I met Ingrid again.'

'That was so cruel!' Lizzie groaned.

No longer did she wonder why he had once admitted to not trusting her sex, for he had been let down by the only two women he had learned to love when he was a child. His mother had walked away through her own personal choice but Ingrid Morgan had had no choice, for she had had no rights over her lover's son.

Why the hell had he told her all that? Sebasten asked himself in strong exasperation. Lizzie's eyes were glistening with tears and, even as he was warmed by her emotional response on his behalf, he was embarrassed by it too.

Ahead of them lay the big, opulent white villa built by Andros Contaxis for his second wife. Lizzie had had a lengthy tour of the house the week before. While a hugely impressive dwelling with as many rooms as a hotel, it lacked character and appeal. Considering that problem and keen to change the subject to one less sensitive, she murmured in a bright upbeat tone, 'I've got so many plans for the house. I can hardly wait to get home to make a start. I really will need the advice of a good interior designer, maybe even an architect.'

Sebasten absorbed that admission in angry, startled bewilderment. He assumed she was referring to the house he had offered her for her own sole occupation in London. How the hell could she exude such enthusiasm for literally throwing him back out of her life again? Had nothing that they had shared in recent days made her reappraise that ambition? What was he? A negotiable part of the old sun, sea and sex vacation aboard? Or just a rebound affair after Connor that was now leading to its natural conclusion? Obviously not much more, for all that he was the father of the baby she carried!

Surprised by his silence, Lizzie coloured, for she had assumed that he would be pleased. But then possibly he believed that when they were only just married she had some nerve announcing that she planned to redesign one of his homes. After all, it should have been *his* suggestion, rather than hers, she thought in sudden mortification. Just because her own father had always preferred to let the women in his life take care of such matters did not mean that Sebasten had a similar outlook.

'Of course,' she added hurriedly, striving to backtrack from her stated intention without losing face, 'change doesn't always mean improvement and it could be a mistake to rush into a project that would be so expensive—'

'Spend what you like when you like,' Sebasten delivered in a derisive undertone. 'I couldn't care less.'

Shock sliced through Lizzie. As they entered the villa she stole a shaken glance at his lean, hard profile, wondering what on earth she had said to deserve such a response. Whatever, it was obvious that Sebasten was angry. Furthermore, once their guests began arriving in a flood, Sebasten roved far and wide from her side, leaving her more than once to assume the guise of a faithful follower. He also talked almost exclusively in Greek, which she supposed was understandable when he was mixing with other Greeks, but on several occasions when she was already aware that their companions spoke English he left her feeling superfluous to their conversations.

'You have all my sympathy,' Candice, a beautiful and elegant brunette, remarked to Lizzie out of the blue.

Having already been informed by Candice that she had once dated Sebasten, Lizzie tensed. 'Why?'

'Sebasten doesn't quite have the look of a male who has taken to marriage like a duck to water.' Exotic dark eyes mocked Lizzie's flush of dismay at that crack. 'But then some men are just born to prefer freedom and it *is* early days yet, isn't it?'

That one stinging comment was sufficient to persuade Lizzie that Sebasten was making a public spectacle of her. Seeing him momentarily alone, she studied him. He looked grim without his social smile, pale beneath his usually vibrant olive skin tone, and concern overcame her annoyance. She hurried over to him and said ruefully, 'Are you going to tell me what's the matter with you?'

'Nothing's the matter.' Hard golden eyes clashed with hers in apparent astonishment.

'But I've hardly seen you this evening—'

'Do we need to stick together like superglue?' Sebasten elevated a sardonic ebony brow. 'I have to confess that after two weeks of round-the-clock togetherness, I'm in need of a breather and looking forward to leading more separate lives when we get home.'

The silence enclosed her like silent thunder.

'Believe me, you're not the only one,' Lizzie breathed, fighting to keep her voice level.

She walked away but inside herself she was tottering in shock and devastation. How could he turn on her like that when she had believed them so close? She loved him to distraction but how could she allow herself to love someone that ruthless in stating his own dissatisfaction with their marriage? What had gone wrong, how it had gone wrong without her noticing seemed unimportant. All that mattered was that once again she herself had been guilty of making a fatal misjudgement about how a man felt about her.

Oh, she knew he didn't love her but she had believed that they were incredibly close for all that. Hadn't he said so himself? But then, what did she believe? What Sebasten said *in* bed or what he said *out* of it? She knew which version her intelligence warned her to place most credence in. She gazed round the crowded room but all the faces were just a blur and the clink of glasses, the chatter and the music seemed distant and subdued. Then, without her even appreciating the fact, the most awful dizziness had taken hold of her. As she lurched in the direction of the nearest seat she was too late to prevent what was already happening, and she folded down on the carpet with a stifled moan of dismay.

Already striding towards her, alerted by her striking pallor and wavering stance, Sebasten was right on the spot to take charge but cool did not distinguish the moments that immediately followed Lizzie's fainting fit. Never an optimist at the best of times, in the guilt-stricken mood he was in, Sebasten was convinced he'd killed her stone-dead and the reality that there were at least three doctors present was of no consolation whatsoever.

Lizzie recovered consciousness to find herself lying on a sofa in another room. Three men were hovering but Sebasten was down on his knees, clutching one of her hands, much as if she were on her deathbed. She blinked, almost smiled as her bemused gaze closed in on his lean, strong face, and then she remembered his words of rejection and what colour she had regained receded again and she turned her head away, sucking in a deep, convulsive breath.

'Only a faint, nothing to really worry about,' Sebasten's best friend from university asserted in bracing Greek. 'A mother-to-be shouldn't be standing for hours on end on such a warm and humid evening—'

'And not without having eaten any supper,' chimed in another friend.

'She has a fragile look about her,' the third doctor remarked, his more pessimistic and cautious nature a perfect match for Sebasten's. 'Entertaining two hundred people tonight may well have been too much for her. This is a warning to you. She needs rest and tender care, and try to keep the stress to a minimum.'

Sebasten was feeling bad enough without the news that his lack of care on almost every possible count had contributed to Lizzie's condition. He scooped her up into his arms. 'I'm taking you up to bed.'

Lizzie made no protest. The more she thought about his rejection, the more anguished she felt, and what self-discipline she had was directed towards thanking the doctors for their assistance and striving to behave normally.

By the time Sebasten had carried Lizzie up to the master-bedroom suite and settled her down on the vast circular bed that had sent her into a fit of giggles when she first saw it, even he was a little out of breath. But so shattered had he been by her collapse and by the gut-wrenching punishment of having been forced to think of what life might be like without her that Sebasten was desperate to dig himself back out of the very deep hole that fierce pride had put him in.

'I was lying in my teeth when I said I was tired of us being together,' Sebasten confessed in a raw, driven undertone.

Thinking that now he felt sorry for her and blamed his own blunt honesty for causing her stupid faint, Lizzie flipped over and presented him with her back. 'I'd like to be on my own.'

'I'm sorry I was such a bastard,' Sebasten framed half under his breath, his dark, deep drawl thick with strain. 'I don't want to score points any more. I *do* want you to be happy—'

'Then go away,' she muttered tightly.

'But I *need* you in my life.' Sebasten forced that admission out with much the same gritty force as a male making a confession while facing a loaded gun.

A solitary tear rolled down Lizzie's taut cheek. Obviously he had recognised just how devastated she was at the concept of having to let go of her dream of a happy, normal marriage. 'I don't need you,' she mumbled flatly.

CHAPTER TWELVE

SEBASTEN had had a hell of a night.

Most of their guests had travelled home. Some who had had to stay overnight at the villa at least retired early, but those who did not kept him up until almost dawn. For what remained of the night he paced the room next to Lizzie's and fought the temptation to disturb her so that they could talk again. While Lizzie breakfasted in bed at his express instruction, he had to assume a cheerful-host act until the merciful moment that the last of their visitors had departed. However, by that stage it was time to embark on their return trip to London.

Lizzie came downstairs dressed in a dark green shift dress, her hair pulled back in a sophisticated style, all but her lush pink lips and the tip of her nose hidden behind a giant pair of sunglasses.

'How do you feel?' Sebasten asked, striving to suppress the recollection of finding her bedroom door locked when he had tried to make the same enquiry earlier in the day.

'Marvellous…can't wait to get home!' Lizzie declared, heading for the helicopter outside at speed.

Behind the sunglasses her reddened eyes were dull with misery but Lizzie had her pride to sustain her. When they boarded the Contaxis jet at Athens, she struck up an animated conversation with the stewardesses, went into several determined fits of laughter at the movie she chose to watch and enjoyed a second dessert after eating a hearty late lunch. And she called *him* insensitive, Sebasten reflected in receipt of that concerted display of indifference.

'I have to call into the office,' Sebasten announced after she had climbed into the limousine waiting to collect them in London. 'I'll see you back at the house...we have to talk.'

But what was there to talk about? Lizzie asked herself wretchedly. He had already spelt out how he felt. She had no option but to go to his London home, for the town house he had purchased had yet to be furnished. So, couldn't she buy some furniture? Surely camping out in bare rooms would be better than staying with Sebasten when her presence was no longer welcome?

How could he get bored with her between one moment and the next? Her throat ached and her rebellious memory served up a dozen images of intimacy that cut her like a knife when she could least bear it. Sebasten dragging her out of bed to breakfast at dawn and enjoy what he called 'the best part of the day' and her struggling to match his vibrant energy and conceal her yawns. Sebasten watching her try on clothes, a smouldering gleam of appreciation in his gaze letting her know exactly what to buy. Sebasten curving her into his arms last thing at night and making her feel so incredibly happy and secure.

No, camping out in bare rooms, she decided with a helpless shiver, would be more comfortable than the chilling prospect of sharing the same household even on a temporary basis, ever conscious of what they had had and then lost. Painful as it was, she knew that some men lost all interest in a woman once the excitement of the chase was over and that those same men could go from desire to uninterest almost overnight. Was that Sebasten's true nature? And had he not already achieved what he had said was most important? Their child would be born a Contaxis. The sad fact was that his parents did not have to live together nor even remain married to meet that requirement.

Infuriated at the crisis that had demanded his presence at Contaxis International, Sebasten got back home just before seven that evening. By then, Lizzie had already cleared out. The dressing room off the master bedroom looked as though a whirlwind by the name of Lizzie had gone through it and his staff had tactfully left the evidence for him to find. She had left a note on the bed. Seeing it, he froze, not wanting to read it.

'I borrowed some of your furniture but I'll return it soon. It's easier this way,' she wrote in her note. 'Stay in touch.'

Stay in touch? Sebasten crunched the note between his fingers. *Easier for whom?* He was in total shock. Nothing he had said the night before had made any impression on her. He had said ' I need you' to a woman who could break down in floods of tears over a sad film, but she had still walked out. Let her go, his stubborn pride urged.

When Sebasten hit the bell on the front door, Lizzie mustered her courage and went to answer it.

Lean, bronzed features taut, he was sheathed in a formal dark business suit. She allowed her gaze to flick over him very fast. He looked sensational, but then he always did, she acknowledged painfully. Heart pounding like a road drill, she crossed the echoing hall and showed him into the only furnished room available.

'Look at me…' Sebasten urged in a roughened undertone.

She was shocked by the haunted strain in his dark gold gaze and the fierce tension stamped into every sculpted line of his hard bone-structure.

'Come home…*please*,' he breathed with fierce emphasis. 'We have to talk.'

'I think that all that needs to be said was said last night,' Lizzie said unevenly.

'No…I tried to give you space while we were in Greece. I went against my own nature.' Sebasten shifted a lean, forceful hand to emphasise that point. 'If I had that two weeks a second time, believe me, I wouldn't make the same mistake again.'

'But you went out of your way to hurt me last night.' Lizzie's mind was in angry, defensive turmoil, for she could no longer understand what he wanted from her.

Sebasten released a ragged laugh. 'What did you expect from me after I had to listen to you telling me that you couldn't *wait* to start renovating this house? How was I supposed to react? You were letting me know that nothing had changed, that you weren't prepared to live with me or even give our marriage a fighting chance!'

Lizzie stared back at him with wide, bewildered eyes. 'But I wasn't talking about *this* house…I was talking about your father's villa on the island!'

Sebasten stilled in his pacing track across the room and frowned in equal bemusement. 'You didn't make that clear. The villa on Isvos?'

'Yes.' Lizzie took in a slow, steadying breath as she grasped that they had been talking at cross purposes the previous night. His aggression had been fired by a simple misconception: his belief that she was still hell-bent on setting up a separate household. 'You picked me up wrong and leapt to the wrong conclusion.'

'I don't think so.' Sebasten had a different viewpoint. 'You've moved in here.'

'Only because I thought that was what *you* wanted!'

'Why would I want to live apart from my wife?' The fierce

glitter in his intent golden eyes challenged her, his jawline clenching hard. 'I thought that I could accept that for a while if it meant that you married me but this feels more like the end of our marriage than the beginning. But I know that I can't force you to feel what I feel.'

'And what *do* you feel?' Lizzie almost whispered, so great was her tension, for what he was telling her was exactly what she had needed to hear from him.

'That maybe you haven't quite got over Connor yet. That maybe this situation is what I asked for when I screwed up our relationship from start to finish…but I still love you and I'll wait for as long as it takes,' Sebasten breathed with fierce conviction.

Lizzie was still as a statue. Shock had made her pale. 'You *love* me?'

Sebasten fixed level, strained golden eyes on her and nodded much as if he had just confessed to a terminal illness.

'Since when?' Lizzie could barely frame the question.

'Probably the first night we met. I did things that night that I would never have done in a normal state of mind,' Sebasten confessed with grim dark eyes, not appearing to register that she was fumbling her way down onto the edge of the sofa she had borrowed. 'I did take *huge* advantage of you. You were very vulnerable that night but I just couldn't let go of you. Love is supposed to make people kinder but at that stage it only made me more selfish and ruthless.'

'Sebasten…' Lizzie was wondering if she could dare to credit what she was hearing when what he was saying was her every dream come true.

'No, I'm determined to tell it like it was, no stone left unturned,' Sebasten asserted with a derision angled at himself. 'After I sobered you up that night, I should've put you in a guest room. On the other hand, if I *had* done that you wouldn't have got pregnant and I could never have persuaded you to marry me. So, I'm afraid I can't even regret that we made love.'

Lizzie could not drag her mesmerised stare from his lean, strong face. 'Yes, he was still very much the focused guy she had fallen in love with. But that he should be grateful that she had conceived because that development had ultimately made her let him back into her life again touched her to the heart.

'And when I suspected that you were a virgin, did I feel guilty?' Sebasten spread rueful hands in emphasis. 'No, I didn't feel guilty even then. That made you feel more like mine, and you're right—where you're concerned I'm very possessive and jealous and I was delighted that I was your first lover.'

'You're being so honest,' Lizzie managed in a shaky voice. 'I really like that.'

'Then I saw your driver's licence and realised you were Lisa Denton and it all just blew up in my face. From there on in, it only got worse,' Sebasten continued heavily.

'The night we met…you *honestly* didn't know who I was?' Lizzie gasped.

'I told you I didn't! I saw you on the dance floor and I couldn't take my eyes off you. I had not the smallest suspicion that you were Connor's ex.'

And she hadn't believed him, Lizzie thought in dismay.

'In fact I thought the little blonde I saw speaking to you was Lisa Denton and I had no intention whatsoever of approaching her.'

'That was Jen,' Lizzie whispered, fully convinced that he was telling her the truth.

'Once I knew your true identity, I couldn't acknowledge how I felt about you. I wrecked everything trying to stay loyal as I believed to Connor's memory.'

'Why, though? You admitted you hardly knew him as an adult.'

Sebasten grimaced. 'The day of the funeral was also the day Ingrid told me that he was my half-brother.'

Lizzie absorbed that fact with a flash of anger in her expressive eyes. 'Oh, that was wicked…to finally tell you *that* when Connor was dead!'

'I wouldn't say it was wicked, but with hindsight I can see that it *was* very manipulative timing,' Sebasten conceded with wry regret. 'But Ingrid was out of her head with grief. It sent me haywire though. I felt a great sense of loss. I felt guilty that I had not made more effort to maintain contact with Connor.'

Lizzie did not believe he would have found very much common ground with his half-brother but she was too kind to say so. Her memory of the younger man had softened but she knew that he had been arrogant and self-centred right to the last in allowing his friends to go on believing that she had broken his heart and driven him to the heavy drinking sessions that finally contributed to his death.

'I've learnt more about Connor through what he did to *you* than I probably ever wanted to know,' Sebasten confided with a grimace, as if he could read her mind. 'What I hate most is that I came along and I hurt you even more.'

'That's behind us now,' Lizzie assured him.

'Time and time again, I told myself that the secret of your incredible attraction was just sex,' Sebasten groaned. 'The minute I realised that you were Lisa Denton, I swore to myself that I wouldn't ever sleep with you again…but I *did* and more than once.'

'I know.' Lizzie was trying hard not to smile.

'That episode in the basement just…' Sebasten threw up both hands in a speaking gesture of rare discomfiture. 'It was crass, crazy. I'm really sorry about that. Afterwards, I couldn't believe I'd lost control to that extent…I mean, I was fighting what I felt for you with everything I had! But I was a pushover every time.'

'That's when you realised how keen I was on you, wasn't it?' Lizzie prompted gently.

Dark colour scored his superb cheekbones. 'I felt like a total bastard and I didn't want to hurt you. So, I decided that I had to dump you because the entire situation had become more than I could handle.'

'You poor love…' Lizzie swallowed hard on the unexpected giggle that bubbled in her throat. 'You've had a really tough time.'

'You dumped me,' Sebasten reminded her. 'I couldn't even do that right!'

Lizzie got up and wrapped her arms round him.

'I thought you were angry with me. Why are you hugging me?' Sebasten asked, his Greek accent very thick.

'For making me feel as irresistible as Cleopatra…for letting me see that loving me has made you suffer a lot too…so now I can forgive you for having made me suffer,' Lizzie confided, locking both arms round his neck.

'You can forgive me?' Some of the raw tension in his big, powerful frame eased and he closed his own arms tightly round her. 'Give me a chance to make everything right from now on?'

'Loads of chances,' she promised, conscious of the anxiety still visible in his dark golden eyes. 'When did you realise you'd fallen in love with me?'

Sebasten tensed. 'I sort of suspected it in Greece but I didn't take those thoughts out and examine them because I didn't know what was going to happen when we came back to London. But when you collapsed last night I panicked and faced how much you meant to me. I had this nightmare vision of my life without you in it—'

'Traumatising? I hope so, because you're not getting a life without me in it.'

'I love you the way I never thought I would love any

woman.' His possessive golden gaze pinned with appreciation to her, he framed her irreverent grin with gentle fingers. 'I love everything about you, *pethi mou*...even the
way you annoy the hell out of me sometimes. So stop teasing me.'

She could not have doubted the rough sincerity in his
every spoken syllable and the direct and steady onslaught of
an adoring scrutiny that made her face warm with colour. 'I
love you too...'

'*Still?*' Sebasten demanded. 'I thought you'd got over
me...you wouldn't give an inch even when I practically
begged you to come back to me!'

'I can be stubborn. But I never stopped loving you.'

His brilliant smile flashed across his lean, devastating features and he hugged her close. 'I feel a very uncool degree
of happiness...say it again.'

She did.

And then he felt he had to match her with the same words.
He felt wonderful. He felt ten feet tall. Lizzie was his, finally,
absolutely his. His wedding ring on her finger, his baby on
the way. Freeing her just when she was about to invite the
kiss that every nerve in her body craved, Sebasten closed his
hand over hers and walked her back out to the hall.

'Where are we going?' Lizzie muttered.

'Home...to where it all began. Any chance of me reliving
the highlights?' Sebasten gave her a wicked look of all-male
anticipation.

As he flipped shut the door in their wake and then tucked
her into his car, Lizzie blushed and smiled. 'I think that's very
possible.'

An hour and more later, Sebasten lay back in what now
felt like a secure marital bed to him and held Lizzie close.
He was in a very upbeat mood, checking out her freckles and
discovering that, in spite of all his efforts to keep her under

sunhats and in the shade, the Greek sun had blessed her with another half-dozen. He knew she wasn't fond of her freckles, so he kept the news to himself. He splayed his fingers over her still non-existent tummy and grinned and secretly rejoiced in feelings of intense possessiveness.

'What are you thinking about?' Lizzie whispered, smiling up at him with complete contentment and trust.

'That you're the best investment I've ever made,' Sebasten confided with quiet satisfaction. 'When you have the baby, I'll have *two* of you.'

'We'll be a family. You'll be totally trapped because I'm not letting go of you ever,' Lizzie teased.

'You'd be amazed how good that sounds to me.' Sebasten looked down at her with all the love he couldn't hide and she knew he meant every word of that assurance. 'As long as you don't expect me to buy any more houses for your sole occupation.'

Lizzie grimaced. 'I feel *so* bad about that.'

'Don't. Just remind yourself that we are the same two people who shared an incredible happy honeymoon and we talked about everything under the sun *but*…neither one of us had the guts to broach the sensitive subject of how we planned to live when we got home again,' Sebasten pointed out with wry amusement.

'I was waiting for you to try and persuade me to change my mind,' Lizzie complained. 'I wasn't expecting you to rush out and buy a house overnight either!'

Sebasten burst out laughing at that and kissed her breathless, and it was another hour before they had dinner and he dropped the bait about it having just occurred to him that perhaps her father might like to consider moving into the surplus dwelling they had acquired.

'That's a *fabulous* idea!' Lizzie exclaimed.

And Sebasten basked without conscience in her pleasure

and admiration and knew that he would never own up to the truth that he had hoped for that conclusion all along.

A year and four months later, Sebasten and Lizzie threw a party to celebrate their baby daughter, Gemma's, christening.

Ingrid Morgan attended and Lizzie and she talked at some length. They had made peace with each other months before: Ingrid had felt very guilty and had urged that meeting, but Lizzie had made the effort initially only for Sebasten's sake. However, when she had got to know the older woman better she had begun to relax and like Ingrid for herself. Ingrid had worked through her grief and admitted that she had had no cause to accuse any woman of driving her son to suicide. She had come to terms with the reality that Connor's death had just been an accident.

When all their guests had gone home, Lizzie changed Gemma into her cute bunny nightwear and laid her daughter with tender hands into her cot. She just adored the baby. Gemma had her father's colouring but was already showing signs of her mother's personality. She was a cheerful baby, who slept a lot and rarely cried. Elbows resting on the cot rail, Lizzie smiled down at Gemma, grateful that her baby girl had not inherited her freckles. It was all very well for Sebasten to have a positive *thing* about freckles but he had to appreciate that not everyone shared that outlook, Lizzie reflected with amusement.

It had been an eventful year for both her and her father. Maurice Denton was already divorced. Felicity had met another man and had been keen to speed up the legal proceedings. Her father's spirits had been low for quite a time but moving house had helped and he very much liked living so close to his daughter and was a regular visitor. His own friends had rallied round him in a very supportive way, but her father had also developed a wonderfully friendly and relaxed relationship with Sebasten.

At times during her pregnancy that closeness between her parent and her husband had been just a little irritating for Lizzie. Both Sebasten and her father had been prone to trying to gang up on her and wrap her up in cotton wool. Stubborn to the last, Lizzie had worked until she was seven months pregnant before deciding to tender her resignation. The PR job had been a lot of fun but it had taken her away from Sebasten too many evenings and it had exhausted her.

Gemma had been born without any fuss or complications but Sebasten had lived on his nerves for the last weeks of Lizzie's pregnancy, striving valiantly to conceal his terror that something might go wrong. But Lizzie herself had been an oasis of calm, secure in the knowledge that Sebasten was doing all her worrying for her. He had fallen instantly in love with Gemma and, if possible, Lizzie had fallen even more deeply in love with Sebasten just watching him with their daughter. The guy who had said he preferred children at a distance used every excuse that had ever been invented to lift his daughter and cuddle her.

'Don't you dare lift her,' Lizzie warned, hearing and recognising the footsteps behind her. 'She shouldn't be disturbed when she's ready to go to sleep.'

Sebasten strolled into view, and at one glimpse of his heartbreaking smile Lizzie's pulses speeded up.

'Just when did you get so bossy?' he mocked, brilliant golden eyes roaming over the very tempting vision Lizzie made in her sleek blue skirt suit with her glorious hair tumbling round her shoulders in sexy disarray.

Lizzie grinned. 'When I met you. Either I lay down and got walked on or I fought back.'

'But you're out of line on this occasion. I spent half the evening holding Gemma,' Sebasten pointed out with amusement. 'I'm in the nursery in search of you.'

Already well-aware of that just from the smouldering

gleam in his vibrant gaze as he surveyed her, Lizzie eased forward in a sinuous move into the hard heat and muscularity of his lean, powerful frame and gave him the most welcoming look of invitation she could manage.

'You're an incredible flirt,' Sebasten commented with satisfaction, surrendering at speed and scooping her up into his arms with an efficiency that spoke of regular practice.

'You like that…' Lizzie was used to being carried off to bed and ravished and she encouraged him in that shameless pursuit of pleasure every step of the way.

'I do. And carrying you around does keep me in the peak of athletic condition,' Sebasten teased as he settled her down on their bed.

Lizzie just laughed and kicked off her shoes. 'Kiss me and prove it.'

Sebasten pitched his jacket aside, dropped his tie where he stood, demonstrating an untidy streak that had once been foreign to him, and came down on the bed to haul her back into his arms. 'You're a wanton hussy and I adore you…'

Lizzie battered her eyelashes but the glow of her own love was there in her softened eyes for his to see. Before she could even tell him she loved him like crazy too, he released an appreciative groan in response to that look and melded her lush mouth to his own.

The Greek Tycoon's Baby

*Turn the page to read Lynne Graham's
bonus short story!*

CHAPTER ONE

WHEN the stretch limo pulled up outside, the executives waiting in the foyer fell silent. The new owner of Devlin Systems, the Greek multimillionaire, Leos Kiriakos, had arrived. His ruthless reputation had preceded him and the tension was electric. Everyone was expecting a huge round of redundancies by the end of the month.

Susie Marshall, the slender redhead on reception, was pale as death, her entire concentration centered on the entrance doors being swept open. In just seconds, she would see him for the first time in fourteen long, endless months...

Her co-worker, Jayne, a chatty blonde, whispered, "Bet he's not anything as attractive as his publicity photos!"

Susie snatched in an unsteady breath and clenched her hands tightly together. From the instant Leos Kiriakos had added Devlin Systems to his global business empire, nobody had been interested in talking about anything else. Frantically trying to calculate how to avoid being seen by Leos when she had the misfortune to work on the front desk had run Susie's nerves ragged.

"In fact, it's my bet that below chin level, our Leos will be short and round, and about as sexy as a socks-wash!" Jayne said ruefully.

In immediate contradiction of that forecast, a male who

was an easy six foot four inches tall strode in. With his wide shoulders, lean hips and long powerful legs, he had the well-honed physique of a natural athlete. From the crown of his proud dark head to the soles of his hand-made shoes, he was, by any standard, spectacular.

"I have just died and gone to heaven…." Jayne swore as the executives engulfed Leos Kiriakos, desperate to make a good first impression. "Drop dead gorgeous and loaded!"

"Yes…" Susie mumbled shakily, unable to drag her eyes from those bold, bronzed features. She was dizzy with a longing that shamed her, for the bitter-sweet memory of the last night she had spent in Leos's arms now felt like a guilty secret.

While Leos appeared fully occupied, Susie left the desk and headed for the cloakroom, intending to stay there until the coast was clear.

"Susie…?"

In shock, she froze in her tracks, the startling intervention of that rich, dark voice on a clear and rising question so horrifically unexpected, she almost died right there and then. Slowly, she turned. The men surrounding Leos had parted like the Red Sea.

Heart racing so fast she was afraid she would faint, Susie collided with glittering tawny-golden eyes set between black, spiky lashes. Having initially moved forward, Leos stilled and moved an authorative hand to indicate that she should come to him. His lean, strong face was as hard as granite.

"You work here?" Leos enquired grimly.

Painfully conscious that they were now the focus of astonished stares and surrounded by total silence, Susie nodded jerkily.

"In what capacity?" His fabulous bone structure was taut, the long-lashed brilliance of his eyes raking over her like slashing shards of ice.

"I'm on reception." Susie practically whispered.

His aggressive jawline squared. With a bleak nod of dismissal, Leos swung away from her—again.

CHAPTER TWO

SUSIE peered at her still-swollen eyes in the vanity mirror and suppressed a groan. She had not slept the night before.

A plaintive cry sent her whirling round. Across the room, her baby son was clutching his crib bars in frustration. His toy keys had fallen to the carpet. As she restored the ring to his tiny grasping hand, she smiled as his cross little face cleared like magic.

Ben was six months old. He had silky dark curls, huge melting brown eyes and dimples. His features were still rounded and indistinct but he already bore a marked resemblance to his father in hair, skin, and eye colour, Susie conceded wretchedly.

And there was no denying that she was wretched. Only yesterday, Leos had looked at her with icy hostility. His attitude had really hurt. But then, she and Leos had not parted the best of friends and the pain of that cruel severance remained, biting deepest whenever she looked at the son she adored.

Coping as a single parent had not been easy. Her brother David, who worked abroad, allowed her to live rent-free in his apartment. Without his generosity, she would have been forced to live on welfare. Having Ben cared for in the Devlin Systems day care swallowed half of her salary. What was left over would not stretch to paying a London rent and living expenses as well.

On the bus to work, Susie thought back uneasily to Jayne's reaction to what she had witnessed.

"Well, you've certainly been a dark horse," Jayne had sniped. "Why didn't you say that you actually knew Leos Kiriakos?"

So Susie had told part of the truth but not the whole. Although she had a business degree, she'd been working as an office temp when she first met Leos Kiriakos. While he was over on London on business, flu had laid low two of his personal staff. Susie had arrived at his hotel suite, proud to have got the opportunity but secretly quaking in her shoes. She had fallen in love at first sight of his breathtaking smile. In a split second, he had gone from being the intimidating and powerful Greek tycoon, whom she wanted to impress with her efficiency, to being simply the man of her dreams.

When Leos had asked her out to dinner, she had been overjoyed. Six weeks of ecstatic happiness followed before everything began to go wro…

Susie hurried into the Devlin Systems building and left Ben in the ground floor nursery. As always, leaving him was a wrench. And like every other employee using the excellent childcare facility, she was anxiously wondering whether Leos Kiriakos would keep such a staff luxury.

When she arrived at reception, Jayne pushed a sheet of paper toward her. "Looks like you're on the way up…"

Susie frowned. "What's this?"

"Personnel sent it down. You have an interview with Leos Kiriakos tomorrow afternoon." Jayne's envy was unconcealed. "You must have made quite an impression the last time you worked for him…"

CHAPTER THREE

At ten to three the next day, Susie presented herself on the top floor, dressed in a dark-green skirt suit, with a longer-length jacket, her streaky red-gold curls caught up in a clip, her emerald eyes were strained, the pallor marking her delicate features pronounced.

Two sleepless nights in a row. She had lain awake fretting about whether or not Leos now knew that she had a child. Leos, who had once angrily given forth on the subject of a friend "trapped for the next 20 years by a pregnant woman on the make!"

Had Leos looked at her personnel file? If he had, he would surely have found out that she had given birth to a premature baby, eight months after they broke up!

She was sent straight down the corridor to the managing director's office. Sick with nervous tension, she knocked on the door and entered.

Leos was on the phone, his hard, chiseled profile intent. He indicated the chair set several feet from his desk and returned to his call. Susie sat down and tried to keep her hands steady. She tried crazily to recall what constituted defensive body language, for Leos was certain to know. As she watched him, an emotional pain that was almost physical held her taut.

He had replaced her with another woman without telling

her. But then there had been extenuating circumstances for his behavior. And the truth was, Susie had yet to get over her affair with Leos Kiriakos.

"Sorry about that." Pushing aside the phone, Leos sprang upright, emanating the megawatt energy that was so much a part of him. "Stop looking at me like a scared little mouse, Susie. I didn't bring you up here either to sack you or abuse you. Believe it or not, I can take having been dumped without behaving like Neanderthal man!"

Was this the guy who had growled down the phone at her 14 months ago, "no woman dumps me!" Connecting with eyes of stunning tawny-gold clarity set below level ebony brows, Susie was mesmerized, her heart hammering, her bewildered mind blank. Fortunately Leos was still talking, his rich-accented drawl like evocative long-missed music on her ears.

"I need a social secretary for the next month." Lithe as a jungle cat, Leos strolled over to the tinted windows. "You're quick, you're clever. You don't irritate the hell out of me with stupid questions. When I move on from here, you'll be an executive assistant on the management team."

Disconcerted by his every word, Susie just sank deeper into shock. Clearly, she had been over-sensitive on the day of his arrival, mistaking his natural surprise at seeing her as hostility. "Social s-secretary?"

Leos quoted a salary that made her head spin and then glanced at his gold watch with impatience. "If you want the position it's yours and you start tomorrow. We'll discuss your duties then. I'm rather pushed for time today."

"I'll take it..." she heard herself say, even though his quite shattering indifference to their former relationship pierced her like a knife....

CHAPTER FOUR

Leos was chairing a board meeting when Susie arrived.

Nervous as a cat on hot bricks, she organized the small office allotted to her. Finally, the phone rang and she was summoned into the boardroom. Leos immediately stood up, provoking a noisy thrusting back of seats as the all-male management team surged to emulate his good manners.

"Not only has Miss Marshall a topflight marketing degree, but she is also fluent in French and Spanish," Leos said, disconcerting Susie a great deal with that introduction. "What was she doing down on reception?"

Looking aghast, the personnel manager froze.

"A business that fails to place promising staff in a key position is wasteful." Leos delivered. "I have also taken note of the fact that there are no female managers, an extraordinary achievement in a firm this size."

On that thought for the day, Leos closed the meeting. Suddenly, Susie understood that there had been nothing personal about his decision to promote her. He had simply used her to highlight his lecture about equal opportunities! A confusing mixture of reluctant admiration, pain and resentment assailed her.

A vision of masculine sophistication in a superb gray business suit, Leos showed Susie into his office. "Last month

Devlin Systems settled two charges of sexual discrimination out of court. There will not be a third—"

"I thought you didn't approve of working women—"

Leos raised a brow. "You were the first working woman I took to my bed and you were often unavailable when I wanted you. What I seek for my own satisfaction in my private life has no relation to my opinions as an employer."

Hotly flushed in receipt of that blunt clarification, Susie tore her gaze from his and regretted her own over-familiar comment. All those months ago, she had only actually worked for Leos for three days before their passionate affair began and she had moved on to another agency placement.

"I have a long list of tasks for you," Leos continued without skipping a beat, the heavy silence not seeming to disturb him in the slightest.

But then, she already knew that he did not have a sensitive bone in his body, didn't she? Everything Leos did merely emphasized that she had never been more than a casual bed partner—on his terms. Her throat convulsed with tears.

He extended an audiotape to her. "It's all on here. First, you send out the invitations to the dinner party. Then you can nip over to Bond Street and choose a bracelet for Brigitte. I'll fill in the gift card."

Powered by a near-agonizing sense of humiliation and pain, Susie lifted her head, green eyes alight with outrage.

"You are asking me to choose jewelry for your current lover?' she exclaimed and flung the tape back at his feet. "You call that work? I call it victimization and revenge. Burn in hell, Leos!'

Leos studied her with incredulous tawny eyes.

"I hate you...I really hate you! You were the biggest mistake I ever made in my whole life!" And on that embittered declaration, Susie stalked out....

CHAPTER FIVE

AN HOUR LATER, Susie's tumultuous emotions calmed enough for her to slowly fill with horror at her own behavior.

She had spent 10 minutes silently sobbing in the cloak-room, 20 minutes trying to pull herself back together and the subsequent 30 minutes hugging Ben in the day care.

Ben, whose comfort and security were dependant on her success in the job market. Ben, whose mother had just lost her foolish head and screamed like a shrew at a monstrously insensitive male. Ben, whose mother now had to eat humble pie for his sake.

Back on the top floor, Susie knocked on Leos's office door with a hand she couldn't keep steady. Infuriated with herself, she whirled back flat against the wall and breathed in deeply before going in.

Lounging back in his desk chair, Leos surveyed her, his lean, powerful face unreadable.

"I owe you an apology. I don't know what came over me." Susie attempted to look through him rather than at him.

"I have a very good idea what came over you," Leos drawled softly.

"Naturally, I'm willing to carry out whatever duties the job entails," Susie stated hurriedly, to avoid him passing an opinion on what had provoked her.

"Including shopping for the woman in my life?" Leos inquired even more silkily.

Susie shivered and her hands knotted into fists. She didn't argue but she couldn't force out a word of agreement.

"To think that while we were together I never once saw that temper." Narrowed tawny eyes were pinned to her with laser light intensity. "You were hysterical earlier."

"And offensive. I'm sorry," she told him tightly. "It won't happen again."

"Brigitte is my brother's wife. The dinner party is to celebrate her birthday…." Leos watched the tide of pink mortification sweep up over Susie's complexion.

But her relief was so intense at that news, it outweighed her embarrassment. Involuntarily, she met his eyes. His wide, passionate mouth curved into a slow, burning smile and her willpower went into free fall, allowing disturbingly intimate memories to surface.

Leos kissing her with driving hunger, sending her out of control with excitement. Heat consumed her entire skin surface. She trembled, heartbeat speeding, pulses racing in concert, as she felt her treacherous body respond as it had always done to his potent sexuality.

And then she recalled the angry, half-naked blonde she had found in his apartment 14 months back. It had been her own fault, rushing over there without an invitation, finally making use of the key he had given her—wanting to surprise him—mercifully failing to do so. Fortunately, Leos had already gone, but his blonde bombshell hadn't got around to putting her clothes back on. That humiliating memory doused the wanton heat inside her as efficiently as a bucket of ice water.

"Susie…?" Leos questioned almost roughly.

Susie wrenched her shamed gaze from him. "Am I still working for you?"

"The tape's in your office, along with an address book. There's a pile of correspondence to take care of as well. I'll be out of the office until Monday…"

CHAPTER SIX

SUSIE went to work, reminding herself that Leos would only be at Devlin Systems for a further three weeks. Almost a week had gone already and he still had no idea that she had a child. Why should he find out? Who, after all, would choose to comment on the fact?

The day before, Susie had kept on endlessly replaying the latest audiotape just to listen to Leos's dark, deep, accented drawl. She had learnt that he had recently bought a house in London and that she was to organize his dinner party. The caterers were already booked but Susie had to see them to organize the finer details. Ruefully wondering why Leos's efficient Greek manservant, Stamatis, was not taking care of such domestic matters for him. Susie's increasingly confused and pained thoughts inevitably took her back nearly 18 months.

She had fallen for Leos Kiriakos like a ton of bricks and had counted no costs when he became her first lover. She had known that Leos had a fast reputation with women. Gorgeous, wealthy, dazzlingly successful and then only 29 years old, Leos had had the world at his feet. However, what hurt Susie most was acknowledging that she could not entirely blame Leos for getting tired of her....

A few weeks into their magical, romantic affair, her

mother had died suddenly. In every way possible, Leos had been supportive. However, Susie had changed into a moody misery. What male wanted to deal with such problems after a mere few weeks? Naturally, Leos had got fed up, but her dependency on him had made it difficult for him to ditch her, so he had let their relationship drift, doubtless hoping that she would get the message on her own.

Unfortunately, Susie recalled, drifting back to the present with her eyes swimming with tears as she fed Ben in the day care over her lunch hour, the first and only message she had received had been the half-naked blonde. Dumping Leos on the phone that same day had been a pitiful attempt to save face, for she hadn't mentioned her humiliating encounter with her replacement.

Late that afternoon an elegant, vivacious brunette strolled into Susie's office. "I'm Alisha James. Get hold of Leos for me and inform him that I'm free this weekend after all." A sultry smile curved her ripe mouth. "Tell him I have the most divine ideas for his bedroom!"

Susie reddened, striving to keep her friendly smile in place. "I'm afraid I only have access to a message service. I don't know where Mr. Kiriakos is, but I'll try to find out."

Alisha laughed throatily. "No need. When Leos gets the message—and don't you dare change a word of it—he'll know where to find me waiting."

As the brunette departed, Susie dialed Leos's message service, loathing him and the position he had put her in with bitter, angry pain. She passed on Alisha's provocative invitation, and then tormenting, humiliating jealousy flooded her and she said with artificial brightness to punish herself, "have a great weekend!"

CHAPTER SEVEN

Susie had spent the weekend in torment at the idea of what Leos might be doing with Alisha James.

Ashamed at the emotional turmoil that had destroyed her ability to sleep a single night through and utterly exhausted, Susie arrived at work. She was so angry with herself. Plenty of women had their hearts broken and got on with their lives. Leos was giving her a terrific career opportunity. That was all she should be concentrating on.

Entering her office, she was dismayed to find Leos waiting for her. Sheathed in a superb charcoal grey suit, lean strong face firm, he settled his dark eyes on her.

She stilled. "Is something wrong?"

"Thee mou…it is well for you that I have had two days to cool down." Hard mouth compressed, jawline squared, Leos surveyed her in angry challenge. "How dare you leave such a message for me? That nonsense from Alisha crowned by your snide comment!"

While now appreciating that Leos did not like provocative messages made through third parties, Susie could not comprehend how wishing him a great weekend could have acquired the label of "snide."

"I don't understand."

"No…?" Derision glittered in his level gaze. "Do you

honestly believe that I can't recognise jealousy when I see and hear it?"

Susie reddened fiercely. She was too honest to lie and too mortified to continue meeting his scrutiny. He had to think that either she was neurotically possessive or still madly keen on him.

Perhaps, had he not hurt her so badly, or had she not given birth to his baby, she would have managed to wholly detach herself from their shared past. However, with Ben around, their affair was still very much a major event in her memory, even it is wasn't in his.

Without warning, Leos abandoned his confrontational stance. He reached down for her hand, thoroughly disconcerting her with that sudden switch in mood. "Susie…I didn't intend to say that. I'm sorry."

Susie stared down at the strong brown hand cradling hers, drawn by the warmth and solidarity of him but sent reeling by memories that tormented her. "That's okay."

"Let's have lunch together and clear the air," he suggested.

Lunch? Wildly conscious of the proximity of his lean, powerful physique, Susie trembled, torn by resentment and longing. If only it were that simple, she thought painfully. If only they could act like sane, civilized people. Evidently he was capable of that feat but, sadly, she was not.

"There is no reason for us to be enemies," Leos continued.

Really? For an insane instant, she wanted to scream back at him in denial. He had gone to bed with another woman while she still believed he was hers. She might have understood but she had not forgiven.

"I'm sorry…" Susie eased free and backed away, exhaustion weighing her down. "I'll be more comfortable if we stick to a working relationship."

Shimmering, dark eyes held hers. The silence seethed. Leos inclined his dark head and strode out of her office.…

CHAPTER EIGHT

SUSIE stretched out a sleepy hand and felt something furry and unfamiliar. Extending her fingers she touched cool...leather? Her eyes opened on a startling view of Leos's office.

Leos strolled into the picture, all fluid grace and cool.

Susie sat up on the leather sofa, hampered by the fake fur rug still wrapped round her. "What on earth—?"

Leos shrugged "I found you asleep at your desk before lunch. I tried to wake you but you were well away—"

"You should have shaken me awake!" Bright hair tumbling loose round her shoulders, Susie fought free of the rug and stood up to look for her shoes. "For goodness sake, why did you bring me in here?"

Leos frowned, "Where else could you sleep in comfort?"

"But you must've carried me in..." Susie protested. "Who knows about this?"

"Nobody. I sneaked you in." His charismatic smile tilted her heart on its axis and left her breathless. "Susie...you looked worn out this morning."

"Nevertheless…" Attempting to disconnect from the magnetic charge of his tawny gaze, Susie combed her hair awkwardly with her fingers. "I feel such a mess—"

"I like your hair down…as you used to wear it." Leos moved closer. "It's pretty, natural. I can see all the colors."

Susie could feel his approach pulse through her every skin-cell. Her mouth was dry, her heart thumping. The atmosphere sizzled with sexual awareness. She quivered but her feet stayed put. Caught unprepared, brain still foggy with sleep, her barriers were down and she could not resist the dark force of his attraction, or her own craving for physical contact.

Leos settled his hands on her taut shoulders. "I'm not into sexually harassing employees. So you choose whether or not to walk away—"

Susie gulped. "I—"

"But if you don't walk away now, there's no going back," Leos warned huskily.

Meeting those brilliant eyes, she told herself it was a dream—a dream from which she did not intend to awaken. He moved one hand to her spine and eased her closer. You're not dreaming, you're wide awake, Susie, her conscience shrieked against her will. But she heard herself mumble, "Just one kiss…"

Leos folded her into his arms and knotted his fingers into her bright hair, satisfaction blazing in his smouldering gaze as he scanned her face. "You are bargaining with me…or yourself?"

He didn't wait for her reply and while she was still trying to fight herself, he brought his expert mouth down on hers. By that stage, weak with anticipation, she felt like a powder keg craving a flame. And whoosh…Leos did not disappoint.

She burned with excitement and joy, wanting, needing to touch him, close her straining fingers into the thick silk of his hair, shape his arrogant dark head, settle her palms to his proud cheekbones, hold him tight. Hold him fast, never, ever let him go again…

Leos lifted his head. "It's almost six. We'll have dinner…talk—"

"Almost six?" Susie exclaimed, tearing herself free and racing for the door. The day care shut at half-past five and she was late picking up Ben!

CHAPTER NINE

SAFELY HOME AGAIN, Susie had just settled Ben for the night when the apartment doorbell sounded.

Peering through the peephole, she saw Leos and panic gripped her. Too late she appreciated that running out on Leos without explanation had been even more stupid than kissing him again. Reminding herself that Ben rarely stirred after he went to sleep, she opened the door.

"Why did you rush off like that?" Leos demanded, strong, dark features taut.

Face burning, conflicting emotions tearing at her, Susie went into the sitting room ahead of him. "Regret…embarrassment—"

"No need for either…" A lean hand closed to her shoulder and turned her back to face him. His eyes sought hers. "I want you back, Susie."

Shock held her still.

With a slumberous sigh, Leos lifted a hand and gently ran a forefinger along the line of her full lower lip. "Why so surprised? You should know I don't play games. What you see is what you get—"

"Is it really?" The question erupted from Susie and she whirled away from him, physical senses singing from his touch but her mind a stormy sea of bewilderment. "Does Alisha James know you're here?"

Leos released a rueful groan. "Where I go or what I do has nothing to do with my decorator—"

"Your…what?"

"Alisha's firm is decorating my house."

Though the brunette evidently aspired to a more intimate connection with Leos then she had yet achieved, Susie was embarrassed at having made yet another false assumption.

"Wrong…again." His lustrous eyes now bright with amusement, Leos studied Susie's expression. "But who cares? I don't. Right now, the only woman I want in my life is you—"

A jarring laugh escaped Susie. "You told me that once before—"

"I don't understand your bitterness. You ditched me." Humor set aside, lean powerful face intent, Leos frowned. "Were you crying wolf when you did that? Was I supposed to run after you and try to change your mind?"

"No—"

"It was a bad time for you because you'd lost your mother. But you slammed the door on what we had as if it meant nothing to you. I need you to explain why you did that."

Susie's eyes widened at his demand. Leos sounded so sincere. Possibly he was not aware that she had found that blonde in his apartment. But he was a clever guy; he had to have suspected that she had discovered his infidelity.

"Why are you doing this to me?" Susie lifted up her chin. "Why are you acting innocent? Did you think I wouldn't find out?"

"Find…out…what?" Leos trailed out with exaggerated frustration.

"You were two-timing me…and you know you were!"

His fabulous bone structure clenched hard. "That's a downright lie—"

"Oh, come on…I used that key you gave me for your apartment. A six-foot-tall blonde dressed in only her underwear walked out of your bedroom!"

Susie recognized the exact moment Leos made the connection. He paled with anger beneath his bronzed skin. He breathed something raw in Greek and swinging on his heel, he strode back out of the hall. "If I stay here I'll say much that I will live to regret!"

CHAPTER TEN

Leos phoned Susie at nine-thirty the next morning.

"I won't be in until later. But I've just remembered that I didn't ask you to keep Wednesday evening free—"

"Why?"

"The dinner party. You'll be acting as my hostess," Leos informed her dryly. "Choice doesn't come into it either, Susie. I want you there."

"But I would prefer—"

"In your current capacity, it's a reasonable request. If you want a working relationship, start treating me like your employer."

At that pointed reminder, Susie's cheeks flamed. She was seriously tempted to put her head down and cry. Last night, she had finally faced up to her emotional turmoil. Being around Leos was tearing her apart because she was still in love with him. Learning that Leos wanted her back was almost more than she could handle.

A second chance, an insane little voice had whispered in the back of her mind, shaming and infuriating her—for what could be more impossible in the current circumstances?

Leos Kiriakos had not the faintest idea that she had given birth to his child! They had parted before she realized that she was pregnant. Even worse, that development could be laid almost exclusively at her own door. She had been grieving for her mother and had twice forgotten to take her contraceptive pills. Leos had then swept her off to Paris in the rather touching last-chance belief that a romantic weekend might magically dry her tears and cheer her up. Well, she hadn't cheered up but she had spent the night in his arms. Ben had been conceived in Paris.

Over her lunch hour, she and Ben made a mad dash out to the shops. As always, it was a struggle to steer the buggy through the crowds but Ben adored getting out and about. Back in the Devlin Systems building, Susie headed for the daycare.

By the time she saw Leos standing by the elevators, it was too late to do anything but just attempt to walk on by with a jerky nod of acknowledgement. Ebony brows pleating at the sight of her pushing a buggy, Leos froze in surprise.

Every scrap of color drained from Susie's complexion. Time was moving in slow motion for her. An elevator arrived with a loud pinging noise. Leos was still staring. She saw his hesitation and then he forced her to a standstill by moving forward. "Where did you steal the baby from?"

Her heart felt like it was hammering inside her throat, making it impossible for her to breathe. "The daycare…"

"What daycare?"

"Devlin Systems has a daycare…"

"Has it really?" Leos frowned. "I wonder why I wasn't shown it when I was getting the official tour."

"It's beside the cafeteria. I imagine people thought you might not be interested," Susie whispered shakily.

"So who does the baby belong to?"

Her own lifetime seemed to stretch in the silence which followed.

Susie parted dry lips. "He's…he's mine."

Leos studied her in stunned silence. Then his tawny eyes darkened with incredulous fury. "Thanks for telling me!" Without another word, he strode into the elevator…

CHAPTER ELEVEN

BY THE TIME Susie got back up to her office, the phone was ringing.

It was Leos. "I want to see you in my office."

Stiff with strain, Susie breathed in deep. Showdown-time had arrived, she conceded heavily. And if Leos's instantaneous rage on the ground floor was anything to go by, she could only dread what was coming next. Could there have been a worse way for Leos discover that he was a father?

Leos was by the window with a glass in his hand. He swung round, bold, bronzed features grim. "Why didn't you just tell me you had a baby?"

"Leos—"

"Don't you think I had the right to know?"

"Well, it was more a matter—"

"You let me kiss you...you let me think..." Leos compressed his lips, lines of strain girding his hard mouth, and then he tossed back the remainder of the whisky in his glass.

"All right, so you're shocked—"

"What did you expect? I've been chasing you like some stupid kid and you sat back and you let me, knowing I didn't have a clue what you were keeping from me!" Outraged eyes challenged her. "How could I have worked out that you'd had a child since I last saw you? It's little more than a year since we were together—"

Susie was rigid, but her legs were starting to tremble. "I never thought of telling you…it was stupid, I believed I could keep Ben a secret—"

Leos released his breath with a stark hiss. "You had the gall to accuse me of infidelity? And all this time, do you know what I believed? I thought you dumped me because you couldn't allow yourself to be happy even with me while you were grieving—"

"What are you getting at?" Leos seemed to be circling round, rather than centering on, the main issue, which was surely Ben.

"—and all along it was because you'd met someone else! The oldest story in the book, only I refused to see it," Leos ground out.

"I'd met…someone else?" Susie stressed in bewilderment.

"The father of your baby. Where is he? Since you're living in your brother's apartment, I assume the father is long gone!"

As Susie finally understood that Leos believed that she had conceived Ben with some other man, dismay and anger filled her. "You assume—"

"Forget it…I don't want to know the sordid details!" Leos proceeded to pour himself another shot of alcohol. "In fact, I don't even know why I said I wanted to talk to you, because really, what is there left to say?"

"You've already said more than enough!" Susie shot back at him in furious pain.

Leos shot her a sardonic appraisal. "You were too scared to tell me you had had a baby. Admit it—"

"I refuse to continue this conversation!"

"You have my permission to leave."

Susie reached the door. She was shaking like a leaf.

"Thee mou…now you're trying to make me feel guilty. But your silence was inexcusable. You deceived me!"

"Just like you once deceived me! Why should I care about how you feel now?" Susie slammed out.

CHAPTER TWELVE

AT NINE the following morning, Susie looked up from her computer monitor, just as Leos came in. In a fluid movement he leaned back against the door to close it.

She had spent the previous evening telling herself that she truly loathed Leos Kiriakos. How could he simply assume that her baby was some other man's? That was the one possibility she had not foreseen. And wasn't it peculiar that Leos had shrugged off being confronted about that blonde? Was that his idea of smart footwork? Just act like the blonde had never happened? Well, her memory was sharp as nails.

So it was unfortunate that no matter how mad and bitter Leos made her, he still took her breath away every time she saw him. Standing there, ruggedly masculine even in a formal business suit, aggressive jawline clenched, stunning eyes screened, Leos exuded a slight but perceptible discomfiture that unexpectedly tugged at her heartstrings.

"If you've got something to say, say it," Susie sighed.

"I suppose a sensitive but self-serving, dishonest guy would have leapt straight on the child and said 'Wow, this is just the cutest baby I ever saw!'"

"Did you even look at Ben?"

"I didn't want to look at him…" A split second after admitting that, Leos gritted even white teeth and spread lean brown hands in frustration. "Scratch that comment—"

"Just sensitively slipped out, did it?" Susie turned back to the computer. "Not into babies, are you?"

"No comment. I'm only here to tell you to go out this morning and buy yourself an evening gown for the dinner party." As she sat there stunned by the concept of Leos paying for anything she wore, he settled a gold credit card down on her dark desk and mentioned the name of an exclusive designer outlet. "It's a legitimate business expense—"

"Is this an order?"

"Yes," Leos confirmed without hesitation. "Appearances are everything in my world. I don't want anybody talking down to you—"

"I am only the hired help, Leos—"

"For how much longer?"

Susie raised shaken eyes to his. "Is that a threat?"

"You should know me better than that." Brilliant tawny-golden eyes flared with exasperation. "Call it like it is, Susie. When I look at you, I ache and you feel the same way—"

Susie quivered with an angry response, but she didn't know whom she was most furious with: herself for her quickened breathing and shameless shivery weakness, or him for making that arrogant claim with such cool. "Did the blonde make you feel like that?"

"Never…"

"Tough…" In the charged silence, Susie tore her anguished gaze from his, shattered by that single word with which he appeared to finally admit his cruel betrayal. "You can't turn the clock back. I could never trust you."

"How good at groveling, are you?" Leos murmured silkily on his way out.

Groveling? Not for all the tea in China, not even for a fresh start with the man she still loved.

But it was time she told him the truth about Ben, Susie conceded with bitter reluctance. Eventually, Ben would ask who his father was and expect answers. How could she allow Leos to continue believing that Ben was another man's son? How had she ever imagined that she could keep quiet forever when it was not just her secret to keep...?

CHAPTER THIRTEEN

"THE WILDEST rumors are flying around about you and the boss!" Jayne's gaze rested on Susie with speculative heat and then dropped to the exclusive designer dress box parked beside the desk. "Watch your back, because the grapevine is exploding around this building!"

"Really?" Susie was appalled to recognize yet another dimension to her problems, one she couldn't believe it had taken someone else to point out. She also wished she'd had the wit to hide the dress box.

"Leos Kiriakos will be moving on, but you have to work here—"

"What kind of wild rumors?"

Jayne winced. "Well, they range from the two of you supposedly spending almost the whole of Monday afternoon in his office without coming out once…to the outer reaches of credibility—"

"And the outer reaches are?" Susie mumbled.

"Nasty…that your Ben…well, you know he's got that lovely dark coloring—"

"Say no more…" Susie dropped her head to hide her horror at the devastating accuracy of the grapevine.

"The management team thinks you're planning to spy on their every move and report back to the boss. The word is that when you're with Leos Kiriakos, the door is always closed."

It was perfectly true, and not all the norm in meetings between a junior employee and a powerful business tycoon. Suffering agonies of self-blame and already pitched to the emotional heights on the knowledge that she had to tell Leos that Ben was his son, Susie swept up the phone and hit Leos's extension number, as soon as Jayne had departed.

"Leos…I need to talk to you but I don't want to come around to your office—"

"Why?"

"I believe our behavior has caused a lot of gossip—"

"I don't take account of that sort of nonsense." Leos sounded very male and very superior. "Neither should you—"

"Look, we need to talk about Ben—"

"No…I'm not ready for that…I may never be ready for that," Leos spelled out with blunt emphasis.

"You don't understand—"

"I understand perfectly. You and your child are a package deal. I may be insensitive but I'm not stupid." Leos drawled with cutting clarity. "I'll send a car over to pick you up this evening at seven."

Click! He'd ended the conversation. Susie groaned in disbelief. Why was Leos so certain that he could get her back? Was it so obvious to him that she still cared? How dare he tell her that he was still working out whether or not he could face taking her back, now that she had a child?

Fifteen minutes later, during her lunch break, it was a shock for Susie to glance out of the daycare's kitchen from where she was collecting Ben's food, and see Leos in conversation with the daycare supervisor. A fixed smile on his lean strong face, he was scanning the busy room, his attention lingering on every baby within view. Finally he asked a question to his companion.

Susie watched the discomfited supervisor indicate Ben. Leos zeroed in on Ben and just paled, his fabulous bone structure rigid. One minute later, he strode back out again.

CHAPTER FOURTEEN

HAD LEOS worked out that Ben was his son? That was all that Susie had thought about since lunchtime. Leos had not only left the daycare, he had left the building, and he had not returned.

At seven, Susie was collected from her apartment by a limo. In the sleek midnight-blue evening gown she had selected earlier that day, she would have felt like a million dollars had her nerves not be strung as tight as piano-wires.

Leos greeted Susie in the magnificent hall of his town house. Spectacular in a well-cut dinner jacket, Leos ran appreciatively dark eyes over her and a brilliant smile slashed his wide, sensual mouth. "I want you to meet my brother and his wife before the other guests arrive."

Susie remembered once seeing a photo of his younger brother, Petros, but right at that moment, Susie would have preferred to speak to Leos alone. But, obviously, it was neither the time nor the place to make a big confession about Ben. She had been foolish to think that Leos might have guessed the truth just by looking at Ben. But she honestly didn't know how she was going to tell Leos she had had his baby.

Leos rested a hand to her taut spine. "You remember that blonde who walked out of my bedroom and shocked you last year?"

Susie froze. "Yes…but what on earth—?"

"Brigitte had just come out of a clinic here in London after a miscarriage. I moved into a hotel to give Petros and Brigitte the privacy of my apartment until they flew back to Greece." Leos explained. "I believe Petros was in the shower when you arrived—"

"Are you trying to convince me that—?"

But Susie got no further for they had reached the drawing room, where a very tall blonde was standing beside Petros Kiriakos. Leos was attempting to convince her that the half-naked angry blonde had been Brigitte, his sister-in-law. She refused to believe it…but right there in front of her was the evidence. Brigitte was the woman whom Susie had found in Leos's apartment and she looked rather embarrassed.

"This is a case of my sins coming back to haunt me, Susie." Brigitte gave her a rueful smile of apology. "I was so rude to you that day that I didn't even mention our meeting to Petros, never mind anybody else! It's no excuse, but I was very emotional at the time and you just walking in; well, I lost my temper…totally forgot that it wasn't our apartment—"

"That's fine…I understand. Really, please don't worry about it!" In severe shock at what Leos had confronted her with, Susie passed his sister-in-law a small gaily wrapped parcel with a reassuring smile. "Happy birthday, Brigitte."

Her legs felt like cottonwool sticks. The crowd of chattering guests arriving provided a welcome distraction, but Susie could not have looked at Leos had her life depended on it.

"How good at groveling, are you?" he had asked earlier. How did one grovel when the very ground had been torn from below one's feet? Susie was reeling…

CHAPTER FIFTEEN

It WAS just after midnight.

Susie saw her babysitter out. Her eyes were burning in her head but the tears refused to come. When Leos's guest had begun leaving, she had sneaked out and caught a cab home. "I'm very sorry that I misjudged you," she had said woodenly to Leos.

"Is that it? Is that all you've got to say?" Leos had demanded.

She had been far too upset to say the right things. Fourteen months ago, it had been so easy for her to believe he had betrayed her. She had just been waiting for it to happen. Being madly in love with a man who never mentioned love and never made a date more than two days ahead had just been too much for her to handle in the wake of losing her mother.

That Leos should have preferred a beautiful blonde to her sad-and-sorry self had made perfect sense. She had believed Leos was a louse, a two-timing louse. Only he wasn't. Now she was the one in the wrong, very much in the wrong.

The doorbell buzzed. She knew it was Leos. That was when her eyes finally filled with scorching tears. She loved him so much. How had everything gone so wrong?

White dress-shirt half unbuttoned to show a bronzed slice of muscular chest, his black hair ruffled and his hard jawline roughened by stubble, Leos looked like a very sexy pirate.

Susie said, "I don't know what to say to you—"

Leos dropped the package he was carrying and caught her into his arms, scanning her damp eyes with frowning censure. And then, without any warning at all, he was kissing her with explosive passion, crushing her soft mouth under his over and over again, until she was clinging to him in shivering excitement, senses singing, her heart racing, mind a total wasteland. Raising his proud dark head, Leos gave her a wolfish grin and lifted her.

But he didn't carry her in search of a bedroom. He settled her on the sofa, and reappeared with the package that he tossed on to her lap.

"What...what's this?"

"It's for Ben—"

"B-Ben?"

"I saw him in the daycare yesterday." Dark blood scoring his fabulous cheekbones, Leos shrugged. "He gave me this big smile...he looked little and helpless...I'm not going to say he's the cutest baby I ever saw. He's probably the first baby I ever really looked at."

Trembling, Susie tugged a blue velvet rabbit from the packaging and her throat convulsed once more with tears.

"I had something similar as a baby..." Leos shared.

Shame and guilt engulfed Susie, making her feel the lowest of the low. "Leos...Ben well, er...Ben is six months old."

Leos continued to survey her steadily.

"Ben is your son," Susie framed shakily. "There wasn't any other man. I fell pregnant in Paris by you."

Heart sinking, she watched comprehension grow in his eyes. Then disbelief, shock, and acceptance, followed by a look of searing condemnation.

"What you have just told me," Leos breathed harshly, "is beyond all forgiveness."

Agonized, Susie watched Leos walk out on her and listened to the slam of her front door.

CHAPTER SIXTEEN

WITHIN MINUTES of Leos's arrival that afternoon at Devlin Systems, Susie was called to his office.

Leos raked chilling dark eyes over her. "Why did you come in today? Are you insane?"

Insane? In the automatic way that most people clung to routine in times of crisis, it had not occurred to Susie to stay home. "I—I—"

"Did you think I would want to meet my son for the first time in the workplace nursery?" His darkly handsome features were lit by the hostility of his gaze. "You go downstairs and you take my son out of there. Then you climb into the car waiting and you take Ben to my home."

Distressed by his bitter antagonism, Susie nodded. It should have dawned on her that Leos would wish to meet Ben. But only when Leos had presented her with the velvet rabbit, signifying his willingness to accept a child he had believed to have been another man's, had Susie appreciated how strongly Leos might feel about his own child.

"You decided I had slept with another woman and you took your revenge by denying me the right to know my son," Leos condemned.

"We broke up long before I knew I was pregnant, " Susie protested. "Do you remember talking about that friend of yours who you said was 'trapped' by a pregnant woman on the make?"

"Don't try to justify yourself on that basis. That woman's child might have been fathered by any one of a half-dozen men! We had something very different…or at least, I thought we did—"

Susie flushed with discomfiture. "But I believed you might accuse me of being on the make because you were rich…I didn't want the same label!"

"You will tender your resignation, " Leos continued as if she hadn't spoken, determined, it seemed, to allow her no defense.

"Sacking me, too?"

"Protecting my son's foolish mother from further damaging her reputation and mine—"

"Only yesterday, you told me you took no heed of such nonsense—"

"You should have told me the minute I entered this building that you had a baby, and that the baby was mine! Then…" Leos vented a humorless laugh, "you should have told me the day you realized you had conceived. I wouldn't leave any woman struggling to raise my child alone—"

"Even if it was my fault it happened in the first place?"

"Surely I'm mature enough to accept that making love can make a baby? And that sometimes that particular creative event is out of our control?"

So she was pond slime. Tried and found guilty. From every angle he made that clear. She had misjudged him, made wrong decisions, assumed the worst, surrendered to her own pessimistic expectations.

Having been assailed by tears since the early hours, Susie's throat ached, but she still had to ask him one question. "So…if I'd come to you a year ago and admitted I was pregnant, what would you have said?"

His stunning eyes cut like golden knives into her. "I would have said it was fate…and I would have married you."

"It's easy to be perfect and self-righteous…after the event." Susie left, feeling that he had ripped her heart out.…

CHAPTER SEVENTEEN

LEOS would have married her.

No mention of love though. No doubt he would have made her feel dreadful if he had married her, Susie told herself, no doubt they would both have been miserable. He had not loved her then and now even his respect for her was gone.

"He's really bright...." Leos was watching their six-month-old son chortle and dig under the cushion to find the velvet rabbit his father had tried to conceal from him.

"Hmm..." Seated bolt upright in the drawing room of the town house, Susie studied man and baby, the black hair, golden skin, dark eyes that made them a matching duo.

Ben sat down on the rug. He'd had a nap earlier and Leos had gotten through that hour by asking constant questions about his son. What he liked, what he ate, how he slept, how big he was in comparison with other babies of his age, how clever he was in comparison with other babies of his age, how advanced in comparison with other babies of his age. For a male, who knew nothing about babies, Leos knew it all, including the fact that Ben had been born prematurely.

Why had she had never realized that Leos might be the sort of guy willing to crawl about the floor in a suit that had cost thousands of pounds and happily pretend to be a airplane, or a horse, or a car? Leos was still surveying Ben with a shell-shocked look of pride and pleasure lightening his lean, strong face. From what she could see, discovering he was a father appeared to be a positive source of joy to Leos Kiriakos.

"He's dropping off again," Leos groaned in disappointment, as Ben's lashes drooped and an enormous yawn showed off his baby teeth.

"This is his bedtime."

"Why didn't you say?" Leos reproved.

"One late night won't harm him—"

"But we should stick to his routine, now that he's out of that daycare and he has your full attention—"

"Yes, I'm sorry I worked and neglected him by doing what thousands of other women do to make a living—"

"Don't be facetious. I wasn't blaming you. I was merely pointing out that Ben will much appreciate having you all day—"

"You're planning to keep us, are you?" Susie viewed him with bleak eyes, willing the storm of angry, wounded conflict inside her to stay down, out of sight.

Leos lifted Ben from the rug with excruciatingly gentle hands and laid him down on a sofa, boxing in his sleeping son with a line of cushions. Then he hovered just in case Ben made a sudden attempt to climb over the safety-barrier and fall. "Obviously, we're getting married. I've already been making enquiries about a special license. We'll have the wedding as soon as possible."

In one sense Leos was offering Susie all her past and present secret dreams but at that moment, all that powered her was the terrible hurt he had caused. "I wouldn't marry you if you were the last man alive on earth!"

CHAPTER EIGHTEEN

"I DON'T want you doing the decent thing and marrying me...okay?" As Susie talked to Leos on the phone at nine the following morning, she was biting back sobs. "And at this hour of the day I do not want to talk about the stigma I am casting on your son by being an unmarried mother!"

"Why are you acting this way?" Leos demanded, being totally unreasonable.

Susie hung up the phone.

Leaving Ben with the neighbor, who babysat for her on the rare occasions that she went anywhere without him, Susie headed for Devlin Systems. She had to clear her desk. Hopefully, slipping in near lunchtime would attract the least attention.

Leos had been incredulous when she'd refused to marry him. Ben's needs featured in his every argument. Sadly, Susie had not heard one word that she wanted to hear. His angry inability to forgive her for the past and his refusal to see both sides of the situation would inevitably wreck any marriage. It wasn't enough for her to love him.

Susie had just finished clearing her desk when Leos appeared in the doorway. Unusually, he hovered. Nervous tension soaring, her heart skipped a beat. Tall, dark, devastatingly sexy, and stubborn as solid steel.

"You've never listened to my side of the story," Susie said.

"Meaning?"

"What it was like having my one and only affair with someone like you." Susie's gaze clashed with his intense dark golden eyes. "You were romantic and caring but you never let me feel secure with you…you were too cool for that, too clever, even too fair to hint at a commitment you weren't planning to make—"

Lean, powerful face taut, Leos frowned. "Susie—"

"By the time I met Brigitte in your apartment, I was already convinced you were getting bored with me. You gave me no reason to believe that we had a future beyond your next phone call," Susie asserted shakily. "Yet, you still believe I should have come running back with my big announcement that I was pregnant—"

"Don't you think there might have been a gulf then between what I was feeling and what I was showing you I felt?" His lean hands clenched his sides.

"No. Even my Valentine card didn't have that four letter word, love, on it, Mr. Cool." Misery was rising like a tidal wave inside Susie.

"I really do want to marry you—"

"You don't have to marry me to see Ben." Emotion threatening to overwhelm her, Susie walked into the corridor.

"Susie…" Leos breathed raggedly.

Susie kept moving, eyes swimming with tears.

"I love you…"

Faltering, Susie blinked.

"I've always loved you!" Leos proclaimed with roughened force.

Fascinated faces appeared at doorways.

Susie turned in a dizzy circle. Meeting the raw vulnerable intensity of his gaze, reading the strain in his bronzed features, she saw that he meant every word. A wild surge of happiness engulfed her. "I love you too—"

"This public enough for you?" A wolfish grin slanting his mouth at the muted burst of applause from an audience that was afraid to be too enthusiastic, Leos strode toward her and swept her into his arms. "Mr. Cool just took a hike…"

CHAPTER NINETEEN

IN THE LIMOUSINE, on the way to pick up Ben, Leos banded both arms around Susie and kept her welded to every line of his hard muscular physique. Having kissed her breathless, he was now frowning with masculine bewilderment. "I assumed you knew how I felt—"

"How? By thought-transference?"

"When we were together last year, I could have told you I loved you the first week but I decided it would be...well—"

"Cooler to keep it quiet?"

"More sensible to go with the flow for a while." His dark tawny-golden eyes scanned her with tender appreciation. "Then you lost your mother and I felt like I lost you—"

"Did you?" That admission shook Susie.

"You shut me out. I didn't know whether to push or stand back...in the end I stood back which was the wrong thing to do—"

Susie groaned. "I though you were getting fed up with me—"

"I was devastated when you dumped me...there, I finally said it! " Leos breathed heavily. "Then I waited a couple of weeks and tried to contact you again but you'd moved—"

"Tell me, why did you just assume that Ben wasn't yours?"

"Ben seemed small to me at first. I thought he was a couple of months younger than he is. I went haywire for a couple of days, I was sick with jealousy," he admitted ruefully.

Something that had been puzzling Susie since Wednesday evening prompted her to change the subject and say, "Stamatis answered the door to me the night of the dinner party. Why didn't he just arrange everything for you?"

At that reference to his manservant, Leos gave her a wicked grin. "Haven't you worked that out yet, yinkeka mou? I had to dream up a job for you!"

"Dream up?"

"Not the promotion…the social secretary angle. If you'd gone straight on to the management team, I would never have had a chance to see you alone. The minute I recovered from the shock of finding you at Devlin Systems, I decided to try and get you back—"

Susie was transfixed by what he was telling her. "But that interview you gave me…you were so impersonal—"

"If I had gotten up close and personal as I am doing now…you'd have taken fright and run!" A teasing light in his lustrous dark eyes, Leos claimed another tender kiss. "I had to convince you that I would treat you like an employee, but I'm afraid that was too much of a challenge—"

"For me too. I just couldn't think of you as my boss—"

"I loved it when you got jealous…then you told me to have a great weekend with Alisha James and I thought you were laughing at me!"

Having long since arrived at its destination, the limo was at a standstill. Emerging from another embrace, Leos and Susie registered that fact about 10 minutes later. They rushed upstairs to Ben and told him what a wonderful baby he was. Secure in his parents' love, Ben yawned and fell asleep, as his parents held hands and dreamed of their future…

CHAPTER TWENTY

FOUR DAYS LATER, the special license having been granted, Susie arrived at the church for their wedding.

Her brother, David, had managed to fly back from the Middle East in time to give her away. Brigitte had volunteered to be her matron of honour and Petros was standing in as Leos's best man. Ben sat back in his new luxury buggy and beamed at all his admirers.

Wearing a gossamer-fine dress of lace and silk, Susie walked down the aisle with shining eyes. She had not a single doubt in her mind that she was loved. The weekend had passed in a non-stop blur of arrangements and excitement. They would live in London and in Corfu, where Leos also has a house. They were spending their wedding night at Leos's London townhouse and then flying off the next day to a Caribbean villa. It was already decided that Ben's birthday would be spent in Paris, possibly with a nanny in tow. Now that Leos got the woman he loved back, he could not plan far enough ahead.

Leos watched Susie approach the altar with a smile that made her heart sing. Leos had decided that this time around everything would be different. When he had set her back from him on Friday evening with a determined air of restraint, she had been surprised but touched when he told her why.

"The next time we make love I want you to be my wife, agape mou…"

By Monday night, restraint, he had freely admitted, had become just about the toughest challenge he had ever set himself and he had indicated a willingness to be talked out of his vow. But Susie had had to rush off and meet her brother at the airport, so pressure of time had overcome that of temptation.

Leaving the church, the ceremony over, Leos kissed her with hungry fervor. "How am I going to get through the photo session and the reception at the house?"

"Like Mr. Cool…" Susie shivered with delicious excitement against him.

Leos couldn't take his dark tawny-golden eyes off her for a moment and she loved it. There were loads of photos of them looking deep into each other's eyes. At the reception, it was quite impossible to separate them. When their guests had finally gone and Ben was asleep in his cot in his new room, the bridal couple finally reached the master bedroom.

Although beautifully furnished, it had yet to be decorated. Susie was surprised.

Leos smiled. "I told Alisha you would be taking care of this room—"

"When was that? Surely not that weekend you were mad at me?"

"I was still hoping to marry you—"

Susie's heart melted.

"No way was I going to lose you a second time." Leos tugged her into rousing contact with his lithe, powerful frame. "I love you like I never thought I could love anybody."

And being loved felt like the best thing that had ever happened to her, Susie reflected dreamily, as she gave herself up to another passionate kiss.

The Unlikely Mistress

Sharon Kendrick

Caius Niger
For my poet, mentor, muse and blue-eyed boy.

CHAPTER ONE

SABRINA looked, and then looked again, her heart beating out a guilty beat while she tried to tell herself that her eyes were playing tricks on her. Because he couldn't possibly be for real.

He was standing close to the water, close enough for her to be able to see the carved symmetry of his features. Chiselled cheekbones and a proud, patrician nose. The mouth was luscious—both hard and sensual—a mouth which looked as though it had kissed a lot of women in its time.

Only the eyes stopped the face from being too beautiful—they were too icily cold for perfection. Even from this distance, they seemed to glitter with a vital kind of energy and a black, irresistible kind of danger...

Oh, Lord, thought Sabrina in despair. What am I *thinking* of? She was not the kind of woman to be transfixed by complete strangers—especially not when she was alone and vulnerable in a foreign country. And while Venice was the most beautiful place on earth—she was there on her own.

On her own. Something she was still having to come to term with. Once again, guilt stabbed at her with piercing accuracy.

But still she watched him...

By the edge of the water, Guy felt his body tense with a sense of the unexpected, aware of the unmistakable sensation of being watched. He narrowed hard slate-grey eyes as they scanned the horizon, and his gaze was suddenly arrested by the sight of the woman who drifted in the gondola towards him. Madonna, he thought suddenly. Madonna.

The pale March sun caught a sheen of bright red-gold hair, drifting like a banner around her shoulders. He could see long, slender limbs and skin so pale it looked almost translucent. She's English, he thought suddenly as their eyes clashed across the glittering water. And for one mad, reckless moment he thought about…what? Following her? Buying her a cup of coffee? His mouth hardened into a brief, cynical smile.

It was reckless to want to pick up a total stranger and he, more than most people, knew the folly of being reckless. Hadn't his whole life been spent making amends for his father's one careless act of desperation? The knock-on effect of impulsive behaviour was something to guard against. Resolutely he turned away from her distractions.

Sabrina felt something approaching pain. *Look at me*, she urged him silently, but her gondolier chose that moment to give an expert twist of his wrist to glide the craft into shore and he was lost to her eyes.

She pushed her guidebook back into her handbag and stood up, allowing the gondolier to steady her elbow, nodding her head vigorously, as if she understood every word of his murmured Italian. But she had paid him before the journey and didn't have a clue what he could be saying to her.

And then there was a shout behind her, a deep, alarming shout, and instinctively she knew that the voice belonged to the man with the dark hair. She automatically turned in response, just in time to feel a great whooshing spray of icy cold water as it splashed over her.

It jetted towards her eyes and the shock made her handbag slip from her fingers. She was aware of her gondolier shouting something furiously, and when she opened her eyes again she could see the zigzag of foam left in the wake of a small speedboat.

And the man with the dark hair.

He was standing on the shore right next to her, holding his hand out, and despite the look of icy anger on his face some instinct made her take it, losing herself immediately in the warmth of his firm grasp.

'Why the hell can't people control the machines they're supposed to be in charge of?' he said, in a voice as coolly beautiful as his face. He gave a brief, hard stare at the retreating spray of the boat, then narrowed his eyes as he looked down at the shivering woman whose fingernails were gripping painfully into the palm of his hand. Her face was so white that it looked almost translucent, and he felt a strange kick to his heart. 'You *are* English?'

Up close, he was even more devastating. Breathtakingly so. Awareness shimmered over her skin like fingertips. 'Y-y-yes, I am,' she replied, from between chattering teeth. 'How c-c-could you tell?'

He carried on holding her hand until he was certain that she was grounded. 'Because pale women with freckles and strawberry-blonde hair look quintessentially English, that's why,' he answered slowly as he allowed his eyes to drift irresistibly over her. 'And you're soaking.'

Sabrina looked down at herself, and saw that he wasn't exaggerating. She was wet right through—her T-shirt stained with dirty lagoon water, the pinpoint thrust of her nipples emphasising her plummeting body temperature as much as the chattering of her teeth.

'Not to mention freezing.' He swallowed as he followed the direction of her eyes, tempted to make a flippant joke about wet T-shirt competitions, then deciding against it. Not his scene to make remarks like that to a complete stranger.

Sabrina suddenly realised what was missing. 'Oh, my goodness—I've dropped my handbag!' she wailed.

'Where?'

'In the w-water. And it's got my purse in it!'

He went to peer over the edge of the lagoon, but the dark waters had claimed it.

'Don't!' Sabrina called, terrified that he would just disappear again, exit from her life for ever.

He turned round with a look of mystification. 'Don't what?'

'D-don't t-t-try and retrieve it!'

'You think I'm about to dive into the canal to hunt around for your handbag?' He smiled again. 'Princess, I'm not that much of a hero!' But the smile died on his lips as he saw that the edges of her mouth were turning a very pale blue. 'You know,' he observed slowly, unable to look away from the ice-blue dazzle of her eyes, 'you're really going to have to get out of those wet clothes before you catch pneumonia!'

The intimacy of his remark drove every sane response clean out of her mind. Sabrina opened her mouth, then chattered it shut again.

Guy frowned. He couldn't believe he'd said that. Crass, or what? 'Where are you staying?'

'M-m-miles away.' Naturally. Rooms this close to St Mark's Square tended to be beyond the reach of anyone other than your average millionaire.

Guy's mouth hardened as he read the unconscious appeal in her eyes. Pity she hadn't mentioned that *before* the gondola had sped away. If the driver hadn't been flirting with her quite so outrageously, then he might have been able to warn her about the speedboat in time. And the least he could have done to recompense would have been to give her a free ride back to her hotel.

Which left it up to *him*.

He had achieved what he had set out to do in Venice—had purchased a superb Italian old master for one of his more demanding clients. The price he had bartered had been better than expected and his client would be pleased.

He had planned a quiet day. Playing knight in shining armour hadn't been top of his agenda. But responsibility was etched deep into Guy's personality. He looked down into her heart-shaped face, and felt his heart kick-start again. She really was very beautiful… 'You can't possibly travel home in that state, but you can clean up at my hotel if you like—it's just around the corner.'

'Your *hotel*?' Sabrina swallowed, guiltily remembering the way she had been unable to tear her eyes away from him on the lagoon. She'd been certain that he hadn't seen her—but what if he had? And what if he'd then imagined that she was the kind of woman who allowed herself to be picked up in the most casual manner possible and taken back for a so-called siesta? 'I don't even know you—and I'm not in the habit of going back to strange men's hotel rooms!'

Guy's eyes glittered with unconcealed irritation. He was offering to do her a favour—did she really think that he was after something else? Desperate enough to make a pass at someone he didn't even know?

He supposed that he could have shrugged and said fine and walked away, but something about her defensive stance struck at his conscience. He forced his mouth into a smile. 'Then how about I introduce myself so I'm no longer a stranger?' He held his hand out. 'Guy Masters,' he said softly.

Something in the way he said it struck at Sabrina's heart like a hammer blow, as though she had been waiting all her life to hear just that name spoken aloud. She felt his hand still warming her frozen fingers, his grey eyes sending their icy light across her face, and tiptoes of some unknown emotion began to tingle their way up her spine. 'S-Sabrina Cooper,' she stumbled.

'Well, you'll be quite safe with me, Sabrina Cooper,' he assured her gravely. 'The alternative, of course, is that you travel halfway across Venice looking like that. It's up to you—I'm only offering to help. Take it or leave it.'

His grey eyes didn't stray from her face, which only seemed to reinforce where he *wasn't* looking. And he didn't really want to spell it out. That wet T-shirt did spectacularly draw the eye. Even if the sopping fabric was stretched over a pair of breasts which could in no way be described as voluptuous. On the contrary, he thought, they were small and neat and deliciously cuppable. She wouldn't be *safe* travelling back on her own, looking as beautifully sexy as she did right now.

Sabrina hesitated. Surely a man who looked like Guy Masters would have no need of ulterior motives. 'Why are you being so…?'

'Chivalrous?' he prompted, a cool fire dancing in his eyes. It amused him that she hadn't seen fit to leap at his offer. That didn't happen a lot, not these days. He shrugged. 'Because you're English, and so am I, and I have an over-developed sense of responsibility which just won't seem to go away. You're cold and wet and you've lost your purse. So what else can I do? Rip the clothes from my back in order to cover you up?'

She eyed the taut torso with alarm as her imagination gave her a disturbingly realistic picture of how he would look if he *did* remove that snowy-white T-shirt. What on earth was the matter with her? She had come to Venice in an attempt to make some sense of the tragedy which had transformed her life. And making sense of things did not involve feeling overwhelmingly attracted to men who had a dangerous air of inaccessibility about them.

'Er, no.' She swallowed. 'That won't be necessary. I'll take up your offer of the bathroom. It's very…sweet of you. Thank you.' But 'sweet' did not seem an appropriate word to use about Guy Masters—he was far too elementally masculine for that.

'Come this way,' he said, and they began to walk through the narrow, dark streets of Venice with the slicking sounds of water all around them.

Sabrina felt the weight of heavy, wet denim chafing uncomfortably against her thighs. 'I don't know how I'm going to get my clothes dry.'

'Don't worry. The hotel will think of something.' Hotels like the Palazzo Regina always did, he thought wryly. Catering for each and every whim of their pampered guests, however bizarre. In life, Guy had realised a long, long time ago, you got what you paid for. And the more you paid, the more impressed the world seemed to be.

Sabrina was aware of the curious looks being cast in their direction, and couldn't decide whether that was because she looked half-drowned or because he looked so beautiful. She felt overpoweringly aware of him as he moved with a kind of restrained power by her side, every pore seeming to exude a vital kind of energy. It was as though that magnificent body had imprinted itself indelibly on every single one of her senses and she could feel the incessant pumping of her heart and the rapid little rush of her breathing as they walked.

'How much money was in your purse?' he asked.

'Only a bit. I've left most of it in my hotel safe, along with my tickets.'

'That's something, I guess. Imagine if you'd come out with your airline tickets.'

'Imagine,' she said faintly.

Something in the way she'd said it made him smile. 'We're here,' he announced, stopping in front of a large, impressive façade overlooking the waterfront itself.

Sabrina screwed her face up in disbelief. 'Here?' He was gorgeous, yes, but in his jeans and T-shirt he had seemed just like her—just another tourist. This couldn't be right, surely? His hotel couldn't be this central—not unless he was staying in some sort of museum or palace. Which was exactly what it looked like. 'You're staying *here*?'

Guy heard the incredulity in her voice and sizzled her a glance of mocking query. 'You think I don't know the way back to my own hotel?'

Sabrina compared it to the tiny, dark *pensione* she was staying in. 'It looks more like a palace than a hotel!'

'Mmm. I believe it was.' He glanced down and saw that the walk had removed that ghastly blue tinge from her lips, and smiled. 'A very long time ago.'

'How long?'

'Fourteenth century, would you believe?'

'Good heavens,' said Sabrina lightly, and the question came out before she had time to think about it. 'How on earth can you afford to stay in a place like this?'

Years of self-preservation against women with dollar signs in their eyes made Guy reply, without missing a beat, 'I'm lucky,' he said coolly. 'The company pays for it. Come on. You've started shivering again.'

As soon as they walked into a lavishly ornate foyer, she heard the faint buzz of comment. One of the men working at the reception desk, who looked handsome enough to be a movie star, fixed Guy Masters with an unctuous smile.

'Sir? I trust you have had an enjoyable morning.'

'Eventful,' Guy murmured. 'I'll just have my key, please, Luigi.'

'Certainly, sir, I'll have someone—'

'No, please, don't bother. I'll see myself up.'

In the mirror-lined lift, Sabrina saw how wet she really was.

The water of the lagoon was obviously much dirtier than its colour suggested, because there were tiny spots of mud spattering her T-shirt. And unfortunately there were two damp circles ringing her breasts, drawing attention to the outline of her bra which was embarrassingly visible. And so, too, were her nipples, tight and hot and aching. Turned on by a man she had only just met...

Appalled by her dark and unwanted thoughts, she quickly crossed her arms and clamped them over her bust. 'That man at Reception gave me a very funny look.'

Guy felt a pulse flicker as he stared at her reflection in the mirror, noting the protective body language and working out for himself the reason for it. 'Well, you must admit you do look pretty spectacular,' he murmured. Like some glorious nymph who had just emerged from the water.

'Mmmm,' she agreed. 'Spectacularly drowned.'

He narrowed his eyes. Her voice was unusually soft. As soft as her lips. The lift pinged to a halt. 'Here's my suite.'

Suite?

Sabrina thought of her own small *pensione*, where she could never find anyone on duty. Like last night, for example, when the water coming from the tap had been nothing more than a dark, brackish trickle. With the aid of her phrasebook, she had been forced to laboriously construct a note to the *manager*, requesting that he do something about the hot water. What if she'd gone back today, dripping from head to toe in filthy lagoon water, to discover that nothing had been resolved?

Thank heavens for the chivalrous Guy Masters, she told herself—but she felt a mixture of nerves and excitement as he unlocked the door to his suite.

He pushed open the door to let her inside and Sabrina had to stifle a small cry of astonishment as she walked into a high-ceilinged sitting room. Because, yes, of course, she'd known that places such as these existed, but it was something so outside her own experience that it was like stepping into a parallel world.

The room was full of furniture which even an idiot could tell was very old. Antique, in fact. And priceless too, she imagined.

Sabrina looked around her. The light was muted because all the shutters were closed, but that made the contents of the room stand out even more.

Silken rugs in jewel-bright colours were scattered on the marble floors, on which stood spindly-legged chairs and tables. There was a faded sofa of crimson and gold and a couple of chairs which matched, all strewn with cushions of the same rich colours. She slowly turned to see an oil painting of a long-dead doge, set against the timeless Venetian backdrop, one of many paintings hung on the crimson walls.

'Oh, but it's beautiful,' she breathed. 'So beautiful.'

Guy watched her slow appraisal, her uninhibited pleasure making her look curiously elegant, despite the damp and dirty clothes.

'Isn't it?' he said softly, but he wasn't even looking at the painting.

And the lack of light was far too intimate, he decided suddenly, striding over to the window to push open the shutters, so the reflected light from the Grand Canal gleamed and glittered back into the room at them.

A view like that was worth a king's ransom, thought Sabrina, suddenly feeling as out of place as some scruffy urchin who had come seeking shelter from the storm.

It brought her quickly to her senses. She wasn't here to enjoy the view. Or to make small-talk. She had better just clean up and be on her way.

She cleared her throat. 'Could you show me—?'

He turned around, noting the sudden pinkness in her

cheeks, the two high spots of colour making her look like some flaxen-plaited doll. 'Sure. The bathroom's that door over there.' He pointed. 'Take as long as you like. Oh, and throw your wet clothes out and I'll send them down and have them laundered.'

'Thank you.'

Sabrina was glad to lock the bathroom door behind her and peel off the freezing clothes from her shivering flesh. They smelt so *dank*!

The jeans were first, and then the T-shirt, and she dropped the sodden garments onto the marble floor. But her bra and panties were damp with canal water, too. Should she risk...?

Risk what? she asked herself impatiently. She couldn't keep sodden underwear on, and this pair of sensible cotton briefs was hardly likely to have him trying to beat the door down!

Sheltering behind the screen of the door, she picked the bundle up.

'Guy?'

'Leave them outside,' came a muffled sort of voice, and she did as he asked, quickly slamming the door shut and sliding the lock home before stepping into the shower, with its industrial-sized head.

Outside, Guy gingerly picked up the deposited items as if he were handling a poisonous snake.

Had it really been necessary for her to take *everything* off? he wondered uncomfortably, while asking himself why some women chose to wear knickers which looked as if they were armour-plated.

He knew almost nothing about Sabrina Cooper, and would never see her again after today, but what he *did* know was that she certainly hadn't come to Venice with seduction in mind.

Not unless she was intending to appeal to the type of man who got turned on by the frumpy gym-mistress look!

Biting back a smile, he wandered over to the telephone and picked up the receiver.

'*Pronto!*' he drawled for courtesy's sake, and then immediately switched to English, in which most of the staff were fluent. His Italian was passable—but in a case concerning a strange woman's underwear he needed no misunderstandings! 'How long will it take to get some clothes laundered?'

There was a short pause. 'Certainly within a couple of hours, sir.'

Guy frowned. That long? And just what were they supposed to do while Sabrina's jeans and T-shirt and bra and panties whizzed around in the washing machine? His time was precious, and his leisure time especially so. There were a million things he would rather be doing than being forced to sit and chat to someone with whom he had nothing in common other than that they both hailed from the same country.

Damn!

'Let's try for half that time, shall we?' he suggested softly. 'And can you have some coffee brought up at the same time?'

Bearing a tray of coffee, the valet came and collected the damp garments and Guy heard the sound of the shower being turned off. He walked over to the bathroom door.

'I'm afraid your clothes won't be back for an hour,' he called.

'An *hour*?' Sabrina's heart plummeted as she stood behind the locked door. What was she supposed to do in the meantime? Stay wrapped in a towel inside this steamy bathroom?

He heard the annoyance in her voice and felt like telling her that the idea pleased him even less than it did her. But he hadn't been forced to bring her back here, had he? No, he'd made that decision all on his own—so he could hardly complain about it now.

'Why don't you use that towelling robe hanging up on the back of the door?' he suggested evenly. 'And there's some coffee out here when you're ready.'

Squinting at herself in the cloudy mirror, Sabrina shrugged on a towelling gown which was as luxuriously thick and fluffy as she would expect in a place like this. She slipped it over her bare, freckled shoulders, and as she did so she became aware of the faint trace of male scent which clung to it.

Guy had been wearing this robe before her, she realised as an unwelcome burst of sexual hunger grew into life inside her. Guy's body had been as naked beneath this as her own now was. She felt the sudden picking up of her heart as the evocative muskiness invaded her nostrils, and she wondered if she might be going slightly mad.

How could a complete stranger—however attractive he undoubtedly was—manage to have such an incapacitating and powerful effect on her? Making her feel like some puppet jerked and manipulated by invisible strings. Was this what the death of her fiancé had turned her into—some kind of predator?

Guy glanced up as she walked in and his grey eyes narrowed, a pulse hammering at his temple. Maybe the robe hadn't been such a good idea after all, he conceded. Because wasn't there something awfully erotic about a woman wearing an oversized masculine garment like that? On him it reached to just below his knees—but on this woman's pale and slender frame it almost skimmed her ankles.

'How about some coffee?' he queried steadily.

'C-coffee would be lovely,' she stumbled, suddenly feeling acutely shy. She perched on the edge of a sofa on the opposite side of the room, telling herself that she had absolutely nothing to worry about. The circumstances might be bizarre, but for some reason she trusted this man. Men of Guy Masters's calibre wouldn't make a clumsy pass at a stranger, despite that brief, hungry darkening of his eyes.

He poured them both coffee and thought that conversation might be safer than silence. 'First time in Venice?'

'First time abroad,' she admitted.

'You're kidding!'

She shook her head. 'No, I'm not. I've never been out of England before.' Michael hadn't earned very much, and neither had she—and saving up to buy a house had seemed more important than trips abroad. Though a man like Guy Masters would probably not understand that.

'And you came here on your own?'

'That's right.'

He looked at her curiously. 'Pretty daring thing to do,' he observed, 'first time in a foreign country on your own?'

Sabrina stared down at the fingers which were laced around her coffee-cup. 'I've never done anything remotely daring before…'

'What, never?' he teased softly.

Sabrina didn't smile back. Hadn't she decided that life was too short to play safe all the time? 'So I thought I'd give it a try,' she said solemnly, and shifted her bottom back a little further on the seat.

Guy sipped his coffee and wished that she would sit still, not keep shifting around on the sofa as if she had ants in her pants. And then he remembered.

She wasn't wearing any.

Dear God. A shaft of desire shot through him, which was as unexpected as it was inappropriate, and he took a huge mouthful of coffee—almost glad when it scalded his lips. He risked a surreptitious glance at his watch. Only forty-five minutes to go. Less if he was lucky. Much more of this and he would be unable to move.

'So why Venice?' he queried, a slight edge of desperation to his voice.

'Oh, it's one of the world's most beautiful cities, and I— I had to…to…'

Something in the quality of her hesitation made him stir with interest. 'Had to what?'

She had been about to say 'get away', but that particular statement always provoked the questions to ask why, and once that question had been asked then the whole sad story would come out. A story she was weary of telling. Weary of living through. She had come to Italy to escape from death and its clutches.

'I had to see St Mark's Square.' She smiled brightly. 'It was something of a life's ambition. So was riding in a gondola.'

'But not taking a bath in the Grand Canal?'

She actually laughed. 'No. Not that. I hadn't bargained on that!'

He thought how the laugh lit up her face. Like sunshine glowing from within. 'And how long are you staying?'

'Only a couple more days. How about you?'

He felt a pulse begin to beat insistently at his temple. Suddenly Venice was getting more attractive by the minute—rather uncomfortably attractive, actually. 'Me, too,' he said huskily, and risked another glance at his watch.

The room seemed much too small. Much too intimate. Again Sabrina shifted self-consciously on the sofa.

'How old are you?' he demanded suddenly, as she crossed one pale, slender thigh over the other.

Old enough to recognise that maybe Guy Masters wasn't completely indifferent to her after all. The quiet, metallic gleam in the cool grey eyes told her that. But that wasn't the kind of answer he was seeking.

'I'm twenty-seven,' she told him.

'You look younger.'

'So people say.' She lifted her eyebrows. 'And you?'

'Thirty-two.'

'You look older.'

Their eyes connected as something primitive shuddered in the air around them.

'I know I do,' he murmured.

His words caressed her and Sabrina stared at him, unable to stop her eyes from committing every exquisite feature to memory. I will never forget you, she thought with an aching sense of sadness. Ever.

They sat in silence for a while as they drank their coffee. Eventually, there was a rap on the door and the valet delivered an exquisitely laundered set of underwear, jeans and T-shirt. Guy handed them over to her. 'There you go,' he said gravely.

She took them, blushingly aware that his fingertips had actually been touching the pressed cotton of her bra and panties. 'I'd better go and get changed.'

And if he'd thought that she'd looked exquisite before, that was nothing to the transformation which had taken place when she emerged, shimmering, from the bathroom. Guy didn't know what the laundry had managed to do with her clothes, but they now looked as if they were brand-new, and her hair had dried to a glorious strawberry-blonde sheen which spilled over her shoulders.

'You'd better take this,' he said as he dug deep into the pocket of his trousers and withdrew a wad of money, seeing her eyes widen in an alarmed question as he gave it to her.

'What's this?' she demanded.

'Didn't you drop your purse into the water?' he queried softly. 'And don't you need to get home?'

'I can't take your money,' she protested.

'Then don't. Think of it as a loan. Pay me back tomorrow if you like.'

Sabrina slid the notes thoughtfully into the back pocket of her jeans. 'OK. I will. Thanks.'

He went down with her in the lift to the foyer, telling himself that he would never see her again.

And wondering why that thought should make him ache so much, and so badly.

CHAPTER TWO

DESPITE telling herself that she was being crazy and un-
realistic, Sabrina couldn't help the decided spring to her step
next morning as she set off to return Guy's money, nor the
flush of anticipation which made her cheeks glow. And why
had she dressed up for him in an ice-blue sundress which very
nearly matched her eyes and peep-toed sandals which made
her legs look longer than they really were?

Surely she didn't imagine for a moment that he would take
one look at her and decide that she was the woman of his
dreams?

She put the stack of lire in an envelope. He probably
wouldn't even be there, she reasoned. She would just have
to leave the money for him at Reception.

The buildings soared up all around her and the water—
which was everywhere—seemed to glimmer and glitter with
some unspoken promise. As her steps drew her closer to
Guy's hotel, she felt the slow prickle of nerves.

She told herself that even if he was there he would probably just take the money with that cool, enigmatic smile and
thank her. Then say goodbye, his faintly quizzical expression
mocking her if she was foolish enough to linger hopefully
over their farewells.

Drawing a deep breath, she walked into the foyer, surprised that the man behind the desk with the movie-star looks should raise his eyebrows in recognition the moment he saw her. He quickly picked up the telephone and started speaking into it.

By the time she had reached the desk he had finished his call and was glancing down at a notepad in front of him. He smiled at her.

'Ah, Signorina Cooper,' he purred.

She raised her eyebrows. 'You know my name?'

The smile widened. 'But of course! Signor Masters asked me to telephone him the moment you arrived.'

Well, that was something. At least he hadn't imagined that she'd just disappeared into the sunset with his money.

She quickly took the envelope from her handbag. 'Can I just leave this here for him?' she said breathlessly. 'I won't stay. I'm—'

'Not planning on running away from me, are you, Miss Cooper?' came a deep voice from just behind her, and Sabrina turned round to find herself caught in the hard, grey crossfire of his eyes. And she was lost. Utterly lost.

'Hello, Guy,' she said weakly.

'Hello, Sabrina,' he mocked, his gaze running over her with pleasure, thinking that she had dressed up for him, and the rapid beat of his heart told him exactly what *that* meant.

'I brought your money back.' She held the envelope out.

'So I see.'

'I can't thank you enough for coming to my rescue. I don't know how I would have managed otherwise.' She swallowed down the constricting lump which was affecting her ability to breathe. 'Anyway, I'd better go—'

But he cut her words short with the restraining touch of his fingertips on her bare arm—a feather-light and innocent enough touch, but one which made sensation skate erotic little whispers all over its surface. He felt suddenly breathless. *Reckless.*

His eyes darkened. 'Why go anywhere?' he questioned softly. It's a beautiful day. We're both on our own. Why don't we go sightseeing together?'

'Together?'

He paused for a dangerous beat, giving her the unthinkable opportunity of saying no. 'Unless you'd rather be on your own?'

Well, that was why she had come to Venice, wasn't it? To get away and escape. To throw off the shackles of anxious eyes which followed her every move.

But Sabrina didn't want to get away. Not from Guy. She tried to keep her voice casual. 'Not especially.'

Guy almost laughed aloud at her lukewarm response. He wondered if she did this all the time—sent out these conflicting messages so that while that flushed look of anticipation and the bright sparkle of her eyes were like a sweet invitation to possess her, the somewhat indifferent responses to his questions were a slammed door in the face. Perplexing. And he hadn't been perplexed by a woman in a long time.

'So is that a yes or a no?'

It was an I'm-not-sure-whether-I'm-doing-the-right-thing, Sabrina thought, but she smiled anyway. 'It's a yes,' she said.

He watched the way she flicked her hair back over her shoulder. The movement made her breasts dance beneath the thin cotton dress, and Guy felt the primitive urge to take her somewhere and impale her and make her his. He hardened his mouth, appalled at himself.

'Why don't you tell me what you've seen already?' he suggested unevenly. 'And where you'd like to eat lunch?'

Sabrina noticed the sudden tension around his mouth, the way his eyes had darkened into a hungry glitter, and while she knew that she ought to be intimidated by the sheer potency of his masculinity she had never felt less intimidated in her life.

'I've seen the Basilica di San Marco,' she said. 'Of course! And the Golden House and the Doges Palace. But that's all. Lunch—I wouldn't have a clue about.' Her budget was tight and she'd been skipping lunch. But that had been no hardship.

Guy noticed the shadowed hollows beneath the high sweep of her cheekbones and wondered if she had been eating properly. 'Then let's go and find the rest of Venice,' he suggested softly.

But it took an effort for Sabrina to concentrate on her surroundings as they walked out into the sunshine. Yesterday the city had seemed like the most magical place on the planet, while today it was difficult to think about anything other than the man at her side.

At least she had some idea of what she was supposed to be looking at. She'd spent the preceding weeks reading every book about Venice that she could lay her hands on—it had been a good kind of displacement therapy—but Guy could more than match her.

'Did you know that the humorist Robert Benchley sent a telegram when he arrived in Venice?' Guy murmured. 'Saying, "Streets full of water. Please advise."'

Sabrina thought that his grey eyes looked soft, soft as the cream silk shirt he wore. 'No, I didn't know that. But Truman Capote said that Venice was like eating an entire box of chocolate liqueurs in one go.'

'Oh, did he?' He liked the quickness of her mind, the way her thoughts matched his own. Liked the fact that she'd researched the place so thoroughly. He felt his heart begin to pick up its beat as he stared down at her, at the strawberry-blonde hair which gleamed like bright gold in the midday sun and the slim, pale column of her neck. There was a fragility about her which was rare in a modern woman, he thought, and wondered what it would be like to take her in his arms. Take her to his bed. Whether she would bend or break…

He realised that they had spent the best part of two hours together and she hadn't asked him a single question about his life back in England. And he noticed that she'd been quietly evasive on the subject of her own life.

But why not? he thought with a sudden sense of liberation. Wasn't anonymity a kind of freedom in itself? Didn't he live the kind of life where people judged him before they had even met him, depending on what they'd heard about him?

The bell of San Marco rang out twice, and Guy looked at his watch. 'We'd better try and find a table for lunch while there's still time.'

Sabrina stared up into dark grey eyes and felt her skin prickle in heated reaction. 'I'm not hungry.'

'Is that why you're so thin?' he demanded. 'Because you skip lunch?'

'Thanks very much!'

'Oh, I'm not complaining,' he murmured, as his eyes drifted over her. 'Your cheekbones are quite exquisitely pronounced and your legs are just the right side of slender. I suppose you have to work at it, the same as every other woman.'

Sabrina let her gaze fall from his face, staring instead at the pink-tipped toes which peeped through her strappy sandals, remembering how she'd forced herself to paint them, telling herself that out of such small, unimportant rituals some kind of normal life would be resumed.

'Sabrina,' he said softly. 'What's the matter? It was supposed to be a compliment. Have I insulted you? Embarrassed you?'

She looked up again. Now would be the perfect time to tell him that the weight had simply fallen away after Michael's death. But tell him that and she would be back playing the unwanted role of the bereaved fiancée. Was it selfish of her to want to play a different part? To want to feel the sun warm and alive on her cheeks and see the unmistakable glint of appreciation in the eyes of the man who stood looking down at her? To feel *alive* again, instead of half-dead herself?

She shook herself out of her reverie and forced a smile which, to her suprise, felt as if it wanted to stay on her mouth. 'By telling me I'm thin? Come on, Guy—did you ever hear of a woman who was offended by that?'

Her smile was like the sun nudging out from behind a cloud, he thought. 'I guess not.' Come to think of it, he didn't have much appetite himself, and certainly not for conventional fare.

Instead, he found himself wondering how her lips would taste and what the scent of her breath would be like against his. He shook his head to dispel the sensual imagery. 'Why don't we have coffee and a pastry at one of these cafés in the square?' he suggested steadily. 'It's warm enough to sit outside in the sunshine.'

They found a vacant table and ordered pastries with their coffee, the lightest and most beautiful cakes imaginable, and Guy thought that they tasted like sawdust in his mouth. And saw that Sabrina had taken exactly two mouthfuls herself.

'It must be the heat.' She shrugged in response to the mocking question in his eyes.

'So it must.' He echoed the lie, knowing that their lack of hunger had nothing to do with the temperature.

He marched her through the city like a professional tour guide, as if determined that he should show her everything. Sabrina wondered what had provoked this sudden, relentless pace, but she was too bewitched by him to care.

They stood side by side on the Bridge of Sighs and stared into the dark waters beneath.

'Look down there,' said Sabrina suddenly. 'And think of the thousands of tourists who have stood here like this and been affected by this amazing city.'

His heart missed a beat as enchantment washed over him. 'You mean the way it's affecting us now?'

'Yes.' She told herself it wasn't *that* remarkable for him to have echoed her thoughts, but still her voice trembled. 'That's exactly what I mean.'

He wanted her, he thought. And she wanted him. 'Are you going to have dinner with me tonight, Sabrina?' he asked suddenly.

She didn't even stop to think about it, or bother to wonder whether she'd made it too easy for him. 'You know I am.'

He nodded, the thrill of anticipation making his heart pick up speed. 'Tell me where you're staying and I'll pick you up at eight.'

'You don't have to do that.'

Her reluctance sharpened an appetite already keenly honed. 'Oh, but I insist,' he contradicted softly.

But pride made her match his determination. He must be some kind of hot-shot to be staying at that hotel. She didn't want him seeing her humble little *pensione*, emphasising how great the differences between them. Just now they were as close to equal as they would ever be and she wanted to hold onto that. 'I'll meet you in the square. Honestly, Guy, I'm an independent woman, you know!'

'Well, sometimes a man doesn't want an independent woman,' he ground out. He couldn't believe he'd just said that, but he had. Or that he'd caught her by the arm to feel the soft tremble of flesh where his fingers burnt so delectably against her bare skin. 'Are you always this damned stubborn?'

Something in the heated frustration of his question made Sabrina's blood sing with a glorious inevitability, and she had the sense of being led towards something which defied all logic. It was liberation at its most intense and powerful, and she was no longer heartbroken, bereaved Sabrina. For one enchanted moment she stood poised on the brink of something magical.

She smiled. 'Only if I need to be.'

There was a long and dangerous pause. 'But I'm used to getting my own way,' he told her steadily.

'I know you are. It shows.'

She looked down at his tanned fingers which still lay against her white skin, and he let his hand fall, perplexed by his own actions. He was a man whose reputation hinged on being in control—so why was he acting as if he were auditioning for the leading role in a Western movie?

'Was I being unbearably high-handed?' he asked her, missing the satin feel of her skin beneath his fingertips.

She took one last look at him as she stepped into the water-taxi which had slid to a halt beside them. Not unbearably anything, she thought. You wouldn't know how to be. 'Only a little.' She shrugged. 'I'll see you tonight at eight.'

And Guy was left staring at the back of her bright blonde head, his heart thundering with a mixture of admiration and frustration.

CHAPTER THREE

SABRINA was twenty minutes late. Guy had never had a woman keep him waiting in his life and he couldn't decide whether to be irritated or intrigued. He glanced down at his watch for the umpteenth time and actually began to wonder whether he'd been stood up.

But then he saw her crossing the square, wearing some slinky little silver-grey dress with a filmy silver stole around her pale shoulders, her legs looking deliciously long in spindly, high-heeled shoes.

Sabrina spotted his tall, brooding figure straight away, as if he had been programmed to dominate her whole horizon. He was wearing a pale grey unstructured suit which did nothing to disguise the hard, muscular body beneath. And, outwardly at least, he looked completely relaxed, but as she grew closer she could see a coiled kind of tension, which gave him the dark, irresistible shimmer of danger. He looked completely relaxed, but there was no mistaking the watchful quality which made his grey eyes gleam with subdued promise.

She had very nearly not come tonight, lifting the telephone to ring Guy's hotel more than once, telling herself that this was fast turning into something she hadn't planned. Something she wasn't sure if she could handle.

Or stop.

But something had prevented her cancelling—something she couldn't quite put her finger on. Maybe it was the memory of that first, glorious sight of him. Leaving behind the knowledge that if she were never to see him again, then the world would never seem quite the same place.

His smile widened as she approached, but he made no move towards her. Let her come to me, he thought. He wanted to watch the way she moved—her hips unconsciously thrusting forward, the fluid sway of her bottom. He imagined those hips crushed beneath the hard contours of his own, and swallowed. *Come to me, baby*, he thought silently. *Come.*

'Hello,' Sabrina said breathlessly, but something in the darkening of his eyes seemed to have robbed her of the ability to suck air into her lungs.

'Hello.' So. No blurted little excuses for being late. No shrugged or coy reasons. Her carelessness sharpened his desire for her even more intensely and he felt his senses clamour into life. 'Where would you like to eat?'

There was a new, dangerous quality about Guy tonight, Sabrina thought. A danger which should have frightened her, but instead filled her with a sense of almost unendurable excitement. And inevitability. 'You know the city far better than I do,' she said huskily. 'You choose.'

'OK,' he said easily, and for a moment felt the penitent shimmer of guilt. As if he hadn't just spent an hour under the hammering power of the shower, deciding exactly where he wanted to take her. He had opened his mouth to the torrent of water which had beaten down on him, his body growing hard with frustration as he remembered that Sabrina had stood naked beneath these same icy jets.

Except that he doubted whether *she* had needed an icecold shower to ward off a desire which was stronger than any desire he could remember.

The restaurant was close by and its menu was famous. It

was private and discreet but not in the least bit stuffy; he wondered whether she would comment on its proximity to his hotel, but she didn't.

And it wasn't until they were seated in the darkened alcove he had expressly requested that he relaxed enough to expel a long, relieved breath. She was here, he thought exultantly. Sabrina was *here*. Her hair was all caught back in a smooth pleat at the back of her head and he wanted to reach out and tumble it all the way down her back.

'You look beautiful,' he said slowly.

The way he was looking at her made her feel beautiful. She savoured the compliment, held onto it and tried it out in her mind. 'Why, thank you,' she said demurely.

'I thought you weren't coming.' He couldn't believe he'd just said that either. Hadn't the hard lessons of his childhood meant that he'd spent his whole life striving for some kind of invulnerability?

'I nearly didn't.' Oh, God, she thought, please don't ask me why. Because I might just have to tell you that I knew, if I came, where I might end up spending the night.

'What changed your mind?'

'I was hungry.'

He laughed as the waiter came over with the menus, and Sabrina took hers with hands which had begun to tremble. She wondered whether Guy had noticed.

He had. But he hadn't needed to see her fingers shaking to know that she was working herself up to a fever pitch of sexual excitement which almost matched his own. That was evident enough from the soft line of colour which suffused the high curve of her cheekbones and the hectic glitter of her eyes. The way her lips looked all swollen and pouting, parting moistly of their own volition, the rosy pink tip of her tongue peeping through. And the way the buds of her tiny breasts pushed like metal studs against the silvery silk of her gown.

His grey eyes glittered into hers as she stared unseeingly at the menu. 'Want me to order for you?'

Strange she should be so grateful for a question which would normally have left her open-mouthed with indignation. 'Yes, please.'

His eyes scanned the menu uninterestedly. About the only things he felt like eating right now were oysters, followed by a great big dish of dark, juicy cherries—and it didn't take a great stretch of the imagination to work out why that was.

Guy shifted his chair a little, relieved that the heavy white damask of the tablecloth concealed the first heavy throbbing of desire. Another first, he thought wryly, unable to remember a time when he'd been so exquisitely aroused by a woman without any touch being involved.

He ordered *Brodetto di pesce* followed by *moleche*. Dessert he would take an option on. He had his own ideas for dessert...

The waiter brought over a bottle of the bone-dry Breganze *bianco*, but Sabrina felt intoxicated just by the lazy promise of his smile.

'I don't know if I need any wine,' she admitted.

'Me neither.' He shrugged, but he poured them half a glass each and signalled for some water.

Sabrina sipped at her drink, feeling suddenly shy, not daring to look up, afraid of what she would see in the grey dazzle of his eyes. Or what he might read in hers...

'You know, we've spent nearly the whole day together—and I don't know a single thing about you,' he observed softly. 'I'm not used to women being quite so mysterious.'

Sabrina put her glass down. Here it came. The getting-to-know-you talk. A talk she most emphatically did not want to have. She'd been touched by a tragedy which had left her tainted, simply by association. People treated you differently once they found out and she didn't want Guy to treat her differently. She wanted him to carry on exactly as he was.

She forced a lightness into her voice. 'What exactly do you want to know?'

Guy narrowed his eyes. Women usually loved talking about themselves. Give them an opener like that and you couldn't shut them up for hours. 'It isn't supposed to be an interrogation session,' he informed her softly, and then he leaned across the table, dark mischief dancing in his eyes. 'Why? Have you got some dark, guilty secret you're keeping from me, Sabrina? Don't tell me—in real life you're a lap-dancer?'

His outrageous question lifted some of the tension, and Sabrina found herself smiling back. 'Much more exciting than that! I work in a bookshop, actually,' she confided, and waited for his reaction.

'A bookshop?' he repeated slowly.

'That's right.' Now it was her turn for mischief. 'You know. They sell those things consisting of pages glued together along one side and bound—'

'And why,' he said, with a smile playing at the corners of his lips, 'do you work in a bookshop?'

She took a sip of her wine. 'Oh, all the usual reasons—I love books. I'm a romantic. I have a great desire to exist on low wages. Do you want me to go on?'

'All night,' he murmured. 'All night.' But then their fish soup arrived and Guy stared at his darkly, wishing that he had known her longer. Wishing that she was already his lover so that he could have suggested that they leave the food untouched and just go straight home to bed. 'And where exactly is this bookshop?'

Sabrina nibbled at a piece of bread. 'In Salisbury. Right next to the Cathedral. Do you know it?'

'Nope. I've never been there,' he said thoughtfully.

She studied the curved dip at the centre of his upper lip and shamelessly found herself wanting to run her tongue along its perfect outline. 'How about you? Where do you live? What kind of work do you do?' She thought of the man she had first seen, in jeans and T-shirt. 'It must be something pretty high-powered for your company to pay for a hotel like that.'

Guy hesitated. When people said that money talked, they didn't realise that it also swore. It sounded ridiculous to consider yourself as being *too* highly paid, but he'd long ago realised that wealth had drawbacks all of its own. And when you were deemed rich—in a world where money was worshipped more than any of the more traditional gods—then lots of people wanted to know you for all the wrong reasons.

Not that he would have put Sabrina into that category. But he liked the sweet, unaffected way she was with him. He hadn't been treated as an equal for a very long time. And if he started hinting at just how much he was really worth, might she not be slightly overawed?

'Oh, I'm just a wheeler-dealer,' he shrugged.

'And what does a wheeler-dealer do?'

He smiled. 'A bit of everything. I buy and sell. Property. Art. Sometimes even cars. Houses occasionally.' But there was no disguising the dismissiveness in his voice as he topped her wine up. 'All pretty boring stuff. Finish your soup.'

'I have finished.'

She'd barely touched it, he noticed as the waiter removed their plates—but, then, neither had he. And he was still aroused. So aroused that…

Sabrina saw the dark colour which had flared over his cheekbones and suddenly she felt weak. Across the table they stared at one another, and the sounds of the other diners retreated so that they might have been alone in the crowded room.

'G-Guy,' she stumbled, through the ragged movement of her breathing.

'What is it?' he murmured.

'The waiter is w-waiting to give us our main course.'

Guy looked up to find the waiter standing beside the table, holding two plates containing crayfish and barely able to contain his smile.

'*Grazie*,' said Guy tightly.

'*Prego*.' The waiter grinned.

Sabrina smoothed her fingers over her flushed cheeks. She didn't speak until the waiter was out of earshot. 'Did you see his face?' she whispered.

'We're in Italy,' he remarked, with a shrug. 'They're used to couples displaying…' he lingered over a wholly inappropriate word '…affection. Now eat your crayfish,' he urged softly.

Like two condemned prisoners eating a last meal, they both silently spooned the crayfish into their mouths. It was fine food, meant to be savoured and enjoyed, but they both ate it quickly, without tasting it. In fact, Guy only just refrained from shovelling it down as if he were on a ten-minute lunch-break.

Sabrina wondered why she didn't feel shy. Or embarrassed. Why being with Guy in an atmosphere so tense with expectation seemed to feel so right. Something she needed more than anything in the world. She put her knife and fork down with a shaky hand and saw that Guy had mirrored her movements.

'Shall I call for the bill?' he queried.

She forced herself to try and respond normally, even though she knew what he meant by his question. 'Don't you want dessert? Or coffee?'

His mouth curved. He heard the delicious thunder of the inevitable. 'I thought we could try somewhere else for coffee.'

'Yes,' she agreed with nervous excitement, because she

knew exactly what he meant—and wouldn't a well-brought up girl be frightened by that? Or outraged? 'I guess we could.'

In a daze she allowed him to drape the wrap around her shoulders, feeling the negligent brush of his fingertips against her bare flesh as he did so, and she felt the breath catch in her throat like dust.

He took her by the hand and led her outside into the starry night, looking down at her with soft, silver light gleaming from his eyes.

'You're shivering,' he observed quietly, tracing a thoughtful fingertip down the slim, pale column of her neck and seeing her tremble even more. 'Again.'

'Y-yes.'

He took his jacket off and draped it around her shoulders; the broad cut of it almost swamped her slender frame. 'Here, take this…'

'You'll get cold yourself,' she objected.

'I don't think there's any danger of that,' he said softly, and, sliding his arms around her waist, he bent his head to kiss her.

Her heart was blazing as her mouth parted to meet the first sweet touch of his lips. She ignored the half-hearted voice of her conscience telling her to stop this, because who could have stopped *this*?

He was breathing life into her, bringing warmth flooding back into her veins. As though she had been some cold, bloodless statue and now…now…

'Oh, Guy,' she whispered, in a distracted plea. 'Guy.' But the words were lost against the honeyed softness of his mouth.

Desire shafted through him like an arrow. 'Oh, God, yes, Sabrina,' he ground out, on a sultry note of hunger. 'Yes, and yes, and yes.' He brought her closer into his body, up to the cradle of his hips, where the hard, lean power of him was un-mistakable. And now it was Guy's turn to make a harsh lit-tle sound. He broke the kiss off with a supreme effort, tearing his mouth away to look down with frustrated perplexity into her disappointed eyes.

'This is all threatening to get out of hand,' he groaned, suck-ing in a shuddering breath which scorched the lining of his lungs. 'I haven't engaged in such a public display of passion for a long time.' He had always liked beds—clean sheets and clini-cal comfort—so why was he having to swallow down the primi-tive urge to lead her to the nearest narrow, dark alleyway, pin her up against some ancient wall and do it to her right there…?

She felt no fear, and no shame. Only an overwhelming need to be near him. She trickled a questing fingertip down the proud, hard lines of his face. 'M-me neither.'

He forced himself to bite out the question, even though it was the most difficult thing he had ever had to say. 'Do you want me to take you back to your hotel, or would you like to…?' The word trailed off temptingly.

'To what?' she asked softly.

'To come back with me? We could have that dessert. Coffee. What do you think? Would you like that, princess?'

'Yes,' she whispered, knowing that he didn't want coffee any more than she did.

He took her hand and led her through the darkened streets. She felt dizzy with the sense of his proximity but she was so disorientated that he could have been leading her to the ends of the earth for all she knew. Or cared.

It wasn't until they found themselves back in the grand elegance of his suite, with the hazy gleam of the lamps fall-ing like moonlight on her flushed cheeks, that something of the enormity of what she was about to embark on began to seep into Sabrina's consciousness. She ought to stop this, she told herself, and stop it right now.

Yet the longer she stared into the mesmerising glitter of those dark-lashed eyes, the harder it was to listen to reason. Because reason was a weak component in the presence of raw need.

And Michael had taught her that nothing was certain. His death had brought the frailty of life crashing home in a way that nothing else could have done. Why, she could walk out of this room right now and something could happen to ensure that she would never see Guy Masters again. And never know the warmth of his embrace, or taste the luxury of his kiss.

She turned her face up to his, but her half-felt protest became a moan of surrender as he drove his mouth down on hers with a hungry kiss which splintered her senses.

He reached out to remove the clip from her hair, murmured his warm pleasure as it fell in a red-blonde gleam around her shoulders. 'See how your hair glows like fire against your skin. And how your eyes sparkle like pure, clear aquamarines.'

She had never been seduced by words before, had never known their sweet, wanton power. 'G-Guy,' she said shakily.

His eyes gleamed like silver and onyx. 'I want to see you, to see your flesh glow in the moonlight. I want to undress you.' He moved his hand distractedly to find the zip of her dress, before sliding it down with unsteady fingers, kissing her neck as the silky material parted for him.

She gasped as she felt the touch of his fingers against her burning skin and the weight of his hands as they moved down to possessively cup the curve of her bottom. Her head fell helplessly against his shoulder as she felt her dress begin to slide down over her thighs.

'God, princess, you're driving me *crazy*,' he ground out on a shudder as the dress pooled with a silken whisper at her feet. He lifted his head to gaze at her, taken aback by the sight of her frivolous underwear.

It was the last thing he had been expecting—she looked like a centrefold. A pure white lace bra through which her nipples peaked rosy and hard, and a matching wisp of a G-string through which he could distinctly see the red-gold blur of hair. And then there was the outrageous little suspender belt, onto which were clipped the sheerest stockings he had ever seen.

He very nearly lost control. What had happened to the plain cotton functional garments she'd been wearing the other day? The ones which he'd sent to the laundry whilst thinking that she was obviously of the gym-mistress persuasion?

He gazed at the slender curves of her body, his hand unsteady as it followed the path of his eyes. 'You wore these for me?' he questioned shakily, his fingers splaying over the barely perceptible curve of her belly.

'Yes.'

'Sweet, sweet torment. You look…wonderful.' He swallowed. 'Quite the most exquisite thing I've ever seen.'

She found herself blushing under that passion-glazed scrutiny. The underwear had been bought as part of her trousseau, for the honeymoon she'd been fated never to have.

Her worried mother had persuaded her to pack them. 'Good underwear always makes a woman feel better about herself,' she'd urged her. 'And it seems such a pity to waste such beautiful lingerie.'

Not wanting a row, Sabrina had weakly agreed to take them and had stuffed them into the bottom of her suitcase, knowing that she would never have the heart to wear them. And yet some instinct had urged her to slide them onto her scented and freshly bathed body before dressing to meet Guy this evening… Had she secretly been imagining that shining look of delight as he looked at her?

He dipped his head and dropped a soft kiss on her mouth. 'Get into bed,' he ordered unsteadily, 'while I undress.'

She slid between the linen sheets immediately, thankful that he wasn't expecting her to undress *him*. Why, her hands were shaking even more than his.

She watched as he slowly began to unbutton his silk shirt, and in a reflex action her fingers slid up to clutch at her throat, their tips colliding with the thin gold chain from which hung a ring.

Her engagement ring!

Guy had bent to remove one of his shoes, and Sabrina took the opportunity to pull the sheet right up to her chin and to unclip the chain without him seeing. She was about to place it unobtrusively on the floor beside her when he glanced up to see her shrouded in the sheet, with only her face and bright hair showing, and he gave a lazy smile.

Maybe he was more old-fashioned than he gave himself credit for—because it pleased him to see that she was a little shy. 'You look sweet,' he murmured. 'Very, very sweet.'

'D-do I?' Whereas he looked the antithesis of sweet. He looked strong and dark and very, very aroused. Maybe she should have been frightened by his hard, masculine body, but she was in too deep now. Too enthralled by him—too chained by the honeyed flutterings of desire.

His shirt fluttered to the ground and he left it where it lay with arrogant disregard. But when he turned his attention to the belt that was holding up his trousers, Sabrina surreptitiously allowed the chain to slither like a slim gold snake onto the carpet.

He kicked his trousers off and Sabrina hastily shut her eyes, only to open them to find him looking down at her, a kind of bemused tenderness on his face.

'You *are* shy,' he observed softly.

'A little,' she answered truthfully.

'I like it.'

'Do you?'

'Mmm. But, then, I think I like everything about you. Your golden hair spread all over my pillow. Your skin as white as milk.' Wearing only a pair of dark, silken boxer shorts, he lifted back the sheet and climbed into bed beside her. 'Come here,' he said softly, pulling her into the warm cradle of his arms.

She felt the shock of sensation as they tangled their limbs, his bare, warm flesh pressing against hers, and she gasped with a heightened sense of recognition.

He dipped his mouth to brush against a tiny, puckered nipple. 'I find myself in the curious position of not knowing where to begin,' he murmured. 'Like a starving man being presented with the most fantastic banquet and being completely spoilt for choice.'

'Guy,' she stumbled helplessly, her eyes huge and dark. 'So, do I kiss you?' he mused. 'Yes, I think so.' His lips brushed lightly over hers, there and gone in an instant, leaving her mouth moistly open and expectant. 'Or touch you here?' A feather-light flicker of finger to nipple which made her shiver. 'Yes, you like that, don't you, my sweet torment?'

'Y-yes,' she gasped.

'Or here?' The tantalising graze of that same finger over the moist, warm centre of her panties and Sabrina gasped aloud. 'You like that, too, don't you?'

He looked down, losing himself in the black distraction of her eyes, and felt himself grow so hard that he thought he actually might explode. He struggled to rein in his feelings and then kissed the tip of her nose.

'On second thoughts,' he said thickly, 'we've got all night.'

Guy awoke to the clear tinge of early morning. He narrowed his eyes in the direction of the unshuttered windows to see the first rose-gold shaft of the new sun. The very early morning.

He didn't stir. By his side, Sabrina lay sleeping, her arms spread out in careless abandon across the rumpled bed. He had no wish to wake her—and not just because they'd fallen into a passion-sated slumber only a couple of hours back. No, he needed a little time to come to terms with what had just happened.

Well, he knew exactly what had happened. He felt his mouth dry. They had spent a whole night indulging every single sexual fantasy he'd ever had—and a few more besides. As if there were infinite variations and dimensions to the act of making love that he had never discovered before.

As if the world were about to end and they had greedily needed to discover every sensual pleasure known to man. Or woman.

He swallowed, his heart beginning a rapid drumming at the slow, inevitable stir of arousal. No, if he woke her now it would happen all over again—and, much as he wanted it to happen, he also needed to think.

Because, if he were being brutally honest, he'd behaved in a way that he'd never imagined he could. Had just spent the night making love to a stranger. To a woman who was beautiful, intelligent and engaging—but a stranger nonetheless.

He gazed again at the sky, which was now being pierced by a soft apricot light, and his mouth hardened. He was old enough and experienced enough to know that what had happened between them last night was rare. And yet he'd been reckless, out of control. He'd enjoyed it, yes, but that didn't mean he approved of his actions.

'Mmm!' Beneath the sheet, Sabrina stretched her body sleepily.

Guy felt his heart rate increase as he looked down at the perfect outline of her slender body and felt the stirrings of desire spring into full and vibrant life. 'And "mmm" to you, too,' he said softly.

Sabrina opened her eyes and felt impaled by that lancing glance of steel-grey as seductive memories of the night danced tantalisingly through her mind. But reality brought with it disbelief. She had given herself to him, no holds barred. So now what? 'What time is it?' she said uncertainly.

'Early.' He leaned over her, his lean, hair-roughened torso just crying out to be touched. 'Is that all you've got to say for yourself?' he teased.

Her doubts fled with the warm reality of his proximity. 'That depends.' Sabrina gave in to temptation and reached one finger up to touch a hard, flat nipple. He groaned, dipping his head to kiss her while one hand trailed down over her flat belly, to where she was hot and moist and ready.

He raised his eyebrows mockingly as he moved to lie over her, dropping tiny kisses on the flutter of her eyelashes and her lips. 'Do you always wake up so pleasingly compliant in the morning?' he murmured, reaching down the side of the bed to open another packet of contraceptives. His fingers came into contact with something hard and metallic and he impatiently shoved it aside until he found what he was looking for.

She could feel the hard tip of him nudging against her and her instant warm, sweet response. Last night he had not only brought her back to life, he'd made her feel his equal. There was nothing she could have done or said that would have shocked him, nor he her.

Sabrina was not about to start making odious comparisons, but she'd never known that lovemaking could be so free or so uninhibited. That it could have so many faces, and so many forms.

With a newly learnt and slumberously provocative pout, she took the condom from him.

'Shall I deal with this for you?' she whispered.

He gave a low laugh of delight, but the laugh was tinged

with a certain amount of apprehension. Right then she could do what she liked with him, and he suspected that he would just lie there like a puppy and grin with pleasure. What the hell had happened to his habitual dominance? His need to orchestrate?

'Deal away, princess,' he drawled.

She pushed him to lie back against the pillow, and knelt over him, her long, bare thighs straddling him. 'Quite appropriate, really,' she said breathily, as she slowly inched the sheath down over the hard, silken length of him. 'As you're a dealer.'

'Oh, God,' he moaned. 'God! Why are you taking so long?'

Her fingernails lightly teased at the delicate protection. 'But it's all your fault, Guy—you shouldn't *be* so long,' she teased.

He let her torment him until the condom was firmly in place and then he swiftly lifted her up and laid her on her back. Again he moved above her, but this time there was an inexplicable mixture of emotions on his face, his eyes so dark that Sabrina didn't have a clue what was going on inside that head of his.

'You know,' he mused, and now it was his turn to tease her, the full tip of him nudging against her, 'I always thought that girls who worked in bookshops would be so timid. So demure.'

'And aren't I?'

He smiled, but there was an odd edge to the smile. 'No, you're not,' he groaned. 'You're a very bad girl indeed and you leave me no alternative than to do *this* to you...'

He thrust into her with such power that stars exploded behind her eyes, and he'd barely moved inside her before she could feel the first slow glimmerings of release. Drowning in honeyed sweetness, she turned her head distractedly from side to side on the pillow as wave upon wave of pure sensation left her shuddering and helpless in their wake.

Guy tried to make it last, but he was lost. This must be some kind of record, he thought as he felt the first sweet tug of his own release.

It was one of the best orgasms of his life, but it left him feeling curiously empty, as though she had taken something from him he had not intended to give. He slowly withdrew from her to find her watching him with dazed disbelief, and his smile was wry as he kissed her.

'Go to sleep now,' he urged. 'Go to sleep.'

And only when her breathing became steady did he slip silently from between the sheets.

CHAPTER FOUR

WHEN Sabrina opened her eyes again, the space on the bed beside her was empty. She gazed around the room, listening out for the sounds of activity in the bathroom, but there was only silence.

She sat up in bed and yawned, noticing that Guy's clothes were gone. She ran her fingers back through her tousled hair and wondered where he was. Rubbing her eyes, she picked up her watch. Ten past seven. Very early. So where could he be?

She clambered out of bed and went into the bathroom, where she found most things she needed, including a courtesy toothbrush, still wrapped in its Cellophane paper.

She wandered back into the bedroom just as the phone started ringing, and she picked it up with a smile on her face.

'Guy?' she said, thinking how pampered she sounded.

But it wasn't Guy. The voice was female—a husky voice which was edged with suspicion.

'Who is this, please?'

Sabrina wondered fleetingly whether she should give her name. No, better not. 'This is a friend of Guy's,' she answered.

'A friend?' The voice sharpened. 'And where is he, please?'

'He's gone out.'

'Where has he gone?' asked the voice impatiently.

Suddenly Sabrina had had enough. The woman was speaking to her as if she were a chambermaid! 'Who would like to know?' she asked softly.

The voice acquired a sudden brittle ring. 'This is one of Prince Raschid's representatives. The Prince is keen to learn whether Mr Masters has managed to acquire the painting he was so anxious to secure.'

Sabrina very nearly dropped the phone. 'I really have no idea where he's gone,' she said slowly, still reeling from the fact that Guy Masters was doing deals for *princes*. 'I'm sorry.'

'The Prince is paying Mr Masters an extremely large commission—for which we would obviously expect him to be instantly accessible,' said the voice icily. 'And whether or not he chooses to jeopardise that commission by using his time in Venice to concentrate on his love affairs, instead of paying attention to the work in hand, is obviously something which the Prince will be very interested to hear about.'

Sabrina drew in a deep breath, trying to remember that the customer was always right. 'Isn't there someone else who can deal with your query?'

There was silence. 'The Prince will only deal with the owner of the company. Not his minions. Goodbye,' said the woman, and put the phone down.

The owner of the company? The company that paid for this hotel room? Sabrina stared down at the receiver, then walked over to the desk, which was covered with neat sheaves of paper.

She hunted around until she found what she was looking for—a letterheaded sheet of business notepaper stating, 'Guy Masters. Dealer in fine art', and an address in what was probably one of the most famous and exclusive streets in London.

Sabrina felt dizzy. Sick. He had lied. Just a little lie—but a lie all the same. What else had he lied to her about? she wondered as she hunted distractedly around the room for her discarded panties. All those things he'd said. He'd implied...

She drew in a deep, unsteady breath as she clipped up her bra. She remembered his words as she'd gazed up with wide-eyed admiration at the hotel's beautifully faded façade. 'The company pays for it.'

He had deliberately played down his wealth and his influence—which begged the question why? Did he think that if she found out just how rich he really was, he might never get rid of her? And was that why he had disappeared so conclusively this morning, despite knowing that she would probably be feeling vulnerable?

She had just slithered into her panties when the phone rang again, and she snatched it up without thinking.

'Signor Masters, please,' said an Italian-accented voice.

Feeling that she'd already been down this road, Sabrina sighed. 'He isn't here.'

'Could you please give him a message?' asked the voice.

Curiosity overrode caution. 'OK,' said Sabrina tentatively.

'This is Air Executive at Venice Airport. We need him to confirm his seat on this afternoon's flight out to London. A water-taxi has been booked for two-thirty, as requested.'

A flight out *today*?

'I'll tell him,' said Sabrina in a dazed and hurt voice, then replaced the receiver.

The bastard! The cheating, lying bastard! Another lie! How many more would she discover? He had told her that he was staying for a few days—just as she was. Maybe he had always planned to leave just as soon as he had taken her to bed—he probably hadn't reckoned on her falling into it quite so quickly.

She felt the sickening plummet of her stomach as the reality of what she had done began to sink in. She had slept with a stranger. It had been the most heart-stoppingly beautiful night, yes, but Guy hadn't even been able to face her this morning. And that was how much he cared about her. At least he was allowing her to make the decision to leave herself, rather than having to eject her.

Face it, she told herself with a bitter pang of regret, you've been used. The classic one-night stand. But what had she expected? No woman would ever receive courtesy and consideration from a man like Guy Masters—not when she had ended up in bed with him on a first date.

Her heart racing, Sabrina slithered the silvery-blue dress over her head and located first one shoe, and then the other.

She looked around at the sumptuous fittings of the room, feeling more out of place with each second that passed. This was not her kind of world. Guy was not her kind of man. Get out now, she told herself—now while you still have some pride left.

He was probably downstairs on the lookout in the huge marble foyer, waiting until she had gone back to her own hotel and the coast was clear for him to return to his suite.

Pausing only to brush through the tangled strands of her hair, she quietly left the room and located the lift, steadfastly ignoring the rather curious expression of a beautiful young Italian woman until it had reached the ground floor.

Stealthily slinking out, she peeped around one of the giant marble pillars to see, to her absolute horror, that Guy was sprawled out on one of the silk sofas, talking into a mobile phone.

He looked, Sabrina thought, completely businesslike. Miles away. Worlds away. Worlds apart. He'd shaved, put on a suit and smoothed down the hair which she had ruffled with her greedy, frantic fingers during the night. He didn't look remotely like a man who had spent the whole night making mad, passionate love to her. Maybe that had been put in the out tray, she thought, her heart thundering like a cannon in her ears.

She waited until he turned his head, giving her a glimpse of that hard, beautiful profile as he gestured for a coffee.

Moving with a quiet and guilty step, Sabrina quietly left the hotel.

Guy opened the door to his suite, wondering whether Sabrina would still be in bed, telling himself that he would not join her there. After recklessness came reason.

But still a slow rise of colour begin to flush its way along his cheeks, and he moved quietly towards the bed and stared down at it with slowly dawning disbelief. Empty.

He stood very still. 'Sabrina?' he called softly, but even as he said her name he knew that it was futile.

She had gone.

He ripped the covers back, as if they were somehow concealing her, as if her slender frame could be hidden away, but there was nothing other than the lingering musky traces of sex marking the sheets.

His mouth twisted as he dropped the sheet as abruptly as if it were contaminated, his grey eyes growing steely as they travelled around the room.

Her clothes had gone. The discarded panties and stockings had disappeared.

Gone, just as if she had never been there.

A slow pulse began to throb unsteadily at his temple, his gaze not missing a thing as he walked round to the other side of the bed. His eyes scanned this way and that for the note which logic told him she had not left. And at first the glint of gold which gleamed so palely against the silken rug held no interest for him.

Until he realised that she had left *something* behind.

He bent and retrieved the delicate chain and stared down at it with dawning realisation as it glittered in the palm of his hand.

And his mouth twisted into a slow, cruel smile as his fingers closed over it and he dropped it deep into the pocket of his trousers.

CHAPTER FIVE

THE old-fashioned bell on the bookshop door clanged loudly as Sabrina stepped in out of the rain. The shop was empty save for a mild-looking man with glasses who glanced up, his face brightening into a smile of welcome.

'Sabrina!' he said in delight. 'Welcome back!'

Sabrina tried to match his smile, and wondered if it looked as lopsided as it felt. 'Thanks, Paul,' she said, and slowly began to unbutton her raincoat, brushing off the drops of rain as she did so. 'It's great to be back!'

'So, how was Venice?'

Sabrina quickly turned to hang the dripping garment on the peg, hoping that he wouldn't see the sudden defensive set of her shoulders. Or the swift shiver of memory which had her biting her lip in consternation. How could you ache so badly for a man you barely knew? she wondered. A man who had given you his body, but not his honesty?

But by the time she turned round again she had managed to compose her face into the kind of dreamy post-holiday smile which Paul would be expecting.

'Venice? Oh, it was...' She swallowed as recollections of mocking grey eyes and a hard, lean body swam unwillingly into her mind. 'It was lovely!' she finished lamely.

'Lovely?' echoed Paul, pulling a face. 'This is the place

that you wanted to visit more than anywhere else on earth and you describe it as "lovely"? What happened in Venice, Sabrina?' He laughed. 'Did you leave your descriptive powers behind?'

'I'm a bit tired after all the travelling, that's all. I went to see my aunt in Scotland as soon as I got back.' She sat down at the desk and began to flick through the morning's post.

'Yes.' Paul frowned. 'You look a little pale. Like some coffee?'

'I'd love some. I'll make it.'

But Paul Bailey shook his head. 'No, you won't. I'll do it. You look bushed. Sit down and I'll bring you something hot and restorative.'

'Thanks, Paul,' said Sabrina gratefully. She dropped a discarded envelope into the bin and looked around.

It was hard to believe that she was back. That everything was just as she'd left it. And nothing had changed.

She bit her lip again and stared down at the pile of manila envelopes on her lap.

Except her. *She* had changed. In the course of those few days in Venice she had discovered some unbelievable things about herself—things she wasn't sure she liked at all.

And now she was having to come to terms with the knowledge that she was the kind of woman who was able to have a passionate fling with a man who was little more than a stranger to her. A stranger who had left her heart breaking for him.

Paul came back into the room, carrying a tray with two steaming mugs of coffee, one of which he deposited in front of her, together with a chocolate bar.

She shook her head. 'You can have the biscuit. I'm not hungry.'

Paul tutted, sounding torn between concern and impatience. 'I thought that one of the reasons behind you going to Italy was to try and tempt yourself back into eating.' His voice softened, along with his eyes. 'Come on—you can't keep pining for Michael for ever, you know, Sabrina. He wouldn't want that.'

Sabrina quickly put down the coffee, terrified that she might drop it. For what would the decent and honourable Paul say if he knew how little she had been pining for Michael? She tried to imagine his reaction if she told him the truth about her holiday, and paled at the thought of how his opinion of her would be reversed if only he knew.

'In fact,' said Paul gently, 'I thought you were going to come back from Venice a new woman—wasn't that the plan?'

She lifted her head. 'And I haven't?' she teased him. 'Is that what you mean?'

He shrugged awkwardly. 'Just as slim and even paler— what *did* you do out there?'

'What does everyone do in Venice?' she asked lightly, as she tried not to remember.

Paul grinned. 'You travelled in a gondola, right?'

Sabrina forced a smile in response. 'You bet I did!' And that was how the whole damned thing had started—blinded by a man with night-dark hair and a body which had stirred a deep, primitive response in her. And she couldn't blame Guy for that. She had set the wheels for that in motion herself. Unless she was planning to blame him for his physical beauty and impact. 'Anyway, that's enough about me, Paul. How has business been?'

Paul shrugged. 'So-so. March is slow, as you know, but it'll be Easter soon. Interestingly enough, I had a phone call yesterday from a man trying to track down a rare first edition.'

Sabrina sipped her coffee. 'Oh?'

'That's right. You must have served him. He asked for you. I told him you weren't due in until today.'

'Really?' she questioned absently.

Once she had drunk her coffee, Sabrina forced herself to get back into the slow and rhythmical pattern of her working day and found it comforting. She would put the whole affair down to experience and not let it get out of hand in her imagination. After all, lots of people had holiday romances which ended badly.

If only Guy Masters wasn't such an unforgettable man. If only she hadn't lost her head. But 'if onlys' wouldn't change a thing—they never did.

Fortunately, work soon took over. Maybe that was because she had become an expert in pushing away disturbing thoughts. She settled down to some long-overdue ordering and soon became immersed in that.

She heard the sound of the shop door clanging open and flourished her signature in the order book before looking up and blinking, her polite smile freezing into disbelief on her lips.

It couldn't be him, she thought, even as her heart responded with an instinctive surge of excitement. But the delight ebbed away as quickly as it had come, to be replaced by a sudden wariness when she saw the dark, forbidding expression on his face.

It couldn't be him. But it was.

She was aware of the fact that Paul was working in the storeroom, and composed her face accordingly.

'Hello, Guy,' she said, her voice sounding astonishingly calm considering that the thundering of her heart was threatening to deafen her. 'This is a surprise.'

'Is it?' He leaned over the desk and the male scent of him reached out to her senses, sending them spinning out of control as she registered his closeness. 'So you *do* remember me?' he drawled silkily. 'Wow—*that's* a relief.'

Sabrina blushed at the implication behind his insulting question. 'Of course I remember you! I... We...'

'Had a night of no-holds-barred sex before you did a runner in the morning?' he remarked insolently.

'You were the one who did a runner, and will you *keep your voice down*?' she hissed furiously.

'Or what?'

'Or I'll have you thrown out of the shop!'

Guy's gaze swivelled to where Paul was busy flicking through a card index, and he raised a laconic eyebrow. 'Oh, really?'

She knew just what he was implying. For a man of similar age to Guy, Paul was no weakling, but comparing him to the angry specimen of manhood who stood just inches away from her would be like comparing a child's chug-chug train to a high-speed express. But even so...

Sabrina raised a stubborn chin to him. No matter what had happened between the two of them, he couldn't just march in here like some autocratic dictator and start jeopardising her very livelihood. Not when he'd already taken out her heart and smashed it into smithereens...

'Yes, really!'

He cocked an arrogant eyebrow at her. 'Going to start talking, then, are we, Sabrina?'

'I can't talk to you now,' she stated levelly. 'I'm working.'

'Then when?'

'I don't know,' she prevaricated.

The grey eyes narrowed. 'What time is your lunch-hour?'

'I don't usually take lunch.'

'House rules?' he drawled.

'No, my rules,' she answered stiffly.

'Then change the rules, baby,' he commanded, with a cool arrogance which infuriated her almost as much as it reminded her of his consummate mastery in bed. 'And change them now.'

Sabrina tried to imagine the worst-case scenario. What if

she agreed to meet him for lunch—in a city where she had lived all her life and where she was known? She wasn't the same woman here as he had met in Venice. Not by any stretch of the imagination. But what if he managed to reduce her to that same mindless being who just cried out for his touch?

And it wasn't difficult to work out how he might go about that. Surely he would only have to take her in his arms again. Just as he'd done before. She couldn't guarantee that she wouldn't succumb, and how could she possibly come back in here after *that* and spend the afternoon working, as if nothing had happened?

'I eat my lunch here,' she told him resolutely.

He rubbed a thoughtful forefinger over his chin, and the movement was accompanied by the unconscious thrust of his hips. 'Then I guess I'll just wait here until you've finished,' he told her softly, and then deliberately raised his voice. 'Perhaps you could point me to the section on erotic literature?'

'Don't you *dare*—'

'Is something wrong, Sabrina?' Paul came through from the storeroom, pushing his spectacles to the back of his nose, looking with distrust at the tall, dark man who was towering over his assistant's desk.

Sabrina sent a look of appeal up at Guy but was met with nothing but an uncompromising glitter. She knew then that he wouldn't be going anywhere until he got what he'd come for. And that there was no way she could get out of this meeting. She swallowed down her reservations and forced a brittle smile.

'Guy is a friend...' She hesitated on the inappropriate word before continuing, seeing the brief, hard twist of his mouth as he registered it, too. 'A friend of mine. Who has dropped into town unexpectedly—'

Guy fixed Paul with a bland smile. 'And I was hoping to persuade her to come to lunch with me, but—'

'Well, we usually eat a sandwich here—but you go to lunch if you want, Sabrina!' said Paul immediately. 'It'll make a nice change.'

Sabrina shook her head and sent Guy a furious look. How dared he be so manipulative in order to get his own way? 'No, thanks, Paul. I've agreed to meet Guy…after work.' She managed to get the words out—even though they almost choked her in the process.

'Yes, she has. I can *hardly wait.*' Guy gave her another wintry smile, but the hungry look of intent which had darkened his eyes told its own story. 'I'm taking you out for dinner, Sabrina.'

That was what he thought! 'Just a drink will be fine,' she said stiffly. 'My mother will be expecting me home for supper.'

'Your mother?' A frown of disbelief criss-crossed his forehead. Surely she didn't still live with her *mother*?

Sabrina read the disappointment in his eyes, and pride and fury warred inside her like a bubbling cauldron. What had he expected? A reenactment of that night in Venice? A half-finished meal and she would fall back into bed with him?

'Yes,' she said, with a demure flutter of her eyelashes. 'I live with my mother.'

'And what time do you finish?'

'Five-thirty.'

'I'll be here,' he promised, on a note of silky threat. 'Waiting.'

'I'll look forward to it,' she responded furiously.

Guy forced himself to give his cool, polite smile as he left the shop. But inside he was raging. *Raging.*

He should have just forgotten all about her. That was what he had told himself over and over on the plane coming back from Italy. He didn't know what had possessed him to track her down like some kind of amateur sleuth. Because, yes, there were a few questions he would like a few honest answers to—but common sense had told him just to cut his losses and run. She was trouble, and he couldn't for the life of him work out why.

He should have just posted her the chain and the ring with a cynical note attached saying, 'Thanks for the memory.'

And left it at that.

But he had been driven by a compulsion to see her again and to challenge her—a compulsion he was certain was driven by nothing more than the fact that she had given him the best sex of his life.

But maybe that had been *because* she'd been a stranger, not *in spite of* that fact. Because she'd had no expectations of him. Or any knowledge. She'd judged him as a man—a well-paid employee, true, but not as a man with megabucks. She had responded to him in the most fundamental way possible, and he to her. It had left him shaken, seeking some kind of explanation which would enable him to let the memory go.

She had been honest and open and giving in his bed—so why the secrets? The hidden chain and a ring which was almost certainly an engagement ring. Why the sudden and dramatic exit—like something out of a bad movie?

Guy walked around Salisbury dodging the showers—but not dodging them accurately enough. So that by the time he arrived at Wells Bookstore at twenty-five minutes past five his thick, ruffled hair was sprinkled with raindrops which glittered like tears amidst the ebony waves.

Sabrina glanced up from her desk and her heart caught in her throat at the sight of his rain-soaked frame. He would, she thought, be all too easy to fall in love with. Women must fall in love with him all the time. Leave me alone, Guy Masters, she urged him silently. Go away and leave me alone.

Paul, who was standing a little space away, followed the troubled direction of her eyes.

'Your friend is waiting,' he said carefully. 'You'd better go.'

Sabrina turned to him, her eyes beseeching him. 'I know what you're thinking.'

Paul shrugged. 'It's not my place to say anything about your private life, Sabrina—but it *is* very soon after Michael, isn't it? Just take it easy, that's all.'

Guilt smote at her with a giant hand. 'He's just a friend.'

Paul gave her an awkward smile. 'Sure he is,' he said, as though he didn't quite believe her. 'Look, it's none of my business.'

'No.' She picked up her coat from the hook. 'I'll see you in the morning, Paul. Goodnight.'

Through the window Guy watched her shrugging her raincoat on, unable to stop himself from marvelling at the innate grace of her movements. She moved like a dream, he thought—all long, slender limbs and that bright, shiny hair shimmering like sunlight in the grey of the rainy afternoon.

He remembered the way she had straddled him, her pale, naked thighs on either side of his waist, and he felt the first uncomfortable stirrings of desire—until he reminded himself that that was not why he was here.

Sabrina pushed the door open and thought how chilly Guy's grey eyes looked, and how unsmiling his mouth. She told herself that this would be one short evening to get through and then she need never see him again. He had lied to her, she told herself bitterly.

'Where would you like to go?' she questioned.

'You live here.' He shrugged. 'How the hell should I know?'

'I meant do you just want coffee—or a drink?'

He remembered that night in Venice and the lack of interest with which he'd greeted the wine. Yet tonight he could have willingly sunk a bucketful of liquor. 'A drink,' he said abruptly.

Me, too, she thought as she led the way across a cobbled courtyard to one of the city's oldest pubs.

Inside, a log fire blazed at each end of the bar and the warmth hit her like a blanket.

'Go and find a seat,' he instructed tersely. 'What do you want to drink?'

'B-brandy.' She shivered violently, despite the heat of the room.

She found a table far away from the others. She suspected that their conversation wouldn't be for general consumption. Then she slipped her coat off and sat there waiting for him, her knees glued primly together—like a girl who had just been to deportment lessons.

He brought two large brandies over to the table and sat down opposite her, aware of the way that she shrank back when their knees brushed.

'Oh? So shy, Sabrina? Don't like me touching you?' He held his glass up in a mocking toast. 'Isn't that a little like shutting the stable door after the horse has bolted? You weren't so shy in my bed, were you, my beauty?'

She gulped down some brandy, the liquid burning welcome fire down her throat, and her cheeks flushed with indignant heat. 'Did you bring me here just so you could insult me?' she demanded. 'Is that what you'd like, Guy?'

He shook his dark head and sipped his own drink more sparingly, surveying her over the rim of his glass with eyes which gave nothing away. 'Not at all.' But he bit back the unexpectedly explicit comment about what he *would* like.

She put the glass down, feeling slightly dizzy with the impact of the burning liquor on an empty stomach. 'What, then?'

He dipped his hand deep into his trouser pocket, aware that her eyes instinctively followed the movement. Aware, too, that she certainly wasn't immune to him either. He watched with fascination as her eyes darkened and he could sense that she was resisting the desire to run her tongue over her lips.

'Recognise this?' he asked casually, as he withdrew the thin gold chain with the pretty little ring and dropped it on the polished surface of the table in front of her.

Sabrina's heart pounded with guilt and shame. 'Don't insult me even more by asking me questions like that!' she said bitterly. 'Of course I recognise it! It's mine—you know it's mine! I left it in your bedroom!'

It lay like an omen before them.

'Then why hide it from me?'

She opened her mouth to deny it, but could not. He knew. He was an intelligent man. She was cornered, and she reacted in the same way that all trapped creatures reacted. She attacked. 'You lied to me, too!' she accused.

His eyes narrowed. 'When?'

'You implied that you were *employed* by the company— you didn't tell me you owned it!'

He nodded and his eyes took on a hard, bright glitter. 'Yes, I heard about your discussion with Prince Raschid's emissary.'

'She insulted me!'

'So I believe.' His lips flattened into a forbidding line.

'She was jealous,' said Sabrina slowly, as she recognised now the emotion which had made the woman's voice so brittle. 'Jealous that I was in your bedroom.'

'Yes.' His gaze didn't waver.

'Have you slept with her, too?'

'That's none of your business!' he snapped, but something about the dark horror written in her eyes made him relent. 'Of course I haven't slept with her! She's a business acquaintance I've met on barely half a dozen occasions!'

'And you met me once,' said Sabrina hollowly.

'That's different!' But he didn't pause to ask himself why.

'So why did you lie to me about owning the company?'

He paused deliberately and met her eyes with a bitter challenge. 'I wanted to be sure that it was me you were turned on by, and not all the trappings.'

'As though I'm some kind of cheap little gold-digger, you mean?' Sabrina glared at him. 'And you lied to me about when you were leaving Venice, too!' she accused.

He raised a dark, arrogant eyebrow. 'Did I?'

'You know you did! You told me you were staying for a few days, yet the airport said you had a flight booked out that afternoon!'

He gave her a look of barely concealed impatience. 'Oh, *that*!' he said dismissively. 'So what? Flights can usually be changed.'

'And if they can't?' she challenged.

'Then you buy another ticket.' His eyes glittered. 'A small price to pay under the circumstances.'

The cool, arrogant statement told her in no uncertain terms his true opinion of her, and Sabrina stared at him with hurt and anger in her eyes. 'These particular circumstances being sex with a stranger, you mean?'

He smiled. He certainly preferred her fighting and spitting to that lost look of despair she'd worn when they'd first walked in here. 'You were there, too, Sabrina. That's what we did—had sex.'

'Yes,' she said bitterly, thinking that he didn't even respect her enough to dress up what had happened by calling it lovemaking.

'And you still haven't answered my question,' he observed coolly. 'About the ring.'

Shakily, she grabbed her glass from the table and drank from it.

He wondered whether she was aware that her tiny breasts moved with such sweetness beneath the fine sweater she wore. A pulse began to beat insistently at his temple and he jabbed an angry finger at the chain. 'So why hide it from me, Sabrina?'

She stared down into the trickle of brandy left in her glass and started to feel nervous. 'Can I have another drink, please?'

'No, you bloody well can't!' He didn't take his gaze from her downcast head. 'Sabrina? I'll ask you again. *Why hide it from me?*'

'I d-don't know.'

'Oh, yes, you do.' He sucked in a deep, painful breath. 'Is it an engagement ring?'

Well, now he would know what type of woman she really was. 'Yes. Yes, it is. You know it is!'

He nodded, unprepared for the jerking pain of jealousy. And a bright, burning anger—as fierce as anything he had ever experienced. It pierced like an arrow through his heart. He tried to stay calm, but it took every shred of self-restraint he possessed. 'I see.'

There was something so wounding about the way he said those two empty words that Sabrina looked at him with a question in her eyes.

'Now I understand,' Guy said heavily. He pushed the chain across the table towards her and gave a hollow, humourless laugh. 'You must have had a lot of explaining to do.'

She stared back at him in genuine confusion. 'Explaining?'

He leaned back in his chair a little, as if close proximity to her might taint him. Or tempt him. 'Well, yes. Hell, I know you're a *liberal* woman, Sabrina—you certainly proved that—but surely your fiancé would be a little jealous if he found out about your little *lapse*?' His mouth curved. 'Though maybe not. Maybe you're the kind of couple who play away.' He lowered his voice into a sexy, insulting whisper. 'Then get turned on by telling each other all about it. There are couples like that, or so I believe.'

The blood left Sabrina's face and she stared at him in horror, scarcely able to make any sense of his words. She would have risen to her feet and walked out there and then, except that her legs felt so unsteady she didn't think she would be able to stand properly. 'How d-dare you insult me?' she whispered.

'You're honestly asking how I dare?' His eyebrows disappeared into the still damp strands of his ebony hair. But now it was his turn to look outraged as he leaned forward, his voice little more than a harsh, accusing whisper. 'Quite easily, actually. When you meet a woman and she does what you did to me that night, it's kind of *disappointing* to discover that she's got some poor sucker of a fiancé waiting on the sidelines.'

His mouth twisted as his anger drove him on remorselessly. 'Maybe you were bored with him, huh? Or were on the lookout for someone a little more…*loaded*.'

He deliberately gave the taunt two meanings, and his dark gaze flickered insultingly in the direction of his lap, seeing her flinch as her eyes followed his. And then he shifted in his seat, angry and uncomfortable, realising that he was starting to get turned on. What the hell did she *do* to him? 'Was that it?' he snarled. 'Were you looking for someone with a little more to offer than your home-spun boy?'

Sabrina felt sick and she shook her head, unable to speak. But he didn't seem to be expecting an answer because he ploughed on, a hard, clipped edge of rage to his voice.

'So what did you tell him? Did you describe in full and graphic detail the things I did to you? The things you did to me? Just what *did* you tell him, Sabrina?'

The unwitting inappropriateness of his question brought her a new kind of strength, and she wanted to reach out and to wound him, just as he had wounded her.

'Nothing!' she choked out. 'I didn't tell him anything! I couldn't, could I? Because he's dead, you see, Guy! Dead, dead, *dead*!'

And the spots which danced before her eyes dissolved into rainbows, and then, thankfully, into darkness.

CHAPTER SIX

GUY knew that Sabrina was going to faint even before the great heavy weight of her eyelids flickered to slump over her eyes. The colour blanched right out of her face and she swayed, slender and blonde as a blade of wheat.

He caught her just before she slid to the ground, pushing her head down to her knees while with his other hand he reached round to undo the top button of her shirt. He felt her wriggle beneath his fingers.

She groaned. 'Guy—'

'Don't try to say anything.' His words were controlled and clipped as he rubbed the back of her neck, while inside his mind raced. A dead fiancé. His eyes narrowed. Why the hell hadn't she told him that right at the beginning?

Sabrina felt dizzy, dazedly aware that the other customers must be staring at her and knowing that the last thing she wanted was to attract more attention to herself. She needed to get out of here. And fast. But Guy's fingers were distracting her so. She tried ineffectually to shrug off the fingertips which massaged so soothingly at the nape of her neck.

He felt her flinch beneath his touch and his mouth hardened. 'Don't worry,' he ground out agitatedly. 'I'm not going to hurt you.'

How could he hurt her any more than she had been hurt

already? As if his words had not wounded her and left her smarting. She felt the salty trickle of a tear as it meandered its way down her cheek and she sucked in a choked kind of sob. As if she were listening through a cotton-wool cloud which had dulled all her senses, she heard Guy talking to someone else. And then he was easing her head back and dabbing at her damp temples with some deliciously cool cloth.

She opened her eyes with difficulty, startled by the flickering gleam of concern which had briefly softened the hard eyes. 'I'm OK.'

'You are not OK,' he contradicted her, crouching down so that his face was on a level with hers. 'Do you want me to take you home?'

In this state? Why, her mother would start fretting about her—and hadn't she had enough to worry about over the last few months? 'Can we wait here for a little bit?' she asked weakly.

Guy made a slow, glittering appraisal of all the curious faces that were turned in their direction and frowned. 'Or somewhere less public? There are rooms upstairs. Why don't I see if we can use one—at least until you recover.'

Sabrina stared at him in undisguised horror. Surely he didn't imagine for a moment that…that…

'Oh, I see.' Guy gave a low, hollow laugh. 'Is that what you think of me, Sabrina?' he questioned. 'So governed by my libido that I'd take any opportunity to pounce on the nearest woman, even though she's only half-conscious?'

'I didn't say that.'

'No, you didn't have to,' he said grimly. 'The accusation was written all over your face. But don't worry, princess— that's not really my thing.'

Sabrina let her head fall back against the rest. 'I don't want to stay here.'

'You don't have to. Come on, let's go upstairs,' he said,

and his arm was strong at the small of her back as he helped her to her feet.

The temptation to just lean back and lose herself in the warm haven of his arms was overwhelming, but Sabrina feebly pushed his guiding hand away from her. Touching him in any way at all was too much like trouble.

'I can do it myself,' she said stubbornly.

He looked as if he didn't believe her, but didn't argue the point, just walked right behind her in case she stumbled and fell.

Gripping the bannister with a grim kind of determination, she was glad when they reached the top and he pushed open the door of one of the rooms.

It was as different from his suite in Venice as it could have been—clean and middle-of-the-road, with a mass of chintz and swagged fabrics—and Sabrina heaved a small sigh of relief. She certainly didn't need reminders in the way of vast, luxuriously appointed beds or priceless paintings.

She flopped down onto the flower-sprigged duvet and heaved a sigh of relief.

Guy stood beside the bed, looking down at her, his face impenetrable as a disturbing thought nagged at his conscience. 'So why the hell did you faint?'

Reproach sparked from her eyes. 'Why do *you* think I fainted, Guy? Don't you imagine that the things you accused me of would make most women feel ill?'

But he shook his head. 'Harsh words are not normally enough to make a healthy young woman pass out.' His eyes threw her a cold, challenging glitter. 'You're not pregnant by any chance, are you?'

She supposed that he had every right to ask her, but that didn't make answering any easier. Especially not when the look of abject horror on his face told her *exactly* what he would think of that particular development.

'No, I'm not.' She lifted her head. 'And please don't imply that that was something in my game plan. We took precautions, remember?'

He wished she hadn't reminded him, though maybe he only had himself to blame—he had been the one who had brought the subject up. But her defiant words only painted the most gloriously explicit picture of the way she had made the putting on of those damned condoms into some of the single most erotic moments of his life.

He forced himself to express the harsh truth. 'And precautions fail. Everyone knows that.'

Sabrina stared at him as life and energy began to warm their way around her veins once more. And anger. 'Then you should have given more thought to that *before* we made love, shouldn't you?'

'Yes,' he said bitterly. 'Maybe I should—only I wasn't thinking too straight at the time.'

'And just how would you be coping now if I told you that, yes, I *was* pregnant?'

He glittered her a chilly look. 'I'm in the fortunate position of being able to support a child—'

'Financially, you mean?' she challenged. 'Certainly not emotionally, by the sound of it.'

'Anyway, you're not pregnant, are you, Sabrina?' he snapped. 'So it's academic!'

But the nagging and worrying thought was that she *could* have allowed herself to get pregnant, and then never seen him again. Because Guy was right. Precautions *did* fail. Yet falling pregnant had been the very last thing on her mind. 'Maybe we both acted like the world's two biggest fools!'

He didn't agree with her blurted declaration, just continued to subject her to a cool, steady scrutiny. 'So, if pregnancy is not the reason for you fainting, what else could it be? Have you been eating properly?'

'I…yes…no,' she admitted eventually. 'Not really.'

'For how long?' he clipped out.

'It's obvious, isn't it? Since Michael died, I guess.'

Guy felt the flicker of a muscle at his cheek, unprepared for the sharp kick of unreasonable jealousy. So the fiancé had had a name, had he? 'And how long ago was that?'

There was no way to answer other than truthfully, but mentally Sabrina prepared herself for his disapproval. 'Four months,' she told him baldly.

There was silence. 'Four months?' he said heavily, as though he must have misheard her.

She didn't look away. 'That's right. I expect I've shocked you,' she said. 'Haven't I?'

He gave a bitter laugh. 'One way and another, I've done a pretty good job of shocking myself lately.' Four *months*? His mouth hardened. It threw what had happened into a completely different perspective. He had wondered about her spectacular and uninhibited response in his arms.

So had he just been a substitute for the man who had died? A warm, living body filling her and reminding her of what life should be?

'You didn't waste much time, did you?' he said flatly.

'And here comes the condemnation,' she said in a low voice.

'It was an observation.' He walked over to study an unimaginative little hunting print and resisted the temptation to punch his fist against the flowered wallpaper. When he turned around to face her, Sabrina could see the fire and the fury that sparked from his eyes. 'Why the hell didn't you tell me about it before?'

She bit her lip, willing her eyes not to fill with tears. 'Why do you think?' she said tremulously, before she had had time to think it through.

Guy stilled, his eyes narrowing perceptively. 'Because I

wouldn't have made love to you,' he said slowly. 'Because even if it had killed me—' and he suspected that it might have gone some way towards doing that '—there is no way that I would have taken a vulnerable woman to bed and seduced her over and over again! But you wanted me badly, didn't you, Sabrina?' he concluded arrogantly. 'So much that you weren't prepared to risk not getting what you wanted! *That's* why you didn't tell me!'

Sabrina shook her head, and it felt as though it were filled with lead. 'You wanted it, too.' She bit her lip guiltily. 'You make me sound passive—and I wasn't. We both know that. We both wanted it…'

'Badly,' he put in softly, seeing the answering colour which flooded her cheeks. 'Very, very badly. Yes, we did.' He shook his head in a gesture which was the closest he had ever come to confusion. 'The question is *why* we both wanted it— so much that it drove reason and sane behaviour clean away.'

'We were sexually attracted,' she said shakily. But it had been much more than that. She forced herself to forget the warm glow of recognition she had experienced the very first time she had set eyes on him. As if she had known him all her life. Or longer. She stared at his handsome face and tried to sound coolly logical. 'I'm sure that kind of thing happens to you all the time, Guy.'

He shook his head in anger. 'But that's just the point, dammit—it doesn't! Oh…' He shrugged as he saw her disbelieving face. 'Women come on to me all the time, sure…'

Sabrina's smile turned into a grimace, wondering if he had any idea how much he had just insulted her.

'But usually it leaves me cold,' he reflected thoughtfully. 'I haven't had casual sex since I was a teenager.' And never like that, he thought achingly. Never like that.

Sabrina flinched. '*I* don't remember coming on to *you*,' she objected, but more out of a sense of pride than conviction. 'I thought it was *you* coming on to *me*!'

He threw her a look of mocking query. 'It was pretty mutual, Sabrina. You're not going to deny that, are you?'

No, she wasn't going to deny it. She looked down at her lap, as if the knotted fingers lying there would provide some kind of inspiration.

'I'm still waiting for an answer, princess.'

The resolve which had deepened his voice made Sabrina frown at him in alarm. 'That sounded like a threat!'

He shook his head. 'Of course it isn't a threat,' he said patiently. 'But surely you aren't deluding yourself that we don't need to talk about what happened.'

She bit her trembling lip. 'C-can't we just call it history, and forget it ever happened?' she croaked.

'No,' he said flatly. 'Of course we can't. I think you owe me some sort of explanation, Sabrina.'

'I owe you nothing!'

He wanted to know. He *needed* to. 'Why did you run away the next morning?'

'Why do you think?' She shuddered as she remembered waking up all warm and replete in his bed. 'Because I realised what I had done! And it was never going to be any more than a one-night stand, was it, Guy? Besides, you lied to me—so how could I trust you?'

'And wouldn't it have been more sensible to have thought all this through before it actually happened?' he demanded. 'I didn't drag you back there with me! You weren't drunk!'

His condemnation was like a slap in the face and Sabrina flinched beneath his accusing stare.

'So what was I?' he demanded. 'A substitute? Did you close your eyes and pretend it was Michael?' He ignored her look of pain, remorselessly grinding the words out. 'Any man would have done for you, wouldn't he, Sabrina? I just happened to come along and press the right buttons.'

She met the dark, accusing fire in his eyes. 'You honestly think that?'

'I don't know what to think. It's not a situation I've ever found myself in before. Thank God.' His gaze narrowed into a piercing grey laser, and then he saw her white, bewildered face and felt a sudden slap of conscience. 'You look terrible,' he said bluntly.

'Thanks.' She sat up a bit and sucked in a breath. 'I'm feeling a bit better, actually.'

'Well, you don't look it. 'I'm going to ring down for some soup for you. You can't go home in that state.'

'Guy, no—'

'Guy, *yes*,' he countered, reaching out to pick up the phone, completely overriding her objections.

Soup and sandwiches arrived with the kind of speed which suggested to Sabrina that he might have already ordered them. Had that been the muffled conversation with the landlord she had overheard?

She told herself that she felt too weak to face food, but the stern look on his dark face warned her that if she refused to eat, he didn't look averse to picking up the spoon and actually feeding her!

Guy sat and watched her. The thick broth sent steam over her pale features, but gradually, as the bowl emptied, some of the roses began to creep back into her cheeks. He saw her half-heartedly bite into a sandwich and then look at it with something approaching awakening—as if she had only just learnt how good food could taste when you were hungry.

Sabrina wiped at her lips with a napkin and sighed, aware of the glittering grey eyes which were following her movements with a steely kind of fascination. He hadn't, she realised, eaten a single thing—he'd just sat there and watched her like a hawk.

She flicked him a questioning look. 'You're not hungry?'

'No, I'm not hungry,' he said flatly. 'And I think it's time I got you home.'

She shook her head. He was too potent a presence, who had demonstrated the depth of his contempt for her. She didn't want him invading any more of her space. She didn't need any more aching reminders of just how devastating he really was.

She had blown it with Guy Masters by being too greedy. She should have given him her telephone number and gone back to her own hotel that night.

But nothing could change the fact that she had been desperate for him, driven on by an unrecognisable hunger she'd been unable to control.

Well, it was too late now. What man wouldn't be filled with contempt at what she had allowed to happen, and so soon?

'Why don't you just call me a cab?' she said tiredly. 'I don't need you to come with me.'

'I'm taking you home,' he said firmly. He saw her open her mouth and shook his head with the kind of dominance that brooked no argument. 'Oh, no, Sabrina,' he said softly. 'This has nothing to do with independence, or pride. You're in no state to go home on your own—'

'Yes, I am!' she protested.

'You are not,' he contradicted impatiently. 'And you can sit there arguing with me all night long, but it won't change a thing. I'm not budging on this—I'm taking you home.'

But her ice-blue eyes looked so helpless as she stared up at him that he found himself unable to resist the temptation to brush a stray strand of hair away from her cheek, feeling its warm tremble beneath his fingertip.

His grey gaze burned into her and for one heart-stopping moment she thought that he had relented. She saw the sudden, impulsive softening of his mouth and the way that his eyes had now brightened to glittering jet and thought that he was about to kiss her.

But all he did was open the door. 'Come on,' he said abruptly. 'Time we were out of here.'

He made her sit down while he went to settle up with the landlord, gently placing her against some cushions as if she really *were* pregnant. And Sabrina bit her lip as an inexplicable yearning to carry his black-haired baby washed over her.

Outside the pub was no ordinary taxi—somehow he had managed to magic up a long, low limousine from somewhere. Sabrina registered the gleaming bodywork with a disbelieving blink as Guy opened the door of the car. She supposed that Salisbury did *have* vehicles like this for hire—it was just that she had never encountered them before. Not in her world.

'Here, put this on,' he said, as he slid into the back seat beside her and buckled up her seat belt, still playing the guardian angel.

'Where are we going?' asked the driver.

'Wilton Street,' she responded quietly.

The driver half turned in his seat and shot a quick look in Guy's direction. 'Wilton Street?' he asked in surprise. 'Are you sure?'

'Of course she's sure!' snapped Guy, and flicked shut the glass partition, immediately distracted by the sweet perfume of her hair.

Sabrina felt the bitter ache of emptiness as the huge car negotiated its way into a tiny road, where the houses were small and boxy, each one looking exactly the same. She stole a glance at the stony perfection of his profile, knowing that she would never see him again after tonight.

And maybe it was best that she didn't. They weren't just from different worlds—more like different universes.

The driver flipped the glass partition open. 'What number Wilton Street?'

'Number th-three,' she stumbled.

Guy heard the tremble in her voice as the car pulled to a halt in front of a tiny house and frowned.

'You're crying!' he exclaimed softly.

'N-no, I'm not.' She gulped, but took the crisp, white handkerchief which he offered her and buried her nose in it.

'Why are you crying? Because I spoke so harshly?'

She heard the self-recrimination which had hardened his voice and shook her head wordlessly as she tried to bring the gulping sobs under control. How could she tell him that she didn't really know why she was crying? That maybe her tears were for Michael—maybe just for herself. Or maybe she was mourning a golden relationship with Guy Masters which had been doomed from the very outset.

He waited until the shuddering of her breathing had slowed down in something approaching calm and then he got out of the car and went round to open the door for her.

'Wait here for me,' he said to the driver.

He led Sabrina up the narrow front path and rang the doorbell. Moments later the door was opened by a woman who was unmistakably Sabrina's mother. She had an amazing pair of identical ice-blue eyes and her hair was still bright—apart from the occasional touch of grey. And Guy had a sudden powerful vision of what Sabrina would look like in her fifties.

Mrs Cooper's eyes flew open in alarm as she saw her daughter's pale and tear-stained face. 'Sabrina, darling!' she exclaimed. 'Whatever is it?' She looked up at the tall, dark man who was supporting her. 'Who are you? What's happened to her?'

'Nothing at all has happened to harm her.' Guy injected calm into his voice as Sabrina shook off his restraining hand

and sat down abruptly at the foot of the staircase. 'She's a little upset,' he said. 'Although I suppose that's understandable, under the circumstances.'

Mrs Cooper nodded. 'So she's told you about Michael?'

Again Guy felt the sharp spear of unreasonable jealousy. 'Yes, she has.'

Sabrina wondered why they were talking about her as if she wasn't there. Or why her mother was staring up at Guy with trust rather than suspicion.

'My name is Guy Masters,' he said. 'Sabrina and I met in Venice.' He took a business card from his coat pocket and gave it to her. 'Will you give this to your daughter in the morning?' he said, moving to the staircase and bending his head down so that it was almost touching Sabrina's.

'Ring me if you need to talk,' he said grimly.

And then he was gone and the hall seemed suddenly so empty—so lacking in the strength and vitality generated by that dark, mocking face and that beautiful, strong body.

Mrs Cooper shut the door behind him, and turned to her daughter. 'Are you going to tell me what happened, darling?'

Sabrina shook her head wearily. 'It's too complicated to explain. I'm OK now.'

'Are you sure?'

Sabrina nodded, and slowly rose to her feet. 'Positive.'

Mrs Cooper cocked her head in the direction of the front door. 'He seems very considerate, dear,' she commented curiously, 'your Mr Guy Masters. Are you going to ring him?'

'No.' But Sabrina actually managed a wan smile. *Considerate?* She could think of about a hundred adjectives which would describe Guy Masters.

And considerate wouldn't even make the list.

CHAPTER SEVEN

RING me if you need to talk. Those had been Guy's last words to her a week or so ago.

Sabrina opened her eyes and stared at the blank white space of the ceiling. What woman would want to admit to being needy? And what could she possibly say if she picked the phone up to ring him? *Hello, Guy, it's me, Sabrina. Remember me? I'm the woman you had the one-night stand with in Venice?*

And then what?

No. There was no point in ringing him. No point in anything really, other than trying to get through each day the best way she could.

'Sabrina?'

Sabrina turned over and yawned as she focussed her eyes on the clock on the locker. Nearly ten o'clock. She loved her Sunday morning lie-ins. 'Yes, Mum?'

'You've got—' there was a rather odd note in her mother's voice as she called up the stairs, Sabrina thought '—a *visitor*, dear!'

Some sixth sense warned her. Sabrina sat bolt upright in bed, her baggy Minnie Mouse nightshirt almost swamping her.

'Who is it?' she demanded hoarsely.

'It's Guy,' called her mother.

Her heart did a somersault. 'Guy M-Masters?'

'Why, how many others do you know?' came a shockingly familiar voice.

'I'm still in bed!' she shouted down, feeling the shiver of nerves beginning to trace chaotic pathways over her skin. There was a split-second pause, and then a sardonic reply.

'Don't worry. I'll wait.'

She told herself that there was no way of getting out of seeing him, even if she'd wanted to. And that was the most disturbing thing of all.

She didn't want to.

Sabrina felt the powerful acceleration of her heart as she quickly showered and dressed.

Instinct told her not to go over the top with her choice of clothes, while pride nagged at her to make *some* sort of effort. If he was simply calling by to check on her welfare—then she refused to have him wondering what he had ever seen in her.

But she was actually shaking as she dressed—in a warm woollen dress which she'd bought at the market, its ice-blue colour matching her eyes exactly. And her knee-high leather boots—absolutely ancient now, but lovingly polished and cared for, so that they had entirely justified their original high price-tag.

Sabrina went downstairs, expecting—no, *hoping*—to feel nothing for him. But she wondered who she had been trying to fool, because the moment she walked into the sitting room and saw him she was incapacitated by his sheer physical beauty.

He looked, she thought with a sharp edge of despair, absolutely wonderful—as wonderful as the first time she had seen him. He was wearing a pair of faded jeans which clung to every millimetre of the longest, most muscular legs she had ever seen. The denim emphasised the jut of his hips and the flat planes of his stomach. And he was wearing a beautiful cashmere sweater in a shade of grey just darker than his eyes. A dark jacket lay heaped over a chair.

There was nothing she could do to stop the primitive leap of pleasure in her heart. But at least she could keep it from showing. 'Hello, Guy,' she said calmly.

He thought how fine and how translucent her skin was—so fine that you could quite clearly see the shadowed definition of her amazing cheekbones. He had not meant to come here today—he had been waiting for a phone call which had never materialised. He had expected her to ring, the way women always did. And he had been unable to get her out of his mind. Out of a determination to forget her had grown a need to know that she was OK. Well, she certainly *looked* OK. More than OK.

'Hello, Sabrina,' he said slowly. 'How are you feeling?'

'Better,' she told him truthfully. 'Much better.'

They stared at one another, like two people meeting for the first time. Well, maybe not quite like that, thought Sabrina. She knew too much about him to ever be like that. The top button of his shirt was open to reveal the tiniest jagged scar which ran alongside his Adam's apple. A scar she distinctly remembered running the tip of her tongue along, so that his big body had writhed with a kind of reluctant pleasure.

'Would you like coffee, or something?'

He looked at the luscious tremble of her lips and the ice-blue dazzle of her eyes. 'No, I'll tell you what I'd really like,' he said slowly.

It was so like something he had murmured at the most intimate point of their lovemaking that Sabrina felt her cheeks begin to burn.

'I've got the car outside,' he said evenly. I thought maybe you could show me something of the city. I'll park close to the centre, and we can walk.'

Sabrina looked around her, at her sweet mother who could never be accused of being uptight. But the house was small, no, tiny, and it would be impossible to do anything other than stumble out pleasantries that neither of them meant.

'I'll go and get my coat,' she said.

'Wrap up warmly, Sabrina,' said her mother. 'It may be sunny outside, but it's bitterly cold in that wind.'

Guy helped her on with the coat, which had a collar of fake fur. Her hair was loose and spilled into the fur, giving her a faintly glamorous appearance, he thought.

His fingers brushed lightly over her shoulders and he felt the dark lickings of temptation scramble at his senses. He remembered how translucent her skin had been, and that his tongue had followed the fine blue tracery of the veins which laced her tiny breasts.

She looked at him, a question darkening the blue of her eyes. 'Where's the car?'

'It's a little way along the street.' He omitted to say that the street was way too narrow for such a powerful car.

'Not the limousine, I hope?' she asked faintly.

He heard the trace of mockery, and gave a wry smile. So she wasn't particularly impressed by status symbols. 'No, not the limousine.' They began to walk up the road together. 'The landlord of the pub ordered that car, not me. He obviously took one look at me and made an assumption about what my requirements were. I wasn't intending to make quite such a statement,' he added drily.

'Well, you did,' Sabrina remarked as they drew alongside a more sedate, but equally luxurious car. 'My mother said that all week the neighbours have been dying to know who the visitor was.'

He paused in the act of unlocking the door, his grey gaze steady and imperturbable. 'And what did you tell them?'

She managed to return his look, though it wasn't easy—

not when it took her mind back to how she had seen it when he'd been in her arms. Stripped of all pretence, darkened and glazed with…lust, she reminded herself painfully. That was all it had been. Lust.

'I said that you were…' She hesitated and now the gaze became laser-sharp, lancing through her. 'A friend.'

His mouth twisted into a cool smile as he held the door open for her. 'A friend?' he mocked.

'What should I have said, then? A lover?'

'That certainly would have been more accurate, wouldn't it?'

'I don't think so, Guy. It's in the past tense now.'

She slid her legs into the car. Actually, she had wanted to say 'acquaintance', because that had seemed more accurate than 'friend', though it hadn't really seemed appropriate either—not in view of what had happened. 'Acquaintance' implied that you didn't know somebody terribly well, and yet she knew Guy Masters exceedingly well. Sabrina swallowed. In certain respects, anyway.

She kept her eyes fixed straight ahead while he drove into the city and parked. And in the dim, ugly light of the concrete car park he looked down at her.

'You haven't asked me why I'm here,' he said suddenly.

'Maybe I'm afraid of what your answer will be.' She lifted her shoulders a little. 'Why *are* you here?'

'That's just it.' He gave a short laugh and shook his head as he locked the car doors. 'I don't know!'

With a chill wind blowing in their faces, they walked right into the centre of the city, with the cathedral spire dominating the skyline and drawing them in like a magnet.

'Want to go inside?' she asked softly.

He glittered her a dark smile. 'You know I do.'

Yes, she had known that, just as she instinctively knew that he didn't want a guided tour, not today. The stiff set of his shoulders said, *Stay away*, quite clearly.

So she walked around the huge empty cathedral with him, quickly turning away when he paused to stare up at the altar and an indescribable sadness seemed to harden his beautiful face into stone.

And that was grief, she recognised painfully, a grief too bitter to intrude into.

Outside, the wind whipped her hair into ribbons which curled over her cheeks and Guy found his fingers itching to brush them away.

'I'll drive you home,' he said abruptly.

She felt the sinking sensation of disappointment. 'OK,' she agreed.

But as he drew up at the end of her street he made no move, taking the key out of the ignition and turning to look at her.

'So what happened?' he asked quietly. 'To Michael?' he persisted softly. 'How did he die?'

There was silence.

'It was a car crash,' she said eventually. 'He wanted to go out for the evening, and I didn't. We were supposed to be saving up. He tried to change my mind, but I wouldn't. He…' This bit was hard, but she forced herself to continue. 'He said that I was a control freak.'

His eyes narrowed with interest. 'A control freak?' he echoed softly. 'Is that so?'

She supposed that he didn't believe her, and how could she blame him? She hadn't exactly behaved like that around him, had she? 'Well, that's the most peculiar thing—I *do* like to be in control, yes. Normally.'

'And so do I,' he said, his voice as bitter as the recrimination in his eyes. 'Perhaps we just bring out the worst in each other.'

And the best, she thought suddenly. The very best.

'We had a row,' she remembered, her voice slowing painfully. 'A blazing row. And Michael got angry and he stormed out, and…and…that's when he crashed. He was killed instantly.'

Guy nodded, his grey eyes narrowing perceptively. 'Oh, I see,' he said slowly. 'So you carry all the guilt, as well as the grief, do you, Sabrina?'

'If only I hadn't been so rigid,' she said bitterly. 'If I'd gone with him then it might not have happened.'

'And it just might. That's a pretty heavy burden to carry, you know, Sabrina. What with that and our little fling you could soon find that feeling guilty becomes too much of a habit.'

She unclipped her seat belt angrily. 'I don't have to stay here and listen to—'

'The truth?' he drawled, and something in the way he said it stopped her in her tracks.

'Do you think I feel good about myself?' she demanded. 'Letting a man who was virtually a stranger make love to me, and so soon—'

And so thoroughly, he thought longingly. 'Yeah, yeah, yeah,' he interrupted coolly. 'I thought we'd already done the regret trip, Sabrina.'

'*We?*' she queried. 'You mean you feel bad about what happened, too?'

'What do *you* think?'

Sabrina looked down at her lap. So now she knew.

'I don't know anything about you,' she realised aloud, but he shook his head.

'Oh, yes, you do,' he said softly. 'You haven't seen my flat, or met my family, or seen where I work—but none of that is important. You've seen me at my most—' He bit the word out as if he didn't like it very much. 'Exposed.'

'Like every woman you've been to bed with, you mean?'

He shook his head. 'That night was something outside my

experience. Like you, Sabrina, I like to be in control—and on that occasion I most definitely wasn't.'

'Guy,' she said suddenly, and something in the way she said it made his eyes narrow.

'What?'

'Who were you thinking about—back there in the cathedral?'

He stilled. Usually he would have blanked such an intrusive question, but hadn't he just been asking her questions just like that?

'I was thinking about my father,' he said slowly, feeling her suck the admission from him. 'He died a long time ago,' he said, and then his face hardened. 'But we're not here to talk about me, are we?'

'Apparently not.' She shrugged listlessly.

'What you need to face up to now is that it *happened*! Everything. Michael died and we made love all night long, and however much you might want to unwish that—you can't. Fact. End of story. The important question is where do you go from here?'

'I don't know,' she admitted brokenly.

His mouth tightened as he saw the dark shadows thrown onto her pale skin by her sharpened cheekbones. 'I'm taking you out to lunch,' he said grimly.

She shook her head, more tempted than she should have been. 'I can't. I usually have lunch with my mother on Sundays.'

'Then bring her along.'

'Are you sure?'

'Why not? She eats lunch, doesn't she?'

Sabrina nodded, surprised and pleased. Michael wouldn't have dreamed of issuing such an invitation—he'd seen parents as nothing but authority figures, just hell-bent on stopping you enjoying yourself. 'I'm sure she'd be delighted,' she said truthfully.

'Then let's go and find her,' he said, still in that same grim voice.

Sabrina's mother was as pleased by the invitation as her daughter had anticipated, especially when Guy chose a restaurant on the very edge of the city, one which neither of the two women had ever visited before.

'Oh, we couldn't possibly—it's much too expensive!' protested Mrs Cooper.

'No, it's not,' said Guy patiently.

'And we'll never get a table,' put in Sabrina.

The grey eyes glittered. 'Want to bet?'

And of course he got a table—how could she have ever doubted for a moment that he wouldn't? Men like Guy Masters always got tables.

Sabrina tried very hard to eat her shrimp salad and lobster with some element of appetite, but it was unbelievably difficult to concentrate on the food when there was such a distraction on the other side of the table.

Her eyes kept straying to the dark gleam of Guy's hair as he sat and chatted to her mother. The top two buttons of his shirt were undone and she could just see the faint shadowing where the dark hair began.

She wiped a damp palm over the napkin which lay on her lap. What on earth would her mother say if she had any idea that the man who was chatting to her so companionably had ravished her daughter more than she'd believed it possible for a woman to be ravished.

Guy studied her from over his wineglass, suddenly registering her tense silence. 'You're very quiet, Sabrina,' he observed.

'Oh, she's quiet like that a lot of the time,' said Mrs Cooper. 'Can't seem to snap out of it, can you, darling?'

'I don't think Guy particularly wants to hear, Mum,' said Sabrina warningly.

But Mrs Cooper was only just warming to her subject. 'I'm dreadfully sorry that Michael is dead—of course I am— and it's hit her very hard, as you would expect.'

Sabrina didn't dare meet Guy's eyes for fear of the derision she might find there. Grief-stricken people didn't tend to behave in the way she had behaved.

'I know what it's like myself,' said Mrs Cooper, and she reached over and patted Sabrina's head. 'After my husband left me, people always saw me just as a divorcee—not as Maureen Cooper in her own right.'

Guy nodded. So Sabrina had no father either.

'No one will give the poor girl a chance to get over it. And the trouble is that this is where she grew up. Everyone knows her, and everyone knew Michael—and she can't escape from their memories. I think she should get out and have a little fun. That's why I persuaded her to go to Venice—she'd always wanted to go there—but when she came back she looked worse than ever.'

'Have you quite finished, Mum?'

'Can't you get away somewhere?' queried Guy thoughtfully.

'Like where?' She met the stormy challenge of his gaze. She had tried fleeing to Venice and look where *that* had got her.

'How about London? That's where most people want to go.'

'London's expensive,' said Sabrina defensively. 'And I don't earn very much. And, besides, I don't really feel like going into a city where I don't know anyone.'

'But you know me, Sabrina,' came the surprising response.

She violently began spearing at a piece of lobster.

'You know you can always come and stay with me.' He'd spoken the words aloud before he'd realised their implication.

For a second Sabrina froze, and then slowly lifted her head to gaze at him in disbelief. 'What did you say?' she whispered.

'I have a flat,' he said. 'A big flat—plenty big enough to accommodate another person. Come and use the spare room for a while.'

She thought of sharing a flat with him, even temporarily, and her heart began to bang against her ribcage—until she forced herself to quash the hopeless dream and replace it with reality. 'It's a crazy idea,' she said woodenly. 'I don't have a job to go to.'

'So find one.' He shrugged.

'It isn't as easy as that, Guy,' said Mrs Cooper gently.

Sabrina found herself thinking that Wells did have another branch, in the capital, but loyally she found herself confirming her mother's words. 'No, it isn't.'

Guy stirred his coffee, as if he didn't really care, and Mrs Cooper got up from the table and beamed. 'Will you excuse me for a minute?'

Guy rose to his feet until Mrs Cooper had disappeared, and Sabrina thought what impeccable manners he had. She stared across the table at him as he sat back down. 'It's very…kind of you, Guy, but you know very well I can't accept your offer.'

He coolly returned her stare. 'Do I?'

She narrowed her eyes in frustration. 'Don't be so obtuse.'

'Then don't be so damned evasive—and come right out with what it is you want to say!'

Surely he wasn't really expecting her to say it out loud. But, from his unhelpful silence, he clearly was. Reminding herself that they had already been as intimate as any couple could be, Sabrina drew in a deep breath.

'How could I come and stay with you, not knowing—' she met his gaze without flinching '—whether we…we…'

'Oh, for God's sake!' he snapped, as the meaning of her words became clear to him. 'Do you really think that I'm about to start extracting rent in the form of sexual favours?'

'That wasn't what I said!'

'That's what you meant, though—isn't it?'

She shook her head, but without conviction.

He leaned back in his chair and looked at her speculatively. 'You told me you like to be in control, didn't you? Is that why you're afraid to come? Afraid that you'll lose it again around me? Scared to risk it?'

She met the challenge in his eyes. 'Do you think you're so irresistible?'

'I don't know. Maybe that's something we should both find out. Maybe we both need this opportunity to redeem ourselves.'

She stared at him in confusion. 'Redeem ourselves?'

'Sure. This is the perfect opportunity to demonstrate that we're not completely ruled by our hormones—'

'That's a very nice way to put it!'

'Sabrina, there isn't,' he told her bluntly, 'a *nice* way to put it.'

'So you're saying that the relationship will be platonic?'

'No, that's not what I'm saying at all,' he countered. 'I'm not promising anything.'

Sabrina began to get a glimmering of understanding about what he meant. Put two people who were sexually attracted to each other in a flat, and in the end it all came down to who cracked first. And who didn't. Control, that was what this was all about. Power and control. But she said nothing more as her mother had begun to walk back towards the table.

Nothing more was said on the subject during the drive back to her house, and Sabrina felt an unwilling sense of emptiness as Guy said goodbye to her mother, then turned to her, his enigmatic grey eyes glittering darkly.

'Goodbye, Sabrina.'

'Goodbye, Guy. Thanks for lunch.'

He gave a brief hard smile before climbing into his car.

Sabrina and her mother stood and watched the powerful car move away.

'You aren't going to go, are you, darling?' asked Mrs Cooper. Sabrina carried on looking, even though the tail-lights had long since disappeared.

'I don't know, Mum,' she said honestly. 'I just don't know.'

CHAPTER EIGHT

SABRINA'S pulse was hammering as she punched out the number, and it hammered even more when the connection was made and a rich, deep voice said, 'Guy Masters.'

She opened her mouth but no words emerged.

The voice sounded impatient now. 'Guy Masters,' he repeated irritatedly.

'Guy. It's me—Sabrina.'

There was a two-second pause which seemed like an eternity.

'Sabrina Cooper,' she rushed on. 'Remember? We met—'

'Yes, of course I remember you, Sabrina. How are you?'

For a moment she was tempted to hang up and forget the whole stupid idea, but she had spent the last few weeks changing her life around. She couldn't back out now.

'I've managed to get a transfer!' she said, and then, in case he had completely forgotten his proposal, rushed on, 'To the London branch of Wells. They've said I can work there for six weeks. The bookshop,' she added, just in case he had forgotten *that*.

'Oh.' There was a pause. 'Good. So, when are you coming to stay?'

He *did* remember. Thank God. 'I can start first thing on Monday.' Sabrina crossed the fingers of her left hand and pulled a ghastly grimace at herself in the mirror. 'If it's all right with you, I thought I'd come on Sunday afternoon.'

'*This* Sunday?'

'If that's a problem—'

'No.' The deep voice sounded thoughtful. 'No, that shouldn't be a problem.'

She thought he might make the effort to sound a little more convincing. Or pleased about it. 'Are you sure?'

'Have you got a pen?' he asked tersely. 'I'll give you directions how to get here.'

She scribbled down his home address, instantly noting that it was in Knightsbridge. So she would be staying in one of London's most affluent areas.

'What time will we see you?'

'We?' she questioned, feeling suddenly frozen by nerves.

'I'm having a few friends for brunch—but they'll probably have gone by teatime.'

'Then I'll come at teatime,' she promised hoarsely.

She struggled onto the train on Sunday with her two suitcases and then onto the tube, where she had to stand for the entire journey because it seemed that the whole world and his brother were heading for Knightsbridge and the museums.

So by the time she reached the outrageously exclusive address which Guy had given her she felt as grimy and bedraggled as a cat which had been left out in the rain all night.

His flat was situated in a quiet square, several streets back from the main thoroughfare of Knightsbridge. In the centre of the square was a gated garden, and Sabrina put her suitcases down and peered in through the railings.

Beneath the trees, daffodils waved their sun-yellow trumpets, and she could hear the sound of birdsong. And despite her misgivings, Sabrina felt a sudden sense of freedom. Picking up her cases with a renewed determination, she walked up the steps of the house, rang the doorbell and waited.

Sabrina glanced down at her watch as she waited. Four-thirty. Most people's idea of teatime, surely? What if the unthinkable had happened and Guy had forgotten that she was coming? What would she do if he wasn't in?

She lifted her finger to the doorbell once more and just at that moment the door opened and there stood Guy. She swallowed down the lump which had risen in her throat.

His dark hair was ruffled, and he wore an old pair of jeans with the top two buttons left undone, revealing a provocative downward arrowing of dark hair. He had clearly just dragged on a black T-shirt which clung to every perfectly defined muscle of his chest. He looked, Sabrina thought with a sudden stab of anxiety, as if he'd just got out of bed.

His eyes narrowed with an unmistakable look of surprise as he stared down at her, and then he said, very steadily, 'Sabrina!'

Her heart thumped faster. 'You *had* forgotten I was coming.'

He didn't miss a beat. 'Of course I hadn't forgotten.' He stole a glance at his watch, which gleamed gold against the faint blur of hair on his wrist, and frowned. Hell, was *that* the time? 'It's later than I thought. Come on in. Let me take your cases. We're just finishing brunch.'

'At this time?'

'Why not?' he said softly. 'It's Sunday. No deadlines.'

'If you're busy I can go away and come back later,' she said, although as soon as the words were out of her mouth she realised how ridiculous they sounded—because where on earth would she go on a late spring afternoon in a city where she knew nobody?

He smiled as he took the suitcases from her, thinking how cold she looked. How she always looked as if she needed protecting. His protection. 'Don't be silly,' he said softly. 'Come on in. You look frozen.'

Well, she was shivering, yes, but that had more to do with the reality of seeing him in the glorious, living flesh. Of hearing his rich, deep voice. It had only been a few weeks, but it seemed like a whole lifetime since she had last seen him. How could she have so easily forgotten the impact he had on her—as compelling now as when she had first set eyes on him?

She followed him inside, but her nerves were jangled even further when she saw just how amazing his home was—all light and space and breathtakingly big windows.

The walls were painted in some pale, cool colour with modern paintings which might have looked out of place in a period building but looked as though they had been designed to hang just there.

He gestured towards a sweeping staircase. 'I'll show you your room in a minute. Come on up and meet the others first.'

Oh, lord, and here she was looking all grubby and windswept. And whilst Guy looked pretty ruffled himself, he managed to look extremely sexy into the bargain.

There was no time to do anything except hastily smooth down her hair, and she followed him upstairs, trying to look anywhere but at the denim which hugged his narrow hips as he walked.

She could hear the muffled notes of lazy laughter—feminine laughter—and the chinking of glasses, and a sense of apprehension washed over her, even though she forced herself to pin a smile onto her lips. They can't eat me, she told herself. They're Guy's friends.

Guy glanced down at her as he put the cases down. She looked bushed. And fragile. And yet…yet…

A pulse began a slow, heavy dance at his temple as he pushed the door open.

'Come on in and say hi. This is Sabrina,' he announced, as three faces looked up. 'Sabrina Cooper.'

The first thing that registered was that two of the three occupants of the room were female. And that one of them was a heart-stoppingly beautiful brunette who was stretched out on a huge lemon sofa, painting her toenails and wearing a lazy smile.

She had on a pair of jeans which had been carefully constructed to emphasise every curve of her delectable bottom. As did the teeny-weeny T-shirt which came to just above her smooth brown navel. So, did she, wondered Sabrina with an unsteady thump of her heart, belong to Guy?

'This is Jenna Jones.' Guy smiled.

Jenna gave a polite smile. 'Hi,' she said shortly.

The other sofa was occupied by a man who was looking at Sabrina with interest. At his feet sat the second woman, her hair twisted into a topknot, and they were both drinking champagne out of long, frosted flutes.

'And this is Tom Roberts, my cousin,' said Guy. 'Our mothers are sisters.'

Sabrina looked at Tom, trying to see any family resemblance, but she couldn't. But, then, Tom's face was neither so haughty nor so aloof as Guy's. 'Hello.'

Tom crinkled her a smile. 'Hello, Sabrina.'

'And Trudi Herley—his fiancée.'

'Come and sit down and have some champagne, Sabrina,' said Trudi. 'Have you eaten?' She pointed to the remains of what Sabrina assumed had been brunch, which lay on trays scattered in the centre of the room.

At least they seemed friendlier than Jenna, who hadn't moved and was staring at Sabrina with a decidedly moody look on her face. She looked over at Guy.

'You haven't told us about Sabrina, Guy, darling.'

'Haven't I?' For no good reason, Guy suddenly resented the implication that he *should* have done.

He poured out a flute of champagne and handed it to Sabrina, putting his hand in the small of her back and propelling her towards one of the chairs. 'Go and sit down over there.'

Feeling a little like a marionette, Sabrina obeyed, gulping nervously at the glass of bubbly as he lowered his long-legged frame into a chair opposite her.

Who *were* these people? And who was Jenna, for goodness' sake? That possessive look she was currently slanting at Guy suggested that the two of them were more than just friends. He hadn't brought *that* into the equation when he'd suggested she come and stay with him.

'So where did you two meet?' persisted Jenna.

Ice-grey eyes glittered coolly in Sabrina's direction. 'We met in Venice,' Guy said slowly, seeing her body stiffen in recollection and feeling his own slow, answering response.

Sabrina studied her glass of champagne intently, feeling as naïve as it was possible to feel. Why had she said she would come here? Because there was a part of her which had been secretly hoping that they might fall into each other's arms again? Why hadn't she considered that he had a life she knew nothing about? With other women and other friends? Who obviously were not about to welcome her with open arms. Not if Jenna's reaction was anything to go by.

'Venice?' echoed Tom, and threw him a curious look. 'When you flew over to buy that painting?'

'That's right,' said Guy succinctly, and drained his glass.

'But I thought you never mixed business and pleasure?'

'I don't,' came Guy's smooth retort. 'Not usually.'

Sabrina saw Tom raise his eyebrows in surprise.

'And what were *you* doing in Venice, Sabrina?' asked Jenna.

'I was there on holiday.'

'On your *own*?'

Sabrina saw Guy frown at the question, and something in the quality of the brief, hard look he sent her gave her the courage to be truthful. Just for once she allowed herself to focus on the pleasure of their lovemaking, instead of the guilt, and a dreamy smile curved her mouth. 'That's right,' she said softly. 'It's the most wonderful place to explore on your own—you never know what you might find there.'

Guy's eyes were arrowed in her direction, their dark glitter telling her that he shared the erotic memory.

'So where *exactly* do you live?' persisted Jenna.

'In Salisbury.'

'Really? Are you on an awayday, or something?'

'Er, not exactly…'

'Sabrina's going to be…' Guy paused, as if seeking an elusive word. 'Staying…with me for a while.'

'*Staying* here?' Jenna's mouth fell open as if he had just confessed to murder. 'You mean she's going to be *living* here?'

'Sure.' He shrugged, and gave a lazy smile. 'Why not?'

Sabrina couldn't miss the swift look of amazement that crossed Trudi's face before she narrowed her eyes, then slowly stood up and nudged Tom with her bare foot. 'Good heavens,' she said faintly. 'Right. Time we were going, I think. Thank goodness Jenna is driving, and not me! Come on, Jen!'

Sabrina drew a deep breath and raised her head, her gaze drawn to the unfathomable grey of Guy's eyes, knowing that she needed to get out of there. Because if Jenna *did* belong to Guy, then she couldn't bear to endure a tender farewell scene between the two of them.

'Could you show me where I'll be sleeping, please, Guy?'

'Would that be the main bedroom, Guy?' Jenna smiled spikily. 'Or the junk room you call the spare?'

There was a brief, frozen silence and then Guy stood up, his mouth tightening with an unmistakable look of irritation.

'If that was intended to embarrass Sabrina, Jenna, then you've succeeded with honours,' he said shortly. 'This way, Sabrina.'

There was a rather stunned silence as the two of them left the room. He picked up her suitcases, a thoughtful glint in his eyes as he observed her set expression.

Neither of them said a word until he threw open a door right at the end of the corridor to reveal a small room cluttered with a desk, a filing cabinet, an exercise bike and, hardly visible beneath a heap of skiing clothes, a narrow, single bed.

Sabrina turned to face him. 'You weren't expecting me,' she observed, and tried to keep the disappointment from her voice as she took in the general chaos.

He gave a half-apologetic shrug. He was letting her have the room, for heaven's sake—was she expecting red-carpet treatment into the bargain? 'I was snowed under when you rang last week, and I just didn't get around to asking my cleaning lady to sort the place out. Let me go and see the others out, and then I'll come and help you tidy up.'

'I can do it myself!'

'You don't know where to store things,' he said evenly, and walked out of the room before she had a chance to reply.

Unable to do anything until he came back, Sabrina went and stood over by the window, gazing out at the darkening sky, at the city lights which were just beginning to flicker on. She thought of how her life had changed, and was changing still, in ways she had never imagined would happen to a girl like her. And there wasn't, she realised, a single thing she could do to stop it. So, was that fate, or destiny?

She was still standing there when he returned, and as he walked into the confined space she suddenly became stupidly aware of the fact that he had now done up the top two buttons of his jeans.

And that they were alone.

'What did your friends say?' she asked him.

Guy's mouth twisted. 'Let's just say that they wanted to know more than I was prepared to tell them.'

She dreaded having to ask, but she needed to know. 'And is Jenna your…your…girlfriend?'

He stared at her in disbelief. 'You really think I'd invite another woman to stay with me, without telling her, if she was?'

'I don't know, do I? That's exactly why I'm asking!'

The challenging look was replaced by one of faint irritation. 'I tend to go for a little more communication in my relationships than that,' he said coldly.

'So you don't have one at the moment?'

'One what, princess?' he mocked.

Suddenly she was aware that they were in a bedroom, and that the space between them yawned like a great, gaping chasm. It was the antithesis of the eager way they had fallen into each other's arms back in Venice… No. She wasn't going to put herself through that kind of torture.

'Relationship,' she said doggedly.

God, but she was persistent! 'No, Sabrina,' he said deliberately. 'I do not have a relationship at the moment.'

She realised then that there was something else she needed to know, something which she really ought to have established before she'd come here.

'And won't I…' she lifted her face to his '…cramp your style?'

He looked down at her, momentarily disorientated by that fierce little look of pride. He frowned. 'What are you talking about?'

Her heart was in her mouth as she said it, but she managed to keep her voice steady. 'Well, if you haven't got a relationship, then presumably you're in the market for one—'

'Why, is that an offer?' he questioned silkily, but the surge of blood to his loins made him wish he could take the question back again.

'It most certainly is not!'

'Pity. Actually, I'm *not* "in the market" for a relationship, as you so delightfully put it.'

Was that a note of warning colouring his tone? A polite but efficient way of telling her not to start concocting any little fantasies of her own?

'You might meet someone else,' Sabrina rushed on. 'And prospective girlfriends might be put off by the presence of another woman. Particularly one with whom…whom…'

'With whom I've already had a relationship?' he challenged coolly.

She felt oddly defiant. 'Do you really think that what we had could be called a relationship, Guy?'

'Well, how would *you* like to describe it?' he mused.

As the most wonderful night of her life, that was how *she* would describe it, but tell Guy that and she would see his gorgeous face freeze with fastidious horror. Men judged events differently. A little light passion. No, scrub that. Very heavy passion.

'Things just got out of hand,' she said, trying not to think about the way he'd smiled a secret kind of smile as he'd bent his dark head to kiss her. 'That's all.

As a blow to his sexual pride, it was quite the most exquisite thrust, and Guy very nearly smiled. But not quite. 'They sure did,' he agreed in a sultry murmur, watching with dark interest as the nipples of her tiny breasts sprang into glorious life beneath the sweater she wore. Almost as if they were reaching out to touch him.

He leaned over the bed and scooped up an armful of ski clothes. 'I'll pack these away,' he groaned. 'And then I'll think about throwing together some supper.'

Guy's idea of 'throwing together some supper' was not what Sabrina understood by the term. For a start, the contents of his fridge could have kept the most dedicated hedonist going for at least a week. Sabrina could see fancy chocolates, champagne and enough different cheeses to stock a delicatessen.

'Do you like smoked salmon?' he asked.

'Er, love it.'

He looked up at her, and frowned. 'Well, do you or don't you?'

'I said yes, didn't I?'

'You sounded unsure.' He gave a little click of irritation. 'Look, Sabrina, let's just get a couple of things straight, shall we? I don't want you agreeing with me for the sake of it—just because it's my flat.'

'OK,' she agreed. 'And while we're on the subject of house rules—'

'Rules?' he interrupted, with a sardonic elevation of his dark brows. 'Goodness me, how very schoolmistressy of you! Are we talking firm and unbending rules, I wonder, or very, very *flexible* ones?'

Sabrina felt a mixture of fury and frustration as she stared into eyes which mocked her. He could stop that right now! 'Oh, do, please, spare me the innuendo!' she snapped.

Guy gave a reluctant smile. Had he actually been worried that all the fire had gone out of her? Not all of it, no. 'OK,' he said slowly.

'I meant rules about things like paying you rent—'

'The rent doesn't matter.'

'It *does* matter,' said Sabrina stubbornly. 'I can't stay here for nothing—and before you tell me that you can afford it—'

'You know very well I can—'

'That's not the point.'

'Then just what is the point?' said Guy steadily, hooking his thumbs into the waistband of his jeans.

The movement distracted her, and suddenly she found his proximity disburbing. More than disturbing. Had she really thought that she would just be able to ignore that blatant sex appeal? 'I'd just like to make a contribution while I'm here.'

Their eyes met.

'Oh?' questioned Guy softly.

She saw the swift darkening of his eyes. 'I'll contribute food,' she told him shakily.

'Food?' Guy queried dazedly.

'Towards the running of the household,' she elaborated.

'Yeah,' he agreed distractedly. 'Whatever you say, Sabrina.'

CHAPTER NINE

SABRINA was woken by a banging on the door, and her eyes flickered open for a few dazed moments before reality clicked in from unconsciousness. Her gaze drifted upwards. A high ceiling. A beautiful flat. Guy's flat.

'Sab*rina*!'

Guy's voice!

'What is it?' she answered groggily.

'Are you awake?'

'I am now.' She yawned and picked up her wristwatch, which was lying on the locker. Six-thirty? What time did he call this? She had never been the best early morning person in the world. Still in the warm haze of sleep, she felt too lazy to be inhibited.

'Why have you woken me up?' She yawned again.

'I wondered why you weren't up. Did you set your alarm? We don't want you to be late on your first day, now, do we, Sabrina?'

That teasing little lilt set her senses fizzing. 'Of course I set my alarm! I don't have to be at work until nine!'

'That late?' he drawled. 'I'll have been at my desk for at least two hours by then.'

'I'll have a medal minted for you, Guy!'

He sounded amused. 'I'm just off now—you'd better come out while I show you how the security system works.'

Sabrina was out of bed and pulling a face at her tousled reflection in an instant. She raked a brush through the unruly locks, pulled on her dressing gown and opened the door.

He was wearing the most beautiful dark pinstriped suit with a matching waistcoat and pure silk tie. The snowy shirt emphasised the blackness of his hair, the faint tan of his skin and the almost indecent length of his legs.

Sabrina couldn't stop her heart from racing at just the sight of him—but it was with pure delight rather than desire, as if seeing Guy in the morning was the most perfect way to start a day. Even though her fingers flew automatically to her chest to clutch together the gaping blue satin of the robe.

Guy didn't miss the movement, nor the tantalising glimpse of pale breast it obscured. He swallowed. 'Let me show you how to set the alarm.'

'Right.' Sabrina tried to listen carefully to what he was saying, but it wasn't easy. It seemed bizarre, crazy, stupid—*tantalising*—for her to be standing half-naked beside him, concentrating fiercely on which numbers his fingers were punching out on the alarm system and not on the delicious lemon and musk scent which drifted from his skin.

'Now, this key,' he told her, deliberately leaning a little bit away from her, because it was more than distracting being this close to the butting little swell of her breasts as they jutted against the slippery satin of her robe, 'is for this lock here. The longer, thicker key…' Oh, God, he thought despairingly, what was she *doing* to him? 'That locks here.' He swallowed. 'Got that?'

'Could you show me again?' She had hardly heard a thing he was saying, and she wished he would just go. But the last thing she needed was for all his expensive paintings and books and furniture to suddenly 'walk'—just because she hadn't had the sense to lock up properly.

'Do you want me to write it down for you, step by step?' he questioned sarcastically.

'That won't be necessary!'

This time she listened as if her life depended on it.

'Understand now?'

'Perfectly, thank you very much.'

He shot a glance at his watch and gave a small click of irritation. 'You've made me late now. I haven't been late in years.'

'Well, you could have shown me all this last night, couldn't you?'

Yeah, he supposed he could have done—it was just that they had opened a bottle of wine during dinner and had then sat and finished it in the sitting room. Bad idea. And Sabrina had kicked her shoes off in front of the fire, perfectly innocuously, but Guy had been riveted by the sight of those spectacularly slender ankles and had found it difficult to tear his eyes away from them. He had never quite understood why the Victorians had considered the ankle such an erogenous zone, but last night the reason had suddenly hit him in a moment of pulse-hammering insight.

He usually did paperwork on Sunday evenings, but last night it had lain neglected. And now he was late.

He glowered. 'I'll be home around seven.'

She looked at him expectantly. 'Will you be eating supper? Or going out?'

He had said that he would meet up for a drink with Philip Caprice—the man who was now working for Prince Raschid—but he couldn't really leave her alone on her first full day in London, could he?

He sighed. 'No, I won't be going out.'

'Then—' she suddenly felt ridiculously and utterly *shy* '—maybe I could cook *you* supper tonight. I'll buy the food and everything—as I said, that can be my contribution towards my upkeep.'

He hid a smile, unwillingly admiring her persistence, as well as her independence. 'OK,' he agreed gravely. He suspected that she would conjure up some bland but rather noble concoction of pulses or brown rice or something. He repressed a shudder. 'I shall look forward to it.'

After her shower, Sabrina went back to her room to get dressed. At least now it looked slightly better than when she had first arrived. Guy had cleared away the clutter on the desk, and had pushed the filing cabinets back against the wall. The exercise bike had been moved from its inconvenient position located slap-bang in the middle of the room. It could do with some decent curtains, she decided suddenly, instead of those rather stark blinds.

She shook her head at herself in the mirror. She was here on a purely temporary basis—she certainly shouldn't start thinking major redecoration schemes!

She dressed in black trousers and a warm black sweater and took the tube to where the London branch of Wells was situated, close to St Paul's Cathedral.

It was an exquisite jewel of a Georgian building, set in the shadow of the mighty church. Sabrina had been there twice while negotiating her transfer and had met the man she would be working for.

Tim Reardon was the archetypal bookshop owner—tall, lean and lanky, with a fall of shiny straight hair which flopped into his eyes most of the time. He was vague, affable, quietly spoken and charmingly polite. He was single, attractive—and the very antithesis of Guy Masters.

And Sabrina could not have gone out with him if he had been the very last man on the planet.

'Come on in, Sabrina.' Tim held his hand out and gave her a friendly smile. 'I'll make us both coffee and then I'll show you the set-up.'

'Thanks.' She smiled and began to unbutton her coat.

'Where are you staying?' he asked, as he hung her coat up for her.

It still made her feel slightly awkward to acknowledge it. 'In Knightsbridge, actually.'

'*Knightsbridge?*' Tom gave her a curious look which clearly wondered how she could afford to live in such an expensive neighbourhood on her modest earnings.

'I'm staying with a...friend,' she elaborated awkwardly.

'Lucky you,' he said lightly, but to her relief, he didn't pursue it.

It was easy to slot in. The shop virtually mirrored its Salisbury counterpart, and after she and Tim had drunk their coffee they set to work, opening the post and filing away all the ordered books which had just come in.

The shop was quiet first thing in the morning, and it wasn't until just after eleven that the first Cathedral tourists began to drift in, looking for their copies of William Shakespeare and Jane Austen.

During her lunch-hour Sabrina managed to locate a supermarket and rushed round buying ingredients. Never had choosing the right thing proved as taxing. She wanted, she realised, to impress Guy.

When he arrived back home that evening, he walked in on an unfamiliar domestic scene, with smells of cooking wafting towards him and loud music blaring from the kitchen.

He moved through the flat in the direction of the noise, pausing first at the dining-room door, where the table had been very carefully laid for dinner for two.

And when he walked into the kitchen, Sabrina didn't notice that he was there, not at first. She was picking up something from the floor, her black trousers stretched tightly over the high curve of her bottom, and Guy felt his throat thicken.

'Hello, Sabrina.'

Half a lemon slid uselessly from her fingers back to the

floor as she heard the soft, rich timbre of his voice. She turned round slowly, trying to compose herself, to see him still wearing the beautiful dark suit, the slight shadowing around his chin the only outward sign that twelve hours had elapsed since she had last seen him. Oh, sweet Lord, she thought despairingly. He is *gorgeous*.

'Hi!' she said brightly. 'Good day at—'

'The office?' he put in curtly. 'Yes, fine, thanks.'

'Shall I fix you a drink? Or would you prefer to get changed first?'

His mouth tightened. 'Any minute now and you're going to offer to bring me my pipe and slippers.'

Sabrina stiffened as she heard his sarcastic tone. 'I was only trying to be friendly—'

'As opposed to coming over as a parody of a wife, you mean?'

'That was certainly not my intention,' she told him primly.

The glittering grey gaze moved around the room to see that his rather cold and clinical kitchen had suddenly come to life. 'This looks quite some feast,' he observed softly.

'Not really.' But she blushed with pleasure. 'And if you're planning to get out of your best suit, could you, please, do it now, Guy? Because dinner will be ready in precisely five minutes.'

Neglected work. Late. And now she was telling him to get changed!

Guy opened his mouth to object and then shut it again. What was the point? And she was right—he didn't want to eat in his 'best' suit, which was actually one of twenty-eight he had hanging neatly in his wardrobe. He sighed. 'Five minutes,' he echoed.

He took slightly longer than five minutes, simply because, to his intense exasperation, he realised that she had managed to turn him on. Had that been her bossiness or her presumption? he wondered achingly as he threw cold water onto his face like a man who had been burning up in the sun all day. Or maybe it had something to do with the fact that he hadn't been with a woman since that amazing night with Sabrina in Venice. Hadn't wanted to. Still didn't want anyone. Except her.

Now, that, he thought, was worrying.

The meal began badly, with Guy frowning at the heap of prawns with mayonnaise which Sabrina had heaped on a plate.

'You don't like prawns?' she asked him nervously.

'Yeah, I love them, but you really shouldn't have gone to all this trouble.'

'Oh, it was no trouble,' she lied, thinking about the beef Wellington which was currently puffing up nicely in the oven. 'Do you want to open the wine? I bought a bottle.'

He shook his head, remembering last night, the way it had loosened him up so that he had spent a heated night tossing and turning and wondering what she would do if he walked just along the corridor and silently slipped into bed beside her. 'Not for me thanks,' he answered repressively. 'You can have some, of course.'

'I'm fine, thanks.' As if she would sit there drinking her way through a bottle of wine while he looked down that haughty and patrician nose of his.

Guy saw the beef Wellington being carried in on an ornate silver platter he'd forgotten he had and which she must have fished out from somewhere.

'Sabrina,' he groaned.

Her fingers tightened on the knife. 'Don't tell me you don't like beef Wellington,' she said, the slight note of desperation making her voice sound edgy.

'Who in their right mind wouldn't?' He sighed. 'It's just that you must have spent a fortune on this meal—'

'It was supposed to be a way of saying thank you—'

'And I've told you before not to thank me!' he said savagely, feeling the sweet, inconvenient rush of desire as her lips trembled in rebuke at him. 'Look, Sabrina, I don't expect you earn very much, working in a bookshop—'

'Certainly nowhere in your league, Guy,' she retorted.

'And I don't want you spending it all on fancy food!'

'I'm not here to accept charity—especially not yours!'

'Sabrina—'

'No, Guy,' she said stubbornly. 'I want to pay my way as much as possible.'

He took the slice she offered him and he stared down at it with grudging reluctance. Pink and perfect. So she could cook, too. He scowled. 'Do that,' he clipped out. 'But this is the last time you buy me steak! Understood?'

That was enough to guarantee the complete loss of her appetite, and it was only pride which made Sabrina eat every single thing on her plate. But by the time they were drinking their coffee his forbidding expression seemed to have thawed a little.

'That was delicious,' he said.

'The pleasure was all mine.'

He heard the sarcasm in her voice, saw the little pout of accusation which hovered on her lips. Maybe he *had* been a little hard on her. 'I'm not used to sharing,' he shrugged.

'It shows.' She risked a question, even if the dark face didn't look particularly forthcoming. 'Have you got any brothers and sisters?'

'One brother; he's younger.'

'And where is he now?'

He sighed as he saw her patient look of interest. These heart-to-heart chats had never really been part of his scene. 'He lives in Paris—he works for a newspaper.'

'That sounds interesting.'

He blanked the conversation with a bland smile. 'Does it?'

But Sabrina wasn't giving up that easily. What were they *supposed* to talk about, night after night—the *weather*?

'So, no live-in girlfriends?' she asked.

The eyes glittered. 'Nope.'

'Oh.' She digested this.

'You sound surprised,' he observed.

'I am, a little.'

'You see me as so devastatingly eligible, do you, Sabrina?'

Her smile stayed as enigmatic as his. 'That's a fairly ego-tistical conclusion to jump to, Guy—that wasn't what I said at all. I just thought that a man in your position would yearn for all the comforts of having a resident girlfriend.'

'You mean regular meals.' His eyes fell to his empty plate. 'And regular sex?'

Sabrina went scarlet. 'Something like that.'

'The comfort and ease of the shared bed?' he mused. 'It's tempting, I give you that. But sex is the easy bit—it's com-munication that causes all the problems. Or rather the lack of it.' His voice grew hard, almost bitter.

Sabrina looked at him and wondered what he wasn't tell-ing her. 'You mean you've never found anyone you could communicate with?'

'Something like that.' No one he'd ever really *wanted* to communicate with. 'Or at least, not unless we both happened to be horizontal at the time.' He looked at her thoughtfully as she blushed. 'But I have a very low boredom threshold, princess,' he added softly.

He was telling her not to come too close—it was as plain as the day itself. And it was the most arrogant warning she had ever heard. 'More coffee?' she asked him coolly.

CHAPTER TEN

'SO HOW has your first week been?'

Guy looked across the sitting room to where Sabrina was curled up like a kitten with a book on her lap—she was always *reading*, though he noticed that not many pages had been turned in the past hour. Snap, he thought with a grim kind of satisfaction. He hadn't made many inroads into his *own* reading.

Sabrina met the piercing grey gaze and repressed a guilty kind of longing. How could she possibly concentrate on her book when she had such a distraction sitting just across the room from her?

'I've enjoyed it,' she told him truthfully. Well, most of it, anyway. It wasn't easy being around him, being plagued by memories of a time it was clear that both of them wished forgotten—but at least she had done her utmost not to show it. She forced a smile. 'How do you rate me as a flatmate?'

Guy thought about it. She was certainly less intrusive than he would have imagined. She kept out of his way in the mornings. She didn't drift around the place in bits of provocative clothing—and she didn't leave panties and tights draped over the radiator, which he understood was one of the major irritations when sharing with a woman.

'Seven out of ten,' he drawled, his smile not quite easy.

'And how's the bookshop surviving with its newest member of staff?'

Sabrina wished he wouldn't stretch his legs out like that. 'The shop is f-fine,' she stumbled. 'In fact, it's very similar to the Salisbury branch—'

'So living in the big city doesn't scare you, Miss Cooper?' he mocked softly, cutting right through her stumbled reply.

'I don't scare easy,' she said, raising a glittering blue gaze, and thinking that it was all too easy to be scared. Scared of her susceptibility to Guy Masters—especially when he looked at her like *that*. Scared of what might happen if he should happen to lazily make a pass at her—because surely *most* men who had already slept with a woman *would* make a pass. Even if they'd said that they wouldn't.

But Guy, of course, hadn't.

In fact, he'd spent the last five evenings behaving as though he had a piece of radioactive equipment in the room with him—keeping a wary and observant distance and occasionally glancing her a look from beneath those sensationally long black lashes. But tonight he seemed edgy.

'Do you want to go out for a drink before supper?' he asked suddenly.

Sabrina snapped her book shut with nervous fingers. 'What, now, tonight?'

He shrugged. 'It's Friday night—it's what people do.'

Anything would be better than having to spend another whole evening watching while she managed to turn reading a book into a very erotic art form indeed. It was all getting a little too cosy for comfort. And Guy had found that leafing through art-world journals had lost most of its allure when he had the infinitely more distracting vision of Sabrina flicking that bright red-gold hair back over her slim shoulders.

But it was a challenge he had set himself and Guy thrived

on challenges. He was determined to resist her—and resist her he damned well would. Unwittingly he had taken advantage of her once before, but once had been enough. 'How about it?' he asked.

She thought about the fine wines he had crowding the vast rack in the dining room. Maybe he wanted to go out because he was bored, just sitting here alone with her night after night. And it was just politeness which had made him invite her to go with him.

'You go out if you like,' she offered. 'I'll stay in. You don't have to have me tagging along with you.'

'You can't sit in here all on your own,' he objected.

She forced a smile. It would do her good. After five evenings she was beginning to enjoy his company a little *too* much. 'Go on! You go, Guy—I'll be fine here. I'll probably have an early night.'

Guy felt an infuriating urge to stay home, yet he hadn't been out a single night this week—and this from the man who was the original party animal. 'Sure?' he asked reluctantly.

'Who else is going?'

'Tom is, and a couple of guys who work with him. Oh, and I expect that Trudi and Jenna might turn up.'

Jenna. Sabrina's smile didn't slip. 'I think I'll pass, if you don't mind. Honestly, Guy, I'm tired.'

Guy rose to his feet, strangely reluctant to move. 'Maybe we should go out for dinner some time?'

She felt a little stab of pleasure, until she reminded herself that it wasn't a date. He was simply making sure that she wasn't bored.

'Dinner?' she asked casually.

'Yeah. There are a couple of clients I need to take out—you might as well come with me.'

'Oh. Right,' she said, her heart sinking despite her intention not to let it. No, it definitely *wasn't* a date—he couldn't have phrased it more unflatteringly if he'd tried. The token female at a client dinner!

He paused by the door and shot her a quick glance. 'Any plans for tomorrow?'

'Not really. I'm working. I work every third Saturday.'

He nodded. 'Me, too. Well, actually, I work *most* Saturdays.'

Sabrina stared at him. 'Why?'

He frowned. 'Why what?'

'Why do you work on Saturdays?' She gave him a slightly waspish smile. He left at the crack of dawn each morning and didn't put in an appearance until at least eight o'clock. Even after five days she had decided that he drove himself too hard. 'You do happen to *own* the company, don't you, Guy?'

'Yes, I do, and I like to make sure that I stay one step ahead of my competitors,' he retorted softly. 'And the only way to do that is to work hard. Number-one lesson in life. Build yourself so high that no one can knock you down. Ever.'

She lifted her eyebrows. He sounded almost *ruthless*. 'Try to be invincible, you mean?'

There was an unmistakable flicker of tension around his mouth. 'It's an achievable goal,' he answered, in a voice which was suddenly harsh.

She was tempted to tell him that he was already top of the heap. And that it didn't look as if anyone was going to knock him anywhere, least of all down, but there was a distinctly warning glitter hardening his slate-grey eyes.

She thought of him as polished and sophisticated, a man who had everything, with his dark good looks and his enormous flat and wealthy lifestyle—and that wasn't even taking into account his consummate skill as a lover. Yet something just now had frozen his face into granite. Had made him look almost savage. Was Guy Masters a man of never-ending ambition—and, if so, then why, when he seemed to have more than most men could only dream of?

'What's so good about being invincible?' she queried softly.

Guy's face tightened. Because it was the opposite of how his father had operated, with his easy come, easy go attitude to life and all the devastation that attitude had brought in its wake. But he had never shared that devastation with any woman and he wasn't about to start now. Even with Sabrina Cooper and her warm, trusting smile and tantalising blue eyes which the devil himself must have given her.

'It all comes down to personal choice,' he said coldly. 'And that's mine.'

Sabrina could recognise a brush-off when she heard one—and more than a reluctance to open up. From the daunting expression in those dark, stormy eyes, it was more like a *refusal* to talk.

Tactically, she retreated.

'Have a nice time,' she said placidly. 'I think I'll have a bath and that early night.'

Guy had to stifle a groan as some of the tension he'd been feeling was replaced by a new and different kind of tension. Images of her long, pale limbs submerged beneath the foaming bubbles of his bathtub crept tantalisingly into his mind as his photographic memory recalled them with breathtaking accuracy. Did she really need to share something like *that* with him?

'Yeah,' he clipped out. 'Do that.'

'Shall I leave you some supper?' she asked. 'I thought I'd make some risotto—I got some amazing oyster mushrooms cheap at the market.'

Guy scowled. Just five days and she seemed to have taken over most of the cooking and most of the shopping—and she insisted on shopping around to save him money—*even when he'd told her that she didn't need to*. With her, it seemed pride as much as parsimony—and she could be so damned *stubborn*.

'You don't have to cook for me every night,' he said shortly. 'I told you that.'

'But it's no trouble if I'm cooking for myself—'

'I'm perfectly capable of fixing myself some eggs when I get home!' Guy snapped, and turned and walked out of the room, because that hurt little tremble of her mouth was enough to crumble a heart of stone.

Sabrina could hear him slamming around in his room; then the telephone began to ring. She waited to see whether Guy would answer it, but it carried on ringing and so she picked it up.

'Hello?'

There was a pause, and then a rather flustered-sounding woman's voice said, 'I'm sorry—I think I must have got the wrong number.'

'Who did you want to speak to?' enquired Sabrina patiently.

'Guy Masters. My son.'

'Your *son*? Oh, I'm sorry, Mrs Masters, I didn't realise—I'll just get him for you.'

'No, no, wait a minute—just who might *you* be?'

Sabrina cleared her throat. 'I'm Sabrina,' she said. 'Sabrina Cooper.' And then, because the voice seemed to be waiting for some kind of clarification, she added, 'I'm staying here. With Guy.'

'*Are* you now?' enquired the voice interestedly.

'Er, just a minute, I'll get him for you,' said Sabrina hastily, but when she looked up it was to find Guy standing in the doorway, his face a dark and daunting study.

Wordlessly, he came and took the phone from her, and Sabrina quickly left the room, but not before she heard his first responses.

'Hi, Ma. Mmm. Mmm. No, no. No—nothing like that.'

A few minutes later, he came and found her in the kitchen, chopping up her mushrooms.

'Don't do that again!' he warned.

She put the knife down. 'Do what?'

'Answer my phone—especially when I'm *around*.'

'I'm sorry,' she said stiffly. 'I didn't realise I was breaking some unwritten rule, but of course it *is* your flat.' His flat, his territory, his control.

But he didn't appear to be listening. 'And now my mother's asking me eight hundred questions about you. Move a woman in and suddenly everyone's thinking rice and confetti!'

'Well, I can assure you that I'm not,' she told him acidly.

'Me, neither!' he snapped.

She turned her back on him and heard him go out, slamming the door behind him, and she viciously decapitated a mushroom. He was bad-tempered and unreasonable, she told herself. And she must have been crazy to agree to come here.

Guy walked into the Kensington wine-bar where his friends had been congregating on Friday evenings for as long as he could remember, surveying the dimly lit and crowded room with an unenthusiastic eye. He asked himself why he had bothered to come out to fight his way to the bar for a glass of champagne when he could have drunk something colder and vastly superior at home. And maybe given Sabrina a glass, too.

He shook his head. What the hell was he thinking of? He *always* went out on a Friday night!

'Guy!' called Tom Roberts, from the other side of the room, and Guy forced himself to smile in response as he wove his way through the crowded room.

'It's obviously been a bad day!' joked his cousin, as Guy joined him.

'On the contrary.' Guy took the proffered glass of champagne and gave it a thoughtful sip. 'I think I may have negotiated a deal on that old schoolhouse over by the river. It's going to make someone a wonderful home.'

'So why the long face?' teased Tom.

'I guess I'm just tired,' said Guy, and that much was true. Sleep didn't come easily when all you could think about was moon-pale flesh and banner-bright hair and a naked body in the room just along the corridor.

Tom topped up his glass. 'So how's the new flatmate working out?' he asked casually.

Guy could recognise a leading question when he heard one. 'Sabrina?' he stalled, equally casually.

Tom smiled. 'Unless you've moved another one in.'

'I must have needed my head examined!' groaned Guy.

'That bad, is it?' Tom threw him a sympathetic glance. 'She seemed sweet.'

'Yeah, she is.' Too damned sweet. Sweet as honey. That night in his bed—all clinging and sticky like honey. A honey *trap*, he thought with a sudden heat, and drained his glass in one. 'Where's Trudi tonight?' he asked.

'She's on a sales conference in Brussels,' explained Tom. 'She's not coming back until tomorrow.'

Guy nodded. Good. Good. 'Fancy going out for a meal in a while?' he asked.

'Oh!' Tom started grinning. 'Diversionary tactics to keep you out of the flat, you mean?'

'I don't know what you're talking about.' Guy shrugged.

'Oh, we've all been there, mate,' said Tom obscurely. 'There's bound to be a woman sooner or later who gets underneath your skin. It's about time it happened to you!'

'Sorry.' Guy's voice was cool but firm. 'You've lost me.'

Tom put his glass down and narrowed his eyes. 'And you still haven't told me anything about Sabrina Cooper…'

'What do you want to know?'

'The obvious. Like, is she a friend, or is she a lover?'

Guy opened his mouth and then shut it again. What was the point in trying to explain the whole bizarre situation, even to a man who had known him nearly all his life? Sabrina's reputation wouldn't emerge from it unscathed. And neither, he realised grimly, would his own.

'We're men, Tom,' he said flippantly, 'so we never talk about things like that, right?'

In Guy's high-tech kitchen, Sabrina unenthusiastically cooked her risotto, and then picked at it without interest. She had made plenty. Enough for two…just in case. But Guy still wasn't back. Should she pop the rest into the fridge and cover it with clingfilm? Or would Guy go mad if she did that? Probably. He'd blanched with horror when she'd suggested frying up some leftover potato for breakfast.

After supper she forced herself to relax in a long, deep bath, and when she came out she looked at the clock to see that it was getting on for ten. So, his 'quick' drink was taking longer than he'd anticipated.

She put her bedroom light out and tried to sleep, but sleep infuriatingly refused to protect her with its mantle of oblivion. In the end she gave up trying and snapped on the light and tried reading her book.

'Tried' being the operative word. The words danced like tiny black beetles in front of her and all she could think about was that it was now nearly midnight and all the bars would be closed.

And Guy still wasn't back.

She pulled on her dressing gown and went to pace up and down the sitting room.

By twelve she was getting frantic, and by one she was just about to pick up the phone and call the hospital when she heard the sound of a key being turned in the lock. She flew out into the hall to find Guy with his back to her, shutting the door with exaggerated care and hanging up his overcoat with the other hand.

Sabrina didn't even stop to think about it. She just blazed right in there. 'Where the hell have you *been*?' she demanded.

He turned round, the grey eyes narrowing to cold chips of slate as he saw Sabrina in her satin dressing gown, her tiny breasts heaving, a look of complete fury on her face. 'I *beg* your pardon?'

That frosty little question should have been enough to stop her in her tracks, and normally it would have done, but, then, this didn't feel normal. None of it did. Surely 'normal' would have meant a complete numbing of her senses until she was properly over Michael?

'You told me you were going out for a quick drink!' she stormed, her breathing coming through in great ragged bursts.

Guy felt torn between incredulty and irritation. 'And?'

'And it *wasn't*, was it? Not quick at all. It's way past midnight—what *time* do you call this?'

'It's none of your damned business what time it is!' he roared. 'I'll live my own life, the way I always have done! I'll go out *when* I want and *where* I want and with *whom* I want—and I'll do it *without* your permission, thank you, princess!'

Through her shuddering breaths Sabrina stared at him, re-alising just how preposterous she must have sounded. And realising that if she didn't get away from him pretty quickly, she risked making even more of a fool of herself.

'I'm sorry,' she said tightly. 'I spoke out of turn.' She half ran along the corridor and into her room and then pressed her forehead to the door, her eyes closed, her breath still shudder-ing.

He'd seen the awful whitening of her face and the brief glimspe of terror which had iced the blue of her eyes, and in an instant he'd begun to comprehend just what had motivated her reaction.

'Damn!' he swore softly. Swiftly following in her footsteps, he went and banged his fist on the door. 'Oh, damn!'

Behind the door, Sabrina froze. Just keep quiet, some instinct of preservation told her. Keep very quiet and just don't answer and he might go away.

'Sabrina! Open the damned door. We both know you can't possibly be asleep.'

She shook her head. 'Go away.'

'I'm not moving from this spot until you open the door and come out and talk to me. That way neither of us will get to sleep and that means we'll both be bad-tempered at work tomorrow.'

You and your precious *work*, thought Sabrina, trying to concentrate on something—*anything*—other than how she wanted to open the door and fall into his arms, and…and…

'Alternatively, I could kick it down,' he promised in a voice of silky intent.

It was such an outrageous proposal that Sabrina very nearly smiled. 'You wouldn't do that,' she sniffed.

'Not unless you make me,' he agreed mockingly. 'So, are you going to open the door now? Or not?'

Slowly, she complied, her fingers clutching onto the handle as if they were petrified, gearing herself up to withstand Guy's fury at her presumptuous behaviour. But when she dared to look up into his face it was to see a look of bitter regret written there, and Sabrina felt the trembling approach of tears. If she weren't careful, she was in terrible danger of exposing all her desperate insecurities to him.

'I'm s-sorry,' she said shakily. 'I had no right—'

'No.' He shook his head. 'I'm sorry. It was the most stupid and insensitive thing to do and, oh, God, Sabrina…' His voice deepened to a caress as he saw her face crumple. 'Princess, don't cry. Please, don't cry.'

'I'm n-not c-crying,' she sobbed quietly, trying simultaneously to push him out of the room and close the door after him, and failing miserably to do either.

Saying something that she couldn't quite make out, Guy just grabbed her by the hand and steered her into the sitting room.

'What do you think you're doing?' she spluttered.

'What does it look like? I'm taking you somewhere where we can talk.' Somewhere that didn't involve a bed. 'I'm damned if I'm going to have you fainting on me for a second time!'

'I'm not going to faint. I want to go to bed,' she said plaintively.

'Well, we need to talk,' he said grimly. 'Or, rather, *you* need to talk, princess.'

He pushed her down very gently on the sofa and covered her with a cashmere throw, which was as light as a feather and as warm as toast.

'That's nice,' she said automatically.

It was also vital, in his opinion, that she cover up. If he wanted to talk to her—or, rather, have her talk to *him*—then he needed to concentrate. And it would be damned nigh impossible trying to concentrate on anything—other than an urgent need to possess her—when that silky robe was clinging like honey to the sweet swell of her limbs and moulding the perfect outline of her tiny breasts.

He sat down next to her and stared into the pale heart of her face. 'It was thoughtless of me. I should have telephoned—told you I was going to be late.'

'It doesn't matter.' She shook her head. 'I had no right to expect—'

'You had every right to expect consideration,' he refuted heatedly. 'And at least a *modicum* of understanding.' There was a grim kind of pause and his grey eyes glittered with self-recrimination. 'And I showed you neither.' He had deliberately stayed out tonight—and he still wasn't sure why—without thinking through the consequences of his actions. 'Neither,' he finished bitterly.

'It doesn't matter,' she repeated, and even managed to raise her shoulders in a shrug, as if it really *didn't* matter, but he shook his head like a man who was onto something and wouldn't give up.

'Why don't you tell me,' he said slowly, 'about the night Michael died? Is that what happened? Were you waiting for him and he never came?'

Something in the burning intensity of his eyes pierced right through the barriers she'd built around herself. She'd pushed the memories of that night to the far recesses of her mind. Deliberately. It had been a defence mechanism to shield her from the bitter pain, and the guilt. She'd refused counsellors and her mother's faltering requests that she open up and talk to someone.

But something in Guy's face completely disarmed her, and her words of defiance and denial died on her lips.

'OK, I'll tell.' She nodded her head slowly. 'I'll tell you everything.' There was a pause while she struggled to find the right words. 'Like I said, Michael wanted to go out that night and I didn't, and it was more than about the fact we couldn't afford it. It was a filthy night. The weather was awful…snow and ice.'

She took a slow, shuddering breath and stared at him as she forced herself to face up to the truth for the first time. 'Just awful. I said that it wasn't a good night to be out driving…but he wouldn't listen… He just wouldn't *listen*!'

Guy nodded as the strands of her story began to be woven together, beginning to make some sense of her guilt.

'I told him to be sure and ring me when he got to the pub, only the phone call didn't come, and I wasn't sure if he was sulking because he was angry with me…and…'

'And?' His voice was soft. Too soft. How could you resist a voice that soft?

'And when I rang the pub...' Sabrina bit her lip '...they said they hadn't seen him. So I thought he must have changed his mind about going there, never dreaming... never dreaming—'

'Never dreaming that the inconceivable had happened,' he said carefully, 'and that he'd never be coming back again?'

His words were edged with anger, and an emotion it took her a moment or two to recognise. Pain. 'That's right,' she agreed slowly.

'So you think that you should have stopped him from driving that night?'

'Of course I should have stopped him!' she shot back bitterly, but Guy shook his dark head.

'Don't you know that we can't govern other people's lives?' he demanded quietly. 'Or decide their destiny. You could have stopped him from going, but how do you know that he wouldn't have been hit by a bus on his way to work the next day? Maybe,' he added, with slow deliberation, 'maybe it was just his time.'

Her lips froze. 'His time?'

'To die.' His mouth hardened.

'Fate,' she elaborated painfully. 'That's fate.'

'Yeah, fate.'

She stared straight into the burning silver gaze, dazzled by it. 'You honestly believe that?' she whispered, and he gave a hollow kind of laugh.

'Sometimes it's easier to think of it that way.' He shrugged. 'Easier for the living to let go and carry on. And you have to let go, Sabrina, you *have* to—you must realise that. Don't you?'

'But I feel so guilty!'

'Because he's dead and you're alive?'

His perception took her breath away. 'Yes.'

He gave a brittle smile. 'But nothing can change that, Sabrina. Nothing can bring him back. You owe it to yourself to let go. And to Michael.'

'Yes.' She sighed with a kind of surrender made all the easier by that luminous look of understanding. 'Yes.'

He watched as the thready breath made her lips tremble, he saw her wide-eyed look of trust, and he knew what she wanted and needed more than anything else at the moment. Pure animal comfort. Even if doing it would half kill him.

He drew her into the circle of his arms and hugged her tightly against his chest, the wetness of her tears warming his skin through his shirt. Her breasts were soft and pointed and her hair was full of the scent of lilac, and it took every bit of his self-control to dampen down his instinctive desire as he smoothed the bright strands down with a distracted hand.

'It's going to be OK,' he muttered, and prayed for his body not to react to her proximity. 'I promise you.'

Through her tears it occurred to Sabrina that his kindness and understanding were just two more facets of a complex personality which perplexed and intrigued her more with each day that passed. And that simply wasn't on the agenda. Her stay here was only temporary, she reminded herself as more tears spilled onto his shirt.

Guy let her cry until her sobs became dry and shuddering, and then he went and made her some hot chocolate, sitting in front of her like a determined nurse while she drank it.

He thought how unselfconsciously provocative her movements were. Thought that she shouldn't look that sexy with eyes bright red from crying and hair which was matted by those tears. But sexy she looked. Extremely sexy.

'So.' He sat back on his heels. 'Are you going to let it go now, Sabrina?'

She couldn't have said no, even if she'd wanted to, not with that silver gaze compelling her to start living her life again. 'Yes,' she said slowly. 'I am.'

'Good.' He smiled. 'And are you going to let me take you out for dinner next week?'

She forced herself to remember that the question wasn't as warmly intimate as it sounded. 'Sure,' she said lightly. 'Is this the client dinner?'

'That's right,' he agreed. 'I have a Middle-Eastern potentate I've just bought a picture for. How would you like to have dinner with Prince Khalim?'

'*Prince* Khalim?' She gulped. 'Just how many princes do you know, Guy?'

He smiled. 'Khalim is my oldest friend. I've known him since schooldays—it was through him I got most of my contacts.'

'But, Guy—'

'Don't worry about it,' he soothed. 'You'll like him—a little old-fashioned perhaps, but he's a nice guy.'

CHAPTER ELEVEN

FOR the next week, Sabrina was in a complete state of nerves. What on earth did you wear if you were going out for dinner with a *prince*?

She rang her mother and explained her predicament.

'Good heavens,' said her mother faintly. 'A *prince*? You'll never want to come home to Salisbury at this rate!'

Sabrina winced at how her mother had unerringly hit on the truth. She couldn't imagine wanting to either, but that had everything to do with Guy and nothing whatsoever to do with a Middle-Eastern potentate.

'What do I *wear*, Mum?' she repeated patiently.

'You've got lots of lovely clothes! Just be yourself,' said her mother. 'My goodness—wait until the neighbours hear about *this*!'

'Well, I don't want you to tell them,' said Sabrina stubbornly. Because however much she wished otherwise, one day soon she was going to have to go back and live at home, and she would do herself no favours whatsoever if she arrived with Guy Masters's magic dust still clinging to her skin.

She even tried to quiz Guy about the correct dress code one evening when he arrived home even later than usual and had been in a snarling temper. She produced a huge tureen of soup, and he stared down at the steaming bowlful and suddenly went very quiet.

'You don't like home-made soup?' she asked nervously.

Guy looked up. The soup looked perfect. Damn it—*she* looked perfect, standing there in a pair of white jeans and a white T-shirt, with her bright hair caught back in a ponytail.

'Haven't had a lot of experience of it,' he said shortly. 'My mother used to open a can.'

Sabrina pushed some cheese across the table towards him. 'Wasn't she keen on cooking, then?'

It was an such an artless question that Guy found himself uncharacteristically answering it. 'Not particularly. And we were always…moving,' he said slowly. 'So a lot of her time was taken up with settling into new places.'

'You make it sound quite nomadic, Guy.'

'Do I? I suppose it was when you compare it with living in one place all your life.'

'Like me, you mean?'

He shrugged. 'Well, you did, didn't you?'

'Yes,' she said carefully, as some warning light in his eyes told her to go back to the safer subject of cooking, rather than the potential minefield of childhood.

She sawed through a crusty loaf and handed him a huge chunk of it. 'My mother was so busy going out to work that she never had time to cook properly, except at weekends.'

He nodded, seeing the sudden, defensive set of her face. Despite his reservations, he found himself asking, 'How old were you when your father left?'

'Eight.' She pulled a face. 'He fell in love with my mum's "best" friend.'

He winced. 'That must have been tough.'

'Yes.' She stared down at the soup without really seeing it. 'For a while it was dreadful.' She looked up and gave him a bright smile. 'But time heals, doesn't it? Corny, but true.'

'Yeah, but you always get left with a scar.' He shrugged, but he shook his head at the silent question in her eyes. 'Tell me more.'

'Just I always vowed that when I grew up I would learn how to cook properly.'

Unexpectedly, he found the thought of Sabrina as a little girl exquisitely touching. He sipped the soup. 'Well, you achieved it with honours,' he murmured.

She glowed with pleasure. 'Guy?'

'Mmm?'

'You know this dinner on Saturday night—'

He put his spoon down. 'Damn!'

'It's been cancelled?' she asked hopefully.

He shook his head. 'Nope—but I haven't organised anything and I'm in Paris all day tomorrow. You'll have to book the restaurant, Sabrina.'

'Like *Where*? I don't really know London at all!'

He reeled off a list of London's most famous eating places and Sabrina shook her head doubtfully.

'We'll never get a table at any of those places *this* late!'

He gave a small smile. 'Just try mentioning my name.'

From anyone else it would have sounded outrageously arrogant—from Guy it just sounded supremely confident.

'And what on earth can I *wear*?' she wailed.

'Wear what you want.' He shrugged. 'You always look pretty good to me.'

She had received better compliments in her life, but none had she embraced as warmly as Guy's careless words and she had to force herself to suppress the guilt. She *was* letting go, and starting to live again—and there was nothing unacceptable about enjoying a compliment.

It still didn't solve the problem of what to wear, of course.

Guy left at the crack of dawn the following morning.

Sabrina heard him moving around the flat and for once came, yawning, out into the hall to say goodbye to him.

His hand tightened around the handle of his briefcase as he saw her hair in all its tousled disarray tumbling down over her shoulders. Was she trying to play the siren? he wondered distractedly. But that was just the thing—he honestly didn't think she *was*.

'Have you remembered your passport?'

'Sabrina!' he exploded. 'I've been flying to Paris at least once a month for the last I don't know how long! How the hell do you think I managed before you came into my life?' It had been a calm, ordered time which was slowly but surely fading from his memory, the end of which had seemed to co-incide with him urging her to let her guilt and her sorrow go. He had only himself to blame, and yet he hadn't realised how familiar it could feel, living with a woman—even if you *weren't* having sex with her. He winced. Why remind himself of *that*?

'Send me a postcard.' Sabrina smiled.

'I won't have time,' he said tightly, because he was having to fight the terrible urge to kiss her goodbye—as if she were his *wife* or something. His smile tasted like acid on his mouth. 'And don't forget to book the damned restaurant!'

'I won't forget.' She stood at the front door until he'd disappeared out of sight, praying that he would turn round and give her that rare and brilliant smile. But he didn't.

Sabrina felt more than a little intimidated at the thought of booking a meal at a place she had only ever read about in magazines. Wouldn't even her best dress look out of place in a venue as upmarket as that? And, when she thought about it, wouldn't Prince Khalim be bored rigid with going to fancy restaurants, and Guy, too, for that matter? Wouldn't they rather try something a little *different*?

She spent her lunch-hour scouring the restaurant section

of the capital's biggest glossy magazine, and eventually found what she'd half thought she'd been looking for. She picked up the phone and booked it.

But Guy was delayed in Paris. He phoned that night.

'This deal is taking longer than I thought,' he said, and she could hear the sounds of people in the background. 'I may even have to stay over for a few days.'

'A few *days*?'

'You'll be OK on your own, won't you?'

Sabrina pulled a face. She couldn't be missing him *already*, could she? 'Yes, of course I will.'

'Just lock up carefully.' There was a pause. 'Ring Tom Roberts if you need anything. Actually, I'll ring him—get him to keep an eye on you.'

'I don't need anyone to keep an eye on me! You make me sound helpless!' she objected, and could hear the smile in his response.

'Not helpless, Sabrina. Maybe just a little vulnerable at the moment.' And make damned sure you remember that, he thought grimly as he hung up before tapping out Tom's number.

Guy arrived back from Paris on Saturday morning, feeling all frazzled and frayed around the edges as he walked into the kitchen to a delicious smell of coffee. Sabrina was already dressed, busy buttering a slice of toast. He paused for a moment which felt dangerous. Because his kitchen had never felt more of a home than it did at that moment.

He'd missed her, he realised with a sudden sense of shock.

'Hi,' he said softly.

Sabrina turned round slowly, trying to compose her face, making sure that every trace of leaping excitement had been eradicated from her features. She smiled instead. 'Welcome home! How was your trip? Would you like some coffee?'

He wanted something a lot more fundamental than coffee, but he nodded his head, sat down at the table and took the mug of coffee she slid towards him.

'You're up early,' he commented.

'I'm working today, remember?'

He frowned. Had it really been three weeks since the last time she'd been in the shop on Saturday morning? 'Yeah.' He sighed. He'd been almost tempted to take the day off himself, and to ask her whether she wanted to go to a gallery with him, but if she was working... 'I guess I might as well go in myself.' He yawned.

Sabrina fixed him with a stern look. 'Oh, for goodness' sake, Guy! You've only just got back from Paris. Give yourself a break!'

He glared at her. 'I've managed to get along just fine for the last thirty-two years without anyone telling me how to live my life, if it's all the same to you, Sabrina.' He paused. 'Did you book the restaurant?'

'I did,' she said steadily, without missing a beat.

'Which one?'

Her bright smiled didn't falter. 'It's a surprise!'

'A surprise?'

She wondered what had caused that sudden hardening of his voice. 'You don't like surprises?'

'No,' he clipped out, and then saw her crestfallen face and relented. It was unpredictability he shied away from. She wasn't to know that surprises made him feel as though the control which was so fundamental to him could be in danger of slipping away. Loosen up, he told himself—just as he'd told her to. He smiled. 'It had better be a good one.'

'Oh, I think it will be.'

'We're picking Khalim up from his hotel at eight.'

She nodded, trying to be helpful. 'So shall I order us a car, too?'

'Yes,' he murmured, wondering why he got the distinct impression that the balance of power had somehow shifted in this relationship without him really noticing. He'd wanted her to try and let the past go, but he hadn't expected such an enchanting switch into sexy and sassy and bossy mode. It was much too irresistible a transformation. 'Thanks,' he added heavily.

Sabrina spent hours in the bathroom getting ready, comfortable in the knowledge that she wouldn't be holding Guy up. Thank heavens there were three, she thought, remembering her initial shock at discovering that one flat had three bathrooms all to itself. Back in Salisbury her mother would have been beating the door down by now.

In the spare room, she pulled out the hanger on which hung the dress she'd bought after work yesterday, and she looked at it with eager eyes. It was a dream—easily the most grown-up and sophisticated thing she had ever owned—but nothing less would do, not for a prince!

It was in deepest violet velvet and it fell to just above the knee, with long, fitted sleeves. In fact, the whole dress accentuated every curve of her body and the rich, vibrant colour contrasted deeply with her red-gold hair. It was a simple dress, possibly a little *too* simple, which was why she'd bought diamanté earrings and an ornate and glittering necklace to go with it.

She stepped back to look at herself in the mirror and gave a nod of satisfaction. The diamanté necklace and earrings sparkled and spangled in the light. She looked good! Maybe the best she had ever looked—and there was an added sparkle to her eyes and a soft flush to her cheeks.

Guy was standing by the window in the sitting room, doing up his cuff-links, and he looked up as she made her entrance, then froze.

Sabrina, who had been watching him expectantly, saw the

sudden stiffening of his body, the swift hard gleam in his eyes, and her heart sank.

'You don't think it's suitable?'

A pulse hammered at his temple. 'Don't be so bloody naïve, Sabrina! Of course it's suitable—' He'd never seen anything more suitable in his life—and the thing it was most suitable for was being ripped off her body... He groaned and tried to pay a gracious compliment. 'It's lovely,' he finished lamely.

'Oh. Right.' She screwed her nose up. 'You don't think it's too over the top?'

'*No*, I don't!' He drew a deep breath. 'And I think we've just about exhausted the subject of what you're wearing. Now, where the hell is this bloody car?'

Sabrina hoped that he was going to moderate his language a little, especially in front of Prince Khalim, but now didn't seem a very good time to say so, especially since at that moment the doorbell rang, and the chauffeur was standing there, telling them that their car was ready. She picked up the same diaphanous silver wrap she'd worn in Venice and turned to Guy.

'Ready?' she asked, thinking that she'd never seen him in formal black tie regalia before, and just how darkly imposing and broad-shouldered it made him appear.

'And waiting,' he said, in a grim kind of voice.

Outside stood a long, gleaming, black car which made the limousine he'd hired in Salisbury look like an ancient old banger. Sabrina felt like a film star as she climbed inside.

But as they were whisked towards the West End Guy seemed to want to avoid all her attempts at conversation, and Sabrina forced herself to look out of the window, trying to appear interested in the sights as they sped by, wondering why he was sitting in such stony silence.

All he could think about was how much he wanted to kiss

her, and it was driving him out of his mind. Since when had *kissing* been his number-one priority?

The car slid to a halt in front of the Granchester Hotel, which was situated right opposite Hyde Park and where a uniformed doorman immediately sprang to attention.

'I'd better go inside and tell him we're here,' said Guy, still in that same, heavy voice.

But at that moment there was some sort of commotion and several burly men in suits emerged from the hotel entrance and stood, looking this way and that.

'That's his security,' said Guy, seeing her expression of bemusement. 'They may want to check the restaurant out so your little "surprise" may have to be unmasked, Sabrina, dearest.'

In the dim light of the early evening, Sabrina blanched. Maybe she had misjudged the whole situation completely, but by then it was too late to do anything about it because the men in suits had all stood up straight to attention. And the most striking man she had ever seen in her life came gliding out of the hotel.

It wasn't just the fact that he was tall—although Guy was actually taller by about a head. Or that he was wearing a long, silky kind of robe which was a cross between white and gold and hinted at a hard body beneath. Or that his hair was darker than the night—much blacker than Guy's—and his skin the deep golden colour of some ancient and lovingly polished piece of wood. Or that his eyes were as black as onyx itself—curiously deep, all-seeing eyes which were as emotionless and as cold as any she had ever seen.

For he was all those things, and more, thought Sabrina. He was a prince—and not just by title. He oozed it from every autocratic pore of his body.

His nose was a cruel, hard curve, and so was his mouth, and something about his whole rather rich and haughty demeanour made Sabrina feel slightly panicky with nerves as she recalled the restaurant booking she'd made. What had she *done*?

As Guy opened the door he felt Sabrina shiver beside him, and he glanced down at her, his mouth tightening. So the old knockout Khalim effect was having its usual reaction, he thought cynically.

'Don't worry, he likes blondes,' he told her cryptically. 'So you should be on to a winner!'

'But I'm a strawberry-blonde!' she objected, stung by that critical note in his voice. 'That's different.'

'And strawberries are rich and luscious,' Guy answered softly. 'Be careful, Sabrina—he eats women like you for breakfast.'

Sabrina glared at his back as he stepped from the car and the two men greeted each other like the old friends they were.

'Guy!' said Khalim, the hard lips curving into a smile.

Guy jerked his head in the direction of the suits. 'Are you bringing this lot with you?'

Khalim glanced a flickering look at the back of the car, where Sabrina was sitting frozen with nerves. The black eyes narrowed.

'They will follow behind us,' he said, 'but they will sit outside in the car. They shall not bother us while we are eating.' His voice softened as another dark, enigmatic glance was directed at the car. 'And who do you have sitting and waiting so beautifully for us, Guy?'

Guy felt an unwelcome flicker of irritation. This was Khalim, Khalim whom he had known since school—when they'd forged an instant friendship after Guy had beaten him at chess. Khalim had never been beaten by anyone before— but, then, as Guy had coolly pointed out, he'd been brought up in an environment where letting Khalim win was paramount.

The two boys had fallen with fists on one another, and had had to be pulled apart—both snarling and glaring like young tiger cubs. And then one of them—they'd each taken the credit afterwards—had started laughing, and the laughter had been contagious and had created a bond which had never been broken down the years.

Khalim's father had given Guy his first big break, and Guy had never forgotten that.

So why did he now feel like the small boy who'd wanted to pulverise his schoolmate?

'This is Sabrina,' said Guy shortly.

He pulled open the car door and Khalim slid inside next to Sabrina, the silken fabric of his robe whispering and clinging to the lean definition of his muscular legs. 'Sabrina Cooper.'

'And Sabrina is your…?' Khalim paused delicately, as if searching for the right word.

'Friend,' said Guy instantly, because in that instant no other word seemed to do. 'She's staying in my flat for a few weeks.'

'Indeed?' murmured Khalim.

Sabrina felt the slow thudding of disappointment. Every word Guy had said was true—but, oh, if he'd wanted to emphasise that their love affair was dead, that her role in his life only transitory, then he couldn't have done it more succinctly. Or more cruelly.

'That's right,' she said staunchly, and attempted to echo his casual tone. 'I'm just passing through.'

'Indeed?' murmured Khalim again. Black eyes glinted as he raised her hand and lightly brushed his lips against the fingertips. 'Khalim,' he purred. 'And I am charmed.'

It was difficult not to be charmed herself by such quaintly old-fashioned manners. And the sight of Guy glowering from the other side of the car had her smiling back at the Prince.

'I've booked the restaurant for tonight,' she babbled. 'I do hope I've made the right choice.'

The curved smile edged upwards. 'Water and bread can be sustenance enough,' said Khalim softly, 'when the company is this spectacular.'

Guy turned his head to look out of the window, thinking that he just might be sick. He'd heard Khalim's chat-up lines over the years—and as far as he knew—they had a one hundred per cent success rate. But this…this… *outrageous* flirting was really too much.

Sabrina had given the restaurant address to the driver when she'd made the phone booking for the car, but as it negotiated its way through Notting Hill and drew up outside a small, colourful café, her heart sank.

The signs, it had to be admitted, didn't look very promising. There was a garish awning outside, beneath which the sign read, THE PIE SHOP.

Guy's eyes narrowed incredulously. 'Just what *is* this place, Sabrina?'

'It got a very good review in the papers,' she defended, determined not to flinch beneath the quiet look of fury in his eyes. 'And I thought it would be…different.'

'It is certainly different,' said Khalim, his voice tilting with amusement. 'Come, let us go and see what delights The Pie Shop has to offer.

It was the kind of place which employed out-of-work actresses as waitresses—so at least the glamour quotient was high. But Khalim didn't seem at all interested in the nubile specimens who ushered them inside. In fact, his attention seemed to be all on Sabrina.

Almost worryingly so, she told herself as they were given a table in the corner.

There were no menus, just a huge blackboard with the dishes of the day printed on it in chalk.

'I'm surprised there isn't sawdust on the floor,' said Guy acidly, but Khalim was gazing around him with the air of a man who had stepped into a different world.

'No, but it is charming,' he murmured. 'Quite charming. And the smell of the food delicious. Every summer my mother used to take me and my sisters into the mountains, and we would eat a meal with an old man who had spent his life caring for the goats and living in a simple dwelling. This place reminds me of that.'

Oh, *great*, thought Guy. He frosted a look at Sabrina across the table. 'Khalim hasn't eaten red meat for years.' He gave a pointed stare at the dish of the day—shepherd's pie. 'Any suggestions, Sabrina?'

She thought that she'd never seen him quite this grumpy before, but it occurred to her that if he hadn't wanted her to come along, then he shouldn't have asked her. 'How about fish pie?' she suggested brightly.

'Fish *pie*,' echoed Khalim, as if she'd just proposed a lavish banquet. 'Do you know—I haven't eaten fish pie since we were at school. Do you remember, Guy? Always on Fridays.' And he gave a wistful smile, which briefly softened his hard, proud face.

How did she *do* it, wondered Guy distractedly. How had she unerringly hit on the one dish which would produce a rare state of nostalgia in a man who'd very probably been offered every delicacy under the sun?

'Three fish pies,' he said to the waitress, and Sabrina, who'd been about to order the shepherd's pie, hastily shut her mouth. It might be considered bad manners to eat meat in front of the Prince.

It wasn't the easiest meal she had ever sat through, mainly because Guy would hardly meet her eye, just chatted to Khalim about the paintings he'd seen recently in Paris.

Khalim listened and ate his meal slowly and with evident

pleasure. Occasionally he would turn to Sabrina and fix her with that hard, black stare as he asked her about her work in the bookshop as if it were the single most fascinating subject in the world.

And Sabrina smiled and tried to look attentive, while miserably ploughing her way through the fish pie.

After she'd pushed her plate away, Khalim leaned forward, his fingertips brushing against the bright glitter of her necklace.

'Who bought you these diamonds, my beauty?' he murmured.

Sabrina smiled. 'Oh, they're not real!'

'Really?' Khalim brushed one of the gems thoughtfully. 'Then it must be your skin which enhances them—for they look absolutely priceless.'

What Khalim didn't know about diamonds could be written on the back of a postage stamp, and Guy watched with increasing fury as the Prince's dark, elegant fingers contrasted against her milk-white skin.

'Shall we skip pudding?' he demanded.

They ordered coffee instead, and Guy was just paying the bill when Khalim lightly placed his hand on Sabrina's wrist.

'I'm in England for another couple of weeks,' he mused. 'Perhaps you would have dinner with me some night?'

Sabrina looked over at Guy, unsure of how you went about saying to a prince that it was a terribly sweet offer but that she was fast falling in love with someone else, thank you.

In love? Her cheeks grew hot, and the pounding in her heart increased. What in heaven's name was she thinking of? She couldn't be falling in love. She *couldn't*. It was too soon after Michael—much too soon.

She glanced over at the object of her affections, who was chatting to the waitress and giving her the benefit of the sunniest smile she'd seen all evening.

'Sabrina?' prompted Khalim softly.

Well, all *right*, she thought furiously, and smiled back at him. 'That would be wonderful,' she agreed shyly.

CHAPTER TWELVE

Guy maintained a simmering silence all the way home, even after they'd left Khalim back at his hotel and the chauffeur had dropped them back at the flat.

In fact, he waited until he'd slammed the front door behind them. He didn't have many neighbours, it was true, but the ones he did have had known him for years. And would probably have gone into extreme shock if they'd heard Guy Masters yelling at a woman, which was exactly what he felt like doing.

'Are you *mad*?' he demanded.

'And are *you* lacking in any social graces?' Sabrina returned hotly.

'You spent the whole night simpering up to Khalim!'

'Only because you could hardly bring yourself to say a civil word to me—and I was *not* simpering!'

He steadied his breath. Stay calm, he told himself. Stay calm. This wasn't like him at all. 'Do you have any idea of that man's reputation with women?'

Sabrina met his eyes with dignity. 'He seemed quite the gentleman—'

'*Quite the gentleman?*' he repeated faintly.

'Besides, I thought he was your friend.'

He heard the rebuke in her voice. 'He *is* my friend! He also has a legendary libido. Legendary. I can't believe that you'd be so naïve, Sabrina.' And he pictured the two of them together, and the black dagger of jealousy cut into him and sent the words spilling out before he could stop them. 'You weren't so naïve when…' But the words died as soon as he saw the look on her face.

'When what, Guy?' she asked coldly.

'Nothing.'

But she wasn't going to let this one rest. 'Oh, yes—*something*,' she contradicted furiously. 'Perhaps you think that if I go out with Khalim, I'll fall straight into bed with him. That he will be able to seduce me with the same ease as you did.'

He saw the hurt which clouded her ice-blue eyes and his mouth tightened. 'That's not what I said.'

'It's what you meant, though, isn't it? Well, *damn* you, Guy Masters, if that's your opinion of me, then there's no point me saying any more, is there? You obviously think I'm a tramp!' And she stalked off down to her bedroom, trembling with rage and distress.

He watched her go, fighting down the urge to run after her because he knew what the only outcome would be if he confronted her when emotions were running so high. God, he'd barely been able to watch Khalim coming on to her all night. And yet with his jealousy he'd offended her. Deeply.

But the time for reconciliation would be in the cold, clear light of logical thinking, not now—not when he was aching for her so badly that if he got within touching distance of her he would just want to haul her into his arms and crush his mouth down on hers and… Stifling a groan, he went off to take a much-needed shower.

Sabrina spent a restless night and woke up remembering the scene of the night before. And Guy's appalling insinuations.

She turned onto her side and gazed sightlessly up at the wall, wondering if those heated words should change things.

She could leave and go back to Salisbury now. Today, if she really wanted to. Maybe that was what a sane, sensible person would do. The trouble was that she felt neither particularly sane nor particularly sensible. She wanted...

She turned onto her other side and stared at the exercise bike, which was now positioned underneath the window. What *did* she want?

Most of her wanted Guy, with a growing love she hardly dared to acknowledge—but what did Guy want?

Nothing, it would appear.

Oh, she suspected that he still felt desire for her—she wasn't *stupid*. She had seen that unmistakable darkening of his eyes, the sudden tension of his body when she'd been close to him sometimes. He certainly wasn't immune to her—but neither did he seem to want to do anything about it.

She sighed. Perhaps she should just be grateful that he was behaving like such a gentleman. Her mother *would* be pleased.

There was a rap on the door, and a voice called out softly, 'Sabrina? Are you awake?'

'I am now!' she replied acidly.

Behind the door, Guy smiled. 'I'm making breakfast.'

'What do you want—a medal?'

'Just your company.'

She pushed the duvet back and stepped out of bed. What was the point in sulking, and pretending she hated him? If she intended to stay—and she did—she couldn't behave like a petulant child simply because he'd lost his temper with her last night. 'You'll have to wait until I'm showered and dressed,' she said.

Guy gave another wry smile. The trouble was that he liked

it when she started laying down the law. And it was novel enough to be very, very stimulating. 'Don't take too long.'

'Then go away and leave me to it.'

'Yes, Sabrina,' he murmured.

She appeared dressed and showered twenty minutes later, to find that he'd put a crisp white cloth on the dining-room table and there were freshly squeezed juice, warm croissants and different jams. And he was sitting, barefooted, in jeans and a T-shirt, reading a newspaper.

He looked up as she came in and their eyes met.

'I'm sorry,' he said, and forced himself to behave like a calm and rational human being instead of some kind of jealous monster. 'I had absolutely no right to talk to you like that. Whether or not you choose to go out with Khalim is entirely up to you.'

'You're absolutely right,' Sabrina agreed coolly as she sat down opposite him and picked up a napkin. 'It is.'

It was not the answer he'd been expecting. Or wanted. But he forced himself to smile. 'I'm going into the office for a couple of hours,' he said.

'But it's Sunday!' She pouted disapprovingly.

'Princess,' he said grimly, because much more of this and he really might lose his head. Or something even more dangerous. Like his heart. 'I just about know my days of the week!'

'You're going to burn out before you're forty,' she warned.

He drummed his fingers on the table. 'Lecture over now, is it, Sabrina?'

They spent the rest of that week being extremely polite to each other. And more than a little wary.

He was home earlier than usual on Thursday. Just as he'd been home earlier on Tuesday. Funny how the office suddenly seemed to have lost some of its old allure. He'd picked up a take-away on the way home, and they'd stood together, unpacking the foil containers, while Guy tried very hard not to be diverted by the sweet sheen of her hair.

'How about dinner tomorrow night?' he asked suddenly.

Sabrina looked up, surprised that he was keen to repeat the experience after what had happened last time. Unless... 'You mean, with you?'

'Yeah, and another client.'

Her heart fell, but she was damned if she would show it. 'Not Khalim?' she posed, wondering guiltily whether she ought to tell him that an exquisite orchid from the Prince had arrived by post yesterday. And it was hidden in all its scented beauty in the one place that Guy would never find it.

Her bedroom.

'No, not Khalim.' He spooned some rice onto his plate. 'Actually, it's a businessman who wants to buy a painting which has just come onto the market.' He shrugged. 'Even though he doesn't particularly like it.'

'Then why on earth is he buying it?'

'As an investment. And as a coup.' The ice-blue eyes were narrowed at him perceptively. She had a strange and infuriating habit of looking at him in that questioning way, and when she did he just couldn't seem to resist telling her what she wanted to know. 'He's a bit of an idiot, actually.'

Sabrina put the spoon down. 'And you want to give up your Friday night to have dinner with an idiot—and mine, too?'

'It's business.'

'Oh, yes—*business*.' She couldn't keep the derision out of her voice. 'Better not miss out, then, Guy—you really need that extra million bucks, don't you?'

Guy froze. He hadn't been the recipient of undiluted criticism for more years than he cared to remember, and even if it had more than a kernel of truth in it, it wasn't *her* damned place to give it to him. 'I take it that's a refusal?' he snapped, thinking that there wasn't a single other woman of his acquaintance who would have turned him down.

'Too right it is! I'd rather stay in and read my book, if you must know.'

'Fine,' he said tightly. 'Then do that.'

'I will!'

They had just sat down in a frosty silence to eat their meal when the telephone began to ring.

'You'd better get that, Guy,' said Sabrina sweetly. 'You virtually bit my head off the last time I answered it when you were here!'

And no wonder. He stood up. Ever since that day his mother had taken to ringing him at work and bombarding him with all kinds of questions about Sabrina. Where had they met, and what was she like? And the more he seemed to protest that she was nothing more than a girl who happened to be staying for a while, the less his mother seemed to believe him.

'You've never had a woman living with you before,' she'd pointed out.

'She's not living *with* me,' he'd explained tersely. 'Just living in the same flat. It's no big deal, Ma—people do it all the time these days.'

'Not someone like you,' his mother had said serenely. 'I know how you like to be in control.'

'So?'

'Well, as every year passes you become more and more eligible—'

'Ma,' he'd objected on a note of drawling humour.

'It's true. And an attractive young woman invading your space would normally have you running screaming in the opposite direction.'

'Who says she's attractive?' Guy had asked suspiciously.

'Well, *is* she?'

'Mmm,' he'd agreed, without thinking. 'She is. Very.'

His mother had sounded oddly triumphant. 'So when are we going to meet her? Your brother and I are itching with curiosity.'

'Then itch away. You are *not* going to meet her,' he'd said patiently. Then, having heard his mother's offended silence, he'd sighed. 'Not just yet, anyway…'

He picked the phone up. 'Guy Masters.'

'Guy? Khalim here.'

'Khalim!' He forced enthusiasm into his voice. 'What can I do for you?'

'May I speak with Sabrina, please?' came the honey-smooth response. 'I was going to ask her out to dinner on Saturday.'

Resisting the urge to slam the phone down, Guy marched back into the dining room. 'It's Khalim on the phone,' he said accusingly. 'For *you*.'

Infuriatingly, Sabrina found herself thinking about the orchid, and felt the blood rush hotly into her cheeks. 'I wonder what he wants.'

'To ask you out for dinner.' He stared at the pink cheeks and wondered what had caused her to blush. 'But we've been invited out to a party on Saturday.'

'We?' she asked disbelievingly.

'Well, I have,' he admitted. 'But I'm sure that Jenna won't mind if I bring someone.'

Oh, sure. Sabrina could just imagine how much Jenna would like *her* there. 'Jenna doesn't like me, Guy—on the only two occasions I've met her, she's looked at me as though I was an insect she found squashed onto the sole of her shoe.'

'She's better with men than with women,' he observed.

Understatement of the year. Sabrina paused by the door, thinking that she was fed up with only being good enough for client dinners with idiots or as the unwanted guest at the party of a predatory woman who obviously wanted Guy for herself.

'Actually, I just might go out with Khalim,' she said. 'It could be rather fun.'

Guy could hear her on the phone to his friend, and his pulse began to hammer. He pushed his barely touched plate of food away, and scowled. She could do what she damned well liked.

Inexplicably, Guy found himself cancelling the client dinner on Friday, and then spent the next evening prowling the sitting room like an edgy jungle cat as he waited for Khalim to arrive. He seethed when Sabrina breezed into the sitting room and he saw that she was wearing that same silky silvery grey dress she'd worn in Venice. The night he'd taken her to his bed.

It was on the tip of his tongue to ask her whether she intended an action replay with his friend, but some last vestige of sanity made him bite back the jealous words that he instinctively knew she would never forgive. Words that deep down he knew he didn't mean—so why the hell did he keep imagining the whole scenario, as if someone were running a film reel through his mind?

Sabrina felt slightly on edge, wondering if she was equipped to cope with a man who, as Guy had already said, ate women like her for breakfast.

Suddenly she wished that she hadn't been so proud, or so stupid. Fancy letting Guy go alone to a party where Jenna would no doubt be waiting to get her hooks in him. 'Aren't you going to be late, Guy?' she asked tentatively, and then almost recoiled from the anger in his eyes.

'Want me to get out from under your feet?' he asked silkily.

'Don't be so insulting!'

He picked up his jacket with a careless finger. 'Just

be careful, huh? You've got the number of my mobile, haven't you?'

'Why, do you think he's about to drag me off to his palace with him to make mad love to me all night?' she asked sarcastically.

'I wouldn't blame him if he did,' he drawled. He looked at the silver-grey fabric, which clung so enticingly to the slender curves of her body, and swallowed. If Khalim attempted to do that then as one man to another he would completely be able to understand it. 'But just remember this, Sabrina— he'll never marry an Englishwoman. His destiny has been mapped out for him since birth.'

'I'm not looking for a husband!' she snapped.

'Good.' He gave the ghost of a smile. 'Have a good time.'

'What, after *that* little pep-talk?' she asked acidly.

After Guy had gone, she felt like ringing up Khalim to cancel—but, apart from the fact that she didn't have a number for him—even Sabrina realised that such a loss of face would be intolerable to a man like the Prince.

Even so, she felt as if the executioner's axe was about to fall while she waited for the doorbell to ring.

Guy walked into the party and wished he could walk straight out again. He narrowed his eyes against the mêlée. Too many people, too much noise, too much smoke, and the music was *hellish*.

'Hello, Guy,' came a low, husky voice by his side, and he turned round to see Jenna, an expression he didn't quite recognise making her lovely face look a little less lovely than usual.

'Hi,' he said, thinking how overly jovial he sounded. He handed her a slim, silver-wrapped present. 'Happy birthday!'

'For me?' she said coyly. 'What is it?'

The question irritated him far more than it had any right to. 'Why not open it and see?'

Jenna's perfectly painted fingernails greedily ripped open the paper. 'Oh,' she said slowly. 'A book.'

She said it, thought Guy wryly, as though he'd just given her a serpent.

'Apparently, if you only read one book for the rest of your life, this is the one. It's up for a prize, and most people in the industry think it's just going to walk away with it.' He was, he realised, repeating Sabrina's enthusiastic praise almost word for word. She had recommended that he read it himself, and maybe he would. Maybe he would.

'Oh,' Jenna said.

The blinkers seemed to drop from his eyes as he surveyed Jenna's look of bemusement. It was going to be, he realised sadly, completely wasted on her. 'Hope you like it,' he finished lamely, and wondered just how long he could stay at this party without looking boorish.

'I'm sure I will!' Jenna's green eyes slanted from side to side. 'On your own?' she quizzed softly.

Something in her tone made his hackles rise. 'Obviously.'

Jenna shrugged. 'Nothing obvious about it at all—I'm surprised you haven't brought your new *flatmate* with you.'

Guy stared at her. Funny how you could know someone for years and years, and a remark which should have been completely inoffensive should suddenly sound like the most intolerable intrusion. His grey eyes gleamed. 'And why should that surprise you, Jenna?'

'Well…' Jenna drank some champagne and left some of the liquid to gleam provocatively on her lips. 'You know what people have been saying, don't you?'

'No, I don't. Why don't you tell me?' he suggested evenly.

Jenna shrugged. 'Oh, just that she's not your flatmate at all—but your lover.' She gave a shrill little laugh. 'As if!'

Some dark kind of explosion seemed to happen inside his head. 'You'd find that such a bizarre scenario, would you?' he asked quietly.

'Well…' Jenna shrugged, seemingly oblivious to the dangerous quality in his tone. 'I think that most people would, don't you? You're…' She gave a foolish, beaming smile, like someone who had decided to bet all their money on an outsider.

'Hmm? What am I?'

'You're…well, you're everything that most women would ever want, I suppose,' she stumbled. 'And she's…'

Guy froze. 'She's what?'

'Well, I'm sure she's very *nice*,' said Jenna insincerely. 'But she's just a small-town girl who works in a *bookshop*, isn't she?'

'As opposed to a small-minded girl who lives off her daddy's trust fund?'

Jenna stared at him. 'Guy!' she protested. 'That was completely uncalled for!'

His grey eyes were as cold as ice. 'What right do you think you have to criticise a sweet, beautiful woman who actually works hard for her living? Who has seen tragedy and looked it in the face, and managed to come to terms with it?'

'I didn't know anything about that!'

'You don't know anything about anything!' he snapped. 'Not about anything that really matters! Forgive me if I don't stay, Jenna, but I have something waiting for me at home!'

Or someone.

Except that he didn't—and why would he expect to? All he'd offered Sabrina had been some lousy dinner with a man he himself had admitted was a fool. And the only additional carrot he'd dangled in front of her had been a trip to the party of a woman who looked down her nose at her.

Was this what his life had become? Some kind of extravagant but superficial game? Going to all the right places but with all the wrong people—and for the wrong reasons, too?

And Sabrina was now out with Khalim—a man he liked and respected, but a man who was a veritable tiger where women were concerned. He had seen for himself that Khalim had been capitivated by Sabrina's easy, uncomplicated charm—just as he had been. He'd also said that Khalim would never marry an Englishwoman—but what if Sabrina's golden bright beauty was the exception to the rule? Khalim was used to getting whatever he wanted in life. Wouldn't he move heaven and earth to possess a woman if she'd touched his heart in a way that no one else had?

He drove like fury back to the flat, but it was, as he'd fully expected, empty.

He'd never spent a longer evening in his life—bar the one where he'd sat with his mother and waited for news which they'd both known in their hearts would be the worst possible news.

He tried reading, but that was useless, and he hated the television with a passion. He realised that he hadn't eaten, but couldn't face preparing any food. Or even eating some of Sabrina's carefully packed leftovers which sat at the back of the fridge. And the sight of her slavish economising made him want to hit something.

Or someone.

Guy forced himself to face the fact that she might not come home at all. That Khalim might now be making love to her with all the skill acquired from having had women offer themselves to him since he'd been barely out of his teens.

And if that *was* the case, then he must force himself to act like a rational man. He had no right to show temper or outrage. They weren't committing any crime. He didn't own her.

He glanced down at his watch. Where the hell *was* she?

He had just sprawled down on the sofa, a glass of wine in front of him, when he heard the sound of a key in the front door. He rose to his feet, but stood right where he was and waited. Because he knew that he might have to face the fact that Sabrina was not alone.

CHAPTER THIRTEEN

SABRINA walked into the sitting room to find Guy standing there, as motionless as if he'd been carved from some beautiful dark and golden stone. His eyes were the only animated part of his body, and they swept over her in a glittering and hectic question.

'Is Khalim with you?'

She shook her head. 'No. He's just driven off.'

Guy expelled a quiet breath of relief, but he didn't move. He had rushed in once before. This time it had to be different. He gestured towards the bottle of claret which stood on the table. 'Would you like some wine?'

It had been an emotional evening. She had drunk mineral water and jasmine tea, but right then she needed a drink. 'I'd love one.'

He poured her a glass and put it down on one of the small tables, keeping his voice deliberately casual. 'So. Good evening, was it?'

Sabrina dropped her shawl over the back of one of the chairs and went to sit down on one of the sofas. It hadn't been the evening she'd been expecting. But then she hadn't expected to find herself weeping quietly on Khalim's shoulder and telling him that she was in love with Guy—and that if he ever said anything to Guy about it, she would never forgive him.

And Khalim, still slightly shell-shocked from the first rejection he had ever encountered, had given a rueful smile and smoothed a tear-soaked strand of hair away from her cheek with a gentle finger.

'You think I would risk you not forgiving me?' he'd mused. 'You know, Guy is a strong man, not a stupid man—and he is behaving like one if he ignores this most precious gift which is his for the taking.'

Sabrina had bitten nervously at her lip. How could she possibly tell Khalim the truth? That she'd fallen into his friend's arms in Venice with such indecent haste that he probably had no respect left for her.

'He's not interested in me that way,' she'd told him stolidly. 'Not any more. I know he's not.'

'Then for the first time in my life I must question his judgement,' Khalim had replied in a hard, cold voice.

'And anyway,' she'd said, in a small voice, 'even if he was, I don't think I could bear to make myself that vulnerable again. If you love someone, then losing them is just unbearable.'

His dark eyes had narrowed. 'Explain,' he'd ordered quietly. And she'd told him all about Michael and he'd listened thoughtfully.

'So you see,' she'd finished, 'it's much too soon for me to fall in love with someone else—it does a disservice to Michael's memory.'

The hard lips had curved briefly into a smile. 'But love has no respect for convention, Sabrina,' he had sighed.

And from that moment on he had behaved almost as though she was sick, and in a way maybe she was. For the pain in her heart was real enough, surely? As real as the sharp pierce of longing which ripped right through her whenever she thought of Guy.

Khalim had made her eat a little something, and told her

something of his homeland. His voice had lulled her and soothed her, and his softly accented descriptions of his up-bringing had transported her to another world.

Just as Guy had transported her to another world.

But it wasn't her world.

'It was certainly different,' she said to Guy, as she remembered.

He forced himself to keep the jealous monster at bay. 'Oh?'

She sat down, picked up her glass and sipped at it grate-fully, acutely aware of the glittering grey gaze which held her fast in its dazzle. She thought that he looked almost strained tonight, with a strange kind of restlessness about him.

'How was Jenna's party?'

'Boring as hell.'

'Really?'

'Really. But I don't want to talk about Jenna's party. I'm much more interested in your evening.'

'Oh, Khalim had hired a private room in the most amaz-ing restaurant you've ever seen,' she said, still slightly reel-ing from the experience. 'Imagine—a whole room to ourselves!'

Behind the hard line of his mouth Guy gritted his teeth. Just a taste of Khalim's average over-the-top seduction tech-nique. 'How very impressive,' he said steadily.

He really *did* seem to be tense, as if he was hanging onto his self-control with difficulty, and Sabrina stared at him, willing her heart not to wrench, but it was hopeless. Every time she looked at him she felt nothing but an unbearable sense of longing.

'It was. Very,' she said simply. No need to tell him that she'd barely eaten a thing, or that the spectacular surround-ings hadn't registered. She might as well have been sitting in some scruffy old café for all that she would have noticed—

because Guy hadn't been there. And the world was just not the same place when Guy wasn't there.

'And are you going to see him again?'

Something in the harshness of the question made her go very still, and she gazed up into the hard contours of his face. 'And if I am?'

There was a dangerous pause. 'I don't like it.'

'*You* don't like it?' Sabrina stared at him. She thought about his rage when she'd told him she was going to accept Khalim's offer of a date. If she thought about it rationally, all the facts added up to jealousy. So, was Guy jealous of Khalim and, if so, why, when he had shown no signs of wanting her for himself? 'Why not?'

'Why do you think?' he snapped. 'Because it's doing my head in to think that he wants you when I want you so badly for myself.'

Joy mingled with disbelief. '*You*...want me?' she repeated, her voice trembling.

'Of course I want you! Haven't I wanted you ever since I made the foolish suggestion that you come and live here?'

'Why was it foolish?' she breathed.

He knew that now was not the time for his habitual evasion. 'Maybe I was just fooling myself into thinking that what happened in Venice was a reckless one-off.' Hadn't part of him secretly hoped it had been? He shook his head. 'But my feelings for you haven't changed.'

Sabrina stared at him. He'd used the word 'feelings', but she suspected that he really meant desire. But, however he chose to phrase it, it didn't really matter—because nothing could change the way she felt about him. Nothing.

'Haven't they?' she whispered.

'Not a bit.'

Guy watched her eyes darken involuntarily as their eyes locked, and saw the soft tremble of her lips. And suddenly he knew that neither logic nor reason could stop what he was about to do.

With a hand that wasn't quite steady he put his glass down on the table, walked over to the sofa and stood looking down at her. He saw the sudden parting of her lips as she read the answering hunger in his eyes.

'Guy?' she said breathlessly.

'Sabrina?' came the soft mocking response. 'Do you think we've played the waiting game for long enough?'

She could barely get the single word out. 'Y-yes.'

He held his hand out to her and she took it. In an instant she was in his arms, and his eyes were hard and bright and hungry as he brought his lips down to kiss her.

And just that first heady contact set her on fire. Blazing. With a tiny moan, she coiled her arms around his neck like a snake and he pulled her hard into his body so that their hips melded, and she could feel the hard, powerful jut of him throught the fine linen of his trousers.

He kissed her with a frustration that went bone-deep, and Guy found himself lost in the sweetness of her mouth, as if he could never get enough of plundering its honeyed moistness. He pulled her even closer, feeling the tips of her nipples as they strained against the sheer, silky fabric of her dress.

With an effort he pulled his lips away from hers, and she made a murmured little protest as he looked down at her, his eyes glittering black, opaque with desire.

'Is this what you really want, princess?' he groaned. 'Because if you don't, we'd better stop this right now.'

Her arms were still around his neck, their hips still intimately meshed. She could feel the growing power of him and realised how much he wanted her. And how much of an effort it must have taken for him to say that.

'Yes, I do,' she said almost shyly—which was crazy when

she considered that she hadn't been in the least shy with him before. But that night and that capitulation had been motivated by passion, pure and sweet and undiluted. While this…

This was love—more potent than any other emotion in the world. But only for *her*, she reminded herself. Only for her. Guy wasn't making any declarations—he was just a man, with a man's libido.

And maybe, knowing that, she should have stopped him, but Sabrina knew that no force in the world could have stopped her. Not when she wanted Guy this badly. 'Yes,' she said again. 'Yes.'

He found the gleam of flesh on her pale shoulder utterly irresistible and trickled a slow finger over its satin curve, watching as she shivered in response.

'Mmm,' he murmured, as he slipped first one strap down and then the other, so that the material fell in soft folds to her waist. Her tiny breasts were thrusting furiously against the soft lavender lace of her bra, the tips rosy and hard, and he nudged the pad of his thumb against one, seeing her body jerk automatically in response.

Her eyelids fluttered to a close. 'Guy!' She uttered his name in choked response to that first touch, feeling the wet, wild warmth of response.

'Feels good, doesn't it?' he murmured, circling his thumb with feather-light torment.

Good? It felt as if she'd just been catapulted straight into a place where nothing existed but pure sensation. 'It feels fantastic,' she moaned.

'No, *you* feel fantastic.' His closed his hand possessively over one tiny breast and her nails immediately dug into his neck as she swayed against him, communicating her heated reaction as clearly as if she'd spoken it.

Guy frowned. She was so damned responsive! He always took his women to bed. Always. And yet suddenly he discovered that he didn't want to break the spell by moving from where they were and taking their clothes off. He wanted to do it to her right here. And right now. It was as simple and as elemental as that.

'I don't know if I can make it to the bedroom,' he groaned.

'Who cares?' she whispered back.

'You mean you don't?'

'No.' She would swing from the chandelier if he wanted her to.

He pushed her down onto the carpet and joined her there, pulling her into his arms and kissing her while his hand slid beneath her dress and smoothed it all the way up to her thighs. He gazed down at their milky pale curves and felt his resolve slipping away. 'I don't know if I can even bear the time to take your clothes off, princess. Or mine.' He grazed her a light stroking touch where she was most responsive, smiling as her body bucked against his hand.

Sabrina's head fell back against the Persian carpet as she felt the first honeyed flutter of his fingers, and her thighs parted for him of their own volition. 'Then don't,' she breathed hoarsely, feeling as wanton right then as she had ever felt. 'Don't. Let's just do it.'

She found herself fumbling at the button of his trousers, then rasping the zip down with difficulty, her hand straying agitatedly over his hard swell, and she heard him suck in a ragged breath.

'Make that a definite,' he moaned as he tugged her panties down right over her thighs, skimming them impatiently over her ankles and then tossing them over his shoulder. 'Now, my little temptress…'

Hearing the slumberous intent in his voice, Sabrina opened her eyes to see him kick off his trousers, exposing the true, daunting power of his arousal, and she shivered as he came to kneel over her.

He bent his head and touched his mouth against hers as he positioned himself close to her. Tantalisingly close. 'Want me?' he whispered.

She couldn't think of a time when she hadn't. Not if she was being honest with herself. 'Oh, God, yes,' she moaned helplessly, as she writhed her hips impatiently beneath his.

'Well, then…' And he groaned as he entered her with one single, powerful thrust. 'You've got me.'

This time was different. This time she knew him—or at least as much of him as he was prepared to let her know. For there was always some sense that Guy was holding something of himself back. But who cared? Maybe she would never have all of him—but no person could ever totally possess another, could they?

But now—physically at least—he was as abandoned as she had only ever dreamed he could be.

In Venice he had been a skilful lover, but they had been strangers. This time his kisses were deeper, his caresses more tender. With each long, deep stroke, she felt enchained by his possession. It *felt* different. As if it really mattered.

No. That was simply an illusion, she forced herself to remember. Just the body's way of tricking the mind into thinking that this was something more than just a basic human need. She tried to keep a hold on her sanity, even as the first waves of orgasm began to shimmer her down into its sweet, shuddering waters. And only sanity prevented her from crying out how much she loved him.

Guy watched the arching of her back and the indolent splaying of her limbs, and only when he saw her body begin to judder and bloom did he allow himself to let go, to the most exquisite release.

Afterwards they lay together on the carpet, dipping in and out of a slumberous doze, their limbs still damp and tangled.

He heard her yawn and looked to where her tousled red-blonde hair lay ribboned across his chest. 'You do realise,' he murmured sleepily, 'that we're still half-dressed?'

She looked down at herself. Then at him.

Her dress lay rucked up to her waist, while Guy was wearing nothing but a T-shirt. She could see the beautifully pale curves of his buttocks and she felt a warm heat begin to suffuse her.

'Oh.'

He rolled on to her and captured her face as his hips crushed hers beneath him. 'Is that all you can say— "Oh"?' He saw her squirm and her agitated look and his eyes narrowed. '*Oh,*' he repeated softly, but he managed to fill the word with a sultry promise. 'Maybe we *had* better go to bed.'

Sabrina swallowed. 'What, right now?'

He smiled. 'Mmm. Right now.' And he pulled her to her feet, shaking his head as he saw her look around the room for her underwear. 'Leave that,' he instructed softly. 'You won't be needing any clothes tonight.' And saw her shivered response.

He took her by the hand and led her to his bedroom, in a section of the large flat she usually avoided, throwing the door open to reveal an airy room dominated by an enormous bed. Huge windows looked down onto the flower-filled square.

'I don't think you've ever been in here before, have you, princess?' he murmured. 'Do you like it?'

'Well, I have seen it,' admitted Sabrina, and saw the question in his eyes. 'I sneaked a look when I first moved in. I was…curious.' More than curious.

She had wanted to see whether the room could tell her more about the man, but it had thrown up few clues. The paintings were superb, the furniture modern and luxurious— but it was an oddly dispassionate room. As though he was wary about expressing too much of his personality through mere fixtures and fittings. Again, there was that distinctive air of containment.

Guy should have been riled at what could definitely have been termed as an intrusion, but found himself smiling instead. He thought that few people would have admitted it. But then wasn't Sabrina's innate innocence one of her sweetest and most appealing features? Well, that and her stubborn insistence and the way she could make him mad and then make him smile an instant later. Even the way she nagged him about working too hard—which his mother had long given up on.

'Do you mind?' she asked. 'That I sneaked a look?'

He saw the uncertainty which had clouded the ice-blue eyes, and a wave of an emotion he didn't recognise washed over him. He forced himself instead to watch the pert thrust of her breasts.

'I'm rather turned on by the thought of you prowling around in here like a pussy-cat,' he said roughly. 'Come on, let's go to bed.'

CHAPTER FOURTEEN

SABRINA opened her eyes to the morning light and closed them again as images of the previous night came flickering back.

What had she *done*? Placed herself in the most precariously vulnerable position in the world—that was what she'd done. Given herself to Guy, heart, body and soul.

'Good morning, princess,' came a murmured greeting, and her eyes snapped open to see Guy standing, towering above her, already shaved and dressed for work in another exquisitely cut dark suit, and she felt a great wrench of longing.

'Hello,' she whispered, her heart thundering at the sight of him.

He smiled. 'You were sleeping so beautifully that I couldn't bear to wake you.'

She sat up and saw his eyes darken as her bare breasts were exposed, and some protective instinct made her gather the sheet around her.

'You're going already?' she asked him.

'Wish I didn't have to, but I have an early meeting,' he said softly, and sat down on the bed beside her.

Of course he did. Guy the workaholic. Guy the driven. He might have spent most of the night making exquisite love to her, but that didn't change his priorities, did it? And work came first. It always would.

Well, she might have been compliant in his arms last night, but that didn't mean that she had to exist in a passive state of insecurity now.

'This changes things, doesn't it?' she said slowly.

There was an imperceptible pause as the grey eyes narrowed. He'd hoped to avoid any kind of analysis. 'How come?'

'Oh, don't be obtuse, Guy, you're much too intelligent for that,' she told him crossly. 'If I'm living with you...' She saw the wariness on his face and wished she'd phrased it better. 'If I'm living here and we're having—'

'Sex?' he put in, with a wicked grin.

Thank goodness he'd interrupted her. She'd been about to say 'a relationship', but his drawled one-word question had brought what had just happened between them down to the lowest common denominator. And shown her more clearly than anything else could have done just how different their agendas were. She might love Guy—but that didn't mean he felt the same way about her. Men didn't need to be *in* love to make love the way he had done.

'Yes, sex.' She swallowed.

'Good sex.' He trickled a finger slowly from shoulder to breast, and she let the sheet fall. 'The very best,' he added slowly.

It should have been a compliment, so why did it sound little short of an insult? 'Thank you,' she said stiffly.

He flicked softly at one rosy nipple, feeling it surge into instant life beneath his finger. God, he felt like just getting back into bed with her and forgetting the damned meeting. His face hardened. He hadn't got where he was today by letting a woman trap him with her honeyed sweetness.

'Why should it change anything, except for the better?' he

questioned softly. 'We carry on as we were, only now you share my bed at night. I can't think of anything I'd rather have.'

'No,' she said sadly. Of course he couldn't. He didn't want commitment, or even a relationship. He wanted sex, pure and simple—and obviously he thought that was all she wanted, too. And who could blame him? Hadn't she always demonstrated the sensual side of her nature around him?

He reluctantly moved his hand from her breast and cupped her face instead. 'What's the problem, Sabrina?' he asked gently. 'Why the long face? Let's just enjoy it, huh?'

And when she came to the end of her stay with him, what then? But consenting adults didn't make unnecessary emotional demands, did they? Guy didn't love *her*—and wouldn't he doubt *her* feelings if he had any idea what they were? Wouldn't he consider her fickle if she told him she'd fallen in love with him—only months after the death of the man she'd been due to spend the rest of her life with?

But love could strike without warning. It wasn't exclusive. Just because she'd been in love once before, that didn't mean it couldn't happen again. What she'd felt for Michael hadn't been what she felt for Guy. Her feelings were different, but that didn't make them any less valid. And they were all-consuming.

She wanted him, she realised, on whatever terms he was prepared to take her.

But he wouldn't know that. She would keep her dignity and play at being a modern woman, not a lovesick fool who would settle for anything—just as long as it included him.

'OK, let's just enjoy it,' she echoed, and slanted him a smile.

Her look was one of pure provocation, and just for one second Guy wavered, itching to undress and climb into bed with her and lose himself in her body.

But he'd broken so many rules where Sabrina was concerned—wouldn't one more be his downfall? Hadn't he controlled his life according to a rigid plan laid down by the circumstances of his youth? It would be nothing short of recklessness to go in deeper than he already was. Her fiancé wasn't long gone, he reminded himself. For Sabrina, this was a purely physical affair on the rebound. It had to be. Logic told him that.

He stood up quickly, not trusting himself to kiss her. Just being this close to her and knowing she was stark naked underneath that sheet was playing havoc with his senses. 'Time I was out of here,' he said abruptly, and then softened to give her a smile. 'I'll see you tonight, princess.'

She watched him go, heard the front door slam, shatteringly aware that he hadn't even kissed her. Maybe she should be grateful for that. At least he wasn't filling her head with false promises of happy-ever-after.

She sighed. They would carry on as before. Living together—only this time, as Guy had so unromantically put it, with sex as part of the equation.

The next three weeks ticked away like a time-bomb, with Sabrina alternating between giddy elation and wild despair but determined to show neither emotion.

Guy took her to the theatre, and to concerts. He even skipped work on the Saturdays when she was off and they explored London together, like tourists.

And at night…

At night he couldn't seem to keep his hands off her. And it was really quite disturbing how one dark, sensual look levelled mockingly at her across the sitting room was enough to send her running straight into his arms.

While sometimes she despised herself for her instant surrender whenever he touched her, at least she had the comfort of knowing that it didn't seem any different for him. She could reduce him to putty in her hands.

Why, she had even made him late for work this morning, and thrown his careful schedule into disarray. All because she had strolled into the bathroom one morning, wearing nothing but a pair of silver camiknickers while he'd been combing his hair.

Guy had stilled as he'd seen her reflection in the mirror, the pale swell of her breasts and the long curve of her legs beneath the frivolous lace trim. A pulse had begun to beat steadily at his temple.

'What are you doing?' he asked, in an odd kind of voice.

She batted him an innocent smile as she bent down to retrieve a book from where she'd been reading it in the bath the previous night while waiting for him to get back from Rome.

'I forgot this,' she said, and straightened up.

But the sight of the silver silk stretching tightly over her bottom had been enough to send his senses into overdrive. He put the comb down with a hand which wasn't quite steady.

'Kiss me goodbye,' he ordered throatily.

She went into his arms without a word, and pressed her lips to his, feeling them part on a sigh to greet her. 'Goodbye,' she whispered, but she couldn't resist moving her body closer and feeling the sudden responding tension in his.

His hand snaked around her waist, drawing her in closer still. He was painfully and erotically aware of her barely clothed state, even through the thickness of the suit he wore.

Trapped against his hard, virile body, Sabrina felt the warm pooling of a desire so strong that she couldn't have resisted it if she had tried. And she certainly wasn't trying.

'I don't want to be late,' he ground out, but once again he drove his mouth down onto hers in a sweet, crushing kiss.

'God forbid,' she murmured, and flicked her tongue inside his mouth, hearing him groan in response.

'Stop it, Sabrina,' he pleaded, but only half-heartedly.

Caught up with longing and compelled by a need to shatter that rigid control, she moulded her breasts brazenly against his torso. 'Stop what?' she murmured, and allowed her fingers to trickle down over the rocky shaft of his erection, feeling him jerk in distracted response. 'Do you want me to stop this?' She ran her hand expertly over him. 'Do you, Guy?'

A shudder ran through him as he felt her begin to unzip him. There would be no stopping now, he realised with a hot, heady rush of blood, and then his hands were on her breasts, feeling them spring into excited life beneath his hungry fingertips.

She struggled to free the zip and the trousers fell redundantly to his ankles. She heard him swear softly, and then, very deliberately, he moved the damp silk panel of her camiknickers aside and delved his fingers deep into the honeyed moistness. She gasped.

'Do you like that?' he murmured, feeling her thighs instantly parting for him. 'Do you?'

Her response was instant and overwhelming. Sabrina swayed as she clasped his dark head against her, murmuring a protest she didn't feel, her knees sagging weakly as she felt the swift heat of need. He lifted his head to glitter her a look of provocative assessment and swiftly turned her over so that she was bending over the bath.

He ripped her camiknickers off without compunction and let his silk boxer shorts fall to his ankles, and she realised that he was going to…going to…

'Oh, Guy!' she gasped ecstatically, as he entered her.

He groaned as he submerged himself in her hot, molten depths, thinking that it shouldn't be this simple—or this out of control. And then he wasn't doing any thinking at all. The world had shifted focus and then hardened, to a brighter focus, and now it splintered out of all recognition as they both cried out at the same time.

He pulled out of her and turned her around, thinking how shaken she looked. Well, hell, he was pretty shaken himself. When had he ever acted like *that* before? In Venice, he reminded himself grimly, that was when.

'You've made me late for work,' was all he said. Then he gave her a hard, crushing kiss before turning and swiftly walking out of the bathroom.

Flushed with orgasm, and a bitter kind of regret, Sabrina slammed the lock home behind him and then sank to her knees on the bathroom floor as dry, shuddering sobs began to tear at her throat. What on earth was happening to them?

As a demonstration of lust, that experience had been in a class of its own. Guy had used her for sex, but hadn't she gone ahead and *allowed* herself to be used? She loved him, yes, but he'd never given any indication that he felt even a *fraction* of love for her. And she didn't want to love again. Not like this. Bad enough that she'd loved and lost Michael—but at least Michael had felt the same way about *her*.

And she had known then with a sinking certainty that this one-sided love would bring her nothing but heartbreak. Far better to begin to distance herself. Starting from now.

It was late-night shopping this evening, and she'd make herself go browsing round after she'd finished work, deliberately make herself late home.

But Guy was even later. He'd had to juggle his day to include the missed meeting, and then had sat through it, bored and distracted, trying not to keep glancing down at his watch and thinking about Sabrina.

This was getting slightly ridiculous, he thought exasperatedly as he let himself into the flat. Going home at night had become the highlight of his day.

But tonight there was no meal cooking.

Just Sabrina sitting on the sofa, looking moody, an unopened book lying on her lap.

He dropped his briefcase and gave her a thoughtful look. 'Hi,' he said softly.

'Hi.'

He thought how wooden her voice sounded. And maybe he deserved it. 'Sabrina, listen—about this morning—'

'No, Guy, please.' She shook her head, her cheeks growing pink as shame vied with remembered pleasure. 'It happened—let's forget it.'

That was the trouble—he couldn't forget it. It had been on his mind all day. And so had she. 'I shouldn't have been so abrupt with you afterwards.'

'No, you shouldn't!' She threw him a furious look. 'And maybe *I* shouldn't have committed the terrible sin of wandering in looking like that when you were getting ready for work. How wicked of me to unwittingly throw temptation in your path, Guy! Heaven forbid that you should ever break your rigid routine and be *late*!'

'Sabrina,' he said softly, 'are we going to fight about this all night?'

'No, we aren't.' She drew a deep breath. They weren't going to fight about anything and she was going to be very calm and grown-up about what she had to say. 'We ought to talk about me going.'

He went very still, as though he hadn't heard her properly. '*Going?*' he echoed. 'What are you talking about?' His voice softened. 'Aren't you taking things a little too far, princess? I know what we did was pretty wham-bam-and-thank-you-ma'am, but there's no need to overreact.'

'This has nothing to do with this morning.' But she forced herself to remember that brutal and loveless kiss, and that somehow made what she had to say all the easier. 'I only came here on a temporary basis, remember? And the six weeks are nearly up.'

If she'd detonated a small bomb on the carpet in front of

him he couldn't have been more shell-shocked. Her stay had merged into one pleasurable and sensual blur. Had she really been here for *that* long? Guy stared at her. 'But you aren't really going?'

It was a million miles away from the 'please, don't go' she'd been hopelessly praying for. She kept her face carefully composed. 'I have to, Guy—I won't have a job after next Friday, and they won't hold my job in Salisbury. Believe it or not, jobs in bookshops are highly sought-after.'

He could believe it quite easily—but then he'd seen her at work. A meeting had been cancelled and he'd called for her unexpectedly one lunchtime, dismissively waving away her protests that she'd brought a sandwich with her.

'We'll feed it to the pigeons,' he'd murmured, thinking that the books and the old polished wood of the shop only seemed to enhance her bright-haired beauty. One look at Sabrina sitting busy at her desk, and any sane person would have thought it the most perfect job in the world.

'So leave.' He shrugged.

Sabrina froze. 'Leave?'

Guy gave a slow smile. 'Sure. I can support you.'

'I don't want your support,' she said stiffly. 'Or your charity.'

'Sabrina.' His voice softened as he walked across the room and sat down beside her on the sofa, not missing the almost imperceptible shift of her body as she leaned away from him. 'It's not charity. I earn obscene amounts of money—'

'You said it, Guy.'

His eyes narrowed. 'You don't *need* to work,' he said quietly.

'*I don't need to work?*' she repeated in disbelief, before leaping to her feet to stare down at him in an angry blaze. 'Says who? Says *you*! Well, if that's the case, you don't know anything, Guy, not really!'

'Oh? This is fast becoming a real home-truth session,' he drawled. 'Do continue, Sabrina—I'm fascinated.'

'Don't you have any idea about my need for independence?' she stormed, ignoring the dangerous note in his voice. 'Or did you think I would just fall to the ground in a grateful heap because you've offered to "support" me?'

'Clearly not,' came the dry retort. A lot of women would have done. His mother, for example, had never forgotten what he'd done for her. But that had been different. That had been called survival.

Jenna, he realised, would have adored the idea. So would many of the other trust-fund babes. Not Sabrina, though, he realised slowly. Her principles were in a different class.

'It's *your* flat!' she stormed. '*You* have all the control here—so just imagine if you started paying for me, too. How unequal would *that* make things? At least buying groceries now and then makes me feel as though I'm doing my bit!'

He looked at her steadily. 'So what do you suggest we do?'

She looked at him sadly, realising that she'd talked herself into a corner. There was no solution—or at least not one that would make her happy. Only one thing could do that, and he wasn't offering her permanence.

Because if she accepted his offer to stay while he supported her, then where would that leave her? Busy clinging on to a relationship which would grow increasingly more one-sided.

Even if she found herself another job here in London, wouldn't that just be postponing the inevitable heartbreak when he tired of her?

'I'll leave at the end of next week,' she said impassively. 'As orginally planned.'

Guy's body quickened, even as his heart felt the unfamiliar pang of rejection. But if she was expecting him to *beg* her to change her mind, she had a lot to learn about him. Needing something enough to beg made you vulnerable, and he had once made a vow never to be vulnerable again. He paused. 'So, until you go, will we continue as…before, Sabrina?'

How very delicately phrased, she thought with a slight tinge of hysteria. 'You mean, will I be sharing your bed at night?'

He thought that there were a few more flattering ways she could have described it. 'That's exactly what I mean,' he answered coolly.

Her hunger for him warred with her self-respect, but it was never going to be much of a battle. She thought about how bleak her future would be without him, and knew that she wanted to savour every last, glorious moment. 'Ask me tonight,' she said flippantly.

He knew from the darkening of her eyes just what her answer would be, but any triumph was eclipsed by a slow, ticking anger. So she thought she could just play cat and mouse with him when it suited her, did she?

He rose to his feet with stealthy grace and pulled her into his arms without warning. 'Why don't I ask you now?' he drawled, before claiming her mouth in a kiss which had her reeling.

CHAPTER FIFTEEN

SABRINA let herself into the flat with a heavy heart and went to put the shopping in the kitchen.

Two more days. Just two.

It was inconceivable. Especially as Guy had spent the last few days seemingly hell-bent on showing her just what she would be missing. He didn't seem satisfied until he had her sobbing out her shuddering pleasure, night after night…but he'd never asked her to stay.

She made herself a coffee and then went to stand at the window, where the bright hues of early summer dazzled from the garden in the square. How on earth could she ever go back to being what she had been?

Or maybe that was the wrong way to look at it. She could never really go back to being the old Sabrina—there was a new one now, ready and willing to take her place. And rebirth, like birth, was always painful. Why else would she feel this terrible, tearing pain at the thought of never seeing Guy Masters again?

Would he miss her? she wondered achingly. Probably, just a little, yes. And certainly in bed. But the missing, like their relationship, would be unequal. Guy called the shots and Guy had all the control. He would miss her for a little while and then move on.

Sabrina glanced down at her watch. It was only just past six, so there was at least an hour and a half before he would grace the flat with his presence.

She had bought a load of cheap vegetables at the market, and she had just begun to chop them in order to make a soup when there was a sharp ring at the doorbell. Wiping her hands down over the apron which she insisted on wearing, and which Guy always teased her about, Sabrina went to answer it, to find Tom Roberts standing on the doorstep.

'Hi, Tom.' She smiled affectionately.

She'd last seen Guy's cousin at a drinks party a couple of weeks ago, and then he'd been sipping at a Bloody Mary and laughing at something Sabrina had said. But today he looked wary.

'Hi, Sabrina—may I come in?'

'Oh, yes, of course, of course,' babbled Sabrina, and pulled the door open. 'Only I'm afraid that Guy isn't back from work yet.'

'I know that. It isn't Guy I've come to see. It's you.'

'Oh.' She smiled. 'That's nice. You'd better come in.'

'Thanks.' He followed her into the sitting room and sat down.

Sabrina looked at him expectantly. 'Can I get you a drink, Tom?'

'No, thanks—I'm out to dinner later and Trudi will kill me if I turn up with an inane grin on my face.' He suddenly grew serious. 'Is it really true? Guy says you're leaving.'

Hearing the words spoken aloud like that by a third person made Sabrina realise just how horribly true it was.

'That's right. I am.'

'But, Sabrina, *why*? I mean, I've never seen him looking so contented—happy, even! And you're the first woman he's ever lived with, even though women have been mounting campaigns to snare him for years. He says that he doesn't want you to go, but that you're going anyway. So why?'

She shook her head. 'I can't go into it, Tom. It's too complicated, and it isn't fair on Guy.'

'Fair on Guy?' Tom repeated slowly. 'Sabrina, look…' He seemed to be having difficulty choosing the right words. 'I've known Guy all my life, but, with him, what you see isn't automatically what you get.'

'You're talking in riddles, Tom.'

He pulled a face. 'Everyone looks at him and thinks that he's Mr Invulnerable—strong and rich and powerful—'

'Maybe that's because he *is*,' observed Sabrina drily.

'Yeah, I know all that. And that's what he likes to project. But that's only part of the package—he keeps a lot of himself hidden. That highly controlled and tough exterior he's cultivated—that's what he shows to the world.'

'You're telling me,' said Sabrina bitterly. 'The man for whom the term, "workaholic" was invented.'

'And have you never stopped to ask yourself why?'

'Tom, you know him better than almost anyone—so you must also know that he doesn't like to talk about himself.'

'Well, maybe it's about time you tried! I mean, like, *really* tried! Have you?'

'When a door is kept locked you give up trying to open it,' she said.

'You could always try kicking it down,' he suggested softly.

'Women don't kick doors down,' Sabrina objected, forgetting for a moment that they were talking metaphorically.

'But they can,' he objected. 'It just takes longer.'

She stared at Tom, taken aback by his vehemence, even though that wary look was still in place on his face. There was, she realised, something he wasn't telling her. And she knew that his loyalty to his cousin meant he wouldn't disclose it. 'Maybe I should,' she agreed slowly.

'Anyway…' Tom rose to his feet. 'Time I was going. And there's no need to mention to Guy that I was here.'

She shook her head. 'Don't worry. I won't.'

After he'd gone, Sabrina prowled the flat, the soup forgotten, and realised that she'd been guilty of some sort of emotional cowardice. She'd fought for her independence, and a kind of equality with Guy, and yet she'd allowed herself to be daunted by that enigmatic, don't-ask-me quality of his.

She had shared his life, and his bed, but had stood on the sidelines when it had come to exploring his feelings—mainly out of a selfish sense of self-preservation. She'd known that he hadn't wanted her to ask, and so she hadn't. She'd wanted Guy, but hadn't been prepared to risk being hurt by him—and you couldn't do that in a relationship. Loving someone automatically made you vulnerable to pain.

I've got to talk to him, she told herself. Whatever happens, I can't leave him without having done that.

Guy cut his meeting short, and it was clear from his secretary's expression that she clearly thought he had taken leave of his senses.

Well, maybe he had.

Or maybe he was just coming to his senses.

He found himself asking why he was prepared to let someone like Sabrina simply walk out of his life without argument. As if he had no control over the future. As though, because of one long-ago act, a pattern had been set in his life and he was powerless to change it. It was ironic, really, that he—the master of control—was allowing events to gather up speed by themselves.

He'd spent his life shielding himself from the prying questions of women on the make. Yet Sabrina was clearly *not* on the make—and neither did she ask him questions.

He was so caught up in his thoughts that he missed his stop on the tube. Another first, he thought wryly as he walked home in the golden summer sunshine. But the idea that Guy

Masters—the cool and controlled Guy Masters—had misjudged a train journey he'd been making for the past who-knew-how-many years actually had him smiling ruefully.

He walked into the flat. 'Sabrina?' He watched while she drifted out of the sitting room, as graceful as that water nymph he'd first compared her to in Venice.

'Hello,' she said softly.

She'd used her waiting hour to shower, and to change and carefully apply her make-up. Because this was important, she realised. Very important. And, like a job interview she was determined to win, she just wanted to look her best. It was as simple as that.

Guy wanted to kiss her. Hell, he wanted to lose himself in the sweet torment of her body. But he didn't trust himself to touch her. Sometimes desire could cloud judgement, and right then he needed every bit of judgement he'd ever possessed.

'I need to talk to you, Sabrina.'

'And I need to talk to you.'

He nodded, but absently, as if he'd scarcely heard her. Like a man with a lot on his mind.

'Let's go into the sitting room,' he said abruptly.

Sabrina nodded as she followed him, vaguely disappointed at something in his tone but determined not to lose her nerve. She would chip, chip, chip away until she found out what she needed to know and what Tom hadn't been able to tell her.

In the sitting room neither of them sat, but instead stood looking at each other warily, like two fighters sizing each other up before a duel.

'Do you want to leave?' he demanded. 'I mean, really?'

Truth? Or lie? Communication? Or hiding behind social niceties? What did she have to lose? 'Of course I don't!'

Relief flooded his veins like a drug, and Guy drew in a

deep breath. 'Well, that's good—because I don't want you to either. I want you to stay here. With me.'

Sabrina stared at him steadily. She had played her part— now she needed to know the truth from *him*. 'Why?'

How else to say this without shooting straight from the hip? But Guy used words carefully—he recognised their power and their significance—and there were certain words that he would not use lightly. Or recklessly. Unless he was certain that he meant them. And he didn't want to frighten her either. Or push her into something before she was ready. 'I...care for you, Sabrina,' he said slowly. 'That's why.'

So he cared for her. It was a curiously colourless way to phrase it, but Sabrina nodded her head slowly, less disappointed than she'd imagined she would be. He wasn't offering her the moon, no, but it was a start. For Guy to even *admit* caring for her was something. Because he was not, she knew, a man who would make a declaration without thinking it through first, or without meaning it.

But if she stayed then there had to be a new honesty between them. 'Why leave it until the day before I was going?' she demanded. 'Why on earth didn't you say something before?'

'Because I was burying my head in the sand and believing in the impossible.' He sighed. 'I imagined that my life would continue in its calm and uncluttered way once you'd gone. I didn't realise that the thought of you not being here was going to drive me out of my mind!'

Well, that was a bit better. A lot better. She actually smiled, but the smile had a hint of reproof about it. 'Hell, Guy, I've virtually packed all my suitcases!'

'Then unpack them,' he drawled silkily, but something in her face made him backtrack. He owed her more than that rather dispassionate request that she stay with him. 'Listen to me, Sabrina. I'm no good at trust—you'll have to help me.

I'm used to women who are...' he paused '...*different* from you.'

Women who wouldn't want to know him if he was just an average guy. Not like Sabrina. She'd fallen under his spell without knowing *who* he was. His gaze was unflickering. 'And I guess my childhood sowed the seeds of distrust almost from the start.'

She held her breath. Here, she was certain, lay the key to the barrier he'd erected around himself. This was what Tom had been hinting at. 'Do you want to tell me about it?' she asked him softly.

He paused only for as long as it took to be mesmerised by the ice-blue dazzle of her eyes. 'Yes,' he said simply, and gave a long sigh. 'You're always complaining that I work too hard...'

Her persistence had, in fact, sown the first seeds of doubt in his mind. Had made him look closely at her accusations. 'And you've made me see how right you are. When you live alone, there's no one to question you—no one to compare yourself with. It's become a habit that's hard to break, a habit that started a long time ago...'

'Tell me, Guy,' she urged quietly, remembering how he'd let her unburden herself over Michael. And suspecting that he now needed to do the same for himself.

His mouth flattened. 'My father was the opposite to the way I am—his whole life was a reckless gamble. He would hear about some sure-fire scheme to make money and he would invest everything he had. Our life became a lottery. My mother and my brother and I used to find ourselves living in mansions. Or hovels, more often than not,' he went on, with a disparaging shrug. 'With my mother trying to feed two growing boys—and next to nothing in the cupboard. I guess it was just fortunate that a family trust paid for our education, or things would have come to a head much sooner.'

'But something happened?' prompted Sabrina, hurting herself at the look of pain which had frozen his features. 'Something really bad?'

Was it that obvious? he wondered. He'd thought that he'd trained his face to hide all emotion—but Sabrina seemed to have the ability to make it come creeping back again. The words he'd locked away for so long came tumbling out as if they couldn't wait to be spoken.

'His schemes became more and more bizarre and my mother grew concerned. She tried to get all our assets put in her name, but he was far cleverer than she was. I guess these days she wouldn't have stayed with him—but things were different then. And she was loyal, too.' Just as you would be, he thought suddenly.

He saw her look of horror and heard himself defending his father. And that was something else he'd only just realised. That, whatever wrong he had done, his father was still his father.

'Oh, it wasn't a malicious action on his part—more a lack of judgement and a sense of misplaced pride. But one day he went too far and lost everything.' Guy shrugged. 'The business, the house, the car. Everything. With debts galore thrown in for good measure. Only this time his spirit was broken, too. I was fifteen, and my brother was twelve.'

There was a grim silence. Sabrina didn't say a word.

'My mother's parents took us in—they had a beautiful big house close to the cliffs in Cornwall.' His eyes grew distant as he thought back to a time he'd buried away deep in the recesses of his mind. 'But accepting charity—even family charity—was anathema to my father. He tried working in paid employment, but he could never cope with working for other people. His mood went down and there seemed to be no way that anyone could reach out and help him. And he and my mother never communicated particularly well.'

Sabrina nodded. That explained a lot, too. Guy's fear of

relationships, his wariness of commitment and sharing. A bad role-model could put you off for life.

His face grew dark as he forced himself to say the words. 'One night he went out and never came back again.'

'What happened?' whispered Sabrina hoarsely.

He didn't coat it with any sugar. 'He went out walking on the cliff-top. It was a wild night and the wind was blowing up a storm. He fell... We'll never know what really happened—whether he lost his footing, or if the wind caught him off balance. Or whether he jumped.'

He met her eyes with such a bleak expression that Sabrina couldn't help herself. In fact, even if he'd been just about to kick her out she still would have gone straight over and put her arms around him and hugged him as tightly as she knew how. Trying, however futilely, to take some of his pain away.

'Oh, Guy,' she whispered brokenly. 'Guy.'

He dropped a kiss onto her beautiful head, but forced himself to continue, feeling the burden lifting even as he shared it with her.

'I determined then that I would never be placed in such a vulnerable position again—and neither would my mother or brother.'

'So how did you manage?'

'Against everyone's advice, I left school at sixteen and started working, and I never really stopped. Khalim's father gave me a break, and I was off.' Off on a merry-go-round of hard work which had continued until this bright-haired temptress had walked into his life.

Sabrina rubbed her cheek against his shirt. He'd told her everything she'd wanted to know, without her having to ask him. He'd trusted her enough to open up to her. Would his trust now spread out and out, like ripples on a pond, so that their relationship got bigger and bigger?

'I didn't plan to feel this way about you, Sabrina,' he admitted huskily as he caught her by the shoulders and forced her to look up at him, his own eyes soft with promise.

She felt the glimmer of tears. 'As if anyone has any control over their feelings.' She gulped. 'I wasn't planning on...' Her words tailed off. To talk of love would frighten him almost as much as it frightened her.

'On what?'

'Needing you like this,' she compromised.

'Need can be a powerful emotion, princess.' He tipped her chin upwards with the tip of his finger and gave a slightly shell-shocked smile. 'I find I need *you* pretty badly myself.'

She recognised what it had cost him to admit that. She stood on tiptoe to plant a soft kiss on his lips, and he sighed.

'So you'll stay?' he asked.

She drew her mouth away, her dreamy expression replaced by one of caution. Should she stay? But did she really have any alternative, when the thought of leaving filled her with a kind of mad despair?

All he'd told her was that he cared for her. He'd made no promise other than an unspoken one, which was that he trusted her enough to open up his heart. And surely trust—coming from a man like Guy—was worth all the most passionate declarations in the world.

'Sabrina?' he prompted softly.

'You know I will.'

'What's the date?' he asked suddenly, stroking a red-gold lock of hair off her cheek.

She thought back to all the order forms she'd filled in at the bookshop that morning. 'June the tenth. Why?'

He kissed the tip of her nose. 'Just remember it,' he urged softly.

EPILOGUE

GUY closed the front door and turned to look at Sabrina, a slow smile lighting up his face as he thought how beautiful she looked in her mint-green dress with her glorious bright hair tied back with a matching green ribbon.

'So, how did that go, do you think?' he asked her.

'I think they enjoyed it.' Her eyes glinted with mischief. 'Your mother kept asking me whether we'd arranged a wedding date.'

'And what did you say?'

'I said no, of course. Because we haven't.' But there was no resentment in her voice. 'And your sister-in-law kept telling me how much she had enjoyed her two pregnancies.'

'I'll bet she did!' He grinned. 'Like some more champagne?'

She'd barely touched a drop all afternoon. She'd been so nervous about meeting Guy's mother and stepfather and his brother and wife and their two children. But the lunch had gone like a dream, and now relief began to seep into her veins. 'Love some.'

He opened up the French doors leading onto the balcony and brought out two fizzing flutes. He handed her one as they sat side by side on the small bench, turning their faces towards the sun.

'Do you know what the date is, princess?' he asked quietly.

The glass was halfway to her mouth, but she quickly put it down on the decking and turned to look at him as a distant memory stirred in her mind. 'But you know the date!' she exclaimed. 'We've had this lunch in the diary for ages. It's June the tenth. Why?'

He put his own glass down to join hers—champagne was the very last thing on his mind. 'It's exactly a year since I persuaded you to stay,' he said softly. 'Remember?'

She nodded, mesmerised by the dawning tenderness on his face. 'I didn't take a lot of persuading,' she said drily.

He smiled. 'It didn't seem like that at the time. I knew then that I loved you, princess.' He lifted her hand to his mouth and kissed one fingertip after another. 'But I didn't want to rush you, or push you into something you weren't ready for. You needed time to recover from Michael's death and time to decide whether you could ever trust yourself to love again.'

'Oh, Guy,' she whispered, shaken by the depth of his understanding. 'Darling, darling Guy.'

'I love you,' he said in a wondering kind of tone, as though he had just discovered a foreign language in which he was fluent.

And Sabrina realised that deep in her heart she'd known that he loved her. Loving wasn't just about saying three little words—Guy had shown her in every way that counted that he cared. His consideration, his softness, his intelligent regard and respect for her and the beautiful power of his lovemaking had left her in no doubt of that whatsoever.

'I love you,' she said softly.

He leaned forward to gently kiss her. He had known that, too. Her love for him was as bright as the June sunshine which was beating down so warmly on their faces.

Their lives together had merged and harmonised. Guy

had stopped working on Saturdays, too. And now he came home at a decent hour in the evenings—sometimes even before her—which was a good thing. Unwilling to lose her, Wells had created a new job for her—enlarging the children's section of the bookshop. Sabrina had organised author signings and related talks, which had been avidly and ecstatically received, and now she had groups of schoolchildren from all over London to enjoy them.

'So will you marry me?' he asked, very, very softly. 'Now that you've had time to heal properly?

'Oh, yes, I'll marry you,' she responded huskily. 'You know I will.'

Sabrina looked at his dear, sweet face and her heart turned over with love for him. It was true that time was a great healer, but in a way Guy had been helping to heal her from the moment she'd met him. Some people didn't believe in love at first sight, but Sabrina did. Something primitive had shimmered down on them from the first moment they'd set eyes on each other, and since then the feeling had just grown and grown.

Some things happened because they were meant to, and she and Guy were meant to. You could call it fate or you could call it destiny, but Sabrina called it pure and perfect love.

In Bed with the Boss

*Turn the page to read Sharon Kendrick's
exclusive short story!*

CHAPTER ONE

HE started with her ankles, which were the most delicious ankles he had ever seen, then his eyes traveled slowly to her knees, and beyond.

From across the room, he made a leisurely appraisal of slim hips and a tiny waist, exquisite breasts and hair the color of fire. He saved the face until last, and when at last his gaze reached the huge emerald eyes and pouty pink lips, he almost choked on his glass of champagne.

"Josephine?" he silently mouthed in incredulous question, and because she hadn't moved, he walked over to where she stood. "Josephine?"

Josephine's heart was racing and her hands felt clammy, but not just because he was the most devastating man in the room—he had always had precisely that effect on her.

"Of course it's me, Blake," she remonstrated. "Surely you recognized me?"

There was a pause. "Not really." Last time he'd seen her, she'd had braces on her teeth and freckles. The little girl next door. In the tiny village they'd lived in he had watched her grow from toddler to teenager. And now? He swallowed, even though he was no longer drinking. "You've…you've grown up all of a sudden."

"But I'm 23 years old now, Blake," she said softly.

"And you live in London now?" he guessed.

"That's right. You, too?"

"Mmm." God, she was beautiful! More than beautiful. "How long since we've seen each other?"

She stared into the ice-blue eyes. She could have told him to the exact minute. "Oh, must be about seven years," she said casually. "Not since you moved away."

He couldn't take his eyes off her. "What kind of work do you do?" he questioned casually.

"I'm a model."

A model. Yes. That would explain the sudden transformation from duckling to dazzling swan.

"A successful model?" he questioned.

She gave a modest smile. "Kind of." She sipped her drink and smiled at him. "How about you?"

The smile beguiled him. "I'm a venture capitalist."

"Sounds like a bandit!"

He laughed. "Does it?" A bandit might have carried her straight off to bed with him, something he—uncharacteristically—felt *just* like doing.

"Do I look like a bandit?"

Kind of, she thought, but shook her head. "No, you look like a venture capitalist!"

"How about another drink?" His lips curved in a smile. "Or would you rather dance?"

There was no choice! But she managed to shrug her shoulders, as if she didn't mind either way. "I love dancing," she admitted.

Normally, he could take it or leave it, and he couldn't remember the last time he had danced with a woman who wasn't Kim. But the opportunity to hold her was too much to miss. "Me, too. Come on, then."

The gods must have been looking down on her, because at that moment the music slowed, and he took her in his arms and she felt almost dizzy, achingly aware of the hard, lean strength of his body.

"I—I like this song," she said, rather shakily.

"Mmm." He liked the drift of her scent even more.

He absently pulled her closer and buried his lips in her hair and Josephine was unprepared for the shimmering of heat that skittered such debilitating sensations across her skin.

Blake felt the sudden jackknifing of desire as her slender curves melted against his flesh like butter, and he had to stifle a moan.

Maybe he'd better just take her home and say good-night.

Sooner, rather than later.

But he was seduced by the moonlight and the way she walked, the way she made him laugh. And a shared past could produce nostalgia...and nostalgia could be pretty potent stuff.

He accepted coffee. And then another, and her eyes mesmerized him with their dazzling green fire.

"Guess I'd better think about leaving," he said reluctantly.

"I guess so. It's been...fun."

"Yeah."

She was lost in the light of his eyes. "Goodbye, Blake."

"Goodbye, Josephine."

She wondered if she would ever see him again, and when she reached up on tiptoe to kiss him goodbye, her lips somehow collided with the faint rasp of his jaw, and it felt so earthy that she shivered against him in unstoppable response.

Something inexplicable exploded inside him and he turned his head and captured her mouth with his, knowing without a shadow of a doubt that this was heading for the bedroom.

"I don't usually do this kind of thing," he groaned, as the kiss got hotter and harder.

Neither did she, but once again his mouth had hungrily covered hers and her words somehow got lost on his lips.

It was the best night of Josephine's life, but in the morning he had left without asking to see her again, and much later she heard that he had gone back to Kim and that they had become engaged.

And soon after that she had met his cousin Luke, and within three months they were married.

CHAPTER TWO

LUKE had gone.

He hadn't even taken his toothbrush, but she knew he had gone. That fact hit her with a certainty even more intense than the blade of lightning that illuminated the bathroom with its harsh blue-white light. Josephine momentarily shrank from its impact, and winced.

The toothbrush was still there, yes, but further investigation showed that her husband of just one year had cleared the rest of the house like a locust.

Gone were the rows of designer suits and the handmade Italian shoes. Gone, too, were the priceless objets d'art which he had always insisted they buy.

Or rather, that *she* buy, Josephine reminded herself bitterly.

The lightning was followed by a thunderbolt that could have deafened the hounds of hell. And then the rain began— a rain so heavy and remorseless that the loud banging on the front door didn't register straight away.

And when it did, she froze with a sinking feeling that felt almost like disappointment.

Had he left, only to return?

She ran into the hall and pulled open the door and the sight of the tall, drenched figure made her heart briefly suspend its frenzied beat.

For it wasn't Luke who stood there like a dark avenging angel, but his cousin Blake. Blake. The man she had not seen for over a year—not since he had stormed round to her flat and told her that she would be a crazy fool to marry a man like Luke.

"B-Blake!" she gasped, but the word dried to sawdust in her mouth.

"Disappointed?" he drawled, but at least she was here. And she seemed to be okay. "Expecting your husband, were you, sweetheart?"

She shook her head, wishing he wouldn't use that word, not when he didn't mean it. "He's taken all his clothes. He's gone."

"I know he has," he said grimly.

Her eyes narrowed. "How can you possibly—"

But Blake wasn't listening. He had unceremoniously pushed his way past her, to stand dripping raindrops onto the beautiful, polished wooden floor.

"Shut the door!" he commanded, his eyes raking reluctantly over her skimpy evening dress. A pulse began to beat at his temple. So she still dressed to kill. "Or were you hoping to freeze to death? Just shut the door, Josephine! *Now!*"

Mutely she obeyed him. There was something about the tone of his voice that was impossible to ignore. But maybe if she had listened to him the last time around, she wouldn't be in this situation.

She stared at him. They said that time healed, but time didn't always change the way someone made you *feel*. She hadn't seen him in over a year, but the sheer force of his personality was devastating as ever. As were his looks. The blue eyes were as vibrant as a summer sky and the hard, lean body as formidably gorgeous as it had ever been.

Lucky Kim, she thought, forcing herself to remember in the most painful way possible that he had a fiancée.

"What are you doing here?" she whispered. "And how on earth did you know that Luke had left, when I've only just found out myself?"

He gave a cynical smile, which iced over her. "Because he rang me from the airport."

"The airport?" she repeated dully. "Where was he going?"

"He didn't say."

"I don't understand," she breathed, and she heard him swear softly beneath his breath.

"I think you're just about to," he gritted. "He's with someone called Sadie." The blue eyes bored into her questioningly. "Know her?"

Josephine nodded. "Yes, I know her," she said dully. Best friends weren't all they were cracked up to be, were they? And yet, deep down, he wasn't telling her anything that she hadn't already guessed.

But despite the fact that Luke had gone, only one question nudged at the edges of her mind.

"So just why are *you* here, Blake?"

CHAPTER THREE

BLAKE shrugged. "I guess I've come to pick up the pieces ."

Still feeling as though she was in the midst of some nightmare, Josephine stared at him uncomprehendingly. "And what's that supposed to mean?"

His eyes moved over her, noting the angular line of her collarbone and the way her hipbones jutted against the filmy material of her dress.

As a model, she had always been slim, but now she looked as though a breath of wind could blow her away. Had marriage to his cousin turned her into a mere shadow of herself?

"How the hell can he afford to take off like that?" he demanded.

Josephine stared at him blankly, because his words didn't make sense. Come to think of it, nothing made sense right now. "What?"

"I think it might be a good idea if you took a look at your accounts," he ground out.

All she could see was his blue eyes burning into her. "Accounts?" she echoed.

It was only a hunch, but Blake knew his cousin well enough to suspect that he had taken more than his clothes with him. "Just do it, will you?" he said quietly. "I doubt whether Luke has financed his trip with the fruit of his own labors."

The rising sense of panic she felt was making her blood run cold, and though she shook her head in denial, she couldn't stop herself from suspecting the worst. But he wouldn't have taken her money, surely? Bad enough that he had walked off with one of her supposed friends—surely it couldn't get any worse than that?

She could feel Blake's eyes on her as she walked to the bureau to find the telephone number of the bank. She picked up the phone and punched in the numbers and when it was answered she said, shakily, "I'd like to know the balance of my current account, please. And could you check my savings account, too, please?"

The sums quoted took her breath away and her fingers were trembling as she turned round to meet the piercing brilliance of his eyes.

"Both accounts are empty," she said in a dead, flat voice. "He's taken everything."

His mouth twisted, ruing an aunt who had showered everything on his pretty, petulant cousin. "It seems that your precious Luke is nothing more than a common thief."

The rising panic was fast turning into a swamping tide. "Oh, my God," she breathed. "He can't have done!"

"Well, it looks as if he damned well has!" He let out a low sigh of frustration. "I told you that you were a fool to marry him, Josephine! I've known the guy for most of my life—I *knew* what he was like! You should have listened to me!"

Yes, she should have listened to him, but how could she have done, when her perception of him had been tainted by the night she had spent in his arms? And the fact that he hadn't wanted her afterward.

"Does it make you feel better to say 'I told you so'?" she questioned, her voice shaking with a sense of anger and outrage.

He shook his head. "You know, you're going to have to contact the police."

"The *police*?" It was unthinkable, surely, to report her husband to the police?

"Of course you will!" he stated impatiently. "Your precious Luke can't be allowed to get away with bleeding you dry! I presume that most of it was *your* money?"

Of course it was. Luke's "acting" career had dried up around about the time she'd married him. They had lived off the small fortune she had earned as a model. And when she had decided to study for an alternative career, her fees at business school and the fact that neither of them had been earning had eaten into a fair bit of it.

"Yes," she said dully. "It was mine."

"Well, surprise, surprise," he murmured.

And then, with threatened tears making her mouth taste salty, she turned to stare up at the impassive man who stood before her. "Oh, Blake," she whispered, because he might be forbidding, but at that moment he looked so damned strong. "What the hell am I going to do?"

CHAPTER FOUR

"YOU could always go back on the catwalk," Blake murmured.

But Josephine shook her head. Her days of hanging around the cattle market, of being judged by the length of her legs and the swell of her breast were long gone. "I'm through with modeling."

Blake's eyes glittered. "You could always come and work for me."

"*You?*" Disbelievingly, Josephine stared at the to-die-for face. "*You'd* give me a job? Just like that?"

"Well, no, not just like that. Didn't I hear that you'd gone back to school? That you were planning to make your mark in the world of high finance?"

She wasn't sure if it was sarcasm she could hear in his voice, but now was hardly the time for nitpicking about his attitude. "But I know virtually nothing about venture capitalism."

Now the blue eyes gleamed. "Oh, so you remember what I do for a living, do you, Josephine?" he questioned softly.

She remembered a whole lot more besides, but that was a trip down memory lane that she did *not* intend taking. "Like I said, it's not something I'm familiar with."

"Well, it isn't exactly brain surgery," he drawled. "And you're a fast learner, aren't you?"

Her cheeks flushed as she wondered whether he was referring to the things he had taught her in bed, but she pushed
the thought away. "Why?" she whispered. "Why would you
go out of your way to help me?"

His mouth curved. Did she think that if she turned those
big, green eyes on him, she could twist him around her little
finger like she'd done once before, and make him act in a way
that was alien to him? Because before Josephine, he'd never
had a one-night stand in his life. Never.

"Oh, don't flatter yourself that it's because your plight is
making my heart bleed for you," he murmured. "You got
yourself into this situation and part of me feels like telling
you to get yourself out of it, but—"

"But?"

"Luke may be a worthless airhead," he mused. "But the
fact remains that he happens to be related to me—and his behavior leaves a rather nasty taste in my mouth."

"And the scandal wouldn't do your reputation any good,
I suppose?"

He gave a cool smile. "Oh, I wouldn't worry your head
about that. My reputation speaks for itself—and some two-
bit marital breakdown wouldn't affect it. No, I'm in a position to offer you a job, that's all. I will give you a job, until
you decide what you want to do."

She eyed him warily. "A job doing what?"

He elevated the elegant curve of his eyebrows. "Why,
doing what you do best, of course—being decorative."

Some women might have taken that as a compliment, but
not Josephine. Men always took her at face value, and never
saw beneath the pretty face, until sometimes even *she* wondered if she were all superficial glamour, with no real sub-
stance beneath. "Decorative in what way?"

His eyes narrowed. Did she think he was going to demand
that she use the potent weapon of her sensuality to please

him? Lie draped around his office, half-naked, perhaps? He felt the jerk of desire.

"My receptionist, Sallie, is going on maternity leave and I need someone to replace her. Someone to sit behind a desk and answer the phone and smile prettily at all the visitors. Using you might work out better than employing a temp. Think you could manage that, Josephine?"

A receptionist! Not exactly what she'd had in mind when she'd sweated over management strategies and long-term projections! But Blake Devlin ran a highly successful company—and wouldn't a foot in the door, however lowly, give her the entrée she needed?

"But your business is in central London," she said haltingly. "And this is much too far to commute." Not that she felt she *could* stay here, not with Luke's ghost haunting the half-empty rooms, mocking her with the knowledge of what a sham their marriage had really been. "So where do I stay?"

"Why not come and stay with me?" He shrugged his broad shoulders, although the beat of his heart queried the wisdom of his next words. "I have a large apartment—there's plenty of room."

Her stomach tied itself up in knots. Once she would have given the world to hear him say those words. "I could always ask one of my girlfriends to put me up—" But her voice trailed off. Most of her girlfriends were cozily cohabiting—could she really just land on one of their doorsteps like Cinderella? While Blake lived slap-bang in the center of London, just a short distance from his offices.

And didn't the thought of sharing with Blake make her heart beat faster with a delicious, illicit kind of pleasure? "I'm not sure," she said uncertainly.

His cool smile mocked her. "You think I'm offering you the other half of my bed? Is that what's worrying you?"

Josephine's cheeks flamed as her mind cruelly conjured

up a forbidding sensual memory. "Of course I don't! And anyway, what about Kim?" she questioned, forcing herself to say the name without her voice shaking. "Won't she object to another woman living in your flat?"

"What I do is not Kim's concern."

She stared at him. "What do you mean?"

"Not anymore." There wasn't a flicker of emotion to disturb the shuttered features. "You see, Kim and I are no longer engaged."

CHAPTER FIVE

JOSEPHINE stared at Blake in disbelief. "You're not engaged to Kim anymore?"

His mouth tightened. "That's what I said."

"But why?"

Blake stared at her, thinking that she ought to give a little more attention to the mess of her own life before she started enquiring about *his*. "I don't think that's any of your business, do you? Now why don't you pack a suitcase, and we'll drive to London?"

Still dazed by the speed of what was happening to her, Josephine threw together the most suitable clothes she had, leaving Blake standing grim-faced in the sitting room.

"I can easily let this place out," she offered, once her packing was done. "That way I'll be able to pay my way." And at least that would give her some kind of financial independence, along with the salary he would be paying her.

He nodded. "Shall we go?"

He took her case from her while she locked the door of the house and settled herself into the leather-lined luxury of his car.

He shot her a brief look as he turned the ignition key, but forced his eyes back onto the road immediately, his hands tightening around the wheel.

He had persuaded her to change out of that ridiculously provocative little evening dress, but jeans and a sweater were proving almost as distractive. How had he allowed himself to forget what a knockout of a woman she was—with her long, rangy limbs, which once she had wrapped so eagerly around his neck?

Forget that, he told himself doggedly. *Forget* it.

Josephine tried to doze on the journey to London, but nothing could stop the thoughts that whirled around her aching head. Luke had stolen her money and her friend and delivered the ultimate slap in the face.

"I can have him traced, you know," said Blake carefully.

She opened her eyes and turned to look at the hard, dark profile. "How?"

"There are ways and means."

She supposed there were, if you were rich enough. "I don't know." Could she bear to see him? What would they have left to say to one another?

Blake looked at the stiff, uptight set of her shoulders and wondered what had happened to the life and the fire that had once burned so brightly within her. Had Luke stamped that out completely? And why the hell had she allowed him to?

"Maybe you're hoping that he'll come to his senses and come running home to you?" he ground out. But he didn't wait for an answer, just drew up in front of a large and elegant apartment block. "We're here," he said shortly.

But once inside the luxury of his home, reality began to hit home and Josephine realized just where she was, and with whom. Had she been out of her mind to agree to live in such close confines with a man who had once made love to her all night, and then walked away without a backward glance?

She looked around her, longing for the escape of sleep. "Where will I be sleeping?"

His mouth hardened. As far away from him as possible.

But the pert thrust of her breasts reminded him of something very elemental indeed, and he felt the hardening of desire.

"I'll show you." He beckoned for her to follow him to the guest bedroom, where a huge bed seemed to dominate the entire room, and as he slung the suitcase down, he wondered what she wore in bed these days.

Josephine looked around, anything to avoid the sudden hectic glittering in his eyes. "This is lovely. Thank you."

"Do you want to go to bed right now?" he questioned silkily.

CHAPTER SIX

CAUGHT in the cross fire of his eyes, Josephine stared across the bed at Blake as fantasy and reality spun her mind into confusion. "B-bed?" she gulped, and felt her heart accelerate.

Was she always this compliant? he wondered furiously. So at ease with her own sexuality that she would turn on for any man who made a move on her? Would she resist him if he pulled her into his arms and began to make love to her right now?

"Yes, bed," he responded mockingly, as he turned to walk away. "It's getting late, and I'm bushed. Good night, Josephine—I'll see you in the morning."

And he shut the door very quietly behind him.

After a largely sleepless night, Josephine was up early the following morning, pulling on a demure sweater and skirt with an unexpected feeling of liberation, despite the situation she found herself in.

She realized how heavy Luke's influence on her had been. He always insisted on vetting her clothes–and the ones he liked had been designed specifically to show off her reed-slim figure to advantage.

Why had she let him dictate to her so?

Because she had wanted to make their partnership work. Because she wanted a marriage just like the one her parents had had. Revealing clothes had seemed a small price to pay for a harmony, which had never quite happened.

She walked into the sitting room and Blake stilled momentarily when he caught that first sight of her—a Josephine he had never seen before.

She was wearing a knee-length skirt in soft, heathery colors of purple and green, with a green sweater, which brought out the color of her eyes. Her hair was scraped back in a chignon that sat neatly on the back of her long neck, but the most surprising thing of all was that she was wearing a pair of wire-rimmed spectacles.

She looked neat and sweet and—astonishingly enough—extremely *efficient*.

"Glasses?" he exclaimed.

She was having a bit of difficulty concentrating–but then she had never seen Blake in an exquisitely cut three-piece suit before, a suit that seemed to make his long legs go on forever. "Men never make passes at girls who wear glasses" was her one irreverent thought before meeting the question in his eyes.

"You don't like them?"

"I didn't say that," he responded steadily. "I just didn't know you wore them, that's all."

"I prefer them. Luke used to like me to wear contact lenses, so I did."

That figured. Glasses made her look almost prim. Aloof. And so at odds with the passionate woman he knew lay beneath. Blake swallowed. Though no less attractive for looking aloof. No way.

"There's coffee in the pot. And some muffins in the basket."

"Th-thanks."

She forced herself to eat something, though it wasn't easy, not with Blake's long legs stretched out underneath the table, only a whisper away from hers.

She wondered just what kind of reception she was going to get at his company, but she waited until they were in the car before she asked him. "What exactly have you told your employees about me?"

He shrugged. "Just that you're an old friend, and that you're standing in for a while."

Friend? He didn't make her feel like his friend. "Not that I was deserted and duped by my ex-husband?"

He shook his head impatiently. "Wouldn't that rather risk you sounding like a victim, Josephine? Or maybe that's how you see yourself?"

"Maybe in the past I allowed myself to be," she said slowly. "But not anymore."

"Good," he murmured, but he was struggling to keep his eyes on the road. With her knees pressed decorously together, he noted that she still had the best pair of legs he had ever seen on a woman.

"You probably *could* walk back into modeling, you know. If you really wanted to," he observed, thinking that maybe it was a crime to deny the world of that much beauty. There was a pause. "Did you resent it when Luke asked you to stop?"

Josephine shook her head. She had been so busy trying to see the wisdom in Luke's objection to her work taking her away from him that there hadn't been the time or the inclination for resentment. Then it had seemed a good idea—only now was she beginning to get an idea of how little she had asserted herself. And only now it occurred to her that Luke's demands may have been motivated more by jealousy of the fact that her career was eclipsing his. "Not really," she sighed, wondering how she could have been so *blind*.

She didn't elaborate, which Blake thought was curiously loyal in view of what Luke had done, but which might also mean that she was still in love with him. Though if she was, then why describe him as her "ex"?

"So are you still in love with Luke, Josephine?" he drawled, as the car glided into the underground car-park.

CHAPTER SEVEN

IT was a question that brought painful memories in its wake and Josephine stared into the steely gleam of Blake's eyes. Just what *did* she feel about Luke now? "I don't know," she said flatly.

He wasn't prepared for the sharp slam of jealousy in his gut. "Come on, Josephine, you can do better than that."

She shrugged. Maybe she could. "You've already guessed that the marriage was a disaster—a fact confirmed that my husband sought to leave me so suddenly."

"That doesn't answer my question. A woman can still love a man, even if he treats her badly."

He didn't appear to have noticed the irony that *his* behavior toward her had hardly been textbook perfect. With a sudden growing sense of resolution, she put all her energy into a smile. "I hope I have a little more pride than that, Blake. I've never really been a fan of masochism. Now, hadn't we better get going?"

He noticed how neatly she had avoided answering the question. "Sure." He watched the way she walked up the stairs in front of him and forced himself to stifle a groan. Demure the skirt might be, yes—but it did absolutely nothing to disguise the high, hard curve of her bottom.

He followed her into Reception and willed the aching to

subside. "This is Sallie!" he announced, smiling at the glow-ingly pregnant blonde at the desk. "Sallie, this is Josephine—who's going to be filling in while you're away. Will you show her the ropes?"

"Yes, Blake. Of course."

He gave a ghost of a smile. "I'll see you later, Josie," he said softly.

Then he was gone, and Josephine found herself watching his retreating back almost wistfully. She was on her own now—and it was up to her to show not just Blake, but every-one else in the company, that she wasn't just a pretty face, but could do the job properly.

Sallie gestured to a chair. "So you know anything about venture capitalists?" she asked.

Josephine shook her head. "Not a thing! But I'm ready to learn!"

"You'll need to be," smiled Sallie.

It was a long time since Josephine had put in a full day's work, and she had never worked in an office before, so by the end of the afternoon she was absolutely dead on her feet.

But by going-home time, she had learnt to use the com-plicated phone system and got to grips with the computer terminal.

She was also beginning to get an inkling of just how vast Blake's empire really was…and how hard he worked…and the contrast between him and his cousin couldn't have been more marked.

"So you're a *friend* of Blake's, are you?" Sallie asked carefully over afternoon tea. "Not a girlfriend, or anything?"

Josephine shook her head. One bout of passionate sex 15 months ago certainly didn't put her in *that* category. "No. Why?"

"Oh, nothing. He hasn't gone out with *anyone* since he

split with Kim, you know," Sallie confided. "We all reckon he's still carrying a torch for her."

"Oh." Stupidly, Josephine felt her heart lurch with disappointment.

So maybe Kim wasn't completely out of the picture.

But at least Sallie's comment reinforced the fact that entertaining any false hopes about a man who despised her, was a complete waste of time.

It was just extremely bad timing that after working nonstop, a shadow should fall over her desk just as she was repairing her lipstick. Josephine blinked as narrow hips swam into her line of vision and she looked up into a pair of ice-blue eyes.

His gaze was cold and distinctly unfriendly—but then, why should it be otherwise? She was just someone he saw as a loser, someone he was reluctantly doing a favor for.

And Josephine realized that she might never have his affection, but that she was damned well going to have to earn his respect. The question was how?

CHAPTER EIGHT

WEEKENDS were going to be the worst, Blake decided. At least during the week, the days were filled by going to the office and evenings spent catching up on the million and one things he needed to do. But Josephine's first Saturday in his apartment had him feeling like a caged tiger with nowhere to go.

He almost collided with her outside the bathroom and his blood pressure shot through the ceiling. No glasses or prissy little skirts and sweaters *now,* he thought furiously. Just long, pale limbs still glistening with tiny beads of water, and hair streaming in rivulets over her shoulders to cling erotically to her breasts.

"Can't you put something on?" he snarled.

"I was just on my way to do exactly that!" she retorted, but her cheeks went very hot. She hadn't missed the sudden darkening of his eyes, nor the fleeting look of hunger that had crossed his face. "I-if you wouldn't mind letting me pass."

"Delighted," he said sarcastically, but even though he pressed himself against the wall, he could still feel the warmth emanating from a body clad only in a large bath sheet.

"Thank you," she said, the close proximity making her only too aware of his raw masculinity, the rugged features, and the muscular shafts of his thighs, which rippled through his jeans.

She shut the bedroom door behind her with a shaking

hand, feeling the guilty sting of blood to her breasts and realizing that he wasn't immune to her—nor she to him. But
deep down she could tell that he hated himself for wanting
a woman he despised so much.

He was drinking coffee in the sitting room when she finished dressing and he looked up as she walked in, wondering where she had acquired the knack of always making him
want to drag her off to the nearest bed. He fought for something conventional to say, and fixed her with a bland smile.

"So how has your first week at work been?"

She narrowed her eyes suspiciously. Was a criticism about
to come winging her way? "I've really enjoyed it."

"Not quite modeling, though, is it?"

"No. But it's rather refreshing to be judged on what you
do, rather than how you look."

He frowned. He'd never thought of it that way. "But the
pay isn't as good."

"Pay isn't everything," she said, with a touch of defiant
pride. And she would show him just how hard she had been
working! "Er, Blake?"

"Josephine?"

How she wished he wouldn't always adopt that horrible
sardonic tone! "I…er…" She met his cool, quizzical stare.
"I have a proposition to put to you. Well, sort of."

His mind played out an aching sexual fantasy. He could
think of a few propositions he wouldn't mind putting to *her.*
"Really? About what?"

"About work actually."

He gave her a look of barely concealed amusement. "I can
hardly wait," he murmured.

"Do you remember Giuseppi Rossi?" she blurted out, seeing his hateful smile.

He frowned as he flipped back through his memory bank.
"The young Italian horticultural chemist?"

"That's right. He's called by the office a few times now."

"And you've had a chat with him, am I right?" His mouth twisted. He could imagine–the Italian looked as if he should be starring in the movies, not bent over a test tube in a laboratory.

"That's right." She drew a deep breath. "Blake, he says you won't see him—"

"Because there's no point," he butted in impatiently, instantly recognizing where this conversation was headed. "I have no intention of bankrolling his company, Josephine—so if that's what you're about to ask me, then you can save your breath."

"But he's *brilliant*!" she argued, ignoring the dangerous light in his eyes. "This organic weed killer he's working on sounds absolutely revolutionary!"

"So, a week into the job and already you're an expert?"

"Please don't patronize me, Blake!"

"I'm trying to tell you how it *is,* Josephine—and it's just not the kind of scheme I involve myself in!"

"So my opinion counts for nothing?"

"Why should it?" he questioned arrogantly.

"What about the fact that I came away from business school with a distinction?"

He was impressed, but he didn't show it. "That's theory, not practice!"

"Or that they told us that sometimes—just sometimes— we should go with our instincts, and my instinct is telling me that this is a brilliant idea."

"I said *no,* Josephine," he growled. "My experience overrules your instinct. Believe me, I'm right."

It felt like being kicked in the teeth. Not just the way he had dismissed her idea out of hand, but his zero lack of faith in her judgment.

"Then I'll just have to prove you wrong, won't I, Blake?" she challenged hotly.

CHAPTER NINE

"So ARE you going to carry on sulking at work, as well?" Blake murmured, leaning over the reception desk only to be punished by the mesmerizing vision of her breasts gloriously outlined in pure cashmere.

Josephine looked up and frowned, and wished he would stop wearing that gorgeous aftershave, or stand farther away. Or something. "I am not sulking."

"Wrong. You've been off with me ever since you asked me about Giuseppi." In fact, she had subjected him to a polite freeze whenever he spoke to her, and infuriatingly, it was having the effect of making him *want* her to talk to him. He wasn't used to women giving him the cold shoulder, he was used to them eating out of his hand. "Are you still mad about *that*?"

She gave him a chilly stare. Of course she was! "It wasn't so much that you failed to look at his proposal in full, it was the fact that you obviously credit me with no intelligence or imagination at all."

The jury on the intelligence part was still out—an intelligent woman wouldn't have rushed headlong into marriage with a man like Luke, surely? But of her imagination, he was in no doubt—she had certainly been as imaginative as a man could want the night he'd made love to her.

"Let's just say I'm giving it some thought," he said placatingly.

And she was supposed to fall to her knees and thank him, was she? Her chilly look didn't waver. Josephine had been working her socks off at Devlin Associates–and while *he* might not have noticed it, the others certainly had. Why, just this morning, his second-in-command had told her that if her people skills could be marketed, then none of them need ever work again!

"And I'm supposed to be grateful for that, am I, Blake?"

"You could try," he answered flippantly and thoughtfully fingered a bright petal of one of the flowers that stood on the desk. He hadn't really noticed flowers there before. "Did you put these here?" he questioned suspiciously.

She nodded. She had jettisoned the rather ugly and very dusty rubber plant. "I thought it added something to the atmosphere of the room. Do you have a problem with that?"

He shook his head. "Just make sure that you use money from petty cash, that's all."

"I did." She smiled, steeling herself against the sheer potency of his appeal. "Was there something else you wanted, Blake?"

"Have you eaten lunch yet?"

"No," she answered repressively.

"Want to grab a sandwich with me?"

It wasn't the most alluring invitation she had ever received, but her curiosity was aroused. He had never asked her to lunch before, so why start now?

"Why not?" she shrugged.

His irritation at her noncommittal response was only increased when the proprietor of the Italian deli around the corner danced besotted attention on her request for beef on rye. He narrowed his eyes as he watched her accept the sandwich. Was she *flirting* with him? He had to say that she wasn't.

Maybe it was just some unconscious message she sent out that had most red-blooded men fawning all over her.

They sat down. "This is very sweet of you, Blake," she murmured.

"Not really. I've got some news for you, and I thought it best if I broke it away from the office."

There was something darkly ominous about the way he spoke, and the hand that held the sandwich froze halfway to her mouth. "What news?" she whispered.

"Just that I've managed to trace your husband," he said. "I've found Luke."

CHAPTER TEN

JOSEPHINE's hand shook uncontrollably. "You've *found* Luke?" she whispered. *"Where?"*

Blake was watching her face carefully. "Your husband is on a beach in Bali." He shrugged in distaste. "He certainly decided to leave you in style!"

Using *her* money. Josephine's ego, which she had been slowly building up all week like a convalescent patient, now collapsed like a day-old soufflé. She let her gaze drop to her half-eaten sandwich, unwilling to meet Blake's eyes, reluctant to see the mockery there—or his triumph at seeing her neatly slotted back into the role marked "victim."

"I can get him back to England, you know."

She did look up then. He looked so sure of himself. So confident. So strong. "How?"

"I could threaten him with the police—"

"That would make him want to stay, surely?"

"Not if I told him you *haven't* yet reported him—but that you damned well will if he doesn't get back here and give you what he hasn't spent."

Josephine shook her head tiredly. Had Blake tracked him down deliberately to undermine her? To force her into contacting the police, as he thought she should?

She had been doing okay before this latest bombshell—

not great—but okay, and part of the reason for that was that Luke's absence had made her feel free. Unburdened by the nagging weight of a marriage on the rocks, a relationship in dire trouble.

"Do you want him back?" he demanded.

"No, of course I don't!"

"I don't mean back with *you,* Josephine," he said, in a voice which for Blake could almost be described as gentle. "I mean to sort the whole business out to some kind of satisfactory conclusion."

She tried to imagine what the reality would be like. Luke back in England. Seeing her living with Blake and putting two and two together to come up 105. She shuddered. "Not yet," she prevaricated.

He stirred his coffee, allowing himself to ask the question that had been bothering him for a long time now. "Why did you marry him?" he asked quietly.

"For the same reason that everyone gets married, I suppose. Because I thought I was in love!"

He silently registered her use of the word "thought." "But you weren't?"

"How could I have been? I barely knew him—it all happened so fast." She had been hurting and vulnerable—her one-night stand with Blake having eaten into her already precarious self-esteem. People thought that models had everything most women wanted, but what no one seemed to realize was that beauty often went hand in hand with a crippling insecurity. Because people wanted you for all the wrong reasons. Luke certainly had—and maybe Blake had, too.

"He rushed you," said Blake slowly.

But Josephine shook her head violently, and a strand of bright-red hair came free of the constricting chignon. "I must have wanted to be rushed," she explained carefully. "And he was fun. Everything with Luke was carefree. He made me laugh." At a time when laughter had been in drastically short supply in her life.

"Did you marry him on the rebound from me?" he asked quietly.

CHAPTER ELEVEN

JOSEPHINE had rarely experienced such a pure and blinding rage as she glared at Blake across the table of the coffee shop. "Of all the arrogant and insufferable things I've ever heard, that really has to take first prize, Blake! Is your ego so over-inflated that you think one night with you—*one night,*" she repeated in disbelief, "would lead me to marry the first man who asked me?"

"So the fact that Luke was my cousin had nothing to do with it?"

She opened her mouth to say something more on the subject of his ego, then shut it again. For wasn't there a tiny kernel of truth in his assumption? She had been swept off her feet by Luke, yes, a handsome actor who could have won an Oscar for his use of manipulative charm. But hadn't the fact that he had been related to a man she had spent her formative years pining over, made her feel a certain sense of *triumph*? And *power*?

Particularly when Blake had come blazing round to her flat and urged her to postpone the marriage. She had decided that he was motivated by sour grapes, nothing more, and certainly not out of concern for her. *He* didn't want her—he had made that abundantly clear–but he was damned if anyone else should have her, either. Hadn't her indignation at his request that she put an end to it only fueled her determination to marry Luke?

"Maybe just a little," she admitted.

Blake expelled a long, low breath, realizing that one-night stands were never as straightforward as they appeared to be at the time. Which he guessed was why he'd only ever had one in his life. You felt good for a while, and then you just felt empty. He had hurt Josephine by the way he'd behaved toward her. He recognized that now.

He sighed, wanting to put a smile back on her lips—and heaven only knew, there had been precious few of those in the past couple of weeks. "Listen, Josie—let's forget about Luke for a minute. What if I told you that I had another look at Giuseppi Rossi's scheme—and you were right—it *did* show potential? Maybe it's time for me to move in different directions." His eyes gleamed. "I think I'm going to back him."

Josephine stared at him, recognizing the sweetener for what it was, but knowing that she could not accept this attempt at an olive branch on Blake's terms alone.

She leaned across the table toward him. "I want to help back him, too. I want to put some money in!"

He frowned. "You don't need to—"

"But I want to!" she interrupted passionately—because it had been her hunch, *her* hunch–not Blake's.

"Why?"

"Because if it's the success that I think it's going to be, then I want part of it. It's my baby, Blake—not yours."

A smile played at the corners of his mouth. "How much money?"

"Enough."

"How much?" The sum she mentioned made him raise his eyebrows. "But you haven't got that kind of money, Josephine. Not unless you're planning to sell the house?"

"No, I don't, but I can get it."

"How?"

"I have a necklace I can sell." A necklace given to her by Luke in the first few heady weeks of their relationship. A garish piece, bought more as a symbol of how much he had been prepared to spend on her than because of any intrinsic beauty. She had never really liked it.

"You're willing to gamble that much on the basis of *what*?" he demanded incredulously.

"I told you. Instinct," she answered slowly and fixed him with a curious look. "Don't you ever act on instinct, Blake?"

"Not usually."

Something unsaid hovered in the air between them. "Ever?" she persisted.

There was a pause. "Just the once."

"When was that?" But even as she asked the question, she knew what the answer was going to be.

His mouth flattened. "The night I slept with you, sweetheart."

CHAPTER TWELVE

JOSEPHINE forced herself to remain impassive. "I thought you'd forgotten all about that night," she said quietly.

"*Forgotten* it?" Blake echoed, in disbelief, because since she'd moved in he'd been remembering it about every two seconds. "Why on earth should you think that?"

"Because you never mention it."

"Well, neither do you," he accused softly.

She didn't look away. "No."

"And anyway—it isn't the easiest subject to bring up, is it?" He adopted a mocking voice. "Josephine, do you remember the night when we tumbled uninhibitedly into bed together?"

She pushed a piece of bread around the plate. "But that's exactly what happened," she said baldly.

"And you badly regretted it, didn't you?"

She looked up. "Not as much as you obviously did!"

His eyes narrowed. "Meaning?"

"You couldn't wait to get away the next morning, could you?"

How honest to be? Totally, he decided. He owed her that, no matter how hurtful his words might be. She had endured enough subterfuge with Luke.

"I thought that we both understood the situation for what it was," he said softly.

Josephine blinked uncomprehendingly. "What was to understand?"

"That sometimes these things happen. A man and woman end up in bed together, even though they hadn't planned for it to happen."

"And it doesn't *mean* anything—is that what you're saying?"

This was proving even harder than he had anticipated and the look of confusion, which was blazing from her eyes, only added to his discomfiture. If he had ever wondered whether there had been other one-night stands in Josephine's life, then she had silently and implicitly answered it by the look on her face.

"I'm saying that it provided a great deal of pleasure at the time." A pulse beat insistently at his temple as he remembered just *how* pleasurable. "But sometimes that's as far as it goes."

Josephine swallowed. How eloquently he had put it, but no less wounding for that. "And you ran straight back to your relationship with Kim, didn't you?"

He shook his head. "I didn't go straight from your bed to Kim's, if that's what you're implying. I wasn't with Kim at the time—"

"For which I suppose I must be grateful."

"But, yes," he sighed, and stared into her hurt and angry face, "I *did* get back with her. We went back a long way and I felt I owed it to both of us to give it one last shot. It wasn't the first time we'd split up. That's the way our relationship was at the time."

And now, she wondered, but pride would not let her ask him that. Just because the girls at work thought he had never gotten over Kim didn't mean anything, did it? There had certainly been no sign of her since Josephine had moved in with him. And Blake himself had told her that the engagement was broken.

As they stood up to leave, she decided that it had been a painful and difficult talk, but maybe it had cleared the air between them.

And their one night of hot sex could now be consigned to history.

CHAPTER THIRTEEN

BLAKE slammed into the flat at just gone eight, his face dark as thunder, to find Josephine grilling chicken, her sensible skirt stretched tight over the cups of her buttocks as she bent to take two plates out of the oven.

"Everything okay?" she asked.

Blake sucked in a breath of frustration. She had taken to cooking dinner some nights, so that he had the torture of watching her move around his kitchen. An exquisite torture he decided, just as she smoothed her hands down over her apron, emphasizing the washboard-flat stomach.

He threw his briefcase onto a chair and averted his eyes. "Yeah, sure," he agreed sardonically. "Perfect as pie! I spoke to your friend Giuseppi this afternoon, who now seems to think he's died and gone to heaven!"

"You told him the good news? That you were going to back him?"

Good for whom, he hazarded, wondering whether she had hopes of her own for the sexy young Italian. "Yeah, I told him."

He sounded as though he had had second thoughts. "You don't seem very happy about it," she ventured.

More than one kind of frustration began to simmer into a boil. "What do you expect, Josephine?" he demanded. "I tell him one thing, and on the strength of what a cub reception-ist says—I go back on everything I said and agree to back him! What do you think that says to him about my profes-sional judgment? My reputation?"

"Your pride?" she teased.

His *pride*? Maybe she was right. And maybe the absence of pride might give him the freedom to ask her what had been bothering him.

"Like a drink?" he questioned.

Something in the darkening of his eyes was making her heart beat a little faster, and she switched the grill off with a shaking hand. "Sure."

He handed her a glass of wine and watched her while she drank some. "You never did answer my question," he said slowly.

She guessed from the deepening of his voice that this was nothing to do with work. "What question was that?"

"About whether you regretted what we did that night?"

"Didn't I?"

"You know you didn't."

"For what it's worth—then, no, I didn't regret it—not re-ally. Just the way it fizzled out, I guess."

"But you recovered pretty quickly—fast enough to marry Luke within three months of meeting him."

"And you went back to Kim," she pointed out. "You had a pretty speedy recovery yourself."

He nodded, and he felt the stir of longing deep in his groin. "But things have changed now, haven't they?" He put his glass down.

She saw the way his eyes had darkened and something deep inside her began to melt. "Wh-what?" she whispered, as he walked across the kitchen to face her.

"You're no longer with Luke." He stared down at her. "And…"

"A-and?" Her lips trembled, and he traced their shivering outline with the tip of his finger.

"I'm no longer with Kim. Which makes us free agents, doesn't it?"

He moved his finger to smooth the curve of her jaw, and from there to her neck, and then farther still to the swell of her tiny breast, and shaking uncontrollably, she let him.

"And free agents can do what the hell they please, don't you think?"

"Blake," she swallowed, because his face was ablaze with hunger.

"And this will please both of us, sweetheart," he murmured huskily, his fingers beginning to undo the buttons of her blouse.

CHAPTER FOURTEEN

"BLAKE!" Josephine gasped, as he impatiently freed the last button and the air washed over her breasts.

He seemed to have been waiting for this moment all his life. "What?" he growled, and bent his dark head, suckling the nipple through the lace of her brassiere and her head jerked back, her eyes closing with helpless pleasure as he pushed one hard thigh between the unprotesting softness of hers.

She gripped his shoulders as the fierce promise of his body began to send sensual messages singing through her blood. "Don't you like what I'm doing?" he murmured.

He brazenly asked this particular question just as he was impatiently pulling the zip of her skirt down, so that moments later it had pooled in a whisper at her feet.

"Do you?" he demanded.

Since *this* question was accompanied by a provocative finger wriggling all the way up her thigh, she could do little other than make a shuddering little sigh, which became a moan when he found what he had clearly been seeking.

He felt the jerk of desire—sweet and sharp and potent—as he delved beneath her lace panties to find her honey sweet and turned on, and he sucked in a disbelieving breath. This was how he remembered her—so instantaneously responsive to everything he did to her.

"Do you know what I want to do to you?" he whispered huskily.

She shook her head, and raised her mouth to nip her teeth at the lobe of his ear, hearing his half-stifled murmur of delight.

"*Everything,*" he breathed. "I want to do everything to you, Josephine, and then a little bit more."

She knew before he began to tug at her panties that he wasn't planning on taking her to the bedroom. Through half-shielded eyes she sneaked a look downward, where his desire could have been daunting if she hadn't wanted him so much. She doubted whether he would even *make* it to the bedroom, not in that kind of aroused state.

She flicked open the belt of his trousers and unzipped him and she heard his sigh of pleasure as he sprang free into the palm of her hand.

"Oh, sweetheart," he ground out unsteadily as he raised his head to look down at her, his blue eyes dazed. "Sweetheart."

His mouth grazed hers, explored it and licked it until she was on fire with him, and when he impatiently shoved aside the supper plates and bent her over the kitchen counter, she felt a wild and dizzyingly sensation of elation.

God, but she made him crazy! He kicked away his trousers and stared down at her, silhouetted against the countertop. Her hair had worked its way free, and was wild and messy—tumbling over the lace-covered strain of her breasts, while her cheeks were pink and her green eyes glittering.

He felt her syrupy moistness as he pushed against her, and then he thrust into her with an exultant kind of groan.

Josephine was unprepared for the sensation of completeness, of this being so *right,* but then, if her thoughts went out of control so did her body, because almost immediately the fiercest, most elemental orgasm had her shaking in his arms just before she heard his own soft, disbelieving sigh.

So the first time had not been an exaggeration. It was always this good with this man. She lifted her lips to his ear. "Thank you," she whispered softly

He was about to ask her what she was thanking him for when the telephone began to ring, and in her disorientated and sleepy state of fulfillment, Josephine automatically reached out her hand to pick it up.

Blake groaned. "You should have ignored it," he whispered, but she smiled.

"Hello?" she yawned, and then stilled as she heard the voice at the other end, a cold, clammy sweat breaking out on her forehead. She handed him the receiver. "It's for you," she said, in a voice that was a hairsbreadth away from shaking. "It's Kim."

CHAPTER FIFTEEN

BLAKE took the receiver and tried to plant a kiss on Josephine's lips along the way, but she was busy wriggling out from underneath him, her face like thunder and her naked breasts brushing tantalizingly against his chest.

He sighed. "Kim? Hi!" He listened for a moment. "Well, it's not exactly the best time—" Kim was speaking rapidly now and he watched helplessly as Josephine flounced across the kitchen, her bare bottom wiggling. He heard her open the bathroom door and slam it shut with an almighty bang.

He listened to what Kim was saying.

"Yeah, okay. I'll see you there," he said. "But it'll have to be quick."

He replaced the phone, pulled on his jeans, and then went and hammered on the bathroom door.

"Josephine!"

"Go to hell!" she yelled.

"I need to talk to you!"

"Go and talk to *Kim* instead, why don't you?"

And then she turned the shower full on to drown out the sound of his voice and the sound of her tears.

She stood beneath the hot jets for a long time so that her skin was pink and wrinkled by the time she emerged, and, though she stood and listened for several minutes—there was no sound from the rest of the apartment.

He had gone.

Gone? Where? To *Kim*?

Like an automaton, she dressed in jeans and a sweater, but she did not bother drying her hair–she couldn't care less what it looked like–and her hands were shaking too much to be of any use.

It hurt, she realized. It hurt like crazy to think that Blake was still so close to Kim that he would rush straight off at her bidding, especially at a time like *that*.

And she realized something else, too.

That somewhere along the way she had fallen in love with her boss. So where did that leave her? Vulnerable and open to all kinds of heartache if all he wanted was a willing bed-partner.

Trying to dull some of the pain, she finished her glass of wine and didn't hear the front door close, didn't register anything at all until she saw Blake standing there in the kitchen, his face not guilty, but full of a quiet suppressed rage.

"I'm surprised you're still here," he said quietly.

She lifted her chin, her eyes glittering but defiant. "I don't have a choice, do I?" she returned. "Where else would I go at this time of night?"

He gave a bitter smile as he poured himself a glass of wine and drank it, before turning to face her, his features set. "And that's the only reason you stayed, is it, Josephine? A kind of emotional prisoner?"

"A *physical* prisoner," she corrected icily. "There was precious little emotion involved in what just happened."

"So, history has repeated itself," he mused. "There was precious little emotion involved the last time, if my memory serves me well."

She turned her face away, afraid that he would see the sudden leap of tears. No emotion? Maybe not for him, but for her, it had been overwhelming. The stupid and indiscriminate kind of emotion that made you love a man who would never love you back.

"How's Kim?" she asked flippantly. "Has she forgiven you your infidelity *this* time? Or has she grown a little tired of your wayward libido?"

Blake glared at Josephine, his breath coming quick and fast. "Kim rang me up to tell me that she's pregnant!"

CHAPTER SIXTEEN

THERE was a long, awful pause and Josephine very nearly passed out. "Oh, my God," she moaned.

Blake understood immediately and stared at her, his eyes glittering furiously. "It isn't *my* baby!" he roared.

"It isn't?"

"Of course it isn't! She's living with a lawyer! She has been for months! She rang me on her mobile to say she was just passing in a taxi, and I went downstairs to congratulate her. And do you really think that I would have made love to you—"

"Oh, please don't dress it up!" she snapped. "Having the minimum amount of clothes removed and being bent over the kitchen counter is hardly what I would call making love!"

Arrogantly, he raised his eyebrows. "I didn't hear you objecting at the time."

Her cheeks went pink. "That was because...because..."

"Because what, Josephine?" he prompted softly.

Because she had been in the throes of a physical response so intense that it had threatened to rock the foundations of her world. But hadn't it always been like that with him?

"I was as carried away as you were at the time!"

It wasn't any kind of loving declaration, but he nodded, badly needing to control his indignation and his fury, because if he wasn't careful then things would get said that they would regret. Or more important, things *wouldn't* get said— things that maybe he should have said a long time ago.

"Do you really think I would go straight from your arms and into Kim's?" he asked again.

She bit her lip. "How should I know? You never talk about her, do you? And you bit my head off when I asked. But the girls at work mention her."

"And what do they say?"

"Just that you never got over her—and that you've never been out with anyone since you split up."

He sucked in a breath. "Well, one part of the equation, at least–is true." He met the wary question in her eyes. "I haven't been out with anyone since Kim."

The other fact penetrated her befuddled brain. "Does that mean you *are* over her?"

"Of course I'm over her!" he exploded. "I'm not the kind of man who can make out with two women at the same time–it's not in my nature!"

Her voice was low. "What about the night of the party?"

He shook his head. "I told you, my relationship with Kim was off at the time. That's how it was—on and off—sometimes for great chunks of time." He could see from the question in her eyes that she wanted—maybe *needed* some kind of explanation. "She was the kind of woman I thought would make a good wife—"

"What kind of woman is that?" she asked, thinking how coldly dispassionate he sounded.

"Someone steady, logical, calm—"

"The 'right type'?" she put in sarcastically. "As opposed to the type of woman who would leap into bed with you without even being asked out for dinner first?"

"Don't put yourself down, Josephine."

"Why? Are you going to do that for me?"

"And stop being so bloody defensive and *listen* to me for once!" he stormed, and then controlled his breathing with an effort. "Kim thought the same about me—intellectually, she could imagine us settling down together—two people with a lot in common who would make good companions."

"So what happened to change your mind?"

He shrugged. "Relationships aren't like a mathematical problem—you can't punch in all the right numbers and come up with the perfect partner. I went back to Kim soon after that night with you, but I discovered—" He wondered whether what had happened between him and Josephine had made him view the world differently. "I discovered that there was no real spark between the two of us, although there was a good deal of respect and affection. And the spark is what keeps a relationship alive."

Josephine stared at him, realizing that things really *were* over between him and Kim, but realizing something else, too.

"Isn't this going to change things at work?"

He frowned. "What things?"

"Do you think we'll still be able to work together now that we're having sex?"

CHAPTER SEVENTEEN

"HAVE you worked out the answer to your question yet, sweetheart?" Blake drawled.

Josephine blinked. He had just rung through to reception saying that he needed to see her urgently, and here she was, in the dauntingly large room of his penthouse office. "What question?"

"About whether we'd be able to carry on working together now that we're having sex."

"What a horrible way to put it!" she said crossly.

"It was *your* choice of words, Josephine," he pointed out and then he gave a slow smile. "I think it's working out just fine, don't you?"

"Yes," she said cautiously. But only by making the huge effort of separating the cool Blake at the office with the hot and passionate Blake at home. Her mouth dried. And if she wasn't careful, she was going to break her cardinal rule of not linking the two men. "Is that what you called me in here to say?"

He rose to his feet, thinking how beautiful she looked when she was trying to be angry with him. "No, I called you in here to ask two things. The first is why you've started sending the press releases round in an email to everyone in the company."

"Because it's instant and because it gives everyone a buzz. And it makes *everyone* feel involved!"

"It's not how we usually work it, Josephine."

She heard the faint note of authority in his voice and decided to ignore it. She stared him out. "So? If we always did things in exactly the same way, we'd never progress, would we, Blake?"

"Are you arguing with me?"

"No, I'm trying to make you see sense!"

"Like you did with Giuseppi, you mean?"

"Exactly," she said smugly.

"Except that it's too early to say if his scheme will take off."

"I'm confident," she answered.

"I know you are." He walked across the office and stared down at her. What a difference a month could make—because the Josephine who sat so glowingly before him was a million miles away from the deflated woman he had brought back to London with him. "Everyone here thinks you're pretty wonderful!"

"And what do *you* think?" she flashed back.

His voice was slightly unsteady. "I think you're pretty wonderful myself."

"Why, *thank* you, Blake," she said demurely, then hastily stood up. Praise was all very well and good, but there was something in the darkening of Blake's eyes that was making her feel distinctly unprofessional, and she had vowed never to be *that*.

"What was the second thing you asked me in here for?"

He raised her hand to his lips. "A kiss."

She shivered and tried to take her hand away, but he had it locked fast in his. "Blake–we mustn't."

"Mustn't what?" he murmured, as he bent his head to nuzzle his mouth against the long line of her neck.

"*You* know!" She tried to wriggle out of his arms, but unfortunately just at the same moment he pulled her against him, so that the wriggle became a sinuous writhe against the hard length of his body.

"Mmm. I know everything," he teased, and bent his head to kiss her.

"Blake, this is going to get out of hand," she protested.

"I intend it to," he said, sliding his hand underneath her skirt.

"I won't be able to resist unless you stop it," she begged.

"Then don't."

There was a moment when she pretended to struggle, but it was as fainthearted as could be, because she wanted him as much as he wanted her.

He made love to her very swiftly and very beautifully on the floor of his office.

"Lock the door!" she gasped, just as he began to unzip his trousers.

"I already did!" he gasped back.

"Oh, my," sighed Josephine afterward, languidly stretching her arms above her head. "That was just *heaven!*"

Blake looked at her where she lay on his office floor, her eyes closed, her clothes awry, an expression of satiated bliss on her face, and he realized that he needed some kind of closure with her past. Hell, they *both* did.

"Fix your clothes, Josephine," he said suddenly. "We're going out."

Josephine opened her eyes. "Out where?"

"To see Luke. He's back in London."

CHAPTER EIGHTEEN

The car crawled along the busy London streets, and Josephine tried to take in the facts. Luke was back. Here in London!

"How long has he been back?"

"A couple of weeks. I guess he thought that he could lie low and not be discovered, but I found out as soon as he had set foot in Britain."

"But you didn't bother telling me?"

Blake shot her a look. "You claimed not to be particularly interested." .

And she hadn't been. That much was true. But then her heart and her mind and her body had been full of the man beside her.

"Besides," he gave a tight smile. "You seem to have blossomed pretty well without him. You've become some woman, Josephine."

It was probably the sweetest thing he had ever said to her. "Why, th-thank you," she responded shakily.

The door to Luke's apartment was opened and Josephine was shocked by the sight of her estranged husband, wearing just a pair of trousers.

He had gained weight and his face was tanned but puffy, with a faint sheen of sweat, his eyes dark-rimmed. In his hand he held a glass half-full of whiskey, and his eyes narrowed with sly perception as he stared from one to the other.

"Well, well, well," he sneered. "So my powerful cousin finally got what he always wanted, did he? Hope she's a bit more responsive in *your* bed, mate, than she was in mine."

Resisting the urge to smack him in the face, Blake looked across at Josephine. Was *that* why she had thanked him after her orgasm, she wondered? He gave her a tender smile. "We've no complaints in that department, have we, sweetheart?"

Luke scowled. "What do you want?"

"Can we come inside?" asked Blake quite calmly.

"If you want," came the ungracious reply.

Inside, the flat was a shambles and the first thing that Josephine saw was a discarded pair of women's high-heeled shoes and a crumpled pair of panties.

Blake stood watching her frozen expression, then turned to Luke.

"So you're still with Sadie, are you?"

"God, no! I traded her in for a newer model, actually." Luke gave a glassy grin. "So what can I do for you, Josephine?"

The unplanned words came tumbling out all by themselves. "I'd—I'd like a divorce please, Luke—just as soon as possible."

He stilled, and a calculating look came into his eyes. "Why, so you can get it together with Mr. Megabucks?" He stared insultingly at her neat, navy suit. "He'll never marry you, you know, Josephine—however much you try to turn yourself into the woman he wants you to be, with the frumpy clothes and the glasses!"

"On the contrary," interjected Blake smoothly. "I love Josephine very much whatever she's wearing—or not wearing—and I intend to marry her as soon as possible—if she'll have me. Oh, and one more thing, Luke."

Luke stilled, as if something in Blake's tone was more than a little threatening. "What?"

"I imagine that even *your* profligate habits haven't been able to blow all the money that you stole from Josephine—"

"For richer or for poorer," mocked Luke. "Those are the words of the wedding vows—"

"Shut up," ground out Blake. "I'm telling you that if the remainder of the money isn't in her bank account by the end of the week, then you will be hit with the full force of the law. And I want everything that you have spent paid back. In full. Understood?"

Luke lasted the blistering blue stare for only about 10 seconds, and then his eyes dropped to his bare feet. "Yeah," he agreed sulkily.

Her heart was pounding so hard that Josephine could barely breath and she clutched at Blake's hand. "C-come on. L-let's j-just get out of here," she stumbled.

They made it back to the car and she sat there with tears streaming down her cheeks.

"Why are you crying, sweetheart?" he asked gently. "Did it upset you to see him looking such a mess?"

She shook her head. "Wh-what did you have to say that for?" she sobbed.

"Which bit in particular?" he asked, smiling.

"The love and flowers bit! To hurry the divorce along? Or to salvage what's left of my pride?"

"Neither. Because it's true. It's always been true—only I was too blind and too stubborn to admit it to myself before. You're the spark I've been missing—the spark that I need. You make me feel *alive,* sweetheart—more alive than I thought it was possible to feel."

She stared at him, knowing deep down that he would not say these things if they were not true.

"So will you marry me?" he murmured silkily.

There was a long pause before she fixed him with an answering stare, her green eyes huge in her face. "No, Blake," she whispered. "I can't."

CHAPTER NINETEEN

BLAKE'S eyes narrowed in disbelief. "Say that again."

"I can't marry you."

There was a pause. "Would you mind telling me why? It isn't because you don't love me, I know that."

It was an arrogant declaration, but at least it was honest. "You're so confident that I love you?" Josephine questioned quietly.

He wondered if she was blind to the way that she looked at him sometimes when she thought she wasn't being observed. Like the sun had suddenly come out. "But you do, don't you?"

What point was there in denying it anymore?

"Yes. Very much."

"So why won't you marry me?"

Josephine let out a long, low sigh. "Because it would be too easy."

"Marriage is *supposed* to be easy," he said gently. "Not difficult."

"Yes, but don't you see, Blake—I've already had one failed marriage. I don't want to rush into another—like a woman crossing a stream and leaping from one emotional rock to the next. This has all been like a roller coaster—"

"What has?"

"The closure with Luke. The relief. The closeness with you—but what if it's all an illusion? What if six months down the line we find it's all played out?"

He shook his head. "It won't be."

"But how can you know that?" she demanded, her voice rising, knowing that she was heaping pain on herself by not giving in to what she wanted more than anything in the world, but knowing, deep down, that she needed the courage to see it through. "You thought that you wanted to marry Kim—you were with her for *years,* and yet in the end you acknowledged that it wasn't right."

"Because I feel differently about you than the way I felt about Kim," he said simply. "With Kim I just felt that I was playing a part—a part I wanted to play, it's true. But none of it felt real, the way it does with you. You're everything I thought I *didn't* want—you're stubborn and fiery. You make me want to make love to you in the most unsuitable of places."

She blushed, remembering them working late last night, and the protracted pleasure of the ride in the lift.

"You make me *respond,*" he continued passionately. "And I don't just mean sexually, I mean emotionally, too. You engage me at a level I didn't think I had in me. I broke every rule in the book the night I took you home from that party. Don't you understand, Josephine, that we *belong* together— in a way that Kim and I never did."

"Oh, darling," she whispered.

"I must have been mad not to have admitted it to myself sooner. I risked losing you—hell, I *did* lose you! I'm just thanking God that your marriage failed and that I had the chance to try again."

It was hard to reconcile Blake—her passionate but contained Blake—coming out with such unequivocal declarations of need and love. She wanted to get on the mobile phone and to demand that Luke give her the quickest divorce in history so that she could become Mrs. Josephine Devlin at the first opportunity.

But she owed it to him to apply the brakes just a little.

Hell, she owed it to *herself*.

She reached for his hand and kissed the tip of each finger in turn, and she thought that she could read a certain sense of victory in the ice-blue eyes. But his words surprised her even more than his wry smile.

"You aren't going to give in on this, are you, sweetheart?"

"How can you tell?"

"I just can." Like he seemed to be able to tell most things about her, and his knowledge of her grew day by day. He sighed, knowing that she was right and respecting her for it, even as it irritated him that she would not bend to his will.

But wasn't that one of the reasons why he loved her?

"Okay." He nodded his dark head. "I'll wait. Just don't make me wait too long, Josephine," he growled.

CHAPTER TWENTY

"So how does it feel to be a millionaire, sweetheart?" Blake asked softly.

Josephine smiled. "Huh! You tell *me*—you should know!"

He laughed. Giuseppi's revolutionary organic weed killer had been launched to ecstatic worldwide response and the shares had been floated on the stock market last week, leaving him with his biggest ever success on his hands.

No. Not his.

"You know, it's your success, sweetheart. All yours." He leaned over to plant a kiss on her lips. "If it hadn't been for your stubbornness and determination—I would never have backed him. I should have listened to you from the outset."

"But why should you have done?" she asked him. "*You* were the expert—"

"Supposedly," he interjected dryly.

"It was just an instinctive feeling that it was all going to come good."

As they had done together. More than good. Blake had once said that Giuseppi had looked as though he had died and gone to heaven—well, he now had a pretty good idea of how he must have felt!

"And yet you ruthlessly refused to be instinctive about marrying me," he mused. "When I knew you wanted to. We keep acting out-of-character around each other, don't we, Josie?"

She considered this. "Or maybe it's just that we bring out the best in each other," she said seriously. "Exploring the sides of ourselves that we'd never really looked at before."

He smiled. "Happy?"

"Ecstatic would be an understatement!"

"That's a 'yes,' is it?" he teased.

They were sitting outside on Blake's roof garden in the glorious, golden summer sunshine, just contemplating whether to eat in or go out for supper.

And contemplating other things, as well.

Josephine's divorce had come through and Luke had paid back most of the money. She was now financially more than solvent and well respected within the company—more important, she now respected *herself*. She sighed. It didn't get much better than this. The board had just agreed to promote her, and she was living with the man she loved.

"It's been well over a year since I first moved in here with you," she observed, a note of surprise in her voice. "Hard to believe, isn't it?"

In some ways, yes—in others, not at all. Time was immeasurable when you were happy, Blake realized, and he was happier than he had imagined it possible to be.

He kissed her again, just for the hell of it. "You know, maybe you were right, sweetheart, maybe we *don't* need a wedding ring to be committed to one another."

Josephine frowned. "I don't remember saying *that*."

"Not in so many words, perhaps." He shrugged. "But marriage to Luke scared you off, I know that, and the last thing I want is for you to enter into an institution that makes you uneasy. I'm not going anywhere, honey—and we don't need a wedding to prove it."

The frown grew deeper. "Are you saying that you no longer want to marry me?"

With great difficulty, he bit back a smile. "That's not what I'm saying at all," he corrected smoothly. "Just I'm perfectly happy with the status quo. Aren't you?"

Suddenly, no she was *not*! "I *do* want to get married, actually," she said sulkily, but the soft blaze from his eyes teased a smile out of her. "I've been waiting for you to ask me again!"

He shook his head and a mischievous light glinted in the blue eyes. "Oh, no—we've done it that way round and you said no. So in the spirit of our wonderful and very equal relationship, I really think you ought to ask me, Josephine."

"I'm not getting down on one knee, if that's what you think!"

"Why not sit on my knee instead?" he suggested gravely.

She did as he asked, perched herself comfortably and erotically over one hard, muscular thigh and looked deep into his eyes. "Will you marry me, Blake?"

"I'll have to think about it."

"For how long?" she cried, trying to keep the alarm from her voice.

He enjoyed the moment. "Oh, for about—say—five seconds." He grinned. "Of course I'll marry you, Josephine—though I thought you'd never ask, you stubborn woman!"

He kissed her for a very long time and as she kissed him back her last rational thought was that Blake knew exactly how to handle her.

In more ways than one!

His Pretend Wife

Lucy Gordon

PROLOGUE

HE WOULD never have known her.

He would have known her anywhere.

Andrew caught only the briefest glimpse of the woman, at the far end of the hospital corridor, but it was enough to revive memory, as soft as a bird's wing fluttering past his face.

She looked nothing like Ellie, who'd been young and luscious as a ripe peach. This was a thin, pale woman, who looked as though life had thrown everything at her, and left her exhausted. Yet there was a hint of Ellie in the resolute set of her head and the angle of her jaw. The bird's wing fluttered again, and vanished.

He couldn't afford sentimentality. He was a busy man, second in command of the Heart Unit of Burdell Hospital. Ultimately he could only be satisfied with heading the team, but there was no shame in being second when the chief was Elmer Rylance, a man of international eminence. Soon he would retire and Andrew would step into his shoes.

He'd fast-tracked, giving everything to his work, allowing no distractions, as a broken marriage could testify. He was young for his position, although he didn't look it. His tall figure was still lean, his features handsome, and there was no grey in his dark hair, but his face had a gaunt look from too many hours spent in work, and not enough spent in living. And there was something about his eyes that spoke of an inner withering.

He had only time for a glimpse of the woman, enough to show that she was with a child, a little girl of about seven, on whom her eyes were fixed with an anguished possessiveness with which he was all too familiar. In this place he'd seen a thousand mothers look at their children like that. And usually his skill sent the two of them home happy. But not always. He turned swiftly into his office.

His secretary was there before him, the list of appointments ready waiting on his desk, along with the necessary files, the coffee being made, exactly as he liked it. She was the best. He only employed the best, just as he only bought the best.

The first patient on his list was seventeen, the age that Ellie had been. There the likeness ended. His patient was weary with illness. Ellie had been an earth nymph, vibrant with life, laughing her way through the world with the confidence of someone who knew she was blessed by the gods, and laughter would last for ever.

'Mr Blake?' Miss Hasting was eyeing him with concern.

He shook himself out of his reverie. 'I'm sorry, did you speak?'

'I asked if you'd seen the test results. They're just here…'

He grunted, annoyed with himself for the moment of inattention. That was a weakness, and he always concealed weakness. Miss Hasting was too well disciplined to notice. She was a perfectly functioning machine. Like himself.

Ellie's beauty had been wild and overflowing, making him think of wine and sun, freedom and splendour: all the good things of life that had been his for such a brief time.

He switched the thought off as easily as he would have switched off the light behind an X-ray. He had a heavy day ahead.

Besides, it hadn't been her.

'Time for me to start on my ward rounds,' he told Miss Hasting briefly. 'Make a call to...' For five minutes he gave brisk instructions.

When he went out into the corridor again the woman was gone.

He was glad of that.

CHAPTER ONE

SHE would have known him anywhere, any time. Down the length of the corridor. Down the length of the years.

Years that had changed her from a flighty, blinkered young girl who'd thought the world danced to her merry tune, to a bitter, grieving woman who knew that the world was something you had to fight. And you could never, ever really win.

She'd been partly prepared, seeing his name on the hospital literature. Andrew Blake was a common name, and it might not have been him, but she knew at once that it was. Just two words on the page, yet they had brought before her the rangy young man, too tense, too thoughtful, a challenge to a girl who'd known any man could have been hers if she'd only snapped her fingers. So she'd snapped. And he'd been hers. And they'd both paid a bitter price.

She'd planned a glamorous, if ill-defined, career for herself. She would earn a fortune and live in a mansion. The reality was 'Comfy 'n' Cosy', a shabby boarding house in a down-at-heel part of London. The paint peeled, the smell of cabbage clung, and the only thing that was 'comfy' was the kindness of her landlady, Mrs Daisy Hentage.

Daisy was peering through the torn lace curtains when the cab drew up, and Elinor helped her daughter onto the pavement. Once Hetta would have protested, 'I can manage, Mummy!' And there would have been a mother/daughter tussle, which would have made Elinor feel desperate. But now Hetta no longer argued, just wearily did as she was told. And that was a thousand times worse.

Daisy had the front door open in readiness as they slowly climbed the stone steps. 'The kettle's on,' she said. 'Come into my room.' She was middle-aged, widowed, and built like a cushion.

She scraped a living from the boarding house, which sheltered, besides Elinor and her daughter, a young married couple, several assorted students, and 'that Mr Jenson' with whom she waged constant war about his smoking in bed.

When the house was full Daisy had only one small room left for herself. But if her room was small her heart was large, and she'd taken Elinor and her little girl right into it. She cared for Hetta while Elinor was out working as a freelance beautician, and there was nobody else the distraught mother would have trusted with her precious child.

After the strain of her journey Hetta was ready to doze off on the sofa. When they were sure she was safely asleep they slipped into the kitchen and Daisy said quietly, 'Did you see the great man in person, or did you get fobbed off?'

'Elmer Rylance saw me. They say he always sees people himself when it's bad news.'

'It's much too soon to talk like that.'

'Hetta's heart is damaged and she needs a new one. But it has to be an exact match, and small enough for a child.' Elinor covered her eyes with her hand and spoke huskily. 'If we don't find one before—'

'You will, you will.' Daisy put her arms around the younger woman's thin body and held her as she wept. 'There's still time.'

'That's what he said, but he's said it so often. He was kind and he tried to be upbeat, but the bottom line is there's no guarantee. It needs a miracle, and I don't believe in miracles.'

'Well, I do,' Daisy said firmly. 'I just know that a miracle is going to happen for you.'

Elinor gave a shaky laugh. 'Have you been reading the tarot cards again, Daisy?'

Daisy's life was divided between the cards, the runes and the stars. She blindly believed everything she read, until it was proved wrong, after which she believed something else. She said it kept her cheerful.

'Yes, I have,' she said now, 'and they say everything's going to be all right. You can scoff, but you'd better believe me. Good luck's coming, and it's going to take you by surprise.'

'Nothing takes me by surprise any more,' Elinor said, drying her eyes. 'Except—'

'What?'

'Oh, it's just that I thought I saw a ghost today.'

'What kind of a ghost?' Daisy said eagerly.

'Nothing, I'm getting as fanciful as you are. How about another cuppa?'

'It's not fair for you to be facing this alone,' Daisy said, starting to pour.

'I'm not alone while I've got you.'

'I meant a feller. Someone who's there for you. Like Hetta's dad.'

'The less said about Tom Landers, the better. He was a disaster. I should never have married him. And before him was my first husband, who was also a disaster. And before him…' Elinor's voice faded.

'Was that one a disaster too?'

'No, *I* was. He loved me. He wanted to marry me, but I threw him over. I didn't mean to be cruel, but I was. And I broke his heart.'

'You couldn't help it if you didn't love him.'

'But I did love him,' Elinor said softly. 'I loved him more than I've ever loved anyone in my whole life, except Hetta. But I didn't realise it then. Not for years. By then it was too late.' Anguish racked her. 'Oh, Daisy, I had the best any woman could have. And I threw it all away.'

There was more than one kind of ghost. Sometimes it was the other person, teasing you with memories of what might have been. But sometimes it was your own younger self, dancing ahead of you through the shadows, asking reproachfully how she'd turned into you.

To Ellie Foster, sixteen going on seventeen, life had been heaven: an impoverished kind of heaven, since there had never been money to spare in her home or those of her friends, and there had been a lot of 'making do'. But there had been the freedom of having left school. Her mother had tried to persuade her to stay on, perhaps even go to college, but Ellie had regarded that idea with horror. Who needed boring lessons when they could work in the cosmetics department of a big store? She'd seized on the job, and had had a wage packet and a kind of independence.

Best of all, she'd been gorgeous. She'd known it without conceit because boys had never stopped following her, trying to snatch a kiss, or just looking at her like gormless puppies. That had been the most fun of all.

She'd been tall, nearly five-foot eight, with a slender, curved figure and endless legs. She'd worn her naturally blonde hair long and luxuriant, letting it flow over her shoulders. To her other blessings had been added a pair of deep blue eyes and a full mouth that had been able to suddenly beam out a brilliant smile. She'd had only to give a man that smile…

What appalled Elinor, as she looked back over the years,

was her own ignorance in those days. With just a few puny weapons she'd thought she could have the universe at her feet. Who had there been to tell her otherwise? Certainly not the love-struck lads who'd followed her about, practically in a convoy.

They'd formed a little gang, Pete and Clive and Johnny, Johnny's sister Grace, and another girl who'd tagged along because Ellie had always been the centre of the action, and being part of her entourage meant status. She'd been a natural leader, that had gone without saying. And she wouldn't be stuck long in Markton, the featureless provincial town where she'd been born. She could be anything she wanted. A model perhaps, or a television presenter, or someone who was famous for being famous. Whatever. The cosmetics counter had only been temporary. The city lights had beckoned, and, after that, the world.

Her seventeenth birthday had been looming, and as Grace had had a birthday in the same week both sets of parents had got together and held the party at Grace's home, which had been bigger. Ellie had a new dress for the occasion. It looked like shimmering gold and was both too sophisticated and too revealing, as her scandalised mother had protested.

'Mum, it's a party,' Ellie said in a voice that settled the matter. 'This is how people dress at parties.'

'It's much too low,' her mother said flatly. 'And too short.'

'Well, if you've got it, flaunt it. I've got it.'

'And you're certainly flaunting it. In my day only a certain kind of woman dressed like that.'

Ellie collapsed laughing. The things mothers said, honestly! But she gave Mrs Foster a hug and asked kindly, 'When you were my age, didn't you ever flaunt it?'

'I didn't have it to flaunt, dear. If I'd had—well, maybe I'd have gone a bit mad, too. But then I'd have lost your father. He didn't like girls who "displayed everything in the shop window".'

Ellie crowed with delight. 'You mean he was as much of a stick-in-the-mud then as he is now?'

'Don't be unkind about your father. He's a very nice, kind man.'

'How can you say that when he wanted to hold you back, stop you having fun?'

'He didn't. He just wanted me to have my fun with him. So did I. We loved each other. You'll find out one day. You'll meet the right man, and you won't want any fun that doesn't include him.'

'OK, OK,' Ellie said, not believing a word of it, but feeling good-natured. 'I just don't want to meet the right man until I've done a bit of living.'

Oh, the irony of having uttered those words, on that evening of all evenings! But she only came to see it later.

'Let's get to this party,' Mrs Foster said indulgently. 'You're only young once.'

Ellie kissed her, delighted, though not surprised, to have got her own way again.

The party overflowed with guests, with noise and merriment. The parents hung around for the first hour, then bowed to the unmistakable hints that were being thrown at them, and departed to the peace of the pub, leaving the young people alone. Someone turned up the music. Someone else produced a bottle of strong cider. Ellie waved it away, preferring to stick to light wine. Life was more enjoyable with a clear head.

The music changed, became smoochy. In the centre of the room couples danced, not touching, because that wasn't 'cool', but writhing in each other's general direction. She beckoned to Pete and he joined her, his eyes fixed longingly on her gyrating form. She was smooth and graceful, moving as though the music were part of her.

At first she barely glimpsed the stranger in the doorway,

but then a turn brought her back to face him, and she saw that he was taller than everyone else in the room, and looked a little older. He wore a shirt and jeans, which were conservative compared to the funky teenage clothes around him.

What struck her most of all was his expression, the lips quirked in a wry smile, like a man showing indulgence to children. Obviously he thought a teenage rave beneath his dignity, and that made her very annoyed.

It wouldn't have mattered if he clearly belonged to another generation. Older people were expected to be stuffy. But he was in his twenties, too young for that slightly lofty look, she thought.

Nor would she have minded if he'd been unattractive. But for a man with those mobile, sensual lips to be above the crowd was a deadly insult. His lean features made matters worse, being slightly irregular in a way that was intriguing. His eyes were a crime too, dark, lustrous and expressive. They should be watching her, filled with admiration, instead of flickering over everyone with a hint of amusement.

'Who's that?' she yelled to her partner above the music.

'That's Johnny's brother, Andrew,' he yelled back, glancing at the door. 'He's a doctor. We don't see much of him here.'

Johnny was weaving his way over to his brother. Ellie couldn't hear them through the music, but she could follow their greeting, the way Johnny indicated for Andrew to join the party, and Andrew's grimace as he mouthed, 'You've gotta be kidding.'

She followed Johnny's reply, 'Aw, c'mon.'

And Andrew's dismissive, 'Thanks, but I don't play with children.'

Children. He might as well have shouted the word. And her response, as she later realised, was childish. She put an extra sensuousness into her writhing, which made the boys shout appreciation and the girls glare. She'd show him who was a child.

But when she looked up he'd gone.

She found him in the kitchen half an hour later, eating bread and cheese and drinking a cup of tea. She'd switched tactics now. Charm would be better.

'What are you hiding out here for?' she asked, smiling. 'It's a party. You should be having fun.'

'I'm sorry, what did you say?' He raised his head from the book he'd been reading. His eyes were unfocused, as though part of him was still buried in the pages, and he didn't seem to have noticed her smile.

'It's a party. Come and have fun. Don't be boring out here.'

'Better than being boring in there,' he said, indicating the noise with his head.

'Who says you're boring?'

He shrugged. 'I would be to them.' His tone suggested that he wasn't breaking his heart over this.

'So live a little.'

'By "live" you mean drink too much and make a fool of myself? No, thanks. I did that in my first year at Uni, and who needs to repeat an experience?'

He was dividing his attention between Ellie and his book, making no secret of the fact that she couldn't go fast enough for him.

'You mean *we're* boring, don't you?' she demanded, nettled.

He shrugged. 'If the cap fits.' Then he looked up from the book, giving her his whole attention. 'I'm sorry, that was rude of me.'

'Yes, it was,' noticing that his smile was gentle and charming.

'What's the party about?'

'It's my birthday—and Grace's.'

'How old are you?'

'Nineteen.' He laid down the book and regarded her, his head on one side. 'All right, not quite nineteen,' she admitted.

He looked her up and down in a way that made her think he was getting the point at last, but when he spoke it was only to say, 'Not quite eighteen, either.'

'I'm seventeen today,' she admitted.

'Don't sound so disappointed. Seventeen is a lot of fun.'

'How would you know? I'll bet you were never seventeen.'

He laughed at that. 'I was, but it's lost in the mists of time.'

When he grinned he was very attractive, she decided. 'Yes, I can see you're very old. You must be at least twenty-one.'

'Twenty-six, actually. Ancient.'

'No way. I like older men.' She was perching on the edge of the table now, crossing her legs so that their silky perfection was on display.

'Really?' he said, meeting her eyes.

'Really,' she said in a husky voice, full of meaning.

He picked up the book. 'Go back to your party, little girl. And be careful what you drink.'

'I think that's up to me,' she said defiantly.

'Sure. Enjoy the hangover.'

She glared but he wasn't looking. There was nothing to do but flounce out of the kitchen, slamming the door behind her. So she did it.

She found Johnny drinking cider.

'Your brother's insufferable,' she snapped.

'I could have told you that. Dull as ditch water. I don't know what made him arrive home tonight of all nights. He's supposed to be studying for his exams.'

'I thought he was already a doctor.'

'He is. He qualified last summer. This is a different lot of exams. He's always studying for something. Forget him and enjoy yourself. Here.' He poured some cider into a glass for her and she drank it in one gulp. Johnny immediately refilled her glass and she drained it again.

Out of sight she clutched the edge of the table. Not for the world would she have done anything so uncool as reveal how it was affecting her. She took a deep breath against the swimming of her head, and held out her glass.

'Fill it up,' she commanded with bravado.

He did so, and from somewhere there was an admiring cheer. Encouraged, she seized the big plastic bottle and drained it.

When she took the floor again she found that something had happened to her. Her limbs were mysteriously light, she danced as if floating on air and her whole body seemed infused with sensuality. Partners came and went. She didn't know who she was dancing with from one moment to the next, but she knew that none of them was the one she wanted.

'Hey,' she said, suddenly aware that there was a pair of unfamiliar arms about her, and she was being urged towards the door. 'Who are you?'

'You know me,' somebody whispered against her mouth. It was a man, but she couldn't think who he was. 'And you fancy me, don't you?'

'Do I?'

"Course you do. You're up for it, I can tell. Hey, what do you think you're doing?' The last words were addressed to someone who'd appeared out of nowhere and was determinedly freeing Ellie from the man's arms. 'Clear off.'

'No, *you* clear off,' came Andrew's voice.

'Now, look here—'

'Get lost before I do something very painful to you,' Andrew said, speaking almost casually.

'He will too,' Ellie remarked to nobody in particular. 'He's a doctor, so he'd know how.' The whole thing suddenly seemed terribly funny and she collapsed in giggles. Strong arms held her up, but now they were Andrew's arms.

'Thank you, kind sir,' she said with dignity, 'for coming to my rescue like a knight in shining armour.'

'What the devil have you been drinking?' Andrew demanded, not sounding at all like a gallant knight.

'Dunno,' she replied truthfully. 'It's a party.'

'So because it's a party you have to pour filthy rubbish down your throat and make a fool of yourself?' he said scathingly.

'Who are you calling a fool?'

'You, because you act like one.'

'Push off,' she said belligerently. The scene wasn't going at all as it should. 'I can take care of myself.'

'Oh, yeah!' he said, not even trying to be polite. 'I've seen children who can take better care of themselves than you. Come on.'

He'd taken a firm hold of her, but not in the way that other young men tried to. More like a man clearing out the rubbish. Ellie found herself being propelled firmly to the door.

'What d'you think you're doing?' she demanded.

'Taking you home.'

'I don't want to go home.' She tried to struggle but he had his hand firmly around her waist. 'Let *go*!'

'Don't waste your energy,' he advised her kindly. 'I'm a lot stronger than you.'

'Help!' she yelled. *'Abduction! Kidnap! Help!'*

That made them sit up, she was glad to see. Heads turned. Pete appeared, blocking their path.

'Where are you taking my girl?' he said belligerently.

'Who said I was your girl?' she demanded, briefly diverted. 'I never—'

'Shut up, the pair of you,' Andrew said without heat. 'She's not your girl because you don't know how to look after her. And you—' he tightened his grip on Ellie as she tried to make a bolt for it '—you aren't old enough to be anybody's girl. You're just a daft little kid who puts on fancy clothes and her mother's make-up and thinks she's grown up. Now, let's get out of here.'

'I don't want to get out of here.'

'Did I ask what you wanted?' he enquired indifferently.

'You'll be sorry you did this.'

'Not half as sorry as you'll be if I don't.'

She redoubled her efforts to escape, but he simply lifted her off the floor and left her kicking helplessly as he pushed Pete aside and strode on. Her head was swimming from the cider and her limbs were growing heavy, but through the gathering mist of tipsiness she could see her friends sniggering at her plight.

But then—relief! Johnny appeared, also trying to block their path.

'Put her down,' he said. 'She's my girl.'

'Another one?' Andrew said ironically. 'Listen, Johnny, I'll deal with you later. Just now I'm taking Ellie home where she'll be safe. What's her address, by the way?'

'Don't tell him,' she raged.

But Johnny had seen his elder brother's face and decided on discretion. He gave Andrew the information with a meekness that made Ellie disgusted with him. Before she could tell him so she found she was being carried out of the room. As the door swung to she was sure she could hear a burst of laughter, and it increased her rage.

Outside the house stood the most disgusting old van she'd ever seen. She couldn't believe he actually meant her to travel in that, but he was opening the door and shovelling her into the passenger seat. Shovelling was the only word for it. She immediately tried to break out and he slammed the door shut again.

'We can do this the easy way, or the hard way,' he said through the half-open window. 'The easy way is for you to sit here quietly. The hard way is for me to chuck you in the back, lock the rear doors and keep you there until we reach the other end.'

'You wouldn't dare.'

He grinned. 'Even you're not stupid enough to believe that.'

'Whaddaya mean? *Even* me?'

'Work it out.'

As he went around to the driver's seat she sat in sullen silence, partly because she knew he meant what he said, and partly because it was becoming hard to move. She leant her head against the back of the seat, just for a moment.

CHAPTER TWO

'ARE you all right, darling?' Mrs Foster's face came into focus.

'Mum? What—?'

Somehow the van had turned into her own bed in her own room. Her head was throbbing and her mother was smiling at her anxiously.

'How did I—? Oh, goodness!'

She bounded out of bed and just reached the bathroom before the storm broke. When it was over and she was feeling a little better she noticed something for the first time.

She was wearing only a bra and panties. They were peach-coloured, flimsy lace, and might as well not have existed for all they concealed. Her golden dress and her tights had been removed.

When? Where? How?

She made her way carefully back to her room, and mercifully her mother was there with strong tea.

'Did you have too much to drink last night, dear? Andrew said you'd come over faint and asked him to bring you home, but I couldn't help wondering—well, not to worry. I could see he's a really nice young man.'

Oh, sure, he's a nice young man. He stripped me almost naked while I was unconscious. And he had the unspeakable nerve to hang my dress up neatly on a hanger.

It was there, on the wardrobe, hung and straightened by skilled hands. Its very perfection was an outrage.

'What did he tell you?' she mumbled into her tea.

'He brought you home, and when you got here you went straight to bed, and he sat downstairs waiting for us so that he could explain that you were already here, and we needn't wait up.'

'He's Johnny's elder brother.'

'He told us. Apparently he's a doctor. I always thought you liked young men to be a bit more colourful than that.'

'He's not a boyfriend. I only met him last night.'

'But he's the one you turned to when you needed help, so he must have made a big impression on you.'

'He did that, all right,' she muttered.

'It's nice to know that you're getting so discerning now you're growing up.'

That was the final insult. *'Mum!'*

'What, dear?'

'I'm seventeen. It'll be years before I'm interested in a boring doctor. He just happened to have a car.'

'You mean that revolting van? You must be really smitten if you liked him for that.'

'I'm not feeling well,' she said hastily. 'I think I'll go back to sleep.'

Her mother tactfully left her and Ellie snuggled down, feeling like a wrung-out rag. As she drifted off she remembered the stranger who'd tried to drag her away. She might have passed out with him instead of with Andrew, and instinct told her that he wouldn't have simply brought her home and put her to bed.

Try as she might she couldn't recall Andrew removing her clothes and putting her to bed. He was rude and insufferable, but he'd saved her from a nasty fate. What was more, he'd seen her almost naked, which none of her boyfriends had. It was maddening to think that he might have looked at her with admiration, and she hadn't known.

But as the waves of sleep came over her again, she began to dream. She was in a moving vehicle that stopped suddenly. The door beside her opened and she was pulled out so that she fell against a man who picked her up in his arms as easily as if she'd weighed nothing.

He was carrying her—there was the click of the front door, then the feel of climbing. It felt good to rest against him—safe and warm. Somehow her arm had found its way around his neck, her face was buried against him, and she could hear the soft thunder of his heartbeat.

They were in her room and she was being lowered gently onto the bed. His face swam in and out of her consciousness, lean, serious, the mobile features full of expression—if only she could read it.

But then the darkness obscured everything, and she was sinking down, down into deep sleep, leaving the dream and its mysteries for another time.

Her very first hangover was a grim experience, but by late afternoon she'd rejoined the human race. Soon Andrew would drop by to see how she was. Their eyes would meet, and each would see in the other's the memory of last night.

She dressed plainly in trousers and top, and applied only the very slightest make-up. This elegant restraint would make him forget the juvenile who'd aroused his scorn. He would be intrigued. They would talk and he would discover that she had a brain and a personality as well as a beautiful shape. He would become her willing slave, and that would serve him right for dismissing her as a kid.

But it wasn't Andrew who called. Only Johnny.

Rats!

'Hallo, Johnny,' she said, trying not to sound as disappointed as she felt.

'You better now? You were looking pretty green when I last saw you.'

'I wonder why,' she said pointedly.

'Yeah, right,' he mumbled. 'It was my fault. No need to keep on. I've had it all from Andrew.'

'Oh?' she said carelessly. 'What did he say?'

'What didn't he say?' Johnny struck a declamatory attitude. '"Pouring cider down the throat of a silly girl who hasn't got two brain cells to rub together—"'

'Who's he calling silly?' she demanded indignantly. This scene wasn't going to plan, but how could it when the leading man was missing?

'Why don't we go back to your home now?' she suggested casually. 'Then I can thank him.'

'He's not there. This morning he took off to visit his girlfriend.'

'*What?* How long for?'

'Dunno! Lilian's studying for medical exams too, so they'll probably work together. I'll bet they study far into the night, and then go to bed to sleep. And that's all he'll do. He's got ice water in his veins.'

As in a flash of lightning she saw Andrew's face leaning over her as he began to remove her clothes. Not ice water.

Then the lightning was gone, and she was here again with Johnny, suddenly realising how young he was. How could she ever have been flattered by the admiration of this boy?

But for the next few days she still hung around with him, had supper at his house, just in case Andrew appeared. But he didn't, and after four days she gave this up. She told Andrew's mother that she was so sorry to have missed him, and she would write him a note of thanks. Sitting at the kitchen table, she applied herself.

Dear Andrew,

I shall give this note to your mother, and ask her to make sure that you get it. I owe you my thanks—for the help you gave me at the party the other night.

Good. Dignified and restrained, and giving no clue to her real thoughts: *You're a dirty, rotten so-and-so for not coming to see me.*

'There are two "esses" in passionate,' said Andrew's voice over her shoulder.

She jumped with sheer astonishment. 'What—? I didn't—'

'And one "y" in undying, and one "u" in gratitude.'

She leapt up to confront him. 'What are you on about?' she demanded. She could have screamed at being caught unawares after all her careful plans. Once again life had handed her the wrong script.

But his face came out of the right script. It was tired and pale, as if he'd studied too long, but his eyes held a glowing light that made her want to smile.

'I was writing you a note to thank you for your help, but I never said anything about passionate, undying gratitude.'

He took it from her and studied the few words regretfully. 'You just hadn't reached that bit yet,' he suggested.

'In your dreams! Just because a person is being polite, that doesn't mean that another person can go creeping up behind them and—and make fun of them—when all a person was doing was—was—'

'Being polite,' he supplied helpfully.

'I'd have thanked you myself if you'd still been around next day.'

'I thought I'd better not be,' he said quietly.

Suddenly she was growing warm, as though he'd openly referred to the way he'd undressed her. She turned away so that he shouldn't see how her cheeks were flaming.

The next moment the rest of the family entered the kitchen. There were greetings, laughter, surprise.

'I thought you were staying until the end of the week,' his mother said.

'Oh, you know me,' Andrew said carelessly. 'Always chopping and changing.'

'You? Once you've decided on something it's like arguing with a rock.'

Andrew merely gave the calm smile that Ellie was to come to know. It meant that other people's opinions washed off him.

'I feel sorry for Lilian, if she marries you,' Grace teased.

'She won't,' Andrew said mildly. 'Too much good sense.'

'Sense?' Grace echoed, aghast. 'Is that what you say about the love of your life? Don't you thrill when you see her? Doesn't your heart beat with anticipation, your pulse—?'

'Whoever invented kid sisters ought to be shot,' Andrew observed without heat.

'Who's a kid?' Grace demanded. 'I'm seventeen.'

'From where I'm standing that's a kid,' Andrew teased.

Grace took hold of Ellie's arm. 'Come on, let's go upstairs and play my new records.'

'No, let's help your mother lay the table,' Ellie said quickly. Anything was better than being bracketed with Andrew's 'kid' sister.

After the meal they all went out into the garden and watched fireflies, talking about nothing in particular. When the rest went in she hung back, touching his arm lightly so that he turned and stayed with her.

'I didn't say thank you properly,' she said.

In the darkness she could just make out his grin. 'You were saying different at the time. Nothing was bad enough for me.'

'Well—I wasn't quite myself.'

'You were smashed. Not a pretty sight. And very dangerous.'

'Yes, I might fall into the hands of a man who'd undress me while I was unconscious,' she pointed out. 'That could be dangerous too.'

She wasn't really annoyed with him for undressing her, but for some reason she wanted to talk about it.

'What are you saying? Are you asking me if I ravished you?'

She smiled at him provocatively. 'Did you?'

'Stop playing games with me, Ellie,' he said quietly. 'You're too young and ignorant about men to risk this kind of conversation.'

'Is it risky?'

'It would be with some men. It's not with me because I know how innocent you really are, and I respect it.'

'You mean I mustn't ask if you "ravished" me?'

He was angry then. 'You know damned well I didn't.'

'How do I know?'

'Because you'd know if I had.'

'So why undress me at all?'

'If I'd just dumped you into bed fully clothed your mother would have guessed that you were incapable. I was trying to make everything look as normal as possible. But I'm a doctor. I'm used to naked bodies, and yours meant nothing to me.'

She glared. It was maddening not to be able to tell him that this was just what she minded most.

Grace put her head out of the window. 'Andrew, Lilian's on the phone.'

She couldn't help overhearing the first part of the call. 'Lilian? Hi, honey, yes, I got here OK—it was a wonderful few days, wasn't it? You know I do—' He gave a soft laugh that seemed to go through Ellie.

She stood still, filled with sensations that she didn't understand and couldn't control. Andrew was a man, not a boy. He excited her and mystified her, and he had all the allure of the unknown. But her chief sensation, although she didn't understand it then, was childish, hurt pride.

There and then she made up her mind that she was going to make him fall in love with her, and that would show everyone. Above all it would show him that he couldn't look down on her from lofty heights.

Oh, God, she thought now, looking back down the tunnel of years, *I was only seventeen. What did I know?*

The house stood well back from the road, almost hidden by trees. It was large and costly, the residence of a wealthy, successful man.

It was dusk as Andrew drove up the winding drive, and there were no lights to greet him. But for himself the house was empty, and even he spent very little time here since his wife and son had departed. He had a bachelor flat near the hospital.

This grandiose place wasn't a home to him. It never had been. He'd bought it three years ago to satisfy Myra, who'd fallen in love with its size and luxury. She'd been the wife of the youngest top-ranking cardiothoracic surgeon in the country, and she'd expected to live appropriately. Andrew had demurred at the house, which was almost a mansion, with a porticoed door and walls covered with ivy. But Myra had insisted, and he'd yielded, as so often, to conceal the fact that his feeling for her had died. If it had ever lived.

For a while she'd enjoyed playing lady of the manor. She'd named the place 'Oaks' after the two magnificent trees in the garden. She'd bought their son, Simon, a pony, and had him taught to ride in the grounds. But by that time their marriage had effectively been over. She hadn't even wanted Oaks as part of the divorce settlement.

He was pouring himself a drink when his mobile went. It was Myra, which made his head immediately start to ache.

'You're no easier to get hold of than you ever were,' she said wryly. 'Where are you?'

'The house.'

'What are you rattling around in that place for?'

'I can't think.'

'Just checking about the weekend. Simon's looking forward to seeing you.'

'Look, I was going to call you about that—'

'Don't you dare!'

'I'll have to work over the weekend. Can't you explain to Simon, make him understand?'

'But he already does understand, Andrew. It's *what* he understands that should be worrying you. He understands that he's always last on your list of priorities.'

'That's not true.'

'Damn, it *is* true! Look, I married you knowing your work always came first. I made that choice. But Simon didn't. He expects to have a father who loves him—'

'Don't dare say I don't love my son,' he barked.

'Do you think I need to say it? Don't you think he knows it every time you let him down?'

'Put him on.'

The talk with his son was a disaster. Simon was quiet and polite, saying, 'Yes, Daddy,' and 'It's all right, Daddy,' at regular intervals. And it wasn't all right. It was all dreadfully wrong, and he didn't know what to do about it.

He was tired to the bone. He microwaved something from the freezer, barely noticing what it was, then settled down in front of his computer. For two hours he worked mechanically and only stopped because his head was aching too badly for him to think. But that was good. He didn't want to think.

He wondered why he suddenly felt so drained and futile.

The demands of work were crushing, but they always were. Pressure, stress, instant decisions, life and death—these were the things he thrived on, without which he wouldn't exist. Suddenly they weren't enough. Or rather, they were too much. For the first time in his career—no, his whole life—he wondered if he could cope with everything that was required of him.

It was absurd to connect this sudden loss of confidence with the brief moment in the hospital corridor when he'd been confronted with a past he'd thought safely dead and buried.

Buried. Not dead.

He hunted in the top drawer of his desk until he found a set of keys, selected one, and used it to open the bottom drawer. At the back, buried under a pile of papers, was an envelope, stuffed with photographs. He laid it on the desk, but made no move to open it, as though reluctant to take the final step.

At last he shook out the contents onto the desk, and spread them out with one hand. They were cheap snaps, nothing special, except for the glowing faces of the two young people in them.

The girl's long blonde hair streamed over her shoulders in glorious profusion, her face was brilliant with life. It was that life, rather than her beauty, that made her striking. All youth and abundance seemed to have gathered in her, as though any man who came near her must be touched by her golden shadow, and be blessed all his days.

Blessed all his days. There was a thought to bring a bitter smile to the face of a man who'd felt that blessing, and seen it die.

He lingered over the girl's laughing face, trying to reconcile it with the weary look he'd seen on the woman in the corridor. Just once her gaze was turned on the young man, and he studied her expression, trying to detect in it some trace of the love he'd once believed in. In every other picture she was looking directly at the camera.

By contrast, the man had eyes only for her, as though nothing else in the world existed for him. His hands were about her waist or on her shoulder, touching her face, his expression one of tender adoration.

Andrew wanted to seize him, shake him, crying, You fool, don't be taken in by her. She's nothing but a cold-hearted little schemer, who'll break your heart and laugh at you.

She'd been laughing when he'd first seen her at the party, dancing with blissful abandon. With her head thrown back in enjoyment, her eyes sparkling, she'd seemed the very embodiment of everything he'd given up on the day he'd decided to be the greatest doctor in the world. He'd devoted himself to study, ignoring the young, heedless pleasures that other medical students had seemed to find time for. They'd been all right for people who'd been satisfied with being ordinary doctors, but he hadn't been satisfied, and he hadn't been going to be ordinary.

Without warning this shimmering pixie had burst on him, and before he'd been able to control the feeling, he'd been filled with fierce regret for the whole side of life he'd rejected. He'd escaped to the kitchen, away from the sight of her.

But then she'd appeared, looking even younger close-up, and he'd known that she'd been dangerous to his peace of mind. He'd assumed an air of lofty indifference, talking to her with one eye still on his book, as though he hadn't been able to tear himself away, although the truth had been that every fibre of him had been aware of her.

He'd have liked to believe her claim of being nineteen, but her air of bravado had given her away. She'd flirted like a kid, crossing her beautiful legs on the table near him, and saying she liked older men in a 'come hither' voice that would have finished him but for his stern resolutions. His advice to 'go back to your party, pretty little girl' had been an act of desperation.

He'd promised himself to avoid her, but when he'd seen boys getting her drunk for a laugh he'd had to step in and rescue her.

He'd taken the house key from her purse and carried her up the stairs to what he'd guessed had been her room. He'd removed her clothes because if her mother had found her fully dressed and asleep she might have guessed the truth. He was a doctor, and impersonal, so he'd thought.

But he'd found himself holding a girl wearing a bra and panties so wispy as to have been almost non-existent. Laying her gently on the bed, he'd been shocked to find how his hands had longed to linger over her silky skin and perfect shape. He'd hung up her dress, using the controlled movements to impose discipline on his mind and, through his mind, his sensations. Discipline, control, order. That was how it had always been with him.

But not this time. Fear had seized him, and he'd got out as fast as he'd been able to.

He'd fled to the imagined safety of Lilian, a girlfriend as sedate and studious as himself. But there had been no safety there, or anywhere. After that it was too late. It had always been too late.

CHAPTER THREE

HETTA and Elinor shared their cramped little room both night and day. It meant that Elinor spent half her night listening for Hetta's breathing, terrified lest her child had slipped away in the darkness. Each dawn she gave thanks that Hetta was still alive, and tried to convince herself that she wasn't losing ground. Every morning she went to work and telephoned home after the first hour, to hear Daisy say, 'She's fine.' In the late afternoon she hurried home at the first chance, anxious to look at Hetta's face and lie to herself that the little girl wasn't really looking paler or more tired.

There were the regular check-ups with the local doctor, who assured her that Hetta was 'holding on'. And there were the further check-ups at the hospital, where Sir Elmer Rylance would make kindly noises.

'I promise you Hetta is top of the list,' he told her once. 'As soon as a suitable heart becomes available…'

But day followed day, week followed week, and no heart ever became available.

If it ever did happen she knew she would be called at home, yet she couldn't help a glimmer of hope as she and Hetta entered the cardiac unit for their April appointment. It was two months since she'd last been here and glimpsed

Andrew Blake from a distance. In that time she'd managed to persuade herself that she'd imagined it.

There was a new nurse today, young and not very confident. She ushered Elinor and Hetta into the consulting room and seemed taken aback to find it empty.

'Oh, yes,' the nurse said quickly, 'I should have told you—'

'It's all right,' came a man's voice from the door. 'I'll explain everything to Mrs Landers.'

She knew the voice at once, just as she had recognised his face, despite the years. As he closed the door behind the nurse and went to the desk Elinor waited for him to look at her, braced herself for the shock in his eyes.

'I apologise for Sir Elmer's absence, Mrs Landers,' he said briskly. 'I'm afraid he's gone down with a touch of flu. My name is Andrew Blake, and I'm taking over his appointments for today.'

He looked up, shook hands with her briefly, and returned to his notes.

He didn't recognise her.

After the first shock she felt an overwhelming relief. Only Hetta mattered. She had no time for distractions.

He talked to the child in a gentle, unemotional voice, listened to her heart, and asked questions. He didn't talk down to her, Elinor was impressed to see, but assumed that she understood a good deal. Hetta didn't disappoint him. She was an old hand at this by now.

'Do you get breathless more often than you used to?' he asked.

Hetta nodded and made a face. 'It's a pig.'

'I'm sure it is. I expect there's lots you can't do.'

'Heaps and heaps,' she said, sensing a sympathetic ear. 'I want a dog, but Mummy says it would be too bois—something.'

'Too boisterous,' Andrew agreed.

'Hetta, that's not really the reason,' Elinor protested. 'We can't have pets in that little room.'

'You live in one room?' Andrew asked.

'In a boarding house. It's just a bit tiny, but everyone's fond of Hetta and kind to her.'

'Do you smoke?'

'No. I never did, but I wouldn't do it around Hetta.'

'Good. What about the other tenants?'

'Mr Jenson smokes like a chimney,' Hetta confided. 'Daisy's very cross with him.'

'Tell me about the others.'

Man and child became absorbed in their talk, giving Elinor the opportunity to watch him, and note the changes of twelve years.

He had always been a tall man, slightly too thin for his height. Now that he'd filled out he was imposing. Perhaps his face had grown sharper, his chin a little more forceful, but he still had a thick shock of dark hair with no sign of thinning. At thirty-eight he was the essence of power and success, exactly as he'd always meant to be.

At last he said, 'Hetta, do you know the play area just along the corridor?'

'Mmm! They've got a rabbit,' she said wistfully.

'Would you like to go along and see the rabbit now?'

Hetta nodded and left the room as eagerly as her constant weariness would allow.

'Is there anyone to help you with her?' Andrew asked. 'Family?'

'My parents are both dead. Daisy helps me a lot. She's the landlady, and like a second mother to me. She cares for Hetta when I'm out working.'

'Is your job very demanding?'

'I'm a freelance beautician. I go into people's homes to

do their hair, nails and make-up. It has the advantage that I can make my own hours.'

'But if you have to take time off you don't get paid, I suppose.'

'It will be different when she's well. Then I can work really hard and make some money to take her away for a holiday. We talk about that—' She stopped, her voice running down wearily. Why was she telling him these unlikely dreams that would never come true?

Now she was passionately glad that he hadn't recognised her as he listened to her tale of defeat and failure.

'Is Hetta any worse?' she asked desperately.

'There's been some slight deterioration but nothing to be too troubled about. I've made a small change in her medication,' he said, scribbling. 'It'll make her breathing a little easier. Call my office if you're alarmed about her condition.'

I'm always alarmed about her condition, she wanted to scream. *I'm alarmed, terrified, despairing. and you can't help. You were going to be the world's greatest doctor, but my child is dying and you can't do anything.*

But all she said was, 'Thank you.'

'Good day to you, Mrs Landers.'

'Good day.'

That night, as always, she sat with Hetta. When the child had fallen asleep she rose and went to the window, looking out onto the unlovely back yards that were so typical of this depressing neighbourhood.

A machine, she thought. *That's what he's become. Just a machine. It was always bound to happen. Even back then he had his life planned out, a straight path, dead ahead, and no distractions to the left or the right. He said so.*

Why did I ever worry? I didn't make any impact on him. Not in the end.

* * *

It had been so simple to promise herself that she would win Andrew's heart. But as week had followed week in silence she'd faced the fact that he'd returned to Lilian and forgotten her. She'd pictured them together, laughing about her.

'You should have seen this silly little kid I met,' he must have said. 'Thought she was grown up, but didn't have a clue.'

He might have telephoned to see how she was, but he didn't.

She could have screamed. How could she make him fall in love with her if he wasn't there?

For lack of anything better to do, she continued going out with the kids in the gang, although after Andrew their conversation sounded juvenile, and their concerns meaningless. The boys talked about the girls, the girls sighed over pop stars and made eyes at the boys. The talk was mildly indecent in an ignorant sort of way.

Then Jack Smith appeared among them. He was a motor mechanic, brashly handsome, and twenty-one. He fixed on Ellie as the best-looking girl in town, and his admiration, following Andrew's departure, warmed her.

'A smasher, that's what you are,' he told her one night when they were all sitting at a table outside a pub. 'Bet you could have any feller you wanted.'

'She could,' Grace agreed. 'You should have seen her at our birthday party. They were all over her. Even Andrew.'

'No, he wasn't,' Ellie's honesty compelled her to say. 'He was saving me from the others.'

'Oh, go on! What happened when he got you alone? You've never told.'

'And I'm never going to.'

There were knowing cries of 'Ooh!'

'Who is this Andrew?' Jack demanded.

'My snooty elder brother,' Grace said. 'He carried Ellie out of the party thrown over his shoulder, like a caveman.'

'No, he didn't,' Ellie corrected. 'He just lifted me off the floor a bit.'

'But he'd have *liked* to throw you over his shoulder, wouldn't he?'

Ellie would have given a lot to know the answer to that question herself.

'Bet he fancies you really,' Grace persisted.

'Don't think so,' Ellie said, clinging onto truthfulness with a touch of desperation. It was hard because her pride was involved. 'Don't forget about Lilian.'

'Bet you could make him forget Lilian,' Grace nagged. 'Bet you could if you set your mind to it.'

'Ellie could make *anyone* fall in love with her,' Jack said admiringly. 'Whether she had a mind to or not.'

'Not Andrew,' Ellie said, to bring the conversation back to him. 'Nobody will ever get under his skin.'

'Bet you could,' Grace obliged.

'Bet I couldn't,' Ellie said, speaking gruffly to hide how much the thought pleased her.

'Bet you could.'

'Bet I couldn't.'

'Could.'

'Couldn't.'

'Could.'

'Couldn't!'

In the end she shrugged and said, 'Well, maybe I could if I set my mind to it. But I'm not going to.'

'Oh, go on! It'll be fun seeing my big brother when he's not being so cocky.'

'Yes,' Ellie murmured with feeling.

'Go on, then.'

'No.'

'You're chicken.'

'I'm not.'

'You are.'

'I'm not.'

'You are.'

Goaded, she said, 'Listen, I could have anyone I want, and that includes your snooty brother. But I'm not interested in him.'

'So pretend.'

'I'll think about it.'

Like children squabbling in the playground, she thought, years later. *That was the level of the conversation that had ultimately broken a man's heart.*

Even as a child Andrew had been orderly about remembering dates and details. For a man of science it was very useful.

But there were times he would have been glad of a little forgetfulness. His brother's birthday, for instance, which came exactly seven weeks and three days after Grace's birthday party; seven weeks and three days after the night he'd met Ellie; seven weeks and two days since he'd fled her, six weeks and five days since he'd returned home to find her there and known that it had been useless to run and a mistake to return.

It would be an even worse mistake to attend Johnny's birthday festivities and risk another meeting. But his mother said it was his family duty, and duty was something Andrew never shirked.

When the day came he set out, armed with a gift for his brother, but as he reached town it occurred to him to buy something for his mother too, and headed for the nearest department store.

And there was Ellie, serving on the cosmetics counter, laughing with a customer as she demonstrated a perfume on her wrist. She didn't see Andrew at first, so that he had time to stand and watch her. And in that moment he knew that all the discipline and control, all the mental tricks to blot her out, had been for nothing, and the truth was that he had thought of her night and day since their last meeting.

She looked up and saw him. Smiled. He smiled back. It was all over.

When the customer had gone he approached her, heart thumping. To cover his confusion he made his face sterner and more rigid than usual.

'Good morning,' he said, almost fiercely.

'Hey, don't bite my head off,' she protested, laughing. 'What have I done wrong?'

'Nothing,' he said hastily. 'I only said good morning.'

'You made it sound like the crack of doom.'

Her smile touched him again, and this time he relaxed a little. 'I'm looking for something for my mother,' he told her. 'I don't see why Johnny should have all the gifts.'

'Johnny?'

'His nineteenth birthday.'

'Is it? I didn't know.'

'But aren't you coming to the party?' he asked, dismayed.

'I haven't seen much of Johnny lately,' she said with a light shrug. 'Do you want perfume, or lipstick, or—?'

'Pardon?'

'For your mother.'

'My mother? Oh, yes, her present.'

Pull yourself together, he thought. *You're burbling like an idiot.*

'What sort of make-up does she wear?' Ellie asked.

'Um…' He looked at her, wild-eyed, and she laughed at his confusion. But not unkindly.

'I'll bet you've never noticed if she wears any at all,' she teased.

'It's not the sort of thing I'm good at,' he confessed.

'You and the rest of the male population.'

'What do you do for the others?'

'Scented soap is pretty safe, especially with some nice gift wrapping.'

She showed him a variety of boxed soaps and he chose the biggest, an astounding pink and mauve creation.

'I thought you'd pick that one,' she said.

'I guess that means everyone does, huh?'

'Not everyone. Only the fellers. I'll gift-wrap it for free. I guess I owe you, and I like to pay my debts.'

'Ah! Now that's a pity because I was hoping you'd pay your debt in another way.'

'How?'

'I'd feel self-conscious turning up alone at this do. Since you and Johnny are—aren't—well, you might come with me. Just to make me look good.'

'You didn't bring Lilian?'

'Why should you ask that?' he demanded, suddenly self-conscious. 'It's what my mother said. I don't know why everyone assumes that—I'm fond of Lilian but we're not joined at the hip—head—' he corrected hastily. He had a horrible feeling that he was blushing like a boy.

'The only problem is that it's the store's late night,' Ellie said. 'We don't close until nine.'

'I'll be outside, waiting.'

When the time came she was late, filling him with dread lest she'd thought better of it and stood him up.

'Did you think I wasn't coming?' Her voice burst through his gloomy reverie. 'I'm so sorry, but the manager wouldn't stop talking.'

'It doesn't matter,' he said, brilliant with joy. 'You're here.'

She tucked her arm in his as they began to walk. 'Have you been to Johnny's party?'

'Yes, and it was noisy. Johnny was talking about going to the funfair in the park later, and most of the food at home has gone now. Why don't we grab a snack somewhere, and join them later?'

'Great.'

He took her to a small French restaurant, formal, but pleasantly quiet. She didn't look out of place here as she would have done in her gold party get-up, Andrew realised. Everything about her was more restrained, more gentle, more delightful.

'Did your mother like her present?' she asked.

'She was over the moon,' he said truthfully. 'You'd have thought I'd bought her a whole bath house instead of a few cakes of soap.'

'It's not the soap. It's because you thought of her.'

'I guess you're right.'

'I know I'm right. You should see some of my male customers, getting all worked up about this perfume or that perfume, treating it like rocket science. And I want to grab their lapels and yell, "Just show her you've thought of her. That's the real present." Gee, men can be so dumb.'

'I guess we can,' he said, entranced, willing her to go on.

She did so, entertaining him for several minutes with a witty description of life at the cosmetics counter, which seemed to be a crash course in human nature. Again he had the feeling that she was more mature than he remembered. The true reason didn't occur to him. This was her subject. She was an expert in it, and therefore at an advantage.

She was a joy to treat, revelling in every new taste with a defenceless candour that went to his heart.

'You aren't eating,' she challenged, looking up from the steak dressed with the chef's 'special' sauce.

'I'm enjoying watching you too much,' he said, and was surprised at himself. Normally he avoided any remark, however trivial, that savoured of self-revelation. It was her, he decided. Her frankness demanded a response.

'It's yummy,' she said blissfully.

'And there's even better to come.'

'Ice cream?'

'That's right. We'll have everything on the menu.'

'Go on, I'm more grown up than that.' She looked at him slyly. 'Well, almost.'

He groaned. 'Am I ever going to be forgiven for the things I said that time?'

'Well, I guess you were right. Mind you, I'd die before admitting it.'

He grinned. She laughed back, and suddenly their first meeting became a shared joke.

'I'm surprised you want to bother with a kids' party,' she said. 'Don't we all seem very juvenile to you?'

'My mother wanted me to come, and I guess I did it to please her.'

'That was kind of you. Like the soap.'

Again he knew the unfamiliar impulse to frankness. After resisting for a moment he yielded and found it unexpectedly easy. 'Not really,' he said. 'Part of me's trying to ease my conscience for being a bad son.'

'A bad son? You? No way. Your mother's terribly proud of you, all you've achieved—top marks in all your exams, really going places.'

'But in a sense I've done it at her expense, or at the expense of the family, which is the same thing. You can only give all of yourself to one thing at a time. I've held back from my family and given myself to work, which is something that benefits me, first and most.'

'But what about the people you heal? You benefit them. If you were only concerned about yourself you could be a banker or—or anything that makes a lot of money.'

'But I'd have been a terrible banker and I'm a good doctor. It makes sense to play to my skills. And by the time I've finished I'll have made a lot of money. But I have to be the best. And I will, whatever the cost.'

He'd gone further than he'd meant to. She was staring at him.

'You really mean that, don't you?'

'Do I sound very cold-blooded? Should I have talked about my mission to do good?'

She shook her head. 'People with missions to do good scare me. They always want to tell other people what to do. As long as you make sick people well, who cares about your reasons?'

'That's what I think,' he said, feeling a load slip away from him at finding someone who understood.

Suddenly he was talking, telling her about the frustrations of his childhood when he'd dreamed of escaping this dull little town where his parents had lived their contented lives.

'They're happy, and that's fine for them, but this place couldn't be enough for me.'

'What would be enough?'

'The top.'

'But which tree? You're working in a hospital now, aren't you?'

'That's right. Long hours, low pay. It's back-breaking and you don't get any sleep. No matter. It's great. I'm learning, and I'll get there.'

'And what then?'

'Then? Then I'll have everything I want.'

He knew, even as he said it, that it couldn't be true unless 'everything' included her. But he shied from the thought. It wasn't in the plan.

'I suppose we ought to put in an appearance at the funfair,' he said.

'Ooh, yes,' she said, becoming young again.

They went on everything, the scenic railway, the dodgems, the carousel, the big wheel. The wheel scared her and he had to put his arm around her. Then she forgot her fear and laughed up into his face, so that everything vanished, leaving just the two of them high up above the world.

And that was when he kissed her, with the stars raining about them and the sound of fireworks all around. He didn't know if the fireworks were real or inside himself, but they glittered and sparkled as she threw her arms about his neck and gave him back kiss for kiss.

'I've been plotting for ages how to kiss you,' he said when they freed their lips, gasping. 'And I'm such a coward that I waited until now, when you can't escape.'

'I don't want to escape,' she said recklessly. 'Kiss me— kiss me—'

He kissed her again and again, revelling in the response he could feel in her eager young body, and promising himself—chivalrous idiot that he was—not to abuse her trust.

Looking back down the years to that night, Andrew judged his young self harshly.

Fool. Bird brain. No common sense, or if you had you'd put it on hold. She was playing with you, laughing at you, and you fell for it like a daft boy, because you wanted to believe all those pretty fairy tales, and that's the stupidest thing of all.

But sometimes he would sigh and murmur, 'Just the same, I was a better man then than I am now.'

CHAPTER FOUR

AT SEVENTEEN Ellie reckoned life should be fun, and romance was part of that fun. You played the field, and if you won the man you'd set your heart on that was wonderful, but there were still other men in the world.

Of course she was crazy about Andrew—for the moment. They would date, and love each other; she would find a job in the same town as his hospital.

But she was startled to discover that his feelings were of a different order. He was a serious, dedicated man in his love as in his work. He offered her total commitment and he demanded the same in return.

Away from him Ellie made firm resolutions about cooling their relationship, refusing to let him make plans for their future. But with him her plans melted in the intensity of his adoration.

'Darling, darling, Ellie, you do love me, don't you?'

And as she looked into his glowing eyes the only possible answer was yes.

He never actually asked her to marry him, simply started talking about it as a foregone conclusion. Her mother was thrilled that she'd found 'a nice, steady young man' so soon, and she didn't know how to tell Mum that Andrew's steadiness was a point against him.

She was flattered, overwhelmed, confused, ecstatic, filled with love, longing and desire. The depth of his feelings touched her heart and made her tender towards him, which increased his love. It was all sweet and wonderful, but down the end of the rose strewn tunnel she saw dirty plates, dirty socks, dirty nappies.

'What's wrong with having children while we're young?' he asked when she managed to voice some doubts.

'Because it's not how I want to spend my youth,' she flung back. 'I want a career first.'

'Darling, one day I'm going to be a top consultant. I don't want my wife doing shampoos and sets.'

'Why you—you dinosaur!' she exploded.

Soon they were in the middle of a blazing row, their first. Ellie was upset, but Andrew was torn apart. His misery shocked her and she flung herself into his arms, longing only to comfort him. Making up was blissful, but afterwards she was more firmly tied to him than ever, and she was beginning to feel like a prisoner.

Yet she couldn't break away. He filled her with bittersweet emotions that she'd never known before, so intense that it was like living in a new, glowing world. She could only cling on and hope for a miracle to make everything right.

His mother was appalled at the prospect of his early marriage to a girl who could bring him no advantages. 'You could do a great deal better for yourself,' she snapped in Ellie's presence.

But Andrew slipped his arm about his beloved's shoulder, drawing her close to his tall, strong body, and said gently, 'She loves me, as much as I love her. Could I do better than that?' Then his voice rose joyfully. 'Mum, be happy for me. I've got the most wonderful girl in the world.'

She wanted him, ached for him, and raged at the old-fashioned chivalry that made him refuse until they were married.

She guessed that her youth preyed on his mind, but she knew too little of the world to respect his strength of will and consideration for her. She only felt that she wanted to be naked with him, make love to him, please him and be pleased by him. Her body was beautiful, but he would do nothing to claim her. It was insulting.

Since they had no money they spent their time together wandering in the park where the funfair had been. One day they took a boat out onto the lake. The weather was hot, and Andrew wore only a pair of shorts. She lay back blissfully and watched the sun turning his skin to gold as he pulled on the oars, making nothing of the task.

She thought of his strength, how she'd sensed it through his kisses, the movements of his hands, both tender and urgent. She knew he desired her and was fighting it. But how long could he hold out against his own feelings?

They pulled into a little island where they could picnic in a secluded spot under the trees. Afterwards she lay in the crook of his arm, listening to his heartbeat.

'Do you love me?' she whispered.

He raised himself, pushing her down onto the blanket and looking down on her. 'How can you ask me that?' he said in a quiet, serious voice. 'Don't you know by now how much I love you? Don't you know that you fill the world for me?'

She reached up and touched his face with her fingertips, trying to smooth away the frown lines that hard work and study were already etching on his face. Slowly she worked her hands around to the back of his head and drew him down until his lips touched hers. Instantly she was afire, filled with need and longing. She pressed against him, kissing him back eagerly, fiercely, willing him to abandon himself to feeling and sensation.

To her delight she could sense it happening. He touched her like a man on the verge of losing control, caressing her face, her neck, her breasts through the thin cotton of her blouse. Where his fingers touched, his lips followed, burning her with their passion and satisfying her deeply. She gasped at the flickering of fire that went across her skin, making every inch of her newly aware.

She ran her hands over his bare back, feeling lean, hard muscles, sensing his strength. She wanted to kiss him everywhere.

He fumbled at the buttons of her blouse and she helped him, freeing her breasts to his adoring gaze. His lips against them sent shudders of delight through her, and then again when the tip of his tongue caressed one peaked nipple.

'Andrew,' she whispered, 'darling, yes—please…'

He was fumbling at the waistband of her shorts, opening the button, drawing down the zipper, slipping his hand lovingly inside to where she was eager for him. In another few moments, she thought blissfully, she would know what love was really all about, and then—

She opened her eyes to find him staring at her with shock. There was no desire on his face, only horror, like a man who'd awakened from a nightmare.

'What is it?' she whispered.

'Dear God, what am I doing?' he said hoarsely. 'I promised myself—'

He drew away and jumped to his feet. The next moment he'd taken to his heels and fled.

'Andrew!' she screamed.

But he kept on running as though the devil were after him. She buried her face in her hands, racked by sobs of frustration and rejection.

She was still weeping when he returned a few minutes later. The sight made him fling himself down beside her, taking her in his arms and murmuring words of love and tenderness.

'Ellie, darling, forgive me. I never meant to make you cry, but I couldn't go on,' he said desperately.

'But *why*?' she cried in a shaking voice.

'Because I want you too much, can't you understand that?'

'No! How can you want me too much if you say you love me? It's all a lie, isn't it? You don't really love me at all.'

He became angry. 'Is that how love looks to you? A man has to grab you selfishly, take what he wants and to hell with you, before you can believe he loves you?'

'But it wouldn't be to hell with me because I want it too.'

'What are you telling me? That I wouldn't be the first?' This was a new Andrew, his face dark with possessiveness. What was his was his.

'No, I'm not saying that,' she cried, losing her temper. 'How dare you?'

'I'm sorry, I didn't mean it. Ellie, please let's not quarrel.'

'If you loved me you'd want to make love to me,' she wept.

'And I do want to make love to you. Hell, if you knew how badly I want that! But not like this, out in the open where someone might come along. A quickie after lunch, as though you were some cheap floozie. I think better of you than that and you should think better of yourself.'

'Stop preaching at me,' she cried. 'Everything I want is wrong according to you. You want to make me old before my time.'

'I want to make you happy,' he said miserably. 'But I'm making a rotten job of it. Forgive me for hurting you.'

That was how it was between them. He was a hard, stubborn man, unshakeable in his resolve to do what he saw was right. She could break herself to bits against that rock. Yet the depth and intensity of his love were such that of the two it was he who was her slave, not the other way around. He wouldn't yield, but he would be the first to apologise.

They made it up, after a fashion. But this time the reconciliation was different, tinged with caution. They had learned how they could hurt each other.

Jack Smith was still hanging around, ignoring Ellie's engagement.

'You won't marry him,' he told her once. 'You want a bloke who knows how to enjoy life, like me.'

She was feeling especially sore with Andrew just then, for his stick-in-the-mud attitudes, and she smiled brilliantly at Jack, and didn't deny.

After that he was often around, always available to escort her when Andrew was away working. One day Andrew turned up unexpectedly and found them having a drink together.

'Don't be stuffy,' she cried, when he complained later.

'Either you're my girl or you're not!'

'Maybe I'm not if you're going to put me on a ball and chain.'

'He's a bad lot, Ellie. Even you should be able to see that.'

'What do you mean, even me?'

'You know what I mean.'

'No, tell me.'

'Someone without two thoughts to rub together,' he snapped in one of his rare flares of temper.

'Then I'm surprised you want to marry me.'

His face had softened. 'Because I love you more than I can say. Sometimes I wish I didn't, but I can't help it.'

She too melted. 'You don't need to be jealous of Jack, honest.'

'Jealous of that beefy idiot!' he exploded. 'Don't make me laugh.'

Perhaps they should have quarrelled properly and left it there. But a week later he arrived with plans.

'I can get two weeks off in August, darling. It can be our honeymoon.'

'But that's next month,' she gasped. Suddenly the socks and nappies had come awfully close, and she could almost see the prison bars.

Was that why she did it? How consciously did she decide to go out in the boat with Jack, to land on the same little island that she'd been with Andrew? Did she secretly know that Jack's idea of a joke would be to push the boat out into the water, so that they were stranded?

Andrew arrived the day before their wedding to find her missing. How accusing his eyes were when she and Jack were finally rescued, after being on the island all night! She faced him in her mother's house, defiant.

'It was an accident, that's all.'

'Was it an accident that you went out there? What did you mean by going with him just before our wedding, anyway?'

'I wanted to enjoy myself. No crime in that.'

'That depends how you wanted to enjoy yourself.'

'What do you mean by that?'

'You know what I mean. We went there once ourselves, and I remember your idea of enjoying yourself. But I wouldn't oblige, would I? I was thinking of you, but I don't think that ever got through to you. Was he any more co-operative?'

How cold and dead his face was, as she'd never seen it before. He'd adored her, worshipped her. Now he was close to hating her.

She could have handled it differently, told him that she'd boxed Jack's ears and forced him to keep his distance, which was the truth. And they would have made it up, and married next day.

Instead she'd defied him. 'Believe what you like. If you don't trust me, that's your problem.'

'Ellie, *darling*—' he was still hers if she wanted '—I want to trust you, but you were there all night with him. Just tell me nothing happened.'

'What do *you* think happened?'

'Tell me!'

'Leave me alone,' she screamed. 'Stop pressurising me. Stop trying to control my life, and telling me what to do. You've got it all planned, we marry this week, we have a baby next year, and I sit at home alone with a screaming kid while you work all hours trying to become the great doctor.'

'But we agreed—'

'You agreed. You decided, you told me and I was supposed to fall in line. I don't like being bullied—'

'I bullied you?' Suddenly he was a sick man, his face the colour of death. 'Is that all my love meant to you? Bullying?'

'You don't let me breathe. You've got my life planned out for me, but I want something more.'

'Oh, yes, shampoos and make-up,' he snapped.

'You can sneer, but it's my choice. I don't want to live in a backwater. I want to go to London and work in a big store, and be someone.'

'And you think you're going to be someone with a pig like Jack Smith?'

'He may be a pig to you but he believes in me—'

'He's probably hoping that you'll support him.'

'And he knows how to give a girl a good time.'

'Tell me about that good time,' he said dangerously.

'What do you want to know?' said a voice from the doorway. It was Jack, who'd forced his way past her mother and heard the last words.

'Nothing from you,' Andrew snapped. 'Get out of here.'

'No way. I'm part of this. I didn't have to force Ellie to come with me. She needed a rest from you preaching at her. I just provided the light entertainment, didn't I, darling? Very appreciative she was, too.'

The next moment he was on the floor, knocked down by

a punch like a hammer. Ellie screamed, not for Jack but for Andrew, who yearned to be a surgeon but had risked his valuable right hand.

'Don't,' she begged him.

'Protecting him, Ellie?'

'No, your hand.'

'Do you think I care about that now?'

Jack had climbed to his feet, an ugly look in his eyes. She thought he was going to punch Andrew back, but he did something much worse.

'C'mon, sweetie, let's go. You won your bet, you don't have to take it to the line.'

'Bet? What bet?' Andrew asked.

'Nothing,' she said hurriedly. A pit was opening at her feet.

'Tell me about this bet,' Andrew said quietly.

'Ellie bet a whole gang of us that she could make you fall in love with her. Boy, was that a laugh! It's been an even bigger laugh watching her at work.'

Andrew looked at her. 'You—did that?'

'No—' she said desperately.

'Are you saying it's not true?'

'No—that is—not like that—'

'You mean the answer's yes?'

'It wasn't like that. Just a silly joke—'

'Don't tell me any more,' he said in a quiet voice that was worse to her than shouting. 'I really only have myself to blame for loving you too much. I should never have lost my sense of proportion. Always a mistake, that.'

'Andrew, please listen to me,' she screamed. 'Let me explain—'

'Explain what? You never really wanted to marry me, did you, Ellie? Now I understand. After you'd made a fool of me there was nowhere else to take it. The trouble is I never had much sense of humour, although with you—' He checked, and a spasm of pain went over his face. 'Well, a lot of things were different with you.'

She'd flinched to see hate in his eyes, but now there was something far more terrible than hate. Disillusion.

'I apologise for wasting so much of your time,' he said politely, 'and also for boring you. I won't do so any longer. I wish you every happiness for the future. Good day to you.'

He walked out with a face of stone.

The following month she ran away to London with Jack Smith. They had a hurried marriage in a shabby register office and after that, as Andrew had foretold, she found herself supporting him. From then on nothing went right for her.

Elinor had awaited the call for so long that when it came one evening she didn't, at first, take it in.

'What—what did you say?'

'This is the Burdell Hospital. We have a heart which would seem to be suitable for your daughter.'

'You've got—?'

'I must caution you not to get your hopes up too high. We need to do some final tests before a decision can be made, but an ambulance is heading for you, so will you—?'

Elinor barely heard the rest. Tears of relief poured down her face. She was shaking so hard that she could hardly move, but she forced herself to be calm as she went to find Hetta, even managing a brilliant smile as she called out, 'All right, darling, we're on our way.'

'Really, Mummy? 'Cos last time—'

'I know,' Elinor said quickly. This had happened twice before and their hopes had soared, but in the end the operation hadn't been possible. 'Let's just cross our fingers.'

In no time at all the ambulance was at the door. The news had spread through the boarding house and everyone who was at home came to wave them off. Daisy flapped about like a mother hen, pouring out concern and criticism alike.

'Call me as soon as you know anything, love. Night or day. Jerry, I hope you went to the Job Centre, today. How are you, my pet? Have you got everything? Where's Samson?'

'Here,' Hetta said, producing a disreputable object that had started life as a bear.

'That's fine, then. Elinor, you tell me if there's anything I can do for you. Anything at all.'

During the short journey to the hospital she and Hetta held hands tightly. There were no words for their shared thoughts, but they didn't need words. And then they were there, and nurses were coming to meet them, smiling, looking hopeful.

Cling to that hope, she thought. *Don't think about the other chance.*

There were questions to answer. A nurse took Hetta's temperature, which was normal. Her current state of health was good.

Except that she's dying.

'I know Sir Elmer hasn't been well,' Elinor said. 'Is he back yet?'

'No, it'll be Mr Blake doing this. He's on his way in now.'

'Can I be with Hetta?'

'Just another few minutes while we finish the tests, then I'll take you in. If you could just wait here—'

That was the worst. Waiting. Walking up and down in the featureless waiting room, trying to look into the future and seeing only a blank. Up and down. Back and forth. Look out of the window into the darkness. Watch her own face shadowed in the window, then the door opening, and another presence in the room. A handsome man in a dinner jacket and black bow-tie, who'd obviously been called away from a pleasant evening.

'Have you got the answer yet?' she demanded harshly, swinging around to face him. 'Can you do it?'

'I'll be getting the results in a minute,' Andrew said. 'But please try not to worry.'

'Try not to worry,' she echoed in anguish. 'Do you know how many doctors have said that to me, and how little it means?'

'I can imagine.'

'This has happened before. Twice. The first time they called us and we rushed to the hospital, but when we got there they'd decided to give it to someone else.'

'That means your daughter was strong enough to stand the wait and the other child wasn't,' Andrew said quietly.

'I know. I rationalised it all the way home. So did Hetta. She's so grown up, and she shouldn't have to be. She kept saying, "Never mind, Mummy. There's next time." And three months later it happened again. This time there was no other candidate but there was a delay in getting the heart there, and by the time it arrived it was unusable. Has the heart arrived yet?'

'No.'

Her voice rose. 'Then it could happen again?'

'Not a chance. It's only coming a few miles.'

'But when it gets here you've got to test it and there might be something wrong—'

'Very unlikely. The other hospital does its own tests and we only hear about the heart when they're satisfied. Mrs. Landers, I know this is very hard, but I'm sure it was explained to you that these false dawns are, sadly, very common. I have patients who were called in five times before all the conditions were right for them. But it did happen in the end. They had successful transplants and now they're healthy. Hetta's chances are still good.'

'Are they? She's a child, they're much harder to match.' Elinor gave a wan smile. 'You see how much I've had time to learn.'

'I know,' he said, speaking gently. 'I know. But please try not to think the worst. I promise you, things are looking hopeful.'

She searched his face to see if he were merely comforting her, but there was only a kindly professional mask. She swung away to the window, trying to sort out her impressions. He still gave no sign of remembering her, and she was glad of it. Only Hetta mattered. She took a deep breath and turned back. She had her ghosts under control now, and they wouldn't be allowed to threaten the future.

A nurse looked in and handed Andrew some papers. They must be the test results, Elinor thought, her heart almost stopping with fear. He studied them, gave a grunt, then looked up.

'Splendid!' he said. 'Now we can get on.'

'You mean—'

'The heart's in excellent condition, and all Hetta's test results are good. We're cleared for take-off.'

She gave a gasp, pressing her hands over her mouth to fight back the sob of relief, and turned away. Her chest was heaving silently and she kept her back to him until she had herself under control. When she looked around he was gone.

CHAPTER FIVE

THE nurse gave Elinor a kindly smile. 'I know,' she said. 'Good news can be just as shattering as bad. Now I'll take you to her.'

Hetta was waiting on a trolley. She smiled and held out her arms to Elinor, and they hugged each other.

'It's really it, this time,' she said.

'Yes, this time.'

'Geronimo!'

'Geronimo!'

Elinor tried to sound strong but the word must have come out wonkier than she meant, because Hetta gave a small frown of concern.

'It's all right, Mummy.' Her voice became severe. 'Stop worrying.'

'Who's worrying?'

'You are. You always fret about things, and it's going to be all right.'

'Of course it is,' Elinor said firmly.

'Of course it is,' said a voice over her head.

Andrew was standing there, still in his dinner jacket, looking as cheerful and unconcerned as a man about to embark on a social evening. 'I'm Andrew,' he told Hetta, holding out his hand to her. 'We met once before.'

'Oh, yes. You looked different then.' She shook his hand, eyeing his expensive dinner jacket. 'You weren't prettied up like now.'

One of the nurses grunted with laughter, but it died under his gaze.

'Did I take you away from something nice?' Hetta asked, like a polite little old lady.

'No, something very boring that I was glad to get out of. It wasn't as important as you.'

'Will my op take very long?'

'It'll be as fast as I can make it, but you won't know anything. It's a doddle, you know. I do them all the time. Now, are you all ready?'

'Yes, thank you.'

Hetta smiled, and the look she gave him was full of trust and confidence.

It's the sedation, Elinor thought. *It's relaxing her already.*

But she knew it was more than that. A transformation had come over Andrew. His stiffness had fallen away, leaving behind a friendly, informal man, with nothing to do but make a little girl feel happy.

'Who's this?' he asked, indicating the furry bear. 'A friend of yours?'

'He's Samson. We've always been together.'

'Then he's a very important bear, and he should stay with you,' Andrew said solemnly, tucking the sheet about the two of them as he spoke. 'Keep him safe.'

Hetta giggled, and Elinor sent silent thanks to Andrew for what he was doing. However all this had come about, Hetta was in the right hands.

The nurses were beginning to wheel the trolley away. Elinor followed, her hand clasped in her child's. There was so much she wanted to say, but Hetta's eyelids were already drooping. All too soon they reached the doors through which

Hetta must go and she could not, to a place from which she might never return.

'Love you, darling.'

'Love you, Mummy. Night, night.'

The doors opened, the corridor swallowed her up. She was gone. Suddenly Elinor was full of fear. She had longed for this moment, and now it was here she faced the reality she'd avoided before. She might never see Hetta alive again. This was make or break.

'Oh, God!' she whispered. 'Hetta—*Hetta*—'

'You've done everything for her that you can,' Andrew said. He'd been walking behind them. 'Now you have to trust someone else.'

'I do, I do trust you,' she said swiftly. 'But she's my baby, it's been just the two of us all her life.'

'What about her father?'

'I divorced Tom Landers soon after she was born and I haven't seen him since. Nor do I want to. It's just Hetta and me. If she dies, there's nothing left for me—nothing, nothing! No hope, or happiness, or anything to believe in. Without her, there's no reason to go on.'

As if in a dream he said, 'And yet it is possible to survive terrible grief. Even if all happiness has died, you can find a way to go on.'

There was a strange note in his voice that told her the words were wrenched from the depths of his own heart. Her head jerked up. Looking straight into his eyes, she saw there everything he'd tried to deny. He'd known her from the first moment. Of course he had.

He strove to recover, engulfing her hands in his strong ones. 'Trust me,' he said firmly. 'I will always do everything I can for her—and for you.'

Abruptly he dropped her hands and stepped back. 'I'll go and get scrubbed up. My assistant does the first part, and they'll need me in about half an hour.' He met her eyes again. 'I'll bring her back to you. I promise.'

He walked away without another word. Elinor watched him go, pressing her hands to her mouth, biting back the words she wanted to cry out.

Don't remember that you offered me the best of yourself, and I threw it back at you. Don't remember that I murdered all happiness for you. I didn't know that until this moment.

She pulled herself together. That was years ago. They were different people, and Andrew hadn't reacted to her because their past was unimportant to him. And that was right, because only Hetta mattered now.

Hours passed. Elinor was oblivious to them although she later learned the operation had taken two and a half hours. But minutes were different. She felt every second of every endless minute.

Outside the windows the darkness began to turn to grey as the night passed. She didn't see it, nor the opening of the door. She'd gone too far into another world where there was only suffering and hope, and was aware of nothing until a cup of tea appeared on the low table before her, and Andrew sat down in a nearby chair. He was still in his operating clothes.

'All done,' he said briefly. 'It went like a dream. She should make a complete recovery.'

'Really? Honestly?'

'I wouldn't say so if it wasn't true.'

Elinor buried her face in her hands and sat shaking in silence. He sipped his tea, pretending not to notice.

'Can I go to her?' she asked, raising her head at last.

'In a minute. They're taking her into Intensive Care, and you can go there and be with her when she comes round.'

'Did you really let her keep that smelly old toy all the time?'

He shook his head. 'It wouldn't be practical. But I never distress a child by saying so. I tell them what they want to hear, take the toy away when they've gone under, then make sure it's with them when they wake up. It's a deception, but it makes them happy and, I believe, helps them pull through.'

'You must have a gift for children.'

He shrugged. 'Not really. It's just a trick Elmer taught me. Drink your tea, and then I'll take you to her. Have you got strong nerves?' He shot out the question abruptly.

'What do you mean?'

'You'll be shocked by the sight. She's attached to a dozen machines and they look terrifying, but they're there to help her. When she wakes up don't let her see you're upset. Bursting into tears is the worst possible thing for her.'

'I don't burst into tears,' Elinor said quietly. 'I did when she first became ill. Not any more.'

'Of course. I shouldn't have said that to you,' he said wearily. 'I'm sorry.'

She wanted to say that he had nothing to be sorry for, but he'd already risen and was walking away, calling, 'Come along,' over his shoulder.

A young nurse admitted them to the intensive care unit and led them to a bed in the far corner. Despite her brave words Elinor experienced a reaction when she saw Hetta, lying still, attached to what seemed like a dozen machines. For a moment she couldn't move while she fought back the tears.

'Steady,' Andrew said quietly beside her. 'Take a deep breath.'

'I'm all right,' she said at last. 'It's just—her colour—' Hetta was a cross between yellow and grey.

'Everyone is that colour at this stage,' Andrew said. 'I know it looks bad, but it's not worrying. Come over and let me explain the machines, then they won't seem so bad. These monitor her heartbeat, her blood pressure, the amount of painkiller she's being given. This one is feeding her through a drip, this one is giving her a blood transfusion.'

'That pipe fixed in her mouth—?'

'It goes to this machine here that's doing her breathing for her. Soon she'll be ready to come off it and take control of her own breathing.'

He went on talking, and Elinor lost track of the individual words. What continued to reach her was the quiet kindliness of his voice, calming her fears, offering her the equivalent of a steadying hand.

But suddenly his voice grew sharper as he demanded, 'Where's Samson?'

'Who?' The young nurse was staring as if he'd gone crazy.

'Samson. He's a toy bear. He must be here when she wakes up. Call the operating theatre. Find out what they did with him.' He was rapping out commands now.

The nurse made the call and elicited the information that Samson had been put aside and gone missing.

'Tell them to find him or heads will roll,' Andrew snapped.

'But, sir—'

'I promised that child, and if the promise is broken it could impede her recovery. I don't intend that to happen. Understood?'

The nurse threw him an alarmed look and turned back to the phone.

'Don't worry,' Andrew told Elinor. 'This will get sorted.'

Samson arrived a few minutes later, much the worse for wear, having fallen on the floor and been kicked into a corner by the busy operating staff. Andrew eyed him, recognising the impossibility of putting this filthy object into Hetta's arms.

'Nurse, have you got some disinfectant soap?' he asked. 'Strong.'

'Yes, sir.'

'Get it, please.'

The nurse hurried back with the soap, but was immediately summoned to another bed. Her face said the washing of toys wasn't part of her job on such a high-tension ward.

'I'll do it,' Elinor said.

'There's a wash basin attached to the wall over there,' Andrew said. 'You can keep Hetta in your sights all the time.'

She hurried across and got to work on Samson, who rapidly became his original bright yellow colour. Even his daft smile seemed to have brightened. As she worked Elinor sometimes glanced over to Hetta, where Andrew was still checking the machines. He seemed satisfied, she noted with relief. Then he looked up, saw her watching, gave a brief nod and strode off.

Elinor crept back to Hetta's side, clutching the damp toy. One of the nurses produced a chair for her. Then there was a light touch on her shoulder. It was another nurse, holding something out to her.

'It belongs to Mr Blake's secretary,' she said. 'She keeps it in the office. He said to lend it to you.'

It was a hair-dryer. He'd even thought of that.

Elinor turned the dryer onto Samson until he was bone-dry, then slipped him gently under Hetta's hand. At once the little fingers flexed and tightened around him, although she gave no other sign of life.

Time ticked past. Hetta lay motionless, tiny, seemingly fixed like this for ever.

Andrew arrived again and spoke to the nurse. 'Let's see if she can breathe by herself. Would you mind standing back, please?' This to Elinor.

She got out of their way and watched tensely as the great tube was untied and drawn out of Hetta's mouth. There was a moment when the world seemed to stand still, then her chest heaved and she gave a big sigh.

'Excellent,' Andrew said. 'Couldn't be better. Mrs Landers, you should go and have some breakfast.'

'How can I leave her?'

'She's passed the first milestone successfully, and you'll do better by her if you keep your own strength up. There's an all-night canteen on the top floor. Go and eat. I don't want you fainting under my feet.'

Having barked at her, he strode out, leaving her with only an impression of how exhausted he'd looked after being up all night, and the day was only just starting.

She didn't know if he managed to grab a nap somewhere, but he looked in at about four-hour intervals after that, and was there when Hetta finally opened her eyes.

"Lo, Mummy.'

'Hallo, darling.' But Hetta's eyes had already closed again. 'Darling,' she repeated urgently.

'Leave her,' Andrew said. 'That's as good as you can hope for now.'

He left. After another hour Hetta stirred again. This time she looked at her mother, smiled and fell back to sleep. The day wore on. It was late afternoon before Hetta awoke properly.

"Lo, Mummy,' she said again, but this time she sounded brighter.

Elinor slipped to the floor so that her face should be closer to Hetta's.

'Darling, welcome back.'

'Have I been away?'

'Yes, but you're back now, thank God.'

Hetta looked around her anxiously. 'Where's Samson?'

'He's here,' Elinor said, lifting him to within her view. 'You were cuddling him.'

'But that's not Samson,' Hetta protested.

'It is, darling.'

'It isn't, it isn't.' Hetta was becoming distressed. A nurse anxiously tried to soothe her, but tears began to roll down Hetta's face. Elinor's attempts to reassure her only made the child cry bitterly. This was the worst possible thing for her wounded chest, and Elinor looked around wildly, desperate for help.

'Hey, what's all this?' Andrew said, appearing out of the blue, it seemed to Elinor.

'I want Samson,' Hetta wept. 'You promised.'

'And I always keep my promises,' Andrew said, lounging by her bed, apparently at ease, although his skin was the colour of parchment and there were black shadows under his eyes. 'Samson's been with you all the time—well, almost all. You see, while we were making you as good as new, we thought we'd do the same for him. So we tidied him up and gave him a bath, which he badly needed.'

Hetta's eyes were on him, and she'd stopped crying. 'He doesn't like being bathed,' she said.

'So I gather. His language was frightful. It made the nurses blush.'

Hetta giggled.

'But it's still Samson,' Andrew said. 'You can see by that little tear in his ear.'

'That was Daisy's cat,' Hetta whispered.

'Uh-huh! I gather it was quite a fight. So you see, it's Samson all right, so why don't you just tuck him up against you—like that—and—?'

Hetta was already asleep.

'That's wonderful,' Elinor said. 'How did you ever—?'

'One moment, please, Mrs Landers. Nurse—'

He became deep in discussion with the nurse for several minutes, and when he'd finished the moment had passed. Elinor had turned back to Hetta, watching her with loving, obsessive eyes, and Andrew slipped away quietly without disturbing her.

* * *

For the first week Elinor barely left Hetta. When she needed sleep there was a side room with basic beds, where she would snatch a nap before hurrying back.

At first she watched her with incredulous delight, hardly able to believe that this delicate little creature had survived such a massive onslaught.

Yet Hetta's frailty was increasingly an illusion. For the first time in two years she had a strong heart, working normally. For days she was woozy and sometimes confused from the massive anaesthetic, but the signs of improvement were coming fast, and already her colour was better.

'She's our star patient,' said the nurse in Intensive Care. 'She took over her own breathing at the first possible moment, and since then she's done everything right on time.'

And Elinor was feeling cheerful enough to smile and say, 'I'll swear it's the first time in her life she's done what anyone wanted without argument.'

Hetta giggled. 'I'm a devil, aren't I, Mummy?'

'I thought you were asleep, you cheeky little madam.'

As she came off the machines she was moved into a larger ward, where there were other children, and promptly brightened life with a feud with a little boy in the next bed. Elinor began returning to the boarding house to sleep. Gradually she found she could leave Hetta without worrying if she would still be alive on her return.

Best of all, Hetta's wicked sense of humour had returned, and she liked nothing so much as to tease her mother. The long wound in her chest, so terrifying to Elinor, filled the child with ghoulish pride.

'Isn't it great?' she demanded when the dressing had been removed and Andrew was examining the dark red line.

'If you like that kind of thing,' Elinor said faintly.

'But we do, don't we?' Andrew said to Hetta.

'Yes, we do,' Hetta said firmly. 'Honestly, Mummy, it was a great big electric saw—'

'What?'

'That's how we get through the breastbone to find the heart,' Andrew explained. 'You can't do this operation by playing peek-a-boo through the ribs.'

Hetta giggled and she and Andrew exchanged the glances of conspirators. It wasn't lost on Elinor that the nurse, standing deferentially behind him, was staring at him with astonishment.

As he walked out she followed him quickly. 'What do you mean by talking like that with a child?' she demanded.

'She loves it. It's adults who are squeamish, not children.' The friendly ease he'd shown the child was gone, and he was tense again. 'Good day, Mrs Landers.'

Elinor had to admit that he was right. Hetta was having the time of her life. In no time she'd become the leader of the children's ward, in the heart of any anarchy that was going. To Elinor it was a joy to see her being occasionally naughty. It was so long since she'd had the energy.

Between her and Andrew there had developed a perfect understanding, and she called him Andrew, with his encouragement. To the little girl he wasn't the figure of awe he presented to his staff. He was the friend who'd understood about Samson, and would understand anything she said to him. So to him she confided her nightmares. He listened, nodding in perfect comprehension. Elinor came upon them one day in time to hear him say, 'Do the rocks ever actually fall on you, or does it just look as if they might?'

'I keep thinking they're going to, but I wake up first.'

'Well, it's only the anaesthetic—you know that, don't you?'

'After all this time?'

'Do you know how much we had to give you to knock you out for a process as big as this?'

'How much?' she demanded, fascinated.

He made a wide gesture with his hands. '*This* much.'

'Wow!'

'So you don't get rid of it all at once. It works its way out gradually, and it gives you funny thoughts and dreams. But that's all it is. So the next time you see those rocks, just tell them you're not scared of them, because they're not real.'

Hetta nodded, reassured.

'Why didn't she tell me she's having nightmares?' Elinor demanded of Andrew outside the ward.

'Because she knows you've been through a lot and she's protecting you from any more.'

'She told you that?'

'She didn't have to. Don't you realise that she's looking after you as much as you're looking after her? She's very like you in many ways.'

Then something seemed to occur to him, and he bid her goodnight. He often did that when their paths crossed, and it saddened her.

After the day of the operation, when they'd made contact, she'd somehow believed that soon they would talk about the past, and how they had met again. Perhaps she would have a chance to tell him that she was sorry, and ask his forgiveness. But as the days until Hetta was discharged from hospital narrowed down to four, then three, she realised that it wasn't going to happen.

And after all, she mused, why should it? Their paths had crossed by accident, and doubtless he would be glad to see the back of her. She probably embarrassed him.

But she would always be grateful to him. Theirs had been a sad, stormy relationship that had ended in anger, but now they'd been given a postscript that softened the bitterness.

She doubted that his bitterness had lasted very long. She knew he'd made a success of his life, just as he'd always vowed. She pictured him married to a brilliant society woman, someone whose sophistication could match his own. How glad he must be to have escaped herself.

As for her, why should she be bitter? It was she who had injured him, and if she'd paid for it with years of disappointment and disaster, perhaps that was only justice.

Elinor's money was running dangerously low, and she started working again, accepting freelance beauty assignments that didn't take her too far away. She had just completed a lucrative job and was feeling cheerful as she headed for the hospital in the early evening. This was Hetta's last night, and tomorrow she would be coming home to the boarding house.

She found Hetta in high spirits, competing with the boy opposite to see who could put their tongue out furthest.

'I should think they'll be glad to see the back of you tomorrow,' she said comically, sitting on Hetta's bed.

Hetta nodded, accepting this as a compliment, and they laughed together.

'Are you all ready to go?'

Hetta nodded vigorously. 'Home!' she carolled. 'I'm going home.'

A sound made Elinor glance up quickly, smiling when she saw Daisy. But the smile faded at the look on her friend's face. Daisy seemed distracted with worry, and she beckoned Elinor urgently into the corridor.

'I'm sorry to land this on you, on top of everything else, luv.'

'Daisy, whatever's happened?'

'That Mr Jenson in number six,' Daisy said with loathing. 'Stayed in bed this morning, with a cold, he said. But he took his smokes with him and fell asleep. We were all lucky to get out alive.'

'You mean—?'

'A terrible fire we had, soon after you left this morning. Top floor burned out. Everything black with smoke. And now the fire service say the building's unsafe. They let us back for a few minutes to get our things, but that's all. I brought your stuff.'

For the first time Elinor noticed her suitcases on the floor, and she began to feel sick as the full implications of this reached her. Daisy read her expression without trouble.

'The insurance will cover it,' she said, 'but in the meantime nobody can live there. The two students have gone to a hostel, Mr Jenson has dumped himself on his sister and she's welcome to him. I've found a little hotel nearby, where I can keep an eye on the rebuilding. But I don't know what you'll do.'

'It's all right,' Elinor said, trying to sound calm. 'We'll find somewhere. You've been wonderful to us, Daisy. Now you've got to think of yourself.'

She maintained a cheerful front until she was alone, but then the shock of her situation came over her. In a few hours Hetta would be discharged, and she had nowhere to take her. Daisy's place had been shabby, but it had also been clean and comfortable. There she could have tended Hetta in peace, with Daisy's kindly help. Now she was alone in a cold desert.

She pulled herself together. Whatever happened Hetta must never suspect anything was wrong. She was smiling as she returned to her child, and sat with her, making their own silly little jokes until Hetta fell asleep.

As darkness fell the night shift began to appear. The nurse in charge swept her eyes over the patients, and frowned at the sight of Elinor, sitting in a chair, her suitcases hidden unconvincingly under the bed. Elinor's nervousness grew. Nurse Stewart was a well-meaning woman, and not deliberately unkind. But her mind was rigid. To her there was only one 'right' way of doing things, and that was the way prescribed by the rules. She was also a busybody, happiest when imposing her views on others.

'Mrs Landers,' she said, 'a moment, if you please.'

She swept on to her desk, and Elinor followed her reluctantly.

'Visiting time is over, you know,' Nurse Stewart said. 'I really must ask you to leave.'

'But I can't,' Elinor said desperately. 'I've nowhere to go. The place I lived burned down today. I've only just heard.'

'Is that why you have your suitcases with you?'

'Yes. Someone rescued my things.'

'I see. Well, that's very unfortunate, of course,' the nurse said in the tone she would have used to describe a shortfall of bandages, 'but this is not a hotel. There are no provisions in the rules for overnight accommodation.'

'But I was allowed to stay just after the operation.'

'Ah, yes, when your little girl was in danger, and in the intensive care unit, but she's on a general ward now, and the danger is long over. In fact, I believe she's due to be discharged tomorrow.'

'But where?' Elinor said desperately. 'I've nowhere to take her now.'

'You'd better start looking for somewhere else first thing.'

Somewhere else meant a place that would demand a deposit, and the money she'd made recently wouldn't run to that. Elinor's despair must have shown in her eyes for the nurse, with a plain attempt to be helpful, said, 'I'm sure the social services will help you. There are homes for children with special needs. I'll find you the number.'

'No,' Elinor choked. 'I don't want anyone taking her over. I want her with me.'

'But I'm sure you realise that Hetta's best interests must come first.'

'Her best interests mean a proper home with her mother.'

'But you don't have one, do you?' Nurse Stewart said, smiling blandly.

To Elinor that smile was horrible. It was the face of the pitiless world that had done its best to crush her, and would keep trying until her strength was exhausted. She felt some frightening, uncontrollable feeling rising in her. If it reached the surface it would emerge as screams, she knew it.

Turning, she ran out of the ward, along the corridor and down the stairs until she reached the ground, then out into the hospital garden. Terror and panic were mounting in her as she ran and ran, until at last she collided with a tree and stayed just as she was, clutching the trunk and giving way to her grief.

She'd fought and fought, and given it everything she had. But it wasn't enough, and suddenly she had no more strength to fight.

CHAPTER SIX

ELINOR had held onto her control through everything, refusing to let herself weep no matter how bad things had become. But now it all caught up with her like a wave that had been growing from a great distance until it crashed over her without mercy, leaving her shaking and helpless in the grip of sobs.

'*No!*' she screamed. 'Not any more, please. There has to be an end somewhere. *No more—no—please—*'

'Is something wrong?' asked a man's voice behind her.

'Go away,' she cried passionately. 'Yes, something's wrong. Everything's wrong and there's nobody to help. *Go away!*'

She heard a step, as though someone had moved closer, and Andrew said, 'There *is* someone to help.'

She swung around, tears pouring down her face. She was beyond speech, beyond dismay that he'd found her like this, beyond hope or fear. She could do nothing but lean against the tree in helpless, shuddering despair.

'I don't know what to do,' she said huskily. 'There's always one more thing and I'm falling apart. I mustn't—for Hetta's sake—but I am, I am, and there's nowhere to go—oh, God!—'

She wept freely, not even trying to cover her face. Her

strength had collapsed all in a moment and there was nothing left.

Andrew took hold of her shoulders gently. 'Has something happened to Hetta?' he asked. 'Do you want me to go to her?'

'No, she's fine,' Elinor choked.

'If she's fine, everything's fine. Ellie, do you hear that? If Hetta is safe and well, nothing else matters. Cling to it. Any other problem can be solved.'

But she could barely hear him. Anguish shook her, wrung her out, drained her. He was so close to her that she could feel his breath, and put up her hands as if to fend him off, shaking her head from side to side.

'No,' she gasped, 'no, it's no use—don't you understand? Nothing's any use because as fast as you cope with one thing—there's always something else—it's like—there's someone up there who's going to throw one thing after another into my path until I give in—and—and—'

'OK, OK,' he said. 'You're having hysterics, and it's no wonder after what you've been through, but it's going to be fine—'

'What do you know?' she demanded, not screaming but speaking in a low, hoarse whisper. 'There's nothing you or anyone can do about this. They're going to take her away from me and I can't stop them.'

All her control had gone and grief poured out of her in ugly hee-hawing sobs. Andrew wasted no more time in talking but put his arms about her and pulled her hard against his chest.

'All right,' he murmured. 'Let it come. You've fought it long enough, don't try any more.'

'I can't cope with anything else,' she sobbed.

'There's no need to. You're not alone.'

'Yes, I am, I've always been alone. Oh, you don't have to tell me it's my own fault—'

'I wasn't going to—'

'I know it, and I can survive if it's just me, but it's not fair on Hetta, she's never had any kind of life—'

'But she's going to have a great life now,' he said, trying to be heard through her torrent of words.

'She should have had a better mother, someone who knew what to do and didn't go blundering through life making mistakes and getting it all wrong, and, oh, God! *Oh, God!*'

He gave up trying to get through to her and held her tightly while the storm raged. When he finally felt her calm down a little he put his hands either side of her face.

'Listen to me,' he said severely. 'Whatever it is, something can be done, *yes, it can,*' he added quickly as she tried to speak. 'This is just nerves because you've been through so much and it's all caught up with you in one go. But it's not like you to give in.'

'You don't know what's like me,' she whispered.

'I know you always had a lot of courage.'

'Not really. Way back then—I was all talk. I didn't know what life was about.'

'And you think you know now?'

'It's about betrayal,' she said quietly, 'and fighting, and things always turning out wrong, and knowing it was your own fault because you're stupid.'

'You're not stupid. Don't talk about yourself like that. Now tell me what brought this on. Why should Hetta be taken away from you?'

'Because I've nowhere for us to live. The guest house where we've been staying burned down today and she's due out of here tomorrow.'

'Then we'll find somewhere else for you to go.'

'How can I? I've no money and Nurse Stewart wants to bring in social services, and they'll take her away from me—'

'Of course they won't,' he said firmly. 'They're not ogres. They know Hetta needs her mother. As for Stewart, what on earth made you confide in that stupid woman?'

'I couldn't help it. She found me—I'm not supposed to be here at night—'

'But you've nowhere else. Right. Leave her to me.'

He relaxed his grip, giving her space to draw back and see his face. In the dark it was hard to make out details, but she could see that it was hard and set, and radiated confidence. Even so, 'You won't make Nurse Stewart back down,' she said.

He raised his eyebrows. 'I'm commonly held to have a little authority around here. Even over her. Come on.'

He took her elbow and led her back through the trees. As they approached the lights of the building he released her and said firmly, 'Keep quiet and leave everything to me.'

'All right.' Her fear had gone. The total confidence and authority of this man was beyond question. He could do anything.

His manner as he entered the ward was impeccably formal, and Nurse Stewart hurried forward, eyeing Elinor suspiciously.

'A very serious problem has developed,' she hurried to say. 'Hetta Landers is suddenly homeless, and I really feel it's my duty to—'

'To inform me,' Andrew interrupted her smoothly. 'You were quite right, but Mrs Landers has already consulted me, and I have the problem in hand.'

'I'm sure you agree that it's a matter for the proper authorities. A vulnerable child must not be—'

'Must not be parted from her mother,' Andrew interrupted again, and this time in a manner that made it plain he was taking charge of the conversation. 'I have a good friend who's highly placed in the social services. I've already contacted him, and there's no need for you to take any action.'

Nurse Stewart's mouth tightened, and Elinor guessed that to be told to do nothing was ashes to her.

'Of course, if you have the matter in hand...' she said reluctantly. 'May I know the name of this friend?'

There was a silence, during which Andrew's face assumed the frozen, stony look that his staff dreaded. Elinor thought she would die if he ever turned that look on her. And then she remembered the night that he had.

'Are you implying that you do not believe me, Nurse?' Andrew asked very, very quietly.

Even Nurse Stewart blenched at his tone, but she rallied. 'Certainly not, but if he should be in touch—'

'It will be with me, not you. Now, Mrs Landers, if you'll collect your things, I'm sure your friends will be here for you soon.'

Dazed, Elinor drew her cases quietly from under the bed, managing not to disturb Hetta. Andrew took one from her and strode out of the ward, with her following.

Not a word was uttered while they went along the corridor and into a lift. But when the doors were safely shut and they were on their way down Elinor ventured to say, 'Suppose she checks up to find out if you told the truth?'

He turned astonished eyes on her. 'Check up? On me?'

There it was again, that total dominating authority that expected no challenge. It wasn't even arrogant. It didn't need to be.

'But all those things you said—what will she do when nothing happens?'

He regarded her with faint amusement. 'But something *will* happen. I'm going to make it happen.' His mouth assumed a sardonic twist. 'Don't you think I can?'

'Oh, yes,' she said, meaning it. 'I think you could do just about anything.'

Two floors down they left the lift and headed along another corridor, and a door.

'This is my office. You can stay here tonight. There's a small bathroom through there, so you won't need to go out for any reason. Stretch out on the sofa, keep the door locked and don't answer to anyone except me. I'll be here at five-thirty in the morning. That way, I'll be ahead of the cleaner, who comes at six. Here's a small travelling alarm. Set it for five o'clock. Have I forgotten anything?'

'I can't imagine you forgetting anything. Thank you so much. I just don't know how to—'

'No need,' he said quickly. 'Goodnight.'

He vanished fast, leaving her regarding the closed door. Slowly she locked it, feeling dizzy after the events of that evening. But as she settled herself on the sofa and turned out the light she felt a strange calm descend on her. On the surface things were no better. She still had nowhere to take Hetta next day. But Andrew had said he would take care of it. And that made her feel safe.

Now she could relax enough to fall asleep. As her consciousness blurred she felt she were back again in the garden, racked with torment, pouring out her heart to him, feeling the comfort of his arms about her.

That shouldn't have happened, she thought. It had reminded her of things best forgotten. For years she'd hidden away the memory of what it had felt like to be held by him. Two husbands had come and gone, both of them bad mistakes. She'd survived by not comparing them to the man whose love she'd thrown away because she'd been too young and stupid to appreciate it.

She'd learned its value when it had been too late, and then she'd buried him deep in the dark places of her mind. It had been that or go mad with regret.

Now an ironic accident had forced her to remember. In the darkness it was as though he were there with her again, warming her, murmuring in her ear, just as once he'd whispered words of love and touched her face with his lips.

It was unendurable. She went into the bathroom, stripped off and got under the shower, trying to wash away all the weariness and desperation of her life. But as she stepped out she passed a long mirror, and what she saw gave her a shock. As a professional beautician Elinor knew how to make the best of herself so that her customers would trust her, and with the excellent cosmetics always within her reach she never looked less than well groomed.

But now, gazing back at her was the truth, and she saw, without defences, what the years had done to her. The last time she'd been in his arms her body had been young, rounded, bursting with life. Now she was too thin, her face drawn, her eyes haunted. The glorious mane of blonde hair that he'd loved and through which he'd run his fingers had long gone, hacked off in bitterness some time in her dreadful second marriage. Now it was short and neat, easy to care for, and that was all.

This haunted, desperate woman was what he'd held against him tonight. If he'd thought at all about the beauty he'd once loved it would be with disgust that it had so faded.

It was only then that she remembered that tonight he'd called her Ellie.

Andrew was there on the dot of five-thirty next morning, knocking softly. Elinor was already up, and she let him in. He'd brought her a cup of tea in a paper cup, which she drank down thankfully.

'Any disturbances?' he asked.

'Not one.'

'Good. Now, here's what's going to happen.'

As he spoke he paced the floor, somehow never looking at her.

'Last night I called a friend of mine, who's about to rush off on a business trip, and doesn't want to leave his house empty. The person who was going to look after it for him has let him down at the last moment, and he would be delighted if you'd take over. It's about ten miles from the hospital, on the edge of the country. And the pay is good, so you wouldn't have to leave Hetta in order to work.'

'Pay? You mean he'd actually pay me when he's giving me accommodation?' she asked, hardly daring to believe this.

'There'd be some work. You'd keep the house clean—although most of it is shut up—keep it warm, make sure everyone knew it wasn't empty.'

'And I could forward his mail,' she said quickly.

That made him turn to her, and a strange look passed over his face, as though he was completely taken aback.

'Yes,' he said vaguely, 'although I don't think there would be much. He has it redirected.'

'But I could answer the telephone, and tell people where he is,' she offered, anxious to do more than the light duties prescribed.

'You could do that,' he agreed, but in the same strange fashion, as though he was thinking of something else. 'So I can tell my friend that you agree?'

'I'd be glad to. But he doesn't know anything about me.'

'He'll accept my recommendation.'

'Can I call him, to say thank you?'

'I'll get him to call you when you're there.'

'What's his name?'

'I think you should go now. You must need food. Go up to the all night canteen, and I'll see you later.'

The canteen was serving an early breakfast. Elinor discovered that she was ravenous, and piled her plate with eggs and bacon. At this hour the place was filled with doctors and nurses, weary-eyed after night duty, or just snatching a mouthful before starting their day. Among them she was dismayed to recognise Nurse Stewart.

The older woman's eyes were like gimlets, and Elinor guessed she was furious at being denied the chance to interfere. She'd had to yield before Andrew's authority, but she was unforgiving. She headed straight for Elinor's table and sat down without asking.

'You're here early, Mrs Landers. May I ask where you spent the night?'

'You may not,' Elinor said angrily. 'You have no more say about my daughter, since I gather your shift has finished. As soon as possible I'll be going to the ward to prepare her to come home.'

'But which home? That *is* a question I may legitimately ask?'

'Good morning, ladies,' came a voice from above their heads, and they both looked up to see Andrew about to sit down with them. 'Mrs Landers, I'm delighted to find you here. I telephoned Mr Martin, and he's delighted with his new housekeeper. The place is ready for your immediate occupation, and if you contact my secretary later this morning she'll give you full details.

'There'll also be a chart explaining Hetta's medication, to prevent her body rejecting her new heart, but I understand you already know a lot about that. The nurses say you always watch carefully when she has her pills. Well done. The district nurse is being informed about your arrival, and will call every day. But I don't expect any problems. Nurse Stewart, how nice to see you again. I hope you're eating well. You need to keep your strength up after a night shift. I always say night work is the most exhausting, because your blood sugar's low. Have you found that, or do you manage to…'

He talked on, barely stopping for breath, giving the nurse no time to raise problems. Watching him with admiration, Elinor realised that this was a consummate performance, done for a purpose. Her instincts told her that this apparently outgoing man wasn't the Andrew she knew, either years ago or now. He was forcing himself, and although his manner was light his intent was deadly serious.

But there was a stubborn look in Nurse Stewart's eyes that said she wouldn't be beaten. However long Andrew stayed, she could stay longer, to poke and probe at Elinor's defences, in order, ultimately, to impose her own 'right' solution. And when Andrew's pager went it seemed that the nurse had won.

'Apparently I'm wanted,' Andrew said. 'Mrs Landers, may I trouble you to come with me? There are some final matters to discuss. Good morning, Nurse Stewart. It was a pleasure talking to you.'

His hand was under her elbow, guiding her into the corridor, and then he was breathing out like a schoolboy who'd successfully brought off a prank.

'Thank heavens you came!' she said.

'I only thought of the danger when you'd gone. Did I get there in time to avoid disaster?'

'By a whisker.'

'You'd best get out of here to a place where she can't follow.'

'Is there such a place?'

'Here's the keys to my car. This is the registration number.' He scribbled it for her. 'Get in the back, pull the rug over you and finish your night's sleep. See my secretary in four hours, and give her the keys.'

'Is that safe?' Elinor asked.

'Completely. She's the most discreet woman in the world.'

His car was brand-new and the very last word in luxury and success. There was room to lie down in comfort in the back seat, and pull the mohair rug over her head so that the outside world couldn't see her. Like this she felt warm and protected.

Protected.

Andrew's doing.

* * *

On the dot of ten Elinor presented herself to Andrew's secretary, who received the keys without comment and gave her
a letter from him that she'd just finished typing.

It began 'Dear Mrs Landers' and informed her, politely
and formally, that all arrangements were in place and a cab
had been arranged to take her to the house. Mr Martin understood about Hetta and she would arrive to find the place already warm. Her salary would be paid directly into her bank,
if she would kindly give the details to his secretary. A set of
keys was enclosed, he wished her well, etc. etc.

Going to the ward, she found the day staff there, under the
charge of Nurse Edwards, a cheerful figure whom Hetta
liked.

'All ready to go?' she said, smiling. 'I gather you're going
to be a housekeeper at a nice place on the edge of town.'

'Aren't we going back to Daisy's?' Hetta asked.

'No, darling. They had a fire yesterday.'

'Mr Jenson,' Hetta said at once, in her wise old lady voice.
'Smoking in bed again. Poor Daisy. What will she do?'

'She's got a room nearby, and the insurance will take care
of the rebuilding,' Elinor explained. 'And we're going to look
after this man's house for him.'

'Why don't you let the nurse finish dressing Hetta while
I give you her medication?' Nurse Edwards suggested.

It was like a dream to be getting ready to leave. Only a
short time ago her skies had been dark. Now she had hope
again, and it was thanks to one person.

'I think I'd better find Andrew and say thank you,' Elinor
said.

'I've said my "thank yous",' Hetta explained. 'He came
earlier. He said he was sorry he couldn't see you, but he was
operating this morning, and would be busy all day.'

So that was that. He'd taken every chance to ensure he

didn't meet her again before she left. And perhaps, on the whole, it was best.

As promised, the cab was waiting for her, and in a few minutes they were gliding away from the hospital. Then the suburbs began to fall away and they were in the country. The houses grew further apart, more luxurious, and she realised that she was in a moneyed district, where the buildings weren't houses at all, but 'residences', with drives, and wrought-iron gates.

At last the car turned into a gate more decorative than the others. She just had time to observe the sign reading 'Oaks' before they began the journey up a winding drive, thickly lined with trees. Then the trees parted without warning, giving her a sudden view of the mansion.

It was awesome. She'd expected a rich man's residence, but this had a style and luxury that trumpeted a message to the world. No wonder Mr Martin, whoever he was, didn't care to leave the place empty.

The cab driver waited while she opened the front door and carried her bags in for her, but waved away her money.

'Already paid, ma'am,' he said. 'Including the tip.'

Then they were alone, looking around and around in awe.

'Goodness, Mummy!' Hetta exclaimed. 'It's like a film set.'

'It is, isn't it?'

'Is it real?'

'I don't think it can be.'

They explored together, first the kitchen, a blue and white masterpiece of luxury and modern equipment.

'It's a bit over-the-top for egg and chips,' was Hetta's down-to-earth comment. This was her favourite dish.

'I rather think it was designed for cordon bleu,' Elinor mused.

'But you could do egg and chips?' Hetta asked anxiously.

'For an army, darling.'

The huge refrigerator was stocked to the roof: eggs, rashers, sausages, vegetables, milk and six different fruit juices. The freezer was likewise packed.

In stunned silence they climbed the broad curved stairway to the realms above, where the corridor branched into two corridors, each covered in thick cream carpet. In one direction every door was locked, but in the other they found two unlocked doors. Opening the first they found a large corner bedroom, with windows on two sides, and a modern four-poster bed, hung with white lace.

'You could really be a film star in that,' Hetta breathed.

They found her room opposite, also large, but more down-to-earth. The bed was covered with a duvet depicting wild-life, which delighted Hetta. A study of the bookshelves produced more about wildlife, especially elephants, which pleased her even more. But even as she eagerly scanned the books Elinor saw her eyes begin to droop. She still had a long way to go before complete recovery, and the short journey had taken it out of her.

'Time for your nap, darling,' she said.

'Can I have something to eat first?'

Elinor dropped to one knee to look Hetta in the eyes. 'Of course you can,' she said. 'Of course you can,' she repeated, gathering the little girl against her in a passion of tenderness.

But Hetta was already nodding off in her arms. Elinor lifted her up.

'You can have anything you want,' she whispered, laying her on the bed and propping her up in a half-sitting position, as the hospital had advised until the wound in her chest had finished healing. 'Anything,' she repeated, pulling the duvet up to her chin, 'just as soon as you wake up.'

She slipped briefly downstairs to collect the bags, and unpacked them with her own and Hetta's doors open, in case the child should awaken and be alarmed at the strange surroundings. But she was deeply asleep. Even when Elinor dropped a heavy bag on the floor with a clatter Hetta did no more than sigh happily.

After watching her for a moment Elinor crept out and went on a tour of the house. As Andrew had explained, most of the doors were locked, which was a relief. Evidently her duties would be confined to their rooms upstairs, the kitchen, and the large living room equipped with satellite television and tuned into every conceivable station.

Hetta slept the afternoon away before awakening with an appetite. Elinor whipped her up an omelette and found some ice cream in the freezer. After that they spent a couple of contented hours exploring children's channels on the sofa, until Hetta dropped off again in her mother's arms.

This time, when she'd put her to bed, Elinor looked around the room and saw that here too was a small television with satellite channels. It was a child's room, as the decor made clear: a boy, she judged, from the cowboys on the wallpaper, and one who was denied nothing.

They had joked about film stars, but it wasn't a joke at all, really. The lace-hung four-poster was big enough to sleep six, and the private bathroom that led off from it was like a Hollywood fantasy, with a circular bath sunk into the floor, its elegant cream colour adorned by a jigsaw pattern all the way around the edge. All accessories were gold-plated, even—Elinor was amused to note—the toilet-roll holder. The soap dish held a new cake of cream soap, so heavily scented that she had to sit down after one sniff.

Before going to bed she tried the shower, and discovered that the water came out with real force and maintained its temperature. That was true luxury, she thought, drying off with one of the thick cream towels, and thinking of Daisy's shower attachment, which had to be tied onto the taps and always came off, no matter how tightly you fixed it.

She checked Hetta once more, before snuggling down blissfully in the soft white sheets of the big bed. She'd left both bedroom doors open again, with a light on in the hall between them, so that Hetta could be immediately reassured should she awaken. And in the middle of the night she heard the soft patter of feet and felt someone climb in beside her.

As they drifted off to sleep she wondered if she'd gone to heaven, for that was the only way to explain how her troubles had been swept away and replaced by this perfect peace and serenity. That was the stuff of fairy tales, not real life.

CHAPTER SEVEN

As ONE day slipped into the next nothing happened to disturb their peace. The district nurse called regularly to check Hetta's progress and confirm that she was doing well. She was a comfortable, motherly woman, and the other two were soon calling her Sally.

'Don't be worried if she still needs to sleep a lot,' she advised Elinor. 'She's been through the mill, and it'll be a long recovery. Take everything at her pace.'

Elinor had found a letter in the kitchen explaining the house's secrets to her, the use of each key, plus a set of keys that fitted a car in the garage that she could use. To her relief it was a modest family saloon rather than a luxurious vehicle that would have intimidated her. They began taking short trips to a nearby village where there were a few little shops. Elinor would buy a newspaper, and a few grocery items. They would have a snack in a small, rustic teashop, and then go home.

On one of these trips she tentatively put her cash card in the machine, fearing to find herself overdrawn. But the machine cheerfully reported a healthy balance. She stared. Obviously her first salary cheque had been paid in, but it seemed much larger than anything she'd expected.

She tried again, this time requesting a mini statement.

Sure enough there had been a credit, which she regarded with disbelief. *That much?*

Obviously that was a month's money in advance, but even so.

What was Mr Martin? A philanthropist? Or just slightly crazy?

In a short time Hetta had become so much at ease that Elinor no longer needed to be there when she awoke from her nap. She would simply come downstairs and find her mother in the grounds where she often lingered to enjoy the summer weather.

The extent of those grounds meant that there was no chance to get acquainted with the neighbours, or even see them. Whoever they were, they existed in their own mansions, deep in their own grounds. Apart from Sally nobody came to the house, and they were completely self-contained. It was like existing in a separate world, where there was only quiet, and the chance to heal.

As the tensions drained away, she wondered when in her life before she'd known such total, spirit-healing peace. Not in her wretched marriage to Tom Landers. 'All teeth and trousers,' her mother had said angrily. 'You're a fool, girl. You've been a fool ever since you played fast and loose with the best man you ever knew, or ever will.'

And she'd laid a desperate hand over her mother's mouth because that had been a truth she hadn't been able to face, even on the eve of her wedding to Tom.

Before that, the short-lived marriage to Jack Smith. No peace there, only rows and bitterness, and a desperate attempt to cope with his drinking.

And before that…

She shut the thought off. She couldn't bear it now.

With the money now at her disposal Elinor was able to pay a few outstanding bills, plus the cost of a taxi to bring Daisy for a visit. There was a joyful reunion, Elinor persuaded her friend to stay the night, and when the taxi returned for her next morning she departed with the promise to return again soon.

There was no doubt that her visit had been good for Hetta, who was becoming bored as her strength increased. As she'd told Andrew, she longed for a dog. Failing that, a playmate of her own age. Elinor kept her amused as best she could and the two of them enjoyed the happiest times they'd ever known. But still, there were times when she knew Hetta needed more.

One morning while they were breakfasting and mulling over what to do with the day, there was a noise from the front hall, and she went out to find a letter on the mat, something that had never happened before. Mr Martin's mail was all re-directed, but this one must have slipped through the net. She picked it up and was about to lay it on the hall table when the name caught her eye.

Andrew Blake.

It was a mistake, of course. Andrew and Mr Martin were friends. He'd simply asked if he could have some of his mail sent here.

But why? And in that case why didn't it say 'care of'? And why had Mr Martin never called her, as Andrew had said he would? Because there was no Mr Martin. This was Andrew's house. Of course it was. How could she have been so blind?

Or had she? Hadn't she at least suspected, and then turned her eyes away from the thought, not wanting to confront the implications?

All this time she'd been living here on his charity. She hadn't known it, but he had known. Had he enjoyed the thought? Despised her? Laughed at her?

Could she blame him?

Now she could see how cleverly he'd arranged matters, redirecting his mail, having his calls diverted, locking so many rooms. He'd had to take a chance with the neighbours but even there he'd been lucky. They were too distant to pose any real problem.

The air around her head seemed to be buzzing, and it was suddenly unbearable to have this hanging over her. She snatched up the phone, called the hospital and left a message on Andrew's voice mail. He came back to her almost at once.

'Is Hetta all right?'

'She's fine. I called because some mail arrived for you.'

There was a short silence that would have told her the truth if nothing else had done.

'I'll be there this evening,' he said shortly, and hung up.

She replaced the receiver, and in that exact moment it came over her what a stupid thing she'd done. She could have screamed. By forcing this out into the open she'd made the place too hot to hold her, but she had nowhere else to take Hetta where she would be safe and happy. She should have endured anything rather than spoil things for Hetta. And she would have done, if she'd stopped to think.

I don't learn, she castigated herself bitterly. *Act first, talk first, and think afterwards, when it's way too late. Just like then.*

She could simply have sent the envelope on to the hospital. Andrew would have guessed what she knew when he opened it, but he could have turned a blind eye. Now she'd forced him into the open.

She would have given anything to turn the time back ten minutes.

Or twelve years.

Still in a daze she wandered out into the garden, where Hetta was piling pebbles on top of each other with fierce concentration, until they collapsed.

'It's lovely having a garden, Mum. I do like it here.'

So did I, she thought. *It was like the Garden of Eden. But now the serpent's poisoned everything.*

'Let's go back in,' she said in a strained voice. 'You mustn't overdo it.'

By ten o'clock that night he hadn't shown up, and there was no message. Ten became eleven. Midnight passed.

It meant nothing. There was an emergency at the hospital.

And he wouldn't think to call me, she thought wryly. *Because he sees only the straight path ahead. No distractions. Why am I such a fool?*

The call came the next morning while she was serving breakfast. As she had thought, it had been an emergency.

'I was going to let you know,' he said, sounding tired. 'But things were desperate. I couldn't call you myself and I— didn't want anyone else to do it. I'll be there tonight, if that's OK?'

She assured him that it was fine. To be on the safe side she went out and bought a newspaper with details of rooms to let. And that evening it was the same, hour following hour with no sign of him. So now she knew where she stood. But why? she wondered despondently. Why be kind and then snub her like this? For the pleasure of it?

When she'd put Hetta to bed she sat downstairs for a long time, trying to make herself do something decisive, but lacking the energy. The world seemed cold and dreary.

Suddenly it was one in the morning. She'd been staring into space for more than two hours. She pulled herself together and went out into the hall to mount the stairs. As she did so, a brilliant light shone through the door window, almost blinding her. There was the sound of a car engine, then the slamming of the door. And finally the doorbell.

It couldn't be Andrew, because he must have a key.

But it was Andrew, frowning and uneasy.

She stood back to let him pass, closed the door behind him and helped him off with his coat.

'I'm sorry to be so late,' he said. 'If I hadn't seen the lights on I'd have left. I've been operating all evening.'

'Then you'd better have something to eat,' she said. She needed time to sort out her thoughts. His face was exhausted and haggard, and he looked so different from the man she'd been picturing that she felt the ground shaking under her feet.

'Just a snack. Don't go to any trouble.'

'Omelette,' she said, heading for the kitchen. 'I've got plenty of milk.'

'Fine, I'll have some.'

She filled a tall glass with milk, and watched him drink it. 'Johnny used to say you drank so much milk because you were preparing for your first ulcer,' she remembered suddenly.

'Yes,' he said, as though the memory had surprised him. 'So he did.'

After that she turned away suddenly to concentrate on the omelette. He asked how Hetta was progressing, and mentioned her next appointment, and in this way they got through the next few minutes.

He ate like a man too tired to know what he was putting into his mouth.

'When did you last eat?' Elinor asked.

'Staff canteen. Lunchtime.'

'Is one omelette enough?'

'Would you mind making another one?' he said at once.

She smiled. 'Of course not. Go into the other room, and I'll bring it in.'

A few minutes later she found him on the sofa. She set the plate down on a low table beside him and he smiled his thanks.

'I'm sorry to do this to you two nights running.'

'Don't be silly. Your patients come first. Was it another emergency?'

'No, the same one. A child. He was rushed in last night, and I thought—it looked like it would be all right. But tonight he took a turn for the worse. We did our best for him, but there was never really any chance.'

'I'm sorry.'

'Don't be,' he said harshly. 'It's part of the job. You just have to go on.' He gave a forced smile and indicated the food. 'This is good.'

'I've got some trifle. You should eat as much as you can.'

He gave a faint grin. 'Fattening me up?'

'You never got fat, whatever you ate. It used to make me so mad.'

'Yes. I know.' He added quickly, 'Some trifle, then.'

Another mine dodged. But still the minefields stretched ahead.

When he'd finished eating he yawned, then leaned his head back against the chair, eyes closed. She could clearly see the shape and line of each feature. The straight, uncompromising nose, the strong chin that could only have belonged to a stubborn man, and the mouth that somehow didn't fit with the rest of the face. It was expressive, mobile, suggesting sensitivity, although it had hardened somewhat since they'd loved each other years ago. There were two deep lines on either side of it now, and more lines at the corners of his eyes. It was the face of a man who spent most of his life being tired, and refusing to admit it.

For years she'd resisted the memory of his kisses, and her own frustrated desire for him. But the really dangerous memory was more recent. Just a few short weeks ago his arms had held her as he'd soothed her sobs in the hospital garden. She could feel him now, drawing her head against his shoulder, murmuring soft words of comfort, and against this memory she had no defence at all.

The mouth that now lay relaxed might, or might not, have kissed her hair that night. She couldn't be sure. At the time she'd had no thought for anything but Hetta. It was only afterwards, reliving the moment, that she'd thought she'd felt the soft pressure of his lips. Or maybe not.

His eyes opened so slowly that she had time to avert her gaze, but she didn't try. Nor did he. He only looked at her sadly, and his mouth quirked wryly as though he could see a joke against them both.

'I still can't believe this,' he said. 'And perhaps it isn't really true.'

'That's how I've felt,' she admitted. 'Since that first day when I saw you in the hospital corridor—I tried not to believe it. I've always wondered what I would say to you if we met again, but in twelve years I've never found the answer. "I'm sorry" sounds so inadequate.'

'Good grief! Skip that! I hate apologies. I don't know how to make them myself and it embarrasses me when other people try. Could I have a cup of coffee?'

Domestic tasks were useful for getting over the awkward moments. She made some fresh coffee and when she returned he was studying the newspaper, open at the 'To Let' page, that she'd left on the sofa.

'It was stupid of me to think that you wouldn't find out.'

'This *is* your house?'

'Yes.'

'And Mr Martin?'

'He doesn't exist.'

'So it was all you, including the money you've been paying into my account?'

He shrugged. 'You really are doing me a favour by occupying the house. I don't like it to be empty.'

'You could have employed a house sitter for a quarter of the price. This was just a device for—for—'

'Helping out an old friend?'

'Is that what you call it? To me it looks like charity.'

He frowned. 'Are you angry with me?'

To her own dismay, she found that she was. She'd resolved to play it cool, but she'd reckoned without the humiliation that burned in her when she thought of living on his handouts.

'It doesn't matter,' she said hastily, trying to control herself.

'It matters to me. As I said, it was for an old friend—'

'We were never friends,' she flashed.

'No, we were lovers, until the day you found another lover that you preferred. But you had every right to do that, and if I can draw a line under it, why can't you?'

'Because you've been giving me money,' she said. 'It's—it's insulting.'

'I didn't mean to insult you. I just did what I thought you needed.' He gave a grunt of laughter. 'One thing hasn't changed. You always had a genius for putting me in the wrong. I never knew where I was. I suppose that was part of your charm.'

She'd pulled herself together. 'It's only charming in a seventeen year old,' she said. 'In a middle-aged woman it's a pesky nuisance.'

'You're not middle-aged,' he said quickly. 'You're not even thirty.'

'I look forty and I feel fifty.' She sighed. 'But I'm acting like a ten year old, aren't I? I'm sorry, Andrew. It's just that there's something about taking money—'

'Will you drop the subject?' He sounded strained.

'Yes.' Casting around for another subject, she said brightly, 'Your house is wonderful.'

'Is it?' He sounded barely interested.

'You know it is. You did it. You got where you said you wanted. I always knew you would.'

'Is that what this place says to you? Success?'

'Of course. And the car.'

'Oh, yes. I never knew that my character included a strain of the flashy and vulgar until I found I could afford the toys to play with. And I enjoyed them for a while. I still enjoy the car.' He shook his head as though trying to clear it. 'Forgive me.'

'Forgive you?'

'For not telling you the truth. I meant it for the best, but I should have known that you wouldn't want anything to do with it.' He shrugged. 'Well, anyway—there's no need for this.' He indicated the paper.

'I thought you'd want me to go when I found out.'

'Why should I?'

'Because you took so much trouble to stop me knowing.'

He gave a faint grin, directed at himself. 'You don't know the half of it. I came back here that night and went through the place, hiding anything that could have betrayed me. I stocked the freezer from an all-night supermarket about a mile away. Then I had my phone calls redirected, and my mail rerouted—not that much usually comes here anyway. I did anything I could think of.'

'But why?'

'Would you have accepted if you'd known it was me?'

'I wouldn't have wanted to,' she said after a moment's thought. 'But I'd have had no choice.'

'Exactly. You'd have come here reluctantly, been horribly embarrassed, and got out as soon as you could. I didn't want that.'

'Was that why you knocked on the door tonight instead of using your key?'

'I don't have a key. That is—I do, but not on me. It's locked in my desk, in the study here. This is your house, while you need it. You couldn't feel like that if I could come and go here without your permission.'

'Andrew, I'm sorry,' she said impulsively. 'I backed you into a corner about this, but I never meant to.'

'What do you mean, backed me into a corner?'

'When you found me having hysterics in the garden that night, it was a kind of emotional blackmail.'

'I never felt that. I just felt that I wanted to help you. I couldn't tell you the truth because I knew I wasn't your favourite person.'

'Shouldn't that be my line? I gave you every reason to hate me.'

'I've never hated you, Ellie. Well, yes, perhaps at the beginning. I was young then, and my pride had been hurt. Pride's damnably important when you're twenty-six. But I recovered my sense of proportion. It's a great leveller, a sense of proportion. It helps you see that the things that once seemed earth-shattering didn't matter so much after all. Certainly not enough to hate someone.'

'I'm glad,' she said quietly.

'And you did me a favour. I wasn't ready to marry. I still had my way to make.'

'I seem to recall your mother warning you about that at the time,' Elinor said.

'Yes, and I wouldn't listen. Which was stupid of me.' Abruptly he changed the subject. 'Are you taking care of yourself?'

'I'm all right. Hetta's the sick one.'

'No, Hetta's the recovering one. If you're not careful you're going to be the sick one. The strain on you has been enormous. You've been fighting to be strong, for her, but who's strong for you?'

Only you, she thought. *Ever. But I can't say that.*

'Just make sure you look after yourself now,' he said firmly. 'You need to heal as well.'

'Well, this is the right place to do it,' she agreed. 'Where are you living? I haven't forced you to move into a hotel, have I?'

'No, I've got a little place near the hospital. I'm used to spending most of my time there. I bought this house for my wife, a few years ago.'

'Your—wife?'

'Until recently. The divorce was finalised a few weeks back. I offered her the house as part of the settlement, but she preferred money, so I still have it. I'll get around to selling it soon.'

'Perhaps it still means something to you?'

'No, I'm not clinging onto "happy memories". There aren't any. We knew it was a mistake fairly soon, and the end was always inevitable. All we've had in common for years has been our son. It was a "good" marriage, but not a happy one.'

'Good?'

'Suitable for a young man with his way to make. I wanted to get onto Elmer Rylance's team because he was the best heart surgeon in the world. Half the techniques in use today were invented, or at least perfected, by him. I could have learned them from others, but that wasn't good enough for me. Only the master would do. Lord, I was conceited in those days!

'The difficulty was, getting myself noticed among so many competing for his attention. Then I met Myra at some medical charity function. She's his niece.'

'Oh, I see,' Elinor said quietly.

'Yes, it was as cynical and planned as that. Not the first meeting. That was accident. But dancing with her, trying to turn her head, establishing myself as her escort, all that was done with a purpose. Not very attractive behaviour, but it's the way the world works. At least it does for a certain kind of man, and that was the kind of man I was. Nice, eh?'

'You're very hard on yourself. Why?'

'Because I like to face the truth, and the truth about myself isn't pretty. When I want something I go for it like a bulldozer, and I don't notice who I'm mowing down in the process. You of all people have reason to know that.'

The hint that he blamed himself for their past, rather than her, took her by surprise. She looked at him sadly, not knowing what to say.

'What happened to you afterwards?' he asked.

'I got married to Jack Smith, and it was a disaster. He was every bad thing you warned me about, and in my heart I knew it all the time.'

'Then why—?'

'Because I'd backed myself into a corner,' she said bitterly. 'I just couldn't admit I was wrong. You warned me he was a bad lot, so I had to marry him to prove he wasn't. But he was. After two years I gave up.'

'And Tom Landers?'

'He was my new start, a demonstration to the world that I didn't foul up every time. Except that he was worse than Jack. Hetta was the only good thing to come out of our marriage. After that I swore no more men.'

'Very wise,' he mused. 'You were always a rotten picker.'

'Not always,' she said, and let it go at that.

CHAPTER EIGHT

ANDREW didn't answer and for a moment an awkward silence fell between them. It was broken by a squeak of delight from the hall and Elinor looked up to see Hetta bounding in.

'I knew you'd come to see me,' she said, jumping on Andrew.

'But of course I did,' he said, giving her a hug, and finding himself embracing Samson as well. 'Good grief, have you still got that revolting bear?'

'He's not a revolting bear,' she reproved. 'He's a nice bear. He stayed with me all the time, except when you were horrible and made him have a bath.'

'Yes, I remember now,' he said hastily. 'Beg pardon, ma'am.'

'Samson's my best friend.'

'Better than me?' He sounded piqued.

'Well—p'raps just a bit. But not much.'

Andrew grinned, and again Elinor marvelled at the change in him.

'What are you doing out of bed?' Elinor demanded, trying to sound severe.

'I had to come down and see Andrew 'cos he came to visit me.'

'Of course,' Andrew agreed.

'Can I have some milk?' Hetta begged, sounding like a starving orphan.

'Will you go straight back to bed afterwards?' Elinor countered.

'She's only just arrived,' Andrew protested.

'Andrew hasn't seen my scar yet.'

'And I haven't seen her scar yet.'

It dawned on Elinor that behind the humour he had a serious purpose. He wanted Hetta to stay for his own reasons: perhaps because he felt more at ease with another person there.

She went into the kitchen for milk, and returned to find the other two deep in discussion of medical matters. Hetta was displaying her scar with immense pride, while Andrew studied it and observed how well it had healed.

'How do you enjoy living here?' he asked.

'Heaps,' Hetta said at once. 'There's a huge garden and a swing, and—' her voice became blissful '—Mummy's here all the time.'

'I haven't been with her enough in the past,' Elinor said quickly. 'I had to work and it took me away a lot. But now we're together all day, just the two of us. As Hetta says, it's lovely.'

'I'm glad,' Andrew said. He looked back to Hetta. 'Do you still have those nightmares?'

'Not really,' she said in a considering tone. 'I have funny dreams with lots of things happening, but I'm not scared any more. Not since you told me about them.' She suddenly looked into his face. 'Do *you* have bad dreams?'

He flinched. 'Why do you ask that?'

'You look as if you do.'

'Hetta,' Elinor protested. 'Manners.'

Andrew was looking uncomfortable and it dawned on her that Hetta had touched a nerve. 'Well, everyone does sometimes,' he said. 'Now it's time you went back to bed. It's very late.'

'Will you tuck me up, and I can show you my room?'

'Darling—' Elinor said in quick dismay, but Andrew had already risen and taken the child's hand.

Elinor guessed that the bedroom had been his son's, but he might have been seeing it for the first time as he let Hetta show it to him. It was strange to watch them. Anyone seeing the three of them, not knowing the truth, would have thought them a perfect family. Hetta herself was overjoyed to have her friend back, blissfully ignorant of the undercurrents and tensions between the adults. And maybe her perspective was the right one.

At last she was asleep and they crept out and down the stairs.

'I must be going now,' Andrew said. 'Please don't think of leaving this house. I won't trouble you.'

'Is that what you think you are? A trouble to me? After what I owe you?'

'I wish you wouldn't talk about owing me. That isn't how I think of it. And I only meant that I'm not going to use your circumstances to force my presence on you. You can't go. She's happy. Don't take that away from her just because we once—because of things that don't matter any more.' He looked at her wryly. 'If they ever really mattered.'

'Didn't they?' she couldn't resist asking.

'I don't know. I don't think I can remember by now. Other things become important, other griefs can be greater, and suddenly you wonder what it was all about. But I know this. There's nothing in our past that should drive you away from here.'

'Thank you,' she said, trying to be as relieved as he plainly meant her to, but feeling only an ache. 'It's kind of you—' She stopped, her gaze fixed on his face. 'Andrew, you're dead on your feet. You can't keep your eyes open, can you?'

'I'll be all right. The night air will wake me up.'

'You won't be in the air, you'll be in the car, and you'll probably crash it.' As if to confirm her words he closed his eyes again. She took his arm and led him firmly back to the living room, and almost pushed him down onto the sofa.

'You were crazy coming out here so late after the day you've had. It could have waited until tomorrow.'

'No, it couldn't, not after I didn't turn up last night. I needed to talk to you, make you understand.'

'I understand that you're not fit to drive.'

'Perhaps if you made me a coffee—'

'The only thing I'm making for you is a bed. You're sleeping here.'

'Am I?'

'Yes. How much sleep did you get last night?'

'Three or four hours. I honestly don't remember.'

'Tell me which room.'

'The one with the pine door,' he said vaguely.

'Key.'

'It's on my keyring.'

'Which is?'

'In the drawer of my desk—in the study.' He seemed to be having trouble thinking of the words.

'And the key to that?' she persisted.

'Oh—yes.'

He felt in an inner pocket and produced some keys. Elinor located the one that opened the study, then the top drawer of the desk, and finally the complete set of house keys.

She found the pine door two along from Hetta's room and opened it quietly. It didn't entirely surprise her to find that it was as plain as her own was ornate. The bed was narrow and looked hard. The furniture was neat and functional. Whatever Andrew had been like once, this was how he was now.

She remembered how he'd shrugged aside the child's

death, with a brusque remark about 'going on'. He was right, but it had given her a chill to hear it put that way. Would he have taken Hetta's death so coolly? It was hard to believe, when he was so easy and friendly with her, but what did she know of him?

By the time she'd finished he'd appeared in the doorway. 'Thank you,' he said briefly.

'When do you want to be called?'

'I normally set my alarm for six, but I guess I can allow myself a little longer tomorrow. I'm not operating.'

'Goodnight, then.'

She finished clearing away downstairs and went up quietly. As always Hetta's door stood open, and she looked in, listening to the soft, even breathing, before going to her own room.

She lay down but sleep wouldn't come. Andrew's words, 'suddenly you wonder what it was all about,' haunted her. In her mind she had invested their meeting with so much significance, and now he'd told her, very kindly, that it meant nothing to him. He'd said, too, that she'd done him a favour by deserting him, freeing him to fulfil himself.

But that's not true, she thought, sitting up suddenly. *He was the one who was desperate to get married. I didn't look further than being in love. That's why I hurt him so much.*

'I couldn't help it,' she whispered now into the darkness. 'You wanted me too much. I couldn't cope. Now you're coping by changing the past so that it didn't mean anything.'

She would try to believe that that was best for both of them, but the pain was still there. It was as though she'd possessed one glorious treasure in all her life. And he'd shown her that it was only made of lead.

It had been foolish of her to feel a brief stab of pleasure at the discovery that he was unmarried. What possible difference could that make to her?

But she couldn't hide from her own heart. Since they'd met she'd seen the man nature had meant him to be, not only brilliant but generous in a way that had gone far beyond the call of duty.

He'd loved her and she'd thrown it away. She'd refused to face her regret but it had always been there, and now there was no hiding from it.

Suddenly she sat up, alerted by an unfamiliar sound, as though someone were crying out. In an instant she was out of bed, hurrying across the corridor to Hetta. But her daughter's room was quiet, her sleep undisturbed. The sounds were coming from further down the hall.

Elinor crept out, closing Hetta's door so that she should hear nothing, and made her way along to the pine door. There was no doubt now that the cries were coming from the man who slept behind it, and she knew he wouldn't be pleased if she disturbed him. But she couldn't leave him like this. Pushing open the door, she slipped in and closed it behind her.

A soft light from the window limned his body. He wore no pyjama top, and the sheet had slipped down far enough for her to suspect that he probably wore nothing else either. Not wanting to embarrass him, she swiftly drew it higher, then dropped down by the bed and put her hands on his shoulders, shaking him hard.

'Andrew—Andrew—wake up.'

His eyes opened fast and immediately flew to the little clock beside him with its luminous figures.

'What is it?' he demanded hoarsely. 'Who needs me? Tell them I'm coming at once.'

'No.' She shook him again. 'There's no need for that.' She put the bedside lamp on. 'It's me, you're not in the hospital.'

His eyes seemed to take a moment to focus. Then she felt the tension drain out of him.

'Thank you,' he said wearily. 'Was I shouting?'

'Yes.'

'I'm sorry. It's abominable of me to disturb you. Hetta—?'

'She's still asleep.'

'Thank God! It's just something that happens now and then when I've been overworking.'

'I think you overwork all the time.'

He gave a mirthless laugh. 'Yes, par for the course. Sometimes it's worse than others, but it doesn't mean anything.'

'That's not true,' she said quietly. 'You know it isn't.'

She became aware that she was still holding him, and took her hands away. He hauled himself up in bed, grasping the sheet firmly, in a way that suggested her suspicions had been correct. Then he sat leaning against the bedhead with an expression that seemed strangely defeated. His hair was tousled and fell over his broad forehead.

'Some things are hard to cope with,' he said at last. 'That child who died tonight—we all fought so hard, but it was no use—' Suddenly he closed his eyes. 'He was six years old,' he said huskily.

She drew a swift breath. Who could empathise with that pain better than herself? But she could see the answer on Andrew's face. He was ravaged by his failure, and it was more than the damaged pride of a man who hated to fail. She was witnessing real misery.

'The worst thing is telling the parents,' he went on. 'They were so happy. They'd thought it was going to be all right, and then—their faces.'

'Must it be you who tells them?'

'Yes. I'm the one who's failed them, you see.'

'But that's not fair. People die. It's not your fault. You can't be held responsible if the odds are too great.'

'But I'm the one they trusted.' He gave her a swift, intent

look. 'If Hetta had died, wouldn't you have felt that I'd let you down?'

'I know heart transplants are risky,' she said carefully, 'and it's not fair to blame the surgeon because luck was against him. I wanted a miracle and you gave it to me. But if not—I hope I'd have understood.'

'You wouldn't,' he said, smiling at her sadly. 'You mightn't have said anything, but you'd have looked at me— and I'd have seen you—'

'She's everything to me. You were our only hope and if things had gone wrong—yes, you're right. I wouldn't have been just or fair about it. What did the parents say to you?'

'Nothing. They just looked betrayed. And I can't wipe that look out of my mind. I wanted to be able to tell them that it was all a dreadful mistake, that their son was alive and would wake up soon. I wanted to promise them a miracle, but the miracles aren't in my hands—' He closed his eyes.

'Andrew—' She reached out and touched him again, gently. He opened his eyes and looked at her with weary despair. 'I'm becoming afraid,' he whispered. 'And how can I work if I'm afraid?'

Never before had she known him admit to fear or doubt. It broke down her defences, and without thinking whether she was being wise she gathered him into her arms. Miracles weren't in her power either, or she would have performed a dozen for him. She would gladly have lifted the weights that were crushing him, given him everything, even herself if that was what he wanted.

She caressed him with passionate tenderness, murmuring anything she could think of to comfort him. 'You're not really afraid, my dear. It's only tiredness.'

'But it goes on and on,' he whispered. 'And there's no rest. It's not the work, it's the responsibility—people's lives in your hands. That's the one thing I never thought of in those days.'

'Those days,' she said longingly.

'Do you remember how it was then?' he murmured against her hair. 'How confident I was—no, not just confident, arrogant, cocky!'

'I thought it was wonderful,' she said with a remembering smile. 'You were like a king, so sure of yourself.'

'But I shouldn't have been. I never saw the traps I was laying for myself.'

'Nor did I,' she said gently. 'I don't suppose we ever do.'

'Not until it's too late.' He rested his head against her.

'Do you have nights like this very often?' she asked, stroking his hair.

'Yes. That's one reason I started to stay at the flat. It's better to be alone when this happens.'

'No,' she said swiftly. 'It's never better to be alone. Haven't you learned that? I have.'

'How?'

'Through being alone,' she said simply.

'Funny. In all those years I never pictured you alone.'

His voice was so quiet that she had to strain to hear it. 'What—did you say?' she asked after a moment.

'You were so lovely and full of life—it was what drew me to you—I couldn't stay away—'

'Did you want to?'

'Yes. I kept trying to be strong, but it was no use.'

'I wish I'd known. I always thought of you as so aloof. Andrew?'

Silence. He had fallen asleep against her shoulder.

Moving very carefully, she swung her legs up onto the bed and lay down, drawing him beside her. He made a sound between a grunt and a sigh, turning slightly so that his weight was half across her, his head between her breasts. The bed was so narrow that she was forced to lie pressed up to him, intensely aware of his hard body, now relaxed against hers.

She held him lightly until he began to mutter again, and then she tightened her arms, whispering wordless comfort until the tension went out of him and he fell silent once more.

She stared into the darkness, thinking how achingly ironic it was that he should lie with her now, and not twelve years ago. Then her young body had clamoured for him. Now the ache of desire was there again, but tempered with understanding, and even compassion. She was no longer a girl thinking of her own wishes, but a woman who'd been through the mill and wanted to give him anything that would make his life sweeter.

When he moved again she kissed him, very softly and tenderly, and was pleased when he immediately calmed again. She kissed him again and felt his arms tighten.

'It's all right,' she whispered. 'I'm here.'

She didn't know if he could hear her but she murmured to him again, not words but wordless sounds of comfort, stroking her fingers gently against his hair, his face.

'This is how it should have been,' she told him softly. 'We should always have been like this—if only I'd understood—'

In her mind she saw again the time they'd landed on the little island and lain blissfully under the trees, until she'd broken their bliss by trying to claim him as a lover, and blaming him when he'd refused. Two selfish husbands had taught her the value of a man who'd loved her more than his own pleasure, a man she'd thrown away.

'You were thinking of me, but I didn't know it,' she murmured. 'And when I understood it was all too late. We had something so wonderful and special. I know it now. I used to tell you that I loved you but I didn't know what the words meant. But I could tell you now, if only I could be sure that you wanted to hear. Oh, darling, such things I could say to you now!'

He stirred again and she held her breath, wondering if he'd heard her. He seemed to be still asleep but his hands moved across her body. She should wake him now, and stop him doing this, but the excitement he was setting off confused her.

She wished that she were wearing something beautiful, a glamorous, flimsy concoction such as a woman chose for her lover. The nightgown she had on was made of cotton, and buttoned up to the neck. Its matronly style fitted the way she saw herself these days, but it was out of keeping with the fierce sensations that were coursing through her.

His fingers had found her buttons, were undoing the top one, then the next and the next. She did the rest herself, wrenching at them so fast that the last one flew off. It was she too who pulled the sheet back so that her nakedness lay next to his.

'Ellie…' The word was a whisper.

'Yes, darling, I'm here. Hold onto me.'

She clung to him too, kissing him without restraint, loving him with the pent-up love of years. 'Hold me,' she repeated.

His mouth covered hers eagerly. She welcomed him in, offering her whole self, keeping nothing back. Whatever he needed now, that was what she wanted to give.

He moved like a man urgently pursuing something he had long desired. His hands seemed to know instinctively how to find her, roving lovingly over the hills and valleys of her shape. Now she too was free to explore him and sense what she'd only suspected before, the power of him, the taut hardness of his muscles. He had been designed to please a woman, and everything in her responded.

He kissed her breasts, first one then the other, his tongue caressing her gently, teasing the nipples to peaks of desire.

She'd never known that anything could feel this good. She was coming into her own, claiming what had always truly been hers. She reached for him.

And then Andrew raised his head. His eyes opened.

And with brutal suddenness the dream was over. She saw the shock in his face as he realised what was happening, heard his horrified cry of, 'My God, *no*!'

CHAPTER NINE

ANDREW wrenched himself out of Elinor's arms and for a moment he covered his eyes with his hand, as though engulfed by some feeling that was too much for him. Bitterly she realised that he couldn't even bear to look at her.

'Andrew—' she said desperately.

'No, for pity's sake! Ellie, this isn't the way I wanted it, can't you understand?'

'I'm sorry,' she said, scarlet with embarrassment. 'I didn't mean to—'

'It's my fault. I shouldn't have come here tonight. It's not fair on you.'

She could hear him talking fast, trying to put a different light on this, anything rather than admit that he'd found himself with a woman he didn't want. It was part of his kindness, she thought wretchedly, to try to make her feel better, but nothing could do that.

She was frantically buttoning up her nightdress, keeping her head down, but she was still aware of hasty movements as he covered his nakedness.

'Dear God!' she wept.

'Ellie, please believe me, I didn't come here for this. When I arrived tonight I was going to explain, and then leave. That would have been best for both of us, and I swear it's what I meant.'

'Stop, stop!' she said in an agony of shame. 'Do you think anything you say now can make it right? You're right, you shouldn't have come here. No, no, I didn't mean that. It was my fault. I shouldn't have called you, I shouldn't have come to this house. I should have realised that "Mr Martin" was an invention. I'm not a child to believe in Santa Claus.'

'Don't blame yourself. It was something I wanted to do for you.'

'Why?' she demanded. 'Why should you do anything at all for me? You hate me. You have done for years.'

'I've never hated you.'

'Oh, no, you rise above that, don't you?' she raged. She didn't know why she was turning her temper on him, except that it made her pain more bearable. 'Simple revenge would be beneath you, but heaping coals of fire on my head is different. Was that what it was all about? Make me realise what I threw away? Make me really regret it? Was that the idea? Because if so it was unworthy of you.'

'Ellie, what is this?'

'You know very well what it's about. I really made a fool of myself, didn't I? Just like I did once before, remember, that day on the island? And you turned away from me then, too. You'd think I'd learn, wouldn't you?'

'That other time was different. There was love then. But this—'

'What about "this"? I made a fool of myself again. Or did you make a fool of me? Because that makes us quits, doesn't it? After all this time you finally did it.'

'Stop it, for pity's sake!'

She didn't hear him. 'So let me tell you the rest, then you can really enjoy it. Jack Smith was a drunk who knocked me around, and Tom Landers was a control freak who walked out on me when Hetta was ill. And all the time I knew it was my own fault and I was being punished for what I did to you—'

His hand over her mouth cut her off. Nothing else would have done so. She was adrift in another world where there was only the sound of her own voice saying terrible things to silence her agony of embarrassment.

'You must be mad to talk like this,' he said, dropping his hand and taking her by the shoulders. 'What have I done to deserve it? You make me sound like a monster of spite, and if that's really what you think then I'm surprised you waste two seconds on me.'

'I didn't mean that,' she choked.

'I think you did. I think you're coming out with all the hostility you spared me twelve years ago. Maybe I really did have a lucky escape. Or maybe we both did.'

Silence. He dropped his hands. They stared at each other, aghast.

A shudder went through him. He moved away from her and spoke over his shoulder.

'Let's call it a day. We've both said things tonight that should never have been said, and we have to forget them. In fact we have to forget everything that's happened. It was a mistake to think we could meet each other as though the past didn't exist.'

'Yes,' she said bleakly.

He turned slightly, making a visible effort to pull himself together. 'I'm sorry for everything. You have enough to bear without me adding to it. Go back and get some sleep now. I apologise for disturbing you.'

'Please don't mention it,' she said politely.

Somehow she got out of the room. She made it along the corridor to her own room, shut the door and sank onto the bed, overtaken by violent shivering. She was cold, so cold.

If only she could cry. But no tears would come. She felt she'd cried her last tear long ago.

She meant to be downstairs first next day, but Andrew was there before her, in the kitchen, making coffee. He smiled briefly and set one before her.

'Thank you for letting me stay,' he said politely. 'I needed that sleep.'

He still looked jaded and she wondered how much sleep he'd managed to get after she'd left.

'You're really doing double duty, aren't you?' she managed to say. 'Isn't Sir Elmer back from the flu yet?'

'It turned nasty and he was away longer than we expected, but with any luck he'll be back this week. It'll give me a chance to catch up with my paperwork.'

'And your sleep,' she suggested.

'True. We're none of us at our best when we're overtired, but it's pointless to dwell on those times.'

He was shifting his armour firmly back in place, telling her to forget that she'd seen his weakness, that he'd briefly clung to her and then calamity had engulfed them both.

'Elinor, I want you to understand—'

'It's all right, I understand perfectly.'

'I don't think you do. You were very kind to me last night. You gave me a warmth and comfort I'd almost forgotten existed. But kindness can only go so far, and I never meant to make demands on you.'

'Andrew, please—'

'Wait, let me finish. Last night I said I wasn't going to use your troubles as an excuse to force my presence on you, and barely a few hours later—it was unforgivable of me, and I apologise for my behaviour.'

'It wasn't your fault,' she said in a dead voice. 'You were asleep.'

'I can't justify myself that easily. Because of Hetta, because I was the one lucky enough to be able to help her, you seem to feel that you owe me something, and that you had to repay it. I promise you that isn't so. You owe me nothing, and the last thing I would ever want is that kind of gratitude.'

He was subtly rewriting the facts. In this new version she hadn't thrown herself at him and earned his contempt. It was he who had imposed on her. She wondered if he thought he was making it easier for her. If so, he was wrong. She felt as though she were dying inside. She would have stopped him if she could, but she had no strength to move or speak.

'I promise you nothing like it will ever happen again,' he continued. 'You'll be glad to know that this will be my last visit.' He checked his watch. 'I must be going. Say goodbye to Hetta for me.'

'Let me fetch her. She'll hate it that she missed you.'

'I examined her last night and found her in good shape. The district nurse will continue to call—'

'That's not what I meant. You've been nice to her; she likes you. Let me fetch her.'

'No, I'm in a bit of a hurry.'

'Then come to see us again.'

'I don't think so,' he said harshly, closing his briefcase and not looking at her. 'I'm glad we got matters sorted out, but there's no need—I mean, it would be better if we didn't see each other again. Wouldn't it?'

'Yes,' she said sadly. 'Perhaps it would.'

She followed him into the hall where he put on his jacket, collected his briefcase and went to the door.

'Thank you again,' he said formally. 'I hope you keep well. Please remain here for as long as you wish.'

In a moment the door of his exquisite car had closed behind him, the engine purred into life, and he vanished down the winding drive. Elinor watched him go with a sense of desolation. She knew he'd finally shut a door on her.

As she turned back into the house she saw her daughter descending the stairs slowly. Hetta's face showed that she'd seen him go.

'He didn't wait, Mummy,' she said in a voice of disillusion.

'No, darling. He couldn't.'

'Doesn't he like us after all?'

'He likes you to bits,' Elinor said, giving Hetta a hug. 'Now come on, let's have breakfast.'

For the first time ever her daughter's company was a strain. She wanted to be alone to think, and to cry. But somehow she got through the day without Hetta suspecting anything amiss, and then it was evening and she could go to her room, shut the door, and give way to her anguish.

If only she could blot out the sight of his eyes when he'd opened them, his horror when he'd seen who had been in his arms, his appalled cry of *'No!'* Perhaps he had another woman now, one he loved. And he'd awoken to find himself in the arms of a woman he hadn't chosen, one he now probably despised. That thought made her curl herself up into a tight little ball, as though by doing so she could vanish from her own eyes.

How could she have thought that she had anything to attract him now? But she hadn't been thinking of herself, only of him and his needs, and she'd opened her arms to him in defenceless love.

Love. She resisted the word, but it wouldn't let her go. It was too late now to protest that her love should never have been allowed to live again.

For it didn't live again. It had never died. Through twelve lonely years it had hidden away in a place she couldn't bear to visit, calling to her with a voice she'd refused to hear, waiting for the day it could seize her again. And this time there would be no escape.

After a few days she no longer strained her ears for the sound of a car. He wasn't coming back, and she couldn't stay here. Hetta was well enough for a move, and Andrew's generosity meant that she had enough money to cushion them for a while. It galled her to have to rely on his money, but at least she wouldn't accept any more.

She called Daisy, living in a comfortable little hotel near the boarding house, now being rebuilt. The hotel would have a twin room vacant next week, and Daisy reserved it for them. Hetta was in two minds over the move, sad to be leaving, but glad to see Daisy again.

She wrote Andrew a polite letter, thanking him for his kindness but explaining that she could no longer impose on him. She ended it, 'Yours sincerely, Elinor Landers (Mrs).'

In return she received a blunt note saying, 'There's no need for this. You should reconsider. A.'

She wrote back, 'Thank you, but my mind is made up. Elinor Landers.'

There was no reply.

The days began to narrow down. Four days, then three, then two, one. She would be gone soon and the last connection between them broken. Hetta would need one more visit to the hospital, but doubtless Andrew would depute another doctor to see her.

On the last day, while Hetta was upstairs, unpacking and repacking some toys for the umpteenth time, Elinor went around the garden, trying to be strong-minded and not let herself feel wretched. She knew she'd done the right, the only thing, but the voice of the tempter whispered that she could have stayed a little longer, and perhaps seen him just once more.

Then she thought how that meeting would be: full of the remembered humiliation of their last encounter. Was that pain worth it, just to see him one more time?

Yes, anything was worth it.

As she headed back to the house Elinor became aware that there was someone else in the garden. It was a tall, dark-haired woman, expensively dressed and with an air of ease that came from always having money. Elinor had seen that look often enough in her customers. The stranger watched her approach, unabashed at being discovered intruding. A few feet away Elinor stopped and the two women regarded each other.

'Who are you?' they both said.

The woman laughed. 'I'll answer first, although I don't know why I should, since it's my home.'

'This—? You're—?'

'I'm Myra Blake. And I should have said this *used* to be my home. I moved most of my things out months ago. It doesn't really bother me who's here now, but, just for the record, who are you?'

'I'm Elinor Landers,' she said carefully.

'And when did Andrew move you in? I must say, this kind of caper isn't normally in his line. Too much of a puritan. In fact, that's what—well, it's old history.'

'I'm only here because he operated on my little girl,' Elinor hastened to say, 'and while she was in hospital our home burned down. I had nowhere else to go, and he was very kind.'

Myra Blake gave a crack of laughter. 'Oh, yes, of course. I was forgetting how often he takes in waifs and strays from the hospital.' Her voice was heavy with irony.

'Mrs Blake, I promise you this isn't how it looks. Besides I shall be l—'

'Good grief, what do I care how it looks? Let's go inside and you can make me some tea.'

She turned and led the way to the house, the picture of confidence. Elinor followed, her head in a spin. But since Myra Blake wasn't flustered by the situation she determined that she wouldn't be either.

She made tea and carried it into the room overlooking the garden where Myra had removed her luxurious cashmere coat and tossed it onto a chair. She'd seated herself on the sofa and now leaned back, surveying Elinor from dark eyes that gleamed with malicious fun. She was lovely, with black shining hair, cut elegantly and just touching her shoulders. As a beautician Elinor had become a connoisseur of other women's looks, and professionally she had to admire Myra. Her legs were long and elegant, sheathed in black silk and ending in impossibly high heels. Her curvaceous figure looked as though she worked hard keeping it trim, her complexion was perfect and her face had been made up with great skill.

So this woman had been Andrew's wife, had shared his life, his home, his bed. He'd said it hadn't been a happy marriage, even implied that he'd married cynically, but at some point he must surely have been enraptured by her beauty, and whispered words of passion into her ears as they'd danced at their wedding.

'Smashing!' Myra said suddenly, and Elinor stared at hearing the down-to-earth word from this picture of elegance. 'Smashing tea! Best I ever tasted.' She was sipping enthusiastically.

'I'm glad you like it, Mrs Blake,' Elinor said politely, seating herself.

'Myra, please.'

'Myra, there's a lot I don't understand.'

'Like how I just managed to walk in? I still have a key.' She leaned forward to put her cup on the low table, but suddenly she stopped, frowning as she looked at Elinor. 'Have we ever met before?'

'No, never.'

'Funny, you look familiar somehow. Never mind. So what am I doing here? I want to collect a few things that I left. And I thought Andrew might be around somewhere, although I can't imagine why. He never *was* around. I need to talk to him. So come on, tell me. What gives?'

'What gives?'

'You and Andrew.'

'There is no me and Andrew,' she said firmly. 'My daughter needed a heart transplant. She was originally a patient of Sir Elmer Rylance.'

'My uncle,' Myra said casually.

'Yes, I know.'

'Andrew told you that much, then. Go on.'

'He was ill when a heart became available for my daughter, so Andrew did the operation. And, as I told you, my home caught fire—'

'And he played the Good Samaritan. Well, well!' Myra was looking her over with a look that was hard to read, amused, cynical, but not unfriendly.

'It's a wonderful place for Hetta,' Elinor urged. 'So quiet and peaceful, which is what she needs to recover—'

'And Andrew here to keep an eye on her.'

'He doesn't live here,' Elinor said quickly.

'But he visits?'

'Only once to see how we were doing. It's just Hetta and me. He says he has this little apartment near the hospital—'

'Oh, sure, I know it. A real monk's cell. He spent most of his time there even when we were officially together. When he did come back it was just to see Simon, our son. Don't look like that. I don't suppose I'm telling you anything you didn't know. Andrew's obviously discussed me with you. Hell, I don't mind! In fact it rather suits me. Did he tell you I was getting married again?'

'No.'

'Well, I am. Cyrus Hellerman from Detroit. He's big in motors, and I mean *big*.'

'A millionaire?'

'Please! A million dollars gets you nowhere these days. Multi-multi-multi, if you know what I mean.'

'I think I do,' Elinor said. 'This wasn't enough, then?' She indicated the house.

'This? Nice little cottage, but I felt the need to spread my wings. Enter Cyrus. His wife had died a few months back, he was lonely, and why hang around?'

'For someone else to snap him up?'

'Right,' Myra said, unabashed. 'Of course, Andrew is very successful in his way, and when I married him I was really in awe of him. Uncle Elmer said he was the best of his generation, but he had some funny ideas. He's never made as much money as he should have done because he does so much for free. Well, I respect that. I really do. But it got kind of boring when I wanted to remodel the house.'

'What did Uncle Elmer say about his unpaid work?'

'He was all for it. Said it enhanced Andrew's reputation.'

'But if he was helping people for nothing surely he was thinking of them, not himself?'

'Oh, please! I got all that high-minded stuff from him. I can't tell you how desperate I was to get away from it.' She looked at Elinor suspiciously. 'Are you high-minded?'

'Andrew has just saved my daughter's life, so I'm bound to be a bit high-minded about what he does.'

'Uh-huh! Well, I guess you can't help it, then,' Myra said, as though excusing some social flaw. 'I'm not that way myself.'

'But don't you come from a medical family?'

'Yes, and I can't tell you how that stuff got on my wick all these years. Andrew briefly made me find it acceptable, but the fact is that I misread him as he misread me, and the best thing we ever did was get a divorce.'

'But what about your son?'

'I'm coming to him. You could do me a favour.' She spoke as though it were a given that Elinor would want to. 'Simon is seven years old. What about your little girl?'

'Seven too. And thanks to Andrew she's going to be eight, and nine, and ten.'

'Uncle Elmer says he's the best surgeon he knows for operating on young children. It's a special skill, because everything's so small. Oddly enough, he's good at talking to them as well.'

'Why is that odd?'

'Because his own son is a closed book to him. Mind you, it would help if he spent some more time with him.'

'But there must be so many demands on him. Surely he manages as much as he can.'

'What do you know about it? Were you there on Simon's fifth birthday? Or his sixth, come to that. Have you seen the look on that child's face when his father has put him last yet again? Andrew's digging the grave of that relationship, and if I was the bitch some people think I am I'd sit back and let him do it. As it is, I'm here to do him a favour.'

CHAPTER TEN

MYRA waited for an answer to this last remark, but Elinor decided to play it safe with silence. She was apprehensive about the 'favour' Myra was proposing to do for Andrew. To her relief Myra didn't pursue the point.

'What do you think of this house?' she asked, going to look out of the window to where the garden was at its best.

'I love it.'

'Where are you sleeping?'

Dangerous ground. 'Well, I—'

'I expect you're in my room. It's a hoot, isn't it? That was my Victorian period, except for the bathroom, which was my Egyptian period. If I'd stayed on here I'd have changed them both. Is your daughter around now?'

'She's upstairs,' Elinor said, disconcerted by the abrupt change of subject. 'Oh, no, I think that's her.'

There was a noise in the hall, and the next moment Hetta wandered in, a toy in each hand, and with a cheerful smile that brightened as she saw a visitor.

'Come here, darling,' Elinor called.

Hetta came to her side and stood regarding the visitor with a wide-eyed stare that would have disconcerted someone less at ease than Myra.

'I'm Myra,' she said. 'I used to live here, and I've just been making friends with your mummy.'

'How do you do?' Hetta said politely.

'Do you like it here?'

Hetta nodded.

'Must be a bit lonely, though,' Myra suggested. 'No kids of your own age. No animals. Do you like dogs?'

Hetta nodded again with unmistakable eagerness.

'Then you'd get on well with my son, Simon. He's your age and he's got a puppy. Care to meet him?'

'And the puppy?' Hetta asked at once.

'And the puppy.' Myra flicked open a cell phone and spoke into it. 'OK, Joe.'

Elinor's suspicions were rising by the minute. 'Now, wait a moment—'

'You don't mind my son meeting your daughter, do you?' Myra asked with a touch of wide-eyed reproach.

'It's not that—'

'I really think they'll like each other, and it would mean a lot to him. Ah, there you are, darling!'

A boy of Hetta's age, accompanied by a uniformed chauffeur, had appeared in the door. Elinor drew a slow breath. This was a younger version of Andrew, not in his looks, which were more like Myra's, but in the stillness with which he held himself, the way he looked around the room, taking everything in, but saying nothing.

'This is Simon,' Myra said.

Elinor went forward to him. 'Hallo, I'm—I'm Ellie.' What had made her say that?

'How do you do?' he said politely. He started to offer his hand and remembered that he was holding the puppy. Hetta was there in a flash to relieve him of it.

Elinor introduced them. They were cautious about each other, but the puppy was an immediate bond and after a moment they drifted into a corner together. Elinor could see that Hetta was delighted, and so could Myra. She was watching them with a satisfied expression.

'This is just perfect,' she said. 'All right, Joe, go and get yourself something to eat in the village. I'll call you when I need you.'

The chauffeur nodded and departed.

'Do you mean,' Elinor asked, outraged, 'that you've kept your son sitting out there in the car while you came in here to—to—?'

'Survey the land,' Myra said. 'Of course. It wouldn't have been very nice to bring him in before I knew what he might find, would it? I brought him with me just in case the things I'd heard about you were true. Be prepared, that's my motto.'

'And just what have you heard about me?'

'That you had a kid of your own, same age as Simon, and that you were a good mother. Looks true to me. Otherwise I'd just have taken him away again.'

'Myra, what have you got in mind?'

'Well, my life is getting a bit complicated. Cyrus wants to get married in the next couple of weeks because of some motor show or other, and I need to get out there fast.'

'So take Simon with you.'

'On my honeymoon? Get real. Besides, it's time Andrew really made an effort with his son. It's always been too easy for him to duck out. This time he isn't going to.'

'And you're just going to dump him?' Elinor demanded, speaking quietly, lest Simon heard.

Instead of answering direct Myra said, 'Nurse Stewart's been talking. I gather it was a bit like a French farce that night, you skulking in Andrew's office or under a blanket in the back seat of his car. That bit didn't come from Stewart, but from someone in the parking lot. And one of the district nurses knows this house is Andrew's. I have friends at the hospital and they've kept me informed. It all became very intriguing and I got curious. It's so unlike him.'

'You mean I've made a scandal for him? Oh, no!'

'I suppose it is potentially scandalous,' Myra mused. 'Of course, you're not Andrew's patient but your daughter is, and all this dodging around in car parks is something his enemies could make something of. Andrew's got a lot of enemies. Brilliant people always do, and especially now that Uncle Elmer's heading for retirement. His illness took a lot out of him, so he'll probably go quite soon now. The contenders are lining up to take his place, and malicious tongues are all ready to wag.'

Elinor listened to this with mounting horror. She'd never meant to harm Andrew, but that was what she seemed to have done. But Myra, watching her, gave a cheeky smile.

'Don't worry, *I'm* not malicious, and I won't make trouble. My word on it, and you really can trust my word. I may be superficial and tinselly—guess who called me that?—but when I make a promise I keep it.'

For some reason Elinor believed her.

'But why are you being like this?' she asked. 'I don't understand.'

'You mean why aren't I jealous that he moved another lady in here?'

'You've nothing to be jea—'

'Skip it. You'd have expected a fit, jealous or otherwise. Sorry. Can't oblige. Oh, there was a time when I thought the sun shone out of Andrew, but that was before I discovered what a bore he was.'

'A bore? Andrew?' The exclamation was jerked out of Elinor.

'There, I knew you were high-minded!' Myra exclaimed as though she'd scored a victory. 'Good luck to you. Actually this rather suits me.'

Elinor pulled herself together. This woman's determination to arrange life to suit herself had a hypnotic quality.

'I'm sorry, but you're under a misapprehension,' she said firmly. 'Hetta and I are leaving tomorrow.'

'Damn! Have you and Andrew quarrelled?'

'No,' Elinor said stiffly.

'Has he thrown you out?'

'No.'

'Then why are you leaving?'

'Because Hetta is greatly improved and it's time to move on.'

'Why?'

'I'm sorry, I can't discuss that with you.'

'Where are you going?'

'I don't see why I should dis—'

'Oh, nonsense, of course you can. This is important. Have you got somewhere better than this?'

'No, we're going to a small hotel where I have a friend living. She owned the boarding house that burned down but it'll soon be rebuilt so—'

'You're dumping Andrew for a boarding house? C'mon! Stay here. It's much nicer.'

'That's not the point,' Elinor said, feeling desperate. It was like trying to argue with a juggernaut. 'Even if I weren't going you couldn't just leave Simon here without telling Andrew first.'

'Then let's tell him. You call him up while I make us something to eat.'

Elinor watched helplessly as Myra whisked herself into the kitchen and set about preparing. There was no doubt she was the expert cook for whom the place had been created. She started with milk shakes for the children, who downed them eagerly.

'Go in the garden, kids, and I'll have something more filling for you in a minute,' she called. To Elinor she said, 'Go on, get calling.'

There was nothing to do but obey, although she flinched at the thought of calling a man who'd made it so clear that she embarrassed him. She used the hall phone, and in a few moments she heard Andrew's voice, terse, commanding. 'Yes?'

'It's me,' she said. 'I'm sorry to disturb you at work but something's happened.'

'Hetta?'

'No, Myra, your ex-wife. She's here, and she's got Simon with her. And I think she means him to stay when she goes.'

'I don't understand.'

'She's going to America to get married, and she's not taking him.'

'Put her on,' he snapped.

Elinor returned to the kitchen. 'Andrew wants to talk to you.'

'Sorry, I'm too busy.'

'You can't be. It's what you came here for.'

'No way. I didn't come here for a phone conversation with Andrew. I can do that anywhere. Where's the raspberry sauce? You've moved it.'

'Top shelf. Please come and talk to him.'

'Nope. It was handier on the middle shelf.'

'Not for me. Hetta doesn't like it.'

'Simon adores it with ice cream and milk shake. I'll have some sent to you, but don't let him make a pig of himself. Better get back to Andrew.'

Elinor gave up and returned to the hall. 'She won't come,' she told Andrew.

She could hear him grinding his teeth. 'Tell her—'

She returned to Myra and spoke in a carefully expressionless voice. 'He says stop playing damn fool games and pick up the phone.'

Myra gave a rich crow of laughter. 'Don't worry, I won't embarrass you by responding in kind.'

To Elinor's relief Myra went out into the hall. But she merely hung up the phone and returned to the kitchen. 'No point in arguing,' she explained airily. 'He just doesn't listen.'

The telephone immediately rang and Elinor raced to snatch it up. 'It's not my fault,' she said, harassed.

'I know that. All right, please tell her I'll be over this evening. Are you all right? Is she making herself unpleasant?'

'No,' Elinor said wryly. 'I think she's a little crazy, but not unpleasant.'

She found Myra in the garden with the children, who were playing with the puppy. She had a moment to watch them unobserved, and hear Hetta's giggles of glee.

Then Myra hailed her. 'You stay here while I finish doing the eats,' she said. 'I'll yell when I'm ready.' She headed back to the house.

'Mummy, look at the puppy,' Hetta called. 'His name's Fudge.'

'That's because he's that pale brown colour,' Simon put in.

Fudge promptly squatted on the ground and produced an enormous puddle.

'He's nervous at being in a new place,' Simon hurried to say. 'And he's out in the garden. He *is* house-trained.' Honesty made him add, 'Well, sort of.'

She felt sad for the child, feeling the need to placate her. This was more his house than hers. What sort of a life had he had, between a distant father and the selfish, manipulative mother?

Hetta and Simon were already at ease with each other. He seemed to be a quiet, gentle child, and she couldn't help realising that he would be the ideal playmate for Hetta. She, for her part, had already given him the ultimate token of friendship, hauling up her T-shirt and displaying her wound with enormous pride. Simon had been suitably impressed.

At last Myra called, 'Come and get it!' and they all trooped to the house where she'd laid the table out on the patio.

The meal was a roaring success. Myra was skilled and imaginative, and she knew how to appeal to children. It was hard to dislike her. She was a tough cookie, who seemed to have little in the way of finer feelings. But she was good-natured, and had an outgoing quality that made her company pleasant for a while. Elinor guessed she liked everyone around her to be happy, and would even put herself out to achieve it— as long as she was sure of getting her own way in the end.

She also had a gift for telling a funny story. Despite her unease about Andrew's imminent arrival, Elinor found herself smiling at the tale of Fudge and a donkey. The children hooted with laughter.

They were like that when Andrew came in.

He'd meant to ring the front doorbell, but finding the side gate to the garden open he'd walked around the house until he'd heard laughing voices. Nobody heard him arrive, and he had a moment to stand, taking in the cheerful scene in which he had no part.

It was Elinor who saw him first, glancing up just before he controlled his expression. She rose and the movement alerted the attention of the others. Hetta beamed. Myra regarded him with a cynical smile. Simon looked pleased but uncertain what to expect. Andrew gave a brief nod in his direction, and an even briefer smile. Unease radiated from him.

'Good evening, Myra,' he said.

'You're just in time for some coffee, Andrew. Let's go in, it's getting a little chilly.'

When they had all moved into the living room Myra said, 'Kids, why don't you go and watch television upstairs?'

'I'll go too,' Elinor said hastily.

'Better if you stay,' Myra observed. 'Andrew and I can only take so much of each other's company undiluted.'

Elinor looked at Andrew. 'Please stay,' he requested.

When the children had gone upstairs, clutching Fudge, the three of them surveyed each other uneasily. Elinor felt almost overwhelmed by the bittersweet shock of Andrew's presence after she had accepted that she would never see him again. But she tried to keep a clear head, sensing she was going to need all her wits about her in the next few minutes.

'Myra, if you've come to make trouble—' Andrew began.

'But I haven't. When did I ever make trouble?'

'I won't answer that.'

'When you two have finished quarrelling, it's the kids' bedtime, and I need to know where Simon's sleeping,' Elinor said firmly.

'But here, of course,' Myra said sweetly. 'In his father's house.'

'With no warning?' Andrew snapped. 'You must be out of your mind.'

'Well, it's very simple. I'm off to Detroit to marry Cyrus, and really I can't take a little boy on my honeymoon, even if he wanted to come, which he very sensibly doesn't. He's thrilled at the thought of staying with you. You've let him down so often, but not this time.'

'Do you think I have time to care for a child?'

'Not you. Your girlfriend.'

'Ellie—Mrs Landers—is not my girlfriend, as you so vulgarly put it.'

'Nothing vulgar in having a girlfriend. It's about time you thought of something other than a scalpel.'

'If anybody's interested, I am leaving tomorrow morning,' Elinor said desperately.

'No, you're not,' Myra said airily. 'We settled all that.'

'Did we?' Elinor asked blankly.

'Be nice to her, Andrew. She's going to get you out of a hole.' She turned to Elinor. 'You don't mind getting him out of a hole, do you, Ellie? I can call you Ellie, can't I?'

'No,' Andrew said harshly.

Myra became businesslike. 'Look, it's very simple. Simon is going to stay with you for a while. He's here now, he's got all his stuff, and he's looking forward to it. But if you refuse, then I'll take him away with me now, and he'll come with me to Detroit, and he'll stay there. For good. I swear you'll never see him again.'

He stared at her in a fury. 'You're bluffing.'

'I'm doing you a favour, forcing you to engage with your son before it's too late. So what happens? Do I take him away from you for good?'

'You know I won't let you do that.'

'Fine. He stays here.'

'You've already heard Mrs Landers say that she's leaving,' Andrew said in a tight voice.

'Then you'll have to persuade her to stay, won't you? I'm making some more coffee. Anybody want some?' She floated into the kitchen, as much at ease as though this were a social occasion.

Andrew could hardly look at Elinor.

'What do you want me to do?' she asked.

'I can't let her take him away for good, but if you leave she'll do that,' he said harshly.

She hesitated, torn. 'I don't think she really means that bit.'

'When she makes a threat she carries it out. *Help me, Ellie, for God's sake!*'

'But what use can I be?'

'Stay here. Let him live with you and Hetta.'

'But it's you he wants.'

'I'll visit as often as I can.'

'That's not enough.'

He met her eyes. 'Then I'll move back in.'

'Let us understand each other,' she said in a voice that was steadier than she felt. 'You wish me to be your housekeeper and child-minder.'

'Whatever you want to call it,' he said impatiently. 'Does it matter?'

'Yes, it matters. It will be impossible unless we define our precise relationship.'

'Very well. Housekeeper and child-minder.'

'And you will give me a proper contract of employment, defining my precise duties, and my salary?'

'Very well.'

'All right,' she said very quietly. 'I'll do it.'

It would be hard. He saw her as a convenience. But at least now she need not leave him for a while. Her heart would break in the end. But not just yet.

Myra returned with coffee, which neither of the others wanted.

'Got it all sorted?' she sang out. 'Jolly good. By the way, Andrew, Simon thinks you invited him. Don't let him guess otherwise.'

'Don't worry, he won't,' Elinor said. 'I'll see to that.' She was beginning to reappraise Myra.

Myra beamed at her. 'I knew you wouldn't let me down.' She flicked open her cell phone. 'Joe? You can come for me in fifteen minutes.' She hung up. 'I'll go and say goodbye to Simon.'

She tripped away, apparently oblivious to the tension between the other two.

'Thank you,' he said. 'I can't think straight. She just sprung this on me—'

'Well, maybe she needed to,' Elinor observed lightly.

'You're on her side?'

'I'm on your little boy's side. I think he's getting a raw deal. He's much too quiet and docile for his age. When is he ever naughty?'

'I don't know.'

'I'll bet he never is. And he ought to be. Come on, let's go.' She headed for the door.

'Where are we going?'

'Upstairs, so that he can see you and Myra together, and know that you're in complete accord about his being here. I think you should stand together, and if possible put your arm around her shoulders. And smile at her.'

'That's a lot to ask.'

'It's not really, but even if it is, he's your son. Isn't he worth the effort?'

'Of course, but—'

'Then do it,' she said in a voice that brooked no argument.

She didn't know what had made her take a high hand with him, unless it was the memory of Simon's face, beaming at the sight of his father, but cautiously holding back.

He followed her unwillingly upstairs and along to the room that had been Simon's and was now Hetta's.

'We're staying here after all,' she told her daughter. 'You don't mind coming in with me, do you? Then Simon can have his room back.'

'It's all right,' the little boy said at once. 'Hetta can have it, honest.'

'No, it's yours,' Hetta responded.

'You can have it.'

'No, *you* can.'

'No, *you* can.'

'We'll fight about it later,' Elinor said.

She gave Andrew a determined look and he came forward. 'How about staying here with me, son?' he said. 'Your mother and I thought it would be a good idea.'

'Can I really, Daddy?'

The child's eager face brought home to Andrew that Elinor had been right. It meant the world to Simon to think that his father wanted him. He put his arm awkwardly around Myra's shoulder. 'You don't mind letting me have him for a while, do you?'

'Not if that's what you want,' she responded.

'It's what I want.'

'Is it what Simon wants?' Elinor asked.

The little boy nodded so vigorously that it seemed as though his head might come off. Suddenly his world was full of sunshine, and his father regarded him with shock.

There was a ring on the doorbell below.

'Time for me to go,' Myra said. She gave Simon a hug, then Hetta. Then she turned her expectant gaze on Andrew, who dutifully pecked her cheek. Finally she enveloped Elinor in a scented embrace.

'Thank you,' she whispered in her ear. 'Good luck.'

'Trust me,' Elinor murmured back.

Then she was gone, whisked away by her chauffeur in her glossy car.

'Hetta, you and I will move your things while Simon catches up with his dad,' Elinor said. 'Why don't you two go downstairs, and talk in peace?'

Andrew took orders from nobody except Elmer Rylance, and these days even Rylance usually deferred to him. But he sensed that Elinor knew what she was doing, and right now that made him grateful, so he followed his son downstairs and prepared to embark on a conversation where he knew he would be awkward and probably make mistakes.

Simon soon made it easier for him, smiling happily at having his father's attention, and chattering of what he'd been doing in the last few weeks. Andrew watched him with a kind of aching delight that this sharp-witted, attractive child was

his. Somewhere there must be a way to tell him so. But for
all the precise, scientific, brilliant words that hummed in his
brain, somehow he couldn't locate the right ones for this.

But tonight a kind fate was with him. Simon was in a
mood to interpret even his father's silences as interest, and
somehow they got through an hour without mishap. But he
was relieved when Elinor came down to fetch the child to
bed.

When she came down alone, twenty minutes later, she
found him pacing restlessly.

'You seemed to manage fairly well there,' she said.

'Mostly due to Simon. I don't understand, he was so different to the way he normally is with me,' he said.

'Because Myra told him you invited him.'

'She said that for her own reasons,' Andrew said scorn-
fully.

'What does it matter what her reasons were? She said
what he needed to hear, and it made him happy. All you have
to do is catch the ball and run with it.'

'If I'm taking advice I'd rather it was yours,' he said curtly.
'You seem more of a success as a mother.'

'All right, think of Samson. You told me that night that you
let your child patients believe their toys had stayed with them
because that was what they needed to think. "It's a deception, but it makes them happy." That's what you said. Why
can't you do the same for Simon?'

He stared. 'Are you suggesting that I'm only pretending
to love him? Because if so, you couldn't be more wrong.'

'Then tell him. If the love's there, *tell* him.'

'It's easy for you. You'd know how to say things like that,
but I—' He made a helpless gesture. 'When I'm dealing with
him I'm all at sea.'

'But why? He's a lovely child, and he adores you. Why
can't you just relate to him in the way that he wants?'

'Because I've never known how. At first it was because I was away so much, but then I didn't know what to say to him to make it right when I did get home.'

'Couldn't Myra have helped you?'

'By the time we realised what was wrong, Myra and I were too far apart to help each other with anything.'

'Well, she helped you this time. Andrew, you don't have very much time left to get this right. Soon he'll look elsewhere for his friends, and have his own life and interests. If you don't catch him now, it'll be too late.'

'*I know that.* But it doesn't mean I can do anything about it.' He looked at her. 'But you're here now, and it'll be all right. You won't try to leave again, will you?'

She was about to make the biggest mistake of her life. She should run now, while she still had a last chance.

'No, I won't leave,' she said. 'I'll stay as long as you need me.'

CHAPTER ELEVEN

LIFE assumed a strange, peaceful rhythm of its own. Andrew moved his things back into the house the next day, but for a while they saw little of him. His hours at the hospital were long and he was repeatedly called away for emergencies. He breakfasted with them when he could, and those meals were easier than Elinor had feared. The kids backchatted each other in a way that relieved tension and if Andrew didn't actually join in at least he listened without impatience.

Oddly there was less tension between herself and him than she had feared, which she attributed to the fact that she'd insisted on proper employment conditions and a contract. It was there in black and white. She was Mrs Elinor Landers, housekeeper and child-minder. The dreadful night he'd awoken in her arms had happened to somebody else.

Daisy had reacted strangely when Elinor had called her to tell her about the change of plan. 'That's right, love,' she said cheerfully. 'You stay there with him. You never know.'

'I'm his housekeeper,' she said firmly. 'And you couldn't be more wrong.'

'If you say so, love.'

The first time Andrew managed a reasonably early night Simon was waiting for him.

'Ellie said you might be early,' he said excitedly.

'Nine o'clock isn't early, you should be in bed, and who said you could call her Ellie?'

Simon became nervous at his father's frown. 'I thought— she said it was her name.'

He dropped to one knee so that he could look his son in the eye.

'She said that? She actually told you that her name was Ellie?'

'Yes. Isn't it?'

'Yes, it is.'

'Then—I don't understand.'

'There's a lot I don't understand myself, son. Never mind. And don't tell her about this conversation.'

As Elinor had guessed Simon was the perfect companion for Hetta. Her nature was boisterous and now that her strength was returning she could give it fuller rein. By contrast he was shy and retiring, and when they got up to mischief it was Hetta who made the running, with Simon making vain efforts to restrain her, and Fudge bringing up the rear.

Hetta had slept in her mother's room for only a couple of nights. Then Elinor had opened up the room next door to Simon's, and made it hers. But her favourite occupation was to sit with Simon at his computer. At seven he was already literate and an expert at information technology. Hetta, whose education had suffered because of her illness, was fascinated by the things he knew, and her admiration drew him out. Several times Elinor would discover a light beneath Simon's door in the late evening. Entering, she would find the two of them deep in earnest conversation, which would stop as soon as they saw her. She would simply point and Hetta would scuttle away.

'There are things we need to discuss,' she told Andrew one evening when the children were in bed.

'You're not happy with the arrangement?'

'No, it's fine, but school will be starting soon, and I'll need to organise something.'

'When Simon lived here before, he went to the school in the village. It's excellent. I suggest you enrol them both.'

'Good. One more thing.' She took a deep breath. 'When can you take some time off?'

'Goodness knows—'

'It should be in the next three weeks, before school starts, so that Simon can have you all to himself for several days.' He looked at her, and she grew annoyed. 'Surely an organised man like you can arrange suitable cover in that time? You carried Sir Elmer's load while he was sick. Tell him it's your turn.'

'This isn't the best moment for that,' he mused.

'You mean because he'll be retiring soon, the sharks are circling and your teeth are sharper than anyone's. Fine. I'll tell Simon that his father's a shark.'

'Aren't you being a little unfair?'

'No.'

He became angry. 'I really want that job. You're acting as though I'm being unreasonable.'

'You *are* being unreasonable. There are a hundred jobs. You've only got one son.'

'And what are we going to say to each other "for several days"?'

'It doesn't matter. Talk about the weather, anything. The point is that he'll know you put yourself out to be with him. That'll cover a multitude of sins, and Hetta and I will fill in the gaps.'

'Oh, you'll be there?'

She looked at him with pity. 'I wasn't planning to despatch the two of you to a desert island. Although it might do you some good.'

'Fine. You'll be here. But people still need to talk. It's hard for me to know what to say to him.'

'Who's asking you to say anything? Maybe he'd rather you listened. I expect when you're at work people listen to you, don't they?'

'Usually,' he admitted. 'Unless it's patients, and then I listen.'

'I don't think that covers this situation. You're not in the listening habit, but if you listened to what Simon wants you to hear you might be able to think of some answers. It's not rocket science.'

'No, it's more complicated than that. But you can do it, can't you?' He frowned. 'How?'

She was amused. 'Andrew, you can't take lessons in it. If you could, you'd be marvellous.'

'Yes, I'm good at anything I·can study,' he said wryly. 'And maybe you can take lessons with a first rate teacher. That's why I watch you so closely. You seem to know everything that I don't.'

'Andrew, will you tell me something? Why didn't you just let Simon go to America with Myra?'

'Because he's all I've got to love,' he said simply. 'I've made a mess of every other important relationship. I don't really know how to talk to anyone who means anything to me. Oh, I'm fine with the patients, not just the children, but the adults too. It's easy, because I know what they expect of me, and it's very limited.'

'Limited? Saving their lives?'

'In a way, yes. They come into the hospital and I can be their best friend. I chat with the children, discuss soccer scores and newspaper stories with the adults. Then we pass out of each other's lives without regret. Emotionally they expect nothing from me.'

'You weren't always like that,' she said.

'Yes, I was, potentially. With you I found a way to be different.'

'You mean, this is what I did to you?'

'I wasn't blaming you. You asked me something, and I tried to find a rational explanation.'

'Must everything be rational?'

'It usually is, in the end.'

'Andrew, do you believe that, or is it what you try to tell yourself?'

He sighed. 'Does it matter?'

When he'd gone upstairs she wandered out into the garden with Fudge, who still had matters to attend to. She waited for him, sitting on a bench under the trees.

'May I join you?' It was Andrew with two glasses of wine.

She received one gratefully and he sat down beside her, looking up at the moon, which hung low in the sky, bright and silver. It was a night for lovers, but just now she felt only contentment.

'By the way,' she said after a moment, 'don't forget a wedding present for Myra.'

'Why would I want to do that? She's getting her hands on the Hellerman millions.'

'It's in the cause of good relations. It'll make Simon happy.'

'Then I'll do it. Or rather you'll do it.'

'No, Simon will do it. He's searched the Internet and found a great store in Detroit. All he needs now is your credit card.'

'Fine. I trust you to make sure he doesn't clean me out.'

Through Simon's daily phone calls with Myra they followed the progress of her wedding. Backed by Cyrus's gold card she'd embarked on a spending spree, not always with happy results. A dozen pictures of her in various prospective wedding outfits turned up on Simon's computer. He and Hetta regarded them with awe, which Elinor fully understood when she joined them. Andrew returned one evening to find the three of them gazing at the screen.

'Something interesting?' he asked, walking over. 'Why is your mother in a scarlet satin dress?'

'To get married in?' Simon said, making it a question.

'Really.' Andrew pursed his lips and said no more. To Elinor's pleasure, man and boy regarded each other in silent masculine sympathy.

With Elinor's guidance Simon had chosen some elegant silver for the wedding gift. Myra was genuinely pleased, pretending to believe the fiction that Andrew had thought of it. She even sent him an email saying thank you, which Simon presented to him with pride.

At last the wedding pictures themselves arrived. Myra had avoided red satin and purple velvet in favour of a comparatively restrained dress of ivory brocade. Everything else was over the top, including six bridesmaids and four pageboys who, for no discernible reason, were dressed in highland kilts.

'Are you sorry you weren't there?' Andrew asked his son.

Simon gave him a speaking look. 'Mum would have wanted me to be a page-boy.'

'Then you were definitely better off out of it.'

Every day Elinor set her mind to finding ways to help Andrew connect with his son. She joined in the children's games, she made Simon talk to her, and he did so with a freedom that showed how badly he longed to confide. She remembered how good Andrew had been at chess, and it was no surprise to discover that at seven Simon was already a skilled player.

Once she'd discovered that she went onto the attack, buying a newspaper with a daily chess problem and getting him to solve it. Then she tried to arrange it so that Simon was sitting over the problem when Andrew arrived home. This was hard as Andrew's arrivals could seldom be predicted, but one night she struck lucky. Best of all Simon was so absorbed that he failed to look up when his father entered, something rare enough to make Andrew stride across to see what was engrossing his son, and had to speak to him twice before he could get his attention. After that they worked on the problem together, and Elinor chalked up a minor victory.

'I didn't even know he could play,' he told Elinor that evening as she was making a late-night snack.

'He's pretty good.'

'Yes, he is.'

'As good as you at that age?'

'I think so.' He looked at her shrewdly. 'Was it an accident, what happened tonight?'

'Of course not. I got him into position a few minutes before you got home. But you did the rest yourself.'

'When I employed you as child-minder I didn't envisage you going this far.'

'I'm like you. I like to do my job properly. Besides, the way I see it, I still owe you for Hetta's life. If I can help you with Simon, we're quits.'

'I see,' he said quietly. 'Yes, I never thought of it like that.'

After that there were some phone calls that she didn't understand, or, rather, didn't ask about. She found herself talking to a woman with a voice like cut glass, who turned out to be the secretary of Sir Elmer Rylance. She fetched Andrew to the phone and returned to the children, trying not to speculate.

She made no further mention of his taking time off, and nor did he. She concluded that he'd either forgotten the matter or dismissed it. She was angry with him. She didn't press the matter, but she had a sense of failure. She'd tried to believe that in this matter at least she could be good for him, but it seemed that he now dismissed her opinions as easily as he did everyone else's.

Only when she'd totally given up hope did he arrive home one evening and say, 'That's it! No more hospital for a week.'

The children bounded about in excitement. Over their heads Andrew met her eyes with a look that startled her. It was almost as though he was asking for her approval.

'Why did you keep it to yourself until now?' she asked when she could make herself heard through the riot.

'I wasn't sure until the last minute. It depended on whether my replacement arrived in time, but he did.'

'Is he as good as you?' she couldn't resist asking.

He looked at her. 'Almost. He thinks he's better.'

'If he's so brilliant, how come he's available?'

'He's been offered three other jobs, but the one he wants is Elmer's, so he's been keeping himself free. He jumped at this.'

Of course he would, Elinor thought. It was the chance to work under Rylance's nose and pip the other candidates to the post. And Andrew had stood back and let him do it, because she'd as good as asked him to. But her stab of pleasure was quickly suppressed. He'd done it for Simon, not her. And it might be a disaster for him.

Too late now to say anything. It was done. And Andrew was already going into the garden with the children.

He joined her later that night for their regular glass of wine while Fudge snuffled in the undergrowth.

'Could your replacement really harm you?' she asked.

'In one week?' he demanded. 'You don't think much of my skill.'

'A determined man can do a lot in a week.'

'He can do his worst,' Andrew said arrogantly. 'I gather you think I might soon be on my uppers. That's a pity, because I was going to suggest that we should get married.'

'*What?*' She tried to see him but there was no moon tonight and she could only make out his shape. His face was hidden from her.

'It makes a lot of sense, Ellie. We make a pretty good family. Simon loves you and he's crazy about Hetta.'

'Just a minute—'

'We have to think where this arrangement is going. If we don't marry then sooner or later we'll split up. You're an excellent employee, but employees leave. I want you to stay.'

'It takes a lot more than that to make a family,' she said in a toneless voice. She'd thought Andrew had hurt her in every possible way, but she hadn't thought of this. Marry her to keep a good employee!

'Of course it does, but I'm sure we can make it work. I'm probably not putting this very well, but if you'll only give it some thought—for everyone's sake—'

'Everyone? Does that include me?'

He stared at her, trying to discern on her face what had disturbed him in her voice. 'You don't think this might be a good idea for you?'

'I don't think there could be a worse idea for me. I've told you I'll stay while you need me, but I'm making a condition. Don't ever, ever mention this again.'

She rose and walked away towards the house, with Fudge trotting after her, leaving him sitting alone in the darkness.

It was Andrew who noticed that there was a funfair about a mile away, and he who suggested that they should go. He was also the one to set the date.

'The day after tomorrow,' he said, 'because that's Ellie's birthday.'

Hetta stared. 'How did you know? I didn't tell you.'

'I'm a magician,' he said, and that satisfied her.

'I don't want to make a fuss about my birthday,' she muttered as soon as they were alone.

'Too late. Give your friend Daisy a call and ask her to stay with us that night.'

It would be good to see Daisy again, but she would inevitably take over the children, leaving her too much with Andrew. She'd been steering clear of him ever since he'd made her that insulting offer of marriage, but it was hard now he was at home for the week. He strode off without waiting for an answer, and a few minutes later he departed on a gift-buying expedition with the children.

When her birthday came they all made the breakfast, then plied her with gifts. From Hetta there was a brooch in the shape of a heart, and from Simon a pair of slippers. Andrew's gift was a scarf, made of wool and silk. It was exquisite and expensive, but not so much as to invite comment. She thanked him quietly, and promised to wear it that evening.

The taxi arrived with Daisy, and now she was glad her old friend was there to shield her from the attention. Her thoughts had been in turmoil ever since the other night. There had been a brief temptation to say yes, marry him anyway and count on her own love to be enough.

Try as she might, she couldn't stop her thoughts wandering down that path. To the outside world they looked like a family, two parents and two children. It was tempting to think that they really were a family, to pretend that she were his wife, as she might once have been.

These days, when he took the children into the village, and the three of them returned to find her getting them a snack in the kitchen, they would greet each other with smiles, and for a moment she could think, *This is how it would be if we were married.*

And it could still happen. She could tell him she'd reconsidered and decided that it was a sensible idea. But the word 'sensible' checked her. Her love alone would never be enough for the two of them, and only misery could come from trying to make it.

On the afternoon of her birthday the phone rang. Elinor

was alone when she answered it, and she was immediately glad.

'Hi, sweetie,' came Myra's voice singing down the line. 'How's tricks?'

'We're doing very well,' Elinor said. 'Do you want to talk to Simon?'

'Thanks, but I just got off the line to him an hour ago.'

'How's Detroit?'

'Hot. Muggy. But Cyrus is letting me have the swimming pool enlarged. I thought of making it like a Roman bath house. What do you think?'

'I think it'll be very "you",' Elinor said.

Myra's crack of laughter showed that she fully understood this tact. 'I called to say happy birthday!' she said.

'Thank you. How did you know?'

'Simon told me. He says you're going out on this great party. Big funfair.'

'That's right. An old friend of mine is here, so there'll be three of us looking out for the children.'

'Good, have a great time. And listen, I have a birthday gift for you.'

'That's very kind. I'll look forward to it.'

'No, I'm going to give it to you now. I knew I'd seen you somewhere before as soon as we met, and now it's come to me. It's you in that photograph.'

'What photograph?'

'The one Andrew keeps with him. Or I should say *one* of the ones he keeps with him. There's about a dozen of them. Him and this girl with masses of blonde hair, sitting together, their arms around each other, kissing. And sometimes just her on her own. He didn't know that I knew. I found them in his desk drawer one day, and I never told him. So you were the ghost.'

'The ghost?'

'Andrew's ghost, the one that's always haunted him. I knew soon after we married that there was someone else. I don't mean another woman in the conventional sense, but a secret ghost in his heart that he visited sometimes, and came back looking sad. I was arrogant enough to think I could drive her away, but I never could, because she was the one he loved.'

'Myra, I'm sure you're wrong about this—'

'No, I'm not wrong. It's your face.'

'Yes, it's me, but the rest—we were children. At least, I was.'

'But he wasn't,' Myra said shrewdly. 'One thing I know about Andrew, he gives all of himself to everything. It's exhausting to live with, but the one who really gets dragged through the mill is Andrew.'

'Yes,' Elinor murmured. 'It was like that. I did love him but I was seventeen and all of him was more than I could cope with. If we'd met later—' She sighed.

'Has he been a ghost for you too, then?'

'All the time,' she said slowly, realising that it was true. 'I never meant to keep thinking of him, but somehow he wouldn't go away. I could never forget how badly I'd treated him and it spoiled everything else. And his face on the last day—yes, I suppose that's been my ghost.'

'And you're not going to look me in the eyes and say you don't still love him, are you?' Myra demanded, blithely ignoring the miles separating them.

'Myra—'

'Of course you're not. It stands out a mile. There was always a third person in our marriage,' she added, without rancour. 'It's fascinating to meet her after all this time.'

'I'm sorry.'

'Don't be. It wasn't your fault. Andrew and I should never have married. Once you'd had the "all" there wasn't much left for anyone else. What happens next is up to you, but for Andrew's sake I hope you get your act together. Bye, sweetie. Have a nice birthday.' She hung up.

Elinor set down the phone, her mind whirling. It couldn't be true. Myra had somehow got it wrong. And yet there was something in the word 'ghost' that had caught at her heart. She'd been haunted since the day of their parting, and of course Andrew had been haunted too.

But he'd been cured when they'd met again and he'd seen how she'd changed. She must remember that.

Both children were persuaded to sleep the afternoon away, under the dire threat of having to leave the funfair early. They set out in the early evening, with both youngsters bright-eyed and eager.

Andrew was an unexpected success. The same skills that made him a surgeon made him score bull's-eyes at the coconut shy, which he did so often that the harassed owner ordered him off, to the children's hilarity.

'Oh, look, Mummy, there's a big wheel.' Hetta tugged on Elinor's hand. 'Can we go on it?'

'It looks awfully big, darling,' Elinor said, looking up doubtfully.

'That's the idea,' Andrew observed, following her gaze. 'You're not scared, are you, Ellie?'

'You know I am,' she said softly.

She wondered what was happening. There was something different about Andrew tonight, as though he was determined to provoke her memories.

'Come along,' Daisy carolled, leading the way to the entrance. Simon and Hetta went with her, and the three of them piled in together.

'Come along,' Andrew said, taking Elinor's hand, and soon they were in the seat just behind the others.

Then they were off, sailing silently upward, higher and

higher, until they reached the top and began the stomach-churning descent. But her nerves seemed unimportant because Andrew's arm was about her shoulders, drawing her close.

'Andrew, we agreed—I'm just an employee.'

'No, you agreed that. Tonight you're Ellie. You've always been Ellie. You always will be. Do you remember?' he whispered as his lips brushed on hers.

'Yes, everything.'

'Do you remember what I said to you that night?'

'You said you'd been plotting for ages how to kiss me.'

'"And I'm such a coward that I waited until now, when you can't escape,"' he quoted. 'I'm no braver now. I had to do it again. Kiss me, Ellie. Kiss me for ever.'

She couldn't resist any longer. She threw her arms about him, kissing him fiercely as she had done that first time, while the wheel spun and the stars rained down on them.

CHAPTER TWELVE

EVERYONE agreed that it had been the best night out ever. At home they toasted the occasion in hot chocolate before Daisy and Elinor chivvied the children upstairs.

'Then I'm going straight to bed myself,' Daisy said.

'Me too,' Elinor agreed. 'Goodnight, Andrew.'

The jollity continued as they climbed the stairs and put their giggling charges to bed. They didn't want the day to end, but at last they dropped off to sleep. Elinor kissed Daisy goodnight and went to her own room.

She undressed mechanically, trying to sort out her turbulent thoughts, but knowing it was impossible. Something had happened tonight that had brought about a change in Andrew. It had been happening gradually, she realised, but tonight was different. On top of the wheel he'd spoken of having no courage, but he'd acted like a man who'd finally decided to take his courage in his hands.

When the soft knock came on her door she knew she'd been listening for it for a long time.

Andrew stood there looking hesitant until she stood back for him to pass. He was still dressed in the trousers and shirt he'd worn all evening, the shirt open at the throat. He had something in his hand.

'There's something you ought to see,' he said, offering it to her.

It was an envelope, containing the very photographs Myra had described to her over the phone. Elinor went through them slowly. There were the two of them in each other's arms, oblivious to whoever had been holding the camera, oblivious to all the world but each other.

'We were so young,' she murmured. 'I always knew that I was, but you too—I never realised. Why do you bring me these now?'

'Because I understand you already know about them.'

She stared at him. 'Myra?'

'She called me and said she'd spoken to you earlier.'

'Did she tell you what she'd said to me?'

'The gist of it. Enough to make it clear that I couldn't put this off any longer. There's so much I want to say to you, and I've delayed saying it in case it drove you away.'

'Is it about the past?'

'Yes.'

'Do you think we should risk it? Is there any more to say?'

'There's this to say. Ellie—do you think you can ever forgive me?'

'Shouldn't it be me asking you for forgiveness?'

'No. Everything that happened was my fault. You were so young. You wanted to enjoy yourself and explore life, as you had every right to. And I tried to tie you down long before you were ready.

'Everything you said about me that day was right. I tried to order your life to suit myself. My only excuse is that I knew how badly I needed you. You were my lifeline to the rest of the world. I'd put work and study before everything, and I'd ignored a whole side of myself to do it. Then you brought that part of me back to life, and I knew I had to keep you with me, at all costs. But what I never saw, or wouldn't let myself see, was that the cost was paid by you.

'I drove you into Jack Smith's arms. But for me you'd never have looked at him. Which means that all the bad things that have happened to you since then have been my fault.'

'No, that's too hard. What about what I did to you?'

'Nothing I didn't deserve. If I'd been more patient, instead of grabbing at you, we might have stayed together, and been together now.'

'Andrew, that time I went to the island with Jack, nothing happened. He tried, but he got his face slapped. I wouldn't have done that to you.'

'Thank you. It's odd, after all these years, how much it still means to hear you say that.'

'I wanted you to be the first, and you should have been.'

'Yes, if I hadn't been so smugly determined that my way was right, we could just have found a flat together until you were ready to commit yourself.'

'Lived as brother and sister, you mean?' she asked, gently teasing.

'Blow that! I could barely keep my hands off you, and you made it as hard as you could.'

She stood still a moment, thinking of that time and the life they might have had. 'If only…' she said longingly.

'There are a million if onlys,' he said, stroking her hair.

'If only we'd met a few years later. Just think—'

'I do think,' he said harshly. 'And then I try not to think of it, because it's the way to go mad. For a while after it happened I believe I actually did go crazy. I turned myself into an automaton. I shut off every softer feeling because I had no use for them any more. When I allowed myself to feel emotions again I made sure they were kept in neat order.

'But then I saw you that day in the hospital corridor, and

my whole orderly world went haywire. When we talked and I heard how you'd been forced to live I knew what I'd done to you. I was beside myself, but at least I had the chance to help you. I thought I'd do the operation, Hetta would recover, we'd go our separate ways and I'd feel better about you.

'But then you were homeless, and the temptation was too much for me. I told you a fairy tale to get you here, and I trapped myself because I didn't dare visit you. I was afraid if you knew the truth you'd run away. But I longed to come here. I wanted to see you in my home, as you always should have been. I used to think of you, living here, and pretend that you were my wife. Foolish, eh?'

'Not so foolish as you think,' she murmured, remembering her own pretence.

'What was that?'

'Nothing,' she said hurriedly. 'Go on.' She was holding her breath for whatever came next.

'Then you called me, and I came over that night, and it all went wrong. You were so upset about the money, and when you came to my bed—you don't know how much I wanted you. But not like that. Not because you felt you owed me.'

She stared. 'Is that what you thought? That it was a kind of payment?'

'What else could I think? You so hated taking anything from me, especially money. And then there you were in bed with me, and I thought I heard you saying all the sweet things I wanted to hear from you. I didn't know whether you were really saying them, or whether it was just a dream. I'd had that kind of dream so often. Then I awoke and you were making love to me, and I thought you were doing it as some kind of duty. It was a nightmare.'

'But it wasn't that at all,' she breathed. 'You were wretched and I wanted to be close to you, and love you.

When you pushed me away I thought I'd embarrassed you because you didn't want me.'

'Didn't want you?' he echoed. 'There hasn't been a moment in the last twelve years when I haven't loved you and wanted you, even when I wouldn't admit it to myself. But after that night I felt I'd driven you off. You started planning to leave, but then Myra turned up with Simon, and suddenly I had a second chance. If you knew how my heart sank when you started talking about being my housekeeper and child-minder, and contracts of employment.'

'I was trying to tell you I wouldn't throw myself at you. I thought it would relieve your mind.'

'But I asked you to marry me.'

'To hold onto a good employee. That's what you said.'

'Yes, that's what I *said*. I thought you didn't care about me. I played it cool just to get that ring on your finger. After we were married I could tell you I'd loved you all the time, and always would. Well, anyway, you didn't fall for it, so I changed tack. There had to be some way to woo you. Then I remembered it was your birthday, the anniversary of the day we'd met, and there was the funfair and maybe I could—' He broke off and sighed. 'I haven't improved, have I? I'm still thinking about what I want, trying to grab you, and never mind whether you love me or not.'

'You thought I didn't love you?'

'I was sure of it—until today, when Myra told me some of the things you'd said to her. And then I began to hope.'

'Hope? I loved you with all my heart. I wouldn't marry you because you just wanted a secure employee.'

Andrew looked at her, his heart in his eyes. 'Oh, Ellie,' he said. 'How we misunderstand each other. We always have. Shall we ever get it right? Or shall we keep getting it wrong and love each other anyway?'

His words had a curious effect on her. It was what she'd

longed for, but suddenly all she could see was that the past had made the future confused, perhaps impossible.

'Andrew—'

'What is it, my darling?'

She backed away from him. 'Don't say things like that.'

'But why? Unless I've fooled myself and you can't love me again.'

'I still love you,' she burst out, 'but maybe it's too late. How can we get it back—what we had? The people we were then don't exist any more.'

'Ellie—Ellie—'

'Don't call me that,' she cried. 'She's dead, gone. I can't be Ellie any more.'

He took hold of her. 'Look at me,' he said, raising her face and brushing back her hair. 'Let me see your face. It's the face I've always loved. It hasn't changed with the years except to become sadder and gentler. It's still beautiful, still Ellie, still my love.'

He kissed her before she could reply. Then kissed her again. She stopped trying to struggle and relaxed in his arms, knowing she had no power to fight something she wanted with all her heart. The problems were still waiting for them, but first she would enjoy her love.

'Ellie…'

'Yes, my love, yes—'

'Do you still want me?'

'Always.'

He slipped off her robe. Underneath was one of her matronly nightgowns, which she wore almost as a uniform these days, but his fingers got to work, undoing the buttons and pushing it so that it fell to the floor, and there was the body he loved.

'Did you think you could hide from me like this?' he murmured, his lips against her skin. 'You could dress like an

Eskimo and I'd still pick you out from a million as the most beautiful woman in the world.'

Twice before she'd offered herself to him, but only now could he accept the gift. She sensed his eagerness as she undressed him in turn. When they were both naked he drew her down onto the bed for the loving that had waited too long.

After all these years they approached this moment as strangers, hopeful but unsure. He was broader, less wiry, more powerful than she recalled, but with a gentleness that was unchanged. Time and sadness had added a new dimension to her, and he searched her face as he made love to her, seeking to fathom her secrets, knowing that in the end it couldn't be done.

She had told him that he should have been the first, but in one sense he was. After two husbands he was still her first true lover, the first man to take her into another world and show her wonders. It was awesome, almost alarming, but when she looked into his face she knew she could never be afraid as long as he was with her.

She saw something else too—that in her arms he'd found the fulfilment no other woman could ever have brought him. When their closest union was over, and they lay side by side, it wasn't the end of love-making, merely a different stage. She had never known that such peace was possible. In the moments after desire was fulfilled and the fire faded, only love and tenderness were left.

'I told you I wouldn't let you go,' he said softly as she lay cradled in his arms. 'And now I never will. Let's get married quickly.'

She stirred. 'Andrew, wait, please. It's a little soon to start talking about marriage. We've only just found each other.'

'That's why it's so important not to lose each other again.'

'I don't want that either—' she tried to sit up but he drew her firmly down beside him '—but we could lose each other again if we're not careful. No, listen to me—' She fended him off as he tried to kiss her. 'After twelve years we're different people, and we don't really know who those other people are. We both have years of secrets.'

'There'll never be any secrets between us from now on, I promise. If we know that we love each other the rest can come. Darling—'

He stopped, seeing the sudden unease in her eyes, and his hands fell from her.

'Oh, no!' he said, in a horrified voice. 'I'm doing it again, aren't I? Trying to hurry you into doing what I want.' He got up with a convulsive movement. 'And if you listen to me it'll end the same way.'

'Darling.' She slid quickly across the bed to where he was sitting on the edge. It hurt her to see him troubled. This was important to her, but she moved swiftly to comfort him, putting her arms about him and resting her head against his back. 'Don't make so much of it. I just want a little time to know you, and not make the same mistakes as last time. I love you. I always will.'

'Then why—?' He checked himself quickly. 'Never mind, we'll do it your way.' He turned back to her, revealing himself at an angle that aroused her immediate interest.

'Whatever I want?' she asked, craning her head to see better. 'Anything at all?'

He stroked her head tenderly. 'Your wish is my command.'

'In that case, come here.' She pulled him towards her.

Andrew tensed suddenly.

'What is it?' she asked.

'I thought I heard a noise.'

They listened together, but there was only silence in the darkened house.

'Come back,' she said, drawing him close again.

But the next moment they both heard the noise, footsteps coming up the stairs and the sound of a voice that they both recognised.

'Thanks a bunch, Daisy. Don't worry, I know my way.'

'I don't believe it,' Andrew said, appalled. 'It can't be.'

'I've got a terrible feeling that it is,' Elinor breathed.

The next moment the door opened. Andrew had just enough time to pull the sheet over him before Myra swept into the room.

'Surprise!' she cried.

'Myra, how did you get here?' Elinor asked, aghast. 'You were in Detroit this afternoon!'

'I didn't actually say I was.'

'No, you never did,' she realised.

'I arrived yesterday to stay with Uncle Elmer. He wanted me here for his big weekend.'

'Never mind that,' Andrew said hastily.

'Which means you haven't told Ellie.'

Elinor looked at Andrew. 'Secrets?' she asked quietly.

'I'll explain later,' he growled. 'Not with her here.'

'I got suspicious when you weren't at Uncle Elmer's weekend,' Myra said.

'Maybe I was trying to avoid you,' Andrew suggested.

'Oh, no, darling. Uncle Elmer's house party is a step up the ladder, and you've never missed one of those. You wouldn't risk damaging your career just to avoid me.'

'Why should a house party affect his career?' Elinor asked.

'Because Uncle Elmer is about to nominate his successor, and he has rather old fashioned ideas about surgeons. He doesn't think medical skill is enough. To him a heart surgeon should be a great man who rides loftily above the rest of society.'

'Rubbish,' Andrew snapped.

'But you should have been there,' Elinor cried.

'Tonight was the big banquet,' Myra said.

'Tonight I had something better to do,' Andrew said.

'Go to a funfair, I believe. And for that, you snubbed his big weekend, full of the medical glitterati. And I asked myself why you'd do that. Not just because you don't believe in his ideas. In the past you've always done whatever came next, so why not now?' Her eyes flickered over Elinor. 'And I thought I knew the answer. So I came over to see if I was right.'

'And now you know you are, I suppose you're going to make hay with it,' Andrew growled. 'Well, do your worst.'

'No,' Elinor protested, 'Andrew, I know what it means to you—'

'It means nothing to me beside you,' he said. 'Let her tell him anything she likes.'

'And I've got a fair bit to tell him, haven't I?' Myra mused. 'Some people might call this little set-up an unprofessional relationship. Ellie isn't your patient but her daughter is. And moving them into your house, bringing Ellie into your bed— I think the General Medical Council would have a field day.'

'Myra, you wouldn't,' Elinor cried in horror. Surely she couldn't have been wrong about Myra, who had seemed good-natured despite her touch of hardness?

'I might,' Myra said. 'I might do anything, unless, of course, you draw my claws before I do it.'

'I see,' Andrew said in disgust. 'Blackmail.'

'Hmm. A kind of.'

'So what do you want?'

'Well, if you two were to tell the world that you were going to get married it would all become quite respectable, wouldn't it? It wouldn't matter what I said. Even Uncle Elmer would approve.'

'But—' Andrew hesitated, then said with difficulty, 'about getting married—there's a problem—'

'Oh, don't be stupid, darling, of course there isn't. Don't tell me the two of you are going to make the same mistake again. Andrew, when we talked this afternoon I gave you the key to Ellie, but something told me you were going fumble it. Why, I can't imagine. She's not going to run out on you this time. She's as nuts about you as you are about her.'

'Myra,' Elinor protested, almost laughing as she realised that Myra was, after all, a good, if unorthodox, friend, 'it's not that simple.'

'Yes, it is. Things usually are simple. You see what you want and go for it. Open your eyes, Ellie. Think what'll happen to Andrew if he loses you again? He isn't a man who loves easily, or often. It was his misfortune, and yours, that he met the "one and only" when she was too young. The time was all wrong. Now it's right.'

'It's just that we thought we'd spend a little time getting to know each other first,' Elinor tried to explain. 'We're older now, and we want to go carefully.'

'Whatever for?' Myra demanded, aghast. 'Honestly, sweetie, that's not the way. Just cut the cackle and get on with it. And make it as soon as possible. Next month would be nice. Cyrus and I are coming over here for a publicity do, and I wouldn't miss your wedding for anything.'

Elinor clutched her head. 'This conversation is making me dizzy. How can you be saying these things to me? You were his wife.'

'But I'm not his wife any more. Or if I am, poor Cyrus is deluding himself. I'm sure I married him. Yes, of course I did, I sent you the pictures. By the way, I've got some wedding cake for you all downstairs. All right, all right,' she said quickly, seeing the fulminating look in Andrew's eye. 'I'm very happy, and I'd like to see you both happy too, which, of course, would be the best thing for Simon.'

'And the best for you,' Andrew observed cynically. 'Cyrus

really doesn't want your son by your first marriage spending too much time with you, does he?'

'That depends where he is,' Myra said thoughtfully. 'It's fine at Disneyland because he and Simon are about the same mental age and they can enjoy it together. But at other times Simon would be distinctly in the way. But he loves it here with both of you and Hetta. He's told me so when we've talked on the phone. OK, OK, I'm a selfish cow who doesn't want her son cramping her style. But I do love him, and I'd like to see him settled in the place *he* wants to be.'

They stared at her, thunderstruck. In the silence Myra's cell phone shrilled and she answered, 'It's all right, Uncle Elmer, he's here, but I don't think he can talk now. He's got some important business going down. You can call him tomorrow and give him the good news.'

She hung up. 'All right, I've said my piece. Now it's up to you two. Just get on with it.'

She embraced Elinor. 'I'm going now, but you and I will be seeing each other quite often in the future, since you're going to be stepmother to my son.'

'Am I?'

'Of course you are. We just settled it. Didn't you notice? Is Simon in the same room, by the way? I'd better drop in on him before I go.'

She blew Andrew a kiss, waved and headed for the door.

'Myra,' he said quietly, 'thank you for everything.'

'Just don't forget to invite me to the wedding,' she told him. 'I want to give you away.'

She slipped out and from the corridor they heard her say, 'Simon, darling, there you are! Guess what. Daddy and Ellie are getting married. Isn't that lovely? Hetta, dear, you'll just love being a bridesmaid. Pink satin, I think. You've got the perfect complexion for it.'

Her voice faded.

Silence.

'Well,' Elinor spoke cautiously, 'pink satin isn't so bad. As long as she doesn't bring Hetta to our wedding in scarlet satin.'

He put his arms around her and spoke beseechingly. 'Darling Ellie, you don't have to—'

'Of course I do. We both do. It's all been decided. And Myra was right. We should just cut the cackle and get on with it. What was I fretting about?'

'You're not angry that I kept the weekend a secret? Telling you would have felt like emotional blackmail.'

'No, I'm not angry. I can just hardly believe that you took such a risk.'

'To blazes with Elmer and his glitzy weekend. I wanted to ride on the big wheel with the girl of my dreams. Just like last time. Some things are still the same, Ellie.'

'But think what it might have cost you?'

He held up his hands before her. 'I'll stand or fall by what these can do, not my ability to wear a dinner jacket.'

'Did I hear right? Did Myra say something about good news? I think you got it anyway.'

'Really? I wasn't listening. This is more important. My dearest love, once I tried to pressure you into marriage. I didn't even ask you properly the first time, but I'm asking now. Ellie, will you marry me?'

She took his face gently between her hands.

'Yes, my dearest. I will.'

Wedding in Venice

*Turn the page to read Lucy Gordon's
exclusive short story!*

CHAPTER ONE

"YOUR TROUBLE is that you never take risks," Dulcie said.

"Who? *Me*?" Justine queried, her face full of innocent indignation.

Below them was a flash of sun on water as the plane from England circled Venice Airport before coming in to land.

"I'm always taking risks," Justine said firmly. "I nearly broke my neck last month, hanging over that cliff to get a picture of a gorilla."

"Oh, gorillas! Cliffs!" Dulcie dismissed all such trivial dangers. "You're a professional photographer. I know you take that sort of risk. I'm talking about people."

"You mean men," Justine said frankly. "Fine, let's talk about men. They're great fun—in their way."

"When you've got time for them, you mean," Dulcie teased.

"I'm always dashing off on assignments. I have to fit male distractions into my schedule. It's just common sense."

"You have too much common sense," Dulcie reproved her. "It's getting in the way of your life. When are you going to let your hair down and throw caution to the wind?"

"Like you, you mean? One wink from a gorgeous Italian and you were a goner."

"Guido isn't Italian. He's Venetian," Dulcie corrected.

"Does it matter?"

"Yes," Dulcie said, considering this seriously. "They wink differently. It's more intense somehow. You'll find out for yourself."

"Not me," Justine said firmly. "I won't keel over just because an Italian—sorry, Venetian—gives me the eye. If he winks at me, I'll wink at him. If he looks me over, I'll look him over. Then I'll decide if he's up to standard. What I won't do is simply go weak at the knees."

Dulcie laughed. "Just wait until you meet a Venetian."

When they left the plane Dulcie cleared Customs fast, racing straight into the arms of her fiancé.

Justine took her time, checking that her photographic equipment was undamaged. She was in Venice to take pictures of Dulcie's wedding. As she emerged from Customs she could see the other two locked in a passionate embrace.

Justine grinned. Since Guido lived in Venice and Dulcie in England they hadn't seen each other for weeks, and she guessed this bit was going to take a while.

To pass the time, she took out a mirror and checked her appearance, which had survived the flight in good condition. Her hair was red, not auburn or sandy, but a true, blazing red. She grew it long, but wore it swept up. It made a striking effect with her green eyes.

The lovers finally drew apart, laughing and happy, and Dulcie introduced Justine. Guido greeted his fiancée's friend warmly and led them out of the airport, which was built on the edge of a large expanse of water.

"This is the lagoon," he explained. "Venice is out there in the center, so we reach it by motorboat. The barges you see there are collecting goods to supply the shops and hotels."

One barge was being loaded just next to them. On the quay stood a pile of boxes filled with bottles of wine. Getting them down should have been a job for two men, but one man was tackling it alone.

One foot on the barge, one on the narrow stone steps, he swung up to lift a heavy box, then down to lay it in the boat. He looked to be in his early thirties, was tall and lithe, with an easy grace and a strength that treated the heavy weights as nothing.

Justine noted his very short black denim shorts, which revealed long, powerful thighs. He wore nothing else. His feet were bare, and so, she noted with interest, was his broad chest, which glistened in the sunlight as he dipped and stretched to reach the boxes.

His black hair was a little too long, and was shaggy and damp from his efforts, clinging to the heavy muscles of his neck. It made her smile just to look at such intense, masculine beauty.

Then he looked up and caught her gazing at him. It was too late now to pretend that she wasn't studying him. He didn't seem fazed, though. Perhaps he was used to women's admiring glances.

His grin seemed to confirm it. He had a wide mouth, which gave the biggest smile she had ever seen. It was blazing, glorious, lusty with life. And he aimed it straight at her. Then he winked. And Justine gasped.

Dulcie was right. They *did* wink more intensely, a blatant invitation that said, "Come on in."

And suddenly she didn't know what to do.

CHAPTER TWO

THE boatman's expression and the whole attitude of his athletic body was an invitation to the party of life, and for a moment Justine was stunned. She turned to Dulcie to see if she had noticed the bold boatman, but her friend was busy helping Guido load their bags into the motorboat.

Stop dithering, she told herself. You enjoy a good party.

She pulled herself together and winked back.

His returning smile said, *Message received and understood*, which irked her slightly. She, herself, wasn't quite sure that she understood.

But she wouldn't be seeing him again, and perhaps that was just as well. He was just a little too sure of himself.

They were almost ready to go. Justine settled herself in the back of the boat and Guido started the motor.

The sudden churning of the water made the barge rock, knocking the stranger off balance and overboard. Immediately he climbed back aboard, pushing the soaking hair back from his eyes, visibly cursing, but unhurt. Justine had a last glimpse of him, covered in water, shining in the sun.

Then she was speeding across the lagoon, looking about her in breathless wonder as Venice came into view.

Suddenly she realized that the barge was overtaking them.

At the back stood the man, almost dry now from the effects of the wind, which blew his dark hair straight back from his face.

It was a powerful face, Justine realized, slightly saturnine, yet still with the quality of humor. The chin was stubborn, the nose slightly hooked. Not a conventionally handsome face, but one that would be remembered when pretty boys were forgotten.

He turned his head to give her that marvelous grin again, and she had a strange feeling that he had caught up especially for her.

She mouthed, "Are you all right?" But then remembered that he probably didn't speak English.

But it seemed that he did, for he raised a thumb and nodded.

"*È Riccardo*," Guido yelled. The man in the barge waved at him, then sped up and passed them.

Justine, who was sitting behind Guido and Dulcie, called, "You know him?"

"Yes, he's—" the rest of the words were drowned out by the noise of the motor.

Then she forgot everything as the boat slowed and they entered Venice, gliding along narrow waterways between ancient buildings in a quiet rhythm unlike the harried tempo of most cities she knew, until they finally reached the Grand Canal. Here was the Palazzo Calvani, where Guido lived with his uncle, Count Calvani.

The count was away until the next day, so Guido entertained them alone. At dinner he was charming company, but he was shooed away when Maria, the dressmaker, arrived late in the evening with Dulcie's wedding gown.

"I came out to Venice for one fitting a few weeks back," Dulcie told Justine, "but this is the moment of truth. Let's go upstairs."

The dress was an extravagant confection in white satin and lace, with a long, wide skirt and floor-length veil. Justine snapped madly with her digital camera as Dulcie turned in front of the mirror.

When the dressmaker had gone, Justine got out her laptop and began downloading the pictures from the camera. Dulcie gasped when she saw them on the screen.

"Tomorrow I want to go outside and take more pictures of you wearing this," Justine said.

The photographer in her was at work now, picturing this gorgeous dress against the canals, the picturesque buildings.

As she worked, she asked casually, "Who was that man who passed us on the water this morning, the one Guido called Riccardo?"

"I've never met him," Dulcie said. "Guido has a lot of boatman friends, so he's probably one of them."

Justine let it go. It would be a mistake to seem too curious.

They set out next morning so that Justine could photograph Dulcie in the lovely dress against the background of Venice. She took picture after picture, exhilarated by the beauty she was capturing.

"Just one more," she said at last as they stopped in a little square by the water. "Stand by that fountain."

She arranged her shot, focused and took a step back, then another, and another.

Totally absorbed, she failed to notice that she was getting closer to the canal. Dulcie's cry of warning came too late, and the next moment Justine was stepping back into nothing, and falling.

She gave a yell of despair as she thought of what the water would do to her precious camera.

But there was no water. Instead she landed on something

that felt relatively soft. Sprawled inelegantly on her back, she had a grandstand view of the man she'd seen yesterday, standing over her, regarding her with recognition and delight.

He gave her a mock bow, reaching forward to pull her into a sitting position, and saying, "It's a pleasure to meet you at last."

CHAPTER THREE

IT WAS definitely the boatman from the previous day, wearing slightly more today: a sleeveless black vest and a pair of threadbare jeans that ended just below the knees.

Close up, he was even more overpowering. Justine had to resist the temptation to stare like a dizzy schoolgirl.

He shouldn't be allowed, she decided. That tan, those white teeth, the strength she could sense in his hand, with its hint of even more strength leashed, the glint of the devil in his dark eyes—there ought to be a law against him.

But if there was a law, he would ignore it. She knew that already. He would ignore anything that didn't suit him.

At the moment it seemed to suit him to keep hold of her hand, although she was sitting upright now, and there was no need.

He sat down beside her.

"Are you all right?" he asked. "That was quite a tumble!" "Not as bad as the one you took yesterday," she reminded him.

"But I landed safely in the water."

"Well, I landed safely on—*cabbages*? I'm sitting on cabbages?"

"And onions and potatoes and lettuces. This barge belongs to the Hotel Busoni, and I'm taking supplies to the kitchens."

"Well, I'm very glad you were passing just then, or it could have been really nasty. The water wouldn't have done my camera any good."

"Then I'm happy to have been of service," he said with an air of chivalry that sat oddly with his threadbare clothes.

He squeezed her hand gently between both of his.

"I hope I haven't squashed the vegetables," she said, reluctantly disengaging her hand and feeling around gingerly. "I don't want to get you into trouble."

"Please don't worry about me," he said gravely.

"You're sure your boss will be okay?"

"Let's say I can handle anything he's likely to throw at me."

"Hey, how do I get out? That ledge is way above me."

"Because this is low tide."

"You mean I'm trapped here?"

"Only until we reach the next flight of steps."

He pointed to where she could see steps cut into the stone, about ten yards ahead.

"But we're not moving," she said.

"That's because we've hit a traffic jam," he pointed out, indicating several other barges, bent on the same errand, that were blocking their way.

"Where's Dulcie?" she asked, looking around.

"Your friend is back there. We moved on for a bit after you fell."

Justine could just make out Dulcie standing by the water, at the place where she had gone in. She waved and caught her attention.

Dulcie doubled up with laughter, and indicated that she would walk along the canal's edge to join her, but Justine firmly waved her back for fear of damage to the lovely wedding dress. Dulcie nodded, agreeing to wait.

"I'm taking the pictures of Dulcie and Guido's wedding," Justine explained. "You know Guido, don't you?"

He grinned.

"Everyone knows Guido. He's crazy." Seeing her puzzled look he added, "In Venice, that is a compliment."

"I see—at least, I think I do."

He extended his hand again.

"I am Riccardo Gardini."

"I am Justine Bentley."

They shook hands.

"Will you remain in Venice for long?" he asked.

"I don't know. I've got a few days before the wedding, then I'll stay on to get some shots of the city, but I'm not sure just how long that will take."

"It will take a lifetime," he said at once. "You will never come to the end of Venice. There is always one more beauty to be seen, one more mystery to tease you. So you must stay here forever."

"Well, it's beautiful enough, I agree, and I really want to see it all."

"Then I shall arrange it so that you do."

The lordly way he said, "I shall arrange it," made her lift her eyebrows. Just who did he think he was? And what did he think *she* was? An easy pickup?

"Say that you will spend some time with me," he coaxed.

He was the most dangerously attractive male that she'd met in a long time. Did anything else matter?

And then she saw something that drove everything else out of her mind.

"Oh my goodness, look at that!" she breathed.

"*Maria Vergine!*" he exclaimed, looking around. "What's the matter?"

"*That!*" she said, pointing over his shoulder. "Oh, help! I've got to get out of here, fast."

CHAPTER FOUR

"WHERE'S THE FIRE?" Riccardo demanded, looking around to see what had agitated Justine.

"Dulcie!" Justine cried. "Look at her! Oh, how can that happen and me not be there?"

Turning to look behind him, Riccardo saw Dulcie standing by the canal in her wedding dress. A sudden breeze had arisen, whisking the long veil high, so that it seemed to stream up to the sky, making a perfect gauze halo about her. Dulcie's face was raised and she was laughing with delight. It would have made a glorious picture. And Justine was missing it.

"Can't you take it from here?" Riccardo asked.

"I am," she said, snapping away madly, "but it won't be the same. I need to get close, but how can I while we're stuck here?"

"Like this," Riccardo said, placing his hands on her waist and hoisting her up.

She had a brief sensation of flying, as though she were no more than a bag of feathers he was tossing. Then she landed and scrambled to her feet, almost in one movement.

"Thank you," she gasped, beginning to run.

"Good luck!" he called, but she was already beyond hearing.

Riccardo watched her, wryly aware that she had completely forgotten him. Only a moment ago the air had seemed to sing with the intensity of something that was starting between them. He had asked her to spend time with him. She had hesitated, but his well-honed instincts told him she was about to fall into his net.

But she had escaped at the last minute through one of those twists of fate that even the best fishers of women could not anticipate.

And she hadn't even glanced back for a last look at him. Faced with a good picture opportunity, she'd wiped him from her existence.

Riccardo wasn't a conceited man, but this was not what he was used to. Honor demanded that he did not leave matters there. They had unfinished business.

As he went on his way, he was smiling.

"I can't believe that happened," Justine wailed as Dulcie's veil floated back down to earth. "That would have been the shot of shots, the big one. *Aaaarrrgh!*"

"It's not fair," Dulcie agreed sympathetically. "Still, you got some lovely pictures before that."

But Justine couldn't be consoled. As they made their way back to the Palazzo Calvani she was still mourning "the one that got away."

It was Riccardo's fault, of course. If he hadn't kept her talking she would have been back to work in moments.

I hope his vegetables rot, she thought grumpily.

As soon as they reached the palazzo, Dulcie changed out of the wedding dress and settled it on its stand to await the big day. Then she went to Justine's room, and found her downloading the morning's work.

"Guido's gone to collect Uncle Francesco and Liza from the airport," she said. "I'm longing for you to meet them."

"They're getting married the day before you, right?"

"Right. It's such a romantic story. They've been in love for fifty years, but Liza wouldn't marry him because he was a count and she was his housekeeper. After all this time, she's finally agreed. It's so sweet to see how much they love each other. Guido and I are going to be exactly the same when we're old."

Justine gave a brief, wry smile that made Dulcie cry out, "What's that for? I know you pretend not to believe in love, but even you have to agree that it's a beautiful story."

"I do believe in love," Justine said. "Love is real. It's the 'eternal' bit that I can't swallow."

"Fifty years sounds pretty eternal to me."

"Sure, a fifty-year courtship!" Justine chuckled. "I believe in that. But you know as well as I do that it's when people get married that things start to go wrong."

"Let's be glad the rest of the world doesn't know it," Dulcie observed, "or the human race would die out. Three cheers for men and women getting together."

"Ah, getting together. That's different," Justine said, her eyes twinkling. "I believe in that."

"That's them," Dulcie said, at a sound from below.

She vanished. Justine waited, giving her friend time to greet her new family. Just when she was thinking she should go down and be introduced, Dulcie came flying back.

"You could be right," she said, sounding agitated. "Maybe love doesn't last. Uncle Francesco and Liza have had the most terrible quarrel."

"After all this time? What about?"

"I don't know, but from the way they're glaring at each other there's big trouble. Maybe there'll only be one wedding after all."

CHAPTER FIVE

COUNT CALVANI was a tall, handsome man in his early seventies. Liza, too, was tall, thin and frail-looking, but with an indomitable face. Just now, as Dulcie had warned, both faces were glowering.

They both greeted Justine warmly, and Liza summoned wine and cakes from the kitchen. But she and the count carried on the battle in low voices.

"They're talking Venetian dialect, which I don't understand," Dulcie said. "Guido, whatever's happened?"

He grinned. "Uncle was thinking of having a last-minute party the day after tomorrow, then he changed his mind, thinking it would be too much work for Liza, with the wedding feasts as well. He was being considerate but she's mad at him for 'not having faith in her.'"

"But can't a hotel do the catering?" Justine asked. "What about—" inspiration seemed to strike her from the blue "—what about the Hotel Busoni?"

Guido's eyes lit up and he immediately spoke to his uncle in rapid Venetian. Dulcie smiled and gave her the thumbs-up sign.

"What an inspiration," she told Justine. "The owner is a friend of Guido's. The hotel hasn't been open long, and he needs all the work he can get."

Justine was amused when Guido turned his charm on Liza, putting his hands together imploringly. At last the old woman smiled and gave him a light slap, clearly telling him to stop his nonsense. Guido grinned and leapt for the telephone.

A swift conversation in Venetian ensued, after which Guido said, "He's coming over after dinner, before Liza changes her mind. Hey, Justine, fancy you thinking of the Busoni!"

"It's the only Venice hotel I know," she said quickly.

Over dinner she had the chance to observe the count and Liza when they weren't squabbling and had to admit that they made a charming couple. The handsome man was so dotingly in love with the plain woman that Justine's cynicism took a knock.

But she settled it back into place, reminding herself that she didn't believe in eternal love. She couldn't afford to believe in it.

They had coffee in the garden overlooking the Grand Canal, with a clear view of the floodlit Rialto Bridge. Justine fixed her eyes on it, concentrating on the beauty so that she didn't have to think too closely about what she had just done.

What had possessed her to suggest the Busoni? Who said that Riccardo would be making the hotel's deliveries anyway? And what did she care whether he did or not?

"He's here," Guido said, jumping up and heading toward the building, from which a figure was just emerging.

"Riccardo!" Guido yelled.

"Justine," Dulcie said excitedly, "isn't that the same man who—?"

"Yes," Justine murmured. "It is."

The light and shadow contrasts of the moonlit garden emphasized everything about him that had made an impact on her. He was just as she remembered, but more so.

"Justine," Guido said eagerly, "do you remember this guy from the journey yesterday?"

"Oh, we've met since then," she said, extending her hand to Riccardo. "I fell into his barge this morning, and I can promise you, his cabbages are the best."

"I'm saving money on staff by doing some of the donkey work myself," Riccardo said.

He was talking to Guido but his eyes were on Justine, and his hand held on to hers longer than necessary.

"I would have told you the truth this morning," he said, "but you ran away without giving me the chance."

"Plus you enjoyed having a joke at my expense."

"Well—yes," he admitted.

"To think I was worried about getting you in trouble with your boss!"

"I did tell you that I could handle anything he threw at me," he reminded her.

"Hmm, so you did!"

He grinned.

"You don't trust me?"

"Where would you get an idea like that?" she asked ironically.

"From your voice, your eyes, your face. It's an interesting question for the two of us to explore. Unfortunately, it must wait until my work is finished."

It was reasonable for him to put work first, but his lordly assumption that she would wait like a doll on a shelf riled her.

"That's sounds fascinating," she said, "but it's been a long day. I'm sure everyone will forgive me if I go to bed."

Riccardo's eyes gleamed, acknowledging a round to her.

"You are wrong," he murmured. "*I* will not forgive you. But I can bide my time."

CHAPTER SIX

JUSTINE slipped away alone the next morning. This was a working trip, and as well as photographing the wedding, she wanted to explore Venice.

She called Dulcie to say she wouldn't be home for lunch.

"I'm in St. Mark's Square. I'll get something to eat here."

"You should go to Florian's," Dulcie told her. "It's a genuine eighteenth-century café, and Casanova used to go there because it was the only one in Venice where women were allowed."

Justine found Florian's and sat in the window drinking a sinfully delicious concoction of coffee, chocolate and cream, and listening to the four-piece orchestra playing just outside. The surroundings were still as they must have been two hundred years ago.

If she closed her eyes she could see Casanova, a tall, elegant man in powdered wig and knee breeches. In her vivid imagination, he paused a moment, smiling before he spoke.

"Can we talk for more than two minutes this time?"

His voice was familiar. Justine opened her eyes to find "Casanova" pulling up a chair beside her—in the form of Riccardo.

No wig or knee breeches. Just black jeans and a black shirt that showed tanned, muscular arms. In these sedate surroundings, his look of having just stepped off the brig of a pirate ship made him riotously out of place.

He hailed a waiter and ordered something for himself and a repeat of her order.

"You shouldn't have done that," she said urgently. "I swore I'd only allow myself one."

"I think you can afford the calories," he said with an admiring look at her tiny waist and long legs.

She was used to that kind of look, but this was different, as though he had taken in everything about her in one instant. She hoped she didn't look self-conscious.

"I'm sorry about my little deception," he said.

She gave a rueful smile.

"You don't expect to find a hotel owner collecting his own vegetables. And you were so convincing as a bargee. You swung me up onto the bank as if I weighed nothing."

He laughed and flexed his biceps theatrically. "No problem. I developed these tossing sacks of potatoes around."

She joined in his laughter, but regarded him wryly.

"I see. Women, potatoes—it's all one, huh?"

His eyes gleamed with pure mischief. "Oh, no! Not at all. Between a sack of potatoes and a woman—well, one is a lot more fun than the other."

She felt a sudden flicker of self-consciousness, and was annoyed at herself. For Pete's sake, she was a woman of the world, not a blushing violet! She'd known where this might lead as soon as their eyes met on the lagoon the first day.

But the word "fun," signposting the way ahead, had almost caught her unaware.

Yes, he would be fun, she thought, considering him. The whipcord strength of that easy, loose-limbed body, the sensual light in his eyes, his air of devilment.

Fun. But also a great deal more.

"It's early days for the hotel," he said, apparently not seeing her turmoil, or choosing not to see it. "I turn my hand to most things. Tomorrow night I shall be serving food at the Calvani party."

He watched as she sipped the sweet drink he had ordered for her.

"You never really answered my question yesterday," he said. "How long do you mean to stay in Venice?"

"You practically answered it yourself."

"Yes, I told you that you should stay forever. I'm afraid I tend to arrange people's lives for them, like a dictator. But only the ones I like."

"I don't know how long I'll be here," she said, not answering this directly.

"Is there nobody waiting for you at home who will object if you stay away too long?"

"No," she said wryly. "There is nobody who will object if I stay away too long."

"There ought to be. Please excuse me—I told you I was a dictator. To me it is so clear that you are a woman who should not live alone—"

"But perhaps it's my choice, and then you really are being a dictator."

"Is it your choice?"

"I'm divorced," she said abruptly.

"Your wish or his?"

"He slept with someone else. I threw him out. End of story."

"Had he been faithless before?"

"If he had, I'd have thrown him out before."

"You didn't want to try to save your marriage?"

"There was nothing to save," she said tensely. "It was over."

"So quickly? So easily? So ruthlessly?"

The last word was like a dagger.

"I really have to go," she said, rising. "Thank you for the coffee."

"Are you offended with me?"

"*Yes*. You have no right to—never mind."

She fled without a backward look.

CHAPTER SEVEN

JUSTINE SPENT the rest of that afternoon in St. Mark's Basilica, judging angles, working hard to put Riccardo out of her mind by sheer force of will.

But when she returned to the Palazzo Calvani, Dulcie was bubbling with the day's events.

"Riccardo came this morning to check things for the party. I was just talking to him when you called."

So their meeting had been no accident. He had known where to find her. The thought gave her a strange feeling.

The palazzo was filling up with guests. On the day of the party several of the count's cousins arrived from distant parts of Italy.

Once, looking out of a window, Justine saw Riccardo arrive in a barge laden with food and two members of his staff. She turned away quickly. She did not want to think about him. He had left her thoughts in turmoil with his casually cruel remarks.

So easily! So ruthlessly!

What did he know?

"You look upset," Dulcie said.

"It's just that I found myself talking about Neil yesterday. Now I wish I hadn't."

"Do you regret divorcing him so fast?"

"Not you, too! I did what had to be done. That was it."

More guests arrived and Dulcie went down to greet them, leaving Justine with her thoughts.

It had been a mistake to marry Neil—she'd known that even on the wedding day. They were in love, but she didn't believe in love—not the lasting kind. How could she when her parents' divorce had left her homeless? Both of them had remarried, and she had been shunted around to a series of aunts, "until things settle down."

But things had never settled down. Eventually she'd realized that there was no place for her in either home. After that she had set her face against the world.

She had an eye for shape and color, which had made her a success as a photographer. As her success grew, so did her social life. She was beautiful. Men wanted her. And that was fine, as long as they didn't ask for her heart as well.

She had locked that up in a safe, bolted, barred and labeled Do Not Touch.

With Neil she'd taken the risk, and it had been a mistake. Luckily they'd both seen the light in time. They'd had a nice, civilized divorce, and in future she would stick to adventures.

Riccardo should have been an adventure. But he wouldn't stay in his right place. A few moments of alarming insight had turned him into a threat.

For dinner she put on a figure-hugging cream dress cunningly contrived to be demure and enticing at once. Around her neck she wore a chain of solid gold. With her dramatic red hair, the effect was striking.

"You'll have them all at your feet," Dulcie had predicted earlier, chuckling.

But the first one at her feet was Riccardo, literally. He was waiting at the foot of the grand staircase as she descended.

He was more formally dressed now, in black trousers, snowy shirt and black tie.

As she neared, she waited for his grin of lusty appreciation, but tonight his demeanor was grave and gentle.

"I won't keep you a moment," he said quietly. "I had to tell you that I'm sorry for having distressed you yesterday."

"You're very kind, but I wasn't distressed," she said, trying to sound cool and indifferent.

"Forgive me, but I know that you were, otherwise you would not have run away."

"I did not run away," she said, her temper rising as she began to feel threatened again. "I had work to do. End of story."

"Do you know how often you use that expression?" he asked softly. "Always you try to bring the story to an end at the moment of your choosing. But nobody can do that. The story ends when it ends."

"And do *you* know how often you lecture me?" she asked, speaking in a furious whisper.

"I'm sorry. Yes, that is a fault of mine."

"Why do you think you have the right?"

"Because you matter," he said simply.

"No, I do not matter to you, and you do not matter to me. Please let me pass."

He stood back and inclined his head politely.

"As the signora pleases."

She stared, shocked. He'd reminded her that tonight he was here as a servant. Perhaps he thought she was a snob who'd cold-shouldered him on that account. But before she could tell him he was wrong, Dulcie called back from the door, "Justine, come and meet somebody."

She smiled, hurried across to where boats were drawing up at the palazzo's landing stage, and was engulfed in cheerful greetings.

When she next looked, Riccardo had gone.

CHAPTER EIGHT

A PARTY in the Palazzo Calvani was a step back into an age of elegance. Thirty people dined at the long rosewood table, eating off Sèvres porcelain and drinking from crystal etched with the Calvani crest.

Riccardo had prepared a banquet fit for a king. It was served by the palazzo servants, but under his eagle eyes. As he had told Justine, tonight he was the headwaiter.

It was Justine's first experience of Venetian cuisine, and she promised herself it wouldn't be the last. A dish of sardines in onions, pine seeds and sultanas was only the start. After that there was squid in tomato sauce, pork loins with Swiss cheese and shallots, with pears in hot chocolate to follow.

Clearly, whatever else he was economizing on, Riccardo had hired a superlative chef. There was more to him, she realized, than a lusty charmer. There was also a serious businessman who knew exactly what he was doing.

She tried to smile at him to show her appreciation, but discovered that it was impossible. He never came near her or met her eyes.

Obviously he'd blanked her out because of his absorption in his work. In which case she could hardly complain, she thought wryly, because it was exactly what she had done to him.

And she would be glad to believe that was the only reason. She didn't like to think of what the other one might be.

After dinner there were toasts, then everyone drifted into the garden to drink coffee under trees hung with colored lights.

There were more toasts to the two brides. Justine watched Liza and Dulcie standing together against the background of the canal. They were the two happiest women she had ever seen, because they loved their men and were loved by them.

Justine's eyes blurred. Just for a moment, it was hard to remember that love was only an illusion.

The evening was breaking up. The guests who were staying in the palazzo began to yawn. Those who had to travel were making movements to leave.

Justine went out to the hall, meaning to go, with everyone else, to the landing stage on the Grand Canal, where the glossy motor boats were waiting. From here she could see the other landing stage, round the side of the building, where Riccardo was preparing to leave, packing his things into the barge. He was alone, having sent his staff on ahead to the hotel.

She knew she must talk to him before he left. As he came inside to collect more boxes she approached him.

"That meal was a masterpiece," she ventured.

"The signora is too kind."

"Don't talk to me like that," she begged. "What I said before—I didn't mean it the way I think you took it. You were right. I was upset with you, and I ran away. Then I was even more upset because you noticed."

The gentle look was back in his face. For a moment she thought he was about to say something, but then—

"Riccardo!" Liza was calling him, hurrying toward him with her arms outstretched. "You did a wonderful job," she said warmly.

"Dear Liza!" He embraced her back. "I couldn't have done it without your help."

Liza laughed and indicated Justine.

"Here's the one you should really thank. She told Guido to give you the job."

Riccardo turned puzzled eyes on her.

"I suggested a hotel to help Liza," she said hastily, "and the Busoni was the only name I knew at the time. I had no idea that it was yours."

"Nonetheless, I am in your debt, Signora. Good night. Good night, Liza."

He turned away and jumped down into the barge. He was going, and she knew that if he left like this she would not see him again.

And she must.

The barge engine was starting up. She had only a split second to decide.

The next moment Liza gave a little shriek as Justine went running out onto the landing stage and leapt.

CHAPTER NINE

THIS TIME there were no comfortable cabbages to break her fall, but Justine managed to land on her feet at the bottom of the barge, steadying herself by seizing hold of Riccardo. He swiftly put his arms about her.

"Signora," he protested, "you cannot go on hurling yourself into my boat whenever the mood takes you. People will talk."

"If you'd waited I wouldn't have had to throw myself at you," she pointed out with impeccable logic. She was feeling light-headed and in good spirits. The crazy impulse had improved her mood.

The barge swerved and with one hand he hastily seized the tiller, which he'd abandoned to clasp her. But he kept his other arm about her.

He did not ask why she had done such a thing, nor did she explain. She would have found it hard to do that, even to herself.

Although it was late, there were still lights on the banks of the Grand Canal. Their reflections glowed in the black water, shivering and dancing as the last boats went home.

"Are you cold?" he asked, looking down at her bare shoulders.

"Not at all."

The night air was growing cool, but she was pervaded by warmth.

Down the long curve from the Rialto Bridge to St. Mark's Square they glided until at last Riccardo pointed upward to a building with an ornate front, and the words Hotel Busoni in neon.

"Mine," he said proudly. "At least, it will be when I've paid off the bank."

"Shouldn't it be the Hotel Gardini?" she asked.

I'll change the name when I feel a little more confident of success."

That touch of diffidence surprised her. Riccardo had seemed confident enough for anything.

He swung left into a tiny canal and tied the boat up at the landing stage. When he had climbed out with one box, she lifted the next one up to him.

"You can't help me with this," he protested.

"Yes, I can," she said firmly, hoisting up another box.

There was a trolley by the landing stage. He piled the boxes onto it and led her down a narrow corridor to the hotel's rear entrance.

It was late and only a few staff were about. The kitchen was empty. By now it was no surprise to Justine when he put on a large white apron and began unpacking the boxes.

"This is something else that you do yourself?" she asked.

"Night staff is expensive. When the last shift has gone home I finish up whatever there is to do."

"You have to work late here every night, all alone?"

"Yes, but I wouldn't have it any other way. This is my best time, when I feel this place is most completely mine."

She found another large apron and put it over her dress. He did not protest this time, but gave her a smile that was different from any smile he had given her before. It was no longer the "come-on" look of the pirate, but the secret signal of a conspirator.

It welcomed her into his world. And she was beginning to feel as if that was where she wanted to be.

While he emptied the washing-up machine of the load that had finished, she scraped plates and handed them to him to fill it up again.

"There's still plenty left to do," she said, "so we'd better do them by hand."

She got busy at the sink, working vigorously, until she looked up and found him regarding her strangely; not with a smile this time, but with a look that was half rueful, half wistful.

"What?" she asked.

"This is not how I planned our first evening alone together to be," he said.

"But you told me yourself, you plan too much," she reminded him. "Sometimes it's better when things just happen."

He nodded. "You are wise."

Still he stood there, eyes fixed on her, until she said gently, "Would you hand me that plate, please?"

"What plate?" He sounded dazed.

"The one just next to you."

He gave it to her. Justine turned back to the sink and got to work, but only half her mind was on what she was doing. The skin at the back of her neck and halfway down her spine seemed to have come alive with the awareness of him behind her.

He was going to kiss her just there, she knew it. The hairs were standing up on her neck with the sense of him moving toward her.

But nothing happened, and when she looked around, he was gone.

CHAPTER TEN

RICCARDO was back in a moment, carrying plates. Justine had returned to work at the sink, apparently unconcerned. But she was aware of him now in a new way. A moment had come and gone, and something sweet and indefinable had happened.

She washed, he dried, and in about an hour they had finished.

"Let me show you my home," he said.

He took her hand and they wandered through the quiet building. It was a beautiful place, furnished in the eighteenth-century style and, apart from a man on the night desk, they were alone downstairs.

"But up there, every room is full," Riccardo said, looking up to the ceiling.

"When you said your home, does that mean you live here?"

"Actually, I do, but I meant more. This building used to belong to my family. I was born here, but when I was six my father lost money on bad speculations and had to sell the house. That was when it became a hotel. Ever since, I've dreamed about reclaiming it, and in the end I managed to raise the money. Now I have to keep it."

"Will that be very hard?" she asked.

"Yes, but it's all I want to do."

"So that's why you double as your own dogsbody? I suppose you live in an attic, too?"

His eyes gleamed. "I live under the stars."

It soon became apparent that Riccardo meant exactly what he said. His home was a tiny apartment at the top of the building, but on top of it he had built a square balcony.

Brick pillars went up through the roof, supporting a wooden platform surrounded by a trellis fence on which roses flowered.

"Here we are up among the stars," he said, "and all around us, Venice is sleeping."

Down below she could just make out the sloping roofs, the little streets, called *calles*, where faint lights still glowed. Straight ahead was the softly lit bell tower of St. Mark's, the only other thing that rose this high. Beyond it, in the far distance, the faint glimpse of water glittering under the moon.

"Wait here," he said, and disappeared back down through the trapdoor that led down to his apartment.

Left alone, Justine looked about her at the dark blue night, with its faint lights winking like jewels against velvet, and marveled at so much beauty. In the distance she could hear the echoing cries of gondoliers going home, calling warnings to each other as they approached corners. It was an unearthly sound, like the music of the spheres. After a moment Riccardo returned with a bottle of champagne and two glasses.

"I think we've earned this," he said.

She sat down on one of the seats he indicated, and found that it stretched back to become a recliner.

"I often go to sleep out here," he said. "On warm summer nights it's the best place."

"I can imagine," she said, sipping the champagne he offered her. "It's so perfect—almost too perfect."

"Why do you say that?" he asked quickly.

"Well, nothing is ever as perfect as it seems, is it?"

"Perhaps it is, once in a blue moon. But even if not, shouldn't we enjoy the illusion of perfection while we can?"

"I think that's dangerous," she said quickly. "Why store up disillusion for yourself?"

"Why deprive yourself of all faith in beauty?" he countered. "Or don't you believe in beauty, either?"

"Of course I do. How could I do my job without it? I believe in it but…I suppose I don't trust it."

She walked to the railing and stood sipping champagne, looking out into the blue and silver night. Now words felt like an intrusion. She wanted only to let the night, and the beauty, take possession of her.

She sensed him coming to stand behind her. This time, she knew that he would not go away unless she told him to. He laid his lips softly against the back of her neck, and the feeling shivered through her.

He kissed her there for a long moment, while she stood quite still, savoring the sweet sensation, the pleasure and the happiness.

She drew a long breath. The situation was slipping out of her control, and of all feelings that was the one she dreaded most.

Somehow she must be strong enough to leave him now, or it would be too late. Or perhaps it was already too late. She turned to face him.

CHAPTER ELEVEN

IT WAS JUSTINE who turned the embrace into a kiss, putting her arms about Riccardo's neck, so that he could be in no doubt of her intentions.

"Justine," he whispered, "Justine…"

Everything he wanted from her was in his voice. He wanted *her*, in every way, and at this moment she would have given him all that she was, if only—

If only she was a different person, a woman who wasn't afraid to give her heart, afraid of her own self, her own feelings.

Dulcie had said to her, "When are you going to throw caution to the wind?"

But she had learned that caution over a lifetime, and it was too late for her now.

He murmured her name again against her lips, deepening the kiss in a way that was part plea, part demand. She responded fiercely, longing for the moment when emotion and sensation would take over.

But it didn't come. Try as she might she could not force her heart to rule her head. The knowledge made her want to cry out in despair, but she couldn't change anything.

"What is it?" he asked, sensing her inner struggle and loosening his grip. "Have I misunderstood? You do not feel as I do?"

"I don't know how I feel. How can I know so soon? How can you?"

"I do know."

"You can't," she said desperately, trying to make it true by the force of her assertion.

"Don't tell me how I feel," he said quietly.

"But we've only known each other a few days, and we've hardly talked at all."

"Perhaps it's as well. Talking is when people make mistakes about each other. I have made no mistake. I know what I feel about you. But if you wish, I'll wait a little while before saying it."

"And then I'll be gone," she said, suddenly wistful.

"You must not go before I tell you that I love you."

She surveyed him wryly. "That's very clever," she said. "Very subtle. Very *Venetian*."

"What do you know of Venetians?"

"I'm learning fast. You're great talkers."

"And you think it means nothing?"

"It means whatever you want it to mean at the time, and then tomorrow it means something else." She attempted a teasing tone. "You can tell me you love me tonight, if you want to."

"Can I indeed?"

"Yes, except that I won't take it seriously. By tomorrow everything will change. But tonight is fine."

"Do you think I need your permission to love you?" His voice was still quiet.

"Hey, lighten up," she said, still trying to turn it all into a joke. "We've got the moon and the stars and Venice. Why spoil it by getting serious?"

He didn't answer, just looked at her strangely, like a man trying to comprehend a baffling enigma.

Justine went very deliberately to the recliner, sat down and reached out to him in invitation. After a moment he came to her and took her hand, then knelt beside her and gathered her in his arms.

Now it would happen, she promised herself. Now the attraction that had drawn them together from their first glimpse outside the airport would take over so completely that she could forget caution.

He kissed her slowly, one hand beginning to trace a path from her face, down her neck to her throat. Excitement leapt in her like fire, sending its message in all directions, to her very fingertips, to the heart and depths of her.

As his hand began to drift lower she took a slow breath, eagerly yielding to her sensations.

And then, just as the world began to dissolve, leaving behind only him, it was all taken away. She felt him freeze, then withdraw from her.

Reluctantly Justine opened her eyes and found him looking at her tensely. His breathing was harsh and uneven, and she could feel the strain that racked his whole body.

"What is it?" she whispered. "What's the matter?"

"The matter is that this is not right," he growled.

"How can it be wrong if it's what we both want?"

"Is it? Can you look me in the eyes and say that you truly want me, as I want you? Or are you saying to yourself, I've gone too far to turn back now? Tell me the truth, Justine. I need to know."

CHAPTER TWELVE

RICCARDO'S WORDS made Justine feel as if he could see right into her. She couldn't bear that scrutiny, and closed her eyes. Understanding everything in that gesture, he rose sharply to his feet and moved away from her.

"This is not how it must be between us," he insisted.

"Why do you have to analyze everything?" she cried. "Leave the inside of my head alone. What happens in there is nothing to you."

"If you were just a brief fling that might be true. But you matter. I want to make love to you more than I've ever wanted anything in my life, but it has to be all of you, your heart and your mind, as well as your body."

"Maybe I don't have all that to give. Why can't you be satisfied with what there is?"

"Because you're worth so much more," he said simply.

He went to the trapdoor and held out his hand to her. "Come."

"Where?"

"I'm taking you home."

There was nothing to do but agree. The night was suddenly dead. On the way down he collected one of his jackets, and slipped it about her shoulders.

"Where are we going?" she asked, for he didn't turn toward the landing stage.

"It's only a short walk. The boat brought us almost in a circle, and now the palazzo is just a few streets away."

"How quiet everything is," she said, listening to their feet echoing on the flagstones.

"This is the best time," he said, "when the people have gone in, and the ghosts come out."

"Ghosts?"

"Venice is full of ghosts. They haunt the corners and the little alleyways in the twilight. But don't be afraid. They're friendly ghosts. In Venice they have known love, and been happy, and now they cannot bear to leave it."

She tried to be sensible. It would be easy to become drunk with the words of this charming dreamer. But being sensible didn't really seem very important any more.

What was important was to stroll through these narrow alleys, letting him weave magic spells around her. There would be time for common sense later.

After a while he fell silent, but the magic continued in the unearthly quiet of a city where there were no cars.

His arm was around her shoulders, drawing her close so that she was intimately aware of the warmth of his body. The stress of the evening fell away, and a blessed calm fell over her. Desire had passed into tenderness, giving her a space that she badly needed.

"Here we are," he said at last.

"Where?"

"The Palazzo Calvani. This is a side door. You must ring the bell, but not just yet."

He stroked her face with gentle fingers.

"When the weddings are over, promise me that you will not leave without seeing me again."

"I promise," she whispered contentedly.

After the evening's stormy, unfulfilled passion, he now kissed her like a boy on his first date, lips caressing hers almost uncertainly, if such a word could be associated with this man.

She relaxed into the warmth and tenderness that he offered, not wanting it to end.

It was he who drew back. "Good night," he murmured.

"Good night," Justine whispered back—with just a hint of wistfulness.

He rang a bell by the door.

"The porter will let you in. Good night."

He moved away swiftly and was out of sight before the porter admitted her. Justine hurried up to her room.

At the turn in the stairs there was a half-open window that looked out over the street where they had said goodbye. She could see the place where they had stood together, and wondered where he was now.

Then she saw something that might have been a shadow, standing by the corner. She blinked, and the shadow vanished, only to reappear. Surely it was her imagination? For a moment she had thought the shadow was familiar, and that he was gazing directly up at the window, as though reluctant to leave her. But when she looked again, he was gone, as elusive as a ghost.

CHAPTER THIRTEEN

GUIDO'S COUSIN Marco arrived from Rome, bringing his English fiancée, Harriet.

Marco was one of the most handsome men Justine had ever seen, but, while perfectly civil, he had a distant air.

"Harriet and Marco are rather cool for an engaged couple," Justine observed to Dulcie. "They're not like you and Guido."

"It's not precisely a love match," Dulcie said. "Harriet is the granddaughter of his mother's oldest friend."

"You mean they're not in love?"

Dulcie chuckled. "They think they aren't."

The last one to arrive was Leo, Guido's half brother, an amiable young giant whom Justine liked immediately. He arrived in Venice direct from Texas, where he'd been visiting a ranching friend, enjoying himself riding and "fooling around" as he put it.

Justine gathered that he'd also met Selena, a rodeo rider who'd made more of an impression on him than he wanted to admit. Dulcie and Harriet promptly settled down to grill him about her, until he grinned sheepishly and escaped.

"I'll swear he was blushing," Justine chuckled.

Dulcie nodded. "I don't think we've heard the last of Selena."

She seemed to be floating to her wedding on a tide of serene happiness. Liza, by contrast, was in a state of nerves, suddenly declaring that she needed help with the food.

"But she wouldn't hear of it the first time," Justine protested.

"I know," said Dulcie, "but she liked Riccardo, so I think it's an excuse to send some more work his way. Also," she added with a significant glance at Justine, "I think she may be doing some matchmaking."

"I can't imagine why," Justine said stiffly.

"Well it's your own fault. If you will hurl yourself into a boat driven by a ludicrously attractive man, spend the night with him—"

"I did not spend the night with him—not the way you mean, anyway."

"Well, you came home with the dawn."

"I bet you were all hanging out of the windows," Justine said wrathfully.

Dulcie chuckled. "Let's just say it's not a secret."

"So he'll be coming here to talk to Liza?" Justine asked, trying to sound indifferent.

"I'll tell Liza you want him," Dulcie said mischievously.

"You do and you're dead!" Justine said quickly.

Her own heart was hidden from her. Did she want to see Riccardo or not? He was dangerous because he wouldn't be pigeonholed, and he wouldn't let her take control of their relationship. But that was the only way that she felt safe.

That day she took her camera and went to explore Venice, thinking that when she returned he would be gone. But suddenly she felt distressed at the thought of missing him, and ran all the way back.

Then, disgusted with herself for shilly-shallying over a man, she refused to go anywhere near the kitchen, where he probably was, and sought the garden.

And there he was, talking and laughing with Guido, Marco and Leo. Worst of all, when the three Calvanis saw her, they immediately vanished with a speed that told her what the palazzo gossip was.

"I had hoped to find you here," he said, when they were alone.

"I have a lot of pictures to take," she said. "I'm hurrying to get everything done before the wedding."

"Of course. I, too, have much work to do, but I couldn't leave without seeing you. Does that make you angry?"

"Of course not. Why should it make me angry?"

He gave his wry smile with the wicked hint of mischief, and she had to work hard not to be melted by it.

"So much that I do seems to annoy you," he said. "I've learned to tread carefully. I'm really very scared of you."

"Don't be absurd," she said, laughing despite herself.

What could you do with a man who talked like this, except smile back at him and feel that the day had become brighter?

To give herself a moment she turned away to lean on the railing overlooking the Grand Canal. Riccardo came to stand close behind her.

"There's something I must tell you," he said quietly.

"What?"

"That I've thought about nothing but you since we said good night."

CHAPTER FOURTEEN

"NOTHING BUT ME?" Justine asked lightly. "I hope you gave some thought to the food as well."

Riccardo didn't answer at first, but turned her to look at him.

"It's no good," he said at last. "You can't make a joke of it. That won't solve the problem. And somehow we have to find a way to solve it."

"So you admit it's a problem?"

"Of course it's a problem when a man has fallen in love with a woman, and she—"

"Don't you dare say that I'm in love with you," she spit out.

"How can I? I don't know, any more than you do. I only know that you're fighting it—fighting me. And you're angry with me. Can't you tell me why?"

"You know why," she murmured. "I don't want to feel what I'm feeling. I've got my life in such good order, and you're threatening everything."

"No, I'm only threatening the bolts and bars with which you try to imprison yourself."

"You think I want to be locked in there?"

"Partly, yes. Prison can be a very comforting place. You know where everything is. But I won't let you cling to it.

When the wedding is over, I shall be back, knocking on the door."

"And you're so sure that I'll open it for you?"

"No, I'm not sure at all. I'm never sure with you. Perhaps that's why it has to be you and no other."

The sound of voices from inside the building drew them back to reality.

"I must go," he said reluctantly. "But I'll be back."

He would have turned away, but Justine detained him with her hands on his shoulders, just long enough to kiss him gently.

"Yes," she said. "You must come back."

The next day saw the first wedding, that of the count and Liza, a small, private occasion that took place in a side chapel of St. Mark's Basilica. The day after, it was Dulcie and Guido's turn.

No city in the world staged a wedding like Venice. It was normal for a bride to go to the church in a gondola, but Guido sometimes amused himself by being a part-time gondolier, and many of his friends had turned out for the occasion. At least twenty gondolas escorted Dulcie down the Grand Canal from the Rialto Bridge to the landing stage at St. Mark's.

Justine took pictures to her heart's content, traveling just ahead of the convoy in a motorboat. Landing first, she was able to witness Dulcie's arrival at the great church.

When the bride and groom emerged from the basilica together Justine took her final pictures and raced for the motorboat, to be whisked back to the palazzo and start frantically downloading. When she'd finished, she joined the reception for her final shots, which she took between mouthfuls of wedding cake.

At last the tables were cleared away for the dancing to

begin. Dulcie and Guido took the floor, to applause. Gradually the other guests joined them, until everyone seemed to be dancing, except Justine.

The music was sweet and sensuous, disturbing her vaguely. Nobody should listen to music like that without dancing to it.

"You look tired," said a sympathetic voice at her shoulder.

She turned and saw Riccardo holding out a glass of champagne to her. She drained it thankfully.

"Hey, Riccardo" came Guido's cheerful voice as he danced past with his bride in his arms. "Your duties are finished. From now on you're our guest.

Riccardo smiled and nodded, taking Justine's hand.

"Dance with me," he said.

As if in a dream she circled the floor with him, feeling the movement of his legs, the closeness of his body to hers, and knowing that she had been waiting for this all day.

She had expected him to talk, trying to dazzle her with words again, but instead he looked at her tenderly, in silence, until she could sense that he was caught in the same dream.

Then there was a small commotion. Marco and Harriet were dancing together, absorbed in each other as she hadn't seen them before.

Justine remembered Dulcie's prediction that they were more in love than they thought, and reckoned it might be true. Everyone else thought so, too, because suddenly they were crowding around them, demanding that they set the date for their own wedding.

Justine didn't stay to hear what happened. Riccardo had clasped her hand and was drawing her out into the garden.

CHAPTER FIFTEEN

THE GARDEN was flooded with light from the colored lamps hung between the trees. Guests milled everywhere.

"Let us escape them," Riccardo said, drawing Justine beneath the trees, and not stopping until they had reached the furthest part of the garden.

Once there he wasted no time before taking her into his arms. Justine went willingly. It was no use pretending to herself that she didn't want to kiss him. She wanted it passionately.

He had said he'd thought of nothing but her, and she knew now that everything that had happened to her in those few days, everything she'd seen or heard or done, had simply been another way of waiting for him.

Once before she had come alive in his arms, high on the roof, under the stars. Some part of her was still living in that moment, ready and eager for his touch.

The words he wanted to hear were hard for her, but her mouth spoke to him just the same, caressing his with skill and joy, saying things that could not be said aloud, and eliciting a response that thrilled her. She could feel the excitement mounting but was no longer sure whether it was his or her own. Where did he end and she begin?

"I mustn't kiss you too much," he said at last, huskily, drawing back. "It's dangerous."

She laughed recklessly. "What's wrong with a little danger? I thought you were the kind of man who enjoyed it."

"Don't provoke me, Justine, I'm almost at the end of my control already."

"Then let's be sedate and well behaved," she said, forcing herself to back away from him. It was hard because she was as fired up as he.

She went to the stone wall and looked out over the water.

"Look there," Riccardo said. "Do you recognize them?"

A solitary gondola was gliding out from the palazzo. Justine could see Dulcie reclining in her wedding gown, while Guido took the oar.

"He's got a tiny apartment tucked away somewhere," she said. "Dulcie said they're spending their honeymoon there, away from the world. What an incredibly romantic way to end a wedding!"

"Romantic. Meaning that you disapprove?"

"I wish them well. I hope they'll be the one couple in the world to prove that it can work the way it's supposed to."

"Don't forget the promise you made me, not to leave without seeing me again," he reminded her.

"I've seen you twice since then."

"Not the way I meant. I'll call for you in the boat tomorrow morning and take you—well, wait and see."

"I may have other things to do tomorrow."

His answer was to wrap his arms tightly about her, taking her prisoner.

"No," he said firmly. "You haven't."

"Oh, yes, I have," she retorted playfully.

"Oh, no, you haven't," he assured her just as playfully.

"Well then, I guess I haven't." She smiled.

He kissed her briefly and released her.

"I'll see you tomorrow."

He slipped away before anyone could see them together,

and Justine wandered back to the wedding, where everyone was toasting Marco and Harriet.

She dressed for boating in dark blue trousers and a white silk top.

Riccardo was waiting for her in Guido's motorboat, borrowed for the occasion.

He was dressed in black shorts and shirt, the black stark against the brown of his skin.

He reached up to help her into the boat.

"Steady, careful," he said.

"I'm not breakable." She laughed. "I could simply jump in. Or fall in. I've done it before."

"Yes, twice," he agreed with comical gravity. "It's causing talk. If you do it a third time you'll have to marry me."

She shook her head, her eyes dancing. "A terrible fate."

"Do you think so?"

"I meant for you. Imagine having to marry me for a reason like that."

"I'd marry you for any reason if I thought I could talk you into it."

CHAPTER SIXTEEN

FOR A WHILE Justine concentrated on enjoying the day out as Riccardo gently urged the motorboat down the Grand Canal and out into the lagoon where there were miles of open water, bounded on the far side by the long islands of the Lido.

"Where are we going?" she asked, standing beside him at the wheel.

"We're going nowhere," he replied, putting his arm about her and drawing her tightly against him.

"Where's nowhere?"

"Wait and see."

That was fine with her. Who could ask for more than to drift across the water, going nowhere with him?

"There's some champagne below," he said.

She went down and found the boat less cramped than she had expected. There was a large cushioned space, almost as big as a double bed. In the picnic hamper she found champagne and glasses, and took them up.

He stopped the boat within sight of some of the smaller islands, and they drank contentedly.

"If this is nowhere, I love it," she said.

He nodded. "The most peaceful place on earth." He brushed her face gently. "I love you."

She shook her head. "Don't."

"Do you find it so hard to believe?"

"So quickly? Yes, it's hard."

His shrug had a touch of helplessness that sat oddly with his usual air of confidence.

"I, too, was taken by surprise. You see, I'm like you. I plan my life ahead. I had not planned for you, and yet there you were, at the airport.

"Justine, I don't understand what's happened to us any more than you do. I only know that it *has* happened, and there's no going back. To say that it's too soon, that we've barely met, is easy. I admit it, but it changes nothing.

"That day I went to the airport, I had nothing on my mind but collecting supplies. Then I looked up and saw the woman I'd been waiting for all my life. She was red-haired and glorious, and she looked me straight in the eye in a way that said, 'Fool with me at your peril.'

"I'd never had a challenge that thrilled me more. There and then I decided to fool with her. And the more I knew her, the more I knew it had to be for the rest of my life."

"Don't I get a say?"

"Of course. Tell me what you want from me. A brief adventure? Fine. We'll have an adventure. And afterward you will stay with me forever."

"Then it wouldn't be an adventure," she countered. "An adventure is brief. That's why it's an adventure."

"And you don't think that spending your life with one man might be an adventure?"

"That's just clever words."

"What you really want is a fling, but flings are for people who can't commit themselves."

"You forget I've been married."

"No, I don't forget. But I don't think you committed yourself to that marriage, otherwise you wouldn't have cast it aside at the first hurdle."

"You know nothing about it," she cried, on the defensive again.

"Then tell me. Show me that I'm wrong."

"I don't have to explain myself to you."

"Not to me, but to yourself. Have you ever tried to do that, beyond believing that all your prejudices had been proved correct?"

"I don't have to listen to this."

"Fine, run away."

Justine looked all around her. Water everywhere.

"Well, I can't, can I?" she seethed. "I'm trapped out here now."

"Ah, yes! I never thought of that."

"Like hell you didn't."

He grinned.

"Will you please start this engine and take me back to Venice?"

"I've got a better idea," he said. "Why don't we go below and have something to eat?"

For a moment she glared at him, then relented. "All right, but it's under protest!"

"Of course. You'll find the smoked salmon tastes just as good under protest."

She aimed a friendly punch at him. It was too glorious a day for anger.

The picnic hamper was full of the very finest from the hotel. As she unpacked and they reclined against the cushions, she asked, "How is it you were able to take the day off?"

"I did well out of those catering assignments, so I could hire some extra help for a few days. This is more important."

As he'd promised, the food was exquisite. For once she forgot about healthy eating and indulged herself. Afterward she was suddenly sleepy, and when he drew her back against his shoulder she nodded off at once.

She awoke to find him watching her and had a sudden conviction that he'd been doing that all the time.

"Now tell me about yourself," he said. "I want to know everything."

CHAPTER SEVENTEEN

HELD IN THE SAFETY of Riccardo's arms, Justine struggled with memories that usually she tried never to think of.

"Until I was eight years old I thought I had a happy home. I knew my parents loved each other more than they loved me, but there was love to spare for everyone, or so I thought." Justine let out a sigh. It was difficult for her to talk about this.

"My mother used to say that being in love was the most important thing in the world, and nothing mattered more than being true to your heart.

"But then she fell in love with another man, and he became the most important thing in the world—enough for her to leave us to be with him."

Justine gave a little wry smile. "She had to be true to her heart, you see. Well, she was. She made a fine romantic heroine, giving up everything for love. But one of the things she gave up was me."

Riccardo was watching her with shocked intensity. "She didn't take you with her?"

"But how could she?" Justine asked in a rallying voice. "Romantic heroines can't have eight-year-old kids in tow."

He gave her hand the smallest squeeze, as if to show that he understood her irony.

"So you stayed with your father?" he asked.

"For a while. Then he dumped me on one of his sisters while he went out on the town. He didn't want me cramping his style, either. In due course he fell in love again.

"They sent me to boarding school for a while. Then there was some mix-up about who was supposed to be collecting me for Christmas. In the end, neither of them did. I spent Christmas in the care of the Social Services."

Riccardo swore violently. Justine didn't understand the words, but from his tone she guessed it was a profanity. She felt vaguely comforted at the fierceness of his empathy.

"I never lived with either of my parents again," she went on. "Neither of their new marriages lasted. My mother is currently being true to her heart in South America with a man ten years younger. We don't keep in touch."

"So that's why your views are jaded," Riccardo said. "And who could blame you?"

"As far as I'm concerned love is just an excuse for selfishness."

"In selfish people, yes. But love doesn't make us what we are. It merely reveals the truth about us. Selfish people love selfishly, generous people love generously. Your parents were spoiled brats, but don't blame love. It didn't make them that way."

"It gave them the excuse," she said stubbornly.

"But you were married. Didn't you love him?"

"So much that it scared me."

"Ah. I see."

"Don't say that. You don't see anything. I wanted our marriage to work, but—I can't explain—"

She could never explain the fear that had pervaded her. Too much happiness, she had thought. One day it would be snatched away. Watch for that moment, be ready for it, go to meet it with a smile, and don't let anyone know you care. Never, never let them know that.

No, she couldn't put these things into words.

But then, looking at Riccardo's face, she knew she didn't have to. He understood everything. He'd seen into her soul with eyes of love and seen the turmoil of rage, bitterness and misery that was insidiously driving out everything else, until the best had all gone.

"He wanted a child," she said abruptly. "I didn't. Not then, anyway. Who am I to be a parent? So we started to quarrel. One day—one day, I realized that the quarrels were destroying us."

"So you quarreled harder, to drive him away," Riccardo said. "You reckoned that would be less painful than waiting for the breakup to occur naturally."

She stared. "How did you know that?"

"It's not magic. Attack sometimes seems the best form of defense. But it leaves you with nothing."

"I can cope with nothing," she said desperately. "It's what I'm used to. What I can't take is believing in something and then learning all over again that it's an illusion."

"I know," he said gently, tightening his arms and drawing her against him.

In the comfort of his embrace it was easy to fall asleep again. When she awoke it was night, and they were speeding back across the lagoon.

"Where are we going now?" she asked, coming to stand beside him at the wheel.

"Home," he said.

She didn't ask where he meant. A few minutes later they had stopped in the small canal that ran by the hotel, and were climbing up to the stars.

CHAPTER EIGHTEEN

THE DAWN came softly and quickly, ushered in by the bell of St Mark's campanile. Justine stood on the balcony on top of Riccardo's apartment, and marveled at the beauty of the morning.

She had spent the night in his arms, not making love, but enclosed in safety. Instinctively he had known what she needed, and had given it to her. A generous man, loving generously.

He came up through the trapdoor, bearing a cup of hot tea.

"You're a magician," she said. "I'm just ready to murder for a cup of tea."

She sipped blissfully, looking around her and down into the narrow alleys. Then she stiffened.

"What's that? It looks like water in the streets."

"It is," Riccardo sighed. "It's high tide and the lagoon has flooded. It used to only happen in winter. Now it can be at any time."

The photographer in her spoke at once. "I must get my camera."

He grinned ruefully. "How did I know you were going to say that? Come on, I'll take you home."

Outside she found the whole aspect of Venice transformed. Wherever she looked the narrow streets seemed to be lakes, and although the water was only four inches deep the effect was still staggering.

Running like children, hand in hand, they splashed their way back to the palazzo and secured all her equipment.

"First we go to St. Mark's Square," he said. "It's an astonishing sight when this happens, and it won't last long because the tide will turn."

It was like that all day. He acted as her caddy and her advisor, telling her where to find the best shots.

"I love this city," she said as they finally sat together at Florian's, drinking chocolate.

He was clever enough to say nothing, letting her work out the implications for herself.

When they came out, the water had gone, and they strolled contentedly back to the hotel. While he saw to some business in the hotel she went up to the apartment and took a shower.

He arrived upstairs later to find her swathed in one of his towel dressing gowns, drinking tea. He held out his hand and led her to bed.

His loving was like himself, generous, skillful, unpredictable. Relaxed at last, Justine responded wholeheartedly, and discovered that she too was unpredictable. It was like finding that you'd turned into a new person.

Dozing in his arms afterward she found her mind traveling along new paths of discovery. Much of her business involved traveling abroad. She could run it as well from Venice as from England.

She woke to find him planting soft kisses on her face.

"Stay with me always," he begged.

It would be so easy to say yes, to believe in the bright dream. She closed her eyes, breathing in the scent of him. Now the last leap seemed not only possible but easy, inevitable.

But before she could speak her cell phone shrilled.

"Answer it," he said. "There's time enough for what we have to say to each other."

It was Dulcie, calling from her honeymoon hideout.

"Blissful," she said in answer to Justine's question. "I can recommend marriage."

Justine laughed. "That's very interesting."

"But something sad has happened. Harriet has left Marco."

"What? But they were setting the date," Justine protested.

"I know. Now it's all over."

When the call ended Justine slowly replaced the receiver, feeling stunned.

"What has happened?" Riccardo asked, with foreboding.

"Harriet and Marco have broken up. Two days after it was going to last forever."

In a daze she saw the bright dream disintegrate and fall with tinkling shivers around her feet. So much for love eternal! What had she been thinking of to believe in such stuff?

She began to laugh, falling back on the bed, contorted with mirth.

"Is it funny?" Riccardo asked.

"Of course it is, don't you see? Oh, what an idiot I've been!"

"Justine, this has nothing to do with us."

"The hell it hasn't! It has to do with everyone who buys into that pretty fantasy. And I came so close—but not any-more. I got confused, but I've seen the light now, and I'm going home before I make a bigger fool of myself than I al-ready have. Don't try to stop me Riccardo."

She waited for him to argue, but there was only silence. It seemed he had accepted her decision and, illogically, she knew a little ache of desolation. If he would only speak a word to dissuade her—

"I'll take you home," he said.

CHAPTER NINETEEN

JUSTINE'S flight was at noon the next day. At ten, while she was finishing packing, Liza looked into her room to say, "The boat is here for you."

The old woman bid her an affectionate goodbye, not hiding her disappointment that Justine was leaving Riccardo. The count also embraced her exuberantly, and escorted her out to the landing stage, where his staff had already piled Justine's bags into the motorboat.

She gave them both a last kiss and, turning, put out her hand for the boatman to help her aboard.

"*Buon giorno!*" Riccardo said.

"You?"

She felt a flash of dismay. They'd said their goodbyes last night, devastated and defeated on her side, quiet and strangely resigned on his. Why couldn't he leave it there?

But in the same moment she knew she hadn't wanted him to do that, and the greater pain would be to leave without seeing him again.

His hand tightened over hers and he drew her into the boat. When he had seen her seated he swung away down the Grand Canal, then across the lagoon to the airport, reversing the journey of the first day.

But something was different this time. Suddenly the engine spluttered and died.

"We seem to have a problem," Riccardo said.

"I don't believe it," Justine said, jumping up and coming to stand beside him. "There's nothing wrong with that engine."

He shrugged. "Let's just say there are things I want to say before you leave. You may ignore them. You probably will. But I can't let you go without saying them."

Before he could say more, a large wave made the boat rock, knocking her off balance so that she had to cling to him. He was as steady as a rock.

"You see?" he said. "The boat lurches but we don't fall because we cling to each other."

"Pretty words, but only words," she said desperately. "You were right when you said that I don't trust love. How can you trust something that's built on such shifting foundations?"

Riccardo's answer astonished her.

"What's wrong with shifting foundations?"

She stared. "Everything's wrong with them. You can't use them to build something that will last."

"You can say that after what you saw yesterday, when we had to wade through high tide? You're wrong, and Venice is the proof that you're wrong. No city was ever built on shakier foundations than this one.

"A thousand years ago our ancestors fled into the tiny islands of the lagoon to escape the barbarians. Here they thrust wooden stakes down into the mud and built a city on top of those stakes that has been the glory of the world.

"You've heard that Venice is sinking, and yesterday you saw it for yourself. She's been sinking for centuries, but she's still here. Why? Because those of us who love her fight and struggle to keep her afloat.

"Does the lagoon flood? We'll build barriers. Does the

humid air rot the pictures? We'll restore them. We never stop patching the old girl up, and she's still with us."

"But love isn't like that—"

"Love is *exactly* like that. People change all the time, because life alters them. The man and woman who fall in love are not the same people they will be when their first child is born, then their first grandchild.

"If the love lasts it's because they've struggled and adjusted to the endless changes. When the foundations move, they move with them, and so the love survives. It alters. After many years it looks different, but it's still there, and *it's still love*. Don't you see?"

"Yes," she said sadly. "I do see. And you're right."

"Well then—"

"My darling, please try to understand. I see everything you want me to see. But I can't do it."

Silence. Only the lapping of the water against the boat. His face was sadder than any human being's she had ever seen.

At last he released her and started the engine again. Soon they were skimming across the water. Gradually the airport came into sight, growing larger every moment, until he slowed and eased into the jetty.

In a few minutes she would be gone, and everything would be over. Her heart was breaking, but she had no idea how to stop what was happening.

CHAPTER TWENTY

RICCARDO carried her bags from the boat to the airport buildings and piled them onto a trolley.

"I'll say goodbye now," he said briefly.

"Won't you come with me to the check-in?"

"There's no need."

"You can't wait to get away from me."

"I thought it was you going away from me."

Justine made a helpless gesture. She was beyond speech.

"Listen, *amor mio*," he said, taking gentle hold of her shoulders. "I thought there was still a chance for us, but there's something in you that I can't get past—fear or stubbornness, or just that you don't really love me—"

"Don't say that," she cried passionately. "You know I love you."

"But it isn't enough, is it? Too many ghosts haunt you, and I can't dispel them. I wish I could, because now I, too, have a ghost that will haunt me all my life."

"Venice is a city of ghosts," she reminded him. "You taught me that."

"Yes, but I didn't want you to be a ghost. I wanted you to be my reality. Instead, you'll be a 'might-have-been,' and that's the worst kind of ghost there is."

She nodded. She couldn't deny it. But neither could she

stop what was happening. It was like being carried on by the irresistible tide that flowed through the lagoon.

"So," he went on, "I won't come any further. I won't watch you get onto the plane, and wave as it vanishes into the sky, because I couldn't bear to."

"It isn't that I don't love you," she said huskily. "Please believe me. It's just that I can't take any more risks."

"What do you mean 'any more'?" he asked with sudden anger. "You've never taken a risk in your life. Even your marriage was hedged around with safety barriers, and they were what destroyed it.

"Do you remember my saying that if you jumped into my boat a third time you'd have to marry me? Do it now. Risk it. Take that third leap, and find my arms outstretched to catch you. Because they always will be."

"I know," she choked. "But it's how I am. I can't help it."

"Then there's no hope for us?"

She shook her head.

"Goodbye, *amor mio*," he said softly. "I shall never forget you."

He took her face between his hands and kissed her with a tenderness that broke her heart.

"Goodbye, goodbye," he whispered.

She clung to him, wanting to prolong the moment forever, but unable to change her mind.

He walked away from her toward the jetty. She waited for him to look back, telling herself that until he did that, it wasn't over.

But he didn't look back, and she realized that he wouldn't do so. He wasn't sentimental, just a man with a powerful, loving heart that she had rejected.

She began to push the trolley toward the check-in, but every step seemed forced.

She had made her decision and must stick with it.

Even if the rest of her life was desolate. And it would be. That wasn't a risk. It was a certainty.

"Defense is the best form of attack, but it leaves you with nothing."

"I can cope with nothing."

Not anymore.

In a few moments he would be gone forever. It only needed a little courage and a lot of faith.

"Take that third leap, and find my arms outstretched...."

She looked around wildly. It was almost too late. She began to run. Outside she could see the water and the queues waiting for motor taxis.

He was there, just getting into the motorboat, starting it up.

"Riccardo!" she screamed. "Riccardo, wait for me."

But he couldn't hear her. The noise of his engine drowned her out. She began to run, frantic as she saw the precious chance slipping away.

The boat was drawing away, but at the last moment something made him look back. Justine saw his face, alight with love and joy as he realized what she meant to do.

"Wait for me, my love. I'm coming. I'm coming!"

The onlookers parted to let her through. She sped the last few feet and took a flying leap off the jetty, soaring high into the air before falling into the arms that were outstretched to receive her forever.

100 Reasons to Celebrate

2008 is a very special year as we celebrate Mills and Boon's Centenary.

Each month throughout the year there will be something new and exciting to mark the centenary, so watch for your favourite authors, captivating new stories, special limited edition collections…and more!

www.millsandboon.co.uk

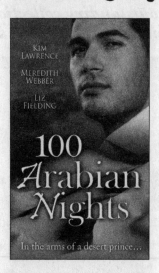

Two men have vowed to protect the women they love...

New York Times bestselling author

DIANA PALMER

Hard to Handle

Hunter

On a top secret operation in the desert, chief of
security Hunter knew Jennifer Marist needed his
protection. Soon he discovered the lure of Jenny's
wild, sweet passion – and a love he'd never
dreamed possible.

Man in Control

Eight years after DEA agent Alexander Cobb had
turned Jodie Clayburn down, Alexander could
hardly believe the beauty that Jodie had become...
or that she'd helped him crack a dangerous
drug-smuggling case. Would the man in control
finally surrender to his desires?

Available 20th June 2008